from *Desert Gold*

The raider tried to sheer Diablo off closer under the wall, to make the slope where his companion had escaped. But Diablo was uncontrollable. He was running wild, with breaking gait. Closer and closer crept that white, smoothly gliding, beautiful machine of speed.

Then, like one white flash following another, the two horses gleamed down the bank of a wash and disappeared in clouds of dust.

★ ZANE GREY ★

DESERT GOLD

and

THE LIGHT of WESTERN STARS

A TOM DOHERTY ASSOCIATES BOOK | NEW YORK

This is a work of fiction. All of the characters, organizations, and events portrayed in these novels are either products of the author's imagination or are used fictitiously.

DESERT GOLD AND THE LIGHT OF WESTERN STARS

A Forge Book
Published by Tom Doherty Associates
175 Fifth Avenue
New York, NY 10010

www.tor-forge.com

Forge® is a registered trademark of Macmillan Publishing Group, LLC.

ISBN 978-0-7653-9842-0

Our books may be purchased in bulk for promotional, educational, or business use. Please contact your local bookseller or the Macmillan Corporate and Premium Sales Department at 1-800-221-7945, extension 5442, or by e-mail at MacmillanSpecialMarkets@macmillan.com.

First Edition: August 2018

Printed in the United States of America

0 9 8 7 6 5 4 3 2 1

CONTENTS

DESERT
GOLD

★

PROLOGUE

A face haunted Cameron—a woman's face. It was there in the white heart of the dying campfire; it hung in the shadows that hovered over the flickering light; it drifted in the darkness beyond.

This hour, when the day had closed and the lonely desert night set in with its dead silence, was one in which Cameron's mind was thronged with memories of a time long past—of a home back in Peoria, of a woman he had wronged and lost, and loved too late. He was a prospector for gold, a hunter of solitude, a lover of the drear, rock-ribbed infinitude, because he wanted to be alone to remember.

A sound disturbed Cameron's reflections. He bent his head, listening. A soft wind fanned the paling embers, blew sparks and white ashes and thin smoke away into the enshrouding circle of blackness. His burro did not appear to be moving about. The quiet split to the cry of a coyote. It rose strange, wild, mournful—not the howl of a prowling upland beast baying the campfire or barking at a lonely prospector, but the wail of a wolf, full-voiced, crying out the meaning of the desert and the night. Hunger throbbed in it—hunger for a mate, for offspring, for life. When it ceased, the terrible desert silence smote Cameron, and the cry echoed in his soul. He and that wandering wolf were brothers.

Then a sharp clink of metal on stone and soft pads of hoofs in sand prompted Cameron to reach for his gun, and to move out of the light of the waning campfire. He was somewhere along the wild borderline between Sonora and Arizona; and the prospector who dared the heat and barrenness of that region risked other dangers sometimes as menacing.

Figures darker than the gloom approached and took shape, and in the light turned out to be those of a white man and a heavily packed burro.

"Hello there," the man called, as he came to a halt and gazed about him. "I saw your fire. May I make camp here?"

Cameron came forth out of the shadow and greeted his visitor, whom he took for a prospector like himself. Cameron resented the breaking of his lonely campfire vigil, but he respected the law of the desert.

The stranger thanked him, and then slipped the pack from his burro. Then he rolled out his pack and began preparations for a meal. His movements were slow and methodical.

Cameron watched him, still with resentment, yet with a curious and growing interest. The campfire burst into a bright blaze, and by its light Cameron saw a man whose gray hair somehow did not seem to make him old, and whose stooped shoulders did not detract from an impression of rugged strength.

"Find any mineral?" asked Cameron, presently.

His visitor looked up quickly, as if startled by the sound of a human voice. He replied, and then the two men talked a little. But the stranger evidently preferred silence. Cameron understood that. He laughed grimly and bent a keener gaze upon the furrowed, shadowy face. Another of those strange desert prospectors in whom there was some relentless driving power besides the lust for gold! Cameron felt that between this man and himself there was a subtle affinity, vague and undefined, perhaps born of the divination that here was a desert wanderer like himself, perhaps born of a deeper, an unintelligible relation having its roots back in the past. A long-forgotten sensation stirred in Cameron's breast, one so long forgotten that he could not recognize it. But it was akin to pain.

II

When he awakened he found, to his surprise, that his companion had departed. A trail in the sand led off to the north. There was no water in that direction. Cameron shrugged his shoulders; it was not his affair; he had his own problems. And straightway he forgot his strange visitor.

Cameron began his day, grateful for the solitude that was now unbroken, for the cañon-furrowed and cactus-spired scene that now showed no sign of life. He traveled southwest, never straying far from the dry streambed; and in a desultory way, without eagerness, he hunted for signs of gold.

The work was toilsome, yet the periods of rest in which he indulged were not taken because of fatigue. He rested to look, to listen, to feel. What the vast silent world meant to him had always been a mystical thing, which he felt in all its incalculable power, but never understood.

That day, while it was yet light, and he was digging in

a moist white-bordered wash for water, he was brought sharply up by hearing the crack of hard hoofs on stone. There down the cañon came a man and a burro. Cameron recognized them.

"Hello, friend," called the man, halting. "Our trails crossed again. That's good."

"Hello," replied Cameron, slowly. "Any mineral sign today?"

"No."

They made camp together, ate their frugal meal, smoked a pipe, and rolled in their blankets without exchanging many words. In the morning the same reticence, the same aloofness characterized the manner of both. But Cameron's companion, when he had packed his burro and was ready to start, faced about and said: "We might stay together, if it's all right with you."

"I never take a partner," replied Cameron.

"You're alone; I'm alone," said the other, mildly. "It's a big place. If we find gold there'll be enough for two."

"I don't go down into the desert for gold alone," rejoined Cameron, with a chill note in his swift reply.

His companion's deep-set, luminous eyes emitted a singular flash. It moved Cameron to say that in the years of his wandering he had met no man who could endure equally with him the blasting heat, the blinding dust storms, the wilderness of sand and rock and lava and cactus, the terrible silence and desolation of the desert. Cameron waved a hand toward the wide, shimmering, shadowy descent of plain and range. "I may strike through the Sonora Desert. I may head for Pinacate or north for the Colorado Basin. You are an old man."

"I don't know the country, but to me one place is the same as another," replied his companion. For moments he seemed to forget himself, and swept his far-reaching gaze out over the colored gulf of stone and sand. Then with gentle slaps he drove his burro in behind Cameron. "Yes, I'm old. I'm lonely, too. It's come to me just lately. But, friend, I can still travel, and for a few days my company won't hurt you."

"Have it your way," said Cameron.

They began a slow march down into the desert. At sunset they camped under the lee of a low mesa. Cameron was glad his comrade had the Indian habit of silence. Another day's travel found the prospectors deep in the wilderness. Then there came a breaking of reserve, noticeable in the elder man, almost imperceptibly gradual in Cameron. Besides the meager mesquite campfire this grayfaced, thoughtful old prospector would remove his black pipe from his mouth to talk a little, and Cameron would listen, and sometimes unlock his lips to speak a word. And so, as Cameron began to respond to the influence of a desert less lonely than habitual, he began to take keener note of his comrade, and found him different from any other he had ever encountered in the wilderness. This man never grumbled at the heat, the glare, the driving sand, the sour water, the scant fare. During the daylight hours he was seldom idle. At night he sat dreaming before the fire or paced to and fro in the gloom. He slept but little, and that long after Cameron had had his own rest. He was tireless, patient, brooding.

Cameron's awakened interest brought home to him the realization that for years he had shunned companionship. In those years only three men had wandered into the desert with him, and these had left their bones to bleach in the shifting sands. Cameron had not cared to know their secrets. But the more he studied this latest comrade the more he began to suspect that he might have missed something in the others. In his own driving passion to take his secret into the limitless abode of silence and desolation, where he could be alone with it, he had forgotten that life dealt shocks to other men. Somehow this silent comrade reminded him.

One afternoon late, after they had toiled up a white, winding wash of sand and gravel, they came upon a dry water hole. Cameron dug deep into the sand, but without avail. He was turning to retrace weary steps back to the last water when his comrade asked him to wait. Cameron watched him search in his pack and bring forth what appeared to be a small, forked branch of a peach tree. He grasped the prongs of the fork and held them before him with the end standing straight out, and then he began to walk along the streambed. Cameron, at first amused, then amazed, then pitying and at last curious, kept pace with the prospector. He saw a strong tension of his comrade's wrists, as if he was holding hard against a considerable force. The end of the peach branch began to quiver and turn. Cameron reached out a hand to touch it, and was astounded at feeling a powerful vibrant force pulling the branch downward. He felt it as a magnetic shock. The branch kept turning, and at length pointed to the ground.

"Dig here," said the prospector.

"What!" ejaculated Cameron. Had the man lost his mind?

Then Cameron stood by while his comrade dug in the sand. Three feet he dug—four—five, and the sand grew dark, then moist. At six feet water began to seep through.

"Get the little basket in my pack," he said.

Cameron complied, and saw his comrade drop the basket into the deep hole, where it kept the sides from caving in and allowed the water to seep through. While Cameron watched, the basket filled. Of all the strange incidents of his desert career this was the strangest. Curiously he picked up the peach branch and held it as he had seen it held. The thing, however, was dead in his hands.

"I see you haven't got it," remarked his comrade. "Few men have."

"Got what?" demanded Cameron.

"A power to find water that way. Back in Illinois an old German used to do that to locate wells. He showed me I had the same power. I can't explain. But you needn't look so dumbfounded. There's nothing supernatural about it."

"You mean it's a simple fact—that some men have a magnetism, a force or power to find water as you did?"

"Yes. It's not unusual on the farms back in Illinois, Ohio, Pennsylvania. The old German I spoke of made money traveling round with his peach fork."

"What a gift for a man in the desert!"

Cameron's comrade smiled—the second time in all those days.

They entered a region where mineral abounded, and their march became slower. Generally they took the course of a wash, one on each side, and let the burros travel leisurely along nipping at the bleached blades of scant grass, or at sage or cactus, while they searched in the cañons and under the ledges for signs of gold. When they found any rock that hinted of gold they picked off a piece and gave it a chemical test. The search was fascinating. They interspersed the work with long, restful moments when they looked afar down the vast reaches and smoky shingles to the line of dim mountains. Some impelling desire, not all the lure of gold, took them to the top of mesas and escarpments; and here, when they had

dug and picked, they rested and gazed out at the wide
prospect. Then, as the sun lost its heat and sank lowering
to dent its red disk behind far-distant spurs, they halted
in a shady cañon or likely spot in a dry wash and tried
for water. When they found it they unpacked, gave drink
to the tired burros, and turned them loose. Dead mesquite
served for the campfire. While the strange twilight deepened into weird night they sat propped against stones,
with eyes on the dying embers of the fire, and soon they
lay on the sand with the light of white stars on their dark
faces.

Each succeeding day and night Cameron felt himself
more and more drawn to this strange man. He found that
after hours of burning toil he had insensibly grown nearer
to his comrade. He reflected that after a few weeks in the
desert he had always become a different man. In civilization, in the rough mining camps, he had been a prey to
unrest and gloom. But once down on the great billowing
sweep of this lonely world, he could look into his unquiet
soul without bitterness. Did not the desert magnify men?
Cameron believed that wild men in wild places, fighting
cold, heat, starvation, thirst, barrenness, facing the elements in all their ferocity, usually retrograded, descended
to the savage, lost all heart and soul and became mere
brutes. Likewise he believed that men wandering or lost
in the wilderness often reversed that brutal order of life
and became noble, wonderful, superhuman. So now he did
not marvel at a slow stir stealing warmer along his veins,
and at the premonition that perhaps he and this man,
alone on the desert, driven there by life's mysterious and
remorseless motive, were to see each other through God's
eyes.

His companion was one who thought of himself last. It

humiliated Cameron that in spite of growing keenness he could not hinder him from doing more than an equal share of the day's work. The man was mild, gentle, quiet, mostly silent, yet under all his softness he seemed to be made of the fiber of steel. Cameron could not thwart him. Moreover, he appeared to want to find gold for Cameron, not for himself. Cameron's hands always trembled at the turning of rock that promised gold; he had enough of the prospector's passion for fortune to thrill at the chance of a strike. But the other never showed the least trace of excitement.

One night they were encamped at the head of a cañon. The day had been exceedingly hot, and long after sundown the radiation of heat from the rocks persisted. A desert bird whistled a wild, melancholy note from a dark cliff, and a distant coyote wailed mournfully. The stars shone white until the huge moon rose to burn out all their whiteness. And on this night Cameron watched his comrade, and yielded to interest he had not heretofore voiced.

"Pardner, what drives you into the desert?"

"Do I seem to be a driven man?"

"No. But I feel it. Do you come to forget?"

"Yes."

"Ah!" softly exclaimed Cameron. Always he seemed to have known that. He said no more. He watched the old man rise and begin his nightly pace to and fro, up and down. With slow, soft tread, forward and back, tirelessly and ceaselessly, he paced that beat. He did not look up at the stars or follow the radiant track of the moon along the cañon ramparts. He hung his head. He was lost in another world. It was a world which the lonely desert made real. He looked a dark, sad, plodding figure, and somehow impressed Cameron with the helplessness of men.

Cameron grew acutely conscious of the pang in his own breast, of the fire in his heart, the strife and torment of his passion-driven soul. He had come into the desert to remember a woman. She appeared to him then as she had looked when first she entered his life—a golden-haired girl, blue-eyed, white-skinned, red-lipped, tall and slender and beautiful. He had never forgotten, and an old, sickening remorse knocked at his heart. He rose and climbed out of the cañon and to the top of a mesa, where he paced to and fro and looked down into the weird and mystic shadows, like the darkness of his passion, and farther on down the moon track and the glittering stretches that vanished in the cold, blue horizon. The moon soared radiant and calm, the white stars shone serene. The vault of heaven seemed illimitable and divine. The desert surrounded him, silver-streaked and black-mantled, a chaos of rock and sand, silent, austere, ancient, always waiting. It spoke to Cameron. It was a naked corpse, but it had a soul. In that wild solitude the white stars looked down upon him pitilessly and pityingly. They had shone upon a desert that might once have been alive and was now dead, and might again throb with life, only to die. It was a terrible ordeal for him to stand there alone and realize that he was only a man facing eternity. But that was what gave him strength to endure. Somehow he was a part of it all, some atom in that vastness, somehow necessary to an inscrutable purpose, something indestructible in that desolate world of ruin and death and decay, something perishable and changeable and growing under all the fixity of heaven. In that endless, silent hall of desert there was a spirit; and Cameron felt hovering near him what he imagined to be phantoms of peace.

He returned to camp and sought his comrade.

"I reckon we're two of a kind," he said. "It was a woman who drove me into the desert. But I come to remember. The desert's the only place I can do that."

"Was she your wife?" asked the elder man.

"No."

A long silence ensued. A cool wind blew up the cañon sifting the sand through the dry sage, driving away the last of the lingering heat. The campfire wore down to a ruddy ashen heap.

"I had a daughter," said Cameron's comrade. "She lost her mother at birth. And I—I didn't know how to bring up a girl. She was pretty and gay. It was the—the old story."

His words were peculiarly significant to Cameron. They distressed him. He had been wrapped up in his remorse. If ever in the past he had thought of any one connected with the girl he had wronged he had long forgotten. But the consequences of such wrong were far-reaching. They struck at the roots of a home. Here in the desert he was confronted by the spectacle of a splendid man, a father, wasting his life because he could not forget—because there was nothing left to live for. Cameron understood better now why his comrade was drawn by the desert.

"Well, tell me more?" asked Cameron, earnestly.

"It was the old, old story. My girl was pretty and free. The young bucks ran after her. I guess she did not run away from them. And I was away a good deal—working in another town. She was in love with a wild fellow. I knew nothing of it till too late. He was engaged to marry her. But he didn't come back. And when the disgrace became plain to all, my girl left home. She went west. After a while I heard from her. She was well—working—living for her baby. A long time passed. I had no ties. I drifted west. Her lover had also gone west. In those days every-body went west. I trailed him, intending to kill him. But I lost his trail. Neither could I find any trace of her. She had moved on, driven, no doubt, by the hound of her past. Since then I have taken to the wilds, hunting gold on the desert."

"Yes, it's the old, old story, only sadder, I think," said Cameron; and his voice was strained and unnatural. "Pardner, what Illinois town was it you hailed from?"

"Peoria."

"And your—your name?" went on Cameron, huskily.

"Warren—Jonas Warren."

That name might as well have been a bullet. Cameron stood erect, motionless, as men sometimes stand momentarily when shot straight through the heart. In an instant, when thoughts resurged like blinding flashes of lightning through his mind, he was a swaying, quivering, terror-stricken man. He mumbled something hoarsely and backed into the shadow. But he needed not have feared discovery, however surely his agitation might have betrayed him. Warren sat brooding over the campfire, oblivious of his comrade, absorbed in the past.

Cameron swiftly walked away in the gloom, with the blood thrumming thick in his ears, whispering over and over:

"Merciful God! Nell was *his* daughter!"

III

As thought and feeling multiplied, Cameron was over-whelmed. Beyond belief, indeed, was it that out of the millions of men in the world two who had never seen each other could have been driven into the desert by memory of the same woman. It brought the past so close. It showed Cameron how inevitably all his spiritual life was governed by what had happened long ago. That which made life significant to him was a wandering in silent places where no eye could see him with his secret. Some fateful chance had thrown him with the father of the girl he had wrecked. It was incomprehensible; it was terrible. It was the one thing of all possible happenings in the world of chance that both father and lover would have found unendurable.

Cameron's pain reached to despair when he felt this relation between Warren and himself. Something within him cried out to him to reveal his identity. Warren would kill him; but it was not fear of death that put Cameron on the rack. He had faced death too often to be afraid. It was the thought of adding torture to this long-suffering man. All at once Cameron swore that he would not augment Warren's trouble, or let him stain his hands with blood. He would tell the truth of Nell's sad story and his own, and make what amends he could.

Then Cameron's thought shifted from father to daughter. She was somewhere beyond the dim horizon line. In those past lonely hours by the campfire his fancy had tortured him with pictures of Nell. But his remorseful and cruel fancy had lied to him. Nell had struggled upward out of menacing depths. She had reconstructed a broken life. And now she was fighting for the name and happiness of her child. Little Nell! Cameron experienced a shuddering ripple in all his being—the physical rack of an emotion born of a new and strange consciousness.

As Cameron gazed out over the bloodred, darkening desert suddenly the strife in his soul ceased. The moment was one of incalculable change, in which his eyes seemed to pierce the vastness of cloud and range, and mystery of gloom and shadow—to see with strong vision the illimitable space before him. He felt the grandeur of the desert, its simplicity, its truth. He had learned at last the lesson it taught. No longer strange was his meeting and wandering with Warren. Each had marched in the steps of destiny; and as the lines of their fates had been inextricably tangled in the years that were gone, so now their steps had crossed and turned them toward one common goal. For years they had been two men marching alone, answering to an inward driving search, and the desert had brought them together. For years they had wandered alone in silence and solitude, where the sun burned white all day and the stars burned white all night, blindly following the whisper of a spirit. But now Cameron knew that he was no longer blind, and in this flash of revelation he felt that it had been given him to help Warren with his burden.

He returned to camp trying to evolve a plan. As always at that long hour when the afterglow of sunset lingered in the west, Warren plodded to and fro in the gloom. All night Cameron lay awake thinking.

In the morning, when Warren brought the burros to camp and began preparations for the usual packing, Cameron broke silence.

"Pardner, your story last night made me think. I want to tell you something about myself. It's hard enough to be driven by sorrow for someone you've loved, as you've been driven; but to suffer sleepless and eternal remorse for the *ruin* of one you've loved as I have suffered—that is hell. . . . Listen. In my younger days—it seems long now, yet it's not so many years—I was wild. I wronged the sweetest and loveliest girl I ever knew. I went away not dreaming that any disgrace might come to her. Along about that time I fell into terrible moods—I changed—I learned I really loved her. Then came a letter I should have gotten months before. It told of her trouble—importuned me to hurry to save her. Half frantic with shame and fear, I got a marriage certificate and rushed back to her town. She was gone—had been gone for weeks, and her disgrace was known. Friends warned me to keep out of reach of her father. I trailed her—found her. I married her. But too late! . . . She would not live with me. She left me— I followed her west, but never found her."

Warren leaned forward a little and looked into Cameron's eyes, as if searching there for the repentance that might make him less deserving of a man's scorn.

Cameron met the gaze unflinchingly, and again began to speak:

"You know, of course, how men out here somehow lose old names, old identities. It won't surprise you much to learn my name really isn't Cameron, as I once told you."

Warren stiffened upright. It seemed that there might have been a blank, a suspension, between his grave interest and some strange mood to come.

Cameron felt his heart bulge and contract in his breast; all his body grew cold; and it took tremendous effort for him to make his lips form words.

"Warren, I'm the man you're hunting. I'm Burton. I was Nell's lover!"

The old man rose and towered over Cameron, and then plunged down upon him, and clutched at his throat with terrible stifling hands. The harsh contact, the pain awakened Cameron to his peril before it was too late. Desperate fighting saved him from being hurled to the ground and stamped and crushed. Warren seemed a maddened giant. There was a reeling, swaying, wrestling struggle before the elder man began to weaken. Then Cameron, buffeted, bloody, half-stunned, panted for speech.

"Warren—hold on! Give me—a minute. I married Nell. Didn't you know that? . . . I saved the child!"

Cameron felt the shock that vibrated through Warren. He repeated the words again and again. As if compelled by some resistless power, Warren released Cameron, and, staggering back, stood with uplifted, shaking hands. In his face was a horrible darkness.

"Warren! Wait—listen!" panted Cameron. "I've got that marriage certificate—I've had it by me all these years. I kept it—to prove to myself I did right."

The old man uttered a broken cry.

Cameron stole off among the rocks. How long he absented himself or what he did he had no idea. When he returned Warren was sitting before the campfire, and once more he appeared composed. He spoke, and his voice had a deeper note; but otherwise he seemed as usual.

They packed the burros and faced the north together.

Cameron experienced a singular exaltation. He had lightened his comrade's burden. Wonderfully it came to him that he had also lightened his own. From that hour it was not torment to think of Nell. Walking with his comrade through the silent places, lying beside him under the serene luminous light of the stars, Cameron began to feel the haunting presence of invisible things that were real to him—phantoms whispering peace. In the moan of the cool wind, in the silken seep of sifting sand, in the distant rumble of a slipping ledge, in the faint rush of a shooting star he heard these phantoms of peace coming with whispers of the long pain of men at the last made endurable. Even in the white noonday, under the burning sun, these phantoms came to be real to him. In the dead silence of the midnight hours he heard them breathing nearer on the desert wind—nature's voices of motherhood, whispers of God, peace in the solitude.

IV

There came a morning when the sun shone angry and red through a dull, smoky haze.

"We're in for sandstorms," said Cameron.

They had scarcely covered a mile when a desert-wide, moaning, yellow wall of flying sand swooped down upon them. Seeking shelter in the lee of a rock, they waited, hoping the storm was only a squall, such as frequently whipped across the open places. The moan increased to a roar, and the dull red slowly dimmed, to disappear in the yellow pall, and the air grew thick and dark. Warren slipped the packs from the burros. Cameron feared the sandstorms had arrived some weeks ahead of their usual season.

The men covered their heads and patiently waited. The long hours dragged, and the storm increased in fury. Cameron and Warren wet scarfs with water from their canteens, and bound them round their faces, and then covered their heads. The steady, hollow bellow of flying sand went on. It flew so thickly that enough sifted down under the shelving rock to weight the blankets and almost bury the men. They were frequently compelled to shake off the sand to keep from being borne to the ground. And it was necessary to keep digging out the packs. The floor of their shelter gradually rose higher and higher. They tried to eat, and seemed to be grinding only sand between their teeth. They lost the count of time. They dared not sleep, for that would have meant being buried alive. They could only crouch close to the leaning rock, shake off the sand, blindly dig out their packs, and every moment gasp and cough and choke to fight suffocation.

The storm finally blew itself out. It left the prospectors heavy and stupid for want of sleep. Their burros had wandered away, or had been buried in the sand. Far as eye could reach the desert had marvelously changed; it was now a rippling sea of sand dunes. Away to the north rose the peak that was their only guiding mark. They headed toward it, carrying a shovel and part of their packs.

At noon the peak vanished in the shimmering glare of the desert. The prospectors pushed on, guided by the sun. In every wash they tried for water. With the forked peach branch in his hands Warren always succeeded in locating water. They dug, but it lay too deep. At length, spent and sore, they fell and slept through that night and part of the next day. Then they succeeded in getting water, and quenched their thirst, and filled the canteens, and cooked a meal.

The burning day found them in an interminably wide plain, where there was no shelter from the fierce sun. The men were exceedingly careful with their water, though there was absolute necessity of drinking a little every hour. Late in the afternoon they came to a cañon that they believed was the lower end of the one in which they had last found water. For hours they traveled toward its head, and, long after night had set, found what they sought. Yielding to exhaustion, they slept, and next day were loath to leave the water hole. Cool night spurred them on with canteens full and renewed strength.

Morning told Cameron that they had turned back miles into the desert, and it was desert new to him. The red sun, the increasing heat, and especially the variety and large size of the cactus plants warned Cameron that he had descended to a lower level. Mountain peaks loomed on all sides, some near, others distant; and one, a blue spur, splitting the glaring sky far to the north, Cameron thought he recognized as a landmark. The ascent toward it was heartbreaking, not in steepness, but in its league-and-league-long monotonous rise. Cameron knew there was only one hope—to make the water hold out and never stop to rest. Warren began to weaken. Often he had to halt. The burning white day passed, and likewise the night, with its white stars shining so pitilessly cold and bright.

Cameron measured the water in his canteen by its weight. Evaporation by heat consumed as much as he drank. During one of the rests, when he had wetted his parched mouth and throat, he found opportunity to pour a little water from his canteen into Warren's.

At first Cameron had curbed his restless activity to accommodate the pace of his elder comrade. But now he felt that he was losing something of his instinctive and passionate zeal to get out of the desert. The thought of water came to occupy his mind. He began to imagine that his last little store of water did not appreciably diminish. He knew he was not quite right in his mind regarding water; nevertheless, he felt this to be more of fact than fancy, and he began to ponder.

When next they rested he pretended to be in a kind of stupor; but he covertly watched Warren. The man appeared far gone, yet he had cunning. He cautiously took up Cameron's canteen and poured water into it from his own.

This troubled Cameron. The old irritation at not being able to thwart Warren returned to him. Cameron reflected, and concluded that he had been unwise not to expect this very thing. Then, as his comrade dropped into weary rest, he lifted both canteens. If there were any water in Warren's, it was only very little. Both men had been enduring the terrible desert thirst, concealing it, each giving his water to the other, and the sacrifice had been useless.

Instead of ministering to the parched throats of one or both, the water had evaporated. When Cameron made sure of this, he took one more drink, the last, and poured the little water left into Warren's canteen. He threw his own away.

Soon afterward Warren discovered the loss.

"Where's your canteen?" he asked.

"The heat was getting my water, so I drank what was left."

"My son!" said Warren.

The day opened for them in a red and green hell of rock and cactus. Like a flame the sun scorched and peeled their faces. Warren went blind from the glare, and Cameron had to lead him. At last Warren plunged down, exhausted, in the shade of a ledge.

Cameron rested and waited, hopeless, with hot, weary eyes gazing down from the height where he sat. The ledge was the top step of a ragged gigantic stairway. Below stretched a sad, austere, and lonely valley. A dim, wide streak, lighter than the bordering gray, wound down the valley floor. Once a river had flowed there, leaving only a forlorn trace down the winding floor of this forlorn valley.

Movement on the part of Warren attracted Cameron's attention. Evidently the old prospector had recovered his sight and some of his strength. For he had arisen, and now began to walk along the arroyo bed with his forked peach branch held before him. He had clung to that precious bit of wood. Cameron considered the prospect for water hopeless, because he saw that the arroyo had once been a cañon, and had been filled with sands by desert winds. Warren, however, stopped in a deep pit, and, cutting his canteen in half, began to use one side of it as a scoop. He scooped out a wide hollow, so wide that Cameron was certain he had gone crazy. Cameron gently urged him to stop, and then forcibly tried to make him. But these efforts were futile. Warren worked with slow, ceaseless, methodical movement. He toiled for what seemed hours. Cameron, seeing the darkening, dampening sand, realized a wonderful possibility of water, and he plunged into the pit with the other half of the canteen. Then both men toiled, round and round the wide hole, down deeper and deeper. The sand grew moist, then wet. At the bottom of the deep pit the sand coarsened, gave place to gravel. Finally water welled in, a stronger volume than Cameron ever remembered finding on the desert. It would soon fill the hole and run over. He marveled at the circumstance. The time was near the end of the dry season. Perhaps an underground stream flowed from the range behind down to the valley floor, and at this point came near to the surface. Cameron had heard of such desert miracles.

The finding of water revived Cameron's flagging hopes. But they were short-lived. Warren had spent himself utterly.

"I'm done. Don't linger," he whispered. "My son, go—go!"

Then he fell. Cameron dragged him out of the sand pit to a sheltered place under the ledge. While sitting beside the failing man Cameron discovered painted images on the wall. Often in the desert he had found these evidences of a prehistoric people. Then, from long habit, he picked up a piece of rock and examined it. Its weight made him closely scrutinize it. The color was a peculiar black. He scraped through the black rust to find a piece of gold. Around him lay scattered heaps of black pebbles and bits of black, weathered rock and pieces of broken ledge, and they showed gold.

"Warren! Look! See it! Feel it! Gold!"

But Warren had never cared, and now he was too blind to see.

"Go—go!" he whispered.

Cameron gazed down the gray reaches of that forlorn valley, and something within him that was neither intelligence nor emotion—something inscrutably strange— impelled him to promise.

Then Cameron built up stone monuments to mark his gold strike. That done, he tarried beside the unconscious Warren. Moments passed—grew into hours. Cameron still had strength left to make an effort to get out of the desert. But that same inscrutable something which had ordered his strange involuntary promise to Warren held him beside his fallen comrade. He watched the white sun turn to gold, and then to red, and sink behind mountains in the west. Twilight stole into the arroyo. It lingered, slowly turning to gloom. The vault of blue-black lightened to the blinking of stars. Then fell the serene, silent, luminous desert night.

Cameron kept his vigil. As the long hours wore on he felt creep over him the comforting sense that he need not forever fight sleep. A wan glow flared behind the dark, uneven horizon, and a melancholy misshapen moon rose to make the white night one of shadows. Absolute silence claimed the desert. It was mute. Then that inscrutable something breathed to him, telling him when he was alone. He need not have looked at the dark, still face beside him.

Another face haunted Cameron's—a woman's face. It was there in the white moonlit shadows; it drifted in the darkness beyond; it softened, changed to that of a young girl, sweet, with the same dark, haunting eyes of her mother. Cameron prayed to that nameless thing within him, the spirit of something deep and mystical as life. He prayed to that nameless thing outside, of which the rocks and the sand, the spiked cactus and the ragged lava, the endless waste, with its vast star-fired mantle, were but atoms. He prayed for mercy to a woman—for happiness to her child. Both mother and daughter were close to him then. Time and distance were annihilated. He had faith—he saw into the future. The fateful threads of the past, so inextricably woven with his error, wound out their tragic length here in this forlorn desert.

Cameron then took a little tin box from his pocket, and, opening it, removed a folded certificate. He had kept a pen, and now he wrote something upon the paper, and in lieu of ink he wrote with blood. The moon afforded him enough light to see; and, having replaced the paper, he laid the little box upon a shelf of rock. It would remain there unaffected by dust, moisture, heat, time. How long had those painted images been there clear and sharp on the dry stone walls? There were no trails in that desert, and always there were incalculable changes. Cameron saw this mutable mood of nature—the sands would fly and seep and carve and bury; the floods would dig and cut; the ledges would weather in the heat and rain; the avalanches would slide; the cactus seeds would roll in the wind to catch in a niche and split the soil with thirsty roots. Years would pass. Cameron seemed to see them, too; and likewise destiny leading a child down into this forlorn waste, where she would find love and fortune, and the grave of her father.

Cameron covered the dark, still face of his comrade from the light of the waning moon.

That action was the severing of his hold on realities. They fell away from him in final separation. Vaguely, dreamily he seemed to behold his soul. Night merged into gray day; and night came again, weird and dark. Then up out of the vast void of the desert, from the silence and illimitableness, trooped his phantoms of peace. Majestically they formed around him, marshaling and mustering in ceremonious state, and moved to lay upon him their passionless serenity.

CHAPTER 1

OLD FRIENDS

Richard Gale reflected that his sojourn in the West had been what his disgusted father had predicted—idling here and dreaming there, with no objective point or purpose.

It was reflection such as this, only more serious and perhaps somewhat desperate, that had brought Gale down to the border. For some time the newspapers had been printing news of Mexican revolution, guerrilla warfare, United States cavalry patrolling the international line, American cowboys fighting with the rebels, and wild stories of bold raiders and bandits. Regarding these rumors Gale was skeptical. But as opportunity, and adventure, too, had apparently given him a wide berth in Montana, Wyoming, Colorado, he had struck southwest for the Arizona border, where he hoped to see some stirring life. He did not care very much what happened. Months of futile wandering in the hope of finding a place where he fitted had inclined Richard to his father's opinion.

It was after dark one evening in early October when Richard arrived in Casita. He was surprised to find that it was evidently a town of importance. There was a jostling, jabbering, sombreroed crowd of Mexicans around the railroad station. He felt as if he were in a foreign country. After a while he saw several men of his nationality, one of whom he engaged to carry his luggage to a hotel. They walked up a wide well-lighted street lined with buildings in which were bright windows. Of the many people encountered by Gale most were Mexicans. His guide explained that the smaller half of Casita lay in Arizona, the other half in Mexico, and of several thousand inhabitants the majority belonged on the southern side of the street, which was the boundary line. He also said that rebels had entered the town that day, causing a good deal of excitement.

Gale was almost at the end of his financial resources, which fact occasioned him to turn away from a pretentious hotel and ask his guide for a cheaper lodging house. When this was found, a sight of the loungers in the office, and also a desire for comfort, persuaded Gale to change his traveling clothes for rough outing garb and boots.

"Well, I'm almost broke," he soliloquized, thoughtfully. "The governor said I wouldn't make any money. He's right—so far. And he said I'd be coming home beaten. There he's wrong. I've got a hunch that something'll happen to me in this Greaser town."

He went out into a wide, whitewashed, high-ceiled corridor, and from that into an immense room which, but for pool tables, bar, and benches, would have been like a courtyard. The floor was cobblestoned, the walls were of adobe, and the large windows opened like doors. A blue cloud of smoke filled the place. Gale heard the click of pool balls and the clink of glasses along the crowded bar. Bare-legged, sandal-footed Mexicans in white rubbed shoulders with Mexicans mantled in black and red. There were others in tight-fitting blue uniforms with gold fringe or tassels at the shoulders. These men wore belts with heavy, bone-handled guns, and evidently were the rurales, or native policemen. There were black-bearded, coarse-visaged Americans, some gambling round the little tables, others drinking. The pool tables were the center of a noisy crowd of younger men, several of whom were unsteady on their feet. There were khaki-clad cavalrymen strutting in and out.

At one end of the room, somewhat apart from the general melee, was a group of six men round a little table, four of whom were seated, the other two standing. These last two drew a second glance from Gale. The sharp-featured, bronzed faces and piercing eyes, the tall, slender, loosely jointed bodies, the quiet, easy, reckless air that seemed to be a part of the men—these things would plainly have stamped them as cowboys without the buckled sombreros, the colored scarfs, the high-topped, high-heeled boots with great silver-roweled spurs. Gale did not fail to note, also, that these cowboys wore guns, and this fact was rather a shock to his idea of the modern West. It caused him to give some credence to the rumors of fighting along the border, and he felt a thrill.

He satisfied his hunger in a restaurant adjoining, and as he stepped back into the saloon a man wearing a military cape jostled him. Apologies from both were instant. Gale was moving on when the other stopped short as if startled, and, leaning forward, exclaimed:

"Dick Gale?"

"You've got me," replied Gale, in surprise. "But I don't know you."

He could not see the stranger's face, because it was wholly shaded by a wide-brimmed hat pulled well down.

"By Jove! It's Dick! If this isn't great! Don't you know me?"

"I've heard your voice somewhere," replied Gale. "Maybe I'll recognize you if you come out from under that bonnet."

For answer the man, suddenly manifesting thought of himself, hurriedly drew Gale into the restaurant, where he thrust back his hat to disclose a handsome, sunburned face.

"George Thorne! So help me—"

"'S-s-ssh. You needn't yell," interrupted the other, as he met Gale's outstretched hand. There was a close, hard, straining grip. "I must not be recognized here. There are reasons. I'll explain in a minute. Say, but it's fine to see you! Five years, Dick, five years since I saw you run down University Field and spread-eagle the whole Wisconsin football team."

"Don't recollect that," replied Dick, laughing. "George, I'll bet you I'm gladder to see you than you are to see me. It seems so long. You went into the army, didn't you?"

"I did. I'm here now with the Ninth Cavalry. But— never mind me. What're you doing way down here? Say, I just noticed your togs. Dick, you can't be going in for mining or ranching, not in this God-forsaken desert?"

"On the square, George, I don't know any more why I'm here than—than you know."

"Well, that beats me!" ejaculated Thorne, sitting back in his chair, amaze and concern in his expression. "What the devil's wrong? Your old man's got too much money

for you ever to be up against it. Dick, you couldn't have
gone to the bad?"

A tide of emotion surged over Gale. How good it was
to meet a friend—someone to whom to talk! He had never
appreciated his loneliness until that moment.

"George, how I ever drifted down here I don't know. I
didn't exactly quarrel with the governor. But—damn it,
Dad hurt me—shamed me, and I dug out for the West. It
was this way. After leaving college I tried to please him by
tackling one thing after another that he set me to do. On
the square, I had no head for business. I made a mess of
everything. The governor got sore. He kept ramming the
harpoon into me till I just couldn't stand it. What little ability I possessed deserted me when I got my back up, and
there you are. Dad and I had a rather uncomfortable half
hour. When I quit—when I told him straight out that I was
going West to fare for myself, why, it wouldn't have been
so tough if he hadn't laughed at me. He called me a rich
man's son—an idle, easygoing, spineless swell. He said I
didn't even have character enough to be out-and-out bad.
He said I didn't have sense enough to marry one of the nice
girls in my sister's crowd. He said I couldn't earn a dollar—
that I'd starve out West, and couldn't get back home unless
I sent to him for money. He said he didn't believe I could
fight—could really make a fight for anything under the
sun. Oh—he—he shot it into me, all right."

Dick dropped his head upon his hands, somewhat
ashamed of the smarting dimness in his eyes. He had not
meant to say so much. Yet what a relief to let out that long-
congested burden!

"Fight!" cried Thorne, hotly. "What's ailing him?
Didn't they call you Biff Gale in college? Dick, you were
one of the best men Stagg ever developed. I heard him say

so—that you were the fastest one-hundred-and-seventy-five-pound man he'd ever trained, the hardest to stop."

"The governor didn't count football," said Dick. "He didn't mean that kind of a fight. When I left home I don't think I had an idea what was wrong with me. But George, I think I know now. I was a rich man's son—spoiled, dependent, absolutely ignorant of the value of money. I haven't yet discovered any earning capacity in me. I seem to be unable to do anything with my hands. That's the trouble. But I'm at the end of my tether now. And I'm going to punch cattle or be a miner, or do some real stunt—like joining the rebels."

"Aha! I thought you'd spring that last one on me," declared Thorne, wagging his head. "Well, you just forget it. Say, old boy, there's something doing in Mexico. The United States in general doesn't realize it. But across that line there are crazy revolutionists, ill-paid soldiers, guerrilla leaders, raiders, robbers, outlaws, bandits galore, starving peons by the thousand, girls and women in terror. Mexico is like some of her volcanoes—ready to erupt fire and hell! Don't make the awful mistake of joining the rebel forces. Americans are hated by Mexicans of the lower class—the fighting class, both rebel and federal. Half the time these crazy Greasers are on one side, then on the other. If you didn't starve or get shot in ambush, or die of thirst, some Greaser would knife you in the back for your belt buckle or boots. There are a good many Americans with the rebels eastward toward Agua Prieta and Juarez. Orozco is operating in Chihuahua, and I guess he has some idea of warfare. But this is Sonora, a mountainous desert, the home of the slave and the Yaqui. There's unorganized revolt everywhere. The American miners and ranchers, those who could get away, have fled across into the States, leaving property. Those who couldn't or wouldn't come must fight for their lives, are fighting now."

"That's bad," said Gale. "It's news to me. Why doesn't the government take action, do something?"

"Afraid of international complications. Don't want to offend the Maderists, or be criticized by jealous foreign nations. It's a delicate situation, Dick. The Washington officials know the gravity of it, you can bet. But the United States in general is in the dark, and the army—well, you ought to hear the inside talk back at San Antonio. We're patrolling the boundary line. We're making a grand bluff. I could tell you of a dozen instances where cavalry should have pursued raiders on the other side of the line. But we won't do it. The officers are a grouchy lot these days. You see, of course, what significance would attach to United States cavalry going into Mexican territory. There would simply be hell. My own colonel is the sorest man on the job. We're all sore. It's like sitting on a powder magazine. We can't keep the rebels and raiders from crossing the line. Yet we don't fight. My commission expires soon. I'll be discharged in three months. You can bet I'm glad for more reasons than I've mentioned."

Thorne was evidently laboring under strong, suppressed excitement. His face showed pale under the tan, and his eyes gleamed with a dark fire. Occasionally his delight at meeting, talking with Gale, dominated the other emotions, but not for long. He had seated himself at a table near one of the door-like windows leading into the street, and every little while he would glance sharply out. Also he kept consulting his watch.

These details gradually grew upon Gale as Thorne talked.

"George, it strikes me that you're upset," said Dick presently. "I seem to remember you as a coolheaded fellow whom nothing could disturb. Has the army changed you?"

Thorne laughed. It was a laugh with a strange, high note. It was reckless—it hinted of exaltation. He rose abruptly; he gave the waiter money to go for drinks; he looked into the saloon, and then into the street. On this side of the house there was a porch opening on a plaza with trees and shrubbery and branches. Thorne peered out one window, then another. His actions were rapid. Returning to the table, he put his hands upon it and leaned over to look closely into Gale's face.

"I'm away from camp without leave," he said.

"Isn't that a serious offense?" asked Dick.

"Serious? For me, if I'm discovered, it means ruin. There are rebels in town. Any moment we might have trouble. I ought to be ready for duty—within call. If I'm discovered it means arrest. That means delay—the failure of my plans—ruin."

Gale was silenced by his friend's intensity. Thorne bent over closer with his dark eyes searchingly bright.

"We were old pals—once?"

"Surely," replied Dick.

"What would you say, Dick Gale, if I told you that you're the one man I'd rather have had come along than any other at this crisis of my life?"

The earnest gaze, the passionate voice with its deep tremor drew Dick upright, thrilling and eager, conscious of strange, unfamiliar impetuosity.

"Thorne, I should say I was glad to be the fellow," replied Dick.

Their hands locked for a moment, and they sat down again with heads close over the table.

"Listen," began Thorne, in low, swift whisper, "a few days, a week ago—it seems like a year!—I was of some assistance to refugees fleeing from Mexico into the States. They were all women, and one of them was dressed as a nun. Quite by accident I saw her face. It was that of a beautiful girl. I observed she kept aloof from the others. I suspected a disguise, and, when opportunity afforded, spoke to her, offered my services. She replied to my poor efforts at Spanish in fluent English. She had fled in terror from her home, someplace down in Sinaloa. Rebels are active there. Her father was captured and held for ransom. When the ransom was paid the rebels killed him. The leader of these rebels was a bandit named Rojas. Long before the revolution began he had been feared by people of class—loved by the peons. Bandits are worshiped by the peons. All of the famous bandits have robbed the rich and given to the poor. Rojas saw the daughter, made off with her. But she contrived to bribe her guards, and escaped almost immediately before any harm befell her. She hid among friends. Rojas nearly tore down the town in his efforts to find her. Then she disguised herself, and traveled by horseback, stage, and train to Casita.

"Her story fascinated me, and that one fleeting glimpse I had of her face I couldn't forget. She had no friends here, no money. She knew Rojas was trailing her. This talk I had with her was at the railroad station, where all was bustle and confusion. No one noticed us, so I thought. I advised her to remove the disguise of a nun before she left the waiting-room. And I got a boy to guide her. But he fetched her to this house. I had promised to come in the evening to talk over the situation with her.

"I found her, Dick, and when I saw her—I went stark, staring, raving mad over her. She is the most beautiful,

wonderful girl I ever saw. Her name is Mercedes Castañeda, and she belongs to one of the old wealthy Spanish
families. She has lived abroad and in Havana. She speaks
French as well as English. She is—but I must be brief.

"Dick, think, think! With Mercedes also it was love at
first sight. My plan is to marry her and get her farther to
the interior, away from the border. It may not be easy. She's
watched. So am I. It was impossible to see her without the
women of this house knowing. At first, perhaps, they had
only curiosity—an itch to gossip. But the last two days
there has been a change. Since last night there's some
powerful influence at work. Oh, these Mexicans are subtle, mysterious! After all, they are Spaniards. They work
in secret, in the dark. They are dominated first by religion, then by gold, then by passion for a woman. Rojas
must have got word to his friends here; yesterday his gang
of cutthroat rebels arrived, and today he came. When I
learned that, I took my chance and left camp; I hunted up
a priest. He promised to come here. It's time he's due. But
I'm afraid he'll be stopped."

"Thorne, why don't you take the girl and get married
without waiting, without running these risks?" said Dick.

"I fear it's too late now. I should have done that last
night. You see, we're over the line—"

"Are we in Mexican territory now?" queried Gale,
sharply.

"I guess yes, old boy. That's what complicates it. Rojas
and his rebels have Casita in their hands. But Rojas without his rebels would be able to stop me, get the girl, and
make for his mountain haunts. If Mercedes is really
watched—if her identity is known, which I am sure is the
case—we couldn't get far from this house before I'd be
knifed and she seized."

"Good Heavens! Thorne, can that sort of thing happen less than a stone's throw from the United States line?" asked Gale, incredulously.

"It *can* happen, and don't you forget it. You don't seem to realize the power these guerrilla leaders, these rebel captains, and particularly these bandits, exercise over the mass of Mexicans. A bandit is a man of honor in Mexico. He is feared, envied, loved. In the hearts of the people he stands next to the national idol—the bullfighter, the matador. The race has a wild, barbarian, bloody strain. Take Quinteros, for instance. He was a peon, a slave. He became a famous bandit. At the outbreak of the revolution he proclaimed himself a leader, and with a band of followers he devastated whole counties. The opposition to federal forces was only a blind to rob and riot and carry off women. The motto of this man and his followers was: 'Let us enjoy ourselves while we may!'

"There are other bandits besides Quinteros, not so famous or such great leaders, but just as bloodthirsty. I've seen Rojas. He's a handsome, bold, sneering devil, vainer than any peacock. He decks himself in gold lace and silver trappings, in all the finery he can steal. He was one of the rebels who helped sack Sinaloa and carry off half a million in money and valuables. Rojas spends gold like he spills blood. But he is chiefly famous for abducting women. The peon girls consider it an honor to be ridden off with. Rojas has shown a penchant for girls of the better class."

Thorne wiped the perspiration from his pale face and bent a dark gaze out of the window before he resumed his talk.

"Consider what the position of Mercedes really is. I can't get any help from our side of the line. If so, I don't know where. The population on that side is mostly Mexican, absolutely in sympathy with whatever actuates those on this side. The whole caboodle of Greasers on both sides belong to the class in sympathy with the rebels, the class that secretly respects men like Rojas and hates an aristocrat like Mercedes. They would conspire to throw her into his power. Rojas can turn all the hidden underground influences to his ends. Unless I thwart him he'll get Mercedes as easily as he can light a cigarette. But I'll kill him or some of his gang or her before I let him get her. . . . This is the situation, old friend. I've little time to spare. I face arrest for desertion. Rojas is in town. I think I was followed to this hotel. The priest has betrayed me or has been stopped. Mercedes is here alone, waiting, absolutely dependent upon me to save her from—from . . . She's the sweetest, loveliest girl! . . . In a few moments—sooner or later there'll be hell here! Dick, are you with me?"

Dick Gale drew a long, deep breath. A coldness, a lethargy, an indifference that had weighed upon him for months had passed out of his being. On the instant he could not speak, but his hand closed powerfully upon his friend's. Thorne's face changed wonderfully, the distress, the fear, the appeal all vanishing in a smile of passionate gratefulness.

Then Dick's gaze, attracted by some slight sound, shot over his friend's shoulder to see a face at the window—a handsome, bold, sneering face, with glittering dark eyes that flashed in sinister intentness.

Dick stiffened in his seat. Thorne, with sudden clenching of hands, wheeled toward the window.

"Rojas!" he whispered.

CHAPTER 2

MERCEDES CASTAÑEDA

The dark face vanished. Dick Gale heard footsteps and the tinkle of spurs. He strode to the window, and was in time to see a Mexican swagger into the front door of the saloon. Dick had only a glimpse; but in that he saw a huge black sombrero with a gaudy band, the back of a short, tight-fitting jacket, a heavy pearl-handled gun swinging with a fringe of sash, and close-fitting trousers spreading wide at the bottom. There were men passing in the street, also several Mexicans lounging against the hitching-rail at the curb.

"Did you see him? Where did he go?" whispered Thorne, as he joined Gale. "Those Greasers out there with the cartridge belts crossed over their breasts—they are rebels."

"I think he went into the saloon," replied Dick. "He had a gun, but for all I can see the Greasers out there are unarmed."

"Never believe it! There! Look, Dick! That fellow's a

guard, though he seems so unconcerned. See, he has a short carbine, almost concealed. . . . There's another Greaser farther down the path. I'm afraid Rojas has the house spotted."

"If we could only be sure."

"I'm sure, Dick. Let's cross the hall; I want to see how it looks from the other side of the house."

Gale followed Thorne out of the restaurant into the high-ceiled corridor which evidently divided the hotel, opening into the street and running back to a patio. A few dim yellow lamps flickered. A Mexican with a blanket round his shoulders stood in the front entrance. Back toward the patio there were sounds of boots on the stone floor. Shadows flitted across that end of the corridor. Thorne entered a huge chamber which was even more poorly lighted than the hall. It contained a table littered with papers, a few high-backed chairs, a couple of couches, and was evidently a parlor.

"Mercedes has been meeting me here," said Thorne. "At this hour she comes every moment or so to the head of the stairs there, and if I am here she comes down. Mostly there are people in this room a little later. We go out into the plaza. It faces the dark side of the house, and that's the place I must slip out with her if there's any chance at all to get away."

They peered out of the open window. The plaza was gloomy, and at first glance apparently deserted. In a moment, however, Gale made out a slow-pacing dark form on the path. Farther down there was another. No particular keenness was required to see in these forms a sentinel-like stealthiness.

Gripping Gale's arm, Thorne pulled back from the window.

"You saw them," he whispered. "It's just as I feared.

Rojas has the place surrounded. I should have taken Mercedes away. But I had no time—no chance! I'm bound! . . . . There's Mercedes now! My God! . . . . Dick, think—think if there's a way to get her out of this trap!"

Gale turned as his friend went down the room. In the dim light at the head of the stairs stood the slim, muffled figure of a woman. When she saw Thorne she flew noiselessly down the stairway to him. He caught her in his arms. Then she spoke softly, brokenly, in a low, swift voice. It was a mingling of incoherent Spanish and English; but to Gale it was mellow, deep, unutterably tender, a voice full of joy, fear, passion, hope, and love. Upon Gale it had an unaccountable effect. He found himself thrilling, wondering.

Thorne led the girl to the center of the room, under the light where Gale stood. She had raised a white hand, holding a black-lace mantilla half aside. Dick saw a small, dark head proudly held, an oval face half hidden, white as a flower, and magnificent black eyes.

Then Thorne spoke.

"Mercedes—Dick Gale, an old friend—the best friend I ever had."

She swept the mantilla back over her head, disclosing a lovely face, strange and striking to Gale in its pride and fire, its intensity.

"Señor Gale—ah! I cannot speak my happiness. His friend!"

"Yes, Mercedes; my friend and yours," said Thorne, speaking rapidly. "We'll have need of him. Dear, there's bad news and no time to break it gently. The priest did not come. He must have been detained. And listen—be brave, dear Mercedes—Rojas is here!"

She uttered an inarticulate cry, the poignant terror of

which shook Gale's nerve, and swayed as if she would faint. Thorne caught her, and in husky voice importuned her to bear up.

"My darling! For God's sake don't faint—don't go to pieces! We'd be lost! We've got a chance. We'll think of something. Be strong! Fight!"

It was plain to Gale that Thorne was distracted. He scarcely knew what he was saying. Pale and shaking, he clasped Mercedes to him. Her terror had struck him helpless. It was so intense—it was so full of horrible certainty of what fate awaited her.

She cried out in Spanish, beseeching him; and as he shook his head, she changed to English:

"Señor, my lover, I will be strong—I will fight—I will obey. But swear by my Virgin, if need be to save me from Rojas—you will kill me!"

"Mercedes! Yes, I'll swear," he replied, hoarsely. "I know—I'd rather have you dead than—But don't give up. Rojas can't be sure of you, or he wouldn't wait. He's in there. He's got his men there—all round us. But he hesitates. A beast like Rojas doesn't stand idle for nothing. I tell you we've a chance. Dick, here, will think of something. We'll slip away. Then he'll take you somewhere. Only—speak to him—show him you won't weaken. Mercedes, this is more than love and happiness for us. It's life or death."

She became quiet, and slowly recovered control of herself.

Suddenly she wheeled to face Gale with proud dark eyes, tragic sweetness of appeal, an exquisite grace.

"Señor, you are an American. You cannot know the Spanish blood—the peon bandit's hate and cruelty. I wish to die before Rojas's hand touches me. If he takes me alive, then the hour, the little day that my life lasts afterward will be torture—torture of hell. If I live two days his brutal men will have me. If I live three, the dogs of his camp. . . . Señor, have you a sister whom you love? Help Señor Thorne to save me. He is a soldier. He is bound. He must not betray his honor, his duty, for me. . . . Ah, you two splendid Americans—so big, so strong, so fierce! What is that little black half-breed slave Rojas to such men? Rojas is a coward. Now, let me waste no more precious time. I am ready. I will be brave."

She came close to Gale, holding out her white hands, a woman all fire and soul and passion. To Gale she was wonderful. His heart leaped. As he bent over her hands and kissed them he seemed to feel himself renewed, remade.

"Señorita," he said, "I am happy to be your servant. I can conceive of no greater pleasure than giving the service you require."

"And what is that?" inquired Thorne, hurriedly.

"That of incapacitating Señor Rojas for tonight, and perhaps several nights to come," repined Gale.

"Dick, what will you do?" asked Thorne, now in alarm.

"I'll make a row in that saloon," returned Dick, bluntly. "I'll start something. I'll rush Rojas and his crowd. I'll—"

"Lord, no; you mustn't, Dick—you'll be knifed!" cried Thorne. He was in distress, yet his eyes were shining.

"I'll take a chance. Maybe I can surprise that slow Greaser bunch and get away before they know what's happened. . . . You be ready watching at the window. When the row starts those fellows out there in the plaza will run into the saloon. Then you slip out, go straight through the plaza down the street. It's a dark street, I remember. I'll catch up with you before you get far."

Thorne gasped, but did not say a word. Mercedes

leaned against him, her white hands now at her breast, her great eyes watching Gale as he went out.

In the corridor Gale stopped long enough to pull on a pair of heavy gloves, to muss his hair, and disarrange his collar. Then he stepped into the restaurant, went through, and halted in the door leading into the saloon. His five feet eleven inches and one hundred and eighty pounds were more noticeable there, and it was part of his plan to attract attention to himself. No one, however, appeared to notice him. The pool-players were noisily intent on their game, the same crowd of motley-robed Mexicans hung over the reeking bar. Gale's roving glance soon fixed upon the man he took to be Rojas. He recognized the huge, high-peaked, black sombrero with its ornamented band. The Mexican's face was turned aside. He was in earnest, excited colloquy with a dozen or more comrades, most of whom were sitting round a table. They were listening, talking, drinking. The fact that they wore cartridge belts crossed over their breasts satisfied Gale that these were the rebels. He had noted the belts of the Mexicans outside, who were apparently guards. A waiter brought more drinks to this group at the table, and this caused the leader to turn so Gale could see his face. It was indeed the sinister, sneering face of the bandit Rojas. Gale gazed at the man with curiosity. He was under medium height, and striking in appearance only because of his dandified dress and evil visage. He wore a lace scarf, a tight, bright-buttoned jacket, a buckskin vest embroidered in red, a sash and belt joined by an enormous silver clasp. Gale saw again the pearl-handled gun swinging at the bandit's hip. Jewels flashed in his scarf. There were gold rings in his ears and diamonds on his fingers.

Gale became conscious of an inward fire that threatened to overrun his coolness. Other emotions harried his self-control. It seemed as if sight of the man liberated or created a devil in Gale. And at the bottom of his feelings there seemed to be a wonder at himself, a strange satisfaction for the something that had come to him.

He stepped out of the doorway, down the couple of steps to the floor of the saloon, and he staggered a little, simulating drunkenness. He fell over the pool tables, jostled Mexicans at the bar, laughed like a maudlin fool, and, with his hat slouched down, crowded here and there. Presently his eye caught sight of the group of cowboys whom he had before noticed with such interest.

They were still in a corner somewhat isolated. With fertile mind working, Gale lurched over to them. He remembered his many unsuccessful attempts to get acquainted with cowboys. If he were to get any help from these silent aloof rangers it must be by striking fire from them in one swift stroke. Planting himself squarely before the two tall cowboys who were standing, he looked straight into their lean, bronzed faces. He spared a full moment for that keen, cool gaze before he spoke.

"I'm not drunk. I'm throwing a bluff, and I mean to start a rough house. I'm going to rush that damned bandit Rojas. It's to save a girl—to give her lover, who is my friend, a chance to escape with her. She's in the house. Rojas is here to get her. When I start a row my friend will try to slip out with her. Every door and window is watched. I've got to raise hell to draw the guards in. . . . Well, you're my countrymen. We're in Mexico. A beautiful girl's honor and life are at stake. Now, gentlemen, watch me!"

One cowboy's eyes narrowed, blinking a little, and his lean jaw dropped; the other's hard face rippled with a fleeting smile.

Gale backed away, and his pulse leaped when he saw the two cowboys, as if with one purpose, slowly stride after him. Then Gale swerved, staggering along, brushed against the tables, kicked over the empty chairs. He passed Rojas and his gang, and out of the tail of his eye saw that the bandit was watching him, waving his hands and talking fiercely. The hum of the many voices grew louder, and when Dick lurched against a table, overturning it and spilling glasses into the laps of several Mexicans, there arose a shrill cry. He had succeeded in attracting attention; almost every face turned his way. One of the insulted men, a little tawny fellow, leaped up to confront Gale, and in a frenzy screamed a volley of Spanish, of which Gale distinguished "Gringo!" The Mexican stamped and made a threatening move with his right hand. Dick swung his leg and with a swift side kick knocked the fellow's feet from under him, whirling him down with a thud.

The action was performed so suddenly, so adroitly, it made the Mexican such a weakling, so like a tumbled tenpin, that the shrill jabbering hushed. Gale knew this to be the significant moment.

Wheeling, he rushed at Rojas. It was his old line-breaking plunge. Neither Rojas nor his men had time to move. The black-skinned bandit's face turned a dirty white; his jaw dropped; he would have shrieked if Gale had not hit him. The blow swept him backward against his men. Then Gale's heavy body, swiftly following with the momentum of that rush, struck the little group of rebels. They went down with table and chairs in a sliding crash.

Gale, carried by his plunge, went with them. Like a cat he landed on top. As he rose his powerful hands fastened on Rojas. He jerked the little bandit off the tangled pile of struggling, yelling men, and, swinging him with terrific force, let go his hold. Rojas slid along the floor, knocking over tables and chairs. Gale bounded back, dragged Rojas up, handling him as if he were a limp sack.

A shot rang out above the yells. Gale heard the jingle of breaking glass. The room darkened perceptibly. He flashed a glance backward. The two cowboys were between him and the crowd of frantic rebels. One cowboy held two guns low down, level in front of him. The other had his gun raised and aimed. On the instant it spouted red and white. With the crack came the crashing of glass, another darkening shade over the room. With a cry Gale slung the bleeding Rojas from him. The bandit struck a table, toppled over it, fell, and lay prone.

Another shot made the room full of moving shadows, with light only back of the bar. A white-clad figure rushed at Gale. He tripped the man, but had to kick hard to disengage himself from grasping hands. Another figure closed in on Gale. This one was dark, swift. A blade glinted—described a circle aloft. Simultaneously with a close, red flash the knife wavered; the man wielding it stumbled backward. In the din Gale did not hear a report, but the Mexican's fall was significant. Then pandemonium broke loose. The din became a roar. Gale heard shots that sounded like dull spats in the distance. The big lamp behind the bar seemingly split, then sputtered and went out, leaving the room in darkness.

Gale leaped toward the restaurant door, which was outlined faintly by the yellow light within. Right and left he pushed the groping men who jostled with him. He vaulted a pool table, sent tables and chairs flying, and gained the door, to be the first of a wedging mob to squeeze through. One sweep of his arm knocked the restaurant lamp from its stand; and he ran out, leaving darkness behind him. A few bounds took him into the parlor. It was deserted. Thorne had gotten away with Mercedes!

It was then Gale slowed up. For the space of perhaps sixty seconds he had been moving with startling velocity. He peered cautiously out into the plaza. The paths, the benches, the shady places under the trees contained no skulking men. He ran out, keeping to the shade, and did not go into the path till he was halfway through the plaza. Under a street lamp at the far end of the path he thought he saw two dark figures. He ran faster, and soon reached the street. The uproar back in the hotel began to diminish, or else he was getting out of hearing. The few people he saw close at hand were all coming his way, and only the foremost showed any excitement. Gale walked swiftly, peering ahead for two figures. Presently he saw them—one tall, wearing a cape; the other slight, mantled. Gale drew a sharp breath of relief. Thorne and Mercedes were not far ahead.

From time to time Thorne looked back. He strode swiftly, almost carrying Mercedes, who clung closely to him. She, too, looked back. Once Gale saw her white face flash in the light of a street lamp. He began to overhaul them; and soon when the last lamp had been passed and the street was dark, he ventured a whistle. Thorne heard it, for he turned, whistled a low reply, and went on. Not for some distance beyond, where the street ended in open country, did they halt to wait. The desert began here. Gale felt the soft sand under his feet and saw the grotesque forms of cactus. Then he came up with the fugitives.

"Dick! Are you—all right?" panted Thorne, grasping Gale.

"I'm—out of breath—but—OK," replied Gale.

"Good! Good!" choked Thorne. "I was scared—

helpless. . . . Dick, it worked splendidly. We had no trouble. What on earth did you do?"

"I made the row, all right," said Dick.

"Good Heavens! It was like a row I once heard made by a mob. But the shots, Dick—were they at you? They paralyzed me. Then the yells. What happened? Those guards of Rojas ran round in front at the first shot. Tell me what happened."

"While I was rushing Rojas a couple of cowboys shot out the lamplights. A Mexican who pulled a knife on me got hurt, I guess. Then I think there was some shooting from the rebels after the room was dark."

"Rushing Rojas?" queried Thorne, leaning close to Dick. His voice was thrilling, exultant, deep with a joy that yet needed confirmation. "What did you do to him?"

"I handed him one off side, tackled, then tried a forward pass," replied Dick, lightly speaking the football vernacular so familiar to Thorne.

Thorne leaned closer, his fine face showing fierce and corded in the starlight. "Tell me straight," he demanded, in thick voice.

Gale then divined something of the suffering Thorne had undergone—something of the hot, wild, vengeful passion of a lover who must have brutal truth.

It stilled Dick's lighter mood, and he was about to reply when Mercedes pressed close to him, touched his hands, and looked up into his face with wonderful eyes. He thought he would not soon forget their beauty—the shadow of pain that had been, the hope dawning so fugitively.

"Dear lady," said Gale, with voice not wholly steady. "Rojas himself will hound you no more tonight, nor for many nights."

She seemed to shake, to thrill, to rise with the intelligence.

She pressed his hand close over her heaving breast. Gale felt the quick throb of her heart.

"Señor! Señor Dick!" she cried. Then her voice failed. But her hands flew up; quick as a flash she raised her face—kissed him. Then she turned and with a sob fell into Thorne's arms.

There ensued a silence broken only by Mercedes's sobbing. Gale walked some paces away. If he were not stunned, he certainly was agitated. The strange, sweet fire of that girl's lips remained with him. On the spur of the moment he imagined he had a jealousy of Thorne. But presently this passed. It was only that he had been deeply moved—stirred to the depths during the last hour—had become conscious of the awakening of a spirit. What remained with him now was the splendid glow of gladness that he had been of service to Thorne. And by the intensity of Mercedes's abandon of relief and gratitude he measured her agony of terror and the fate he had spared her.

"Dick, Dick, come here!" called Thorne, softly. "Let's pull ourselves together now. We've got a problem yet. What to do? Where to go? How to get anyplace? We don't dare risk the station—the corrals where Mexicans hire out horses. We're on good old U.S. ground this minute, but we're not out of danger."

As he paused, evidently hoping for a suggestion from Gale, the silence was broken by the clear, ringing peal of a bugle. Thorne gave a violent start. Then he bent over, listening. The beautiful notes of the bugle floated out of the darkness, clearer, sharper, faster.

"It's a call, Dick! It's a call!" he cried.

Gale had no answer to make. Mercedes stood as if stricken. The bugle call ended. From a distance another faintly pealed. There were other sounds too remote to recognize. Then scattering shots rattled out.

"Dick, the rebels are fighting somebody," burst out Thorne, excitedly. "The little federal garrison still holds its stand. Perhaps it is attacked again. Anyway, there's something doing over the line. Maybe the crazy Greasers are firing on our camp. We've feared it—in the dark. . . . And here I am, away without leave—practically a deserter!"

"Go back! Go back, before you're too late!" cried Mercedes.

"Better make tracks, Thorne," added Gale. "It can't help our predicament for you to be arrested. I'll take care of Mercedes."

"No, no, no," replied Thorne. "I can get away—avoid arrest."

"That'd be all right for the immediate present. But it's not best for the future. George, a deserter is a deserter! . . . Better hurry. Leave the girl to me till to-morrow."

Mercedes embraced her lover, begged him to go. Thorne wavered.

"Dick, I'm up against it," he said. "You're right. If only I can run back in time. But, oh, I hate to leave her! Old fellow, you've saved her! I already owe you everlasting gratitude. Keep out of Casita, Dick. The U.S. side might be safe, but I'm afraid to trust it at night. Go out in the desert, up in the mountains, in some safe place. Then come to me in camp. We'll plan. I'll have to confide in Colonel Weede. Maybe he'll help us. Hide her from the rebels—that's all."

He wrung Dick's hand, clasped Mercedes tightly in his arms, kissed her, and murmured low over her, then released her to rush off into the darkness. He disappeared in the gloom. The sound of his dull footfalls gradually died away.

For a moment the desert silence oppressed Gale. He was unaccustomed to such strange stillness. There was a low stir of sand, a rustle of stiff leaves in the wind. How white the stars burned! Then a coyote barked, to be bayed by a dog. Gale realized that he was between the edge of an unknown desert and the edge of a hostile town. He had to choose the desert, because, though he had no doubt that in Casita there were many Americans who might befriend him, he could not chance the risks of seeking them at night.

He felt a slight touch on his arm, felt it move down, felt Mercedes slip a trembling cold little hand into his. Dick looked at her. She seemed a white-faced girl now, with staring, frightened black eyes that flashed up at him. If the loneliness, the silence, the desert, the unknown dangers of the night affected him, what must they be to this hunted, driven girl? Gale's heart swelled. He was alone with her. He had no weapon, no money, no food, no drink, no covering, nothing except his two hands. He had absolutely no knowledge of the desert, of the direction or whereabouts of the boundary line between the republics; he did not know where to find the railroad, or any road or trail, or whether or not there were towns near or far. It was a critical, desperate situation. He thought first of the girl, and groaned in spirit, prayed that it would be given him to save her. When he remembered himself it was with the stunning consciousness that he could conceive of no situation which he would have exchanged for this one—where fortune had set him a perilous task of loyalty to a friend, to a helpless girl.

"Señor, señor!" suddenly whispered Mercedes, clinging to him. "Listen! I hear horses coming!"

CHAPTER 3

A FLIGHT INTO
THE DESERT

Uneasy and startled, Gale listened and, hearing nothing, wondered if Mercedes's fears had not worked upon her imagination. He felt a trembling seize her, and he held her hands tightly.

"You were mistaken, I guess," he whispered.

"No, no, señor."

Dick turned his ear to the soft wind. Presently he heard, or imagined he heard, low beats. Like the first faint, far-off beats of a drumming grouse, they recalled to him the Illinois forests of his boyhood. In a moment he was certain the sounds were the padlike steps of hoofs in yielding sand. The regular tramp was not that of grazing horses.

On the instant, made cautious and stealthy by alarm, Gale drew Mercedes deeper into the gloom of the shrubbery. Sharp pricks from thorns warned him that he was pressing into a cactus growth, and he protected Mercedes as best he could. She was shaking as one with a severe chill. She breathed with little hurried pants and leaned upon him almost in collapse. Gale ground his teeth in helpless rage at the girl's fate. If she had not been beautiful she might still have been free and happy in her home. What a strange world to live in—how unfair was fate!

The sounds of hoofbeats grew louder. Gale made out a dark moving mass against a background of dull gray. There was a line of horses. He could not discern whether or not all the horses carried riders. The murmur of a voice struck his ear—then a low laugh. It made him tingle, for it sounded American. Eagerly he listened. There was an interval when only the hoofbeats could be heard.

"It shore was, Laddy, it shore was," came a voice out of the darkness. "Rough house! Laddy, since wire fences drove us out of Texas we ain't seen the like of that. An' we never had such a call."

"Call? It was a burnin' roast," replied another voice. "I felt low down. He vamoosed some sudden, an' I hope he an' his friends shook the dust of Casita. That's a rotten town, Jim."

Gale jumped up in joy. What luck! The speakers were none other than the two cowboys whom he had accosted in the Mexican hotel.

"Hold on, fellows," he called out, and strode into the road.

The horses snorted and stamped. Then followed swift rustling sounds—a clinking of spurs, then silence. The figures loomed clearer in the gloom. Gale saw five or six horses, two with riders, and one other, at least, carrying a pack. When Gale got within fifteen feet of the group the foremost horseman said:

"I reckon that's close enough, stranger."

Something in the cowboy's hand glinted darkly bright in the starlight.

"You'd recognize me, if it wasn't so dark," replied Gale, halting. "I spoke to you a little while ago—in the saloon back there."

"Come over an' let's see you," said the cowboy, curtly.

Gale advanced till he was close to the horse. The cowboy leaned over the saddle and peered into Gale's face. Then, without a word, he sheathed the gun and held out his hand. Gale met a grip of steel that warmed his blood. The other cowboy got off his nervous, spirited horse and threw the bridle. He, too, peered closely into Gale's face.

"My name's Ladd," he said. "Reckon I'm some glad to meet you again."

Gale felt another grip as hard and strong as the other had been. He realized he had found friends who belonged to a class of men whom he had despaired of ever knowing.

"Gale—Dick Gale is my name," he began, swiftly. "I dropped into Casita tonight hardly knowing where I was. A boy took me to that hotel. There I met an old friend whom I had not seen for years. He belongs to the cavalry stationed here. He had befriended a Spanish girl—fallen in love with her. Rojas had killed this girl's father—tried to abduct her . . . You know what took place at the hotel. Gentlemen, if it's ever possible, I'll show you how I appreciate what you did for me there. I got away, found my friend with the girl. We hurried out here beyond the edge of the town. Then Thorne had to make a break for camp. We heard bugle calls, shots, and he was away without leave. That left the girl with me. I don't know what to do. Thorne swears Casita is no place for Mercedes at night."

"The girl ain't no peon, no common Greaser?" interrupted Ladd.

"No. Her name is Castañeda. She belongs to an old Spanish family, once rich and influential."

"Reckoned as much," replied the cowboy. "There's more than Rojas's wantin' to kidnap a pretty girl. Shore he does that every day or so. Must be somethin' political or feelin' against class. Well, Casita ain't no place for your friend's girl at night or day, or any time. Shore, there's Americans who'd take her in an' fight for her, if necessary. But it ain't wise to risk that. Lash, what do you say?"

"It's been gettin' hotter round this Greaser corral for some weeks," replied the other cowboy. "If that two-bit of a garrison surrenders, there's no tellin' what'll happen. Orozco is headin' west from Agua Prieta with his guerrillas. Campo is burnin' bridges an' tearin' up the railroad south of Nogales. Then there's all these bandits callin' themselves revolutionists just for an excuse to steal, burn, kill, an' ride off with women. It's plain facts, Laddy, an' bein' across the U.S. line a few inches or so don't make no hell of a difference. My advice is, don't let Miss Castañeda ever set foot in Casita again."

"Looks like you've shore spoke sense," said Ladd. "I reckon, Gale, you an' the girl ought to come with us. Casita shore would be a little warm for us to-morrow. We didn't kill anybody, but I shot a Greaser's arm off, an' Lash strained friendly relations by destroyin' property. We know people who'll take care of the señorita till your friend can come for her."

Dick warmly spoke his gratefulness, and, inexpressibly relieved and happy for Mercedes, he went toward the clump of cactus where he had left her. She stood erect, waiting, and, dark as it was, he could tell she had lost the terror that had so shaken her.

"Señor Gale, you are my good angel," she said, tremulously.

"I've been lucky to fall in with these men, and I'm glad with all my heart," he replied. "Come."

He led her into the road up to the cowboys, who now stood bareheaded in the starlight. They seemed shy, and Lash was silent while Ladd made embarrassed, unintelligible reply to Mercedes's thanks.

There were five horses—two saddled, two packed and the remaining one carried only a blanket. Ladd shortened the stirrups on his mount, and helped Mercedes up into the saddle. From the way she settled herself and took the few restive prances of the mettlesome horse Gale judged that she could ride. Lash urged Gale to take his horse. But this Gale refused to do.

"I'll walk," he said. "I'm used to walking. I know cowboys are not."

They tried again to persuade him, without avail. Then Ladd started off, riding bareback. Mercedes fell in behind, with Gale walking beside her. The two pack animals came next, and Lash brought up the rear.

Once started with protection assured for the girl and a real objective point in view, Gale relaxed from the tense strain he had been laboring under. How glad he would have been to acquaint Thorne with their good fortune! Later, of course, there would be some way to get word to the cavalryman. But till then what torments his friend would suffer!

It seemed to Dick that a very long time had elapsed since he stepped off the train; and one by one he went over every detail of incident which had occurred between that arrival and the present moment. Strange as the facts were, he had no doubts. He realized that before that night he had never known the deeps of wrath undisturbed in him; had never conceived even a passing idea that it was possible for him to try to kill a man. His right hand was swollen stiff, so sore that he could scarcely close it. His knuckles were bruised and bleeding, and ached with a sharp pain. Considering the thickness of his heavy glove, Gale was of the opinion that so to bruise his hand he must have struck Rojas a powerful blow. He remembered that for him to give or take a blow had been nothing. This blow to Rojas, however, had been a different matter. The hot wrath which had been his motive was not puzzling; but the effect on him after he had cooled off, a subtle difference, something puzzled and eluded him. The more it baffled him the more he pondered. All those wandering months of his had been filled with dissatisfaction, yet he had been too apathetic to understand himself. So he had not been much of a person to try. Perhaps it had not been the blow to Rojas any more than other things that had wrought some change in him.

His meeting with Thorne; the wonderful black eyes of a Spanish girl; her appeal to him; the hate inspired by Rojas, and the rush, the blow, the action; sight of Thorne and Mercedes hurrying safely away; the girl's hands pressing his to her heaving breast; the sweet fire of her kiss; the fact of her being alone with him, dependent upon him—all these things Gale turned over and over in his mind, only to fail of any definite conclusion as to which had affected him so remarkably, or to tell what had really happened to him.

Had he fallen in love with Thorne's sweetheart? The idea came in a flash. Was he, all in an instant, and by one of those incomprehensible reversals of character, jealous of his friend? Dick was almost afraid to look up at Mercedes. Still he forced himself to do so, and as it chanced Mercedes was looking down at him. Somehow the light was better, and he clearly saw her white face, her black and starry eyes, her perfect mouth. With a quick, graceful impulsiveness she put her hand upon his shoulder. Like her appearance, the action was new, strange, striking to Gale; but it brought home suddenly to him the nature of gratitude and affection in a girl of her blood. It was sweet and sisterly. He knew then that he had not fallen in love with her. The feeling that was akin to jealousy seemed to be of the beautiful something for which Mercedes stood in Thorne's life. Gale then grasped the bewildering possibilities, the infinite wonder of what a girl could mean to a man.

The other haunting intimations of change seemed to be elusively blended with sensations—the heat and thrill of action, the sense of something done and more to do, the utter vanishing of an old weary hunt for he knew not what. Maybe it had been a hunt for work, for energy, for spirit, for love, for his real self. Whatever it might be, there appeared to be now some hope of finding it.

The desert began to lighten. Gray openings in the border of shrubby growths changed to paler hue. The road could be seen some rods ahead, and it had become a stony descent down, steadily down. Dark, ridged backs of mountains bounded the horizon, and all seemed near at hand, hemming in the plain. In the east a white glow grew brighter and brighter, reaching up to a line of cloud, defined sharply below by a rugged notched range. Presently a silver circle rose behind the black mountain, and the gloom of the desert underwent a transformation. From a gray mantle it changed to a transparent haze. The moon was rising.

"Señor, I am cold," said Mercedes.

Dick had been carrying his coat upon his arm. He had felt warm, even hot, and had imagined that the steady walk had occasioned it. But his skin was cool. The heat came from an inward burning. He stopped the horse and raised the coat up, and helped Mercedes put it on.

"I should have thought of you," he said. "But I seemed to feel warm. . . . The coat's a little large; we might wrap it around you twice."

Mercedes smiled and lightly thanked him in Spanish. The flash of mood was in direct contrast to the appealing, passionate, and tragic states in which he had successively viewed her; and it gave him a vivid impression of what vivacity and charm she might possess under happy conditions. He was about to start when he observed that Ladd had halted and was peering ahead in evident caution. Mercedes's horse began to stamp impatiently, raised his ears and head, and acted as if he was about to neigh.

A warning "hist" from Ladd bade Dick put a quieting hand on the horse. Lash came noiselessly forward to join his companion. The two then listened and watched.

An uneasy yet thrilling stir ran through Gale's veins. This scene was not fancy. These men of the ranges had heard or seen or scented danger. It was all real, as tangible and sure as the touch of Mercedes's hand upon his arm. Probably for her the night had terrors beyond Gale's power to comprehend. He looked down into the desert, and would have felt no surprise at anything hidden away among the bristling cactus, the dark, winding arroyos, the shadowed rocks with their moonlit tips, the ragged plain leading to the black bold mountains. The wind appeared to blow softly, with an almost imperceptible moan, over the desert. That was a new sound to Gale. But he heard nothing more.

Presently Lash went to the rear and Ladd started ahead. The progress now, however, was considerably slower, not owing to a bad road—for that became better—but probably owing to caution exercised by the cowboy guide. At the end of a half hour this marked deliberation changed, and the horses followed Ladd's at a gait that put Gale to his best walking-paces.

Meanwhile the moon soared high above the black corrugated peaks. The gray, the gloom, the shadow whitened. The clearing of the dark foreground appeared to lift a distant veil and show endless aisles of desert reaching down between dim horizon-bounding ranges.

Gale gazed abroad, knowing that as this night was the first time for him to awake to consciousness of a vague, wonderful other self, so it was one wherein he began to be aware of an encroaching presence of physical things—the immensity of the star-studded sky, the soaring moon, the bleak, mysterious mountains, and limitless slope, and plain, and ridge, and valley. These things in all their magnificence had not been unnoticed by him before; only now they spoke a different meaning. A voice that he had never heard called him to see, to feel the vast hard externals of heaven and earth, all that represented the open, the free, silence and solitude and space.

Once more his thoughts, like his steps, were halted by Ladd's actions. The cowboy reined in his horse, listened a moment, then swung down out of the saddle. He raised a cautioning hand to the others, then slipped into the gloom and disappeared. Gale marked that the halt had been made in a ridged and cut-up pass between low mesas. He could see the columns of cactus standing out black against the moon-white sky. The horses were evidently tiring, for they showed no impatience. Gale heard their panting breaths, and also the bark of some animal—a dog or a coyote. It sounded like a dog, and this led Gale to wonder if there was any house near at hand. To the right, up under the ledges some distance away, stood two square black objects, too uniform, he thought, to be rocks. While he was peering at them, uncertain what to think, the shrill whistle of a horse pealed out, to be followed by the rattling of hoofs on hard stone. Then a dog barked. At the same moment that Ladd hurriedly appeared in the road a light shone out and danced before one of the square black objects.

"Keep close an' don't make no noise," he whispered, and led his horse at right angles off the road.

Gale followed, leading Mercedes's horse. As he turned he observed that Lash also had dismounted.

To keep closely at Ladd's heels without brushing the cactus or stumbling over rocks and depressions was a task Gale found impossible. After he had been stabbed several times by the bayonetlike spikes, which seemed invisible, the matter of caution became equally one of self-preservation. Both the cowboys, Dick had observed, wore leather chaps. It was no easy matter to lead a spirited horse through the dark, winding lanes walled by thorns. Mercedes's horse often balked and had to be coaxed and carefully guided. Dick concluded that Ladd was making a wide detour. The position of certain stars grown familiar during the march veered round from one side to another. Dick saw that the travel was fast, but by no means noiseless. The pack animals at times crashed and ripped through the narrow places. It seemed to Gale that any one within a mile could have heard these sounds. From the tops of knolls or ridges he looked back, trying to locate the mesas where the light had danced and the dog had barked alarm. He could not distinguish these two rocky eminences from among many rising in the background.

Presently Ladd led out into a wider lane that appeared to run straight. The cowboy mounted his horse, and this fact convinced Gale that they had circled back to the road. The march proceeded then once more at a good, steady, silent walk. When Dick consulted his watch he was amazed to see the hour was still early. How much had happened in little time! He now began to be aware that the night was growing colder; and, strange to him, he felt something damp that in a country he knew he would have recognized as dew. He had not been aware there was dew on the desert. The wind blew stronger, the stars shone whiter, the sky grew darker, and the moon climbed toward the zenith. The road stretched level for miles, then crossed arroyos and ridges, wound between mounds of broken ruined rock, found a level again, and then began a long ascent. Dick asked Mercedes if she was cold, and she answered that she was, speaking especially of her feet, which were growing numb. Then she asked to be helped down to walk awhile. At first she was cold and lame, and accepted the helping hand Dick proffered. After a little, however, she recovered and went on without assistance. Dick could scarcely believe his eyes, as from time to time he stole a sidelong glance at this silent girl, who walked with lithe and rapid stride. She was wrapped in his long coat, yet it did not hide her slender grace. He could not see her face, which was concealed by the black mantle.

A low-spoken word from Ladd recalled Gale to the question of surroundings and of possible dangers. Ladd had halted a few yards ahead. They had reached the summit of what was evidently a high ridge which sloped with much greater steepness on the far side. It was only after a few more forward steps, however, that Dick could see down the slope. Then full in view flashed a bright campfire around which clustered a group of dark figures. They were encamped in a wide arroyo, where horses could be seen grazing in black patches of grass between clusters of trees. A second look at the campers told Gale they were Mexicans. At this moment Lash came forward to join Ladd, and the two spent a long, uninterrupted moment studying the arroyo. A hoarse laugh, faint yet distinct, floated up on the cool wind.

"Well, Laddy, what 'r you makin' of that outfit?" inquired Lash, speaking softly.

"Same as any of them raider outfits," replied Ladd. "They're across the line for beef. But they'll run off any good stock. As hoss thieves these rebels have got 'em all beat. That outfit is waitin' till it's late. There's a ranch up the arroyo."

Gale heard the first speaker curse under his breath.

"Sure, I feel the same," said Ladd. "But we've got a girl an' the young man to look after, not to mention our pack outfit. An' we're huntin' for a job, not a fight, old hoss. Keep on your chaps!"

"Nothin' to it but head south for the Rio Forlorn."

"You're talkin' sense now, Jim. I wish we'd headed that way long ago. But it ain't strange I'd want to travel away from the border, thinkin' of the girl. Jim, we can't go round this Greaser outfit an' strike the road again. Too rough. So we'll have to give up gettin' to San Felipe."

"Perhaps it's just as well, Laddy. Rio Forlorn is on the borderline, but it's country where these rebels ain't been yet."

"Wait till they learn of the oasis an' Beldin's hosses!" exclaimed Laddy. "I'm not anticipatin' peace anywhere along the border, Jim. But we can't go ahead; we can't go back."

"What'll we do, Laddy? It's a hike to Beldin's ranch. An' if we get there in daylight some Greaser will see the girl before Beldin' can hide her. It'll get talked about. The news'll travel to Casita like sage balls before the wind."

"Shore we won't ride into Rio Forlorn in the daytime. Let's slip the packs, Jim. We can hide them off in the cactus an' come back after them. With the young man ridin' we—"

The whispering was interrupted by a loud ringing neigh that whistled up from the arroyo. One of the horses had scented the travelers on the ridge-top. The indifference of the Mexicans changed to attention.

Ladd and Lash turned back and led the horses into the first opening on the south side of the road. There was nothing more said at the moment, and manifestly the cowboys were in a hurry. Gale had to run in the open places to keep up. When they did stop it was welcome to Gale, for he had begun to fall behind.

The packs were slipped, securely tied and hidden in a mesquite clump. Ladd strapped a blanket around one of the horses. His next move was to take off his chaps.

"Gale, you're wearin' boots, an' by liftin' your feet you can beat the cactus," he whispered. "But the—the—Miss Castañeda, she'll be torn all to pieces unless she puts these on. Please tell her—an' hurry."

Dick took the chaps, and, going up to Mercedes, he explained the situation. She laughed, evidently at his embarrassed earnestness, and slipped out of the saddle.

"Señor, chapparejos and I are not strangers," she said.

Deftly and promptly she equipped herself, and then Gale helped her into the saddle, called to her horse, and started off. Lash directed Gale to mount the other saddled horse and go next.

Dick had not ridden a hundred yards behind the trotting leaders before he had sundry painful encounters with reaching cactus arms. The horse missed these by a narrow margin. Dick's knees appeared to be in line, and it became necessary for him to lift them high and let his boots take the onslaught of the spikes. He was at home in the saddle, and the accomplishment was about the only one he possessed that had been of any advantage during his sojourn in the West.

Ladd pursued a zigzag course southward across the desert, trotting down the aisles, cantering in wide, bare patches, walking through the clumps of cacti. The desert seemed all of a sameness to Dick—a wilderness of rocks and jagged growths hemmed in by lowering ranges, always looking close, yet never growing any nearer. The moon slanted back toward the west, losing its white radiance, and the gloom of the earlier evening began to creep into the washes and to darken under the mesas. By and by Ladd entered an arroyo, and here the travelers turned and twisted with the meanderings of a dry streambed. At the head of the cañon they had to take once more to the rougher ground. Always it led down, always it grew rougher, more rolling, with wider bare spaces, always the black ranges loomed close.

Gale became chilled to the bone, and his clothes were damp and cold. His knees smarted from the wounds of the poisoned thorns, and his right hand was either swollen stiff or too numb to move. Moreover, he was tiring. The excitement, the long walk, the miles on miles of jolting trot—these had wearied him. Mercedes must be made of steel, he thought, to stand all that she had been subjected to and yet, when the stars were paling and dawn perhaps not far away, stay in the saddle.

So Dick Gale rode on, drowsier for each mile, and more and more giving the horse a choice of ground. Sometimes a prod from a murderous spine roused Dick. A grayness had blotted out the waning moon in the west and the clear, dark, starry sky overhead. Once when Gale, thinking to fight his weariness, raised his head, he saw that one of the horses in the lead was riderless. Ladd was carrying Mercedes. Dick marveled that her collapse had not come sooner. Another time, rousing himself again, he imagined they were now on a good hard road.

It seemed that hours passed, though he knew only little time had elapsed, when once more he threw off the spell of weariness. He heard a dog bark. Tall trees lined the open lane down which he was riding. Presently in the gray gloom he saw low, square houses with flat roofs. Ladd turned off to the left down another lane, gloomy between trees. Every few rods there was one of the squat houses. This lane opened into wider, lighter space. The cold air bore a sweet perfume—whether of flowers or fruit Dick could not tell. Ladd rode on for perhaps a quarter of a mile, though it seemed interminably long to Dick. A grove of trees loomed dark in the gray of morning. Ladd entered it and was lost in the shade. Dick rode on among trees. Presently he heard voices, and soon another house, low and flat like the others, but so long he could not see the farther end, stood up blacker than the trees. As he dismounted, cramped and sore, he could scarcely stand. Lash came alongside. He spoke, and someone with a big, hearty voice replied to him. Then it seemed to Dick that he was led into blackness like pitch, where, presently, he felt blankets thrown on him, and then his drowsy faculties faded.

CHAPTER 4

FORLORN RIVER

When Dick opened his eyes a flood of golden sunshine streamed in at the open window under which he lay. His first thought was one of blank wonder as to where in the world he happened to be. The room was large, square, adobe-walled. It was littered with saddles, harness, blankets. Upon the floor was a bed spread out upon a tarpaulin. Probably this was where someone had slept. The sight of huge dusty spurs, a gun belt with sheath and gun, and a pair of leather chaps bristling with broken cactus thorns recalled to Dick the cowboys, the ride, Mercedes, and the whole strange adventure that had brought him there.

He did not recollect having removed his boots; indeed, upon second thought, he knew he had not done so. But there they stood upon the floor. Ladd and Lash must have taken them off when he was so exhausted and sleepy that he could not tell what was happening. He felt a dead weight of complete lassitude, and he did not want to move.

A sudden pain in his hand caused him to hold it up. It was black and blue, swollen to almost twice its normal size, and stiff as a board. The knuckles were skinned and crusted with dry blood. Dick soliloquized that it was the worst-looking hand he had seen since football days, and that it would inconvenience him for some time.

A warm, dry, fragrant breeze came through the window. Dick caught again the sweet smell of flowers or fruit. He heard the fluttering of leaves, the murmur of running water, the twittering of birds, then the sound of approaching footsteps and voices. The door at the far end of the room was open. Through it he saw poles of peeled wood upholding a porch roof, a bench, rosebushes in bloom, grass, and beyond these bright-green foliage of trees.

"He shore was sleepin' when I looked in an hour ago," said a voice that Dick recognized as Ladd's.

"Let him sleep," came the reply in deep, good-natured tones. "Mrs. B. says the girl's never moved. Must have been a tough ride for them both. Forty miles through cactus!"

"Young Gale hoofed darn near half the way," replied Ladd. "We tried to make him ride one of our hosses. If we had, we'd never got here. A walk like that'd killed me an' Jim."

"Well, Laddy, I'm right down glad to see you boys, and I'll do all I can for the young couple," said the other. "But I'm doing some worry here; don't mistake me."

"About your stock?"

"I've got only a few head of cattle at the oasis now. I'm worrying some, mostly about my horses. The U.S. is doing some worrying, too, don't mistake me. The rebels have worked west and north as far as Casita. There are no cavalrymen along the line beyond Casita, and there can't be. It's practically waterless desert. But these rebels are desert men. They could cross the line beyond the Rio Forlorn and smuggle arms into Mexico. Of course, my job is to keep tab on Chinese and Japs trying to get into the U.S. from Magdalena Bay. But I'm supposed to patrol the borderline. I'm going to hire some rangers. Now, I'm not so afraid of being shot up, though out in this lonely place there's danger of it; what I'm afraid of most is losing that bunch of horses. If any rebels come this far, or if they ever hear of my horses, they're going to raid me. You know what those guerrilla Mexicans will do for horses. They're crazy on horseflesh. They know fine horses. They breed the finest in the world. So I don't sleep nights any more."

"Reckon me an' Jim might as well tie up with you for a spell, Beldin'. We've been ridin' up an' down Arizona tryin' to keep out of sight of wire fences."

"Laddy, it's open enough around Forlorn River to satisfy even an old-time cowpuncher like you," laughed Belding. "I'd take your staying on as some favor, don't mistake me. Perhaps I can persuade the young man Gale to take a job with me."

"That's shore likely. He said he had no money, no friends. An' if a scrapper's all you're lookin' for he'll do," replied Ladd, with a dry chuckle.

"Mrs. B. will throw some broncho capers round this ranch when she hears I'm going to hire a stranger."

"Why?"

"Well, there's Nell—And you said this Gale was a young American. My wife will be scared to death for fear Nell will fall in love with him."

Laddy choked off a laugh, then evidently slapped his knee or Belding's, for there was a resounding smack.

"He's a fine-spoken, good-looking chap, you said?" went on Belding.

"Shore he is," said Laddy, warmly. "What do you say, Jim?"

By this time Dick Gale's ears began to burn and he was trying to make himself deaf when he wanted to hear every little word.

"Husky young fellow, nice voice, steady, clear eyes, kinda proud, I thought, an' some handsome, he was," replied Jim Lash.

"Maybe I ought to think twice before taking a stranger into my family," said Belding, seriously. "Well, I guess he's all right, Laddy, being the cavalryman's friend. No bum or lunger? He must be all right?"

"Bum? Lunger? Say, didn't I tell you I shook hands with this boy an' was plumb glad to meet him?" demanded Laddy, with considerable heat. Manifestly he had been affronted. "Tom Beldin', he's a gentleman, an' he could lick you in—in half a second. How about that, Jim?"

"Less time," replied Lash. "Tom, here's my stand. Young Gale can have my hoss, my gun, anythin' of mine."

"Aw, I didn't mean to insult you, boys, don't mistake me," said Belding. "Course he's all right."

The object of this conversation lay quiet upon his bed, thrilling and amazed at being so championed by the cowboys, delighted with Belding's idea of employing him, and much amused with the quaint seriousness of the three.

"How's the young man?" called a woman's voice. It was kind and mellow and earnest.

Gale heard footsteps on flagstones.

"He's asleep yet, wife," replied Belding. "Guess he was

pretty much knocked out. . . . I'll close the door there so we won't wake him."

There were slow, soft steps, then the door softly closed. But the fact scarcely made a perceptible difference in the sound of the voices outside.

"Laddy and Jim are going to stay," went on Belding. "It'll be like the old Panhandle days a little. I'm powerful glad to have the boys, Nellie. You know I meant to send to Casita to ask them. We'll see some trouble before the revolution is ended. I think I'll make this young man Gale an offer."

"He isn't a cowboy?" asked Mrs. Belding, quickly.

"No."

"Shore he'd make a darn good one," put in Laddy.

"What is he? Who is he? Where did he come from? Surely you must be—"

"Laddy swears he's all right," interrupted the husband. "That's enough reference for me. Isn't it enough for you?"

"Humph! Laddy knows a lot about young men, now doesn't he, especially strangers from the East? . . . Tom, you must be careful!"

"Wife, I'm only too glad to have a nervy young chap come along. What sense is there in your objection, if Jim and Laddy stick up for him?"

"But, Tom—he'll fall in love with Nell!" protested Mrs. Belding.

"Well, wouldn't that be regular? Doesn't every man who comes along fall in love with Nell? Hasn't it always happened? When she was a schoolgirl in Kansas didn't it happen? Didn't she have a hundred moon-eyed ninnies after her in Texas? I've had some peace out here in the desert, except when a Greaser or a prospector or a Yaqui would come along. Then same old story—in love with Nell!"

"But, Tom, Nell might fall in love with this young man!" exclaimed the wife, in distress.

"Laddy, Jim, didn't I tell you?" cried Belding. "I knew she'd say that. . . . My dear wife, I would be simply overcome with joy if Nell did fall in love once. Real good and hard! She's wilder than any antelope out there on the desert. Nell's nearly twenty now, and so far as we know she's never cared a rap for any fellow. And she's just as gay and full of the devil as she was at fourteen. Nell's as good and lovable as she is pretty, but I'm afraid she'll never grow into a woman while we live out in this lonely land. And you've always hated towns where there was a chance for the girl—just because you were afraid she'd fall in love. You've always been strange, even silly, about that. I've done my best for Nell—loved her as if she were my own daughter. I've changed many business plans to suit your whims. There are rough times ahead, maybe. I need men. I'll hire this chap Gale if he'll stay. Let Nell take her chance with him, just as she'll have to take chances with men when we get out of the desert. She'll be all the better for it."

"I hope Laddy's not mistaken in his opinion of this newcomer," replied Mrs. Belding, with a sigh of resignation.

"Shore I never made a mistake in my life figger'n' people," said Laddy, stoutly.

"Yes, you have, Laddy," replied Mrs. Belding. "You're wrong about Tom. . . . Well, supper is to be got. That young man and the girl will be starved. I'll go in now. If Nell happens around don't—don't flatter her, Laddy, like you did at dinner. Don't make her think of her looks."

Dick heard Mrs. Belding walk away.

"Shore she's powerful particular about that girl," observed Laddy. "Say, Tom, Nell knows she's pretty, doesn't she?"

"She's liable to find it out unless you shut up, Laddy. When you visited us out here some weeks ago, you kept paying cowboy compliments to her."

"An' it's your idee that cowboy compliments are plumb bad for girls?"

"Downright bad, Laddy, so my wife says."

"I'll be darned if I believe any girl can be hurt by a little sweet talk. It pleases 'em. . . . But say, Beldin', speaking of looks, have you got a peek yet at the Spanish girl?"

"Not in the light."

"Well, neither have I in daytime. I had enough by moonlight. Nell is some on looks, but I'm regretful passin' the ribbon to the lady from Mex. Jim, where are you?"

"My money's on Nell," replied Lash. "Gimme a girl with flesh an' color, an' blue eyes a-laughin'. Miss Castañeda is some peach, I'll not gainsay. But her face seemed too white. An' when she flashed those eyes on me, I thought I was shot! When she stood up there at first, thankin' us, I felt as if a—a princess was round somewhere. Now, Nell is kiddish an' sweet an'—"

"Chop it," interrupted Belding. "Here comes Nell now."

Dick's tingling ears took in the pattering of light footsteps, the rush of some one running.

"Here you are," cried a sweet, happy voice. "Dad, the Señorita is perfectly lovely. I've been peeping at her. She sleeps like—like death. She's so white. Oh, I hope she won't be ill."

"Shore she's only played out," said Laddy. "But she had

spunk while it lasted. . . . I was just arguin' with Jim an'
Tom about Miss Castañeda."

"Gracious! Why, she's beautiful. I never saw any one
so beautiful. . . . How strange and sad, that about her! Tell
me more, Laddy. You promised. I'm dying to know. I
never hear anything in this awful place. Didn't you say
the Señorita had a sweetheart?"

"Shore I did."

"And he's a cavalryman?"

"Yes."

"Is he the young man who came with you?"

"Nope. That fellow's the one who saved the girl from
Rojas."

"Ah! Where is he, Laddy?"

"He's in there asleep."

"Is he hurt?"

"I reckon not. He walked about fifteen miles."

"Is he—nice, Laddy?"

"Shore."

"What is he like?"

"Well, I'm not long acquainted, never saw him by day,
but I was some tolerable took with him. An' Jim here, Jim
says the young man can have his gun an' his hoss."

"Wonderful! Laddy, what on earth did this stranger do
to win you cowboys in just one night?"

"I'll shore have to tell you. Me an' Jim was watchin' a
game of cards in the Del Sol saloon in Casita. That's
across the line. We had acquaintances—four fellows from
the Cross Bar outfit, where we worked a while back. This
Del Sol is a billiard hall, saloon, restaurant, an' the like.
An' it was full of Greasers. Some of Campo's rebels were
there drinkin' an' playin' games. Then pretty soon in
come Rojas with some of his outfit. They were packin'

guns an' kept to themselves off to one side. I didn't give them a second look till Jim said he reckoned there was somethin' in the wind. Then, carelesslike, I began to peek at Rojas. They call Rojas the 'dandy rebel,' an' he shore looked the part. It made me sick to see him in all that lace an' glitter, knowin' him to be the cutthroat robber he is. It's no oncommon sight to see excited Greasers. They're all crazy. But this bandit was shore some agitated. He kept his men in a tight bunch round a table. He talked an' waved his hands. He was actually shakin'. His eyes had a wild glare. Now I figgered that trouble was brewin', most likely for the little Casita garrison. People seemed to think Campo an' Rojas would join forces to oust the federals. Jim thought Rojas's excitement was at the hatchin' of some plot. Anyway, we didn't join no card games, an' without pretendin' to, we was some watchful.

"A little while afterward I seen a fellow standin' in the restaurant door. He was a young American dressed in corduroys an' boots, like a prospector. You know it's no onusual fact to see prospectors in these parts. What made me think twice about this one was how big he seemed, how he filled up that door. He looked round the saloon, an' when he spotted Rojas he sorta jerked up. Then he pulled his slouch hat lopsided an' began to stagger down, down the steps. First off I made shore he was drunk. But I remembered he didn't seem drunk before. It was some queer. So I watched that young man.

"He reeled around the room like a fellow who was drunker'n a lord. Nobody but me seemed to notice him. Then he began to stumble over pool-players an' get his feet tangled up in chairs an' bump against tables. He got some pretty hard looks. He came round our way, an' all of a sudden he seen us cowboys. He gave another start, like the one when he first seen Rojas, then he made for us. I tipped Jim off that some-thin' was doin'.

"When he got close he straightened up, put back his slouch hat, an' looked at us. Then I saw his face. It sorta electrified yours truly. It was white, with veins standin' out an' eyes flamin'—a face of fury. I was plumb amazed, didn't know what to think. Then this queer young man shot some cool, polite words at me an' Jim.

"He was only bluffin' at bein' drunk—he meant to rush Rojas, to start a rough house. The bandit was after a girl. This girl was in the hotel, an' she was the sweetheart of a soldier, the young fellow's friend. The hotel was watched by Rojas's guards, an' the plan was to make a fuss an' get the girl away in the excitement. Well, Jim an' me got a hint of our bein' Americans—that cowboys generally had a name for loyalty to women. Then this amazin' chap— you can't imagine how scornful—said for me an' Jim to watch him.

"Before I could catch my breath an' figger out what he meant by 'rush' an' 'rough house' he had knocked over a table an' crowded some Greaser half off the map. One little funny man leaped up like a wild monkey an' began to screech. An' in another second he was in the air upside down. When he lit, he laid there. Then, quicker'n I can tell you, the young man dove at Rojas. Like a mad steer on the rampage he charged Rojas an' his men. The whole outfit went down—smash! I figgered then what 'rush' meant. The young fellow came up out of the pile with Rojas, an' just like I'd sling an empty sack along the floor he sent the bandit. But swift as that went he was on top of Rojas before the chairs an' tables had stopped rollin'.

"I woke up then, an' made for the center of the room, Jim with me. I began to shoot out the lamps. Jim throwed his guns on the crazy rebels, an' I was afraid there'd be blood spilled before I could get the room dark. Bein' shore busy, I lost sight of the young fellow for a second or so, an' when I got an eye free for him I seen a Greaser about to knife him. Think I was some considerate of the Greaser by only shootin' his arm off. Then I cracked the last lamp, an' in the hullabaloo me an' Jim vamoosed.

"We made tracks for our hosses an' packs, an' was hittin' the San Felipe road when we run right plumb into the young man. Well, he said his name was Gale—Dick Gale. The girl was with him safe an' well; but her sweetheart, the soldier bein' away without leave, had to go back sudden. There shore was some trouble, for Jim an' me heard shootin'. Gale said he had no money, no friends, was a stranger in a desert country; an' he was distracted to know how to help the girl. So me an' Jim started off with them for San Felipe, got switched, an' then we headed for the Rio Forlorn."

"Oh, I think he was perfectly splendid!" exclaimed the girl.

"Shore he was. Only, Nell, you can't lay no claim to bein' the original discoverer of that fact."

"But, Laddy, you haven't told me what he looks like."

At this juncture Dick Gale felt it absolutely impossible for him to play the eavesdropper any longer. Quietly he rolled out of bed. The voices still sounded close outside, and it was only by effort that he kept from further listening. Belding's kindly interest, Laddy's blunt and sincere cowboy eulogy, the girl's sweet eagerness and praise—these warmed Gale's heart. He had fallen among simple people, into whose lives the advent of an unknown man was welcome. He found himself in a singularly agitated mood. The excitement, the thrill, the difference felt in himself, experienced the preceding night, had extended on into his present. And the possibilities suggested by the conversation he had unwittingly overheard added sufficiently to the other feelings to put him into a peculiarly receptive state of mind. He was wild to be one of Belding's rangers. The idea of riding a horse in the open desert, with a dangerous duty to perform, seemed to strike him with an appealing force. Something within him went out to the cowboys, to this blunt and kind Belding. He was afraid to meet the girl. If every man who came along fell in love with this sweet-voiced Nell, then what hope had he to escape—now, when his whole inner awakening betokened a change of spirit, hope, a finding of real worth, real good, real power in himself? He did not understand wholly; yet he felt ready to ride, to fight, to love the desert, to love these outdoor men, to love a woman. That beautiful Spanish girl had spoken to something dead in him, and it had quickened to life. The sweet voice of an audacious, unseen girl warned him that presently a still more wonderful thing would happen to him.

Gale imagined he made noise enough as he clumsily pulled on his boots; yet the voices, split by a merry laugh, kept on murmuring outside the door. It was awkward for him, having only one hand available to lace up his boots. He looked out of the window. Evidently this was at the end of the house. There was a flagstone walk, beside which ran a ditch full of swift, muddy water. It made a pleasant sound. There were trees strange of form and color to him. He heard bees, birds, chickens, saw the red of roses and green of grass. Then he saw, close to the wall, a tub full of water, and a bench upon which lay basin, soap, towel, comb, and brush. The window was also a door, for under it there was a step.

Gale hesitated a moment, then went out. He stepped naturally, hoping and expecting that the cowboys would hear him. But nobody came. Awkwardly, with his left hand, he washed his face. Upon a nail in the wall hung a little mirror, by the aid of which Dick combed and brushed his hair. He imagined he looked a most haggard wretch. With that he faced forward, meaning to go round the corner of the house to greet the cowboys and these new-found friends.

Dick had taken but one step when he was halted by laughter and the patter of light feet.

From close around the corner pealed out that sweet voice. "Dad, you'll have your wish, and Mama will be wild!"

Dick saw a little foot sweep into view, a white dress, then the swiftly moving form of a girl. She was looking backward.

"Dad, I shall fall in love with your new ranger. I will—I have—"

Then she plumped squarely into Dick's arms.

She started back violently.

Dick saw a fair face and dark-blue, audaciously flashing eyes. Swift as lightning their expression changed to surprise, fear, wonder. For an instant they were level with Dick's grave questioning. Suddenly, sweetly, she blushed.

"Oh-h!" she faltered.

Then the blush turned to a scarlet fire. She whirled past him, and like a white gleam was gone.

Dick became conscious of the quickened beating of his heart. He experienced a singular exhilaration. That moment had been the one for which he had been ripe, the event upon which strange circumstances had been rushing him.

With a couple of strides he turned the corner. Laddy and Lash were there talking to a man of burly form. Seen by day, both cowboys were gray-haired, red-skinned, and weather-beaten, with lean, sharp features, and gray eyes so much alike that they might have been brothers.

"Hello, there's the young fellow," spoke up the burly man. "Mr. Gale, I'm glad to meet you. My name's Belding."

His greeting was as warm as his handclasp was long and hard. Gale saw a heavy man of medium height. His head was large and covered with grizzled locks. He wore a short-cropped mustache and chin beard. His skin was brown, and his dark eyes beamed with a genial light.

The cowboys were as cordial as if Dick had been their friend for years.

"Young man, did you run into anything as you came out?" asked Belding, with twinkling eyes.

"Why, yes; I met something white and swift flying by," replied Dick.

"Did she see you?" asked Laddy.

"I think so; but she didn't wait for me to introduce myself."

"That was Nell Burton, my girl—stepdaughter, I should say," said Belding. "She's sure some whirlwind, as Laddy calls her. Come, let's go in and meet the wife."

The house was long, like a barracks, with porch extending all the way, and doors every dozen paces. When Dick was ushered into a sitting-room, he was amazed at the light and comfort. This room had two big windows and a door opening into a patio, where there were luxuriant grass, roses in bloom, and flowering trees. He heard a slow splashing of water.

In Mrs. Belding, Gale found a woman of noble proportions and striking appearance. Her hair was white. She had a strong, serious, well-lined face that bore haunting evidences of past beauty. The gaze she bent upon him was almost piercing in its intensity. Her greeting, which seemed to Dick rather slow in coming, was kind though not cordial. Gale's first thought, after he had thanked these good people for their hospitality, was to inquire about Mercedes. He was informed that the Spanish girl had awakened with a considerable fever and nervousness. When, however, her anxiety had been allayed and her thirst relieved, she had fallen asleep again. Mrs. Belding said the girl had suffered no great hardship, other than mental, and would very soon be rested and well.

"Now, Gale," said Belding, when his wife had excused herself to get supper, "the boys, Jim and Laddy, told me about you and the mix-up at Casita. I'll be glad to take care of the girl till it's safe for your soldier friend to get her out of the country. That won't be very soon, don't mistake me. . . . I don't want to seem overcurious about you—Laddy has interested me in you—and straight out I'd like to know what you propose to do now."

"I haven't any plans," replied Dick; and, taking the moment as propitious, he decided to speak frankly concerning himself. "I just drifted down here. My home is in Chicago. When I left school some years ago—I'm twenty-five now—I went to work for my father. He's—he has business interests there. I tried all kinds of inside jobs. I couldn't please my father. I guess I put no real heart in my work. The fact was I didn't know how to work. The governor and I didn't exactly quarrel; but he hurt my feelings, and I quit. Six months or more ago I came West, and have knocked about from Wyoming southwest to the border. I tried to find congenial work, but nothing came my way. To tell you frankly, Mr. Belding, I suppose I didn't much care. I believe, though, that all the time I didn't know what I wanted. I've learned—well, just lately—"

"What do you want to do?" interposed Belding.

"I want a man's job. I want to do things with my hands. I want action. I want to be outdoors."

Belding nodded his head as if he understood that, and he began to speak again, cut something short, then went on, hesitatingly:

"Gale—you could go home again—to the old man— it'd be all right?"

"Mr. Belding, there's nothing shady in my past. The governor would be glad to have me home. That's the only consolation I've got. But I'm not going. I'm broke. I won't be a tramp. And it's up to me to do something."

"How'd you like to be a border ranger?" asked Belding, laying a hand on Dick's knee. "Part of my job here is United States Inspector of Immigration. I've got that boundary line to patrol—to keep out Chinks and Japs. This revolution has added complications, and I'm looking for smugglers and raiders here any day. You'll not be hired by the U.S. You'll simply be my ranger, same as Laddy and Jim, who have promised to work for me. I'll pay you well, give you a room here, furnish everything down to guns, and the finest horse you ever saw in your life. Your job won't be safe and healthy, sometimes, but it'll be a man's job—don't mistake me! You can gamble on having things to do outdoors. Now, what do you say?"

"I accept, and I thank you—I can't say how much," replied Gale, earnestly.

"Good! That's settled. Let's go out and tell Laddy and Jim."

Both boys expressed satisfaction at the turn of affairs, and then with Belding they set out to take Gale around the ranch. The house and several outbuildings were constructed of adobe, which, according to Belding, retained the summer heat on into winter, and the winter cold on into summer. These gray-red mud habitations were hideous to look at, and this fact, perhaps, made their really comfortable interiors more vividly a contrast. The wide grounds were covered with luxuriant grass and flowers and different kinds of trees. Gale's interest led him to ask about fig trees and pomegranates, and especially about a beautiful specimen that Belding called *palo verde*.

Belding explained that the luxuriance of this desert place was owing to a few springs and the dammed-up waters of the Rio Forlorn. Before he had come to the oasis it had been inhabited by a Papago Indian tribe and a few peon families. The oasis lay in an arroyo a mile wide, and sloped southwest for some ten miles or more. The river went dry most of the year; but enough water was stored in flood season to irrigate the gardens and alfalfa fields.

"I've got one never-failing spring on my place," said Belding. "Fine, sweet water! You know what that means in the desert. I like this oasis. The longer I live here the better I like it. There's not a spot in southern Arizona that'll compare with this valley for water or grass or wood. It's beautiful and healthy. Forlorn and lonely, yes, especially for women like my wife and Nell; but I like it. . . . And between you and me, boys, I've got something up my sleeve. There's gold dust in the arroyos, and there's mineral up in the mountains. If we only had water! This hamlet has steadily grown since I took up a station here.

Why, Casita is no place beside Forlorn River. Pretty soon the Southern Pacific will shoot a railroad branch out here. There are possibilities, and I want you boys to stay with me and get in on the ground floor. I wish this rebel war was over. . . . Well, here are the corrals and the fields. Gale, take a look at that bunch of horses!"

Belding's last remark was made as he led his companions out of shady gardens into the open. Gale saw an adobe shed and a huge pen fenced by strangely twisted and contorted branches or trunks of mesquite, and, beyond these, wide, flat fields, green—a dark, rich green—and dotted with beautiful horses. There were whites and blacks, and bays and grays. In his admiration Gale searched his memory to see if he could remember the like of these magnificent animals, and had to admit that the only ones he could compare with them were the Arabian steeds.

"Every rancher loves his horses," said Belding. "When I was in the Panhandle I had some fine stock. But these are Mexican. They came from Durango, where they were bred. Mexican horses are the finest in the world, bar none."

"Shore I reckon I savvy why you don't sleep nights," drawled Laddy. "I see a Greaser out there—no, it's an Indian."

"That's my Papago herdsman. I keep watch over the horses now day and night. Lord, how I'd hate to have Rojas or Salazar or any of those bandit rebels—find my horses! . . . Gale, can you ride?"

Dick modestly replied that he could, according to the Eastern idea of horsemanship.

"You don't need to be half horse to ride one of that bunch. But over there in the other field I've iron-jawed bronchos I wouldn't want you to tackle—except to see the fun. I've an outlaw I'll gamble even Laddy can't ride."

"So. How much'll you gamble?" asked Laddy, instantly.

The ringing of a bell, which Belding said was a call to supper, turned the men back toward the house. Facing that way, Gale saw dark, beetling ridges rising from the oasis and leading up to bare, black mountains. He had heard Belding call them No Name Mountains, and somehow the appellation suited those lofty, mysterious, frowning peaks.

It was not until they reached the house and were about to go in that Belding chanced to discover Gale's crippled hand.

"What an awful hand!" he exclaimed. "Where the devil did you get that?"

"I stove in my knuckles on Rojas," replied Dick.

"You did that in one punch? Say, I'm glad it wasn't me you hit! Why didn't you tell me? That's a bad hand. Those cuts are full of dirt and sand. Inflammation's setting in. It's got to be dressed. Nell!" he called.

There was no answer. He called again, louder.

"Mother, where's the girl?"

"She's there in the dining room," replied Mrs. Belding.

"Did she hear me?" he inquired, impatiently.

"Of course."

"Nell!" roared Belding.

This brought results. Dick saw a glimpse of golden hair and a white dress in the door. But they were not visible longer than a second.

"Dad, what's the matter?" asked a voice that was still as sweet as formerly, but now rather small and constrained.

"Bring the antiseptics, cotton, bandages—and things out here. Hurry now."

Belding fetched a pail of water and a basin from the kitchen. His wife followed him out, and, upon seeing Dick's hand, was all solicitude. Then Dick heard light, quick footsteps, but he did not look up.

"Nell, this is Mr. Gale—Dick Gale, who came with the boys last night," said Belding. "He's got an awful hand. Got it punching that greaser Rojas. I want you to dress it. . . . Gale, this is my stepdaughter, Nell Burton, of whom I spoke. She's some good when there's somebody sick or hurt. Shove out your fist, my boy, and let her get at it. Supper's nearly ready."

Dick felt that same strange, quickening heart throb, yet he had never been cooler in his life. More than anything else in the world he wanted to look at Nell Burton; however, divining that the situation might be embarrassing to her, he refrained from looking up. She began to bathe his injured knuckles. He noted the softness, the deftness of her touch, and then it seemed her fingers were not quite as steady as they might have been. Still, in a moment they appeared to become surer in their work. She had beautiful hands, not too large, though certainly not small, and they were strong, brown, supple. He observed next, with stealthy, upward-stealing glance, that she had rolled up her sleeves, exposing fine, round arms graceful in line. Her skin was brown—no, it was more gold than brown. It had a wonderful clear tint. Dick stoically lowered his eyes then, putting off as long as possible the alluring moment when he was to look into her face. That would be a fateful moment. He played with a certain strange joy of anticipation. When, however, she sat down beside him and rested his injured hand in her lap as she cut bandages, she was so thrillingly near that he yielded to an irrepressible desire to look up. She had a sweet, fair face warmly tinted with that same healthy golden-brown sunburn. Her hair was light gold and abundant, a waving mass. Her eyes were shaded by long, downcast lashes, yet through them he caught a gleam of blue.

Despite the stir within him, Gale, seeing she was now absorbed in her task, critically studied her with a second closer gaze. She was a sweet, wholesome, joyous, pretty girl.

"Shore it musta hurt?" inquired Laddy, who sat an interested spectator.

"Yes, I confess it did," replied Dick, slowly, with his eyes on Nell's face. "But I didn't mind."

The girl's lashes swept up swiftly in surprise. She had taken his words literally. But the dark-blue eyes met his for only a fleeting second. Then the warm tint in her cheeks turned as red as her lips. Hurriedly she finished tying the bandage and rose to her feet.

"I thank you," said Gale, also rising.

With that Belding appeared in the doorway, and, finding the operation concluded, called them in to supper. Dick had the use of only one arm, and he certainly was keenly aware of the shy, silent girl across the table; but in spite of these considerable handicaps he eclipsed both hungry cowboys in the assault upon Mrs. Belding's bounteous supper. Belding talked, the cowboys talked more or less, Mrs. Belding put in a word now and then, and Dick managed to find brief intervals when it was possible for him to say yes or no. He observed gratefully that no one round the table seemed to be aware of his enormous appetite.

After supper, having a favorable opportunity when for a moment no one was at hand, Dick went out through the yard, past the gardens and fields, and climbed the first knoll. From that vantage point he looked out over the little hamlet, somewhat to his right, and was surprised at its extent, its considerable number of adobe houses. The overhanging mountains, ragged and darkened, a great heave of splintered, sundered rock, rather chilled and affronted him.

Westward the setting sun gilded a spiked, frost-colored, limitless expanse of desert. It awed Gale. Everywhere rose blunt, broken ranges or isolated groups of mountains. Yet the desert stretched away down between and beyond them. When the sun set and Gale could not see so far, he felt a relief.

That grand and austere attraction of distance gone, he saw the desert nearer at hand—the valley at his feet. What a strange, gray, somber place! There was a lighter strip of gray winding down between darker hues. This he realized presently was the riverbed, and he saw how the pools of water narrowed and diminished in size till they lost themselves in gray sand. This was the rainy season near its end, and here a little river struggled hopelessly, forlornly to live in the desert. He received a potent impression of the nature of that blasted age-worn waste which he had divined was to give him strength and work and love.

CHAPTER 5

A DESERT ROSE

Belding assigned Dick to a little room which had no windows but two doors, one opening into the patio, the other into the yard on the west side of the house. It contained only the barest necessities for comfort. Dick mentioned the baggage he had left in the hotel at Casita, and it was Belding's opinion that to try to recover this property would be rather risky; at the moment Richard Gale was probably not popular with the Mexicans at Casita. So Dick bade good-by to fine suits of clothes and linen with a feeling that, as he had said farewell to an idle and useless past, it was just as well not to have any old luxuries as reminders. As he possessed, however, not a thing save the clothes on his back, and not even a handkerchief, he expressed regret that he had come to Forlorn River a beggar.

"Beggar hell!" exploded Belding, with his eyes snapping in the lamplight. "Money's the last thing we think of out here. All the same, Gale, if you stick you'll be rich."

"It wouldn't surprise me," replied Dick, thoughtfully. But he was not thinking of material wealth. Then, as he viewed his stained and torn shirt, he laughed and said: "Belding, while I'm getting rich I'd like to have some respectable clothes."

"We've a little Mex store in town, and what you can't get there the womenfolks will make for you."

When Dick lay down he was dully conscious of pain and headache, that he did not feel well. Despite this, and a mind thronging with memories and anticipations, he succumbed to weariness and soon fell asleep.

It was light when he awoke, but a strange brightness seen through what seemed blurred eyes. A moment passed before his mind worked clearly, and then he had to make an effort to think. He was dizzy. When he essayed to lift his right arm, an excruciating pain made him desist. Then he discovered that his arm was badly swollen, and the hand had burst its bandages. The injured member was red, angry, inflamed, and twice its normal size. He felt hot all over, and a raging headache consumed him.

Belding came stamping into the room.

"Hello, Dick. Do you know it's late? How's the busted fist this morning?"

Dick tried to sit up, but his effort was a failure. He got about half up, then felt himself weakly sliding back.

"I guess—I'm pretty sick," he said.

He saw Belding lean over him, feel his face, and speak, and then everything seemed to drift, not into darkness, but into some region where he had dim perceptions of gray moving things, and of voices that were remote. Then there came an interval when all was blank. He knew not whether it was one of minutes or hours, but after it he had a clearer mind. He slept, awakened during nighttime, and slept again. When he again unclosed his eyes the room was sunny, and cool with a fragrant breeze that blew through the open door. Dick felt better; but he had no particular desire to move or talk or eat. He had, however, a burning thirst. Mrs. Belding visited him often; her husband came in several times, and once Nell slipped in noiselessly. Even this last event aroused no interest in Dick.

On the next day he was very much improved.

"We've been afraid of blood poisoning," said Belding. "But my wife thinks the danger's past. You'll have to rest that arm for a while."

Ladd and Jim came peeping in at the door.

"Come in, boys. He can have company—the more the better—if it'll keep him content. He mustn't move, that's all."

The cowboys entered, slow, easy, cool, kind-voiced.

"Shore it's tough," said Ladd, after he had greeted Dick. "You look used up."

Jim Lash wagged his half-bald, sunburned head. "Musta been more'n tough for Rojas."

"Gale, Laddy tells me one of our neighbors, fellow named Carter, is going to Casita," put in Belding. "Here's a chance to get word to your friend the soldier."

"Oh, that will be fine!" exclaimed Dick. "I declare I'd forgotten Thorne. . . . How is Miss Castañeda? I hope—"

"She's all right, Gale. Been up and around the patio for two days. Like all the Spanish—the real thing—she's made of Damascus steel. We've been getting acquainted. She and Nell made friends at once. I'll call them in."

He closed the door leading out into the yard, explaining that he did not want to take chances of Mercedes's presence becoming known to neighbors. Then he went to the patio and called.

Both girls came in, Mercedes leading. Like Nell, she wore white, and she had a red rose in her hand. Dick would scarcely have recognized anything about her except her eyes and the way she carried her little head, and her beauty burst upon him strange and anew. She was swift, impulsive in her movements to reach his side.

"Señor, I am so sorry you were ill—so happy you are better."

Dick greeted her, offering his left hand, gravely apologizing for the fact that, owing to a late infirmity, he could not offer the right. Her smile exquisitely combined sympathy, gratitude, admiration. Then Dick spoke to Nell, likewise offering his hand, which she took shyly. Her reply was a murmured, unintelligible one; but her eyes were glad, and the tint in her cheeks threatened to rival the hue of the rose she carried.

Everybody chatted then, except Nell, who had apparently lost her voice. Presently Dick remembered to speak of the matter of getting news to Thorne.

"Señor, may I write to him? Will someone take a letter? . . . I shall hear from him!" she said; and her white hands emphasized her words.

"Assuredly. I guess poor Thorne is almost crazy. I'll write to him. . . . No, I can't with this crippled hand."

"That'll be all right, Gale," said Belding. "Nell will write for you. She writes all my letters."

So Belding arranged it, and Mercedes flew away to her room to write, while Nell fetched pen and paper and seated herself beside Gale's bed to take his dictation.

What with watching Nell and trying to catch her glance,

and listening to Belding's talk with the cowboys, Dick was hard put to it to dictate any kind of a creditable letter. Nell met his gaze once, then no more. The color came and went in her cheeks, and sometimes when he told her to write so and so, there was a demure smile on her lips. She was laughing at him. And Belding was talking over the risks involved in a trip to Casita.

"Shore I'll ride in with the letters," Ladd said.

"No you won't," replied Belding. "That bandit outfit will be laying for you."

"Well, I reckon if they was I wouldn't be oncommon grieved."

"I'll tell you, boys, I'll ride in myself with Carter. There's business I can see to, and I'm curious to know what the rebels are doing. Laddy, keep one eye open while I'm gone. See the horses are locked up. . . . Gale, I'm going to Casita myself. Ought to get back to-morrow sometime. I'll be ready to start in an hour. Have your letter ready. And say—if you want to write home it's a chance. Sometimes we don't go to the P.O. in a month."

He tramped out, followed by the tall cowboys, and then Dick was enabled to bring his letter to a close. Mercedes came back, and her eyes were shining. Dick imagined a letter received from her would be something of an event for a fellow. Then, remembering Belding's suggestion, he decided to profit by it.

"May I trouble you to write another for me?" asked Dick, as he received the letter from Nell.

"It's no trouble, I'm sure—I'd be pleased," she replied.

That was altogether a wonderful speech of hers, Dick thought, because the words were the first coherent ones she had spoken to him.

"May I stay?" asked Mercedes, smiling.

"By all means," he answered, and then he settled back and began.

Presently Gale paused, partly because of genuine emotion, and stole a look from under his hand at Nell. She wrote swiftly, and her downcast face seemed to be softer in its expression of sweetness. If she had in the very least been drawn to him—But that was absurd—impossible!

When Dick finished dictating, his eyes were upon Mercedes, who sat smilingly curious and sympathetic. How responsive she was! He heard the hasty scratch of Nell's pen. He looked at Nell. Presently she rose, holding out his letter. He was just in time to see a wave of red recede from her face. She gave him one swift gaze, unconscious, searching, then averted it and turned away. She left the room with Mercedes before he could express his thanks.

But that strange, speaking flash of eyes remained to haunt and torment Gale. It was indescribably sweet, and provocative of thoughts that he believed were wild without warrant. Something within him danced for very joy, and the next instant he was conscious of wistful doubt, a gravity that he could not understand. It dawned upon him that for the brief instant when Nell had met his gaze she had lost her shyness. It was a woman's questioning eyes that had pierced through him.

During the rest of the day Gale was content to lie still on his bed thinking and dreaming, dozing at intervals, and watching the lights change upon the mountain peaks, feeling the warm, fragrant desert wind that blew in upon him. He seemed to have lost the faculty of estimating time. A long while, strong in its effect upon him, appeared to have passed since he had met Thorne. He accepted things as he felt them, and repudiated his intelligence. His old inquisitive habit of mind returned. Did he love Nell? Was he only attracted for the moment? What was the use of worrying about her or himself? He refused to answer, and deliberately gave himself up to dreams of her sweet face and of that last dark-blue glance.

Next day he believed he was well enough to leave his room; but Mrs. Belding would not permit him to do so. She was kind, soft-handed, motherly, and she was always coming in to minister to his comfort. This attention was sincere, not in the least forced; yet Gale felt that the friendliness so manifest in the others of the household did not extend to her. He was conscious of something that a little thought persuaded him was antagonism. It surprised and hurt him. He had never been much of a success with girls and young married women, but their mothers and old people had generally been fond of him. Still, though Mrs. Belding's hair was snow-white, she did not impress him as being old. He reflected that there might come a time when it would be desirable, far beyond any ground of everyday friendly kindliness, to have Mrs. Belding be well disposed toward him. So he thought about her, and pondered how to make her like him. It did not take very long for Dick to discover that he liked her. Her face, except when she smiled, was thoughtful and sad. But it seemed too strong, too intense, too nobly lined. It was a face to make one serious. Like a haunting shadow, like a phantom of happier years, the sweetness of Nell's face was there, and infinitely more of beauty than had been transmitted to the daughter. Dick believed Mrs. Belding's friendship and motherly love were worth much striving to win, entirely aside from any more selfish motive. He decided both would be hard to get. Often he felt her deep, penetrating gaze upon him; and, though this in no wise embarrassed him—for he had no shameful secrets of past or present—it showed him how useless it would be to try to conceal anything from her. Naturally, on first impulse, he wanted to hide his interest in the daughter; but he resolved to be absolutely frank and true, and through that win or lose. Moreover, if Mrs. Belding asked him any questions about his home, his family, his connections, he would not avoid direct and truthful answers.

Toward evening Gale heard the tramp of horses and Belding's hearty voice. Presently the rancher strode in upon Gale, shaking the gray dust from his broad shoulders and waving a letter.

"Hello, Dick! Good news and bad!" he said, putting the letter in Dick's hand. "Had no trouble finding your friend Thorne. Looked like he'd been drunk for a week! Say, he nearly threw a fit. I never saw a fellow so wild with joy. He made sure you and Mercedes were lost in the desert. He wrote two letters which I brought. Don't mistake me, boy, it was some fun with Mercedes just now. I teased her, wouldn't give her the letter. You ought to have seen her eyes. If ever you see a black-and-white desert hawk swoop down upon a quail, then you'll know how Mercedes pounced upon her letter. . . . Well, Casita is one hell of a place these days. I tried to get your baggage, and think I made a mistake. We're going to see travel toward Forlorn River. The federal garrison got reinforcements from somewhere, and is holding out. There's been fighting for three days. The rebels have a string of flat railroad cars, all iron, and they ran this up within range of the barricades. They've got some machine guns, and they're going to lick the federals sure. There are dead soldiers in the ditches, Mexican noncombatants lying dead in the streets—and buzzards everywhere! It's reported that Campo, the rebel leader, is on the way up from Sinaloa, and Huerta, a federal general, is coming to relieve the garrison. I don't take much stock in reports. But there's hell in Casita, all right."

"Do you think we'll have trouble out here?" asked Dick, excitedly.

"Sure. Some kind of trouble sooner or later," replied Belding, gloomily. "Why, you can stand on my ranch and step over into Mexico. Laddy says we'll lose horses and other stock in night raids. Jim Lash doesn't look for any worse. But Jim isn't as well acquainted with Greasers as I am. Anyway, my boy, as soon as you can hold a bridle and a gun you'll be on the job, don't mistake me."

"With Laddy and Jim?" asked Dick, trying to be cool.

"Sure. With them and me, and by yourself."

Dick drew a deep breath, and even after Belding had departed he forgot for a moment about the letter in his hand. Then he unfolded the paper and read:

Dear Dick,

You've more than saved my life. To the end of my days you'll be the one man to whom I owe everything. Words fail to express my feelings.

This must be a brief note. Belding is waiting, and I used up most of the time writing to Mercedes. I like Belding. He was not unknown to me, though I never met or saw him before. You'll be interested to learn that he's the unadulterated article, the real Western goods. I've heard of some of his stunts, and they made my hair curl. Dick, your luck is staggering. The way Belding spoke of you was great. But you deserve it, old man.

I'm leaving Mercedes in your charge, subject, of course, to advice from Belding. Take care of her, Dick, for my life is wrapped up in her. By all means keep her from being seen by Mexicans. We are sitting tight here—nothing doing. If some action doesn't come soon it'll be darned strange. Things are centering this way. There's scrapping right along, and people have begun to move. We're still patrolling the line eastward of Casita. It'll be impossible to keep any tab on the line west of Casita, for it's too rough. That cactus desert is awful. Cowboys or rangers with desert-bred horses might keep raiders and smugglers from crossing. But if cavalrymen could stand that waterless wilderness, which I doubt much, their horses would drop under them.

If things do quiet down before my commission expires, I'll get leave of absence, run out to Forlorn River, marry my beautiful Spanish princess, and take her to a civilized country, where, I opine, every son of a gun who sees her will lose his head, and drive me mad. It's my great luck, old pal, that you are a fellow who never seemed to care about pretty girls. So you won't give me the double cross and run off with Mercedes—carry her off, like the villain in the play, I mean.

That reminds me of Rojas. Oh, Dick, it was glorious! You didn't do anything to the Dandy Rebel! Not at all! You merely caressed him—gently moved him to one side. Dick, harken to these glad words: Rojas is in the hospital. I was interested to inquire. He had a smashed finger, a dislocated collarbone, three broken ribs, and a fearful gash on his face. He'll be in the hospital for a month. Dick, when I meet that pigheaded dad of yours I'm going to give him the surprise of his life.

Send me a line whenever any one comes in from F.R., and inclose Mercedes's letter in yours. Take care of her, Dick, and may the future hold in store for you some of the sweetness I know now!

Faithfully yours,
Thorne.

Dick reread the letter, then folded it and placed it under his pillow.

"Never cared for pretty girls, huh?" he soliloquized. "George, I never saw any till I struck Southern Arizona! Guess I'd better make up for lost time."

While he was eating his supper, with appetite rapidly returning to normal, Ladd and Jim came in, bowing their tall heads to enter the door. Their friendly advances were singularly welcome to Gale, but he was still backward. He allowed himself to show that he was glad to see them, and he listened. Jim Lash had heard from Belding the result of the mauling given to Rojas by Dick. And Jim talked about what a grand thing that was. Ladd had a good deal to say about Belding's horses. It took no keen judge of human nature to see that horses constituted Ladd's ruling passion.

"I've had wimmen go back on me, but never no hoss!" declared Ladd, and manifestly that was a controlling truth with him.

"Shore it's a cinch Beldin' is agoin' to lose some of them hosses," he said. "You can search me if I don't think there'll be more doin' on the border here than along the Rio Grande. We're just the same as on Greaser soil. Mebbe we don't stand no such chance of bein' shot up as we would across the line. But who's goin' to give up his hosses without a fight? Half the time when Beldin's stock is out of the alfalfa it's grazin' over the line. He thinks he's careful about them hosses, but he ain't."

"Look a-here, Laddy; you cain't believe all you hear," replied Jim, seriously. "I reckon we mightn't have any trouble."

"Back up, Jim. Shore you're standin' on your bridle. I ain't goin' much on reports. Remember that American we met in Casita, the prospector who'd just gotten out of Sonora? He had some story, he had. Swore he'd killed seventeen Greasers breakin' through the rebel line round the mine where he an' other Americans were corralled. The next day when I met him again, he was drunk, an' then he told me he'd shot thirty Greasers. The chances are he did kill some. But reports are exaggerated. There are miners fightin' for life down in Sonora, you can gamble on that. An' the truth is bad enough. Take Rojas's harryin' of the Señorita, for instance. Can you beat that? Shore, Jim, there's more doin' than the raidin' of a few hosses. An' Forlorn River is goin' to get hers!"

Another dawn found Gale so much recovered that he arose and looked after himself, not, however, without considerable difficulty and rather disheartening twinges of pain.

Some time during the morning he heard the girls in the patio and called to ask if he might join them. He received one response, a mellow, "*Sí*, señor." It was not as much as he wanted, but considering that it was enough, he went out. He had not as yet visited the patio, and surprise and delight were in store for him. He found himself lost in a labyrinth of green and rose-bordered walks. He strolled around, discovering that the patio was a courtyard, open at an end; but he failed to discover the young ladies. So he called again. The answer came from the center of the square. After stooping to get under shrubs and wading through bushes he entered an open sandy circle, full of magnificent and murderous cactus plants, strange to him. On the other side, in the shade of a beautiful tree, he found the girls, Mercedes sitting in a hammock, Nell upon a blanket.

"What a beautiful tree!" he exclaimed. "I never saw one like that. What is it?"

"Palo verde," replied Nell.

"Señor, *palo verde* means 'green tree,'" added Mercedes.

This desert tree, which had struck Dick as so new and strange and beautiful, was not striking on account of size, for it was small, scarcely reaching higher than the roof; but rather because of its exquisite color of green, trunk and branch alike, and owing to the odd fact that it seemed not to possess leaves. All the tree from ground to tiny flat twigs was a soft polished green. It bore no thorns.

Right then and there began Dick's education in desert growths; and he felt that even if he had not had such charming teachers he would still have been absorbed. For the patio was full of desert wonders. A twisting-bunked tree with full foliage of small gray leaves Nell called a mesquite. Then Dick remembered the name, and now he saw where the desert got its pale-gray color. A huge, lofty, fluted column of green was a *saguaro,* or giant cactus. Another odd-shaped cactus, resembling the legs of an inverted devil-fish, bore the name *ocatillo.* Each branch rose high and symmetrical, furnished with sharp blades that seemed to be at once leaves and thorns. Yet another cactus interested Gale, and it looked like a huge, low barrel covered with green-ribbed cloth and long thorns. This was the *bisnaga,* or barrel cactus. According to Nell and Mercedes, this plant was a happy exception to its desert neighbors, for it secreted water which had many times saved the lives of men. Last of the cacti to attract Gale, and the one to make him shiver, was a low plant, consisting of stem and many rounded protuberances of a frosty, steely white, and covered with long, murderous spikes. From this plant the desert got its frosty glitter. It was as stiff, as unyielding as steel, and bore the name *cholla*.

Dick's enthusiasm was contagious, and his earnest desire to learn was flattering to his teachers. When it came to assimilating Spanish, however, he did not appear to be so apt a pupil. He managed, after many trials, to acquire *"buenos días"* and *"buenos tardes,"* and *"señorita"* and *"gracias,"* and a few other short terms. Dick was indeed eager to get a little smattering of Spanish, and perhaps he was not really quite so stupid as he pretended to be. It was delightful to be taught by a beautiful Spaniard who was so gracious and intense and magnetic of personality, and by a sweet American girl who moment by moment forgot her shyness. Gale wished to prolong the lessons.

So that was the beginning of many afternoons in which he learned desert lore and Spanish verbs, and something else that he dared not name.

Nell Burton had never shown to Gale that daring side of her character which had been so suggestively defined in Belding's terse description and Ladd's encomiums, and in her own audacious speech and merry laugh and flashing eye of that never-to-be-forgotten first meeting. She might have been an entirely different girl. But Gale remembered; and when the ice had been somewhat broken between them, he was always trying to surprise her into her real self. There were moments that fairly made him tingle with expectation. Yet he saw little more than a ghost of her vivacity, and never a gleam of that individuality which Belding had called a devil. On the few occasions that Dick had been left alone with her in the patio Nell had grown suddenly unresponsive and restrained, or she had left him on some transparent pretext. On the last occasion Mercedes returned to find Dick staring disconsolately at the rose-bordered path, where Nell had evidently vanished. The Spanish girl was wonderful in her divination.

"Señor Dick!" she cried.

Dick looked at her, soberly nodded his head, and then he laughed. Mercedes had seen through him in one swift glance. Her white hand touched his in wordless sympathy and thrilled him. This Spanish girl was all fire and passion and love. She understood him, she was his friend, she pledged him what he felt would be the most subtle and powerful influence.

Little by little he learned details of Nell's varied life. She had lived in many places. As a child she remembered moving from town to town, of going to school among schoolmates whom she never had time to know. Lawrence, Kansas, where she studied for several years, was the later exception to this changeful nature of her schooling. Then she moved to Stillwater, Oklahoma, from there to Austin, Texas, and on to Waco, where her mother met and married Belding. They lived in New Mexico awhile, in Tucson, Arizona, in Douglas, and finally had come to lonely Forlorn River.

"Mother could never live in one place any length of time," said Nell. "And since we've been in the Southwest she has never ceased trying to find some trace of her father. He was last heard of in Nogales fourteen years ago. She thinks Grandfather was lost in the Sonora Desert. . . . And every place we go is worse. Oh, I love the desert. But I'd like to go back to Lawrence—or to see Chicago or

New York—some of the places Mr. Gale speaks of . . . I remember the college at Lawrence, though I was only twelve. I saw races—and once real football. Since then I've read magazines and papers about big football games, and I was always fascinated. . . . Mr. Gale, of course, you've seen games?"

"Yes, a few," replied Dick; and he laughed a little. It was on his lips then to tell her about some of the famous games in which he had participated. But he refrained from exploiting himself. There was little, however, of the color and sound and cheer, of the violent action and rush and battle incidental to a big college football game that he did not succeed in making Mercedes and Nell feel just as if they had been there. They hung breathless and wide-eyed upon his words.

Someone else was present at the latter part of Dick's narrative. The moment he became aware of Mrs. Belding's presence he remembered fancying he had heard her call, and now he was certain she had done so. Mercedes and Nell, however, had been and still were oblivious to everything except Dick's recital. He saw Mrs. Belding cast a strange, intent glance upon Nell, then turn and go silently through the patio. Dick concluded his talk, but the brilliant beginning was not sustained.

Dick was haunted by the strange expression he had caught on Mrs. Belding's face, especially the look in her eyes. It had been one of repressed pain liberated in a flash of certainty. The mother had seen just as quickly as Mercedes how far he had gone on the road of love. Perhaps she had seen more—even more than he dared hope. The incident roused Gale. He could not understand Mrs. Belding, nor why that look of hers, that seeming baffled, hopeless look of a woman who saw the inevitable forces of life and could not thwart them, should cause him perplexity and distress. He wanted to go to her and tell her how he felt about Nell, but fear of absolute destruction of his hopes held him back. He would wait. Nevertheless, an instinct that was perhaps akin to self-preservation prompted him to want to let Nell know the state of his mind. Words crowded his brain seeking utterance. Who and what he was, how he loved her, the work he expected to take up soon, his longings, hopes, and plans—there was all this and more. But something checked him. And the repression made him so thoughtful and quiet, even melancholy, that he went outdoors to try to throw off the mood. The sun was yet high, and a dazzling white light enveloped valleys and peaks. He felt that the wonderful sunshine was the dominant feature of that arid region. It was like white gold. It had burned its color in a face he knew. It was going to warm his blood and brown his skin. A hot, languid breeze, so dry that he felt his lips shrink with its contact, came from the desert; and it seemed to smell of wide-open, untainted places where sand blew and strange, pungent plants gave a bittersweet tang to the air.

When he returned to the house, some hours later, his room had been put in order. In the middle of the white coverlet on his table lay a fresh red rose. Nell had dropped it there. Dick picked it up, feeling a throb in his breast. It was a bud just beginning to open, to show between its petals a dark-red, unfolding heart. How fragrant it was, how exquisitely delicate, how beautiful its inner hue of red, deep and dark, the crimson of lifeblood!

Had Nell left it there by accident or by intent? Was it merely kindness or a girl's subtlety? Was it a message couched elusively, a symbol, a hope in a half-blown desert rose?

CHAPTER 6

THE YAQUI

Toward evening of a lowering December day, some fifty miles west of Forlorn River, a horseman rode along an old, dimly defined trail. From time to time he halted to study the lay of the land ahead. It was bare, somber, ridgy desert, covered with dun-colored greasewood and stunted prickly pear. Distant mountains hemmed in the valley, raising black spurs above the round lomas and the square-walled mesas.

This lonely horseman bestrode a steed of magnificent build, perfectly white except for a dark bar of color running down the noble head from ears to nose. Sweat-caked dust stained the long flanks. The horse had been running. His mane and tail were laced and knotted to keep their length out of reach of grasping cactus and brush. Clumsy homemade leather shields covered the front of his forelegs and ran up well to his wide breast. What otherwise would have been muscular symmetry of limb was marred by many a scar and many a lump. He was lean, gaunt, worn, a huge machine of muscle and bone, beautiful only in head and mane, a weight-carrier, a horse strong and fierce like the desert that had bred him.

The rider fitted the horse as he fitted the saddle. He was a young man of exceedingly powerful physique, wide-shouldered, long-armed, big-legged. His lean face, where it was not red, blistered, and peeling, was the hue of bronze. He had a dark eye, a falcon gaze, roving and keen. His jaw was prominent and set, mastiff-like; his lips were stern. It was youth with its softness not yet quite burned and hardened away that kept the whole cast of his face from being ruthless.

This young man was Dick Gale, but not the listless traveler, nor the lounging wanderer who, two months before, had by chance dropped into Casita. Friendship, chivalry, love—the deep-seated, unplumbed emotions that had been stirred into being with all their incalculable power for spiritual change, had rendered different the meaning of life. In the moment almost of their realization the desert had claimed Gale, and had drawn him into its crucible. The desert had multiplied weeks into years. Heat, thirst, hunger, loneliness, toil, fear, ferocity, pain—he knew them all. He had felt them all—the white sun, with its glazed, coalescing, lurid fire; the caked split lips and rasping, dry-puffed tongue; the sickening ache in the pit of his stomach; the insupportable silence, the empty space, the utter desolation, the contempt of life; the weary ride, the long climb, the plod in sand, the search, search, search for water; the sleepless night alone, the watch and wait, the dread of ambush, the swift flight; the fierce pursuit of men wild as Bedouins and as fleet, the willingness to deal sudden death, the pain of poison thorn, the stinging tear of lead through flesh; and that strange paradox of the burning desert, the cold at night, the piercing icy wind, the dew that penetrated to the marrow, the numbing desert cold of the dawn.

Beyond any dream of adventure he had ever had, beyond any wild story he had ever read, had been his experience with those hard-riding rangers, Ladd and Lash. Then he had traveled alone the hundred miles of desert between Forlorn River and the Sonoyta Oasis. Ladd's prophecy of trouble on the border had been mild compared to what had become the actuality. With rebel occupancy of the garrison at Casita, outlaws, bandits, raiders in rioting bands had spread westward. Like troops of Arabs, magnificently mounted, they were here, there, everywhere along the line; and if murder and worse were confined to the Mexican side, pillage and raiding were perpetrated across the border. Many a dark-skinned raider bestrode one of Belding's fast horses; and, indeed, all except his selected white thoroughbreds had been stolen. So the job of the rangers had become more than a patrolling of the boundary line to keep Japanese and Chinese from being smuggled into the United States. Belding kept close at home to protect his family and to hold his property. But the three rangers, in fulfilling their duty, had incurred risks on their own side of the line, had been outraged, robbed, pursued, and injured on the other. Some of the few water holes that had to be reached lay far across the border in Mexican territory. Horses had to drink, men had to drink; and Ladd and Lash were not of the stripe that forsook a task because of danger. Slow to wrath at first, as became men who had long lived peaceful lives, they had at length revolted; and desert vultures could have told a gruesome story. Made a comrade and ally of these bordermen, Dick Gale had leaped at the desert action and strife with an intensity of heart and a rare physical ability which accounted for the remarkable fact that he had not yet fallen by the way.

On this December afternoon the three rangers, as often were separated. Lash was far to the westward of Sonoyta, somewhere along Camino del Diablo, that terrible Devil's Road, where many desert wayfarers had perished. Ladd had long been overdue in a prearranged meeting with Gale. The fact that Ladd had not shown up miles west of the Papago Well was significant.

The sun had hidden behind clouds all the latter part of that day, an unusual occurrence for that region even in winter. And now, as the light waned suddenly, telling of the hidden sunset, a cold, dry, penetrating wind sprang up and blew in Gale's face. Not at first, but by imperceptible degrees it chilled him. He untied his coat from the back of the saddle and put it on. A few cold drops of rain touched his cheek.

He halted upon the edge of a low escarpment. Below him the narrowing valley showed bare, black ribs of rock, long, winding gray lines leading down to a central floor where mesquite and cactus dotted the barren landscape. Moving objects, diminutive in size, gray and white in color, arrested Gale's roving sight. They bobbed away for a while, then stopped. They were antelope, and they had seen his horse. When he rode on they started once more, keeping to the lowest level. These wary animals were often desert watchdogs for the ranger; they would betray the proximity of horse or man. With them trotting forward, he made better time for some miles across the valley. When he lost them, caution once more slowed his advance.

The valley sloped up and narrowed, to head into an ar-

royo where grass began to show gray between the clumps
of mesquite. Shadows formed ahead in the hollows, along
the walls of the arroyo, under the trees, and they seemed
to creep, to rise, to float into a veil cast by the background
of bold mountains, at last to claim the skyline. Night was
not close at hand; but it was there in the east, lifting upward, drooping downward, encroaching upon the west.

Gale dismounted to lead his horse, to go forward more
slowly. He had ridden sixty miles since morning, and he
was tired, and a not entirely healed wound in his hip
made one leg drag a little. A mile up the arroyo, near its
head, lay the Papago Well. The need of water for his horse
entailed a risk that otherwise he could have avoided.
The well was on Mexican soil. Gale distinguished a faint
light flickering through the thin, sharp foliage. Campers
were at the well, and, whoever they were, no doubt they
had prevented Ladd from meeting Gale. Ladd had gone
back to the next water-hole, or maybe he was hiding in
an arroyo to the eastward, awaiting developments.

Gale turned his horse, not without urge of iron arm and
persuasive speech, for the desert steed scented water, and
plodded back to the edge of the arroyo, where in a secluded circle of mesquite he halted. The horse snorted
his relief at the removal of the heavy, burdened saddle and
accoutrements, and sagging, bent his knees, lowered himself with slow heave, and plunged down to roll in the
sand. Gale poured the contents of his larger canteen into
his hat and held it to the horse's nose.

"Drink, Sol," he said.

It was but a drop for a thirsty horse. However, Blanco
Sol rubbed a wet muzzle against Gale's hand in appreciation. Gale loved the horse, and was loved in return. They
had saved each other's lives, and had spent long days and

nights of desert solitude together. Sol had known other masters, though none so kind as this new one; but it was certain that Gale had never before known a horse.

The spot of secluded ground was covered with bunches of galleta grass upon which Sol began to graze. Gale made a long halter of his lariat to keep the horse from wandering in search of water. Next Gale kicked off the cumbersome chapparejos, with their flapping, tripping folds of leather over his feet, and drawing a long rifle from its saddle-sheath, he slipped away into the shadows.

The coyotes were howling, not here and there, but in concerted volume at the head of the arroyo. To Dick this was no more reassuring than had been the flickering light of the campfire. The wild desert dogs, with their characteristic insolent curiosity, were baying men round a campfire. Gale proceeded slowly, halting every few steps, careful not to brush against the stiff greasewood. In the soft sand his steps made no sound. The twinkling light vanished occasionally, like a Jack-o'-lantern, and when it did show it seemed still a long way off. Gale was not seeking trouble or inviting danger. Water was the thing that drove him. He must see who these campers were, and then decide how to give Blanco Sol a drink.

A rabbit rustled out of brush at Gale's feet and thumped away over the sand. The wind pattered among dry, broken stalks of dead *ocatilla*. Every little sound brought Gale to a listening pause. The gloom was thickening fast into darkness. It would be a night without starlight. He moved forward up the pale, zigzag aisles between the mesquite. He lost the light for a while, but the coyotes' chorus told him he was approaching the campfire. Presently the light danced through the black branches, and soon grew into a flame. Stooping low, with bushy mesquites between him and the fire, Gale advanced. The coyotes were in full cry. Gale heard the tramping, stamping thumps of many hoofs. The sound worried him. Foot by foot he advanced, and finally began to crawl. The wind favored his position, so that neither coyotes nor horses could scent him. The nearer he approached the head of the arroyo, where the well was located, the thicker grew the desert vegetation. At length a dead *palo verde,* with huge, black clumps of its parasite mistletoe thick in the branches, marked a distance from the well that Gale considered close enough. Noiselessly he crawled here and there until he secured a favorable position, and then rose to peep from behind his covert.

He saw a bright fire, not a cooking fire, for that would have been low and red, but a crackling blaze of mesquite. Three men were in sight, all close to the burning sticks. They were Mexicans and of the coarse type of raiders, rebels, bandits that Gale had expected to see. One stood up, his back to the fire; another sat with shoulders enveloped in a blanket, and the third lounged in the sand, his feet almost in the blaze. They had cast off belts and weapons. A glint of steel caught Gale's eye. Three short, shiny carbines leaned against a rock. A little to the left, within the circle of light, stood a square house made of adobe bricks. Several untrimmed poles upheld a roof of brush, which was partly fallen in. This house was a Papago Indian habitation, and a month before had been occupied by a family that had been murdered or driven off by a roving band of outlaws. A rude corral showed dimly in the edge of firelight, and from a black mass within came the snort and stamp and whinny of horses.

Gale took in the scene in one quick glance, then sank down at the foot of the mesquite. He had naturally expected to see more men. But the situation was by no means new. This was one, or part of one, of the raider bands harrying the border. They were stealing horses, or driving a herd already stolen. These bands were more numerous than the water holes of northern Sonora; they never camped long at one place; like Arabs, they roamed over the desert all the way from Nogales to Casita. If Gale had gone peaceably up to this campfire there were a hundred chances that the raiders would kill and rob him to one chance that they might not. If they recognized him as a ranger comrade of Ladd and Lash, if they got a glimpse of Blanco Sol, then Gale would have no chance.

These Mexicans had evidently been at the well some time. Their horses being in the corral meant that grazing had been done by day. Gale revolved questions in his mind. Had this trio of outlaws run across Ladd? It was not likely, for in that event they might not have been so comfortable and carefree in camp. Were they waiting for more members of their gang? That was very probable. With Gale, however, the most important consideration was how to get his horse to water. Sol must have a drink if it cost a fight. There was stern reason for Gale to hurry eastward along the trail. He thought it best to go back to where he had left his horse and not make any decisive move until daylight.

With the same noiseless care he had exercised in the advance, Gale retreated until it was safe for him to rise and walk on down the arroyo. He found Blanco Sol contentedly grazing. A heavy dew was falling, and, as the grass was abundant, the horse did not show the usual restlessness and distress after a dry and exhausting day. Gale carried his saddle, blankets, and bags into the lee of a little greasewood-covered mound, from around which the wind had cut the soil; and here, in a wash, he risked building a small fire. By this time the wind was piercingly cold. Gale's hands were numb, and he moved them to and fro in the little blaze. Then he made coffee in a cup, cooked some slices of bacon on the end of a stick, and took a couple of hard biscuits from a saddle-bag. Of these his meal consisted. After that he removed the halter from Blanco Sol, intending to leave him free to graze for a while.

Then Gale returned to his little fire, replenished it with short sticks of dead greasewood and mesquite, and, wrapping his blanket round his shoulders, he sat down to warm himself and to wait till it was time to bring in the horse and tie him up.

The fire was inadequate, and Gale was cold and wet with dew. Hunger and thirst were with him. His bones ached, and there was a dull, deep-seated pain throbbing in his unhealed wound. For days unshaven, his beard seemed like a million pricking needles in his blistered skin. He was so tired that, once having settled himself, he did not move hand or foot. The night was dark, dismal, cloudy, windy, growing colder. A moan of wind in the mesquites was occasionally pierced by the high-keyed yelp of a coyote. There were lulls in which the silence seemed to be a thing of stifling, encroaching substance—a thing that enveloped, buried the desert.

Judged by the great average of ideals and conventional standards of life, Dick Gale was a starved, lonely, suffering, miserable wretch. But in his case the judgment would have hit only externals, would have missed the vital inner truth. For Gale was happy with a kind of strange, wild glory in the privations, the pains, the perils, and the silence and solitude to be endured on this desert land. In the past he had not been of any use to himself or others; and he had never known what it meant to be hungry, cold, tired, lonely. He had never worked for anything. The needs of the day had been provided, and to-morrow and the future looked the same. Danger, peril, toil—these had been words read in books and papers.

In the present he used his hands, his senses, and his wits. He had a duty to a man who relied on his services. He was a comrade, a friend, a valuable ally to riding, fighting rangers. He had spent endless days, weeks that seemed years, alone with a horse, trailing over, climbing over, hunting over a desert that was harsh and hostile by nature, and made more perilous by the invasion of savage men. That horse had become human to Gale. And with him Gale had learned to know the simple needs of existence. Like dead scales the superficialities, the falsities, the habits that had once meant all of life dropped off, useless things in this stern waste of rock and sand.

Gale's happiness, as far as it concerned the toil and strife, was perhaps a grim and stoical one. But love abided with him, and it had engendered and fostered other undeveloped traits—romance and a feeling for beauty, and a keen observation of nature. He felt pain, but he was never miserable. He felt the solitude, but he was never lonely.

As he rode across the desert, even though keen eyes searched for the moving black dots, the rising puffs of white dust that were warnings, he saw Nell's face in every cloud. The clean-cut mesas took on the shape of her straight profile, with its strong chin and lips, its fine nose and forehead. There was always a glint of gold or touch of red or graceful line or gleam of blue to remind him of her. Then at night her face shone warm and glowing, flushing and paling, in the campfire.

Tonight, as usual, with a keen ear to the wind, Gale listened as one on guard; yet he watched the changing phantom of a sweet face in the embers, and as he watched he thought. The desert developed and multiplied thought. A thousand sweet faces glowed in the pink and white ashes of his campfire, the faces of other sweethearts or wives that had gleamed for other men. Gale was happy in his thought of Nell, for something, when he was alone this way in the wilderness, told him she was near him, she thought of him, she loved him. But there were many men alone on that vast southwestern plateau, and when they saw dream faces, surely for some it was a fleeting flash, a gleam soon gone, like the hope and the name and the happiness that had been and was now no more. Often Gale thought of those hundreds of desert travelers, prospectors, wanderers who had ventured down the Camino del Diablo, never to be heard of again. Belding had told him of that most terrible of all desert trails—a trail of shifting sands. Lash had traversed it, and brought back stories of buried water holes, of bones bleaching white in the sun, of gold mines as lost as were the prospectors who had sought them, of the merciless Yaqui and his hatred for the Mexican. Gale thought of this trail and the men who had camped along it. For many there had been one night, one campfire that had been the last. This idea seemed to creep in out of the darkness, the loneliness, the silence, and to find a place in Gale's mind, so that it had strange fascination for him. He knew now as he had never dreamed before how men drifted into the desert, leaving behind graves, wrecked homes, ruined lives, lost wives and sweethearts. And for every wanderer every campfire had a phantom face. Gale measured the agony of these men at their last campfire by the joy and promise he traced in the ruddy heart of his own.

By and by Gale remembered what he was waiting for; and, getting up, he took the halter and went out to find Blanco Sol. It was pitch-dark now, and Gale could not see a rod ahead. He felt his way, and presently as he rounded a mesquite he saw Sol's white shape outlined against the blackness. The horse jumped and wheeled, ready to run. It was doubtful if any one unknown to Sol could ever have caught him. Gale's low call reassured him, and he went on grazing. Gale haltered him in the likeliest patch of grass and returned to his camp. There he lifted his saddle into a protected spot under a low wall of the mound, and, laying one blanket on the sand, he covered himself with the other and stretched himself for the night.

Here he was out of reach of the wind; but he heard its melancholy moan in the mesquite. There was no other sound. The coyotes had ceased their hungry cries. Gale dropped to sleep, and slept soundly during the first half of the night; and after that he seemed always to be partially awake, aware of increasing cold and damp. The dark mantle turned gray, and then daylight came quickly. The morning was clear and nipping cold. He threw off the wet blanket and got up cramped and half frozen. A little brisk action was all that was necessary to warm his blood and loosen his muscles, and then he was fresh, tingling, eager. The sun rose in a golden blaze, and the descending valley took on wondrous changing hues. Then he fetched up Blanco Sol, saddled him, and tied him to the thickest clump of mesquite.

"Sol, we'll have a drink pretty soon," he said, patting the splendid neck.

Gale meant it. He would not eat till he had watered his horse. Sol had gone nearly forty-eight hours without a sufficient drink, and that was long enough, even for a desert-bred beast. No three raiders could keep Gale away from that well. Taking his rifle in hand, he faced up the arroyo. Rabbits were frisking in the short willows, and some were so tame he could have kicked them. Gale walked swiftly for a goodly part of the distance, and then, when he saw blue smoke curling up above the trees, he proceeded slowly, with alert eye and ear. From the lay of the land and position of trees seen by daylight, he found an easier and safer course than the one he had taken in the dark. And by careful work he was enabled to get closer to the well, and somewhat above it.

The Mexicans were leisurely cooking their morning meal. They had two fires, one for warmth, the other to cook over. Gale had an idea these raiders were familiar to him. It seemed all these border hawks resembled one another—being mostly small of build, wiry, angular, swarthy-faced, and blackhaired, and they wore the oddly styled Mexican clothes and sombreros. A slow wrath stirred in Gale as he watched the trio. They showed not the slightest indication of breaking camp. One fellow, evidently the leader, packed a gun at his hip, the only weapon in sight. Gale noted this with speculative eyes. The raiders had slept inside the little adobe house, and had not yet brought out the carbines. Next Gale swept his gaze to the corral, in which he saw more than a dozen horses, some of them fine animals. They were stamping and whistling, fighting one another, and pawing the dirt. This was entirely natural behavior for desert horses penned in when they wanted to get at water and grass.

But suddenly one of the blacks, a big, shaggy fellow, shot up his ears and pointed his nose over the top of the fence. He whistled. Other horses looked in the same direction, and their ears went up, and they, too, whistled.

Gale knew that other horses or men, very likely both, were approaching. But the Mexicans did not hear the alarm, or show any interest if they did. These mescal-drinking raiders were not scouts. It was notorious how easily they could be surprised or ambushed. Mostly they were ignorant, thick-skulled peons. They were wonderful horsemen, and could go long without food or water; but they had no other accomplishments or attributes calculated to help them in desert warfare. They had poor sight, poor hearing, poor judgment, and when excited they resembled crazed ants running wild.

Gale saw two Indians on burros come riding up the other side of the knoll upon which the adobe house stood; and apparently they were not aware of the presence of the Mexicans, for they came on up the path. One Indian was a Papago. The other, striking in appearance for other reasons than that he seemed to be about to fall from the burro, Gale took to be a Yaqui. These travelers had absolutely nothing for an outfit except a blanket and a half-empty bag. They came over the knoll and down the path toward the well, turned a corner of the house, and completely surprised the raiders.

Gale heard a short, shrill cry, strangely high and wild, and this came from one of the Indians. It was answered by hoarse shouts. Then the leader of the trio, the Mexican who packed a gun, pulled it and fired point-blank. He missed once—and again. At the third shot the Papago shrieked and tumbled off his burro to fall in a heap. The other Indian swayed, as if the taking away of the support lent by his comrade had brought collapse, and with the fourth shot he, too, slipped to the ground.

The reports had frightened the horses in the corral; and the vicious black, crowding the rickety bars, broke them down. He came plunging out. Two of the Mexicans ran for him, catching him by nose and mane, and the third ran to block the gateway.

Then, with a splendid vaulting mount, the Mexican with the gun leaped to the back of the horse. He yelled and waved his gun, and urged the black forward. The manner of all three was savagely jocose. They were having sport. The two on the ground began to dance and jabber. The mounted leader shot again, and then stuck like a leech upon the bare back of the rearing black. It was a vain show of horsemanship. Then this Mexican, by some strange grip, brought the horse down, plunging almost upon the body of the Indian that had fallen last.

Gale stood aghast with his rifle clutched tight. He could not divine the intention of the raider, but suspected something strikingly brutal. The horse answered to that cruel, guiding hand, yet he swerved and bucked. He reared aloft, pawing the air, wildly snorting, then he plunged down upon the prostrate Indian. Even in the act the intelligent animal tried to keep from striking the body with his hoofs. But that was not possible. A yell, hideous in its passion, signaled this feat of horsemanship.

The Mexican made no move to trample the body of the Papago. He turned the black to ride again over the other Indian. That brought into Gale's mind what he had heard of a Mexican's hate for a Yaqui. It recalled the barbarism of these savage peons, and the war of extermination being waged upon the Yaquis.

Suddenly Gale was horrified to see the Yaqui writhe and raise a feeble hand. The action brought renewed and more savage cries from the Mexicans. The horse snorted in terror.

Gale could bear no more. He took a quick shot at the

rider. He missed the moving figure, but hit the horse. There was a bound, a horrid scream, a mighty plunge, then the horse went down, giving the Mexican a stunning fall. Both beast and man lay still.

Gale rushed from his cover to intercept the other raiders before they could reach the house and their weapons. One fellow yelled and ran wildly in the opposite direction; the other stood stricken in his tracks. Gale ran in close and picked up the gun that had dropped from the raider leader's hand. This fellow had begun to stir, to come out of his stunned condition. Then the frightened horses burst the corral bars, and in a thundering, dust-mantled stream fled up the arroyo.

The fallen raider sat up, mumbling to his saints in one breath, cursing in his next. The other Mexican kept his stand, intimidated by the threatening rifle.

"Go, Greasers! Run!" yelled Gale. Then he yelled it in Spanish. At the point of his rifle he drove the two raiders out of the camp. His next move was to run into the house and fetch out the carbines. With a heavy stone he dismantled each weapon. That done, he set out on a run for his horse. He took the shortest cut down the arroyo, with no concern as to whether or not he would encounter the raiders. Probably such a meeting would be all the worse for them, and they knew it. Blanco Sol heard him coming and whistled a welcome, and when Gale ran up the horse was snorting war. Mounting, Gale rode rapidly back to the scene of the action, and his first thought, when he arrived at the well, was to give Sol a drink and to fill his canteens.

Then Gale led his horse up out of the water hole, and decided before remounting to have a look at the Indians. The Papago had been shot through the heart, but the Yaqui was still alive. Moreover, he was conscious and staring up at Gale with great, strange, somber eyes, black as volcanic slag.

"Gringo good—no kill," he said, in husky whisper.

His speech was not affirmative so much as questioning.

"Yaqui, you're done for," said Gale, and his words were positive. He was simply speaking aloud his mind.

"Yaqui—no hurt—much," replied the Indian, and then he spoke a strange word—repeated it again and again.

An instinct of Gale's, or perhaps some suggestion in the husky, thick whisper or dark face, told Gale to reach for his canteen. He lifted the Indian and gave him a drink, and if ever in all his life he saw gratitude in human eyes he saw it then. Then he examined the injured Yaqui, not forgetting for an instant to send wary, fugitive glances on all sides. Gale was not to be surprised. The Indian had three wounds—a bullet-hole in his shoulder, a crushed arm, and a badly lacerated leg. What had been the matter with him before being set upon by the raider Gale could not be certain.

The ranger thought rapidly. This Yaqui would live unless left there to die or be murdered by the Mexicans when they found courage to sneak back to the well. It never occurred to Gale to abandon the poor fellow. That was where his old training, the higher order of human feeling, made impossible the following of any elemental instinct of self-preservation. All the same, Gale knew he multiplied his perils a hundredfold by burdening himself with a crippled Indian. Swiftly he set to work, and with rifle ever under his hand, and shifting glance spared from his task, he bound up the Yaqui's wounds. At the same time he kept keen watch.

The Indians' burros and the horses of the raiders were all out of sight. Time was too valuable for Gale to use any

in what might be vain search. Therefore, he lifted the
Yaqui upon Sol's broad shoulders and climbed into the
saddle. At a word Sol dropped his head and started eastward up the trail, walking swiftly, without resentment for
his double burden.

Far ahead, between two huge mesas where the trail
mounted over a pass, a long line of dust clouds marked
the position of the horses that had escaped from the corral. Those that had been stolen would travel straight and
true for home, and perhaps would lead the others with
them. The raiders were left on the desert without guns or
mounts.

Blanco Sol walked or jog-trotted six miles to the hour.
At that gait fifty miles would not have wet or turned a hair
of his dazzling white coat. Gale, bearing in mind the ever-
present possibility of encountering more raiders and of
being pursued, saved the strength of the horse. Once out
of sight of Papago Well, Gale dismounted and walked beside the horse, steadying with one firm hand the helpless,
dangling Yaqui.

The sun cleared the eastern ramparts, and the coolness
of morning fled as if before a magic foe. The whole desert changed. The grays wore bright; the mesquites glistened; the cactus took the silver hue of frost, and the rocks
gleamed gold and red. Then, as the heat increased, a wind
rushed up out of the valley behind Gale, and the hotter
the sun blazed down the swifter rushed the wind. The
wonderful transparent haze of distance lost its bluish hue
for one with a tinge of yellow. Flying sand made the peaks
dimly outlined.

Gale kept pace with his horse. He bore the twinge of
pain that darted through his injured hip at every stride.
His eye roved over the wide, smoky prospect seeking the

landmarks he knew. When the wild and bold spurs of No Name Mountains loomed through a rent in flying clouds of sand he felt nearer home. Another hour brought him abreast of a dark, straight shaft rising clear from a beetling escarpment. This was a monument marking the international boundary line. When he had passed it he had his own country underfoot. In the heat of midday he halted in the shade of a rock, and, lifting the Yaqui down, gave him a drink. Then, after a long, sweeping survey of the surrounding desert, he removed Sol's saddle and let him roll, and took for himself a welcome rest and a bite to eat.

The Yaqui was tenacious of life. He was still holding his own. For the first time Gale really looked at the Indian to study him. He had a large head nobly cast, and a face that resembled a shrunken mask. It seemed chiseled in the dark-red, volcanic lava of his Sonora wilderness. The Indians' eyes were always black and mystic, but this Yaqui's encompassed all the tragic desolation of the desert. They were fixed on Gale, moved only when he moved. The Indian was short and broad, and his body showed unusual muscular development, although he seemed greatly emaciated from starvation or illness.

Gale resumed his homeward journey. When he got through the pass he faced a great depression, as rough as if millions of gigantic spikes had been driven by the hammer of Thor into a seamed and cracked floor. This was Altar Valley. It was a chaos of arroyos, cañons, rocks, and ridges all mantled with cactus, and at its eastern end it claimed the dry bed of Forlorn River and water when there was any.

With a wounded, helpless man across the saddle, this stretch of thorny and contorted desert was practically impassable. Yet Gale headed into it unflinchingly. He would carry the Yaqui as far as possible, or until death made the burden no longer a duty. Blanco Sol plodded on over the dragging sand, up and down the steep, loose banks of washes, out on the rocks, and through the rows of white-toothed *chollas.*

The sun sloped westward, bending fiercer heat in vengeful, parting reluctance. The wind slackened. The dust settled. And the bold, forbidding front of No Name Mountains changed to red and gold. Gale held grimly by the side of the tireless, implacable horse, holding the Yaqui on the saddle, taking the brunt of the merciless thorns. In the end it became heartrending toil. His heavy chaps dragged him down; but he dared not go on without them, for, thick and stiff as they were, the terrible, steel-bayoneted spikes of the *chollas* pierced through to sting his legs.

To the last mile Gale held to Blanco Sol's gait and kept ever-watchful gaze ahead on the trail. Then, with the low, flat houses of Forlorn River shining red in the sunset, Gale flagged and rapidly weakened. The Yaqui slipped out of the saddle and dropped limp in the sand. Gale could not mount his horse. He clutched Sol's long tail and twisted his hand in it and staggered on.

Blanco Sol whistled a piercing blast. He scented cool water and sweet alfalfa hay. Twinkling lights ahead meant rest. The melancholy desert twilight rapidly succeeded the sunset. It accentuated the forlorn loneliness of the gray, winding river of sand and its grayer shores. Night shadows trooped down from the black and looming mountains.

CHAPTER 7

WHITE HORSES

Acrippled Yaqui! Why the hell did you saddle yourself with him?" roared Belding, as he laid Gale upon the bed.

Belding had grown hard these late, violent weeks.

"Because I chose," whispered Gale, in reply. "Go after him—he dropped in the trail—across the river—near the first big *saguaro.*"

Belding began to swear as he fumbled with matches and the lamp; but as the light flared up he stopped short in the middle of a word.

"You said you weren't hurt?" he demanded, in sharp anxiety, as he bent over Gale.

"I'm only—all in. . . . Will you go—or send someone—for the Yaqui?"

"Sure, Dick, sure," Belding replied, in softer tones. Then he stalked out; his heels rang on the flagstones; he opened a door and called: "Mother—girls, here's Dick back. He's done up. . . . Now—no, no, he's not hurt or in bad shape. You women! . . . Do what you can to make him comfortable. I've got a little job on hand."

There were quick replies that Gale's dulling ears did not distinguish. Then it seemed Mrs. Belding was beside his bed, her very presence so cool and soothing and helpful; and Mercedes and Nell, wide-eyed and white-faced, were fluttering around him. He drank thirstily, but refused food. He wanted rest. And with their faces drifting away in a kind of haze, with the feeling of gentle hands about him, he lost consciousness.

He slept twenty hours. Then he arose, thirsty, hungry, lame, overworn, and presently went in search of Belding and the business of the day.

"Your Yaqui was near dead, but guess we'll pull him through," said Belding. "Dick, the other day that Indian came here by rail and foot and Lord only knows how else, all the way from New Orleans! He spoke English better than most Indians, and I know a little Yaqui. I got some of his story and guessed the rest. The Mexican government is trying to root out the Yaquis. A year ago his tribe was taken in chains to a Mexican port on the Gulf. The fathers, mothers, children, were separated and put in ships bound for Yucatán. There they were made slaves on the great henequen plantations. They were driven, beaten, starved. Each slave had for a day's rations a hunk of sourdough, no more. Yucatán is low, marshy, damp, hot. The Yaquis were bred on the high, dry Sonoran plateau, where the air is like a knife. They dropped dead in the henequen fields, and their places were taken by more. You see, the Mexicans won't kill outright in their war of extermination of the Yaquis. They get use out of them. It's a horrible thing. . . . Well, this Yaqui you brought in escaped from his captors, got aboard ship, and eventually reached New Orleans. Somehow he traveled way out here. I gave him a bag of food, and he went off with a Papago Indian. He was a sick man then. And he must have fallen foul of some Greasers."

Gale told of his experience at Papago Well.

"That raider who tried to grind the Yaqui under a horse's hoofs—he was a hyena!" concluded Gale, shuddering. "I've seen some blood spilled and some hard sights, but that inhuman devil took my nerve. Why, as I told you, Belding, I missed a shot at him—not twenty paces!"

"Dick, in cases like that the sooner you clean up the bunch the better," said Belding, grimly. "As for hard sights—wait till you've seen a Yaqui do up a Mexican. Bar none, that is the limit! It's bloodlust, a racial hate, deep as life, and terrible. The Spaniards crushed the Aztecs four or five hundred years ago. That hate has had time to grow as deep as a cactus root. The Yaquis are mountain Aztecs. Personally, I think they are noble and intelligent, and if let alone would be peaceable and industrious. I like the few I've known. But they are a doomed race. Have you any idea what ailed this Yaqui before the raider got in his work?"

"No, I haven't. I noticed the Indian seemed in bad shape; but I couldn't tell what was the matter with him."

"Well, my idea is another personal one. Maybe it's off color. I think that Yaqui was, or is, for that matter, dying of a broken heart. All he wanted was to get back to his mountains and die. There are no Yaquis left in that part of Sonora he was bound for."

"He had a strange look in his eyes," said Gale, thoughtfully.

"Yes, I noticed that. But all Yaquis have a wild look. Dick, if I'm not mistaken, this fellow was a chief. It was a waste of strength, a needless risk for you to save him, pack him back here. But, damn the whole Greaser outfit generally, I'm glad you did!"

Gale remembered then to speak of his concern for Ladd.

"Laddy didn't go out to meet you," replied Belding. "I knew you were due in any day, and, as there's been trouble between here and Casita, I sent him that way. Since you've been out our friend Carter lost a bunch of horses and a few steers. Did you get a good look at the horses those raiders had at Papago Well?"

Dick had learned, since he had become a ranger, to see everything with keen, sure, photographic eye; and, being put to the test so often required of him, he described the horses as a dark-colored drove, mostly bays and blacks, with one spotted sorrel.

"Some of Carter's—sure as you're born!" exclaimed Belding. "His bunch has been split up, divided among several bands of raiders. He has a grass ranch up here in Three Mile Arroyo. It's a good long ride in U.S. territory from the border."

"Those horses I saw will go home, don't you think?" asked Dick.

"Sure. They can't be caught or stopped."

"Well, what shall I do now?"

"Stay here and rest," bluntly replied Belding. "You need it. Let the women fuss over you—doctor you a little. When Jim gets back from Sonoyta I'll know more about what we ought to do. By Lord! it seems our job now isn't keeping Japs and Chinks out of the U.S. It's keeping our property from going into Mexico."

"Are there any letters for me?" asked Gale.

"Letters! Say, my boy, it'd take something pretty important to get me or any man here back Casita way. If the town is safe these days the road isn't. It's a month now since any one went to Casita."

Gale had received several letters from his sister Elsie, the last of which he had not answered. There had not been much opportunity for writing on his infrequent returns to Forlorn River; and, besides, Elsie had written that her father had stormed over what he considered Dick's falling into wild and evil ways.

"Time flies," said Dick. "George Thorne will be free before long, and he'll be coming out. I wonder if he'll stay here or try to take Mercedes away?"

"Well, he'll stay right here in Forlorn River, if I have any say," replied Belding. "I'd like to know how he'd ever get that Spanish girl out of the country now, with all the trails overrun by rebels and raiders. It'd be hard to disguise her. Say, Dick, maybe we can get Thorne to stay here. You know, since you've discovered the possibility of a big water supply, I've had dreams of a future for Forlorn River. . . . If only this war was over! Dick, that's what it is—war—scattered war along the northern border of Mexico from gulf to gulf. What if it isn't our war? We're on the fringe. No, we can't develop Forlorn River until there's peace."

The discovery that Belding alluded to was one that might very well lead to the making of a wonderful and agricultural district of Altar Valley. While in college Dick Gale had studied engineering, but he had not set the scientific world afire with his brilliance. Nor after leaving college had he been able to satisfy his father that he could hold a job. Nevertheless, his smattering of engineering skill bore fruit in the last place on earth where anything might have been expected of it—in the desert. Gale had always wondered about the source of Forlorn River. No white man or Mexican, or, so far as known, no Indian, had climbed those mighty broken steps of rock called No Name Mountains, from which Forlorn River was supposed to come. Gale had discovered a long, narrow, rock-bottomed and rock-walled gulch that could be dammed at the lower end by the dynamiting of leaning cliffs above. An inexhaustible supply of water could be stored there. Furthermore, he had worked out an irrigation plan to bring the water down for mining uses, and to make a paradise out of that part of Altar Valley which lay in the United States. Belding claimed there was gold in the arroyos, gold in the gulches, not in quantities to make a prospector rejoice, but enough to work for. And the soil on the higher levels of Altar Valley needed only water to make it grow anything the year round. Gale, too, had come to have dreams of a future for Forlorn River.

On the afternoon of the following day Ladd unexpectedly appeared leading a lame and lathered horse into the yard. Belding and Gale, who were at work at the forge, looked up and were surprised out of speech. The legs of the horse were raw and red, and he seemed about to drop. Ladd's sombrero was missing; he wore a bloody scarf round his head; sweat and blood and dust had formed a crust on his face; little streams of powdery dust slid from him; and the lower half of his scarred chaps were full of broken white thorns.

"Howdy, boys," he drawled. "I shore am glad to see you all."

"Where'n hell's your hat?" demanded Belding, furiously. It was a ridiculous greeting. But Belding's words signified little. The dark shade of worry and solicitude crossing his face told more than his blank amaze.

The ranger stopped unbuckling the saddle girths, and, looking at Belding, broke into his slow, cool laugh.

"Tom, you recollect that whopper of a *saguaro* up here where Carter's trail branches off the main trail to Casita? Well, I climbed it an' left my hat on top for a woodpecker's nest."

"You've been running—fighting?" queried Belding, as if Ladd had not spoken at all.

"I reckon it'll dawn on you after a while," replied Ladd, slipping the saddle.

"Laddy, go in the house to the women," said Belding. "I'll tend to your horse."

"Shore, Tom, in a minute. I've been down the road. An' I found hoss tracks an' steer tracks goin' across the line. But I seen no sign of raiders till this mornin'. Slept at Carter's last night. That raid the other day cleaned him out. He's shootin' mad. Well, this mornin' I rode plumb into a bunch of Carter's hosses, runnin' wild for home. Some Greasers were tryin' to head them round an' chase them back across the line. I rode in between an' made matters embarrassin'. Carter's hosses got away. Then me an' the Greasers had a little game of hide-an'-seek in the cactus. I was on the wrong side, an' had to break through their line to head toward home. We run some. But I had a closer call than I'm stuck on havin'."

"Laddy, you wouldn't have any such close calls if you'd ride one of my horses," expostulated Belding. "This broncho of yours can run, and Lord knows he's game. But you want a big, strong horse, Mexican bred, with cactus in his blood. Take one of the bunch—Bull, White Woman, Blanco José."

"I had a big, fast horse a while back, but I lost him," said Ladd. "This bronch ain't so bad. Shore Bull an' that white devil with his Greaser name—they could run down my bronch, kill him in a mile of cactus. But, somehow, Tom, I can't make up my mind to take one of them grand white hosses. Shore I reckon I'm kinda soft. An' mebbe I'd better take one before the raiders clean up Forlorn River."

Belding cursed low and deep in his throat, and the sound resembled muttering thunder. The shade of anxiety on his face changed to one of dark gloom and passion. Next to his wife and daughter there was nothing so dear to him as those white horses. His father and his grandfather—all his progenitors of whom he had trace—had been lovers of horses. It was in Belding's blood.

"Laddy, before it's too late can't I get the whites away from the border?"

"Mebbe it ain't too late; but where can we take them?"

"To San Felipe?"

"No. We've more chance to hold them here."

"To Casita and the railroad?"

"Afraid to risk gettin' there. An' the town's full of rebels who need hosses."

"Then straight north?"

"Shore man, you're crazy. There's no water, no grass for a hundred miles. I'll tell you, Tom, the safest plan would be to take the white bunch south into Sonora, into some wild mountain valley. Keep them there till the raiders have traveled on back east. Pretty soon there won't be any rich pickin' left for these Greasers. An' then they'll ride on to new ranges."

"Laddy, I don't know the trails into Sonora. An' I can't trust a Mexican or a Papago. Between you and me, I'm afraid of this Indian who herds for me."

"I reckon we'd better stick here, Tom. . . . Dick, it's some good to see you again. But you seem kinda quiet. Shore you get quieter all the time. Did you see any sign of Jim out Sonoyta way?"

Then Belding led the lame horse toward the watering-trough while the two rangers went toward the house. Dick was telling Ladd about the affair at Papago Well when they turned the corner under the porch. Nell was sitting in the door. She rose with a little scream and came flying toward them.

"Now I'll get it," whispered Ladd. "The women'll make a baby of me. An' shore I can't help myself."

"Oh, Laddy, you've been hurt!" cried Nell, as with white cheeks and dilating eyes she ran to him and caught his arm.

"Nell, I only run a thorn in my ear."

"Oh, Laddy, don't lie! You've lied before. I know you're hurt. Come in to Mother."

"Shore, Nell, it's only a scratch. My bronch throwed me."

"Laddy, no horse ever threw you." The girl's words and accusing eyes only hurried the ranger on to further duplicity.

"Mebbe I got it when I was ridin' hard under a mesquite, an' a sharp snag—"

"You've been shot! . . . Mamma, here's Laddy, and he's been shot! . . . . Oh, these dreadful days we're having! I can't bear them! Forlorn River used to be so safe and quiet. Nothing happened. But now! Jim comes home with a bloody hole in him—then Dick—then Laddy! . . . Oh, I'm afraid someday they'll *never* come home."

The morning was bright, still, and clear as crystal. The heat waves had not yet begun to rise from the desert. A soft gray, white, and green tint perfectly blended lay like a mantle over mesquite and sand and cactus. The cañons of distant mountain showed deep and full of lilac haze.

Nell sat perched high upon the topmost bar of the corral gate. Dick leaned beside her, now with his eyes on her face, now gazing out into the alfalfa field where Belding's thoroughbreds grazed and pranced and romped and whistled. Nell watched the horses. She loved them, never tired of watching them. But her gaze was too consciously averted from the yearning eyes that tried to meet hers to be altogether natural.

A great fenced field of velvety green alfalfa furnished a rich background for the drove of about twenty white horses. Even without the horses the field would have presented a striking contrast to the surrounding hot, glaring blaze of rock and sand. Belding had bred a hundred or more horses from the original stock he had brought up from Durango. His particular interest was in the almost unblemished white, and these he had given especial care. He made a good deal of money selling this strain to friends among the ranchers back in Texas. No mercenary consideration, however, could have made him part with the great, rangy white horses he had gotten from the Durango breeder. They were named Blanco Diablo (White Devil), Blanco Sol (White Sun), Blanca Reina (White Queen), Blanca Mujer (White Woman), and El

Grande Blanco Torres (The Big White Bull). Belding had been laughed at by ranchers for preserving the sentimental Durango names, and he had been unmercifully ridiculed by cowboys. But the names had never been changed.

Blanco Diablo was the only horse in the field that was not free to roam and graze where he listed. A stake and a halter held him to one corner, where he was severely let alone by the other horses. He did not like this isolation. Blanco Diablo was not happy unless he was running, or fighting a rival. Of the two he would rather fight. If anything white could resemble a devil, this horse surely did. He had nothing beautiful about him, yet he drew the gaze and held it. The look of him suggested discontent, anger, revolt, viciousness. When he was not grazing or prancing, he held his long, lean head level, pointing his nose and showing his teeth. Belding's favorite was almost all the world to him, and he swore Diablo could stand more heat and thirst and cactus than any other horse he owned, and could run down and kill any horse in the Southwest. The fact that Ladd did not agree with Belding on these salient points was a great disappointment, and also a perpetual source for argument. Ladd and Lash both hated Diablo; and Dick Gale, after one or two narrow escapes from being brained, had inclined to the cowboys' side of the question.

El Grande Blanco Torres upheld his name. He was a huge, massive, thick-flanked stallion, a kingly mate for his full-bodied, glossy consort, Blanca Reina. The other mare, Blanca Mujer, was dazzling white, without a spot, perfectly pointed, racy, graceful, elegant, yet carrying weight and brawn and range that suggested her relation to her forebears.

The cowboys admitted some of Belding's claims for

Diablo, but they gave loyal and unshakable allegiance to Blanco Sol. As for Dick, he had to fight himself to keep out of arguments, for he sometimes imagined he was unreasonable about the horse. Though he could not understand himself, he knew he loved Sol as a man loved a friend, a brother. Free of heavy saddle and the clumsy leg shields, Blanco Sol was somehow all-satisfying to the eyes of the rangers. As long and big as Diablo was, Sol was longer and bigger. Also, he was higher, more powerful. He looked more a thing for action—speedier. At a distance the honorable scars and lumps that marred his muscular legs were not visible. He grazed aloof from the others, and did not cavort nor prance; but when he lifted his head to whistle, how wild he appeared, and proud and splendid! The dazzling whiteness of the desert sun shone from his coat; he had the fire and spirit of the desert in his noble head, its strength and power in his gigantic frame.

"Belding swears Sol never beat Diablo," Dick was saying.

"He believes it," replied Nell. "Dad is queer about that horse."

"But Laddy rode Sol once—made him beat Diablo. Jim saw the race."

Nell laughed. "I saw it, too. For that matter, even I have made Sol put his nose before Dad's favorite."

"I'd like to have seen that. Nell, aren't you ever going to ride with me?"

"Someday—when it's safe."

"Safe!"

"I—I mean when the raiders have left the border."

"Oh, I'm glad you mean that," said Dick, laughing. "Well, I've often wondered how Belding ever came to give Blanco Sol to me."

"He was jealous. I think he wanted to get rid of Sol."

"No? Why, Nell, he'd give Laddy or Jim one of the whites any day."

"Would he? Not Devil or Queen or White Woman. Never in this world! But Dad has lots of fast horses the boys could pick from. Dick, I tell you Dad wants Blanco Sol to run himself out—lose his speed on the desert. Dad is just jealous for Diablo."

"Maybe. He surely has strange passion for horses. I think I understand better than I used to. I owned a couple of racers once. They were just animals to me, I guess. But Blanco Sol!"

"Do you love him?" asked Nell; and now a warm, blue flash of eyes swept his face.

"Do I? Well, rather."

"I'm glad. Sol has been finer, a better horse since you owned him. He loves you, Dick. He's always watching for you. See him raise his head. That's for you. I know as much about horses as Dad or Laddy any day. Sol always hated Diablo, and never had much use for Dad."

Dick looked up at her.

"It'll be—be pretty hard to leave Sol—when I go away."

Nell sat perfectly still.

"Go away?" she asked, presently, with just the faintest tremor in her voice.

"Yes. Sometimes when I get blue—as I am today—I think I'll go. But, in sober truth, Nell, it's not likely that I'll spend all my life here."

There was no answer to this. Dick put his hand softly over hers; and, despite her halfhearted struggle to free it, he held on.

"Nell!"

Her color fled. He saw her lips part. Then a heavy step

on the gravel, a cheerful, complaining voice interrupted him, and made him release Nell and draw back. Belding strode into view round the adobe shed.

"Hey, Dick, that darned Yaqui Indian can't be driven or hired or coaxed to leave Forlorn River. He's well enough to travel. I offered him horse, gun, blanket, grub. But no go."

"That's funny," replied Gale, with a smile. "Let him stay—put him to work."

"It doesn't strike me funny. But I'll tell you what I think. That poor, homeless, heartbroken Indian has taken a liking to you, Dick. These desert Yaquis are strange folk. I've heard strange stories about them. I'd believe 'most anything. And that's how I figure his case. You saved his life. That sort of thing counts big with any Indian, even with an Apache. With a Yaqui maybe it's of deep significance. I've heard a Yaqui say that with his tribe no debt to friend or foe ever went unpaid. Perhaps that's what ails this fellow."

"Dick, don't laugh," said Nell. "I've noticed the Yaqui. It's pathetic the way his great gloomy eyes follow you."

"You've made a friend," continued Belding. "A Yaqui could be a real friend on this desert. If he gets his strength back he'll be of service to you, don't mistake me. He's welcome here. But you're responsible for him, and you'll have trouble keeping him from massacring all the Greasers in Forlorn River."

The probability of a visit from the raiders, and a dash bolder than usual on the outskirts of a ranch, led Belding to build a new corral. It was not sightly to the eye, but it was high and exceedingly strong. The gate was a massive affair, swinging on huge hinges and fastening with heavy chains and padlocks. On the outside it had been completely covered with barbed wire, which would make it a troublesome thing to work on in the dark.

At night Belding locked his white horses in this corral. The Papago herdsman slept in the adobe shed adjoining. Belding did not imagine that any wooden fence, however substantially built, could keep determined raiders from breaking it down. They would have to take time, however, and make considerable noise; and Belding relied on these facts. Belding did not believe a band of night raiders would hold out against a hot rifle fire. So he began to make up some of the sleep he had lost. It was noteworthy, however, that Ladd did not share Belding's sanguine hopes.

Jim Lash rode in, reporting that all was well out along the line toward the Sonoyta Oasis. Days passed, and Belding kept his rangers home. Nothing was heard of raiders at hand. Many of the newcomers, both American and Mexican, who came with wagons and pack trains from Casita stated that property and life were cheap back in that rebel-infested town.

One January morning Dick Gale was awakened by a shrill, menacing cry. He leaped up bewildered and frightened. He heard Belding's booming voice answering shouts, and rapid steps on flagstones. But these had not awakened him. Heavy breaths, almost sobs, seemed at his very door. In the cold and gray dawn Dick saw something white. Gun in hand, he bounded across the room. Just outside his door stood Blanco Sol.

It was not unusual for Sol to come poking his head in at Dick's door during daylight. But now in the early dawn, when he had been locked in the corral, it meant raiders—no less. Dick called softly to the snorting horse; and, hurriedly getting into clothes and boots, he went out with a gun in each hand. Sol was quivering in every muscle. Like a dog he followed Dick around the house. Hearing shouts in the direction of the corrals, Gale bent swift steps that way.

He caught up with Jim Lash, who was also leading a white horse.

"Hello, Jim! Guess it's all over but the fireworks," said Dick.

"I cain't say just what has come off," replied Lash. "I've got the Bull. Found him runnin' in the yard."

They reached the corral to find Belding shaking, roaring like a madman. The gate was open, the corral was empty. Ladd stooped over the ground, evidently trying to find tracks.

"I reckon we might jest as well cool off an' wait for daylight," suggested Jim.

"Shore. They've flown the coop, you can gamble on that. Tom, where's the Papago?" said Ladd.

"He's gone, Laddy—gone!"

"Double-crossed us, eh? I see here's a crowbar lyin' by the gatepost. That Indian fetched it from the forge. It was used to pry out the bolts an' steeples. Tom, I reckon there wasn't much time lost forcin' that gate."

Belding, in shirtsleeves and barefooted, roared with rage. He said he had heard the horses running as he leaped out of bed.

"What woke you?" asked Laddy.

"Sol. He came whistling for Dick. Didn't you hear him before I called you?"

"Hear him! He came thunderin' right under my window. I jumped up in bed, an' when he let out that blast Jim lit square in the middle of the floor, an' I was scared stiff. Dick, seein' it was your room he blew into, what did you think?"

"I couldn't think. I'm shaking yet, Laddy."

"Boys, I'll bet Sol spilled a few raiders if any got hands on him," said Jim. "Now, let's sit down an' wait for daylight. It's my idea we'll find some of the hosses runnin' loose. Tom, you go an' get some clothes on. It's freezin' cold. An' don't forget to tell the womenfolks we're all right."

Daylight made clear some details of the raid. The cowboys found tracks of eight raiders coming up from the riverbed where their horses had been left. Evidently the Papago had been false to his trust. His few personal belongings were gone. Lash was correct in his idea of finding more horses loose in the fields. The men soon rounded up eleven of the whites, all more or less frightened, and among the number were Queen and Blanca Mujer. The raiders had been unable to handle more than one horse for each man. It was bitter irony of fate that Belding should lose his favorite, the one horse more dear to him than all the others. Somewhere out on the trail a raider was fighting the iron-jawed savage Blanco Diablo.

"I reckon we're some lucky," observed Jim Lash.

"Lucky ain't enough word," replied Ladd. "You see, it was this way. Some of the raiders piled over the fence while the others worked on the gate. Mebbe the Papago went inside to pick out the best hosses. But it didn't work except with Diablo, an' how they ever got him I don't know. I'd have gambled it'd take all of eight men to steal him. But Greasers have got us skinned on handlin' hosses."

Belding was unconsolable. He cursed and railed, and finally declared he was going to trail the raiders.

"Tom, you just ain't agoin' to do nothin' of the kind," said Laddy, coolly.

Belding groaned and bowed his head.

"Laddy, you're right," he replied, presently. "I've got to stand it. I can't leave the women and my property. But it's sure tough. I'm sore way down deep, and nothin' but blood would ever satisfy me."

"Leave that to me an' Jim," said Ladd.

"What do you mean to do?" demanded Belding, starting up.

"Shore I don't know yet. . . . Give me a light for my pipe. An' Dick, go fetch out your Yaqui."

CHAPTER 8

THE RUNNING OF
BLANCO SOL

The Yaqui's strange dark glance roved over the corral, the swinging gate with its broken fastenings, the tracks in the road, and then rested upon Belding.

"Malo," he said, and his Spanish was clear.

"Shore Yaqui, about eight bad men, an' a traitor Indian," said Ladd.

"I think he means my herder," added Belding. "If he does, that settles any doubt it might be decent to have— Yaqui—malo Papago—*Sí?*"

The Yaqui spread wide his hands. Then he bent over the tracks in the road. They led everywhither, but gradually he worked out of the thick net to take the trail that the cowboys had followed down to the river. Belding and the rangers kept close at his heels. Occasionally Dick lent a helping hand to the still feeble Indian. He found a trampled spot where the raiders had left their horses. From this point a deeply defined narrow trail led across the dry riverbed.

Belding asked the Yaqui where the raiders would head for in the Sonora Desert. For answer the Indian followed the trail across the stream of sand, through willows and mesquite, up to the level of rock and cactus. At this point he halted. A sand-filled, almost obliterated trail led off to the left, and evidently went round to the east of No Name Mountains. To the right stretched the road toward Papago Well and the Sonoyta Oasis. The trail of the raiders took a southeasterly course over untrodden desert. The Yaqui spoke in his own tongue, then in Spanish.

"Think he means slow march," said Belding. "Laddy, from the looks of that trail the Greasers are having trouble with the horses."

"Tom, shore a boy could see that," replied Laddy. "Ask Yaqui to tell us where the raiders are headin', an' if there's water."

It was wonderful to see the Yaqui point. His dark hand stretched; he sighted over his stretched finger at a low white escarpment in the distance. Then with a stick he traced a line in the sand, and then at the end of that another line at right angles. He made crosses and marks and holes, and as he drew the rude map he talked in Yaqui, in Spanish, with a word here and there in English. Belding translated as best he could. The raiders were heading southeast toward the railroad that ran from Nogales down into Sonora. It was four days' travel, bad trail, good sure water hole one day out; then water not sure for two days. Raiders traveling slow; bothered by too many horses, not looking for pursuit; were never pursued, could be headed and ambushed that night at the first water hole, a natural trap in a valley.

The men returned to the ranch. The rangers ate and drank while making hurried preparations for travel. Blanco Sol and the cowboys' horses were fed, watered, and saddled. Ladd again refused to ride one of Belding's whites. He was quick and cold.

"Get me a long-range rifle an' lots of shells. Rustle now," he said.

"Laddy, you don't want to be weighted down?" protested Belding.

"Shore I want a gun that'll outshoot the dinky little carbines an' muskets used by the rebels. Trot one out an' be quick."

"I've got a .405, a long-barreled heavy rifle that'll shoot a mile. I use it for mountain sheep. But Laddy, it'll break that bronch's back."

"His back won't break so easy. . . . Dick, take plenty of shells for your Remington. An' don't forget your field glass."

In less than an hour after the time of the raid the three rangers, heavily armed and superbly mounted on fresh horses, rode out on the trail. As Gale turned to look back from the far bank of Forlorn River, he saw Nell waving a white scarf. He stood high in his stirrups and waved his sombrero. Then the mesquite hid the girl's slight figure, and Gale wheeled grim-faced to follow the rangers.

They rode in single file with Ladd in the lead. He did not keep to the trail of the raiders all the time. He made short cuts. The raiders were traveling leisurely, and they evinced a liking for the most level and least cactus-covered stretches of ground. But the cowboy took a beeline course for the white escarpment pointed out by the Yaqui; and nothing save deep washes and impassable patches of cactus or rocks made him swerve from it. He kept the broncho at a steady walk over the rougher places and at a swinging Indian canter over the hard and level ground. The sun grew hot and the wind began to blow. Dust clouds rolled along the blue horizon. Whirling columns of sand, like water spouts at sea, circled up out of white arid basins, and swept away and spread aloft before the wind. The escarpment began to rise, to change color, to show breaks upon its rocky face.

Whenever the rangers rode out on the brow of a knoll or ridge or an eminence, before starting to descend, Ladd required of Gale a long, careful, sweeping survey of the desert ahead through the field glass. There were streams of white dust to be seen, streaks of yellow dust, trailing low clouds of sand over the glistening dunes, but no steadily rising, uniformly shaped puffs that would tell a tale of moving horses on the desert.

At noon the rangers got out of the thick cactus. Moreover, the gravel-bottomed washes, the low weathering, rotting ledges of yellow rock gave place to hard sandy rolls and bare clay knolls. The desert resembled a rounded hummocky sea of color. All light shades of blue and pink and yellow and mauve were there dominated by the glaring white sun. Mirages glistened, wavered, faded in the shimmering waves of heat. Dust as fine as powder whiffed from under the tireless hoofs.

The rangers rode on and the escarpment began to loom. The desert floor inclined perceptibly upward. When Gale got an unobstructed view of the slope of the escarpment he located the raiders and horses. In another hour's travel the rangers could see with naked eyes a long, faint moving streak of black and white dots.

"They're headin' for that yellow pass," said Ladd, pointing to a break in the eastern end of the escarpment.

"When they get out of sight we'll rustle. I'm thinkin' that water hole the Yaqui spoke of lays in the pass."

The rangers traveled swiftly over the remaining miles of level desert leading to the ascent of the escarpment. When they achieved the gateway of the pass the sun was low in the west. Dwarfed mesquite and greasewood appeared among the rocks. Ladd gave the word to tie up horses and go forward on foot.

The narrow neck of the pass opened and descended into a valley half a mile wide, perhaps twice that in length. It had apparently unscalable slopes of weathered rock leading up to beetling walls. With floor bare and hard and white, except for a patch of green mesquite near the far end, it was a lurid and desolate spot, the barren bottom of a desert bowl.

"Keep down, boys," said Ladd. "There's the water hole, an' hosses have sharp eyes. Shore the Yaqui figgered this place. I never seen its like for a trap."

Both white and black horses showed against the green, and a thin curling column of blue smoke rose lazily from amid the mesquites.

"I reckon we'd better wait till dark, or mebby daylight," said Jim Lash.

"Let me figger some. Dick, what do you make of the outlet to this hole? Looks rough to me."

With his glass Gale studied the narrow construction of walls and roughened rising floor.

"Laddy, it's harder to get out at that end than here," he replied.

"Shore that's hard enough. Let me have a look. . . . Well, boys, it don't take no figgerin' for this job. Jim, I'll want you at the other end blockin' the pass when we're ready to start."

"When'll that be?" inquired Jim.

"Soon as it's light enough in the mornin'. That Greaser outfit will hang till to-morrow. There's no sure water ahead for two days, you remember."

"I reckon I can slip through to the other end after dark," said Lash, thoughtfully. "It might get me in bad to go round."

The rangers stole back from the vantage point and returned to their horses, which they untied and left farther round among broken sections of cliff. For the horses it was a dry, hungry camp, but the rangers built a fire and had their short though strengthening meal.

The location was high, and through a break in the jumble of rocks the great colored void of desert could be seen rolling away endlessly to the west. The sun set, and after it had gone down the golden tips of mountains dulled, their lower shadows creeping upward.

Jim Lash rolled in his saddle blanket, his feet near the fire, and went to sleep. Ladd told Gale to do likewise while he kept the fire up and waited until it was late enough for Jim to undertake circling round the raiders. When Gale awakened the night was dark, cold, windy. The stars shone with white brilliance. Jim was up saddling his horse, and Ladd was talking low. When Gale rose to accompany them both rangers said he need not go. But Gale wanted to go, because that was the thing Ladd or Jim would have done.

With Ladd leading, they moved away into the gloom. Advance was exceedingly slow, careful, silent. Under the walls the blackness seemed impenetrable. The horse was as cautious as his master. Ladd did not lose his way, nevertheless he wound between blocks of stone and clumps of mesquite, and often tried a passage to abandon it. Finally the trail showed pale in the gloom, and eastern stars twinkled between the lofty ramparts of the pass.

The advance here was still as stealthily made as before, but not so difficult or slow. When the dense gloom of the pass lightened, and there was a wide space of sky and stars overhead, Ladd halted and stood silent a moment.

"Luck again!" he whispered. "The wind's in your face, Jim. The horses won't scent you. Go slow. Don't crack a stone. Keep close under the wall. Try to get up as high as this at the other end. Wait till daylight before riskin' a loose slope. I'll be ridin' the job early. That's all."

Ladd's cool, easy speech was scarcely significant of the perilous undertaking. Lash moved very slowly away, leading his horse. The soft pads of hoofs ceased to sound about the time the gray shape merged into the black shadows. Then Ladd touched Dick's arm, and turned back up the trail.

But Dick tarried a moment. He wanted a fuller sense of that ebony-bottomed abyss, with its pale encircling walls reaching up to the dusky blue sky and the brilliant stars. There was absolutely no sound.

He retraced his steps down, soon coming up with Ladd; and together they picked a way back through the winding recesses of cliff. The campfire was smoldering. Ladd replenished it and lay down to get a few hours' sleep, while Gale kept watch. The after part of the night wore on till the paling of stars, the thickening of gloom indicated the dark hour before dawn. The spot was secluded from wind, but the air grew cold as ice. Gale spent the time stripping wood from a dead mesquite, in pacing to and fro, in listening. Blanco Sol stamped occasionally, which sound was all that broke the stillness. Ladd awoke before the faintest gray appeared. The rangers ate and drank. When the black did lighten to gray they saddled the horses and led them out to the pass and down to the point where they had parted with Lash. Here they awaited daylight.

To Gale it seemed long in coming. Such a delay always aggravated the slow fire within him. He had nothing of Ladd's patience. He wanted action. The gray shadow below thinned out, and the patch of mesquite made a blot upon the pale valley. Then day dawned.

Still Ladd waited. He grew more silent, grimmer as the time of action approached. Gale wondered what the plan of attack would be. Yet he did not ask. He waited ready for orders.

The valley grew clear of gray shadow except under leaning walls on the eastern side. Then a straight column of smoke rose from among the mesquites. Manifestly this was what Ladd had been awaiting. He took the long .405 from its sheath and tried the lever. Then he lifted a cartridge belt from the pommel of his saddle. Every ring held a shell and these shells were four inches long. He buckled the belt round him.

"Come on, Dick."

Ladd led the way down the slope until he reached a position that commanded the rising of the trail from a level. It was the only place a man or horse could leave the valley for the pass.

"Dick, here's your stand. If any raider rides in range take a crack at him. . . . Now I want the lend of your hoss."

"Blanco Sol!" exclaimed Gale, more in amaze that Ladd should ask for the horse than in reluctance to lend him.

"Will you let me have him?" Ladd repeated, almost curtly.

"Certainly, Laddy."

A smile momentarily chased the dark cold gloom that had set upon the ranger's lean face.

"Shore I appreciate it, Dick. I know how you care for that hoss. I guess mebbe Charlie Ladd has loved a hoss! An' one not so good as Sol. I was only tryin' your nerve, Dick, askin' you without tellin' my plan. Sol won't get a scratch, you can gamble on that! I'll ride him down into the valley an' pull the Greasers out in the open. They've got short-ranged carbines. They can't keep out of range of the .405, an' I'll be takin' the dust of their lead. *Sabe,* señor?"

"Laddy! You'll run Sol away from the raiders when they chase you? Run him after them when they try to get away?"

"Shore. I'll run all the time. They can't gain on Sol, an' he'll run them down when I want. Can you beat it?"

"No. It's great! . . . But suppose a raider comes out on Blanco Diablo?"

"I reckon that's the one weak place in my plan. I'm figgerin' they'll never think of that till it's too late. But if they do, well, Sol can outrun Diablo. An' I can always kill the white devil!"

Ladd's strange hate of the horse showed in the passion of his last words, in his hardening jaw and grim set lips.

Gale's hand went swiftly to the ranger's shoulder.

"Laddy. Don't kill Diablo unless it's to save your life."

"All right. But, by God, if I get a chance I'll make Blanco Sol run him off his legs!"

He spoke no more and set about changing the length of Sol's stirrups. When he had them adjusted to suit he mounted and rode down the trail and out upon the level.

He rode leisurely as if merely going to water his horse. The long black rifle lying across his saddle, however, was ominous.

Gale securely tied the other horse to a mesquite at hand, and took a position behind a low rock over which he could easily see and shoot when necessary. He imagined Jim Lash in a similar position at the far end of the valley blocking the outlet. Gale had grown accustomed to danger and the hard and fierce feelings peculiar to it. But the coming drama was so peculiarly different in promise from all he had experienced, that he awaited the moment of action with thrilling intensity. In him stirred long, brooding wrath at these border raiders—affection for Belding, and keen desire to avenge the outrages he had suffered—warm admiration for the cold, implacable Ladd and his absolute fearlessness, and a curious throbbing interest in the old, much-discussed and never-decided argument as to whether Blanco Sol was a fleeter, stronger horse than Blanco Diablo. Gale felt that he was to see a race between these great rivals—the kind of race that made men and horses terrible.

Ladd rode a quarter of a mile out upon the flat before anything happened. Then a whistle rent the still, cold air. A horse had seen or scented Blanco Sol. The whistle was prolonged, faint, but clear. It made the blood thrum in Gale's ears. Sol halted. His head shot up with the old, wild, spirited sweep. Gale leveled his glass at the patch of mesquites. He saw the raiders running to an open place, pointing, gesticulating. The glass brought them so close that he saw dark faces. Suddenly they broke and fled back among the trees. Then he got only white and dark gleams of moving bodies. Evidently that moment was one of boots, guns, and saddles for the raiders.

Lowering the glass, Gale saw that Blanco Sol had started forward again. His gait was now a canter, and he had covered another quarter of a mile before horses and raiders appeared upon the outskirts of the mesquites. Then Blanco Sol stopped. His shrill, ringing whistle came distinctly to Gale's ears. The raiders were mounted on dark horses, and they stood abreast in a motionless line. Gale chuckled as he appreciated what a puzzle the situation presented for them. A lone horseman in the middle of the valley did not perhaps seem so menacing himself as the possibilities his presence suggested.

Then Gale saw a raider gallop swiftly from the group toward the farther outlet of the valley. This might have been owing to characteristic cowardice; but it was more likely a move of the raiders to make sure of retreat. Undoubtedly Ladd saw this galloping horseman. A few waiting moments ensued. The galloping horseman reached the slope, began to climb. With naked eyes Gale saw a puff of white smoke spring out of the rocks. Then the raider wheeled his plunging horse back to the level, and went racing wildly down the valley.

The compact bunch of bays and blacks seemed to break apart and spread rapidly from the edge of the mesquites. Puffs of white smoke indicated firing, and showed the nature of the raiders' excitement. They were far out of ordinary range; but they spurred toward Ladd, shooting as they rode. Ladd held his ground; the big white horse stood like a rock in his tracks. Gale saw little spouts of dust rise in front of Blanco Sol and spread swift as sight to his rear. The raiders' bullets, striking low, were skipping along the hard, bare floor of the valley. Then Ladd raised the long rifle. There was no smoke, but three high, spanging reports rang out. A gap opened in the dark line of advancing horsemen; then a riderless steed sheered off to the right. Blanco Sol seemed to turn as on a pivot and charged back toward the lower end of the valley. He circled over to Gale's right and stretched out into his run. There were now five raiders in pursuit, and they came sweeping down, yelling and shooting, evidently sure of their quarry. Ladd reserved his fire. He kept turning from back to front in his saddle.

Gale saw how the space widened between pursuers and pursued, saw distinctly when Ladd eased up Sol's running. Manifestly Ladd intended to try to lead the raiders round in front of Gale's position, and, presently, Gale saw he was going to succeed. The raiders, riding like vaqueros, swept on in a curve, cutting off what distance they could. One fellow, a small, wiry rider, high on his mount's neck like a jockey, led his companions by many yards. He seemed to be getting the range of Ladd, or else he shot high, for his bullets did not strike up the dust behind Sol. Gale was ready to shoot. Blanco Sol pounded by, his rapid, rhythmic hoofbeats plainly to be heard. He was running easily.

Gale tried to still the jump of heart and pulse, and turned his eye again on the nearest pursuer. This raider was crossing in, his carbine held muzzle up in his right hand, and he was coming swiftly. It was a long shot, upward of five hundred yards. Gale had not time to adjust the sights of the Remington, but he knew the gun and, holding coarsely upon the swiftly moving blot, he began to shoot. The first bullet sent up a great splash of dust beneath the horse's nose, making him leap as if to hurdle a fence. The rifle was automatic; Gale needed only to pull the trigger. He saw now that the raiders behind were in line. Swiftly he worked the trigger. Suddenly the leading horse leaped convulsively, not up nor aside, but straight ahead, and then he crashed to the ground, throwing his rider like a catapult, and then slid and rolled. He half got up, fell back, and kicked; but his rider never moved.

The other rangers sawed the reins of plunging steeds and whirled to escape the unseen battery. Gale slipped a fresh clip into the magazine of his rifle. He restrained himself from useless firing and gave eager eye to the duel below. Ladd began to shoot while Sol was running. The .405 rang out sharply—then again. The heavy bullets streaked the dust all the way across the valley. Ladd aimed deliberately and pulled slowly, unmindful of the kicking dust-puffs behind Sol, and to the side. The raiders spurred madly in pursuit, loading and firing. They shot ten times while Ladd shot once, and all in vain; and on Ladd's sixth shot a raider toppled backward, threw his carbine, and fell with his foot catching in a stirrup. The frightened horse plunged away, dragging him in a path of dust.

Gale had set himself to miss nothing of that fighting race, yet the action passed too swiftly for clear sight of all. Ladd had emptied a magazine, and now Blanco Sol quickened and lengthened his running stride. He ran away from his pursuers. Then it was that the ranger's ruse was divined by the raiders. They hauled sharply up and seemed to be conferring. But that was a fatal mistake. Blanco Sol was seen to break his gait and slow down in several jumps, then square away and stand stock-still. Ladd fired at the closely grouped raiders. An instant passed. Then Gale heard the spat of a bullet out in front, saw a puff of dust, then heard the lead strike the rocks and go whining away. And it was after this that one of the raiders fell prone from his saddle. The steel-jacketed .405 had gone through him on its uninterrupted way to hum past Gale's position.

The remaining two raiders frantically spurred their horses and fled up the valley. Ladd sent Sol after them. It seemed to Gale, even though he realized his excitement, that Blanco Sol made those horses seem like snails. The raiders split, one making for the eastern outlet, the other circling back of the mesquites. Ladd kept on after the latter. Then puffs of white smoke and rifle shots faintly crackling told of Jim Lash's hand in the game. However, he succeeded only in driving the raider back into the valley. But Ladd had turned the other horseman, and now it appeared the two raiders were between Lash above on the stony slope and Ladd below on the level. There was desperate riding on part of the raiders to keep from being hemmed in closer. Only one of them got away, and he came riding for life down under the eastern wall. Blanco Sol settled into his graceful, beautiful swing. He gained steadily, though he was far from extending himself. By Gale's actual count the raider fired eight times in that race down the valley, and all his bullets went low and wide. He pitched the carbine away and lost all control in headlong flight.

Some few hundred rods to the left of Gale the raider put his horse to the weathered slope. He began to climb. The horse was superb, infinitely more courageous than his rider. Zigzag they went up and up, and when Ladd reached the edge of the slope they were high along the cracked and guttered rampart. Once—twice Ladd raised the long rifle, but each time he lowered it. Gale divined that the ranger's restraint was not on account of the Mexican, but for that valiant and faithful horse. Up and up he went, and the yellow dust clouds rose, and an avalanche rolled rattling and cracking down the slope. It was beyond belief that a horse, burdened or unburdened, could find footing and hold it upon that wall of narrow ledges and inverted, slanting gullies. But he climbed on, sure-footed as a mountain goat, and, surmounting the last rough steps, he stood a moment silhouetted against the white sky. Then he disappeared. Ladd sat astride Blanco Sol gazing upward. How the cowboy must have honored that raider's brave steed!

Gale, who had been too dumb to shout the admiration he felt, suddenly leaped up, and his voice came with a shriek:

"LOOK OUT, LADDY!"

A big horse, like a white streak, was bearing down to the right of the ranger. Blanco Diablo! A matchless rider swung with the horse's motion. Gale was stunned. Then he remembered the first raider, the one Lash had shot at and driven away from the outlet. This fellow had made for the mesquite and had put a saddle on Belding's favorite. In the heat of the excitement, while Ladd had been intent upon the climbing horse, this last raider had come down with the speed of the wind straight for the western outlet. Perhaps, very probably, he did not know Gale was there to block it; and certainly he hoped to pass Ladd and Blanco Sol.

A touch of the spur made Sol lunge forward to head off the raider. Diablo was in his stride, but the distance and angle favored Sol. The raider had no carbine. He held aloft a gun ready to level it and fire. He sat the saddle as if it were a stationary seat. Gale saw Ladd lean down and drop the .405 in the sand. He would take no chances of wounding Belding's best-loved horse.

Then Gale sat transfixed with suspended breath watching the horses thundering toward him. Blanco Diablo was speeding low, fleet as an antelope, fierce and terrible in his devilish action, a horse for war and blood and death. He seemed unbeatable. Yet to see the magnificently running Blanco Sol was but to court a doubt. Gale stood spellbound. He might have shot the raider; but he never thought of such a thing. The distance swiftly lessened. Plain it was the raider could not make the opening ahead of Ladd. He saw it and swerved to the left, emptying his six-shooter as he turned. His dark face gleamed as he flashed by Gale.

Blanco Sol thundered across. Then the race became straight away up the valley. Diablo was cold and Sol was hot: therein lay the only handicap and vantage. It was a fleet, beautiful, magnificent race. Gale thrilled and exulted and yelled as his horse settled into a steadily swifter run and began to gain. The dust rolled in a funnel-shaped cloud from the flying hoofs. The raider wheeled with gun puffing white and Ladd ducked low over the neck of his horse.

The gap between Diablo and Sol narrowed yard by yard. At first it had been a wide one. The raider beat his mount and spurred, beat and spurred, wheeled round to shoot, then bent forward again. In his circle at the upper end of the valley he turned far short of the jumble of rocks.

All the devil that was in Blanco Diablo had its running on the downward stretch. The strange, cruel urge of bit and spur, the crazed rider who stuck like a burr upon him, the shots and smoke added terror to his natural violent temper. He ran himself off his feet. But he could not elude that relentless horse behind him. The running of Blanco Sol was that of a sure, remorseless driving power—steadier—stronger—swifter with every long and wonderful stride.

The raider tried to sheer Diablo off closer under the wall, to make the slope where his companion had escaped.

But Diablo was uncontrollable. He was running wild, with breaking gait. Closer and closer crept that white, smoothly gliding, beautiful machine of speed.

Then, like one white flash following another, the two horses gleamed down the bank of a wash and disappeared in clouds of dust.

Gale watched with strained and smarting eyes. The thick throb in his ears was pierced by faint sounds of gunshots. Then he waited in almost unendurable suspense.

Suddenly something whiter than the background of dust appeared above the low roll of valley floor. Gale leveled his glass. In the clear circle shone Blanco Sol's noble head with its long black bar from ears to nose. Sol's head was drooping now. Another second showed Ladd still in the saddle.

The ranger was leading Blanco Diablo—spent—broken—dragging—riderless.

CHAPTER 9

AN INTERRUPTED SIESTA

No man ever had a more eloquent and beautiful pleader for his cause than had Dick Gale in Mercedes Castañeda. He peeped through the green, shining twigs of the *palo verde* that shaded his door. The hour was high noon, and the patio was sultry. The only sounds were the hum of bees in the flowers and the low murmur of the Spanish girl's melodious voice. Nell lay in the hammock, her hands behind her head, with rosy cheeks and arch eyes. Indeed she looked rebellious. Certain it was, Dick reflected, that the young lady had fully recovered the willful personality which had lain dormant for a while. Equally certain it seemed that Mercedes's earnestness was not apparently having the effect it should have had.

Dick was inclined to be rebellious himself. Belding had kept the rangers in off the line, and therefore Dick had been idle most of the time, and, though he tried hard, he had been unable to stay far from Nell's vicinity. He believed she cared for him; but he could not catch her alone long enough to verily his tormenting hope. When alone she was as elusive as a shadow, as quick as a flash, as mysterious as a Yaqui. When he tried to catch her in the garden or fields, or corner her in the patio, she eluded him, and left behind a memory of dark-blue, haunting eyes. It was that look in her eyes which lent him hope. At other times, when it might have been possible for Dick to speak, Nell clung closely to Mercedes. He had long before enlisted the loyal Mercedes in his cause; but in spite of this Nell had been more than a match for them both.

Gale pondered over an idea he had long revolved in his mind, and which now suddenly gave place to a decision that made his heart swell and his cheek burn. He peeped again through the green branches to see Nell laughing at the fiery Mercedes.

"Quién sabe," he called, mockingly, and was delighted with Nell's quick, amazed start.

Then he went in search of Mrs. Belding, and found her busy in the kitchen.

The relation between Gale and Mrs. Belding had subtly and incomprehensibly changed. He understood her less than when at first he divined an antagonism in her. If such a thing were possible she had retained the antagonism while seeming to yield to some influence that must have been fondness for him. Gale was in no wise sure of her affection, and he had long imagined she was afraid of him, or of something that he represented. He had gone on, openly and fairly, though discreetly, with his rather one-sided love affair; and as time passed he had grown less conscious of what had seemed her unspoken opposition. Gale had come to care greatly for Nell's mother. Not only was she the comfort and strength of her home, but also of the inhabitants of Forlorn River. Indian, Mexican, American were all the same to her in trouble or illness; and then she was nurse, doctor, peacemaker, helper. She was good and noble, and there was not a child or grownup in Forlorn River who did not love and bless her. But Mrs. Belding did not seem happy. She was brooding, intense, deep, strong, eager for the happiness and welfare of others; and she was dominated by a worship of her daughter that was as strange as it was pathetic. Mrs. Belding seldom smiled, and never hugged. There was always a soft, sad, hurt look in her eyes. Gale often wondered if there had been other tragedy in her life than the supposed loss of her father in the desert. Perhaps it was the very unsolved nature of that loss which made it haunting.

Mrs. Belding heard Dick's step as he entered the kitchen and, looking up, greeted him.

"Mother," began Dick, earnestly. Belding called her that, and so did Ladd and Lash, but it was the first time for Dick. "Mother—I want to speak to you."

The only indication Mrs. Belding gave of being startled was in her eyes, which darkened, shadowed with multiplying thought.

"I love Nell," went on Dick, simply, "and I want you to let me ask her to be my wife."

Mrs. Belding's face blanched to a deathly white. Gale, thinking with surprise and concern that she was going to faint, moved quickly toward her, took her arm.

"Forgive me. I was blunt. . . . But I thought you knew."

"I've known for a long time," replied Mrs. Belding. Her voice was steady, and there was no evidence of agitation except in her pallor. "Then you—you haven't spoken to Nell?"

Dick laughed. "I've been trying to get a chance to tell her. I haven't had it yet. But she knows. There are other ways besides speech. And Mercedes has told her. I hope, I almost believe Nell cares a little for me."

"I've known that, too, for a long time," said Mrs. Belding, low almost as a whisper.

"You know!" cried Dick, with a glow and rush of feeling.

"Dick, you must be very blind not to see what has been plain to all of us. . . . I guess—it couldn't have been helped. You're a splendid fellow. No wonder she loves you."

"Mother! You'll give her to me?"

She drew him to the light and looked with strange, piercing intentness into his face. Gale had never dreamed a woman's eyes could hold such a world of thought and feeling. It seemed all the sweetness of life was there, and all the pain.

"Do you love her?" she asked.

"With all my heart."

"You want to marry her?"

"Ah, I want to! As much as I want to live and work for her."

"*When* would you marry her?"

"Why! . . . Just as soon as she will do it. To-morrow!" Dick gave a wild, exultant little laugh.

"Dick Gale, you want my Nell? You love her just as she is—her sweetness—her goodness? Just herself, body and soul? . . . There's nothing could change you—nothing?"

"Dear Mrs. Belding, I love Nell for herself. If she loves me I'll be the happiest of men. There's absolutely nothing that could make any difference in me."

"But your people? Oh, Dick, you come of a proud

family. I can tell. I—I once knew a young man like you. A few months can't change pride—blood. Years can't change them. You've become a ranger. You love the adventure—the wild life. That won't last. Perhaps you'll settle down to ranching. I know you love the West. But, Dick, there's your family—"

"If you want to know anything about my family, I'll tell you," interrupted Dick, with strong feeling. "I've no secrets about them or myself. My future and happiness are Nell's to make. No one else shall count with me."

"Then, Dick—you may have her. God—bless—you—both."

Mrs. Belding's strained face underwent a swift and mobile relaxation, and suddenly she was weeping in strangely mingled happiness and bitterness.

"Why, Mother!" Gale could say no more. He did not comprehend a mood seemingly so utterly at variance with Mrs. Belding's habitual temperament. But he put his arm around her. In another moment she had gained command over herself, and, kissing him, she pushed him out of the door.

"There! Go tell her, Dick. . . . And have some spunk about it!"

Gale went thoughtfully back to his room. He vowed that he would answer for Nell's happiness, if he had the wonderful good fortune to win her. Then remembering the hope Mrs. Belding had given him, Dick lost his gravity in a flash, and something began to dance and ring within him. He simply could not keep his steps turned from the patio. Every path led there. His blood was throbbing, his hopes mounting, his spirit soaring. He knew he had never before entered the patio with that inspirited presence.

"Now for some spunk!" he said, under his breath.

Plainly he meant his merry whistle and his buoyant step to interrupt this first languorous stage of the siesta which the girls always took during the hot hours. Nell had acquired the habit long before Mercedes came to show how fixed a thing it was in the life of the tropics. But neither girl heard him. Mercedes lay under the *palo verde,* her beautiful head dark and still upon a cushion. Nell was asleep in the hammock. There was an abandonment in her deep repose, and a faint smile upon her face. Her sweet, red lips, with the soft, perfect curve, had always fascinated Dick, and now drew him irresistibly. He had always been consumed with a desire to kiss her, and now he was overwhelmed with his opportunity. It would be a terrible thing to do, but if she did not awaken at once— No, he would fight the temptation. That would be more than spunk. It would— Suddenly an ugly green fly sailed low over Nell, appeared about to alight on her. Noiselessly Dick stepped close to the hammock bent under the tree, and with a sweep of his hand chased the intruding fly away. But he found himself powerless to straighten up. He was close to her—bending over her face—near the sweet lips. The insolent, dreaming smile just parted them. Then he thought he was lost. But she stirred—he feared she would awaken.

He had stepped back erect when she opened her eyes. They were sleepy, yet surprised until she saw him. Then she was wide awake in a second, bewildered, uncertain.

"Why—you here?" she asked, slowly.

"Large as life!" replied Dick, with unusual gayety.

"How long have you been here?"

"Just got here this fraction of a second," he replied, lying shamelessly.

It was evident that she did not know whether or not to believe him, and as she studied him a slow blush dyed her cheek.

"You are absolutely truthful when you say you just stepped there?"

"Why, of course," answered Dick, right glad he did not have to lie about that.

"I thought—I was—dreaming," she said, and evidently the sound of her voice reassured her.

"Yes, you looked as if you were having pleasant dreams," replied Dick. "So sorry to wake you. I can't see how I came to do it, I was so quiet. Mercedes didn't wake. Well, I'll go and let you have your siesta and dreams."

But he did not move to go. Nell regarded him with curious, speculative eyes.

"Isn't it a lovely day?" queried Dick.

"I think it's hot."

"Only ninety in the shade. And you've told me the mercury goes to one hundred and thirty in midsummer. This is just a glorious golden day."

"Yesterday was finer, but you didn't notice it."

"Oh, yesterday was somewhere back in the past—the inconsequential past."

Nell's sleepy blue eyes opened a little wider. She did not know what to make of this changed young man. Dick felt gleeful and tried hard to keep the fact from becoming manifest.

"What's the inconsequential past? You seem remarkably happy today."

"I certainly am happy. *Adiós*. Pleasant dreams."

Dick turned away then and left the patio by the opening into the yard. Nell was really sleepy, and when she had fallen asleep again he would return. He walked around for a while. Belding and the rangers were shoeing a broncho. Yaqui was in the field with the horses. Blanco Sol grazed contentedly, and now and then lifted his head to watch. His long ears went up at sight of his master, and he whistled. Presently Dick, as if magnet-drawn, retraced his steps to the patio and entered noiselessly.

Nell was now deep in her siesta. She was inert, relaxed, untroubled by dreams. Her hair was damp on her brow.

Again Nell stirred, and gradually awakened. Her eyes unclosed, humid, shadowy, unconscious. They rested upon Dick for a moment before they became clear and comprehensive. He stood back fully ten feet from her, and to all outside appearances regarded her calmly.

"I've interrupted your siesta again," he said. "Please forgive me. I'll take myself off."

He wandered away, and when it became impossible for him to stay away any longer he returned to the patio.

The instant his glance rested upon Nell's face he divined she was feigning sleep. The faint rose-blush had paled. The warm, rich, golden tint of her skin had fled. Dick dropped upon his knees and bent over her. Though his blood was churning in his veins, his breast laboring, his mind whirling with the wonder of that moment and its promise, he made himself deliberate. He wanted more than anything he had ever wanted in his life to see if she would keep up that pretense of sleep and let him kiss her. She must have felt his breath, for her hair waved off her brow. Her cheeks were now white. Her breast swelled and sank. He bent down closer—closer. But he must have been maddeningly slow, for as he bent still closer Nell's eyes opened, and he caught a swift purple gaze of eyes as she whirled her head. Then, with a little cry, she rose and fled.

CHAPTER 10

ROJAS

No word from George Thorne had come to Forlorn River in weeks. Gale grew concerned over the fact, and began to wonder if anything serious could have happened to him. Mercedes showed a slow, wearing strain.

Thorne's commission expired the end of January, and if he could not get his discharge immediately, he surely could obtain leave of absence. Therefore, Gale waited, not without growing anxiety, and did his best to cheer Mercedes. The first of February came bringing news of rebel activities and bandit operations in and around Casita, but not a word from the cavalryman.

Mercedes became silent, mournful. Her eyes were great black windows of tragedy. Nell devoted herself entirely to the unfortunate girl; Dick exerted himself to persuade her that all would yet come well; in fact, the whole household could not have been kinder to a sister or a daughter. But their united efforts were unavailing. Mercedes seemed to accept with fatalistic hopelessness a last and crowning misfortune.

A dozen times Gale declared he would ride in to Casita and find out why they did not hear from Thorne; however, older and wiser heads prevailed over his impetuosity. Belding was not sanguine over the safety of the Casita trail. Refugees from there arrived every day in Forlorn River, and if the tales they told were true, real war would have been preferable to what was going on along the border. Belding and the rangers and the Yaqui held a consultation. Not only had the Indian become a faithful servant to Gale, but he was also of value to Belding. Yaqui had all the craft of his class, and superior intelligence. His knowledge of Mexicans was second only to his hate of them. And Yaqui, who had been scouting on all the trails, gave information that made Belding decide to wait some days before sending any one to Casita. He required promises from his rangers, particularly Gale, not to leave without his consent.

It was upon Gale's coming from this conference that he encountered Nell. Since the interrupted siesta episode she had been more than ordinarily elusive, and about all he had received from her was a tantalizing smile from a distance. He got the impression now, however, that she had awaited him. When he drew close to her he was certain of it, and he experienced more than surprise.

"Dick," she began, hurriedly. "Dad's not going to send any one to see about Thorne?"

"No, not yet. He thinks it best not to. We all think so. I'm sorry. Poor Mercedes!"

"I knew it. I tried to coax him to send Laddy or even Yaqui. He wouldn't listen to me. Dick, Mercedes is dying by inches. Can't you see what ails her? It's more than love or fear. It's uncertainty—suspense. Oh, can't we find out for her?"

"Nell, I feel as badly as you about her. I wanted to ride in to Casita. Belding shut me up quick, the last time."

Nell came close to Gale, clasped his arm. There was no color in her face. Her eyes held a dark, eager excitement.

"Dick, will you skip off without Dad's consent? Risk it! Go to Casita and find out what's happened to Thorne—at least if he ever started for Forlorn River?"

"No, Nell, I won't do that."

She drew away from him with passionate suddenness. "Are you afraid?"

This certainly was not the Nell Burton that Gale knew.

"No, I'm not afraid," Gale replied, a little nettled.

"Will you go—for my sake?" Like lightning her mood changed and she was close to him again, hands on his, her face white, her whole presence sweetly alluring.

"Nell, I won't disobey Belding," protested Gale. "I won't break my word."

"Dick, it'll not be so bad as that. But—what if it is? . . . Go, Dick, if not for poor Mercedes's sake, then for mine—to please me. I'll—I'll. . . . you won't lose anything by going. I think I know how Mercedes feels. Just a word from Thorne or about him would save her. Take Blanco Sol and go, Dick. What rebel outfit could ever ride you down on that horse? Why, Dick, if I was up on Sol I wouldn't be afraid of the whole rebel army."

"My dear girl, it's not a question of being afraid. It's my word—my duty to Belding."

"You said you loved me. If you do love me you will go. . . . You don't love me!"

Gale could only stare at this transformed girl.

"Dick, listen! . . . If you go—if you fetch some word of Thorne to comfort Mercedes, you—well, you will have your reward."

"*Nell!*"

Her dangerous sweetness was as amazing as this newly revealed character.

"Dick, will you go?"

"No—no!" cried Gale, in violence, struggling with himself. "Nell Burton, I'll tell you this. To have the reward I want would mean pretty near heaven for me. But not even for that will I break my word to your father."

She seemed the incarnation of girlish scorn and willful passion.

"*Gracias*, señor," she replied, mockingly. "*Adiós.*" Then she flashed out of his sight.

Gale went to his room at once, disturbed and thrilling, and did not soon recover from that encounter.

The following morning at the breakfast table Nell was not present. Mrs. Belding evidently considered the fact somewhat unusual, for she called out into the patio and then into the yard. Then she went to Mercedes's room. But Nell was not there, either.

"She's in one of her tantrums lately," said Belding. "Wouldn't speak to me this morning. Let her alone, Mother. She's spoiled enough, without running after her. She's always hungry. She'll be on hand presently, don't mistake me."

Notwithstanding Belding's conviction, which Gale shared, Nell did not appear at all during the hour. When Belding and the rangers went outside, Yaqui was eating his meal on the bench where he always sat.

"Yaqui—*Lluvia d'oro, sí?*" asked Belding, waving his hand toward the corrals. The Indian's beautiful name for Nell meant "shower of gold," and Belding used it in asking Yaqui if he had seen her. He received a negative reply.

Perhaps half an hour afterward, as Gale was leaving his room, he saw the Yaqui running up the path from the fields. It was markedly out of the ordinary to see the Indian run. Gale wondered what was the matter. Yaqui ran straight to Belding, who was at work at his bench under the wagon shed. In less than a moment Belding was bellowing for his rangers. Gale got to him first, but Ladd and Lash were not far behind.

"Blanco Sol gone!" yelled Belding, in a rage.

"Gone? In broad daylight, with the Indian a-watchin'?" queried Ladd.

"It happened while Yaqui was at breakfast. That's sure. He'd just watered Sol."

"Raiders!" exclaimed Jim Lash.

"Lord only knows. Yaqui says it wasn't raiders."

"Mebbe Sol's just walked off somewheres."

"He was haltered in the corral."

"Send Yaqui to find the hoss's trail, an' let's figger," said Ladd. "Shore this's no raider job."

In the swift search that ensued Gale did not have anything to say; but his mind was forming a conclusion. When he found his old saddle and bridle missing from the peg in the barn his conclusion became a positive conviction, and it made him, for the moment, cold and sick and speechless.

"Hey, Dick, don't take it so much to heart," said Belding. "We'll likely find Sol, and if we don't, there's other good horses."

"I'm not thinking of Sol," replied Gale.

Ladd cast a sharp glance at Gale, snapped his fingers, and said:

"Damn me if I ain't guessed it, too!"

"What's wrong with you locoed gents?" bluntly demanded Belding.

"Nell has slipped away on Sol," answered Dick.

There was a blank pause, which presently Belding broke.

"Well, that's all right, if Nell's on him. I was afraid we'd lost the horse."

"Belding, you're trackin' bad," said Ladd, wagging his head.

"Nell has started for Casita," burst out Gale. "She has gone to fetch Mercedes some word about Thorne. Oh, Belding, you needn't shake your head. I know she's gone. She tried to persuade me to go, and was furious when I wouldn't."

"I don't believe it," replied Belding, hoarsely. "Nell may have her temper. She's a little devil at times, but she always had good sense."

"Tom, you can gamble she's gone," said Ladd.

"Aw, hell, no! Jim, what do you think?" implored Belding.

"I reckon Sol's white head is pointed level an' straight down the Casita trail. An' Nell can ride. We're losin' time."

That roused Belding to action.

"I say you're all wrong," he yelled, starting for the corrals. "She's only taking a little ride, same as she's done often. But rustle now. Find out. Dick, you ride cross the valley. Jim, you hunt up and down the river. I'll head up San Felipe way. And you, Laddy, take Diablo and hit the

Casita trail. If she really has gone after Thorne you can catch her in an hour or so."

"Shore I'll go," replied Ladd. "But, Beldin', if you're not plumb crazy you're close to it. That big white devil can't catch Sol. Not in an hour or a day or a week! What's more, at the end of any runnin' time, with an even start, Sol will be farther in the lead. An' now Sol's got an hour's start."

"Laddy, you mean to say Sol is a faster horse than Diablo?" thundered Belding, his face purple.

"Shore. I mean to tell you just that there," replied the ranger.

"I'll—I'll bet a—"

"We're wastin' time," curtly interrupted Ladd. "You can gamble on this if you want to. I'll ride your Blanco Devil as he never was rid before, 'cept once when a damn sight better hossman than I am couldn't make him out-run Sol."

Without more words the men saddled and were off, not waiting for the Yaqui to come in with possible information as to what trail Blanco Sol had taken. It certainly did not show in the clear sand of the level valley where Gale rode to and fro. When Gale returned to the house he found Belding and Lash awaiting him. They did not mention their own search, but stated that Yaqui had found Blanco Sol's tracks in the Casita trail. After some consultation Belding decided to send Lash along after Ladd.

The interminable time that followed contained for Gale about as much suspense as he could well bear. What astonished him and helped him greatly to fight off actual distress was the endurance of Nell's mother.

Early on the morning of the second day, Gale, who had acquired an unbreakable habit of watching, saw three white horses and a bay come wearily stepping down the road. He heard Blanco Sol's familiar whistle, and he leaped up wild with joy. The horse was riderless. Gale's sudden joy received a violent check, then resurged when he saw a limp white form in Jim Lash's arms. Ladd was supporting a horseman who wore a military uniform.

Gale shouted with joy and ran into the house to tell the good news. It was the ever-thoughtful Mrs. Belding who prevented him from rushing in to tell Mercedes. Then he hurried out into the yard, closely followed by the Beldings.

Lash handed down a ragged, travel-stained, wan girl into Belding's arms.

"Dad! Mama!"

It was indeed a repentant Nell, but there was spirit yet in the tired blue eyes. Then she caught sight of Gale and gave him a faint smile.

"Hello—Dick."

"Nell!" Gale reached for her hand, held it tightly, and found speech difficult.

"You needn't worry—about your old horse," she said, as Belding carried her toward the door. "Oh, Dick! Blanco Sol is—glorious!"

Gale turned to greet his friend. Indeed, it was but a haggard ghost of the cavalryman. Thorne looked ill or wounded. Gale's greeting was also a question full of fear.

Thorne's answer was a faint smile. He seemed ready to drop from the saddle. Gale helped Ladd hold Thorne upon the horse until they reached the house. Belding came out again. His welcome was checked as he saw the condition of the cavalryman. Thorne reeled into Dick's arms. But he was able to stand and walk.

"I'm not—hurt. Only weak—starved," he said. "Is Mercedes— Take me to her."

"She'll be well the minute she sees him," averred Belding, as he and Gale led the cavalryman to Mercedes's room. There they left him; and Gale, at least, felt his ears ringing with the girl's broken cry of joy.

When Belding and Gale hurried forth again the rangers were tending the tired horses. Upon returning to the house Jim Lash calmly lit his pipe, and Ladd declared that, hungry as he was, he had to tell his story.

"Shore, Beldin'," began Ladd, "that was funny about Diablo catchin' Blanco Sol. Funny ain't the word. I nearly laughed myself to death. Well, I rode in Sol's tracks all the way to Casita. Never seen a rebel or a raider till I got to town. Figgered Nell made the trip in five hours. I went straight to the camp of the cavalrymen, an' found them just coolin' off an' dressin' down their hosses after what looked to me like a big ride. I got there too late for the fireworks.

"Some soldier took me to an officer's tent. Nell was there, some white an' all in. She just said, 'Laddy!' Thorne was there, too, an' he was bein' worked over by the camp doctor. I didn't ask no questions, because I seen quiet was needed round that tent. After satisfying myself that Nell was all right, an' Thorne in no danger, I went out.

"Shore there was so darn many fellers who wanted to an' tried to tell me what'd come off, I thought I'd never find out. But I got the story piece by piece. An' here's what happened.

"Nell rode Blanco Sol a-tearin' into camp, an' had a crowd round her in a jiffy. She told who she was, where she'd come from, an' what she wanted. Well, it seemed a day or so before Nell got there the cavalrymen had heard word of Thorne. You see, Thorne had left camp on leave of absence some time before. He was shore mysterious, they said, an' told nobody where he was goin'. A week or so after he left camp some Greaser give it away that Rojas had a prisoner in a dobe shack near his camp. Nobody paid much attention to what the Greaser said. He wanted money for mescal. An' it was usual for Rojas to have prisoners. But in a few more days it turned out pretty sure that for some reason Rojas was holdin' Thorne.

"Now it happened when this news came Colonel Weede was in Nogales with his staff, an' the officer left in charge didn't know how to proceed. Rojas's camp was across the line in Mexico, an' ridin' over there was serious business. It meant a whole lot more than just scatterin' one Greaser camp. It was what had been botherin' more'n one colonel along the line. Thorne's feller soldiers was anxious to get him out of a bad fix, but they had to wait for orders.

"When Nell found out Thorne was bein' starved an' beat in a dobe shack no more'n two mile across the line, she shore stirred up that cavalry camp. Shore! She told them soldiers Rojas was holdin' Thorne—torturin' him to make him tell where Mercedes was. She told about Mercedes—how sweet an' beautiful she was—how her father had been murdered by Rojas—how she had been hounded by the bandit—how ill an' miserable she was, waitin' for her lover. An' she begged the cavalrymen to rescue Thorne.

"From the way it was told to me I reckon them cavalrymen went up in the air. Fine fiery lot of youngbloods, I thought, achin' for a scrap. But the officer in charge, bein' in a ticklish place, still held out for higher orders.

"Then Nell broke loose. You-all know Nell's tongue is sometimes like a *cholla* thorn. I'd have give somethin' to see her work up that soldier outfit. Nell's never so pretty as when she's mad. An' this last stunt of hers was no girly tantrum, as Beldin' calls it. She musta been ragin' with all the hell there's in a woman. . . . Can't you fellers see her on Blanco Sol with her eyes turnin' black?"

Ladd mopped his sweaty face with his dusty scarf. He was beaming. He was growing excited, hurried in his narrative.

"Right out then Nell *swore* she'd go after Thorne. If them cavalrymen couldn't ride with a Western girl to save a brother American—let them hang back! One feller, under orders, tried to stop Blanco Sol. An' that feller invited himself to the hospital. Then the cavalrymen went flyin' for their hosses. Mebbe Nell's move was just foxy—woman's cunnin'. But I'm thinkin' as she felt then she'd have sent Blanco Sol straight into Rojas's camp, which, I'd forgot to say, was in plain sight.

"It didn't take long for every cavalryman in that camp to get wind of what was comin' off. Shore they musta been wild. They strung out after Nell in a thunderin' troop.

"Say, I wish you fellers could see the lane that bunch of hosses left in the greasewood an' cactus. Looks like there'd been a cattle stampede on the desert. . . . Blanco Sol stayed out in front, you can gamble on that. Right into Rojas's camp! *Sabe,* you señors? Gawd Almighty! I never had a grief that'd hold a candle to this one of bein' too late to see Nell an' Sol in their one best race.

"Rojas an' his men vamoosed without a shot. That ain't surprisin'. There wasn't a shot fired by anybody. The cavalrymen soon found Thorne an' hurried with him back on Uncle Sam's land. Thorne was half naked, black an' blue all over, thin as a rail. He looked mighty sick when I seen him first. That was a little after midday. He was given food an' drink. Shore he seemed a starved man. But he picked up wonderful, an' by the time Jim came along he was wantin' to start for Forlorn River. So was Nell. By main strength as much as persuasion we kept the two of them quiet till next evenin' at dark.

"Well, we made as sneaky a start in the dark as Jim an' me could manage, an' never hit the trail till we was miles from town. Thorne's nerve held him up for a while. Then all at once he tumbled out of his saddle. We got him back, an' Lash held him on. Nell didn't give out till daybreak."

As Ladd paused in his story Belding began to stutter, and finally he exploded. His mighty utterances were incoherent. But plainly the wrath he had felt toward the wilful girl was forgotten. Gale remained gripped by silence.

"I reckon you'll all be some surprised when you see Casita," went on Ladd. "It's half burned an' half tore down. An' the rebels are livin' fat. There was rumors of another federal force on the road from Case Grandes. I seen a good many Americans from interior Mexico, an' the stories they told would make your hair stand up. They all packed guns, was fightin' mad at Greasers, an' sore on the good old U.S. But shore glad to get over the line! Some were waitin' for trains, which don't run reg'lar no more, an' others were ready to hit the trails north."

"Laddy, what knocks me is Rojas holding Thorne prisoner, trying to make him tell where Mercedes had been hidden," said Belding.

"Shore. It'd knock anybody."

"The bandit's crazy over her. That's the Spanish of it," replied Belding, his voice rolling. "Rojas is a peon. He's been a slave to the proud Castilian. He loves Mercedes as he hates her. When I was down in Durango I saw something of these peons' insane passions. Rojas wants this girl only to have her, then kill her. It's damn strange, boys, and even with Thorne here our troubles have just begun."

"Tom, you spoke correct," said Jim Ladd, in his cool drawl.

"Shore I'm not sayin' what I think," added Ladd. But the look of him was not indicative of a tranquil optimism.

Thorne was put to bed in Gale's room. He was very weak, yet he would keep Mercedes's hand and gaze at her with unbelieving eyes. Mercedes's failing hold on hope and strength seemed to have been a fantasy; she was again vivid, magnetic, beautiful, shot through and through with intense and throbbing life. She induced him to take food and drink. Then, fighting sleep with what little strength he had left, at last he succumbed.

For all Dick could ascertain his friend never stirred an eyelash nor a finger for twenty-seven hours. When he awoke he was pale, weak, but the old Thorne.

"Hello, Dick, I didn't dream it then," he said. "There you are, and my darling with the proud, dark eyes—she's here?"

"Why, yes, you locoed cavalryman."

"Say, what's happened to you? It can't be those clothes and a little bronze on your face. . . . Dick, you're older—you've changed. You're not so thickly built. By Gad, if you don't look fine!"

"Thanks. I'm sorry I can't return the compliment. You're about the seediest, hungriest-looking fellow I ever saw. . . . Say, old man, you must have had a tough time."

A dark and somber fire burned out the happiness in Thorne's eyes.

"Dick, don't make me—don't let me think of that fiend

Rojas! . . . I'm here now. I'll be well in a day or two. Then! . . ."

Mercedes came in, radiant and soft-voiced. She fell upon her knees beside Thorne's bed, and neither of them appeared to see Nell enter with a tray. Then Gale and Nell made a good deal of unnecessary bustle in moving a small table close to the bed. Mercedes had forgotten for the moment that her lover had been a starving man. If Thorne remembered it he did not care. They held hands and looked at each other without speaking.

"Nell, I thought I had it bad," whispered Dick. "But I'm not—"

"Hush. It's beautiful," replied Nell, softly; and she tried to coax Dick from the room.

Dick, however, thought he ought to remain at least long enough to tell Thorne that a man in his condition could not exist solely upon love.

Mercedes sprang up blushing with pretty, penitent manner and moving white hands eloquent of her condition.

"Oh, Mercedes—don't go!" cried Thorne, as she stepped to the door.

"Señor Dick will stay. He is not *mucha malo* for you—as I am."

Then she smiled and went out.

"Good Lord!" exclaimed Thorne. "How I love her! Dick, isn't she the most beautiful, the loveliest, the finest—"

"George, I share your enthusiasm," said Dick, dryly, "but Mercedes isn't the only girl on earth."

Manifestly this was a startling piece of information, and struck Thorne in more than one way.

"George," went on Dick, "did you happen to observe the girl who saved your life—who incidentally just fetched in your breakfast?"

"Nell Burton! Why, of course. She's brave, a wonderful girl, and really nice-looking."

"You long, lean, hungry beggar! That was the young lady who might answer the raving eulogy you just got out of your system. . . . I—well, you haven't cornered the love market!"

Thorne uttered some kind of a sound that his weakened condition would not allow to be a whoop.

"Dick! Do you mean it?"

"I shore do, as Laddy says."

"I'm glad, Dick, with all my heart. I wondered at the changed look you wear. Why, boy, you've got a different front. . . . Call the lady in, and you bet I'll look her over right. I can see better now."

"Eat your breakfast. There's plenty of time to dazzle you afterward."

Thorne fell to upon his breakfast and made it vanish with magic speed. Meanwhile Dick told him something of a ranger's life along the border.

"You needn't waste your breath," said Thorne. "I guess I can see. Belding and those rangers have made you the real thing—the real Western goods. . . . What I want to know is all about the girl."

"Well, Laddy swears she's got your girl roped in the corral for looks."

"That's not possible. I'll have to talk to Laddy. . . . But she must be a wonder, or Dick Gale would never have fallen for her. . . . Isn't it great, Dick? I'm here! Mercedes is well—safe! You've got a girl! Oh! . . . But say, I haven't a dollar to my name. I had a lot of money, Dick, and those robbers stole it, my watch—everything. Damn that little black Greaser! He got Mercedes's letters. I wish you could have seen him trying to read them. He's simply nutty over her, Dick. I could have borne the loss of money and valuables—but those beautiful, wonderful letters—they're gone!"

"Cheer up. You have the girl. Belding will make you a proposition presently. The future smiles, old friend. If this rebel business was only ended!"

"Dick, you're going to be my savior twice over. . . . Well, now, listen to me." His gay excitement changed to earnest gravity. "I want to marry Mercedes at once. Is there a padre here?"

"Yes. But are you wise in letting any Mexican, even a priest, know Mercedes is hidden in Forlorn River?"

"It couldn't be kept much longer."

Gale was compelled to acknowledge the truth of this statement.

"I'll marry her first, then I'll face my problem. Fetch the padre, Dick. And ask our kind friends to be witnesses at the ceremony."

Much to Gale's surprise neither Belding nor Ladd objected to the idea of bringing a padre into the household, and thereby making known to at least one Mexican the whereabouts of Mercedes Castañeda. Belding's caution was wearing out in wrath at the persistent unsettled condition of the border, and Ladd grew only the cooler and more silent as possibilities of trouble multiplied.

Gale fetched the padre, a little, wizened, timid man who was old and without interest or penetration. Apparently he married Mercedes and Thorne as he told his beads or mumbled a prayer. It was Mrs. Belding who kept the occasion from being a merry one, and she insisted on not exciting Thorne. Gale marked her unusual pallor and the singular depth and sweetness of her voice.

"Mother, what's the use of making a funeral out of a

marriage?" protested Belding. "A chance for some fun doesn't often come to Forlorn River. You're a fine doctor. Can't you see the girl is what Thorne needed? He'll be well to-morrow, don't mistake me."

"George, when you're all right again we'll add something to present congratulations," said Gale.

"We shore will," put in Ladd.

So with parting jests and smiles they left the couple to themselves.

Belding enjoyed a laugh at his good wife's expense, for Thorne could not be kept in bed, and all in a day, it seemed, he grew so well and so hungry that his friends were delighted, and Mercedes was radiant. In a few days his weakness disappeared and he was going the round of the fields and looking over the ground marked out in Gale's plan of water development. Thorne was highly enthusiastic, and at once staked out his claim for one hundred and sixty acres of land adjoining that of Belding and the rangers. These five tracts took in all the ground necessary for their operations, but in case of the success of the irrigation project the idea was to increase their squatter holding by purchase of more land down the valley. A hundred families had lately moved to Forlorn River; more were coming all the time; and Belding vowed he could see a vision of the whole Altar Valley green with farms.

Meanwhile everybody in Belding's household, except the quiet Ladd and the watchful Yaqui, in the absence of disturbance of any kind along the border, grew freer and more unrestrained, as if anxiety was slowly fading in the peace of the present. Jim Lash made a trip to the Sonoyta Oasis, and Ladd patrolled fifty miles of the line eastward without incident or sight of raiders. Evidently all the border hawks were in at the picking of Casita.

The February nights were cold, with a dry, icy, penetrating coldness that made a warm fire most comfortable. Belding's household usually congregated in the sitting-room, where burning mesquite logs crackled in the open fireplace. Belding's one passion besides horses was the game of checkers, and he was always wanting to play. On this night he sat playing with Ladd, who never won a game and never could give up trying. Mrs. Belding worked with her needle, stopping from time to time to gaze with thoughtful eyes into the fire. Jim Lash smoked his pipe by the hearth and played with the cat on his knee. Thorne and Mercedes were at the table with pencil and paper; and he was trying his best to keep his attention from his wife's beautiful, animated face long enough to read and write a little Spanish. Gale and Nell sat in a corner watching the bright fire.

There came a low knock on the door. It may have been an ordinary knock, for it did not disturb the women; but to Belding and his rangers it had a subtle meaning.

"Who's that?" asked Belding, as he slowly pushed back his chair and looked at Ladd.

"Yaqui," replied the ranger.

"Come in," called Belding.

The door opened, and the short, square, powerfully built Indian entered. He had a magnificent head, strangely staring, somber black eyes, and very darkly bronzed face. He carried a rifle and strode with impressive dignity.

"Yaqui, what do you want?" asked Belding, and repeated his question in Spanish.

"Señor Dick," replied the Indian.

Gale jumped up, stifling an exclamation, and he went outdoors with Yaqui. He felt his arm gripped, and allowed himself to be led away without asking a question. Yaqui's presence was always one of gloom, and now his stern action boded catastrophe. Once clear of trees he pointed to the level desert across the river, where a row of campfires shone bright out of the darkness.

"Raiders!" ejaculated Gale.

Then he cautioned Yaqui to keep sharp lookout, and, hurriedly returning to the house, he called the men out and told them there were rebels or raiders camping just across the line.

Ladd did not say a word. Belding, with an oath, slammed down his cigar.

"I knew it was too good to last. . . . Dick, you and Jim stay here while Laddy and I look around."

Dick returned to the sitting-room. The women were nervous and not to be deceived. So Dick merely said Yaqui had sighted some lights off in the desert, and they probably were campfires. Belding did not soon return, and when he did he was alone, and saying he wanted to consult with the men, he sent Mrs. Belding and the girls to their rooms. His gloomy anxiety had returned.

"Laddy's gone over to scout around and try to find out who the outfit belongs to and how many are in it," said Belding.

"I reckon if they're raiders with bad intentions we wouldn't see no fires," remarked Jim, calmly.

"It'd be useless, I suppose, to send for the cavalry," said Gale. "Whatever's coming off would be over before the soldiers could be notified, let alone reach here."

"Hell, fellows! I don't look for an attack on Forlorn River," burst out Belding. "I can't believe that possible. These rebel-raiders have a little sense. They wouldn't spoil their game by pulling U.S. soldiers across the line from Yuma to El Paso. But, as Jim says, if they wanted to steal a few horses or cattle they wouldn't build fires. I'm afraid it's—"

Belding hesitated and looked with grim concern at the cavalryman.

"What?" queried Thorne.

"I'm afraid it's Rojas."

Thorne turned pale but did not lose his nerve.

"I thought of that at once. If true, it'll be terrible for Mercedes and me. But Rojas will never get his hands on my wife. If I can't kill him, I'll kill her! . . . Belding, this is tough on you—this risk we put upon your family. I regret—"

"Cut that kind of talk," replied Belding, bluntly. "Well, if it is Rojas he's acting damn strange for a raider. That's what worries me. We can't do anything but wait. With Laddy and Yaqui out there we won't be surprised. Let's take the best possible view of the situation until we know more. That'll not likely be before to-morrow."

The women of the house might have gotten some sleep that night, but it was certain the men did not get any. Morning broke cold and gray, the 19th of February. Breakfast was prepared earlier than usual, and an air of suppressed waiting excitement pervaded the place. Otherwise the ordinary details of the morning's work continued as on any other day. Ladd came in hungry and cold, and said the Mexicans were not breaking camp. He reported a good-sized force of rebels, and was taciturn as to his idea of forthcoming events.

About an hour after sunrise Yaqui ran in with the information that part of the rebels were crossing the river.

"That can't mean a fight yet," declared Belding. "But get in the house, boys, and make ready anyway. I'll meet them."

"Drive them off the place same as if you had a company of soldiers backin' you," said Ladd. "Don't give them an inch. We're in bad, and the bigger bluff we put up the more likely our chance."

"Belding, you're an officer of the United States. Mexicans are much impressed by show of authority. I've seen that often in camp," said Thorne.

"Oh, I know the white-livered Greasers better than any of you, don't mistake me," replied Belding. He was pale with rage, but kept command over himself.

The rangers, with Yaqui and Thorne, stationed themselves at the several windows of the sitting-room. Rifles and smaller arms and boxes of shells littered the tables and window seats. No small force of besiegers could overcome a resistance such as Belding and his men were capable of making.

"Here they come, boys," called Gale, from his window. "Rebel-raiders I should say, Laddy."

"Shore. An' a fine outfit for buzzards!"

"Reckon there's about a dozen in the bunch," observed the calm Lash. "Some hosses they're ridin'. Where'n the hell do they get such hosses, anyhow?"

"Shore, Jim, they work hard an' buy 'em with real silver pesos," replied Ladd, sarcastically.

"Do any of you see Rojas?" whispered Thorne.

"Nix. No dandy bandit in that outfit."

"It's too far to see," said Gale.

The horsemen halted at the corrals. They were orderly and showed no evidence of hostility. They were, however, fully armed. Belding stalked out to meet them. Apparently a leader wanted to parley with him, but Belding would hear nothing. He shook his head, waved his arms, stamped to and fro, and his loud, angry voice could be heard clear back at the house. Whereupon the detachment of rebels retired to the bank of the river, beyond the white post that marked the boundary line, and there they once more drew rein. Belding remained by the corrals watching them, evidently still in a threatening mood. Presently a single rider left the troop and trotted his horse back down the road. When he reached the corrals he was seen to halt and pass something to Belding. Then he galloped away to join his comrades.

Belding looked at whatever it was he held in his hand, shook his burly head, and started swiftly for the house. He came striding into the room holding a piece of soiled paper.

"Can't read it and don't know as I want to," he said, savagely.

"Beldin', shore we'd better read it," replied Ladd. "What we want is a line on them Greasers. Whether they're Campo's men or Salazar's, or just a wanderin' bunch of rebels—or Rojas's bandits. *Sabe,* señor?"

Not one of the men was able to translate the garbled scrawl.

"Shore Mercedes can read it," said Ladd.

Thorne opened a door and called her. She came into the room followed by Nell and Mrs. Belding. Evidently all three divined a critical situation.

"My dear, we want you to read what's written on this paper," said Thorne, as he led her to the table. "It was sent in by rebels, and—and we fear contains bad news for us."

Mercedes gave the writing one swift glance, then fainted in Thorne's arms. He carried her to a couch, and with Nell and Mrs. Belding began to work over her.

Belding looked at his rangers. It was characteristic of the man that, now when catastrophe appeared inevitable, all the gloom and care and angry agitation passed from him.

"Laddy, it's Rojas all right. How many men has he out there?"

"Mebbe twenty. Not more."

"We can lick twice that many Greasers."

"Shore."

Jim Lash removed his pipe long enough to speak.

"I reckon. But it ain't sense to start a fight when mebbe we can avoid it."

"What's your idea?"

"Let's stave the Greasers off till dark. Then Laddy an' me an' Thorne will take Mercedes an' hit the trail for Yuma."

"Camino del Diablo! That awful trail with a woman! Jim, do you forget how many *hundreds of men* have perished on the Devil's Road?"

"I reckon I ain't forgettin' nothin'," replied Jim. "The water-holes are full now. There's grass, an' we can do the job in six days."

"It's three hundred miles to Yuma."

"Beldin', Jim's idea hits me pretty reasonable," interposed Ladd. "Lord knows that's about the only chance we've got except fightin'."

"But suppose we do stave Rojas off, and you get safely away with Mercedes. Isn't Rojas going to find it out quick? Then what'll he try to do to us who're left here?"

"I reckon he'd find out by daylight," replied Jim. "But, Tom, he ain't agoin' to start a scrap then. He'd want time an' hosses an' men to chase us out on the trail. You see, I'm figgerin' on the crazy Greaser wantin' the girl. I reckon he'll try to clean up here to get her. But he's too smart to fight you for nothin'. Rojas may be nutty about women, but he's afraid of the U.S. Take my word for it he'd discover the trail in the mornin' an' light out on it. I reckon with ten hours' start we could travel comfortable."

Belding paced up and down the room. Jim and Ladd whispered together. Gale walked to the window and looked out at the distant group of bandits, and then turned his gaze to rest upon Mercedes. She was conscious now, and her eyes seemed all the larger and blacker for the whiteness of her face. Thorne held her hands, and the other women were trying to still her tremblings. No one but Gale saw the Yaqui in the background looking down upon the Spanish girl. All of Yaqui's looks were strange; but this was singularly so. Gale marked it, and felt he would never forget. Mercedes's beauty had never before struck him as being so exquisite, so alluring as now when she lay stricken. Gale wondered if the Indian was affected by her loveliness, her helplessness, or her terror. Yaqui had seen Mercedes only a few times, and upon each of these he had appeared to be fascinated. Could the strange Indian, because his hate for Mexicans was so great, be gloating over her misery? Something about Yaqui—a noble austerity of countenance—made Gale feel his suspicion unjust.

Presently Belding called his rangers to him, and then Thorne.

"Listen to this," he said, earnestly. "I'll go out and have a talk with Rojas. I'll try to reason with him; tell him to think a long time before he sheds blood on Uncle Sam's soil. That he's now after an American's wife! I'll not commit myself, nor will I refuse outright to consider his demands, nor will I show the least fear of him. I'll play for time. If my bluff goes through . . . well and good. . . . After dark the four of you, Laddy, Jim, Dick and Thorne, will

take Mercedes and my best white horses, and, with
Yaqui as guide, circle round through Altar Valley to the
trail, and head for Yuma.... Wait now, Laddy. Let me
finish. I want you to take the white horses for two reasons—to save them and to save you. Savvy? If Rojas
should follow on my horses he'd be likely to catch you.
Also, you can pack a great deal more than on the bronchs.
Also, the big horses can travel faster and farther on little
grass and water. I want you to take the Indian, because in
a case of this kind he'll be a godsend. If you get headed
or lost or have to circle off the trail, think what it'd mean
to have a Yaqui with you. He knows Sonora as no Greaser
knows it. He could hide you, find water and grass, when
you would absolutely believe it impossible. The Indian is
loyal. He has his debt to pay, and he'll pay it, don't mistake me. When you're gone I'll hide Nell so Rojas won't
see her if he searches the place. Then I think I could sit
down and wait without any particular worry."

The rangers approved of Belding's plan, and Thorne
choked in his effort to express his gratitude.

"All right, we'll chance it," concluded Belding. "I'll
go out now and call Rojas and his outfit over.... Say, it
might be as well for me to know just what he said in that
paper."

Thorne went to the side of his wife.

"Mercedes, we've planned to outwit Rojas. Will you
tell us just what he wrote?"

The girl sat up, her eyes dilating, and with her hands
clasping Thorne's, she said:

"Rojas swore—by his saints and his virgin—that if
I wasn't given—to him—in twenty-four hours—he
would set fire to the village—kill the men—carry off the
women—hang the children on cactus thorns!"

A moment's silence followed her last halting whisper.

"By his saints an' his virgin!" echoed Ladd. He laughed—a cold, cutting, deadly laugh—significant and terrible.

Then the Yaqui uttered a singular cry. Gale had heard this once before, and now he remembered it was at the Papago Well.

"Look at the Indian," whispered Belding, hoarsely. "Damn if I don't believe he understood every word Mercedes said. And, gentlemen, don't mistake me, if he ever gets near Señor Rojas there'll be some gory Aztec knife work."

Yaqui had moved close to Mercedes, and stood beside her as she leaned against her husband. She seemed impelled to meet the Indian's gaze, and evidently it was so powerful or hypnotic that it wrought irresistibly upon her. But she must have seen or divined what was beyond the others, for she offered him her trembling hand. Yaqui took it and laid it against his body in a strange motion, and bowed his head. Then he stepped back into the shadow of the room.

Belding went outdoors while the rangers took up their former position at the west window. Each had his own somber thoughts, Gale imagined, and knew his own were dark enough. A slow fire crept along his veins. He saw Belding halt at the corrals and wave his hand. Then the rebels mounted and came briskly up the road, this time to rein in abreast.

Wherever Rojas had kept himself upon the former advance was not clear; but he certainly was prominently in sight now. He made a gaudy, almost a dashing figure. Gale did not recognize the white sombrero, the crimson scarf, the velvet jacket, nor any feature of the dandy's costume;

but their general effect, the whole ensemble, recalled vividly to mind his first sight of the bandit. Rojas dismounted and seemed to be listening. He betrayed none of the excitement Gale had seen in him that night at the Del Sol. Evidently this composure struck Ladd and Lash as unusual in a Mexican supposed to be laboring under stress of feeling. Belding made gestures, vehemently bobbed his big head, appeared to talk with his body as much as with his tongue. Then Rojas was seen to reply, and after that it was clear that the talk became painful and difficult. It ended finally in what appeared to be mutual understanding. Rojas mounted and rode away with his men, while Belding came tramping back to the house.

As he entered the door his eyes were shining, his big hands were clenched, and he was breathing audibly.

"You can rope me if I'm not locoed!" he burst out. "I went out to conciliate a red-handed little murderer, and damn me if I didn't meet a—a—well, I've no suitable name handy. I started my bluff and got along pretty well, but I forgot to mention that Mercedes was Thorne's wife. And what do you think? Rojas swore he loved Mercedes—swore he'd marry her right here in Forlorn River—swore he would give up robbing and killing people, and take her away from Mexico. He has gold—jewels. He swore if he didn't get her nothing mattered. He'd die anyway without her. . . . And here's the strange thing. I believe him! He was cold as ice, and all hell inside. Never saw a Greaser like him. Well, I pretended to be greatly impressed. We got to talking friendly, I suppose, though I didn't understand half he said, and I imagine he gathered less what I said. Anyway, without my asking he said for me to think it over for a day and then we'd talk again."

"Shore we're born lucky!" ejaculated Ladd.

"I reckon Rojas'll be smart enough to string his outfit across the few trails leadin' out of Forlorn River," remarked Jim.

"That needn't worry us. All we want is dark to come," replied Belding. "Yaqui will slip through. If we thank any lucky stars let it be for the Indian. . . . Now, boys, put on your thinking caps. You'll take eight horses, the pick of my bunch. You must pack all that's needed for a possible long trip. Mind, Yaqui may lead you down into some wild Sonora valley and give Rojas the slip. You may get to Yuma in six days, and maybe in six weeks. Yet you've got to pack light—a small pack in saddles—larger ones on the two free horses. You may have a big fight. Laddy, take the .405. Dick will pack his Remington. All of you go gunned heavy. But the main thing is a pack that'll be light enough for swift travel, yet one that'll keep you from starving on the desert."

The rest of that day passed swiftly. Dick had scarcely a word with Nell, and all the time, as he chose and deliberated and worked over his little pack, there was a dull pain in his heart.

The sun set, twilight fell, then night closed down, fortunately a night slightly overcast. Gale saw the white horses pass his door like silent ghosts. Even Blanco Diablo made no sound, and that fact was indeed a tribute to the Yaqui. Gale went out to put his saddle on Blanco Sol. The horse rubbed a soft nose against his shoulder. Then Gale returned to the sitting room. There was nothing more to do but wait and say good-by. Mercedes came clad in leather chaps and coat, a slim stripling of a cowboy, her dark eyes flashing. Her beauty could not be hidden, and now hope and courage had fired her blood.

Gale drew Nell off into the shadow of the room. She

was trembling, and as she leaned toward him she was very different from the coy girl who had so long held him aloof. He took her into his arms.

"Dearest, I'm going—soon. . . . And maybe I'll never—"

"Dick, do—don't say it," sobbed Nell, with her head on his breast.

"I might never come back," he went on, steadily. "I love you—I've loved you ever since the first moment I saw you. Do you care for me—a little?"

"Dear Dick—de-dear Dick, my heart is breaking," faltered Nell, as she clung to him.

"It might be breaking for Mercedes—for Laddy and Jim. I want to hear something for myself. Something to have on long marches—round lonely campfires. Something to keep my spirit alive. Oh, Nell, you can't imagine that silence out there—that terrible world of sand and stone! . . . Do you love me?"

"Yes, yes. Oh, I love you so! I never knew it till now. I love you so. Dick, I'll be safe and I'll wait—and hope and pray for your return."

"If I come back—no—*when* I come back, will you marry me?"

"I—I—oh yes!" she whispered, and returned his kiss.

Belding was in the room speaking softly.

"Nell, darling, I must go," said Dick.

"I'm a selfish little coward," cried Nell. "It's so splendid of you all. I ought to glory in it, but I can't. . . . Fight if you must, Dick. Fight for that lovely persecuted girl. I'll love you—the more. . . . Oh! Good-by! Good-by!"

With a wrench that shook him Gale let her go. He heard Belding's soft voice.

"Yaqui says the early hour's best. Trust him, Laddy. Remember what I say—Yaqui's a godsend."

Then they were all outside in the pale gloom under the trees. Yaqui mounted Blanco Diablo; Mercedes was lifted upon White Woman; Thorne climbed astride Queen; Jim Lash was already upon his horse, which was as white as the others but bore no name; Ladd mounted the stallion Blanco Torres, and gathered up the long halters of the two pack horses; Gale came last with Blanco Sol.

As he toed the stirrup, hand on mane and pommel, Gale took one more look in at the door. Nell stood in the gleam of light, her hair shining, face like ashes, her eyes dark, her lips parted, her arms outstretched. That sweet and tragic picture etched its cruel outlines into Gale's heart. He waved his hand and then fiercely leaped into the saddle.

Blanco Sol stepped out.

Before Gale stretched a line of moving horses, white against dark shadows. He could not see the head of that column; he scarcely heard a soft hoofbeat. A single star shone out of a rift in thin clouds. There was no wind. The air was cold. The dark space of desert seemed to yawn. To the left across the river flickered a few campfires. The chill night, silent and mystical, seemed to close in upon Gale; and he faced the wide, quivering, black level with keen eyes and grim intent, and an awakening of that wild rapture which came like a spell to him in the open desert.

CHAPTER 11

ACROSS CACTUS AND LAVA

Blanco Sol showed no inclination to bend his head to the alfalfa which swished softly about his legs. Gale felt the horse's sensitive, almost human alertness. Sol knew as well as his master the nature of that flight.

At the far corner of the field Yaqui halted, and slowly the line of white horses merged into a compact mass. There was a trail here leading down to the river. The campfires were so close that the bright blazes could be seen in movement, and dark forms crossed in front of them. Yaqui slipped out of his saddle. He ran his hand over Diablo's nose and spoke low, and repeated this action for each of the other horses. Gale had long ceased to question the strange Indian's behavior. There was no explaining or understanding many of his maneuvers. But the results of them were always thought provoking. Gale had never seen horses stand so silently as in this instance; no stamp—no champ of bit—no toss of head—no shake of saddle or pack—no heave or snort! It seemed they had become imbued with the spirit of the Indian.

Yaqui moved away into the shadows as noiselessly as if he were one of them. The darkness swallowed him. He had taken a direction parallel with the trail. Gale wondered if Yaqui meant to try to lead his string of horses by the rebel sentinels. Ladd had his head bent low, his ear toward the trail. Jim's long neck had the arch of a listening deer. Gale listened, too, and as the slow, silent moments went by his faculty of hearing grew more acute from strain. He heard Blanco Sol breathe; he heard the pound of his own heart; he heard the silken rustle of the alfalfa; he heard a faint, far-off sound of voice, like a lost echo. Then his ear seemed to register a movement of air, a disturbance so soft as to be nameless. Then followed long, silent moments.

Yaqui appeared as he had vanished. He might have been part of the shadows. But he was there. He started off down the trail leading Diablo. Again the white line stretched slowly out. Gale fell in behind. A bench of ground, covered with sparse greasewood, sloped gently down to the deep, wide arroyo of Forlorn River. Blanco Sol shied a few feet out of the trail. Peering low with keen eyes, Gale made out three objects—a white sombrero, a blanket, and a Mexican lying facedown. The Yaqui had stolen upon this sentinel like a silent wind of death. Just then a desert coyote wailed, and the wild cry fitted the darkness and the Yaqui's deed.

Once under the dark lee of the river bank Yaqui caused another halt, and he disappeared as before. It seemed to Gale that the Indian started to cross the pale level sand-bed of the river, where stones stood out gray, and the darker line of opposite shore was visible. But he vanished, and it was impossible to tell whether he went one way or another. Moments passed. The horses held heads up, looked toward the glimmering campfires, and listened. Gale thrilled with the meaning of it all—the night—the silence—the flight—and the wonderful Indian stealing with the slow inevitability of doom upon another sentinel. An hour passed and Gale seemed to have become deadened to all sense of hearing. There were no more sounds in the world. The desert was as silent as it was black. Yet again came that strange change in the tensity of Gale's ear-strain, a check, a break, a vibration—and this time the sound did not go nameless. It might have been moan of wind or wail of far-distant wolf, but Gale imagined it was the strangling death-cry of another guard, or that strange, involuntary utterance of the Yaqui. Blanco Sol trembled in all his great frame, and then Gale was certain the sound was not imagination.

That certainty, once and for all, fixed in Gale's mind the mood of his flight. The Yaqui dominated the horses and the rangers. Thorne and Mercedes were as persons under a spell. The Indian's strange silence, the feeling of mystery and power he seemed to create, all that was incomprehensible about him were emphasized in the light of his slow, sure, and ruthless action. If he dominated the others, surely he did more for Gale—colored his thoughts—presaged the wild and terrible future of that flight. If Rojas embodied all the hatred and passion of the peon—scourged slave for a thousand years—then Yaqui embodied all the darkness, the cruelty, the white, sun-heated blood, the ferocity, the tragedy of the desert.

Suddenly the Indian stalked out of the gloom. He mounted Diablo and headed across the river. Once more the line of moving white shadows stretched out. The soft sand gave forth no sound at all. The glimmering campfires sank behind the western bank. Yaqui led the way into the willows, and there was faint swishing of leaves; then into the mesquite, and there was faint rustling of branches. The glimmering lights appeared again, and grotesque forms of *saguaros* loomed darkly. Gale peered sharply along the trail, and, presently, on the pale sand under a cactus, there lay a blanketed form, prone, outstretched, a carbine clutched in one hand, a cigarette, still burning, in the other.

The cavalcade of white horses passed within five hundred yards of campfires, around which dark forms moved in plain sight. Soft pads in sand, faint metallic tickings of steel on thorns, low, regular breathing of horses—these were all the sounds the fugitives made, and they could not have been heard at one-fifth the distance. The lights disappeared from time to time, grew dimmer, more flickering, and at last they vanished altogether. Belding's fleet and tireless steeds were out in front; the desert opened ahead wide, dark, vast. Rojas and his rebels were behind, eating, drinking, careless. The somber shadow lifted from Gale's heart. He held now an unquenchable faith in the Yaqui. Belding would be listening back there along the river. He would know of the escape. He would tell Nell, and then hide her safely. As Gale had accepted a strange and fatalistic foreshadowing of toil, blood, and agony in this desert journey, so he believed in Mercedes's ultimate freedom and happiness, and his own return to the girl who had grown dearer than life.

A cold, gray dawn was fleeing before a rosy sun when Yaqui halted the march at Papago Well. The horses were taken to water, then led down the arroyo into the grass. Here packs were slipped, saddles removed. Mercedes was cold, lame, tired, but happy. It warmed Gale's blood to look at her. The shadow of fear still lay in her eyes, but it was passing. Hope and courage shone there, and affection for her ranger protectors and the Yaqui, and unutterable love for the cavalryman. Jim Lash remarked how cleverly they had fooled the rebels.

"Shore they'll be comin' along," replied Ladd.

They built a fire, cooked and ate. The Yaqui spoke only one word: "Sleep." Blankets were spread. Mercedes dropped into a deep slumber, her head on Thorne's shoulder. Excitement kept Thorne awake. The two rangers dozed beside the fire. Gale shared the Yaqui's watch. The sun began to climb and the icy edge of dawn to wear away. Rabbits bobbed their cotton tails under the mesquite. Gale climbed a rocky wall above the arroyo bank, and there, with command over the miles of the back-trail, he watched.

It was a sweeping, rolling, wrinkled, and streaked range of desert that he saw, ruddy in the morning sunlight, with patches of cactus and mesquite rough-etched in shimmering gloom. No Name Mountains split the eastern sky, towering high, gloomy, grand, with purple veils upon their slopes. They were forty miles away and looked five. Gale thought of the girl who was there under their shadow.

Yaqui kept the horses bunched, and he led them from one little park of galleta grass to another. At the end of three hours he took them to water. Upon his return Gale clambered down from his outlook, the rangers grew active, Mercedes was awakened; and soon the party faced westward, their long shadows moving before them. Yaqui led with Blanco Diablo in a long, easy lope. The arroyo washed itself out into flat desert, and the greens began to shade into gray, and then the gray into red. Only sparse cactus and weathered ledges dotted the great low roll of a rising escarpment. Yaqui suited the gait of his horse to the lay of the land, and his followers accepted his pace. There were canter and trot, and swift walk and slow climb, and long swing—miles up and down and forward. The sun soared hot. The heated air lifted, and incoming currents from the west swept low and hard over the barren earth. In the distance, all around the horizon, accumulations of dust seemed like ranging, mushrooming yellow clouds.

Yaqui was the only one of the fugitives who never looked back. Mercedes did it the most. Gale felt what compelled her; he could not resist it himself. But it was a vain search. For a thousand puffs of white and yellow dust rose from that backward sweep of desert, and any one of them might have been blown from under horses' hoofs. Gale had a conviction that when Yaqui gazed back toward the well and the shining plain beyond, there would be reason for it. But when the sun lost its heat and the wind died down Yaqui took long and careful surveys westward from the high points on the trail. Sunset was not far off, and there in a bare, spotted valley lay Coyote Tanks, the only water hole between Papago Well and the Sonoyta Oasis. Gale used his glass, told Yaqui there was no smoke, no sign of life; still the Indian fixed his falcon eyes on distant spots and looked long. It was as if his vision could not detect what reason or cunning, or intuition, perhaps an instinct, told him was there. Presently in a sheltered spot, where blown sand had not obliterated the trail, Yaqui found the tracks of horses. The curve of the iron shoes pointed westward. An intersecting trail from the north came in here. Gale thought the tracks either one or two days old. Ladd said they were one day. The Indian shook his head.

No farther advance was undertaken. The Yaqui headed south and traveled slowly, climbing to the brow of a bold height of weathered mesa. There he sat his horse and waited. No one questioned him. The rangers dismounted to stretch their legs, and Mercedes was lifted to a rock, where she rested. Thorne had gradually yielded to the desert's influence for silence. He spoke once or twice to Gale, and occasionally whispered to Mercedes. Gale fancied his friend would soon learn that necessary speech in desert travel meant a few greetings, a few words to make real the fact of human companionship, a few short, terse terms for the business of day or night, and perhaps a stern order or a soft call to a horse.

The sun went down, and the golden, rosy veils turned to blue and shaded darker till twilight was there in the valley. Only the spurs of mountains, spiring the near and far horizon, retained their clear outline. Darkness approached, and the clear peaks faded. The horses stamped to be on the move.

"Malo!" exclaimed the Yaqui.

He did not point with his arm, but his falcon head was outstretched, and his piercing eyes gazed at the blurring spot which marked the location of Coyote Tanks.

"Jim, can you see anything?" asked Ladd.

"Nope, but I reckon he can."

Darkness increased momentarily till night shaded the deepest part of the valley.

Then Ladd suddenly straightened up, turned to his horse, and muttered low under his breath.

"I reckon so," said Lash, and for once his easy, good-natured tone was not in evidence. His voice was harsh.

Gale's eyes, keen as they were, were last of the rangers

to see tiny needle-points of light just faintly perceptible in the blackness.

"Laddy! Campfires?" he asked, quickly.

"Shore's you're born, my boy."

"How many?"

Ladd did not reply; but Yaqui held up his hand, his fingers wide. Five campfires! A strong force of rebels or raiders or some other desert troop was camping at Coyote Tanks.

Yaqui sat his horse for a moment, motionless as stone, his dark face immutable and impassive. Then he stretched wide his right arm in the direction of No Name Mountains, now losing their last faint traces of the afterglow, and he shook his head. He made the same impressive gesture toward the Sonoyta Oasis with the same somber negation.

Thereupon he turned Diablo's head to the south and started down the slope. His manner had been decisive, even stern. Lash did not question it, nor did Ladd. Both rangers hesitated, however, and showed a strange, almost a sullen reluctance which Gale had never seen in them before. Raiders were one thing, Rojas was another; Camino del Diablo still another; but that vast and desolate and unwatered waste of cactus and lava, the Sonora Desert, might appall the stoutest heart. Gale felt his own sink—felt himself flinch.

"Oh, where is he going?" cried Mercedes. Her poignant voice seemed to break a spell.

"Shore, lady, Yaqui's goin' home," replied Ladd gently. "An' considerin' our troubles I reckon we ought to thank God he knows the way."

They mounted and rode down the slope toward the darkening south.

Not until night travel was obstructed by a wall of cactus did the Indian halt to make a dry camp. Water and grass for the horses and fire to cook by were not to be had. Mercedes bore up surprisingly; but she fell asleep almost the instant her thirst had been allayed. Thorne laid her upon a blanket and covered her. The men ate and drank. Diablo was the only horse that showed impatience; but he was angry, and not in distress. Blanco Sol licked Gale's hand and stood patiently. Many a time had he taken his rest at night without a drink. Yaqui again bade the men sleep. Ladd said he would take the early watch; but from the way the Indian shook his head and settled himself against a stone, it appeared if Ladd remained awake he would have company. Gale lay down weary of limb and eye. He heard the soft thump of hoofs, the sough of wind in the cactus—then no more.

When he awoke there was bustle and stir about him. Day had not yet dawned, and the air was freezing cold. Yaqui had found a scant bundle of greasewood which served to warm them and to cook breakfast. Mercedes was not aroused till the last moment.

Day dawned with the fugitives in the saddle. A picketed wall of cactus hedged them in, yet the Yaqui made a tortuous path, that, zigzag as it might, in the main always headed south. It was wonderful how he slipped Diablo through the narrow aisles of thorns, saving the horse and saving himself. The others were torn and clutched and held and stung. The way was a flat, sandy pass between low mountain ranges. There were open spots and aisles and squares of sand; and hedging rows of prickly pear and the huge spider-legged *ocatillo* and hummocky masses of clustered *bisnagi*. The day grew dry and hot. A fragrant wind blew through the pass. Cactus flowers bloomed, red and yellow and magenta. The sweet, pale Ajo lily gleamed in shady corners.

Ten miles of travel covered the length of the pass. It opened wide upon a wonderful scene, an arboreal desert, dominated by its pure light green, yet lined by many merging colors. And it rose slowly to a low dim and dark-red zone of lava, spurred, peaked, domed by volcano cones, a wild and ragged region, illimitable as the horizon.

The Yaqui, if not at fault, was yet uncertain. His falcon eyes searched and roved, and became fixed at length at the southwest, and toward this he turned his horse. The great, fluted *saguaros,* fifty, sixty feet high, raised columnal forms, and their branching limbs and curving lines added a grace to the desert. It was the low-bushed cactus that made the toil and pain of travel. Yet these thorny forms were beautiful.

In the basins between the ridges, to right and left along the floor of low plains the mirage glistened, wavered, faded, vanished—lakes and trees and clouds. Inverted mountains hung suspended in the lilac air and faint tracery of white-walled cities.

At noon Yaqui halted the cavalcade. He had selected a field of *bisnagi* cactus for the place of rest. Presently his reason became obvious. With long, heavy knife he cut off the tops of these barrel-shaped plants. He scooped out soft pulp and with stone and hand then began to pound the deeper pulp into a juicy mass. When he threw this out there was a little water left, sweet, cool water which man and horse shared eagerly. Thus he made even the desert's fiercest growths minister to their needs.

But he did not halt long. Miles of gray-green spiked walls lay between him and that line of ragged, red lava which manifestly he must reach before dark. The travel became faster, straighter. And the glistening thorns clutched and clung to leather and cloth and flesh. The horses reared, snorted, balked, leaped—but they were sent on. Only Blanco Sol, the patient, the plodding, the indomitable, needed no goad or spur. Waves and scarfs and wreaths of heat smoked up from the sand. Mercedes reeled in her saddle. Thorne bade her drink, bathed her face, supported her, and then gave way to Ladd, who took the girl with him on Torres's broad back. Yaqui's unflagging purpose and iron arm were bitter and hateful to the proud and haughty spirit of Blanco Diablo. For once Belding's great white devil had met his master. He fought rider, bit, bridle, cactus, sand—and yet he went on and on, zigzagging, turning, winding, crashing through the barbed growths. The middle of the afternoon saw Thorne reeling in his saddle, and then, wherever possible, Gale's powerful arm lent him strength to hold his seat.

The giant cactus came to be only so in name. These *saguaros* were thinning out, growing stunted, and most of them were single columns. Gradually other cactus forms showed a harder struggle for existence, and the spaces of sand between were wider. But now the dreaded, glistening *cholla* began to show pale and gray and white upon the rising slope. Round-topped hills, sunset-colored above, blue-black below, intervened to hide the distant spurs and peaks. Mile and mile long tongues of red lava streamed out between the hills and wound down to stop abruptly upon the slope.

The fugitives were entering a desolate, burned-out world. It rose above them in limitless, gradual ascent and spread wide to east and west. Then the waste of sand began to yield to cinders. The horses sank to their fetlocks as they toiled on. A fine, choking dust blew back from the leaders, and men coughed and horses snorted. The huge, round hills rose smooth, symmetrical, colored as if the setting sun was shining on bare, blue-black surfaces. But the sun was now behind the hills. In between ran the streams of lava. The horsemen skirted the edge between slope of hill and perpendicular ragged wall. This red lava seemed to have flowed and hardened there only yesterday. It was broken, sharp, dull rust color, full of cracks and caves and crevices, and everywhere upon its jagged surface grew the white-thorned *cholla*.

Again twilight encompassed the travelers. But there was still light enough for Gale to see the constricted passage open into a wide, deep space where the dull color was relieved by the gray of gnarled and dwarfed mesquite. Blanco Sol, keenest of scent, whistled his welcome herald of water. The other horses answered, quickened their gait. Gale smelled it, too, sweet, cool, damp on the dry air.

Yaqui turned the corner of a pocket in the lava wall. The file of white horses rounded the corner after him. And Gale, coming last, saw the pale, glancing gleam of a pool of water beautiful in the twilight.

Next day the Yaqui's relentless driving demand on the horses was no longer in evidence. He lost no time, but he did not hasten. His course wound between low cinder dunes which limited their view of the surrounding country. These dunes finally sank down to a black floor as hard as flint with tongues of lava to the left, and to the right the slow descent into the cactus plain. Yaqui was now traveling due west. It was Gale's idea that the Indian was skirting the first sharp-toothed slope of a vast volcanic plateau which formed the western half of the Sonora Desert and extended to the Gulf of California. Travel was slow, but not exhausting for rider or beast. A little sand and meager grass gave a grayish tinge to the strip of black ground between lava and plain.

That day, as the manner rather than the purpose of the Yaqui changed, so there seemed to be subtle differences in the others of the party. Gale himself lost a certain sickening dread, which had not been for himself, but for Mercedes and Nell, and Thorne and the rangers. Jim, good-natured again, might have been patrolling the boundary line. Ladd lost his taciturnity and his gloom changed to a cool, careless air. A mood that was almost defiance began to be manifested in Thorne. It was in Mercedes, however, that Gale marked the most significant change. Her collapse the preceding day might never have been. She was lame and sore; she rode her saddle sidewise, and often she had to be rested and helped; but she had found a reserve fund of strength, and her mental condition was not the same that it had been. Her burden of fear had been lifted. Gale saw in her the difference he always felt in himself after a few days in the desert. Already Mercedes and he, and all of them, had begun to respond to the desert spirit. Moreover, Yaqui's strange influence must have been a call to the primitive.

Thirty miles of easy stages brought the fugitives to another water hole, a little round pocket under the heaved-up edge of lava. There was spare, short, bleached grass for the horses, but no wood for a fire. This night there were question and reply, conjecture, doubt, opinion, and conviction expressed by the men of the party. But the Indian, who alone could have told where they were, where they were going, what chance they had to escape, main-

tained his stoical silence. Gale took the early watch, Ladd
the midnight one, and Lash that of the morning.

The day broke rosy, glorious, cold as ice. Action was
necessary to make useful benumbed hands and feet.
Mercedes was fed while yet wrapped in blankets. Then,
while the packs were being put on and horses saddled, she
walked up and down, slapping her hands, warming her
ears. The rose color of the dawn was in her cheeks,
and the wonderful clearness of desert light in her eyes.
Thorne's eyes sought her constantly. The rangers watched
her. The Yaqui bent his glance upon her only seldom; but
when he did look it seemed that his strange, fixed, and inscrutable face was about to break into a smile. Yet that
never happened. Gale himself was surprised to find how
often his own glance found the slender, dark, beautiful
Spaniard. Was this because of her beauty? he wondered.
He thought not altogether. Mercedes was a woman. She
represented something in life that men of all races for
thousands of years had loved to see and own, to revere
and debase, to fight and die for.

It was a significant index to the day's travel that Yaqui
should keep a blanket from the pack and tear it into strips
to bind the legs of the horses. It meant the dreaded *cholla*
and the knife-edged lava. That Yaqui did not mount Diablo was still more significant. Mercedes must ride; but the
others must walk.

The Indian led off into one of the gray notches between the tumbled streams of lava. These streams were
about thirty feet high, a rotting mass of splintered lava,
rougher than any other kind of roughness in the world. At
the apex of the notch, where two streams met, a narrow
gully wound and ascended. Gale caught sight of the
dim, pale shadow of a onetime trail. Near at hand it was

invisible; he had to look far ahead to catch the faint tracery. Yaqui led Diablo into it, and then began the most laborious and vexatious and painful of all slow travel.

Once up on top of that lava bed, Gale saw stretching away, breaking into millions of crests and ruts, a vast, red-black field sweeping onward and upward, with ragged, low ridges and mounds and spurs leading higher and higher to a great, split escarpment wall, above which dim peaks shone hazily blue in the distance.

He looked no more in that direction. To keep his foot-hold, to save his horse, cost him all energy and attention. The course was marked out for him in the tracks of the other horses. He had only to follow. But nothing could have been more difficult. The disintegrating surface of a lava bed was at once the roughest, the hardest, the mean-est, the cruelest, the most deceitful kind of ground to travel.

It was rotten, yet it had corners as hard and sharp as pikes. It was rough, yet as slippery as ice. If there was a foot of level surface, that space would be one to break through under a horse's hoofs. It was seamed, lined, cracked, ridged, knotted iron. This lava bed resembled a tremendously magnified blinker. It had been a running sea of molten flint, boiling, bubbling, spouting, and it had burst its surface into a million sharp facets as it hardened. The color was dull, dark, angry red, like no other red, in-flaming to the eye. The millions of minute crevices were dominated by deep fissures and holes, ragged and rough beyond all comparison.

The fugitives made slow progress. They picked a cautious, winding way to and fro in little steps here and there along the many twists of the trail, up and down the un-avoidable depressions, round and round the holes. At noon, so winding back upon itself had been their course, they appeared to have come only a short distance up the lava slope.

It was rough work for them; it was terrible work for the horses. Blanco Diablo refused to answer to the power of the Yaqui. He balked, he plunged, he bit and kicked. He had to be pulled and beaten over many places. Mercedes's horse almost threw her, and she was put upon Blanco Sol. The white charger snorted a protest, then, obedient to Gale's stern call, patiently lowered his noble head and pawed the lava for a footing that would hold.

The lava caused Gale toil and worry and pain, but he hated the *chollas*. As the travel progressed this species of cactus increased in number of plants and in size. Everywhere the red lava was spotted with little round patches of glistening frosty white. And under every bunch of *cholla*, along and in the trail, were the discarded joints, like little frosty pinecones covered with spines. It was utterly impossible always to be on the lookout for these, and when Gale stepped on one, often as not the steel-like thorns pierced leather and flesh. Gale came almost to believe what he had heard claimed by desert travelers— that the *cholla* was alive and leaped at man or beast. Certain it was when Gale passed one, if he did not put all attention to avoiding it, he was hooked through his chaps and held by barbed thorns. The pain was almost unendurable. It was like no other. It burned, stung, beat— almost seemed to freeze. It made useless arm or leg. It made him bite his tongue to keep from crying out. It made the sweat roll off him. It made him sick.

Moreover, bad as the *cholla* was for man, it was infinitely worse for beast. A jagged stab from this poisoned cactus was the only thing Blanco Sol could not stand.

Many times that day, before he carried Mercedes, he had wildly snorted, and then stood trembling while Gale picked broken thorns from the muscular legs. But after Mercedes had been put upon Sol Gale made sure no *cholla* touched him.

The afternoon passed like the morning, in ceaseless winding and twisting and climbing along this abandoned trail. Gale saw many water holes, mostly dry, some containing water, all of them catch-basins, full only after rainy season. Little ugly bunched bushes, that Gale scarcely recognized as mesquites, grew near these holes; also stunted greasewood and prickly pear. There was no grass, and the *cholla* alone flourished in that hard soil.

Darkness overtook the party as they unpacked beside a pool of water deep under an overhanging shelf of lava. It had been a hard day. The horses drank their fill, and then stood patiently with drooping heads. Hunger and thirst were appeased, and a warm fire cheered the weary and footsore fugitives. Yaqui said, "Sleep." And so another night passed.

Upon the following morning, ten miles or more up the slow-ascending lava slope, Gale's attention was called from his somber search for the less rough places in the trail.

"Dick, why does Yaqui look back?" asked Mercedes.

Gale was startled.

"Does he?"

"Every little while," replied Mercedes.

Gale was in the rear of all the other horses, so as to take, for Mercedes's sake, the advantage of the broken trail. Yaqui was leading Diablo, winding around a break.

His head was bent as he stepped slowly and unevenly upon the lava. Gale turned to look back, the first time in several days. The mighty hollow of the desert below seemed a wide strip of red—wide strip of green—wide strip of gray—streaking to purple peaks. It was all too vast, too mighty to grasp any little details. He thought, of course, of Rojas in certain pursuit; but it seemed absurd to look for him.

Yaqui led on, and Gale often glanced up from his task to watch the Indian. Presently he saw him stop, turn, and look back. Ladd did likewise, and then Jim and Thorne. Gale found the desire irresistible. Thereafter he often rested Blanco Sol, and looked back the while. He had his field glass, but did not choose to use it.

"Rojas will follow," said Mercedes.

Gale regarded her in amaze. The tone of her voice had been indefinable. If there were fear then he failed to detect it. She was gazing back down the colored slope, and something about her, perhaps the steady, falcon gaze of her magnificent eyes, reminded him of Yaqui.

Many times during the ensuing hour the Indian faced about, and always his followers did likewise. It was high noon, with the sun beating hot and the lava radiating heat, when Yaqui halted for a rest. The place selected was a ridge of lava, almost a promontory, considering its outlook. The horses bunched here and drooped their heads. The rangers were about to slip the packs and remove saddles when Yaqui restrained them.

He fixed a changeless, gleaming gaze on the slow descent, but did not seem to look afar.

Suddenly he uttered his strange cry—the one Gale considered involuntary, or else significant of some tribal trait or feeling. It was incomprehensible, but no one could have doubted its potency. Yaqui pointed down the lava slope, pointing with finger and arm and neck and head—his whole body was instinct with direction. His whole being seemed to have been animated and then frozen. His posture could not have been misunderstood, yet his expression had not altered. Gale had never seen the Indian's face change its hard, red-bronze calm. It was the color and the flintiness and the character of the lava at his feet.

"Shore he sees somethin'," said Ladd. "But my eyes are no good."

"I reckon I ain't sure of mine," replied Jim. "I'm bothered by a dim movin' streak down there."

Thorne gazed eagerly down as he stood beside Mercedes, who sat motionless facing the slope. Gale looked and looked till he hurt his eyes. Then he took his glass out of its case on Sol's saddle.

There appeared to be nothing upon the lava but the innumerable dots of *cholla* shining in the sun. Gale swept his glass slowly forward and back. Then into a nearer field of vision crept a long white-and-black line of horses and men. Without a word he handed the glass to Ladd. The ranger used it, muttering to himself.

"They're on the lava fifteen miles down in an air line," he said, presently. "Jim, shore they're twice that an' more accordin' to the trail."

Jim had his look and replied: "I reckon we're a day an' a night in the lead."

"Is it Rojas?" burst out Thorne, with set jaw.

"Yes, Thorne. It's Rojas and a dozen men or more," replied Gale, and he looked up at Mercedes.

She was transformed. She might have been a medieval princess embodying all the Spanish power and passion of that time, breathing revenge, hate, unquenchable spirit of fire. If her beauty had been wonderful in her helpless and appealing moments, now, when she looked back white-faced and flame-eyed, it was transcendent.

Gale drew a long, deep breath. The mood which had presaged pursuit, strife, blood on this somber desert, returned to him tenfold. He saw Thorne's face corded by black veins, and his teeth exposed like those of a snarling wolf. These rangers, who had coolly risked death many times, and had dealt it often, were white as no fear or pain could have made them. Then, on the moment, Yaqui raised his hand, not clenched or doubled tight, but curled rigid like an eagle's claw; and he shook it in a strange, slow gesture which was menacing and terrible.

It was the woman that called to the depths of these men. And their passion to kill and to save was surpassed only by the wild hate which was yet love, the unfathomable emotion of a peon slave. Gale marveled at it, while he felt his whole being cold and tense, as he turned once more to follow in the tracks of his leaders. The fight predicted by Belding was at hand. What a fight that must be! Rojas was traveling light and fast. He was gaining. He had bought his men with gold, with extravagant promises, perhaps with offers of the body and blood of an aristocrat hateful to their kind. Lastly, there was the wild, desolate environment, a tortured wilderness of jagged lava and poisoned *cholla,* a lonely, fierce, and repellent world, a red stage most somberly and fittingly colored for a supreme struggle between men.

Yaqui looked back no more. Mercedes looked back no more. But the others looked, and the time came when Gale saw the creeping line of pursuers with naked eyes.

A level line above marked the rim of the plateau. Sand began to show in the little lava pits. On and upward toiled the cavalcade, still very slowly advancing. At last Yaqui reached the rim. He stood with his hand on Blanco Diablo; and both were silhouetted against the sky. That was the outlook for a Yaqui. And his great horse, dazzlingly white in the sunlight, with head wildly and proudly erect, mane and tail flying in the wind, made a magnificent picture. The others toiled on and upward, and at last Gale led Blanco Sol over the rim. Then all looked down the red slope.

But shadows were gathering there and no moving line could be seen.

Yaqui mounted and wheeled Diablo away. The others followed. Gale saw that the plateau was no more than a vast field of low, ragged circles, levels, mounds, cones, and whirls of lava. The lava was of a darker red than that down upon the slope, and it was harder than flint. In places fine sand and cinders covered the uneven floor. Strange varieties of cactus vied with the omnipresent *cholla*. Yaqui, however, found ground that his horse covered at a swift walk.

But there was only an hour, perhaps, of this comparatively easy going. Then the Yaqui led them into a zone of craters. The top of the earth seemed to have been blown out in holes from a few rods in width to large craters, some shallow, others deep, and all red as fire. Yaqui circled close to abysses which yawned sheer from a level surface, and he appeared always to be turning upon his course to avoid them.

The plateau had now a considerable dip to the west. Gale marked the slow heave and ripple of the ocean of lava to the south, where high, rounded peaks marked the center of this volcanic region. The uneven nature of the slope westward prevented any extended view, until suddenly the fugitives emerged from a rugged break to come upon a sublime and awe-inspiring spectacle.

They were upon a high point of the western slope of the plateau. It was a slope, but so many leagues long in its descent that only from a great height could any slant have been perceptible. Yaqui and his white horse stood upon the brink of a crater miles in circumference, a thousand feet deep, with its red walls patched in frost-colored spots by the silvery *cholla*. The giant tracery of lava streams waved down the slope to disappear in undulating sand dunes. And these bordered a seemingly endless arm of blue sea. This was the Gulf of California. Beyond the Gulf rose dim, bold mountains, and above them hung the setting sun, dusky red, flooding all that barren empire with a sinister light.

It was strange to Gale then, and perhaps to the others, to see their guide lead Diablo into a smooth and well-worn trail along the rim of the awful crater. Gale looked down into that red chasm. It resembled an inferno. The dark cliffs upon the opposite side were veiled in blue haze that seemed like smoke. Here Yaqui was at home. He moved and looked about him as a man coming at last into his own. Gale saw him stop and gaze out over that red-ribbed void to the Gulf.

Gale divined that somewhere along this crater of hell the Yaqui would make his final stand; and one look into his strange, inscrutable eyes made imagination picture a fitting doom for the pursuing Rojas.

CHAPTER 12

THE CRATER OF HELL

The trail led along a gigantic fissure in the side of the crater, and then down and down into a red-walled, blue-hazed labyrinth.

Presently Gale, upon turning a sharp corner, was utterly amazed to see that the split in the lava sloped out and widened into an arroyo. It was so green and soft and beautiful in all the angry, contorted red surrounding that Gale could scarcely credit his sight. Blanco Sol whistled his welcome to the scent of water. Then Gale saw a great hole, a pit in the shiny lava, a dark, cool, shady well. There was evidence of the fact that at flood seasons the water had an outlet into the arroyo. The soil appeared to be a fine sand, in which a reddish tinge predominated; and it was abundantly covered with a long grass, still partly green. Mesquites and *palo verdes* dotted the arroyo and gradually closed in thickets that obstructed the view.

"Shore it all beats me," exclaimed Ladd. "What a place

to hole up in! We could have hid here for a long time. Boys, I saw mountain sheep, the real old genuine Rocky Mountain bighorn. What do you think of that?"

"I reckon it's a Yaqui hunting ground," replied Lash. "That trail we hit must be hundreds of years old. It's worn deep and smooth in the iron lava."

"Well, all I got to say is—Beldin' was shore right about the Indian. An' I can see Rojas's finish somewhere up along that awful hellhole."

Camp was made on a level spot. Yaqui took the horses to water, and then turned them loose in the arroyo. It was a tired and somber group that sat down to eat. The strain of suspense equaled the wearing effects of the long ride. Mercedes was calm, but her great dark eyes burned in her white face. Yaqui watched her. The others looked at her with unspoken pride. Presently Thorne wrapped her in his blankets, and she seemed to fall asleep at once. Twilight deepened. The campfire blazed brighter. A cool wind played with Mercedes's black hair, waving strands across her brow.

Little of Yaqui's purpose or plan could be elicited from him. But the look of him was enough to satisfy even Thorne. He leaned against a pile of wood, which he had collected, and his gloomy gaze pierced the campfire, and at long intervals strayed over the motionless form of the Spanish girl.

The rangers and Thorne, however, talked in low tones. It was absolutely impossible for Rojas and his men to reach the water hole before noon of the next day. And long before that time the fugitives would have decided on a plan of defense. What that defense would be, and where it would be made, were matters over which the men considered gravely. Ladd averred the Yaqui would put them into an impregnable position, that at the same time would prove a death trap for their pursuers. They exhausted every possibility, and then, tired as they were, still kept on talking.

"What stuns me is that Rojas stuck to our trail," said Thorne, his lined and haggard face expressive of dark passion. "He has followed us into this fearful desert. He'll lose men, horses, perhaps his life. He's only a bandit, and he stands to win no gold. If he ever gets out of here it'll be by herculean labor and by terrible hardship. All for a poor little helpless woman—just a woman! My God, I can't understand it."

"Shore—just a woman," replied Ladd, solemnly nodding his head.

Then there was a long silence during which the men gazed into the fire. Each, perhaps, had some vague conception of the enormity of Rojas's love or hate—some faint and amazing glimpse of the gulf of human passion. Those were cold, hard, grim faces upon which the light flickered.

"Sleep," said the Yaqui.

Thorne rolled in his blanket close beside Mercedes. Then one by one the rangers stretched out, feet to the fire. Gale found that he could not sleep. His eyes were weary, but they would not stay shut; his body ached for rest, yet he could not lie still. The night was so somber, so gloomy, and the lava-encompassed arroyo full of shadows. The dark velvet sky, fretted with white fire, seemed to be close. There was an absolute silence, as of death. Nothing moved—nothing outside of Gale's body appeared to live. The Yaqui sat like an image carved out of lava. The others lay prone and quiet. Would another night see any of them lie that way, quiet forever? Gale felt a ripple pass over him that was at once a shudder and a contraction of muscles. Used as he was to the desert and its oppression, why should he feel tonight as if the weight of its lava and the burden of its mystery were bearing him down?

He sat up after a while and again watched the fire. Nell's sweet face floated like a wraith in the pale smoke—glowed and flushed and smiled in the embers. Other faces shone there—his sister's—that of his mother. Gale shook off the tender memories. This desolate wilderness with its forbidding silence and its dark promise of hell on the morrow—this was not the place to unnerve oneself with thoughts of love and home. But the torturing paradox of the thing was that this was just the place and just the night for a man to be haunted.

By and by Gale rose and walked down a shadowy aisle between the mesquites. On his way back the Yaqui joined him. Gale was not surprised. He had become used to the Indian's strange guardianship. But now, perhaps because of Gale's poignancy of thought, the contending tides of love and regret, the deep, burning premonition of deadly strife, he was moved to keener scrutiny of the Yaqui. That, of course, was futile. The Indian was impenetrable, silent, strange. But suddenly, inexplicably, Gale felt Yaqui's human quality. It was aloof, as was everything about this Indian; but it was there. This savage walked silently beside him, without glance or touch or word. His thought was as inscrutable as if mind had never awakened in his race. Yet Gale was conscious of greatness, and, somehow, he was reminded of the Indian's story. His home had been desolated, his people carried off to slavery, his wife and children separated from him to die. What had life meant to the Yaqui? What had been in his heart? What was now in his mind? Gale could not answer these questions.

But the difference between himself and Yaqui, which he had vaguely felt as that between savages and civilized men, faded out of his mind forever. Yaqui might have considered he owed Gale a debt, and, with a Yaqui's austere and noble fidelity to honor, he meant to pay it. Nevertheless, this was not the thing Gale found in the Indian's silent presence. Accepting the desert with its subtle and inconceivable influence, Gale felt that the savage and the white man had been bound in a tie which was no less brotherly because it could not be comprehended.

Toward dawn Gale managed to get some sleep. Then the morning broke with the sun hidden back of the uplift of the plateau. The horses trooped up the arroyo and snorted for water. After a hurried breakfast the packs were hidden in holes in the lava. The saddles were left where they were, and the horses allowed to graze and wander at will. Canteens were filled, a small bag of food was packed, and blankets made into a bundle. Then Yaqui faced the steep ascent of the lava slope.

The trail he followed led up on the right side of the fissure, opposite to the one he had come down. It was a steep climb, and encumbered as the men were they made but slow progress. Mercedes had to be lifted up smooth steps and across crevices. They passed places where the rims of the fissure were but a few yards apart. At length the rims widened out and the red, smoky crater yawned beneath. Yaqui left the trail and began clambering down over the rough and twisted convolutions of lava which formed the rim. Sometimes he hung sheer over the precipice. It was with extreme difficulty that the party followed him. Mercedes had to be held on narrow, foot-wide ledges. The *cholla* was there to hinder passage. Finally the Indian halted upon a narrow bench of flat, smooth lava, and his followers worked with exceeding care and effort down to his position.

At the back of this bench, between bunches of *cholla,* was a niche, a shallow cave with floor lined apparently with mold. Ladd said the place was a refuge which had been inhabited by mountain sheep for many years. Yaqui spread blankets inside, left the canteen and the sack of food, and with a gesture at once humble, yet that of a chief, he invited Mercedes to enter. A few more gestures and fewer words disclosed his plan. In this inaccessible nook Mercedes was to be hidden. The men were to go around upon the opposite rim, and block the trail leading down to the water hole.

Gale marked the nature of this eyrie. It was the wildest and most rugged place he had ever stepped upon. Only a sheep could have climbed up the wall above or along the slanting shelf of lava beyond. Below glistened a whole bank of *cholla,* frosty in the sunlight, and it overhung an apparently bottomless abyss.

Ladd chose the smallest gun in the party and gave it to Mercedes.

"Shore it's best to go the limit on bein' ready," he said, simply. "The chances are you'll never need it. But if you do—"

He left off there, and his break was significant. Mercedes answered him with a fearless and indomitable flash of eyes. Thorne was the only one who showed any shaken nerve. His leave-taking of his wife was affecting and hurried. Then he and the rangers carefully stepped in the tracks of the Yaqui.

They climbed up to the level of the rim and went along the edge. When they reached the fissure and came upon its narrowest point, Yaqui showed in his actions that he meant to leap it. Ladd restrained the Indian. They then continued along the rim till they reached several bridges of lava which crossed it. The fissure was deep in some parts, choked in others. Evidently the crater had no direct outlet into the arroyo below. Its bottom, however, must have been far beneath the level of the water hole.

After the fissure was crossed the trail was soon found. Here it ran back from the rim. Yaqui waved his hand to the right, where along the corrugated slope of the crater there were holes and crevices and coverts for a hundred men. Yaqui strode on up the trail toward a higher point, where presently his dark figure stood motionless against the sky. The rangers and Thorne selected a deep depression, out of which led several ruts deep enough for cover. According to Ladd it was as good a place as any, perhaps not so hidden as others, but freer from the dreaded *cholla*. Here the men laid down rifles and guns, and, removing their heavy cartridge belts, settled down to wait.

Their location was close to the rim wall and probably five hundred yards from the opposite rim, which was now seen to be considerably below them. The glaring red cliff presented a deceitful and baffling appearance. It had a thousand ledges and holes in its surfaces, and one moment it looked perpendicular and the next there seemed to be a long slant. Thorne pointed out where he thought Mercedes was hidden; Ladd selected another place, and Lash still another. Gale searched for the bank of the *cholla* he had seen under the bench where Mercedes's retreat lay, and when he found it the others disputed his opinion. Then Gale brought his field glass into requisition, proving that he was right. Once located and fixed in sight, the white patch of *cholla,* the bench, and the sheep eyrie stood out from the other features of that rugged wall. But all the men were agreed that Yaqui had hidden Mercedes where only the eyes of a vulture could have found her.

Jim Lash crawled into a little strip of shade and bided the time tranquilly. Ladd was restless and impatient and watchful, every little while rising to look up the far-reaching slope, and then to the right, where Yaqui's dark figure stood out from a high point of the rim. Thorne grew silent, and seemed consumed by a slow, sullen rage. Gale was neither calm nor free of a gnawing suspense nor of a waiting wrath. But as best he could he put the pending action out of mind.

It came over him all of a sudden that he had not grasped the stupendous nature of this desert setting. There was the measureless red slope, its lower ridges finally sinking into white sand dunes toward the blue sea. The cold, sparkling light, the white sun, the deep azure of sky, the feeling of boundless expanse all around him—these meant high altitude. Southward the barren red simply merged into distance. The field of craters rose in high, dark wheels toward the dominating peaks. When Gale withdrew his gaze from the magnitude of these spaces and heights the crater beneath him seemed dwarfed. Yet while he gazed it spread and deepened and multiplied its ragged lines. No, he could not grasp the meaning of size or distance here. There was too much to stun the sight. But the mood in which nature had created this convulsed world of lava seized hold upon him.

Meanwhile the hours passed. As the sun climbed the clear, steely lights vanished, the blue hazes deepened, and slowly the glistening surfaces of lava turned redder. Ladd was concerned to discover that Yaqui was missing from his outlook upon the high point. Jim Lash came out of the shady crevice, and stood up to buckle on his cartridge belt.

His narrow, gray glance slowly roved from the height of lava down along the slope, paused in doubt, and then swept on to resurvey the whole vast eastern dip of the plateau.

"I reckon my eyes are pore," he said. "Mebbe it's this damn red glare. Anyway, what's them creepin' spots up there?"

"Shore I seen them. Mountain sheep," replied Ladd.

"Guess again, Laddy. Dick, I reckon you'd better flash the glass up the slope."

Gale adjusted the field glass and began to search the lava, beginning close at hand and working away from him. Presently the glass became stationary.

"I see half a dozen small animals, brown in color. They look like sheep. But I couldn't distinguish mountain sheep from antelope."

"Shore they're bighorn," said Laddy.

"I reckon if you'll pull around to the east an' search under that long wall of lava—there—you'll see what I see," added Jim.

The glass climbed and circled, wavered an instant, then fixed steady as a rock. There was a breathless silence.

"Fourteen horses—two packed—some mounted—others without riders, and lame," said Gale slowly.

Yaqui appeared far up the trail, coming swiftly. Presently he saw the rangers and halted to wave his arms and point. Then he vanished as if the lava had opened beneath him.

"Lemme have that glass," suddenly said Jim Lash. "I'm seein' red, I tell you. . . . Well, pore as my eyes are they had it right. Rojas an' his outfit have left the trail."

"Jim, you ain't meanin' they've taken to that awful slope?" queried Ladd.

"I sure do. There they are—still comin', but goin' down, too."

"Mebbe Rojas is crazy, but it begins to look like he—"

"Laddy, I'll be danged if the Greaser bunch hasn't va-moosed. Gone out of sight! Right there not a half mile away, the whole caboodle—gone!"

"Shore they're behind a crust or have gone down into a rut," suggested Ladd. "They'll show again in a minute. Look sharp, boys, for I'm figgerin' Rojas'll spread his men."

Minutes passed, but nothing moved upon the slope. Each man crawled up to a vantage point along the crest of rotting lava. The watchers were careful to peer through little notches or from behind a spur, and the constricted nature of their hiding place kept them close together. Ladd's muttering grew into a growl, then lapsed into the silence that marked his companions. From time to time the rangers looked inquiringly at Gale. The field glass, however, like the naked sight, could not catch the slight-est moving object out there upon the lava. A long hour of slow, mounting suspense wore on.

"Shore it's all goin' to be as queer as the Yaqui," said Ladd.

Indeed, the strange mien, the silent action, the somber character of the Indian had not been without effect upon the minds of the men. Then the weird, desolate, tragic scene added to the vague sense of mystery. And now the disappearance of Rojas's band, the long wait in the si-lence, the boding certainty of invisible foes crawling, circling closer and closer, lent to the situation a final touch that made it unreal.

"I'm reckonin' there's a mind behind them Greasers," replied Jim. "Or mebbe we ain't done Rojas credit. . . . If somethin' would only come off!"

That Lash, the coolest, most provokingly nonchalant of men in times of peril, should begin to show a nervous strain was all the more indicative of a subtle pervading unreality.

"Boys, look sharp!" suddenly called Lash. "Low down to the left—mebbe three hundred yards. See, along by them seams of lava—behind the *chollas*. First off I thought it was a sheep. But it's the Yaqui! . . . Crawlin' swift as a lizard! Can't you see him?"

It was a full moment before Jim's companions could locate the Indian. Flat as a snake Yaqui wound himself along with incredible rapidity. His advance was all the more remarkable for the fact that he appeared to pass directly under the dreaded *chollas*. Sometimes he paused to lift his head and look. He was directly in line with a huge whorl of lava that rose higher than any point on the slope. This spur was a quarter of a mile from the position of the rangers.

"Shore he's headin' for that high place," said Ladd. "He's going slow now. There, he's stopped behind some *chollas*. He's gettin' up—no' he's kneelin'. . . . Now what the hell!"

"Laddy, take a peek at the side of that lava ridge," sharply called Jim. "I guess mebbe somethin' ain't comin' off. See! There's Rojas an' his outfit climbin'. Don't make out no hosses. . . . Dick, use your glass an' tell us what's doin'. I'll watch Yaqui an' tell you what his move means."

Clearly and distinctly, almost as if he could have touched them, Gale had Rojas and his followers in sight. They were toiling up the rough lava on foot. They were heavily armed. Spurs, chaps, jackets, scarfs were not in evidence. Gale saw the lean, swarthy faces, the black straggly hair, the ragged, soiled garments which had once been white.

"They're almost up now," Gale was saying. "There! They halt on top. I see Rojas. He looks wild. By—! Fellows, an Indian! . . . It's a Papago. Belding's old herder! . . . The Indian points—this way—then down. He's showing Rojas the lay of the trail."

"Boys, Yaqui's in range of that bunch," said Jim, swiftly. "He's raisin' his rifle slow—Lord, how slow he is! . . . He's covered someone. Which one I can't say. But I think he'll pick Rojas."

"The Yaqui can shoot. He'll pick Rojas," added Gale, grimly.

"Rojas—yes—yes!" cried Thorne, in passion of suspense.

"Not on your life!" Ladd's voice cut in with scorn. "Gentlemen, you can gamble Yaqui'll kill the Papago. That traitor Indian knows these sheep haunts. He's tellin' Rojas—"

A sharp rifle shot rang out.

"Laddy's right," called Gale. "The Papago's hit—his arm falls— There, he tumbles!"

More shots rang out. Yaqui was seen standing erect firing rapidly at the darting Mexicans. For all Gale could make out no second bullet took effect. Rojas and his men vanished behind the bulge of lava. Then Yaqui deliberately backed away from his position. He made no effort to run or hide. Evidently he watched cautiously for signs of pursuers in the ruts and behind the *chollas*. Presently he turned and came straight toward the position of the rangers, sheered off perhaps a hundred paces below it, and disappeared in a crevice. Plainly his intention was to draw pursuers within rifle shot.

"Shore, Jim, you had your wish. Somethin' come off," said Ladd. "An' I'm sayin' thank God for the Yaqui! That Papago'd have ruined us. Even so, mebbe he's told Rojas more'n enough to make us sweat blood."

"He had a chance to kill Rojas," cried out the drawn-faced, passionate Thorne. "He didn't take it! . . . He didn't take it!"

Only Ladd appeared to be able to answer the cavalryman's poignant cry.

"Listen, son," he said, and his voice rang. "We-all know how you feel. An' if I'd had that one shot never in the world could I have picked the Papago guide. I'd have had to kill Rojas. That's the white man of it. But Yaqui was right. Only an Indian could have done it. You can gamble the Papago alive meant slim chance for us. Because he'd lead straight to where Mercedes is hidden, an' then we'd have left cover to fight it out. . . . When you come to think of the Yaqui's hate for Greasers, when you just seen him pass up a shot at one—well, I don't know how to say what I mean, but damn me, my som-brer-ro is off to the Indian!"

"I reckon so, an' I reckon the ball's opened," rejoined Lash, and now that former nervous impatience so unnatural to him was as if it had never been. He was smilingly cool, and his voice had almost a caressing note. He tapped the breach of his Winchester with a sinewy brown hand, and he did not appear to be addressing any one in particular. "Yaqui's opened the ball. Look up your pardners there, gents, an' get ready to dance."

Another wait set in then, and judging by the more direct rays of the sun and a receding of the little shadows cast by the *chollas,* Gale was of the opinion that it was a long wait. But it seemed short. The four men were lying under the bank of a half circular hole in the lava. It was notched and cracked, and its rim was fringed by *chollas.* It sloped down and opened to an unobstructed view of the crater. Gale had the upper position, farthest to the right, and therefore was best shielded from possible fire from the higher ridges of the rim, some three hundred yards distant. Jim came next, well hidden in a crack. The positions of Thorne and Ladd were most exposed. They kept sharp lookout over the uneven rampart of their hiding place.

The sun passed the zenith, began to slope westward, and to grow hotter as it sloped. The men waited and waited. Gale saw no impatience even in Thorne. The sultry air seemed to be laden with some burden or quality that was at once composed of heat, menace, color, and silence. Even the light glancing up from the lava seemed red, and the silence had substance. Sometimes Gale felt that it was unbearable. Yet he made no effort to break it.

Suddenly this dead stillness was rent by a shot, clear and stinging, close at hand. It was from a rifle, not a carbine. With startling quickness a cry followed—a cry that pierced Gale—it was so thin, so high-keyed, so different from all other cries. It was the involuntary human shriek of death.

"Yaqui's called out another pardner," said Jim Lash, laconically.

Carbines began to crack. The reports were quick, light, like sharp spats without any ring. Gale peered from behind the edge of his covert. Above the ragged wave of lava floated faint whitish clouds, all that was visible of smokeless powder. Then Gale made out round spots, dark against the background of red, and in front of them leaped out small tongues of fire. Ladd's .405 began to "spang" with its beautiful sound of power. Thorne was firing, somewhat wildly Gale thought. Then Jim Lash pushed his Winchester over the rim under a *cholla,* and between shots Gale could hear him singing: "Turn the lady, turn—turn the lady, turn! . . . Alaman left! Swing your pardners! . . . Forward an' back! . . . Turn the lady, turn!" Gale got into the fight himself, not so sure that he hit any of the round, bobbing objects he aimed at, but growing sure of himself as action liberated something forced and congested within his breast.

Then over the position of the rangers came a hail of steel bullets. Those that struck the lava hissed away into the crater; those that came biting through the *chollas* made a sound which resembled a sharp ripping of silk. Bits of cactus stung Gale's face, and he dreaded the flying thorns more than he did the flying bullets.

"Hold on, boys," called Ladd, as he crouched down to reload his rifle. "Save your shells. The Greasers are spreadin' on us, some goin' down below Yaqui, others movin' up for that high ridge. When they get up there I'm damned if it won't be hot for us. There ain't room for all of us to hide here."

Ladd raised himself to peep over the rim. Shots were now scattering, and all appeared to come from below. Emboldened by this he rose higher. A shot from in front, a rip of bullet through the *cholla,* a spat of something hitting Ladd's face, a steel missile hissing onwards—these inseparably blended sounds were all registered by Gale's sensitive ear.

With a curse Ladd tumbled down into the hole. His face showed a great gray blotch, and starting blood. Gale felt a sickening assurance of desperate injury to the ranger. He ran to him calling: "Laddy! Laddy!"

"Shore I ain't plugged. It's a damn *cholla* burr. The bullet knocked it in my face. Pull it out!"

The oval, long-spiked cone was firmly imbedded in Ladd's cheek. Blood streamed down his face and neck.

Carefully, yet with no thought of pain to himself, Gale tried to pull the cactus joint away. It was as firm as if it had been nailed there. That was the damnable feature of the barbed thorns: once set, they held on as that strange plant held to its desert life. Ladd began to writhe, and sweat mingled with the blood on his face. He cursed and raved, and his movements made it almost impossible for Gale to do anything.

"Put your knife-blade under an' tear it out!" shouted Ladd, hoarsely.

Thus ordered, Gale slipped a long blade in between the imbedded thorns, and with a powerful jerk literally tore the *cholla* out of Ladd's quivering flesh. Then, where the ranger's face was not red and raw, it certainly was white.

A volley of shots from a different angle was followed by the quick ring of steel bullets striking the lava all around Gale. His first idea, as he heard the projectiles sing and hum and whine away into the air, was that they were coming from above him. He looked up to see a number of low, white and dark knobs upon the high point of lava. They had not been there before. Then he saw little, pale, leaping tongues of fire. As he dodged down he distinctly heard a bullet strike Ladd. At the same instant he seemed to hear Thorne cry out and fall, and Lash's boots scrape rapidly away.

Ladd fell backward still holding the .405. Gale dragged him into the shelter of his own position, and dreading to look at him, took up the heavy weapon. It was with a kind of savage strength that he gripped the rifle; and it was with a cold and deadly intent that he aimed and fired. The first Greaser huddled low, let his carbine go clattering down, and then crawled behind the rim. The second and third jerked back. The fourth seemed to flop up over the crest of lava. A dark arm reached for him, clutched his leg, tried to drag him up. It was in vain. Wildly grasping at the air the bandit fell, slid down a steep shelf, rolled over the rim, to go hurtling down out of sight.

Fingering the hot rifle with close-pressed hands, Gale watched the skyline along the high point of lava. It remained unbroken. As his passion left him he feared to look back at his companions, and the cold chill returned to his breast.

"Shore—I'm damn glad—them Greasers ain't usin' soft-nose bullets," drawled a calm voice.

Swift as lightning Gale whirled.

"Laddy! I thought you were done for," cried Gale, with a break in his voice.

"I ain't a-mindin' the bullet much. But that *cholla* joint took my nerve, an' you can gamble on it. Dick, this hole's pretty high up, ain't it?"

The ranger's blouse was open at the neck, and on his right shoulder under the collarbone was a small hole just beginning to bleed.

"Sure it's high, Laddy," replied Gale, gladly. "Went clear through, clean as a whistle!"

He tore a handkerchief into two parts, made wads, and pressing them close over the wounds he bound them there with Ladd's scarf.

"Shore it's funny how a bullet can floor a man an' then not do any damage," said Ladd. "I felt a zip of wind an' somethin' like a pat on my chest an' down I went. Well, so much for the small caliber with their steel bullets. Supposin' I'd connected with a .405!"

"Laddy, I—I'm afraid Thorne's done for," whispered Gale. "He's lying over there in that crack. I can see part of him. He doesn't move."

"I was wonderin' if I'd have to tell you that. Dick, he went down hard hit, fallin', you know, limp an' soggy. It was a moral cinch one of us would get it in this fight; but God! I'm sorry Thorne had to be the man."

"Laddy, maybe he's not dead," replied Gale. He called aloud to his friend. There was no answer.

Ladd got up, and, after peering keenly at the height of lava, he strode swiftly across the space. It was only a dozen steps to the crack in the lava where Thorne had fallen in headfirst. Ladd bent over, went to his knees, so that Gale saw only his head. Then he appeared rising with arms round the cavalryman. He dragged him across the hole to the sheltered corner that alone afforded protection. He had scarcely reached it when a carbine cracked and a bullet struck the flinty lava, striking sparks, then singing away into the air.

Thorne was either dead or unconscious, and Gale, with a contracting throat and numb heart, decided for the former. Not so Ladd, who probed the bloody gash on Thorne's temple, and then felt his breast.

"He's alive an' not bad hurt. That bullet hit him glancin'. Shore them steel bullets are some lucky for us. Dick, you needn't look so glum. I tell you he ain't bad hurt. I felt his skull with my finger. There's no hole in it. Wash him off an' tie— Wow! did you get the wind of that one? An' mebbe it didn't sing off the lava! . . . Dick, look after Thorne now while I—"

The completion of his speech was the stirring ring of the .405, and then he uttered a laugh that was unpleasant.

"Shore, Greaser, there's a man's size bullet for you. No slim, sharp-point, steel-jacket nail! I'm takin' it on me to believe you're appreciatin' of the .405, seein' as you don't make no fuss."

It was indeed a joy to Gale to find that Thorne had not received a wound necessarily fatal, though it was serious enough. Gale bathed and bound it, and laid the cavalryman against the slant of the bank, his head high to lessen the probability of bleeding.

As Gale straightened up Ladd muttered low and deep, and swung the heavy rifle around to the left. Far along the slope a figure moved. Ladd began to work the lever of the Winchester and to shoot. At every shot the heavy firearm sprang up, and the recoil made Ladd's shoulder give back. Gale saw the bullets strike the lava behind, beside, before the fleeing Mexican, sending up dull puffs of dust. On the sixth shot he plunged down out of sight, either hit or frightened into seeking cover.

"Dick, mebbe there's one or two left above; but we needn't figger much on it," said Ladd, as, loading the rifle, he jerked his fingers quickly from the hot breech. "Listen! Jim an' Yaqui are hittin' it up lively down below. I'll sneak down there. You stay here an' keep about half an eye peeled up yonder, an' keep the rest my way."

Ladd crossed the hole, climbed down into the deep crack where Thorne had fallen, and then went stooping along with only his head above the level. Presently he disappeared. Gale, having little to fear from the high ridge, directed most of his attention toward the point beyond which Ladd had gone. The firing had become desultory, and the light carbine shots outnumbered the sharp rifle shots five to one. Gale made a note of the fact that for some little time he had not heard the unmistakable report of Jim Lash's automatic. Then ensued a long interval in which the desert silence seemed to recover its grip. The .405 ripped it asunder—*spang—spang—spang*. Gale fancied he heard yells. There were a few pattering shots still farther down the trail. Gale had an uneasy conviction that Rojas and some of his band might go straight to the water hole. It would be hard to dislodge even a few men from that retreat.

There seemed a lull in the battle. Gale ventured to stand high, and, screened behind *chollas,* he swept the three-quarter circle of lava with his glass. In the distance he saw horses, but no riders. Below him, down the slope along the crater rim and the trail, the lava was bare of all except tufts of *cholla.* Gale gathered assurance. It looked as if the day was favoring his side. Then Thorne, coming partly to consciousness, engaged Gale's care. The cavalryman stirred and moaned, called for water, and then for Mercedes. Gale held him back with a strong hand, and presently he was once more quiet.

For the first time in hours, as it seemed, Gale took note of the physical aspect of his surroundings. He began to look upon them without keen gaze strained for crouching form, or bobbing head, or spouting carbine. Either Gale's sense of color and proportion had become deranged during the fight, or the encompassing air and the desert had changed. Even the sun had changed. It seemed lowering, oval in shape, magenta in hue, and it had a surface that gleamed like oil on water. Its red rays shone through red haze. Distances that had formerly been clearly outlined were now dim, obscured. The yawning chasm was not the same. It circled wider, redder, deeper. It was a weird, ghastly mouth of hell. Gale stood fascinated, unable to tell how much he saw was real, how much the exaggeration of overwrought emotions. There was no beauty here, but an unparalleled grandeur, a sublime scene of devastation and desolation which might have had its counterpart upon the burned-out moon. The mood that gripped Gale now added to its somber portent an unshakable foreboding of calamity.

He wrestled with the spell as if it were a physical foe. Reason and intelligence had their voices in his mind; but the moment was not one wherein these things could wholly control. He felt life strong within his breast, yet there, a step away, was death, yawning, glaring, smoky, red. It was a moment—an hour for a savage, born, bred, developed in this scarred and blasted place of jagged depths and red distances and silences never meant to be broken. Since Gale was not a savage he fought that call of the red gods which sent him back down the long ages toward his primitive day. His mind combated his sense of sight and the hearing that seemed useless; and his mind did not win all the victory. Something fatal was here, hanging in the balance, as the red haze hung along the vast walls of that crater of hell.

Suddenly harsh, prolonged yells brought him to his feet, and the unrealities vanished. Far down the trails where the crater rims closed in the deep fissure he saw moving forms. They were three in number. Two of them ran nimbly across the lava bridge. The third staggered far behind. It was Ladd. He appeared hard hit. He dragged at the heavy rifle, which he seemed unable to raise. The yells came from him. He was calling the Yaqui.

Gale's heart stood still momentarily. Here, then, was the catastrophe! He hardly dared sweep that fissure with his glass. The two fleeing figures halted—turned to fire at Ladd. Gale recognized the foremost one—small, compact, gaudy—Rojas! The bandit's arm was outstretched. Puffs of white smoke rose, and shots rapped out. When Ladd went down Rojas threw his gun aside and with a wild yell bounded over the lava. His companion followed.

A tide of passion, first hot as fire, then cold as ice, rushed over Gale when he saw Rojas take the trail toward Mercedes's hiding place. The little bandit appeared to have the sure-footedness of a mountain sheep. The Mexican following was not so sure or fast. He turned back. Gale heard the trenchant bark of the .405. Ladd was kneeling. He shot again—again. The retreating bandit seemed to run full into an invisible obstacle, then fell lax, inert, lifeless. Rojas sped on unmindful of the spurts of dust about him. Yaqui, high above Ladd, was also firing at the bandit. Then both rifles were emptied. Rojas turned at a high break in the trail. He shook a defiant hand, and his exulting yell pealed faintly to Gale's ears. About him there was something desperate, magnificent. Then he clambered down the trail.

Ladd dropped the .405, and rising, gun in hand, he staggered toward the bridge of lava. Before he had crossed it Yaqui came bounding down the slope, and in one splendid leap he cleared the fissure. He ran beyond the trail and disappeared on the lava above. Rojas had not seen this sudden, darting move of the Indian.

Gale felt himself bitterly powerless to aid in that pursuit. He could only watch. He wondered, fearfully, what had become of Lash. Presently, when Rojas came out of the cracks and ruts of lava there might be a chance of disabling him by a long shot. His progress was now slow. But he was making straight for Mercedes's hiding place. What was it leading him there—an eagle eye, or hate, or instinct? Why did he go on when there could be no turning back for him on that trail? Ladd was slow, heavy, staggering on the trail; but he was relentless. Only death could stop the ranger now. Surely Rojas must have known that when he chose the trail. From time to time Gale caught glimpses of Yaqui's dark figure stealing along the higher rim of the crater. He was making for a point above the bandit.

Moments—endless moments dragged by. The lowering sun colored only the upper half of the crater walls. Far down the depths were murky blue. Again Gale felt the insupportable silence. The red haze became a transparent veil before his eyes. Sinister, evil, brooding, waiting, seemed that yawning abyss. Ladd staggered along the trail, at times he crawled. The Yaqui gained; he might have had wings; he leaped from jagged crust to jagged crust; his sure-footedness was a wonderful thing.

But for Gale the marvel of that endless period of watching was the purpose of the bandit Rojas. He had now no weapon. Gale's glass made this fact plain. There was death behind him, death below him, death before him, and though he could not have known it, death above him. He never faltered—never made a misstep upon the narrow, flinty trail. When he reached the lower end of the level ledge Gale's poignant doubt became a certainty. Rojas had seen Mercedes. It was incredible, yet Gale believed it. Then, his heart clamped as in an icy vise, Gale threw forward the Remington, and sinking on one knee, began to shoot. He emptied the magazine. Puffs of dust near Rojas did not even make him turn.

As Gale began to reload he was horror-stricken by a low cry from Thorne. The cavalryman had recovered consciousness. He was half raised, pointing with shaking hand at the opposite ledge. His distended eyes were riveted upon Rojas. He was trying to utter speech that would not come.

Gale wheeled, rigid now, steeling himself to one last forlorn hope—that Mercedes could defend herself. She had a gun. He doubted not at all that she would use it. But, remembering her terror of this savage, he feared for her.

Rojas reached the level of the ledge. He halted. He crouched. It was the act of a panther. Manifestly he saw Mercedes within the cave. Then faint shots patted the air, broke in quick echo. Rojas went down as if struck a heavy blow. He was hit. But even as Gale yelled in sheer madness the bandit leaped erect. He seemed too quick, too supple to be badly wounded. A slight, dark figure flashed out of the cave. Mercedes! She backed against the wall. Gale saw a puff of white—heard a report. But the bandit lunged at her. Mercedes ran, not to try to pass him, but straight for the precipice. Her intention was plain. But Rojas outstripped her, even as she reached the verge. Then a piercing scream pealed across the crater—a scream of despair.

Gale closed his eyes. He could not bear to see more.

Thorne echoed Mercedes's scream. Gale looked round just in time to leap and catch the cavalryman as he staggered, apparently for the steep slope. And then, as Gale dragged him back, both fell. Gale saved his friend, but he plunged into a *cholla*. He drew his hands away full of the great glistening cones of thorns.

"For God's sake, Gale, shoot! Shoot! *Kill her! Kill her!* . . . Can't—you—see—Rojas—"

Thorne fainted.

Gale, stunned for the instant, stood with uplifted hands and gazed from Thorne across the crater. Rojas had not killed Mercedes. He was overpowering her. His actions seemed slow, wearing, purposeful. Hers were violent. Like a trapped she-wolf, Mercedes was fighting. She tore, struggled, flung herself.

Rojas's intention was terribly plain.

In agony now, both mental and physical, cold and sick and weak, Gale gripped his rifle and aimed at the struggling forms on the ledge. He pulled the trigger. The bullet struck up a cloud of red dust close to the struggling couple. Again Gale fired, hoping to hit Rojas, praying to kill Mercedes. The bullet struck high. A third—fourth—fifth time the Remington spoke—in vain! The rifle fell from Gale's racked hands.

How horribly plain that fiend's intention! Gale tried to close his eyes, but could not. He prayed wildly for a sudden blindness—to faint as Thorne had fainted. But he was transfixed to the spot with eyes that pierced the red light.

Mercedes was growing weaker, seemed about to collapse.

"Oh, Jim Lash, are you dead?" cried Gale. "Oh, Laddy! . . . Oh, Yaqui!"

Suddenly a dark form literally fell down the wall behind the ledge where Rojas fought the girl. It sank in a heap, then bounded erect.

"Yaqui!" screamed Gale, and he waved his bleeding hands till the blood bespattered his face. Then he choked. Utterance became impossible.

The Indian bent over Rojas and flung him against the wall. Mercedes, sinking back, lay still. When Rojas got up the Indian stood between him and escape from the ledge. Rojas backed the other way along the narrowing shelf of lava. His manner was abject, stupefied. Slowly he stepped backward.

It was then that Gale caught the white gleam of a knife in Yaqui's hand. Rojas turned and ran. He rounded a corner of wall where the footing was precarious. Yaqui followed slowly. His figure was dark and menacing. But he was not in a hurry. When he passed off the ledge Rojas was edging farther and farther along the wall. He was clinging now to the lava, creeping inch by inch. Perhaps he had thought to work around the buttress or climb over it. Evidently he went as far as possible, and there he clung, an unscalable wall above, the abyss beneath.

The approach of the Yaqui was like a slow dark shadow of gloom. If it seemed so to the stricken Gale what must it have been to Rojas? He appeared to sink against the wall. The Yaqui stole closer and closer. He was the savage now, and for him the moment must have been glorified. Gale saw him gaze up at the great circling walls of the crater, then down into the depths. Perhaps the red haze hanging above him, or the purple haze below, or the deep caverns in the lava, held for Yaqui spirits of the desert, his gods to whom he called. Perhaps he invoked shadows of his loved ones and his race, calling them in this moment of vengeance.

Gale heard—or imagined he heard—that wild, strange Yaqui cry.

Then the Indian stepped close to Rojas and bent low, keeping out of reach. How slow were his motions! Would Yaqui never—never end it? . . . A wail drifted across the crater to Gale's ears.

Rojas fell backward and plunged sheer. The bank of white *chollas* caught him, held him upon their steel spikes. How long did the dazed Gale sit there watching Rojas wrestling and writhing in convulsive frenzy? The bandit now seemed mad to win the delayed death.

When he broke free he was a white patched object no longer human, a ball of *cholla* burrs, and he slipped off the bank to shoot down and down into the purple depths of the crater.

CHAPTER 13

CHANGES AT
FORLORN RIVER

The first of March saw the federal occupation of the garrison at Casita. After a short, decisive engagement the rebels were dispersed into small bands and driven eastward along the boundary line toward Nogales.

It was the destiny of Forlorn River, however, never to return to the slow, sleepy tenor of its former existence. Belding's predictions came true. That straggling line of homeseekers was but a forerunner of the real invasion of Altar Valley. Refugees from Mexico and from Casita spread the word that water and wood and grass and land were to be had at Forlorn River; and as if by magic the white tents and red adobe houses sprang up to glisten in the sun.

Belding was happier than he had been for a long time. He believed that evil days for Forlorn River, along with the apathy and lack of enterprise, were in the past. He hired a couple of trustworthy Mexicans to ride the boundary line, and he settled down to think of ranching and irrigation and mining projects. Every morning he expected to receive some word from Sonoyta or Yuma, telling him that Yaqui had guided his party safely across the desert.

Belding was simpleminded, a man more inclined to action than reflection. When the complexities of life hemmed him in, he groped his way out, never quite understanding. His wife had always been a mystery to him. Nell was sunshine most of the time, but, like the sun-dominated desert, she was subject to strange changes, wilful, stormy, sudden. It was enough for Belding now to find his wife in a lighter, happier mood, and to see Nell dreamily turning a ring round and round the third finger of her left hand and watching the west. Every day both mother and daughter appeared further removed from the past darkly threatening days. Belding was hearty in his affections, but undemonstrative. If there was any sentiment in his makeup it had an outlet in his memory of Blanco Diablo and a longing to see him. Often Belding stopped his work to gaze out over the desert toward the west. When he thought of his rangers and Thorne and Mercedes he certainly never forgot his horse. He wondered if Diablo was running, walking, resting; if Yaqui was finding water and grass.

In March, with the short desert winter over, the days began to grow warm. The noon hours were hot, and seemed to give promise of the white summer blaze and blasting furnace wind soon to come. No word was received from the rangers. But this caused Belding no concern, and it seemed to him that his womenfolks considered no news good news.

Among the many changes coming to pass in Forlorn

River were the installing of post-office service and the building of a mescal drinking-house. Belding had worked hard for the post office, but he did not like the idea of a saloon for Forlorn River. Still, that was an inevitable evil. The Mexicans would have mescal. Belding had kept the little border hamlet free of an establishment for distillation of the fiery cactus drink. A good many Americans drifted into Forlorn River—miners, cowboys, prospectors, outlaws, and others of nondescript character; and these men, of course, made the saloon, which was also an inn, their headquarters. Belding, with Carter and other old residents, saw the need of a sheriff for Forlorn River.

One morning early in this spring month, while Belding was on his way from the house to the corrals, he saw Nell running Blanco José down the road at a gait that amazed him. She did not take the turn of the road to come in by the gate. She put José at a four-foot wire fence, and came clattering into the yard.

"Nell must have another tantrum," said Belding. "She's long past due."

Blanco José, like the other white horses, was big of frame and heavy, and thunder rolled from under his great hoofs. Nell pulled him up, and as he pounded and slid to a halt in a cloud of dust she swung lightly down.

It did not take more than half an eye for Belding to see that she was furious.

"Nell, what's come off now?" asked Belding.

"I'm not going to tell you," she replied, and started away, leading José toward the corral.

Belding leisurely followed. She went into the corral, removed José's bridle, and led him to the watering trough. Belding came up and without saying anything began to unbuckle José's saddle girths. But he ventured a look at

Nell. The red had gone from her face, and he was surprised to see her eyes brimming with tears. Most assuredly this was not one of Nell's tantrums. While taking off José's saddle and hanging it in the shed Belding pondered in his slow way. When he came back to the corral Nell had her face against the bars, and she was crying. He slipped a big arm around her and waited. Although it was not often expressed, there was a strong attachment between them.

"Dad, I don't want you to think me a—a baby any more," she said. "I've been insulted."

With a specific fact to make clear thought in Belding's mind he was never slow.

"I knew something unusual had come off. I guess you'd better tell me."

"Dad, I will, if you promise."

"What?"

"Not to mention it to Mother, not to pack a gun down there, and never, never tell Dick."

Belding was silent. Seldom did he make promises readily.

"Nell, sure something must have come off, for you to ask all that."

"If you don't promise I'll never tell, that's all," she declared, firmly.

Belding deliberated a little longer. He knew the girl.

"Well, I promise not to tell Mother," he said, presently; "and seeing you're here safe and well, I guess I won't go packing a gun down there, wherever that is. But I won't promise to keep anything from Dick that perhaps he ought to know."

"Dad, what would Dick do if—if he were here and I were to tell him I'd—I'd been horribly insulted?"

"I guess that'd depend. Mostly, you know, Dick does what you want. But you couldn't stop him—nobody could—if there was reason, a man's reason, to get started. Remember what he did to Rojas! . . . Nell, tell me what's happened."

Nell, regaining her composure, wiped her eyes and smoothed back her hair.

"The other day, Wednesday," she began, "I was coming home, and in front of that mescal drinking-place there was a crowd. It was a noisy crowd. I didn't want to walk out into the street or seem afraid. But I had to do both. There were several young men, and if they weren't drunk they certainly were rude. I never saw them before, but I think they must belong to the mining company that was run out of Sonora by rebels. Mrs. Carter was telling me. Anyway, these young fellows were Americans. They stretched themselves across the walk and smiled at me. I had to go out in the road. One of them, the rudest, followed me. He was a big fellow, red-faced, with prominent eyes and a bold look. He came up beside me and spoke to me. I ran home. And as I ran I heard his companions jeering.

"Well, to-day, just now, when I was riding up the valley road I came upon the same fellows. They had instruments and were surveying. Remembering Dick, and how he always wished for an instrument to help work out his plan for irrigation, I was certainly surprised to see these strangers surveying—and surveying upon Laddy's plot of land. It was a sandy road there, and José happened to be walking. So I reined in and asked these engineers what they were doing. The leader, who was that same bold fellow who had followed me, seemed much pleased at being addressed. He was swaggering—too friendly, not my idea of a gentleman at all. He said he was glad to tell me he was going to run water all over Altar Valley. Dad, you can bet that made me wild. That was Dick's plan, his discovery, and here were surveyors on Laddy's claim.

"Then I told him that he was working on private land and he'd better get off. He seemed to forget his flirty proclivities in amazement. Then he looked cunning. I read his mind. It was news to him that all the land along the valley had been taken up.

"He said something about not seeing any squatters on the land, and then he shut up tight on that score. But he began to be flirty again. He got hold of José's bridle, and before I could catch my breath he said I was a peach, that he wanted to make a date with me, that his name was Chase, that he owned a gold mine in Mexico. He said a lot more I didn't gather, but when he called me 'Dearie' I—well, I lost my temper.

"I jerked on the bridle and told him to let go. He held on and rolled his eyes at me. I dare say he imagined he was a gentleman to be infatuated with. He seemed sure of conquest. One thing was certain, he didn't know the least bit about horses. It scared me the way he got in front of José. I thanked my stars I wasn't up on Blanco Diablo. Well, Dad, I'm a little ashamed now, but I was mad. I slashed him across the face with my quirt. José jumped and knocked Mr. Chase into the sand. I didn't get the horse under control till I was out of sight of those surveyors, and then I let him run home."

"Nell, I guess you punished the fellow enough. Maybe he's only a conceited softy. But I don't like that sort of thing. It isn't Western. I guess he won't be so smart next time. Any fellow would remember being hit by Blanco José. If you'd been up on Diablo we'd have to bury Mr. Chase."

"Thank goodness I wasn't! I'm sorry now, Dad. Perhaps the fellow was hurt. But what could I do? Let's forget all about it, and I'll be careful where I ride in the future. . . . Dad, what does it mean, this surveying around Forlorn River?"

"I don't know, Nell," replied Belding, thoughtfully. "It worries me. It looks good for Forlorn River, but bad for Dick's plan to irrigate the valley. Lord, I'd hate to have someone forestall Dick on that!"

"No, no, we won't let anybody have Dick's rights," declared Nell.

"Where have I been keeping myself not to know about these surveyors?" muttered Belding. "They must have just come."

"Go see Mrs. Carter. She told me there were strangers in town, Americans, who had mining interests in Sonora, and were run out by Orozco. Find out what they're doing, Dad."

Belding discovered that he was, indeed, the last man of consequence in Forlorn River to learn of the arrival of Ben Chase and son, mine owners and operators in Sonora. They, with a force of miners, had been besieged by rebels and finally driven off their property. This property was not destroyed, but held for ransom. And the Chases, pending developments, had packed outfits and struck for the border. Casita had been their objective point, but, for some reason which Belding did not learn, they had arrived instead at Forlorn River. It had taken Ben Chase just one day to see the possibilities of Altar Valley, and in three days he had men at work.

Belding returned home without going to see the Chases and their operations. He wanted to think over the situation. Next morning he went out to the valley to see for himself. Mexicans were hastily erecting adobe houses upon Ladd's one hundred and sixty acres, upon Dick Gale's, upon Jim Lash's and Thorne's. There were men staking the valley floor and the riverbed. That was sufficient for Belding. He turned back toward town and headed for the camp of these intruders.

In fact, the surroundings of Forlorn River, except on the river side, reminded Belding of the mushroom growth of a newly discovered mining camp. Tents were everywhere; adobe shacks were in all stages of construction; rough clapboard houses were going up. The latest of this work was new and surprising to Belding, all because he was a busy man, with no chance to hear village gossip. When he was directed to the headquarters of the Chase Mining Company he went thither in slow-growing wrath.

He came to a big tent with a huge canvas fly stretched in front, under which sat several men in their shirtsleeves. They were talking and smoking.

"My name's Belding. I want to see this Mr. Chase," said Belding, gruffly.

Slow-witted as Belding was, and absorbed in his own feelings, he yet saw plainly that his advent was disturbing to these men. They looked alarmed, exchanged glances, and then quickly turned to him. One of them, a tall, rugged man with sharp face and shrewd eyes and white hair, got up and offered his hand.

"I'm Chase, senior," he said. "My son Radford Chase is here somewhere. You're Belding, the line inspector, I take it? I meant to call on you."

He seemed a rough-and-ready, loud-spoken man, withal cordial enough.

"Yes, I'm the inspector," replied Belding, ignoring the proffered hand, "and I'd like to know what in the hell you mean by taking up land claims—staked ground that belongs to my rangers?"

"Land claims?" slowly echoed Chase, studying his man. "We're taking up only unclaimed land."

"That's a lie. You couldn't miss the stakes."

"Well, Mr. Belding, as to that, I think my men did run across some staked ground. But we recognize only squatters. If your rangers think they've got property just because they drove a few stakes in the ground they're much mistaken. A squatter has to build a house and live on his land so long, according to law, before he owns it."

This argument was unanswerable, and Belding knew it.

"According to law!" exclaimed Belding. "Then you own up; you've jumped our claims."

"Mr. Belding, I'm a plain businessman. I come along. I see a good opening. Nobody seems to have tenable grants. I stake out claims, locate squatters, start to build. It seems to me your rangers have overlooked certain precautions. That's unfortunate for them. I'm prepared to hold my claim and to back all the squatters who work for me. If you don't like it you can carry the matter to Tucson. The law will uphold me."

"The law? Say, on this southwest border we haven't any law except a man's word and a gun."

"Then you'll find United States law has come along with Ben Chase," replied the other, snapping his fingers. He was still smooth, outspoken, but his mask had fallen.

"You're not a Westerner?" queried Belding.

"No, I'm from Illinois."

"I thought the West hadn't bred you. I know your kind. You'd last a long time on the Texas border; now, wouldn't you? You're one of the land and water hogs that has come to root in the West. You're like the timber sharks—

take it all and leave none for those who follow. Mr. Chase, the West would fare better and last longer if men like you were driven out."

"You can't drive me out."

"I'm not so sure of that. Wait till my rangers come back. I wouldn't be in your boots. Don't mistake me. I don't suppose you could be accused of stealing another man's ideas or plan, but sure you've stolen these four claims. Maybe the law might uphold you. But the spirit, not the letter counts with us bordermen."

"See here, Belding, I think you're taking the wrong view of the matter. I'm going to develop this valley. You'd do better to get in with me. I've a proposition to make you about that strip of land of yours facing the river."

"You can't make any deals with me. I won't have anything to do with you."

Belding abruptly left the camp and went home. Nell met him, probably intended to question him, but one look into his face confirmed her fears. She silently turned away. Belding realized he was powerless to stop Chase, and he was sick with disappointment for the ruin of Dick's hopes and his own.

CHAPTER 14

A LOST SON

Time passed. The population of Forlorn River grew apace. Belding, who had once been the head of the community, found himself a person of little consequence. Even had he desired it he would not have had any voice in the selection of postmaster, sheriff, and a few other officials. The Chases divided their labors between Forlorn River and their Mexican gold mine, which had been restored to them. The desert trips between these two places were taken in automobiles. A month's time made the motorcars almost as familiar a sight in Forlorn River as they had been in Casita before the revolution.

Belding was not so busy as he had been formerly. As he lost ambition he began to find less work to do. His wrath at the usurping Chases increased as he slowly realized his powerlessness to cope with such men. They were promoters, men of big interests and wide influence in the Southwest. The more they did for Forlorn River the less reason there seemed to be for his own grievance. He had to admit that it was personal; that he and Gale and the rangers would never have been able to develop the resources of the valley as these men were doing it.

All day long he heard the heavy booming blasts and the rumble of avalanches up in the gorge. Chase's men were dynamiting the cliffs in the narrow box cañon. They were making the dam just as Gale had planned to make it. When this work of blasting was over Belding experienced a relief. He would not now be continually reminded of his and Gale's loss. Resignation finally came to him. But he could not reconcile himself to misfortune for Gale.

Moreover, Belding had other worry and strain. April arrived with no news of the rangers. From Casita came vague reports of raiders in the Sonoyta country—reports impossible to verify until his Mexican rangers returned. When these men rode in, one of them, Gonzales, an intelligent and reliable half-breed, said he had met prospectors at the oasis. They had just come in on the Camino del Diablo, reported a terrible trip of heat and drought, and not a trace of the Yaqui's party.

"That settles it," declared Belding. "Yaqui never went to Sonoyta. He's circled round to the Devil's Road, and the rangers, Mercedes, Thorne, the horses—they—I'm afraid they have been lost in the desert. It's an old story on Camino del Diablo."

He had to tell Nell that, and it was an ordeal which left him weak.

Mrs. Belding listened to him, and was silent for a long time while she held the stricken Nell to her breast. Then she opposed his convictions with that quiet strength so characteristic of her arguments.

"Well, then," decided Belding, "Rojas headed the rangers at Papago Well or the Tanks."

"Tom, when you are down in the mouth you use poor judgment," she went on. "You know only by a miracle could Rojas or anybody have headed those white horses. Where's your old stubborn confidence? Yaqui was up on Diablo. Dick was up on Sol. And there were the other horses. They could not have been headed or caught. Miracles don't happen."

"All right, Mother, it's sure good to hear you," said Belding. She always cheered him, and now he grasped at straws. "I'm not myself these days, don't mistake that. Tell us what you think. You always say you feel things when you really don't know them."

"I can say little more than what you said yourself the night Mercedes was taken away. You told Laddy to trust Yaqui, that he was a godsend. He might go south into some wild Sonora valley. He might lead Rojas into a trap. He would find water and grass where no Mexican or American could."

"But Mother, they're gone seven weeks. Seven weeks! At the most I gave them six weeks. Seven weeks in the desert!"

"How do the Yaquis live?" she asked.

Belding could not reply to that, but hope revived in him. He had faith in his wife, though he could not in the least understand what he imagined was something mystic in her.

"Years ago when I was searching for my father I learned many things about this country," said Mrs. Belding. "You can never tell how long a man may live in the desert. The fiercest, most terrible and inaccessible places often have their hidden oasis. In his later years my father became a prospector. That was strange to me, for he never cared for gold or money. I learned that he was often gone in the desert for weeks, once for months. Then the time came when he never came back. That was years before I reached the southwest border and heard of him. Even then I did not for long give up hope of his coming back. I know now—something tells me—indeed, it seems his spirit tells me—he was lost. But I don't have that feeling for Yaqui and his party. Yaqui has given Rojas the slip or has ambushed him in some trap. Probably that took time and a long journey into Sonora. The Indian is too wise to start back now over dry trails. He'll curb the rangers; he'll wait. I seem to know this, dear Nell, so be brave, patient. Dick Gale will come back to you."

"Oh, Mother!" cried Nell. "I can't give up hope while I have you."

That talk with the strong mother worked a change in Nell and in Belding. Nell, who had done little but brood and watch the west and take violent rides, seemed to settle into a waiting patience that was sad, yet serene. She helped her mother more than ever; she was a comfort to Belding; she began to take active interest in the affairs of the growing village. Belding, who had been breaking under the strain of worry, recovered himself so that to outward appearance he was his old self. He alone knew, however, that his humor was forced, and that the slow burning wrath he felt for the Chases was flaming into hate.

Belding argued with himself that if Ben Chase and his son, Radford, had turned out to be big men in other ways than in the power to carry on great enterprises he might have become reconciled to them. But the father was greedy, grasping, hard, cold; the son added to those traits an overbearing disposition to rule, and he showed a fondness for drink and cards. These men were developing the valley, to be sure, and a horde of poor Mexicans and many Americans were benefiting from that development; nevertheless these Chases were operating in a way which proved they cared only for themselves.

Belding shook off a lethargic spell and decided he had better set about several by no means small tasks, if he wanted to get them finished before the hot months. He made a trip to the Sonoyta Oasis. He satisfied himself that matters along the line were favorable, and that there was absolutely no trace of his rangers. Upon completing this trip he went to Casita with a number of his white thoroughbreds and shipped them to ranchers and horse-breeders in Texas. Then, being near the railroad, and having time, he went up to Tucson. There he learned some interesting particulars about the Chases. They had an office in the city; influential friends in the Capitol. They were powerful men in the rapidly growing finance of the West. They had interested the Southern Pacific Railroad, and in the near future a branch line was to be constructed from San Felipe to Forlorn River. These details of the Chase development were insignificant when compared to a matter striking close home to Belding. His responsibility had been subtly attacked. A doubt had been cast upon his capability of executing the duties of immigration inspector to the best advantage of the state. Belding divined that this was only an entering wedge. The Chases were bent upon driving him out of Forlorn River; but, perhaps to serve better their own ends, they were proceeding at leisure. Belding returned home consumed by rage. But he controlled it. For the first time in his life he was afraid of himself. He had his wife and Nell to think of; and the old law of the West had gone forever.

"Dad, there's another Rojas round these diggings," was Nell's remark, after the greetings were over and the usual questions and answers passed.

Belding's exclamation was cut short by Nell's laugh. She was serious with a kind of amused contempt.

"Mr. Radford Chase!"

"Now Nell, what the—" roared Belding.

"Hush, Dad! Don't swear," interrupted Nell. "I only meant to tease you."

"Humph! Say, my girl, that name Chase makes me see red. If you must tease me hit on some other way. *Sabe*, señorita?"

"*Sí, sí*, Dad."

"Nell, you may as well tell him and have it over," said Mrs. Belding, quietly.

"You promised me once, Dad, that you'd not go packing a gun off down there, didn't you?"

"Yes, I remember," replied Belding; but he did not answer her smile.

"Will you promise again?" she asked, lightly. Here was Nell with arch eyes, yet not the old arch eyes, so full of fun and mischief. Her lips were tremulous; her cheeks seemed less round.

"Yes," rejoined Belding; and he knew why his voice was a little thick.

"Well, if you weren't such a good old blind Dad you'd have seen long ago the way Mr. Radford Chase ran round after me. At first it was only annoying, and I did not want to add to your worries. But these two weeks you've been gone I've been more than annoyed. After that time I struck

Mr. Chase with my quirt he made all possible efforts to meet me. He did meet me wherever I went. He sent me letters till I got tired of sending them back.

"When you left home on your trips I don't know that he grew bolder but he had more opportunity. I couldn't stay in the house all the time. There were Mama's errands and sick people and my Sunday school, and whatnot. Mr. Chase waylaid me every time I went out. If he works any more I don't know when, unless it's when I'm asleep. He followed me until it was less embarrassing for me to let him walk with me and talk his head off. He made love to me. He begged me to marry him. I told him I was already in love and engaged to be married. He said that didn't make any difference. Then I called him a fool.

"Next time he saw me he said he must explain. He meant I was being true to a man who, everybody on the border knew, had been lost in the desert. That—that hurt. Maybe—maybe it's true. Sometimes it seems terribly true. Since then, of course, I have stayed in the house to avoid being hurt again.

"But, Dad, a little thing like a girl sticking close to her mother and her room doesn't stop Mr. Chase. I think he's crazy. Anyway, he's a most persistent fool. I want to be charitable, because the man swears he loves me, and maybe he does, but he is making me nervous. I don't sleep. I'm afraid to be in my room at night. I've gone to Mother's room. He's always hanging round. Bold! Why, that isn't the thing to call Mr. Chase. He's absolutely without a sense of decency. He bribes our servants. He comes into our patio. Think of that! He makes the most ridiculous excuses. He bothers Mother to death. I feel like a poor little rabbit holed by a hound. And I daren't peep out."

Somehow the thing struck Belding as funny, and he

laughed. He had not had a laugh for so long that it made him feel good. He stopped only at sight of Nell's surprise and pain. Then he put his arms round her.

"Never mind dear. I'm an old bear. But it tickled me, I guess. I sure hope Mr. Radford Chase *has* got it bad. . . . Nell, it's only the old story. The fellows fall in love with you. It's your good looks, Nell. What a price women like you and Mercedes have to pay for beauty! I'd a d— good deal rather be ugly as a mud fence."

"So would I, Dad, if—if Dick would still love me."

"He wouldn't, you can gamble on that, as Laddy says. . . . Well, the first time I catch this locoed Romeo sneaking round here I'll—I'll—"

"Dad, you promised."

"Confound it, Nell, I promised not to pack a gun. That's all. I'll only shoot this fellow off the place, gently, mind you, gently. I'll leave the rest for Dick Gale!"

"Oh, Dad!" cried Nell; and she clung to him wistful, frightened, yet something more.

"Don't mistake me, Nell. You have your own way, generally. You pull the wool over Mother's eyes, and you wind me round your little finger. But you can't do either with Dick Gale. You're tenderhearted; you overlook the doings of this hound, Chase. But when Dick comes back, you just make up your mind to a little hell in the Chase camp. Oh, he'll find it out. And I sure want to be round when Dick hands Mr. Radford the same as he handed Rojas!"

Belding kept a sharp lookout for young Chase, and then, a few days later, learned that both son and father had gone off upon one of their frequent trips to Casa Grandes, near where their mines were situated.

April grew apace, and soon gave way to May. One

morning Belding was called from some garden work by the whirring of an automobile and a "Holloa!" He went forward to the front yard and there saw a car he thought resembled one he had seen in Casita. It contained a familiar-looking driver, but the three figures in gray coats and veils were strange to him. By the time he had gotten to the road he decided two were women and the other a man. At the moment their faces were emerging from dusty veils. Belding saw an elderly, sallow-faced, rather frail-appearing man who was an entire stranger to him; a handsome dark-eyed woman whose hair showed white through her veil; and a superbly built girl, whose face made Belding at once think of Dick Gale.

"Is this Mr. Tom Belding, inspector of immigration?" inquired the gentleman, courteously.

"I'm Belding, and I know who you are," replied Belding in hearty amaze, as he stretched forth his big hand. "You're Dick Gale's Dad—the Governor, Dick used to say. I'm sure glad to meet you."

"Thank you. Yes, I'm Dick's governor, and here, Mr. Belding—Dick's mother and his sister Elsie."

Beaming his pleasure, Belding shook hands with the ladies, who showed their agitation clearly.

"Mr. Belding, I've come west to look up my lost son," said Mr. Gale. "His sister's letters were unanswered. We haven't heard from him in months. Is he still here with you?"

"Well, now, sure I'm awful sorry," began Belding, his slow mind at work. "Dick's away just now—been away for a considerable spell. I'm expecting him back any day. . . . Won't you come in? You're all dusty and hot and tired. Come in, and let Mother and Nell make you comfortable. Of course you'll stay. We've a big house. You must stay till Dick comes back. Maybe that'll be— Aw, I guess it won't be long. . . . Let me handle the baggage, Mr. Gale. . . . Come in. I sure am glad to meet you all."

Eager, excited, delighted, Belding went on talking as he ushered the Gales into the sitting-room, presenting them in his hearty way to the astounded Mrs. Belding and Nell. For the space of a few moments his wife and daughter were bewildered. Belding did not recollect any other occasion when a few callers had thrown them off their balance. But of course this was different. He was a little flustered himself—a circumstance that dawned upon him with surprise. When the Gales had been shown to rooms, Mrs. Belding gained the poise momentarily lost; but Nell came rushing back, wilder than a deer, in a state of excitement strange even for her.

"Oh! Dick's mother, his sister!" whispered Nell.

Belding observed the omission of the father in Nell's exclamation of mingled delight and alarm.

"His mother!" went on Nell. "Oh, I knew it! I always guessed it! Dick's people are proud, rich; they're somebody. I thought I'd faint when she looked at me. She was just curious—curious, but so cold and proud. She was wondering about me. Dick has never written her that he's—he's engaged to me. I'm wearing his ring. It was his mother's, he said. I won't—I can't take it off. And I'm scared. . . . But the sister—oh, she's lovely and sweet— proud, too. I felt warm all over when she looked at me. I—I wanted to kiss her. She looks like Dick when he first came to us. But he's changed. They'll hardly recognize him. . . . To think they've come! And I had to be looking a fright, when of all times on earth I'd want to look my best."

Nell, out of breath, ran away evidently to make herself

presentable, according to her idea of the exigency of the case. Belding caught a glimpse of his wife's face as she went out, and it wore a sad, strange, anxious expression. Then Belding sat alone, pondering the contrasting emotions of his wife and daughter. It was beyond his understanding. Women were creatures of feeling. Belding saw reason to be delighted to entertain Dick's family; and for the time being no disturbing thought entered his mind.

Presently the Gales came back into the sitting-room, looking very different without the long gray cloaks and veils. Belding saw distinction and elegance. Mr. Gale seemed a grave, troubled, kindly person, ill in body and mind. Belding received the same impression of power that Ben Chase had given him, only here it was minus any harshness or hard quality. He gathered that Mr. Gale was a man of authority. Mrs. Gale rather frightened Belding, but he could not have told why. The girl was just like Dick as he used to be.

Their manner of speaking also reminded Belding of Dick. They talked of the ride from Ash Fork down to the border, of the ugly and torn-up Casita, of the heat and dust and cactus along the trail. Presently Nell came in, now cool and sweet in white, with a red rose at her breast. Belding had never been so proud of her. He saw that she meant to appear well in the eyes of Dick's people, and began to have a faint perception of what the ordeal was for her. Belding imagined the sooner the Gales were told that Dick was to marry Nell the better for all concerned, and especially for Nell. In the general conversation that ensued he sought for an opening in which to tell this important news, but he was kept so busy answering questions about his position on the border, the kind of place Forlorn

River was, the reason for so many tents, etc., that he was unable to find opportunity.

"It's interesting, very interesting," said Mr. Gale. "At another time I want to learn all you'll tell me about the West. It's new to me. I'm surprised, amazed, sir, I may say. . . . But, Mr. Belding, what I want to know most is about my son. I'm broken in health. I've worried myself ill over him. I don't mind telling you, sir, that we quarreled. I laughed at his threats. He went away. And I've come to see I didn't know Richard. I was wrong to upbraid him. For a year we've known nothing of his doings, and now for almost six months we've not heard from him at all. Frankly, Mr. Belding, I weakened first, and I've come to hunt him up. My fear is that I didn't start soon enough. The boy will have a great position someday— God knows, perhaps soon! I should not have allowed him to run over this wild country for so long. But I hope, though I hardly believed, that he might find himself. Now I'm afraid he s—"

Mr. Gale paused, and the white hand he raised expressively shook a little.

Belding was not so thick-witted where men were concerned. He saw how the matter lay between Dick Gale and his father.

"Well, Mr. Gale, sure most young bucks from the East go to the bad out here," he said, bluntly.

"I've been told that," replied Mr. Gale, and a shade overspread his worn face.

"They blow their money, then go to punching cows, take to whisky."

"Yes," rejoined Mr. Gale, feebly nodding.

"Then they get to gambling, lose their jobs," went on Belding.

Mr. Gale lifted haggard eyes.

"Then it's bumming around, regular tramps, and to the bad generally." Belding spread wide his big arms, and when one of them dropped round Nell, who sat beside him, she squeezed his hand tight. "Sure, it's the regular thing," he concluded, cheerfully.

He rather felt a little glee at Mr. Gale's distress, and Mrs. Gale's crushed I-told-you-so woe in no wise bothered him; but the look in the big, dark eyes of Dick's sister was too much for Belding.

He choked off his characteristic oath when excited and blurted out, "Say, but *Dick Gale* never went to the bad! . . . Listen!"

Belding had scarcely started Dick Gale's story when he perceived that never in his life had he such an absorbed and breathless audience. Presently they were awed, and at the conclusion of that story they sat white-faced, still, amazed beyond speech. Dick Gale's advent in Casita, his rescue of Mercedes, his life as a border ranger certainly lost no picturesque or daring or even noble detail in Belding's telling. He kept back nothing but the present doubt of Dick's safety.

Dick's sister was the first of the three to recover herself.

"Oh, Father!" she cried; and there was a glorious light in her eyes. "Deep down in my heart I knew Dick was a man!"

Mr. Gale rose unsteadily from his chair. His frailty was now painfully manifest.

"Mr. Belding, do you mean my son—Richard Gale—has done all that you told us?" he asked, incredulously.

"I sure do," replied Belding, with hearty good-will.

"Martha, do you hear?" Mr. Gale turned to question his wife. She could not answer. Her face had not yet regained its natural color.

"He faced that bandit and his gang alone—he *fought* them?" demanded Mr. Gale, his voice stronger.

"Dick mopped up the floor with the whole outfit!"

"He rescued a Spanish girl, went into the desert without food, weapons, anything but his hands? Richard Gale, whose hands were always useless?"

Belding nodded with a grin.

"He's a ranger now—riding, fighting, sleeping on the sand, preparing his own food?"

"Well, I should smile," rejoined Belding.

"He cares for his horse, with his own hands?" This query seemed to be the climax of Mr. Gale's strange hunger for truth. He had raised his head a little higher, and his eye was brighter.

Mention of a horse fired Belding's blood.

"Does Dick Gale *care* for his horse? Say, there are not many *men* as well loved as that white horse of Dick's. Blanco Sol he is, Mr. Gale. That's Mex for White Sun. Wait till you see Blanco Sol! Bar one, the whitest, biggest, strongest, fastest, grandest horse in the Southwest!"

"So he loves a horse! I shall not know my own son. . . . Mr. Belding, you say Richard works for you. May I ask, at what salary?"

"He gets forty dollars, board and outfit," replied Belding, proudly.

"Forty dollars?" echoed the father. "By the day or week?"

"The month, of course," said Belding, somewhat taken aback.

"Forty dollars a month for a young man who spent five hundred in the same time when he was at college, and who ran it into thousands when he got out!"

Mr. Gale laughed for the first time, and it was the laugh of a man who wanted to believe what he heard yet scarcely dared to do it.

"What does he do with so much money—money earned by peril, toil, sweat, and blood? Forty dollars a month!"

"He saves it," replied Belding.

Evidently this was too much for Dick Gale's father, and he gazed at his wife in sheer speechless astonishment. Dick's sister clapped her hands like a little child.

Belding saw that the moment was propitious.

"Sure he saves it. Dick's engaged to marry Nell here. My stepdaughter, Nell Burton."

"Oh-h, Dad!" faltered Nell; and she rose, white as her dress.

How strange it was to see Dick's mother and sister rise, also, and turn to Nell with dark, proud, searching eyes. Belding vaguely realized some blunder he had made. Nell's white, appealing face gave him a pang. What had he done? Surely this family of Dick's ought to know his relation to Nell. There was a silence that positively made Belding nervous.

Then Elsie Gale stepped close to Nell.

"Miss Burton, are you really Richard's betrothed?"

Nell's tremulous lips framed an affirmative, but never uttered it. She held out her hand, showing the ring Dick had given her. Miss Gale's recognition was instant, and her response was warm, sweet, gracious.

"I think I am going to be very, very glad," she said, and kissed Nell.

"Miss Burton, we are learning wonderful things about

Richard," added Mr. Gale, in an earnest though shaken voice. "If you have had to do with making a man of him—and now I begin to see, to believe so—may God bless you! . . . My dear girl, I have not really looked at you. Richard's fiancée! . . . Mother, we have not found him yet, but I think we've found his secret. We believed him a lost son. But here is his sweetheart!"

It was only then that the pride and hauteur of Mrs. Gale's face broke into an expression of mingled pain and joy. She opened her arms. Nell, uttering a strange little stifled cry, flew into them.

Belding suddenly discovered an unaccountable blur in his sight. He could not see perfectly, and that was why, when Mrs. Belding entered the sitting room, he was not certain that her face was as sad and white as it seemed.

CHAPTER 15

BOUND IN THE DESERT

Far away from Forlorn River Dick Gale sat stunned, gazing down into the purple depths where Rojas had plunged to his death. The Yaqui stood motionless upon the steep red wall of lava from which he had cut the bandit's hold. Mercedes lay quietly where she had fallen. From across the depths there came to Gale's ear the Indian's strange, wild cry.

Then silence, hollow, breathless, stony silence enveloped the great abyss and its upheaved lava walls. The sun was setting. Every instant the haze reddened and thickened.

Action on the part of the Yaqui loosened the spell which held Gale as motionless as his surroundings. The Indian was edging back toward the ledge. He did not move with his former lithe and sure freedom. He crawled, slipped, dragged himself, rested often, and went on again. He had been wounded. When at last he reached the ledge where Mercedes lay Gale jumped to his feet, strong and thrilling, spurred to meet the responsibility that now rested upon him.

Swiftly he turned to where Thorne lay. The cavalryman was just returning to consciousness. Gale ran for a canteen, bathed his face, made him drink. The look in Thorne's eyes was hard to bear.

"Thorne! Thorne! It's all right, it's all right!" cried Gale, in piercing tones. "Mercedes is safe! Yaqui saved her! Rojas is done for! Yaqui jumped down the wall and drove the bandit off the ledge. Cut him loose from the wall, foot by foot, hand by hand! We've won the fight, Thorne."

For Thorne these were marvelous strength-giving words. The dark horror left his eyes, and they began to dilate, to shine. He stood up, dizzily but unaided, and he gazed across the crater. Yaqui had reached the side of Mercedes, was bending over her. She stirred. Yaqui lifted her to her feet. She appeared weak, unable to stand alone. But she faced across the crater and waved her hand. She was unharmed. Thorne lifted both arms above his head, and from his lips issued a cry. It was neither call nor holler nor welcome nor answer. Like the Yaqui's, it could scarcely be named. But it was deep, husky, prolonged, terribly human in its intensity. It made Gale shudder and made his heart beat like a trip-hammer. Mercedes again waved a white hand. The Yaqui waved, too, and Gale saw in the action an urgent signal.

Hastily taking up canteen and rifles, Gale put a supporting arm around Thorne.

"Come, old man. Can you walk? Sure you can walk! Lean on me, and we'll soon get out of this. Don't look across. Look where you step. We've not much time before dark. Oh Thorne, I'm afraid Jim has cashed in! And the last I saw of Laddy he was badly hurt."

Gale was keyed up to a high pitch of excitement and alertness. He seemed to be able to do many things. But once off the ragged notched lava into the trail he had not such difficulty with Thorne, and could keep his keen gaze shifting everywhere for sight of enemies.

"Listen, Thorne! What's that?" asked Gale, halting as they came to a place where the trail led down through rough breaks in the lava. The silence was broken by a strange sound, almost unbelievable considering the time and place. A voice was droning: "Turn the lady, turn! Turn the lady, turn! Alaman left. All swing; turn the lady, turn!"

"Hello, Jim," called Gale, dragging Thorne round the corner of lava. "Where are you? Oh, you son of a gun! I thought you were dead. Oh, I'm glad to see you! Jim, are you hurt?"

Jim Lash stood in the trail leaning over the butt of his rifle, which evidently he was utilizing as a crutch. He was pale but smiling. His hands were bloody. A scarf had been bound tightly round his left leg just above the knee. The leg hung limp, and the foot dragged.

"I reckon I ain't injured much," replied Jim. "But my leg hurts like hell, if you want to know."

"Laddy! Oh, where's Laddy?"

"He's just across the crack there. I was trying to get to him. We had it hot and heavy down here. Laddy was pretty bad shot up before he tried to head Rojas off the trail. . . . Dick, did you see the Yaqui go after Rojas?"

"Did I!" exclaimed Gale, grimly.

"The finish was all that saved me from runnin' loco plumb over the rim. You see I was closer'n you to where Mercedes was hid. When Rojas an' his last Greaser started across, Laddy went after them, but I couldn't. Laddy did for Rojas's man, then went down himself. But he got up an' fell, got up, went on, an' fell again. Laddy kept doin' that till he dropped for good. I reckon our chances are against findin' him alive. . . . I tell you, boys, Rojas was hell-bent. An' Mercedes was game. I saw her shoot him. But mebbe bullets couldn't stop him then. If I didn't sweat blood when Mercedes was fightin' him on the cliff! Then the finish! Only a Yaqui could have done that. . . . Thorne, you didn't miss it?"

"Yes, I was down and out," replied the cavalryman.

"It's a shame. Greatest stunt I ever seen! Thorne, you're standin' up pretty fair. How about you? Dick, is he bad hurt?"

"No, he's not. A hard knock on the skull and a scalp wound," replied Dick. "Here, Jim, let me help you over this place."

Step by step Gale got the two injured men down the uneven declivity and then across the narrow lava bridge over the fissure. Here he bade them rest while he went along the trail on that side to search for Laddy. Gale found the ranger stretched out, face downward, a reddened hand clutching a gun. Gale thought he was dead. Upon examination, however, it was found that Ladd still lived, though he had many wounds. Gale lifted him and carried him back to the others.

"He's alive, but that's all," said Dick, as he laid the ranger down. "Do what you can. Stop the blood. Laddy's tough as cactus, you know. I'll hurry back for Mercedes and Yaqui."

Gale, like a fleet, sure-footed mountain sheep, ran along the trail. When he came across the Mexican, Rojas's last ally, Gale had evidence of the terrible execution of the .405. He did not pause. On the first part of that descent he made faster time than had Rojas. But he exercised care along the hard, slippery, ragged slope leading to the ledge. Presently he came upon Mercedes and the Yaqui. She ran right into Dick's arms, and there her strength, if not her courage, broke, and she grew lax.

"Mercedes, you're safe! Thorne's safe. It's all right now."

"Rojas!" she whispered.

"Gone! To the bottom of the crater! A Yaqui vengeance, Mercedes."

He heard the girl whisper the name of the Virgin. Then he gathered her up in his arms.

"Come, Yaqui."

The Indian grunted. He had one hand pressed close over a bloody place in his shoulder. Gale looked keenly at him. Yaqui was inscrutable, as of old, yet Gale somehow knew that wound meant little to him. The Indian followed him.

Without pausing, moving slowly in some places, very carefully in others, and swiftly on the smooth part of the trail, Gale carried Mercedes up to the rim and along to the others. Jim Lash worked awkwardly over Ladd. Thorne was trying to assist. Ladd, himself, was conscious, but he was pallid, apparently a death-stricken man. The greeting between Mercedes and Thorne was calm—strangely so, it seemed to Gale. But he was now calm himself. Ladd smiled at him, and evidently would have spoken had he the power. Yaqui then joined the group, and his piercing eyes roved from one to the other, lingering longest over Ladd.

"Dick, I'm figger'n' hard," said Jim, faintly. "In a minute it'll be up to you an' Mercedes. I've about shot my bolt. . . . Reckon you'll do—best by bringin' up blankets—water—salt—fire-wood. Laddy's got—one chance—in a hundred. Fix him up—first. Use hot salt water. If my leg's broken—set it best you can. That hole in Yaqui—only'll bother him a day. Thorne's bad hurt. . . . Now rustle—Dick, old—boy."

Lash's voice died away in a husky whisper, and he quietly lay back, stretching out all but the crippled leg. Gale examined it, assured himself the bones had not been broken, and then rose ready to go down the trail.

"Mercedes, hold Thorne's head up, in your lap—so. Now I'll go."

On the moment Yaqui appeared to have completed the binding of his wounded shoulder, and he started to follow Gale. He paid no attention to Gale's order for him to stay back. But he was slow, and gradually Gale forged ahead. The lingering brightness of the sunset lightened the trail, and the descent to the arroyo was swift and easy. Some of the white horses had come in for water. Blanco Sol spied Gale and whistled and came pounding toward him. It was twilight down in the arroyo. Yaqui appeared and began collecting a bundle of mesquite sticks. Gale hastily put together the things he needed; and, packing them all in a tarpaulin, he turned to retrace his steps up the trail.

Darkness was setting in. The trail was narrow, exceedingly steep, and in some places fronted on precipices. Gale's burden was not very heavy, but its bulk made it unwieldy, and it was always overbalancing him or knocking against the wall side of the trail. Gale found it necessary to wait for Yaqui to take the lead. The Indian's eyes must have seen as well at night as by day. Gale toiled upward, shouldering, swinging, dragging the big pack; and, though the ascent of the slope was not really long, it seemed endless. At last they reached a level, and were soon on the spot with Mercedes and the injured men.

Gale then set to work. Yaqui's part was to keep the fire blazing and the water hot, Mercedes's to help Gale in what way she could. Gale found Ladd had many wounds, yet not one of them was directly in a vital place. Evidently, the ranger had almost bled to death. He remained unconscious through Gale's operations. According to Jim Lash, Ladd had one chance in a hundred, but Gale considered it one in a thousand. Having done all that was possible for the ranger, Gale slipped blankets under and around him, and then turned his attention to Lash.

Jim came out of his stupor. A mushrooming bullet had torn a great hole in his leg. Gale, upon examination, could not be sure the bones had been missed, but there was no bad break. The application of hot salt water made Jim groan. When he had been bandaged and laid beside Ladd, Gale went on to the cavalryman. Thorne was very weak and scarcely conscious. A furrow had been plowed through his scalp down to the bone. When it had been dressed, Mercedes collapsed. Gale laid her with the three in a row and covered them with blankets and the tarpaulin.

Then Yaqui submitted to examination. A bullet had gone through the Indian's shoulder. To Gale it appeared serious. Yaqui said it was a fleabite. But he allowed Gale to bandage it, and obeyed when he was told to lie quiet in his blanket beside the fire.

Gale stood guard. He seemed still calm, and wondered at what he considered a strange absence of poignant feeling. If he had felt weariness it was now gone. He coaxed the fire with as little wood as would keep it burning; he sat beside it; he walked to and fro close by; sometimes he stood over the five sleepers, wondering if two of them, at least, would ever awaken.

Time had passed swiftly, but as the necessity for immediate action had gone by, the hours gradually assumed something of their normal length. The night wore on. The air grew colder, the stars brighter, the sky bluer, and, if such could be possible, the silence more intense. The fire burned out, and for lack of wood could not be rekindled. Gale patrolled his short beat, becoming colder and damper as dawn approached. The darkness grew so dense that he could not see the pale faces of the sleepers. He dreaded the gray dawn and the light. Slowly the heavy black belt close to the lava changed to a pale gloom, then to gray, and after that morning came quickly.

The hour had come for Dick Gale to face his great problem. It was natural that he hung back a little at first; natural that when he went forward to look at the quiet sleepers he did so with a grim and stern force urging him. Yaqui stirred, roused, yawned, got up; and, though he did not smile at Gale, a light shone swiftly across his dark face. His shoulder drooped and appeared stiff, otherwise he was himself. Mercedes lay in deep slumber. Thorne had a high fever, and was beginning to show signs of restlessness. Ladd seemed just barely alive. Jim Lash slept as if he was not much the worse for his wound.

Gale rose from his examination with a sharp breaking of his cold mood. While there was life in Thorne and Ladd there was hope for them. Then he faced his problem, and his decision was instant.

He awoke Mercedes. How wondering, wistful, beautiful was that first opening flash of her eyes! Then the dark, troubled thought came. Swiftly she sat up.

"Mercedes—come. Are you all right? Laddy is alive. Thorne's not—not so bad. But we've got a job on our hands! You must help me."

She bent over Thorne and laid her hands on his hot face. Then she rose—a woman such as he had imagined she might be in an hour of trial.

Gale took up Ladd as carefully and gently as possible.

"Mercedes, bring what you can carry and follow me,"

he said. Then, motioning for Yaqui to remain there, he turned down the slope with Ladd in his arms.

Neither pausing nor making a misstep nor conscious of great effort, Gale carried the wounded man down into the arroyo. Mercedes kept at his heels, light, supple, lithe as a panther. He left her with Ladd and went back. When he had started off with Thorne in his arms he felt the tax on his strength. Surely and swiftly, however, he bore the cavalry-man down the trail to lay him beside Ladd. Again he started back, and when he began to mount the steep lava steps he was hot, wet, breathing hard. As he reached the scene of that night's camp a voice greeted him. Jim Lash was sitting up.

"Hello, Dick. I woke some late this mornin'. Where's Laddy? Dick, you ain't a-goin' to say—"

"Laddy's alive—that's about all," replied Dick.

"Where's Thorne an' Mercedes? Look here, man! I reckon you ain't packin' this crippled outfit down that aw-ful trail?"

"Had to, Jim. An hour's sun—would kill—both Laddy and Thorne. Come on now."

For once Jim Lash's cool good nature and careless in-difference gave precedence to amaze and concern.

"Always knew you was a husky chap. But, Dick, you're no hoss! Get me a crutch an' give me a lift on one side."

"Come on," replied Gale. "I've no time to monkey."

He lifted the ranger, called to Yaqui to follow with some of the camp outfit, and once more essayed the steep descent. Jim Lash was the heaviest man of the three, and Gale's strength was put to enormous strain to carry him on that broken trail. Nevertheless, Gale went down, down, walking swiftly and surely over the bad places; and at last he staggered into the arroyo with bursting heart and red-blinded eyes. When he had recovered he made a final trip up the slope for the camp effects which Yaqui had been unable to carry.

Then he drew Jim and Mercedes and Yaqui, also, into an earnest discussion of ways and means whereby to fight for the life of Thorne. Ladd's case Gale now considered hopeless, though he meant to fight for him, too, as long as he breathed.

In the labor of watching and nursing it seemed to Gale that two days and two nights slipped by like a few hours. During that time the Indian recovered from his injury, and became capable of performing all except heavy tasks. Then Gale succumbed to weariness. After his much-needed rest he relieved Mercedes of the care and watch over Thorne which, up to that time, she had absolutely re-fused to relinquish. The cavalryman had high fever, and Gale feared he had developed blood poisoning. He required constant attention. His condition slowly grew worse, and there came a day which Gale thought surely was the end. But that day passed, and the night, and the next day, and Thorne lived on, ghastly, stricken, raving. Mercedes hung over him with jealous, passionate care and did all that could have been humanly done for a man. She grew wan, absorbed, silent. But suddenly, and to Gale's amaze and thanksgiving, there came an abatement of Thorne's fever. With it some of the heat and redness of the inflamed wound disappeared. Next morning he was conscious, and Gale grasped some of the hope that Mer-cedes had never abandoned. He forced her to rest while he attended to Thorne. That day he saw that the crisis was past. Recovery for Thorne was now possible, and would perhaps depend entirely upon the care he received.

Jim Lash's wound healed without any aggravating symptoms. It would be only a matter of time until he had the use of his leg again. All these days, however, there was little apparent change in Ladd's condition, unless it was that he seemed to fade away as he lingered. At first his wounds remained open; they bled a little all the time outwardly, perhaps internally also; his blood did not seem to clot, and so the bullet-holes did not close. Then Yaqui asked for the care of Ladd. Gale yielded it with opposing thoughts—that Ladd would waste slowly away till life ceased, and that there never was any telling what might lie in the power of this strange Indian. Yaqui absented himself from camp for a while, and when he returned he carried the roots and leaves of desert plants unknown to Gale. From these the Indian brewed an ointment. Then he stripped the bandages from Ladd and applied the mixture to his wounds. That done, he let him lie with the wounds exposed to the air, at night covering him. Next day he again exposed the wounds to the warm, dry air. Slowly they closed, and Ladd ceased to bleed externally.

Days passed and grew into what Gale imagined must have been weeks. Yaqui recovered fully. Jim Lash began to move about on a crutch; he shared the Indian's watch over Ladd. Thorne lay a haggard, emaciated ghost of his former rugged self, but with life in the eyes that turned always toward Mercedes. Ladd lingered and lingered. The life seemingly would not leave his bullet-pierced body. He faded, withered, shrunk till he was almost a skeleton. He knew those who worked and watched over him, but he had no power of speech. His eyes and eyelids moved; the rest of him seemed stone. All those days nothing except water was given him. It was marvelous how tenaciously, however feebly, he clung to life. Gale imagined it was the Yaqui's spirit that held back death. That tireless, implacable, inscrutable savage was ever at the ranger's side. His great somber eyes burned. At length he went to Gale, and, with that strange light flitting across the hard bronzed face, he said Ladd would live.

The second day after Ladd had been given such thin nourishment as he could swallow he recovered the use of his tongue.

"Shore—this's—hell," he whispered.

That was a characteristic speech for the ranger, Gale thought; and indeed it made all who heard it smile while their eyes were wet.

From that time forward Ladd gained, but he gained so immeasurably slowly that only the eyes of hope could have seen any improvement. Jim Lash threw away his crutch, and Thorne was well, if still somewhat weak, before Ladd could lift his arm or turn his head. A kind of long, immovable gloom passed, like a shadow, from his face. His whispers grew stronger. And the day arrived when Gale, who was perhaps the least optimistic, threw doubt to the winds and knew the ranger would get well. For Gale that joyous moment of realization was one in which he seemed to return to a former self long absent. He experienced an elevation of soul. He was suddenly overwhelmed with gratefulness, humility, awe. A gloomy black terror had passed by. He wanted to thank the faithful Mercedes, and Thorne for getting well, and the cheerful Lash, and Ladd himself, and that strange and wonderful Yaqui, now such a splendid figure. He thought of home and Nell. The terrible encompassing red slopes lost something of their fearsomeness, and there was a good spirit hovering near.

* * *

Boys, come round," said Ladd, in his low voice. "An' you, Mercedes. An' call the Yaqui."

Ladd lay in the shade of the brush shelter that had been erected. His head was raised slightly on a pillow. There seemed little of him but long lean lines, and if it had not been for his keen, thoughtful, kindly eyes, his face would have resembled a death mask of a man starved.

"Shore I want to know what day is it an' what month?" asked Ladd.

Nobody could answer him. The question seemed a surprise to Gale, and evidently was so to the others.

"Look at that cactus," went on Ladd.

Near the wall of lava a stunted *saguaro* lifted its head. A few shriveled blossoms that had once been white hung along the fluted column.

"I reckon according to that giant cactus it's somewheres along the end of March," said Jim Lash, soberly.

"Shore it's April. Look where the sun is. An' can't you feel it's gettin' hot?"

"Supposin' it is April?" queried Lash, slowly.

"Well, what I'm drivin' at is it's about time you all was hittin' the trail back to Forlorn River, before the water holes dry out."

"Laddy, I reckon we'll start soon as you're able to be put on a hoss."

"Shore that'll be too late."

A silence ensued, in which those who heard Ladd gazed fixedly at him and then at one another. Lash uneasily shifted the position of his lame leg, and Gale saw him moisten his lips with his tongue.

"Charlie Ladd, I ain't reckonin' you mean we're to ride off an' leave you here?"

"What else is there to do? The hot weather's close.

Pretty soon most of the water holes will be dry. You can't travel then. . . . I'm on my back here, an' God only knows when I could be packed out, Not for weeks, mebbe. I'll never be any good again, even if I was to get out alive. . . . You see, shore this sort of case comes round sometimes in the desert. It's common enough. I've heard of several cases where men had to go an' leave a feller behind. It's reasonable. If you're fightin' the desert you can't afford to be sentimental. . . . Now, as I said, I'm all in. So what's the sense of you waitin' here, when it means the old desert story? By goin' now mebbe you'll get home. If you wait on a chance of takin' me, you'll be too late. Pretty soon this lava'll be one roastin' hell. Shore now, boys, you'll see this the right way? Jim, old pard?"

"No, Laddy, an' I can't figger how you could ever ask me."

"Shore then leave me here with Yaqui an' a couple of the hosses. We can eat sheep meat. An' if the water holds out—"

"No!" interrupted Lash, violently.

Ladd's eyes sought Gale's face.

"Son, you ain't bullheaded like Jim. You'll see the sense of it. There's Nell a-waitin' back at Forlorn River. Think what it means to her! She's a damn fine girl, Dick, an' what right have you to break her heart for an old worn-out cow-puncher? Think how she's watchin' for you with that sweet face all sad an' troubled, an' her eyes turnin' black. You'll go son, won't you?"

Dick shook his head.

The ranger turned his gaze upon Thorne, and now the keen, glistening light in his gray eyes had blurred.

"Thorne, it's different with you. Jim's a fool, an' young Gale has been punctured by *cholla* thorns. He's got the desert poison in his blood. But you now—you've no call to stick—you can find that trail out. It's easy to follow, made by so many shod hosses. Take your wife an' go. . . . Shore you'll go, Thorne?"

Deliberately and without an instant's hesitation the cavalryman replied, "No."

Ladd then directed his appeal to Mercedes. His face was now convulsed, and his voice, though it had sunk to a whisper, was clear, and beautiful with some rich quality that Gale had never before heard in it.

"Mercedes, you're a woman. You're the woman we fought for. An' some of us are shore goin' to die for you. Don't make it all for nothin'. Let us feel we saved the woman. Shore you can make Thorne go. He'll have to go if you say. They'll all have to go. Think of the years of love an' happiness in store for you. A week or so an' it'll be too late. Can you stand for me seein' you? . . . Let me tell you, Mercedes, when the summer heat hits the lava we'll all wither an' curl up like shavin's near a fire. A wind of hell will blow up this slope. Look at them mesquites. See the twist in them. That's the torture of heat an' thirst. Do you want me or all us men seein' you like that? . . . Mercedes, don't make it all for nothin'. Say you'll persuade Thorne, if not the others."

For all the effect his appeal had to move her Mercedes might have possessed a heart as hard and fixed as the surrounding lava.

"Never!"

White-faced, with great black eyes flashing, the Spanish girl spoke the word that bound her and her companions in the desert.

The subject was never mentioned again. Gale thought that he read a sinister purpose in Ladd's mind. To his astonishment, Lash came to him with the same fancy. After that they made certain there never was a gun within reach of Ladd's clutching, clawlike hands.

Gradually a somber spell lifted from the ranger's mind. When he was entirely free of it he began to gather strength daily. Then it was as if he had never known patience—he who had shown so well how to wait. He was in a frenzy to get well. His appetite could not be satisfied.

The sun climbed higher, whiter, hotter. At midday a wind from gulfward roared up the arroyo, and now only the *palo verdes* and the few *saguaros* were green. Every day the water in the lava hole sank an inch.

The Yaqui alone spent the waiting time in activity. He made trips up on the lava slope, and each time, he returned with guns or boots or sombreros, or something belonging to the bandits that had fallen. He never fetched in a saddle or bridle, and from that the rangers concluded Rojas's horses had long before taken their back trail. What speculation, what consternation those saddled horses would cause if they returned to Forlorn River!

As Ladd improved there was one story he had to hear every day. It was the one relating to what he had missed—the sight of Rojas pursued and plunged to his doom. The thing had a morbid fascination for the sick ranger. He reveled in it. He tortured Mercedes. His gentleness and consideration, heretofore so marked, were in abeyance to some sinister, ghastly joy. But to humor him Mercedes racked her soul with the sensations she had suffered when Rojas hounded her out on the ledge; when she shot him; when she sprang to throw herself over the precipice; when she fought him; when with half-blinded eyes she looked up to see the merciless Yaqui reaching for the bandit. Ladd fed his cruel longing with Thorne's poignant recollections, with the keen, clear, never-to-be-forgotten shocks to Gale's eye and ear. Jim Lash, for one at least, never tired of telling how he had seen and heard the tragedy, and every time in the telling it gathered some more tragic and gruesome detail. Jim believed in satiating the ranger. Then in the twilight, when the campfire burned, Ladd would try to get the Yaqui to tell his side of the story. But this the Indian would never do. There was only the expression of his fathomless eyes and the set passion of his massive face.

Those waiting days grew into weeks. Ladd gained very slowly. Nevertheless, at last he could walk about, and soon he averred that, strapped to a horse, he could last out the trip to Forlorn River.

There was rejoicing in camp, and plans were eagerly suggested. The Yaqui happened to be absent. When he returned the rangers told him they were now ready to undertake the journey back across lava and cactus.

Yaqui shook his head. They declared again their intention.

"No!" replied the Indian, and his deep, sonorous voice rolled out upon the quiet of the arroyo. He spoke briefly then. They had waited too long. The smaller water holes back in the trail were dry. The hot summer was upon them. There could be only death waiting down in the burning valley. Here was water and grass and wood and shade from the sun's rays and sheep to be killed on the peaks. The water would hold unless the season was that dreaded *año seco* of the Mexicans.

"Wait for rain," concluded Yaqui, and now as never before he spoke as one with authority. "If no rain—" Silently he lifted a speaking hand.

CHAPTER 16

MOUNTAIN SHEEP

What Gale might have thought an appalling situation, if considered from a safe and comfortable home away from the desert, became, now that he was shut in by the red-ribbed lava walls and great dry wastes, a matter calmly accepted as inevitable. So he imagined it was accepted by the others. Not even Mercedes uttered a regret. No word was spoken of home. If there was thought of loved ones, it was locked deep in their minds. In Mercedes there was no change in womanly quality, perhaps because all she had to love was there in the desert with her.

Gale had often pondered over this singular change in character. He had trained himself, in order to fight a paralyzing something in the desert's influence, to oppose with memory and thought an insidious primitive retrogression to what was scarcely consciousness at all, merely a savage's instinct of sight and sound. He felt the need now of redoubled effort. For there was a sheer happiness in drifting. Not only was it easy to forget, it was hard to remember. His idea was that a man laboring under a great wrong, a great crime, a great passion might find the lonely desert a fitting place for either remembrance or oblivion, according to the nature of his soul. But an ordinary, healthy, reasonably happy mortal who loved the open with its blaze of sun and sweep of wind would have a task to keep from going backward to the natural man as he was before civilization.

By tacit agreement Ladd again became the leader of the party. Ladd was a man who would have taken all the responsibility whether or not it was given him. In moments of hazard, of uncertainty, Lash and Gale, even Belding, unconsciously looked to the ranger. He had that kind of power.

The first thing Ladd asked was to have the store of food that remained spread out upon a tarpaulin. Assuredly, it was a slender enough supply. The ranger stood for long moments gazing down at it. He was groping among past experiences, calling back from his years of life on range and desert that which might be valuable for the present issue. It was impossible to read the gravity of Ladd's face, for he still looked like a dead man, but the slow shake of his head told Gale much. There was a grain of hope, however, in the significance with which he touched the bags of salt and said, "Shore it was sense packin' all that salt!"

Then he turned to face his comrades.

"That's little grub for six starvin' people corralled in the desert. But the grub end ain't worryin' me. Yaqui can get sheep up the slopes. Water! That's the beginnin' an' middle an' end of our case."

"Laddy, I reckon the water hole here never goes dry," replied Jim.

"Ask the Indian."

Upon being questioned, Yaqui repeated what he had said about the dreaded *año seco* of the Mexicans. In a dry year this water hole failed.

"Dick, take a rope an' see how much water's in the hole."

Gale could not find bottom with a thirty-foot lasso. The water was as cool, clear, sweet as if it had been kept in a shaded iron receptacle.

Ladd welcomed this information with surprise and gladness.

"Let's see. Last year was shore pretty dry. Mebbe this summer won't be. Mebbe our wonderful good luck'll hold. Ask Yaqui if he thinks it'll rain."

Mercedes questioned the Indian.

"He says no man can tell surely. But he thinks the rain will come," she replied.

"Shore it'll rain, you can gamble on that now," continued Ladd. "If there's only grass for the hosses! We can't get out of here without hosses. Dick, take the Indian an' scout down the arroyo. To-day I seen the hosses were gettin' fat. Gettin' fat in this desert! But mebbe they've about grazed up all the grass. Go an' see, Dick. An' may you come back with more good news!"

Gale, upon the few occasions when he had wandered down the arroyo, had never gone far. The Yaqui said there was grass for the horses, and until now no one had given the question more consideration. Gale found that the arroyo widened as it opened. Near the head, where it was narrow, the grass lined the course of the dry streambed.

But farther down this streambed spread out. There was every indication that at flood seasons the water covered the floor of the arroyo. The farther Gale went the thicker and larger grew the gnarled mesquites and *palo verdes,* the more cactus and greasewood there were, and other desert growths. Patches of gray grass grew everywhere. Gale began to wonder where the horses were. Finally the trees and brush thinned out, and a milewide gray plain stretched down to reddish sand dunes. Over to one side were the white horses, and even as Gale saw them both Blanco Diablo and Sol lifted their heads and, with white manes tossing in the wind, whistled clarion calls. Here was grass enough for many horses; the arroyo was indeed an oasis.

Ladd and the others were awaiting Gale's report, and they received it with calmness, yet with a joy no less evident because it was restrained. Gale, in his keen observation at the moment, found that he and his comrades turned with glad eyes to the woman of the party.

"Señor Laddy, you think—you—believe—we shall—" she faltered, and her voice failed. It was the woman in her, weakening in the light of real hope, of the happiness now possible beyond that desert barrier.

"Mercedes, no white man can tell what'll come to pass out here," said Ladd, earnestly. "Shore I have hopes now I never dreamed of. I was pretty near a dead man. The Indian saved me. Queer notions have come into my head about Yaqui. I don't understand them. He seems when you look at him only a squalid, sullen, vengeful savage. But Lord! that's far from truth. Mebbe Yaqui's different from most Indians. He *looks* the same, though. Mebbe the trouble is we white folks never knew the Indian. Anyway, Beldin' had it right. Yaqui's our godsend. Now as to the future, I'd like to know mebbe as well as you if we're ever to get home. Only bein' what I am, I say *Quién sabe?* But somethin' tells me Yaqui knows. Ask him, Mercedes. Make him tell. We'll all be the better for knowin'. We'd be stronger for havin' more'n our faith in him. He's a silent Indian, but make him tell."

Mercedes called to Yaqui. At her bidding there was always a suggestion of hurry, which otherwise was never manifest in his actions. She put a hand on his bared muscular arm and began to speak in Spanish. Her voice was low, swift, full of deep emotion, sweet as the sound of a bell. It thrilled Gale, though he understood scarcely a word she said. He did not need translation to know that here spoke the longing of a woman for life, love, home, the heritage of a woman's heart.

Gale doubted his own divining impression. It was that the Yaqui understood this woman's longing. In Gale's sight the Indian's stoicism, his inscrutability, the lavalike hardness of his face, although they did not change, seemed to give forth light, gentleness, loyalty. For an instant Gale seemed to have a vision; but it did not last, and he failed to hold some beautiful illusive thing.

"Si!" rolled out the Indian's reply, full of power and depth.

Mercedes drew a long breath, and her hand sought Thorne's.

"He says yes," she whispered. "He answers he'll save us; he'll take us all back—he knows!"

The Indian turned away to his tasks, and the silence that held the little group was finally broken by Ladd.

"Shore I said so. Now all we've got to do is use sense. Friends, I'm the commissary department of this outfit, an' what I say goes. You all won't eat except when I tell you. Mebbe it'll not be so hard to keep our health. Starved beggars don't get sick. But there's the heat comin', an' we can all go loco, you know. To pass the time! Lord, that's our problem. Now if you all only had a hankerin' for checkers. Shore I'll make a board an' make you play. Thorne, you're the luckiest. You've got your girl, an' this can be a honeymoon. Now with a few tools an' little material see what a grand house you can build for your wife. Dick, you're lucky, too. You like to hunt, an' up there you'll find the finest bighorn huntin' in the West. Take Yaqui and the .405. We need the meat, but while you're gettin' it have your sport. The same chance will never come again. I wish we all was able to go. But crippled men can't climb the lava. Shore you'll see some country from the peaks. There's no wilder place on earth, except the poles. An' when you're older, you an' Nell, with a couple of fine boys, think what it'll be to tell them about bein' lost in the lava, an' about huntin' sheep with a Yaqui. Shore I've hit it. You can take yours out in huntin' and thinkin'. Now if I had a girl like Nell I'd never go crazy. That's your game, Dick. Hunt, an' think of Nell, an' how you'll tell those fine boys about it all, an' about the old cowman you knowed, Laddy, who'll by then be long past the divide. Rustle now, son. Get some enthusiasm. For shore you'll need it for yourself an' us."

Gale climbed the lava slope, away round to the right of the arroyo, along an old trail that Yaqui said the Papagos had made before his own people hunted there. Partway it led through spiked, crested, upheaved lava that would have been almost impassable even without its silver coating of *cholla* cactus. There were benches and ledges and ridges bare and glistening in the sun. From the crests of these Yaqui's searching falcon gaze roved near and far for signs of sheep, and Gale used his glass on the reaches of lava that slanted steeply upward to the corrugated peaks, and down over endless heave and roll and red-waved slopes. The heat smoked up from the lava, and this, with the red color and shiny *chollas,* gave the impression of a world of smoldering fire.

Farther along the slope Yaqui halted and crawled behind projections to a point commanding a view over an extraordinary section of country. The peaks were off to the left. In the foreground were gullies, ridges, cañons, arroyos, all glistening with *chollas* and some other and more numerous white bushes, and here and there towered a green cactus. This region was only a splintered and more devastated part of the volcanic slope, but it was miles in extent. Yaqui peeped over the top of a blunt block of lava and searched the sharp-billowed wilderness. Suddenly he grasped Gale and pointed across a deep wide gully.

With the aid of his glass Gale saw five sheep. They were much larger than he had expected, dull brown in color, and two of them were rams with great curved horns. They were looking in his direction. Remembering what he had heard about the wonderful eyesight of these mountain animals, Gale could only conclude that they had seen the hunters.

Then Yaqui's movements attracted and interested him. The Indian had brought with him a red scarf and a mesquite branch. He tied the scarf on the stick, and propped this up in a crack of the lava. The scarf waved in the wind. That done, the Indian bade Gale watch.

Once again he leveled the glass at the sheep. All five now were motionless, standing like statues, heads pointed across the gully. They were more than a mile distant. When Gale looked without his glass they merged into the roughness of the lava. He was intensely interested. Did the sheep see the red scarf? It seemed incredible, but nothing else could account for that statuesque alertness. The sheep held this rigid position for perhaps fifteen minutes. Then the leading ram started to approach. The others followed. He took a few steps, then halted. Always he held his head up, nose pointed.

"By George, they're coming!" exclaimed Gale. "They see that flag. They're hunting us. They're curious. If this doesn't beat me!"

Evidently the Indian understood, for he grunted.

Gale found difficulty in curbing his impatience. The approach of the sheep was slow. The advances of the leader and the intervals of watching had a singular regularity. He worked like a machine. Gale followed him down the opposite wall, around holes, across gullies, over ridges. Then Gale shifted the glass back to find the others. They were coming also, with exactly the same pace and pause of their leader. What steppers they were! How sure-footed! What leaps they made! It was thrilling to watch them. Gale forgot he had a rifle. The Yaqui pressed a heavy hand down upon his shoulder. He was to keep well hidden and to be quiet. Gale suddenly conceived the idea that the sheep might come clear across to investigate the puzzling red thing fluttering in the breeze. Strange, indeed, would that be for the wildest creatures in the world.

The big ram led on with the same regular persistence, and in half an hour's time he was in the bottom of the great gulf, and soon he was facing up the slope. Gale knew then that the alluring scarf had fascinated him. It was no longer necessary now for Gale to use his glass. There was a short period when an intervening crest of lava hid the sheep from view. After that the two rams and their smaller followers were plainly in sight for perhaps a quarter of an hour. Then they disappeared behind another ridge. Gale kept watching, sure they would come out farther on. A tense period of waiting passed, then a sudden electrifying pressure of Yaqui's hand made Gale tremble with excitement.

Very cautiously he shifted his position. There, not fifty feet distant upon a high mound of lava, stood the leader of the sheep. His size astounded Gale. He seemed all horns. But only for a moment did the impression of horns overbalancing body remain with Gale. The sheep was graceful, sinewy, slender, powerfully built, and in poise magnificent. As Gale watched, spellbound, the second ram leaped lightly upon the mound, and presently the three others did likewise.

Then, indeed, Gale feasted his eyes with a spectacle for a hunter. It came to him suddenly that there had been something he expected to see in this Rocky Mountain bighorn, and it was lacking. They were beautiful, as wonderful as even Ladd's encomiums had led him to suppose. He thought perhaps it was the contrast these soft, sleek, short-furred, graceful animals afforded to what he imagined the barren, terrible lava mountains might develop.

The splendid leader stepped closer, his round, protruding amber eyes, which Gale could now plainly see, intent upon that fatal red flag. Like automatons the other four crowded into his tracks. A few little slow steps, then the leader halted.

At this instant Gale's absorbed attention was directed by Yaqui to the rifle, and so to the purpose of the climb. A little cold shock affronted Gale's vivid pleasure. With it dawned a realization of what he had imagined was lacking in these animals. They did not look wild! The so-called wildest of wild creatures appeared tamer than sheep he had followed on a farm. It would be little less than murder to kill them. Gale regretted the need of slaughter. Nevertheless, he could not resist the desire to show himself and see how tame they really were.

He reached for the .405, and as he threw a shell into the chamber the slight metallic click made the sheep jump. Then Gale rose quickly to his feet.

The noble ram and his band simply stared at Gale. They had never seen a man. They showed not the slightest indication of instinctive fear. Curiosity, surprise, even friendliness, seemed to mark their attitude of attention. Gale imagined that they were going to step still closer. He did not choose to wait to see if this were true. Certainly it already took a grim resolution to raise the heavy .405.

His shot killed the big leader. The others bounded away with remarkable nimbleness. Gale used up the remaining four shells to drop the second ram, and by the time he had reloaded the others were out of range.

The Yaqui's method of hunting was sure and deadly and saving in energy, but Gale never would try it again. He chose to stalk the game. This entailed a great expenditure of strength, the eyes and the lungs of a mountaineer, and, as Gale put it to Ladd, the need of seven-league boots. After being hunted a few times and shot at, the sheep became exceedingly difficult to approach. Gale learned to know that their fame as the keenest-eyed of all animals was well founded. If he worked directly toward a flock, crawling over the sharp lava, always a sentinel ram espied him before he got within range. The only method of attack that he found successful was to locate sheep with his glass, work round to windward of them, and then, getting behind a ridge or buttress, crawl like a lizard to a vantage point. He failed often. The stalk called forth all that was in him of endurance, cunning, speed. As the days grew hotter he hunted in the early morning hours and a while before the sun went down. More than one night he lay out on the lava, with the great stars close overhead and the immense void all beneath him. This pursuit he learned to love. Upon those scarred and blasted slopes the wild spirit that was in him had free rein. And like a shadow the faithful Yaqui tried ever to keep at his heels.

One morning the rising sun greeted him as he surmounted the higher cone of the volcano. He saw the vastness of the east aglow with a glazed rosy whiteness, like the changing hue of an ember. At this height there was a sweeping wind, still cool. The western slopes of lava lay dark, and all that world of sand and gulf and mountain barrier beyond was shrouded in the mystic cloud of distance. Gale had assimilated much of the loneliness and the sense of ownership and the love of lofty heights that might well belong to the great condor of the peak. Like this wide-winged bird, he had an unparalleled range of vision. The very corners whence came the winds seemed pierced by Gale's eyes.

Yaqui spied a flock of sheep far under the curved broken rim of the main crater. Then began the stalk. Gale had taught Yaqui something—that speed might win as well as patient cunning. Keeping out of sight, Gale ran over the spike-crusted lava, leaving the Indian far behind. His feet were magnets, attracting supporting holds, and he passed over them too fast to fall. The wind, the keen air of the heights, the red lava, the boundless surrounding blue, all seemed to have something to do with his wildness. Then, hiding, slipping, creeping, crawling, he closed in upon his quarry until the long rifle grew like stone in his grip, and the whipping "spang" ripped the silence, and the strange echo boomed deep in the crater, and rolled around, as if in hollow mockery at the hopelessness of escape.

Gale's exultant yell was given as much to free himself of some bursting joy of action as it was to call the slower Yaqui. Then he liked the strange echoes. It was a maddening whirl of sound that bored deeper and deeper along the whorled and caverned walls of the crater. It was as if these aged walls resented the violating of their silent sanctity. Gale felt himself a man, a thing alive, something superior to all this savage, dead, upflung world of iron, a master even of all this grandeur and sublimity because he had a soul.

He waited beside his quarry, and breathed deep, and swept the long slopes with searching eyes of habit.

When Yaqui came up they set about the hardest task of all, to pack the best of that heavy sheep down miles of steep, ragged, *cholla*-covered lava. But even in this Gale rejoiced. The heat was nothing, the millions of little pits which could hold and twist a foot were nothing; the blade-edged crusts and the deep fissures and the choked cañons and the tangled, dwarfed mesquites, all these were as nothing but obstacles to be cheerfully overcome. Only the *cholla* hindered Dick Gale.

When his heavy burden pulled him out of sure-footedness, and he plunged into a *cholla,* or when the strange, deceitful, uncanny, almost invisible frosty thorns caught and pierced him, then there was call for all of his fortitude and endurance. For this cactus had a malignant power of torture. Its pain was a stinging, blinding, burning, sickening poison in the blood. If thorns pierced his legs he felt the pain all over his body; if his hands rose from a fall full of the barbed joints, he was helpless and quivering till Yaqui tore them out.

But this one peril, dreaded more than dizzy height of precipice or sunblindness on the glistening peak, did not daunt Gale. His teacher was the Yaqui, and always before him was an example that made him despair of a white man's equality. Color, race, blood, breeding—what were these in the wilderness? Verily, Dick Gale had come to learn the use of his hands.

So in a descent of hours he toiled down the lava slope, to stalk into the arroyo like a burdened giant, wringing wet, panting, clear-eyed and dark-faced, his ragged clothes and boots white with *cholla* thorns.

The gaunt Ladd rose from his shaded seat, removed his pipe from smiling lips, and turned to nod at Jim, and then looked back again.

The torrid summer heat came imperceptibly, or it could never have been borne by white men. It changed the lives of the fugitives, making them partly nocturnal in habit. The nights had the balmy coolness of spring, and would have been delightful for sleep, but that would have made the blazing days unendurable.

The sun rose in a vast white flame. With it came the blasting, withering wind from the gulf. A red haze, like that of earlier sunsets, seemed to come sweeping on the wind, and it roared up the arroyo, and went bellowing into the crater, and rushed on in fury to lash the peaks.

During these hot, windy hours the desert-bound party slept in deep recesses in the lava; and if necessity brought them forth they could not remain out long. The sand burned through boots, and a touch of bare hand on lava raised a blister.

A short while before sundown the Yaqui went forth to build a campfire, and soon the others came out, heat-dazed, half blinded, with parching throats to allay and hunger that was never satisfied. A little action and a cooling of the air revived them, and when night set in they were comfortable round the campfire.

As Ladd had said, one of their greatest problems was the passing of time. The nights were interminably long, but they had to be passed in work or play or dream—anything except sleep. That was Ladd's most inflexible command. He gave no reason. But not improbably the ranger thought that the terrific heat of the day spent in slumber lessened a wear and strain, if not a real danger of madness.

Accordingly, at first the occupations of this little group were many and various. They worked if they had something to do, or could invent a pretext. They told and retold stories until all were wearisome. They sang songs. Mercedes taught Spanish. They played every game they knew. They invented others that were so trivial children would scarcely have been interested, and these they played seriously. In a word, with intelligence and passion, with all that was civilized and human, they fought the ever-infringing loneliness, the savage solitude of their environment.

But they had only finite minds. It was not in reason to expect a complete victory against this mighty Nature, this abounding horizon of death and desolation and decay. Gradually they fell back upon fewer and fewer occupations, until the time came when the silence was hard to break.

Gale believed himself the keenest of the party, the one who thought most, and he watched the effect of the desert upon his companions. He imagined that he saw Ladd grow old sitting around the campfire. Certain it was that the ranger's gray hair had turned white. What had been at times hard and cold and grim about him had strangely vanished in sweet temper and a vacant-mindedness that held him longer as the days passed. For hours, it seemed, Ladd would bend over his checkerboard and never make a move. It mattered not now whether or not he had a part-ner. It was always glad of being spoken to, as if he were called back from some vague region of mind. Jim Lash, the calmest, coolest, most nonchalant, best-humored Westerner Gale had ever met, had by slow degrees lost that cheerful character which would have been of such infinite good to his companions, and always he sat brooding, silently brooding. Jim had no ties, few memories, and the desert was claiming him.

Thorne and Mercedes, however, were living, wonderful proof that spirit, mind, and heart were free—free to soar in scorn of the colossal barrenness and silence and space of that terrible hedging prison of lava. They were young; they loved; they were together; and the oasis was almost a paradise. Gale believed he helped himself by watching them. Imagination had never pictured real happiness to him. Thorne and Mercedes had forgotten the outside world. If they had been existing on the burned-out desolate moon they could hardly have been in a harsher, grimmer, lonelier spot than this red-walled arroyo. But it might have been a statelier Eden than that of the primitive day.

Mercedes grew thinner, until she was a slender shadow of her former self. She became hard, brown as the rangers, lithe and quick as a panther. She seemed to live on water and the air—perhaps, indeed, on love. For of the scant fare, the best of which was continually urged upon her, she partook but little. She reminded Gale of a wild brown creature, free as the wind on the lava slopes. Yet, despite the great change, her beauty remained undiminished. Her eyes, seeming so much larger now in her small face, were great black, starry gulfs. She was the life of that camp. Her smiles, her rapid speech, her low laughter, her quick movements, her playful moods with the rangers, the dark and passionate glance, which rested so often on her lover, the whispers in the dusk as hand in hand they paced the campfire beat—these helped Gale to retain his loosening hold on reality, to resist the lure of a strange beckoning life where a man stood free in the golden open, where emotion was not, nor trouble, nor sickness, nor anything but the savage's rest and sleep and action and dream.

Although the Yaqui was as his shadow, Gale reached a point when he seemed to wander alone at twilight, in the night, at dawn. Far down the arroyo, in the deepening red twilight, when the heat rolled away on slow-dying wind, Blanco Sol raised his splendid head and whistled for his master. Gale reproached himself for neglect of the noble horse. Blanco Sol was always the same. He loved four things—his master, a long drink of cool water, to graze at will, and to run. Time and place, Gale thought, meant little to Sol if he could have those four things. Gale put his arm over the great arched neck and laid his cheek against the long white mane, and then even as he stood there forgot the horse. What was that dull, red-tinged, horizon-wide mantle creeping up the slope? Through it the copper sun glowed, paled, died. Was it only twilight?

Was it gloom? If he thought about it he had a feeling that it was the herald of night, and the night must be a vigil, and that made him tremble.

At night he had formed a habit of climbing up the lava slope as far as the smooth trail extended, and there on a promontory he paced to and fro, and watched the stars, and sat stone-still for hours looking down at the vast void with its moving, changing shadows. From that promontory he gazed up at a velvet-blue sky, deep and dark, bright with millions of cold, distant, blinking stars, and he grasped a little of the meaning of infinitude. He gazed down into the shadows, which, black as they were and impenetrable, yet gave a conception of immeasurable space.

Then the silence! He was dumb, he was awed, he bowed his head, he trembled, he marveled at the desert silence. It was the one thing always present. Even when the wind roared there seemed to be silence. But at night, in this lava world of ashes and canker, he waited for this terrible strangeness of nature to come to him with the secret. He seemed at once a little child and a strong man, and something very old. What tortured him was the incomprehensibility that the vaster the space the greater the silence! At one moment Gale felt there was only death here, and that was the secret; at another he heard the slow beat of a mighty heart.

He came at length to realize that the desert was a teacher. He did not realize all that he had learned, but he was a different man. And when he decided upon that, he was not thinking of the slow, sure call to the primal instincts of man; he was thinking that the desert, as much as he had experienced and no more, would absolutely overturn the whole scale of a man's values, break old habits, form new ones, remake him. More of desert experience,

Gale believed, would be too much for intellect. The desert did not breed civilized man, and that made Gale ponder over a strange thought: after all, was the civilized man inferior to the savage?

Yaqui was the answer to that. When Gale acknowledged this he always remembered his present strange manner of thought. The past, the old order of mind, seemed as remote as this desert world was from the haunts of civilized men. A man must know a savage as Gale knew Yaqui before he could speak authoritatively, and then something stilled his tongue. In the first stage of Gale's observation of Yaqui he had marked tenaciousness of life, stoicism, endurance, strength. These were the attributes of the desert. But what of that second stage wherein the Indian had loomed up a colossal figure of strange honor, loyalty, love? Gale doubted his convictions and scorned himself for doubting.

There in the gloom sat the silent, impassive, inscrutable Yaqui. His dark face, his dark eyes were plain in the light of the stars. Always he was near Gale, unobtrusive, shadowy, but there. Why? Gale absolutely could not doubt that the Indian had heart as well as mind. Yaqui had from the very first stood between Gale and accident, toil, peril. It was his own choosing. Gale could not change him or thwart him. He understood the Indian's idea of obligation and sacred duty. But there was more, and that baffled Gale. In the night hours, alone on the slope, Gale felt in Yaqui, as he felt the mighty throb of that desert pulse, a something that drew him irresistibly to the Indian. Sometimes he looked around to find the Indian, to dispel these strange, pressing thoughts of unreality, and it was never in vain.

Thus the nights passed, endlessly long, with Gale fighting for his old order of thought, fighting the fascination of that infinite sky, and the gloomy insulating whirl of the wide shadows, fighting for belief, hope, prayer, fighting against that terrible ever-recurring idea of being lost, lost, lost in the desert, fighting harder than any other thing the insidious, penetrating, tranquil, unfeeling self that was coming between him and his memory.

He was losing the battle, losing his hold on tangible things, losing his power to stand up under this ponderous, merciless weight of desert space and silence.

He acknowledged it in a kind of despair, and the shadows of the night seemed whirling fiends. Lost! Lost! Lost! What are you waiting for? *Rain?* . . . Lost! Lost! Lost in the desert! So the shadows seemed to scream in voiceless mockery.

At the moment he was alone on the promontory. The night was far spent. A ghastly moon haunted the black volcanic spurs. The winds blew silently. Was he alone? No, he did not seem to be alone. The Yaqui was there. Suddenly a strange, cold sensation crept over Gale. It was new. He felt a presence. Turning, he expected to see the Indian, but instead, a slight shadow, pale, almost white, stood there, not close nor yet distant. It seemed to brighten. Then he saw a woman who resembled a girl he had seemed to know long ago. She was white-faced, golden-haired, and her lips were sweet, and her eyes were turning black. *Nell!* He had forgotten her. Over him flooded a torrent of memory. There was tragic woe in this sweet face. Nell was holding out her arms—she was crying aloud to him across the sand and the cactus and the lava. She was in trouble, and he had been forgetting.

That night he climbed the lava to the topmost cone, and never slipped on a ragged crust nor touched a *cholla* thorn.

A voice had called to him. He saw Nell's eyes in the stars, in the velvet blue of sky, in the blackness of the engulfing shadows. She was with him, a slender shape, a spirit, keeping step with him, and memory was strong, sweet, beating, beautiful. Far down in the west, faintly golden with light of the sinking moon, he saw a cloud that resembled her face. A cloud on the desert horizon! He gazed and gazed. Was that a spirit face like the one by his side? No—he did not dream.

In the hot, sultry morning Yaqui appeared at camp, after long hours of absence, and he pointed with a long, dark arm toward the west. A bank of clouds was rising above the mountain barrier.

"Rain!" he cried; and his sonorous voice rolled down the arroyo.

Those who heard him were as shipwrecked mariners at sight of a distant sail.

Dick Gale, silent, grateful to the depths of his soul, stood with his arm over Blanco Sol and watched the transforming west, where clouds of wondrous size and hue piled over one another, rushing, darkening, spreading, sweeping upward toward that white and glowing sun.

When they reached the zenith and swept round to blot out the blazing orb, the earth took on a dark, lowering aspect. The red of sand and lava changed to steely gray. Vast shadows, like ripples on water, sheeted in from the gulf with a low, strange moan. Yet the silence was like death. The desert was awaiting a strange and hated visitation—storm! If all the endless torrid days, the endless mystic nights had seemed unreal to Gale, what, then, seemed this stupendous spectacle?

"Oh! I felt a drop of rain on my face!" cried Mercedes; and, whispering the name of a saint, she kissed her husband.

The white-haired Ladd, gaunt, old, bent, looked up at the maelstrom of clouds, and he said, softly, "Shore we'll get in the hosses, an' pack light, an' hit the trail, an' make night marches!"

Then up out of the gulf of the west swept a bellowing wind and a black pall and terrible flashes of lightning and thunder like the end of the world—fury, blackness, chaos, the desert storm.

CHAPTER 17

THE WHISTLE OF A HORSE

At the ranch house at Forlorn River Belding stood alone in his darkened room. It was quiet there and quiet outside; the sickening midsummer heat, like a hot heavy blanket, lay upon the house.

He took up the gun belt from his table and with slow hands buckled it around his waist. He seemed to feel something familiar and comfortable and inspiring in the weight of the big gun against his hip. He faced the door as if to go out, but hesitated, and then began a slow, plodding walk up and down the length of the room. Presently he halted at the table, and with reluctant hands he unbuckled the gun belt and laid it down.

The action did not have an air of finality, and Belding knew it. He had seen border life in Texas in the early days; he had been a sheriff when the law in the West depended on a quickness of wrist; he had seen many a man lay down his gun for good and all. His own action was not final. Of late he had done the same thing many times, and this last time it seemed a little harder to do, a little more indicative of vacillation. There were reasons why Belding's gun held for him a gloomy fascination.

The Chases, those grasping and conscienceless agents of a new force in the development of the West, were bent upon Belding's ruin, and, so far as his fortunes at Forlorn River were concerned, had almost accomplished it. One by one he lost points for which he contended with them. He carried into the Tucson courts the matter of the staked claims, and mining claims, and water claims, and he lost all. Following that he lost his government position as inspector of immigration; and this fact, because of what he considered its injustice, had been a hard blow. He had been made to suffer a humiliation equally as great. It came about that he actually had to pay the Chases for water to irrigate his alfalfa fields. The never-failing spring upon his land answered for the needs of household and horses, but no more.

These matters were unfortunate for Belding, but not by any means wholly accountable for his worry and unhappiness and brooding hate. He believed Dick Gale and the rest of the party taken into the desert by the Yaqui had been killed or lost. Two months before a string of Mexican horses, riderless, saddled, starved for grass and wild for water, had come in to Forlorn River. They were a part of the horses belonging to Rojas and his band. Their arrival complicated the mystery and strengthened convictions of the loss of both pursuers and pursued. Belding was wont to say that he had worried himself gray over the fate of his rangers.

Belding's unhappiness could hardly be laid to material loss. He had been rich and was now poor, but change of fortune such as that could not have made him unhappy. Something more somber and mysterious and sad than the loss of Dick Gale and their friends had come into the lives of his wife and Nell. He dated the time of this change back to a certain day when Mrs. Belding recognized in the elder Chase an old schoolmate and a rejected suitor. It took time for slow-thinking Belding to discover anything wrong in his household, especially as the fact of the Gales lingering there made Mrs. Belding and Nell, for the most part, hide their real and deeper feelings. Gradually, however, Belding had forced on him the fact of some secret cause for grief other than Gale's loss. He was sure of it when his wife signified her desire to make a visit to her old home back in Peoria. She did not give many reasons, but she did show him a letter that had found its way from old friends. This letter contained news that may or may not have been authentic; but it was enough, Belding thought, to interest his wife. An old prospector had returned to Peoria, and he had told relatives of meeting Robert Burton at the Sonoyta Oasis fifteen years before, and that Burton had gone into the desert never to return. To Belding this was no surprise, for he had heard that before his marriage. There appeared to have been no doubts as to the death of his wife's first husband. The singular thing was that both Nell's father and grandfather had been lost somewhere in the Sonora Desert.

Belding did not oppose his wife's desire to visit her old home. He thought it would be a wholesome trip for her, and did all in his power to persuade Nell to accompany her. But Nell would not go.

It was after Mrs. Belding's departure that Belding discovered in Nell a condition of mind that amazed and distressed him. She had suddenly become strangely wretched, so that she could not conceal it from even the Gales, who, of all people, Belding imagined, were the ones to make Nell proud. She would tell him nothing. But after a while, when he had thought it out, he dated this further and more deplorable change in Nell back to a day on which he had met Nell with Radford Chase. This indefatigable wooer had not in the least abandoned his suit. Something about the fellow made Belding grind his teeth. But Nell grew not only solicitously, but now strangely, entreatingly earnest in her importunities to Belding not to insult or lay a hand on Chase. This had bound Belding so far; it had made him think and watch. He had never been a man to interfere with his women-folks. They could do as they liked, and usually that pleased him. But a slow surprise gathered and grew upon him when he saw that Nell, apparently, was accepting young Chase's attentions. At least, she no longer hid from him. Belding could not account for this, because he was sure Nell cordially despised the fellow. And toward the end he divined, if he did not actually know, that these Chases possessed some strange power over Nell, and were using it. That stirred a hate in Belding—a hate he had felt at the first and had manfully striven against, which now gave him over to dark brooding thoughts.

Midsummer passed, and the storms came late. But when they arrived they made up for tardiness. Belding did not remember so terrible a storm of wind and rain as that which broke the summer's drought.

In a few days, it seemed, Altar Valley was a bright and green expanse, where dust clouds did not rise. Forlorn River ran, a slow, heavy, turgid torrent. Belding never saw the river in flood that it did not give him joy; yet now, des-ert man as he was, he suffered a regret when he thought

of the great Chase reservoir full and overflowing. The
dull thunder of the spillway was not pleasant. It was the
first time in his life that the sound of falling water jarred
upon him.

Belding noticed workmen once more engaged in the
fields bounding his land. The Chases had extended a main
irrigation ditch down to Belding's farm, skipped the width
of his ground, then had gone on down through Altar Valley. They had exerted every influence to obtain right to
connect these ditches by digging through his land, but
Belding had remained obdurate. He refused to have any
dealings with them. It was therefore with some curiosity
and suspicion that he saw a gang of Mexicans once more
at work upon these ditches.

At daylight next morning a tremendous blast almost
threw Belding out of his bed. It cracked the adobe walls of
his house and broke windows and sent pans and crockery
to the floor with a crash. Belding's idea was that the store
of dynamite kept by the Chases for blasting had blown up.
Hurriedly getting into his clothes, he went to Nell's room
to reassure her; and, telling her to have a thought for their
guests, he went out to see what had happened.

The villagers were pretty badly frightened. Many of the
poorly constructed adobe huts had crumbled almost into
dust. A great yellow cloud, like smoke, hung over the
river. This appeared to be at the upper end of Belding's
plot, and close to the river. When he reached his fence the
smoke and dust were so thick he could scarcely breathe,
and for a little while he was unable to see what had happened. Presently he made out a huge hole in the sand just
about where the irrigation ditch had stopped near his line.
For some reason or other, not clear to Belding, the Mexi-

cans had set off an extraordinarily heavy blast at that point.

Belding pondered. He did not now for a moment consider an accidental discharge of dynamite. But why had this blast been set off? The loose sandy soil had yielded readily to shovel; there were no rocks; as far as construction of a ditch was concerned such a blast would have done more harm than good.

Slowly, with reluctant feet, Belding walked toward a green hollow, where in a cluster of willows lay the never-failing spring that his horses loved so well, and, indeed, which he loved no less. He was actually afraid to part the drooping willows to enter the little cool, shady path that led to the spring. Then, suddenly seized by suspense, he ran the rest of the way.

He was just in time to see the last of the water. It seemed to sink as in quicksand. The shape of the hole had changed. The tremendous force of the blast had obstructed or diverted the underground stream of water.

Belding's never-failing spring had been ruined. What had made this little plot of ground green and sweet and fragrant was now no more. Belding's first feeling was for the pity of it. The pale Ajo lilies would bloom no more under those willows. The willows themselves would soon wither and die. He thought how many times in the middle of hot summer nights he had come down to the spring to drink. Never again!

Suddenly he thought of Blanco Diablo. How the great white thoroughbred had loved this spring! Belding straightened up and looked with tear-blurred eyes out over the waste of desert to the west. Never a day passed that he had not thought of the splendid horse; but this moment, with its significant memory, was doubly keen, and there came a dull pang in his breast.

"Diablo will never drink here again!" muttered Belding.

The loss of Blanco Diablo, though admitted and mourned by Belding, had never seemed quite real until this moment.

The pall of dust drifting over him, the din of the falling water up at the dam, diverted Belding's mind to the Chases. All at once he was in the harsh grip of a cold certainty. The blast had been set off intentionally to ruin his spring. What a hellish trick! No Westerner, no Indian or Mexican, no desert man could have been guilty of such a crime. To ruin a beautiful clear, cool, never-failing stream of water in the desert!

It was then that Belding's worry and indecision and brooding were as if they had never existed. As he strode swiftly back to the house, his head, which had long been bent thoughtfully and sadly, was held erect. He went directly to his room, and with an air that was now final he buckled on his gun belt. He looked the gun over and tried the action. He squared himself and walked a little more erect. Some long-lost individuality had returned to Belding.

"Let's see," he was saying. "I can get Carter to send the horses I've got left back to Waco to my brother. I'll make Nell take what money there is and go hunt up her mother. The Gales are ready to go—today, if I say the word. Nell can travel with them partway East. That's your game, Tom Belding, don't mistake me."

As he went out he encountered Mr. Gale coming up the walk. The long sojourn at Forlorn River, despite the fact that it had been laden with a suspense which was gradually changing to a sad certainty, had been of great benefit to Dick's father. The dry air, the heat, and the quiet had made him, if not entirely a well man, certainly stronger than he had been in many years.

"Belding, what was that terrible roar?" asked Mr. Gale. "We were badly frightened until Miss Nell came to us. We feared it was an earthquake."

"Well, I'll tell you, Mr. Gale, we've had some quakes here, but none of them could hold a candle to this jar we just had."

Then Belding explained what had caused the explosion, and why it had been set off so close to his property.

"It's an outrage, sir, an unspeakable outrage," declared Mr. Gale, hotly. "Such a thing would not be tolerated in the East. Mr. Belding, I'm amazed at your attitude in the face of all this trickery."

"You see—there was Mother and Nell," began Belding, as if apologizing. He dropped his head a little and made marks in the sand with the toe of his boot. "Mr. Gale, I've been sort of half hitched, as Laddy used to say. I'm planning to have a little more elbow room round this ranch. I'm going to send Nell East to her mother. Then I'll— See here, Mr. Gale, would you mind having Nell with you partway when you go home?"

"We'd all be delighted to have her go all the way and make us a visit," replied Mr. Gale.

"That's fine. And you'll be going soon? Don't take that as if I wanted to—" Belding paused, for the truth was that he did want to hurry them off.

"We would have been gone before this, but for you," said Mr. Gale. "Long ago we gave up hope of—of Richard ever returning. And I believe, now we're sure he was lost, that we'd do well to go home at once. You wished us to remain till the heat was broken—till the rains came to make traveling easier for us. Now I see no need for further delay. My stay here has greatly benefited my health. I shall never forget your hospitality. This Western trip would have made me a new man if—only—Richard—"

"Sure. I understand," said Belding, gruffly. "Let's go in and tell the women to pack up."

Nell was busy with the servants preparing breakfast. Belding took her into the sitting room while Mr. Gale called his wife and daughter.

"My girl, I've some news for you," began Belding. "Mr. Gale is leaving today with his family. I'm going to send you with them—partway, anyhow. You're invited to visit them. I think that'd be great for you—help you to forget. But the main thing is—you're going East to join Mother."

Nell gazed at him, white-faced, without uttering a word.

"You see, Nell, I'm about done in Forlorn River," went on Belding. "That blast this morning sank my spring. There's no water now. It was the last straw. So we'll shake the dust of Forlorn River. I'll come on a little later—that's all."

"Dad, you're packing your gun!" exclaimed Nell, suddenly pointing with a trembling finger. She ran to him, and for the first time in his life Belding put her away from him. His movements had lost the old slow gentleness.

"Why, so I am," replied Belding, coolly, as his hand moved down to the sheath swinging at his hip. "Nell, I'm that absentminded these days!"

"Dad!" she cried.

"That'll do from you," he replied, in a voice he had never used to her. "Get breakfast now, then pack to leave Forlorn River."

"Leave Forlorn River!" whispered Nell, with a thin

white hand stealing up to her breast. How changed the girl was! Belding reproached himself for his hardness, but did not speak his thought aloud. Nell was fading here, just as Mercedes had faded before the coming of Thorne.

Nell turned away to the west window and looked out across the desert toward the dim blue peaks in the distance. Belding watched her; likewise the Gales; and no one spoke. There ensued a long silence. Belding felt a lump rise in his throat. Nell laid her arm against the window frame, but gradually it dropped, and she was leaning with her face against the wood. A low sob broke from her. Elsie Gale went to her, embraced her, took the drooping head on her shoulder.

"We've come to be such friends," she said. "I believe it'll be good for you to visit me in the city. Here—all day you look out across that awful lonely desert. . . . Come, Nell."

Heavy steps sounded outside on the flagstones, then the door rattled under a strong knock. Belding opened it. The Chases, father and son, stood beyond the threshold.

"Good morning, Belding," said the elder Chase. "We were routed out early by that big blast and came up to see what was wrong. All a blunder. The Greaser foreman was drunk yesterday, and his ignorant men made a mistake. Sorry if the blast bothered you."

"Chase, I reckon that's the first of your blasts I was ever glad to hear," replied Belding, in a way that made Chase look blank.

"So? Well, I'm glad you're glad," he went on, evidently puzzled. "I was a little worried—you've always been so touchy—we never could get together. I hurried over, fearing maybe you might think the blast—you see, Belding—"

"I see this, Mr. Ben Chase," interrupted Belding, in curt and ringing voice. "The blast *was* a mistake, the biggest you ever made in your life."

"What do you mean?" demanded Chase.

"You'll have to excuse me for a while, unless you're dead set on having it out right now. Mr. Gale and his family are leaving, and my daughter is going with them. I'd rather you'd wait a little."

"Nell going away!" exclaimed Radford Chase. He reminded Belding of an overgrown boy in disappointment.

"Yes. But—*Miss Burton* to you, young man—"

"Mr. Belding, I certainly would prefer a conference with you right now," interposed the elder Chase, cutting short Belding's strange speech. "There are other matters—important matters to discuss. They've got to be settled. May we step in, sir?"

"No, you may not," replied Belding, bluntly. "I'm sure particular who I invite into my house. But I'll go with you."

Belding stepped out and closed the door. "Come away from the house so the women won't hear the—the talk."

The elder Chase was purple with rage, yet seemed to be controlling it. The younger man looked black, sullen, impatient. He appeared not to have a thought of Belding. He was absolutely blind to the situation, as considered from Belding's point of view. Ben Chase found his voice about the time Belding halted under the trees out of earshot from the house.

"Sir, you've insulted me—my son. How dare you? I want you to understand that you're—"

"Chop that kind of talk with me, you——!" interrupted Belding. He had always been profane, and now he certainly did not choose his language. Chase turned livid, gasped, and seemed about to give way to fury. But something about Belding evidently exerted a powerful quieting influence. "If you talk sense I'll listen," went on Belding.

Belding was frankly curious. He did not think any argument or inducement offered by Chase could change his mind on past dealings or his purpose of the present. But he believed by listening he might get some light on what had long puzzled him. The masterly effort Chase put forth to conquer his aroused passions gave Belding another idea of the character of this promoter.

"I want to make a last effort to propitiate you," began Chase, in his quick, smooth voice. That was a singular change to Belding—the dropping instantly into an easy flow of speech. "You've had losses here, and naturally you're sore. I don't blame you. But you can't see this thing from my side of the fence. Business is business. In business the best man wins. The law upheld those transactions of mine the honesty of which you questioned. As to mining and water claims, you lost on this technical point— that you had nothing to prove you had held them for five years. Five years is the time necessary in law. A dozen men might claim the source of Forlorn River, but if they had no house or papers to prove their squatters' rights any man could go in and fight them for the water. . . . Now I want to run that main ditch along the river, through your farm. Can't we make a deal? I'm ready to be liberal—to meet you more than halfway. I'll give you an interest in the company. I think I've influence enough up at the Capitol to have you reinstated as inspector. A little reasonableness on your part will put you right again in Forlorn River, with a chance of growing rich. There's a big future here. . . . My interest, Belding, has become personal.

Radford is in love with your stepdaughter. He wants to marry her. I'll admit now if I had foreseen this situation I wouldn't have pushed you so hard. But we can square the thing. Now let's get together not only in business, but in a family way. If my son's happiness depends upon having this girl, you may rest assured I'll do all I can to get her for him. I'll absolutely make good all your losses. Now what do you say?"

"No," replied Belding. "Your money can't buy a right of way across my ranch. And Nell doesn't want your son. That settles that."

"But you could persuade her."

"I won't, that's all."

"May I ask why?" Chase's voice was losing its suave quality but it was even swifter than before.

"Sure I don't mind your asking," replied Belding, in slow deliberation. "I wouldn't do such a low-down trick. Besides, if I would, I'd want it to be a man I was persuading for. I know Greasers—I know a Yaqui I'd rather give Nell to than your son."

Radford Chase began to roar in inarticulate rage. Belding paid no attention to him; indeed, he never glanced at the young man. The elder Chase checked a violent start. He plucked at the collar of his gray flannel shirt, opened it at the neck.

"My son's offer of marriage is an honor—more an honor, sir, than you perhaps are aware of."

Belding made no reply. His steady gaze did not turn from the long lane that led down to the river. He waited coldly, sure of himself.

"Mrs. Belding's daughter has no right to the name of Burton," snapped Chase. "Did you know that?"

"I did not," replied Belding, quietly.

"Well, you know it now," added Chase, bitingly.

"Sure you can prove what you say?" queried Belding, in the same cool, unemotional tone. It struck him strangely at the moment what little knowledge this man had of the West and of Western character.

"Prove it? Why, yes, I think so, enough to make the truth plain to any reasonable man. I come from Peoria—was born and raised there. I went to school with Nell Warren. That was your wife's maiden name. She was a beautiful, gay girl. All the fellows were in love with her. I knew Bob Burton well. He was a splendid fellow, but wild. Nobody ever knew for sure, but we all supposed he was engaged to marry Nell. He left Peoria, however, and soon after that the truth about Nell came out. She ran away. It was at least a couple of months before Burton showed up in Peoria. He did not stay long. Then for years nothing was heard of either of them. When word did come Nell was in Oklahoma, Burton was in Denver. There's a chance, of course, that Burton followed Nell and married her. That would account for Nell Warren taking the name of Burton. But it isn't likely. None of us ever heard of such a thing and wouldn't have believed it if we had. The affair seemed destined to end unfortunately. But Belding, while I'm at it, I want to say that Nell Warren was one of the sweetest, finest, truest girls in the world. If she drifted to the Southwest and kept her past a secret that was only natural. Certainly it should not be held against her. Why, she was only a child—a girl—seventeen—eighteen years old. . . . In a moment of amazement—when I recognized your wife as an old schoolmate—I blurted the thing out to Radford. You see now how little it matters to me when I ask your stepdaughter's hand in marriage for my son."

Belding stood listening. The genuine emotion in Chase's

voice was as strong as the ring of truth. Belding knew truth when he heard it. The revelation did not surprise him. Belding did not soften, for he divined that Chase's emotion was due to the probing of an old wound, the recalling of a past both happy and painful. Still, human nature was so strange that perhaps kindness and sympathy might yet have a place in this Chase's heart. Belding did not believe so, but he was willing to give Chase the benefit of the doubt.

"So you told my wife you'd respect her secret—keep her dishonor from husband and daughter?" demanded Belding, his dark gaze sweeping back from the lane.

"What! I—I—" stammered Chase.

"You made your son swear to be a man and die before he'd hint the thing to Nell?" went on Belding, and his voice rang louder.

Ben Chase had no answer. The red left his face. His son slunk back against the fence.

"I say you never held this secret over the heads of my wife and her daughter?" thundered Belding.

He had his answer in the gray faces, in the lips that fear made mute. Like a flash Belding saw the whole truth of Mrs. Belding's agony, the reason for her departure; he saw what had been driving Nell; and it seemed that all the dogs of hell were loosed within his heart. He struck out blindly, instinctively in his pain, and the blow sent Ben Chase staggering into the fence corner. Then he stretched forth a long arm and whirled Radford Chase back beside his father.

"I see it all now," went on Belding, hoarsely. "You found the woman's weakness—her love for the girl. You found the girl's weakness—her pride and fear of shame. So you drove the one and hounded the other. God, what a base thing to do! To *tell* the girl was bad enough, but to *threaten* her with betrayal; there's no name for that!"

Belding's voice thickened, and he paused, breathing heavily. He stepped back a few paces; and this, an ominous action for an armed man of his kind, instead of adding to the fear of the Chases, seemed to relieve them. If there had been any pity in Belding's heart he would have felt it then.

"And now, gentlemen," continued Belding, speaking low and with difficulty, "seeing I've turned down your proposition, I suppose you think you've no more call to keep your mouths shut?"

The elder Chase appeared fascinated by something he either saw or felt in Belding, and his gray face grew grayer. He put up a shaking hand. Then Radford Chase, livid and snarling, burst out: "I'll talk till I'm black in the face. You can't stop me!"

"You'll go black in the face, but it won't be from talking," hissed Belding.

His big arm swept down, and when he threw it up the gun glittered in his hand. Simultaneously with the latter action pealed out a shrill, penetrating whistle.

The whistle of a horse! It froze Belding's arm aloft. For an instant he could not move even his eyes. The familiarity of that whistle was terrible in its power to rob him of strength. Then he heard the rapid, heavy pound of hoofs, and again the piercing whistle.

"Blanco Diablo!" he cried, huskily.

He turned to see a huge white horse come thundering into the yard. A wild, gaunt, terrible horse; indeed, the loved Blanco Diablo. A bronzed, long-haired Indian bestrode him. More white horses galloped into the yard, pounded to a halt, whistling home. Belding saw a slim shadow of a girl who seemed all great black eyes.

Under the trees flashed Blanco Sol, as dazzling white, as beautiful as if he had never been lost in the desert. He slid to a halt, then plunged and stamped. His rider leaped, throwing the bridle. Belding saw a powerful, spare, ragged man, with dark, gaunt face and eyes of flame.

Then Nell came running from the house, her golden hair flying, her hands outstretched, her face wonderful.

"Dick! Dick! Oh-h-h, Dick!" she cried. Her voice seemed to quiver in Belding's heart.

Belding's eyes began to blur. He was not sure he saw clearly. Whose face was this now close before him—a long thin, shrunken face, haggard, tragic in its semblance of torture, almost of death? But the eyes were keen and kind. Belding thought wildly that they proved he was not dreaming.

"I shore am glad to see you all," said a well-remembered voice in a slow, cool drawl.

CHAPTER 18

REALITY AGAINST DREAMS

Ladd, Lash, Thorne, Mercedes, they were all held tight in Belding's arms. Then he ran to Blanco Diablo. For once the great horse was gentle, quiet, glad. He remembered this kindest of masters and reached for him with warm, wet muzzle.

Dick Gale was standing bowed over Nell's slight form, almost hidden in his arms. Belding hugged them both. He was like a boy. He saw Ben Chase and his son slip away under the trees, but the circumstance meant nothing to him then.

"Dick! Dick!" he roared. "Is it you? . . . Say, who do you think's here—here, in Forlorn River?"

Gale gripped Belding with a hand as rough and hard as a file and as strong as a vise. But he did not speak a word. Belding thought Gale's eyes would haunt him forever.

It was then three more persons came upon the scene—
Elsie Gale, running swiftly, her father assisting Mrs. Gale,
who appeared about to faint.

"Belding! Who on earth's that?" cried Dick, hoarsely.

"Quién sabe, my son," replied Belding; and now his
voice seemed a little shaky. "Nell, come here. Give him a
chance."

Belding slipped his arm round Nell, and whispered in
her ear. "This'll be great!"

Elsie Gale's face was white and agitated, a face express-
ing extreme joy.

"Oh, Brother! Mama saw you—Papa saw you, and
never knew you! But I knew you when you jumped
quick—that way—off your horse. And now I don't know
you. You wild man! You giant! You splendid barbarian! . . . Mama, Papa, hurry! It *is* Dick! Look at him. Just
look at him! Oh-h, thank God!"

Belding turned away and drew Nell with him. In
another second she and Mercedes were clasped in each
other's arms. Then followed a time of joyful greetings all
round.

The Yaqui stood leaning against a tree watching the
welcoming home of the lost. No one seemed to think of
him, until Belding, ever mindful of the needs of horses,
put a hand on Blanco Diablo and called to Yaqui to bring
the others. They led the string of whites down to the
barn, freed them of wet and dusty saddles and packs, and
turned them loose in the alfalfa, now breast-high. Diablo
found his old spirit; Blanco Sol tossed his head and
whistled his satisfaction; White Woman pranced to and
fro; and presently they all settled down to quiet grazing.
How good it was for Belding to see those white shapes

against the rich background of green! His eyes glistened. It was a sight he had never expected to see again. He lingered there many moments when he wanted to hurry back to his rangers.

At last he tore himself away from watching Blanco Diablo and returned to the house. It was only to find that he might have spared himself the hurry. Jim and Ladd were lying on the beds that had not held them for so many months. Their slumber seemed as deep and quiet as death. Curiously Belding gazed down upon them. They had removed only boots and chaps. Their clothes were in tatters. Jim appeared little more than skin and bones, a long shape, dark and hard as iron. Ladd's appearance shocked Belding. The ranger looked an old man, blasted, shriveled, starved. Yet his gaunt face, though terrible in its records of tortures, had something fine and noble, even beautiful to Belding, in its strength, its victory.

Thorne and Mercedes had disappeared. The low murmur of voices came from Mrs. Gale's room, and Belding concluded that Dick was still with his family. No doubt he, also, would soon seek rest and sleep. Belding went through the patio and called in at Nell's door. She was there sitting by her window. The flush of happiness had not left her face, but she looked stunned, and a shadow of fear lay dark in her eyes. Belding had intended to talk. He wanted someone to listen to him. The expression in Nell's eyes, however, silenced him. He had forgotten. Nell read his thought in his face, and then she lost all her color and dropped her head. Belding entered, stood beside her with a hand on hers. He tried desperately hard to think of the right thing to say, and realized so long as he tried that he could not speak at all.

"Nell—Dick's back safe and sound," he said, slowly. "That's the main thing. I wish you could have seen his eyes when he held you in his arms out there. . . . Of course, Dick's coming knocks out your trip East and changes plans generally. We haven't had the happiest time lately. But now it'll all be different. Dick's as true as a Yaqui. He'll chase that Chase fellow, don't mistake me. . . . Then Mother will be home soon. She'll straighten out this—this mystery. And Nell—however it turns out—I know Dick Gale will feel just the same as I feel. Brace up now, girl."

Belding left the patio and traced thoughtful steps back toward the corrals. He realized the need of his wife. If she had been at home he would not have come so close to killing two men. Nell would never have fallen so low in spirit. Whatever the real truth of the tragedy of his wife's life, it would not make the slightest difference to him. What hurt him was the pain mother and daughter had suffered, were suffering still. Somehow he must put an end to that pain.

He found the Yaqui curled up in a corner of the barn in as deep a sleep as that of the rangers. Looking down at him, Belding felt again the rush of curious thrilling eagerness to learn all that had happened since the dark night when Yaqui had led the white horses away into the desert. Belding curbed his impatience and set to work upon tasks he had long neglected. Presently he was interrupted by Mr. Gale, who came out, beside himself with happiness and excitement. He flung a hundred questions at Belding and never gave him time to answer one, even if that had been possible. Finally, when Mr. Gale lost his breath, Belding got a word in. "See here, Mr. Gale, you know as much as I know. Dick's back. They're all back—a hard lot, starved, burned, torn to pieces, worked out to the limit I never saw in desert travelers, but they're alive—alive and well, man! Just wait. Just gamble I won't sleep or eat till I hear that story. But *they've* got to sleep and eat."

Belding gathered with growing amusement that besides the joy, excitement, anxiety, impatience expressed by Mr. Gale there was something else which Belding took for pride. It pleased him. Looking back, he remembered some of the things Dick had confessed his father thought of him. Belding's sympathy had always been with the boy. But he had learned to like the old man, to find him kind and wise, and to think that perhaps college and business had not brought out the best in Richard Gale. The West had done that, however, as it had for many a wild youngster; and Belding resolved to have a little fun at the expense of Mr. Gale. So he began by making a few remarks that appeared to rob Dick's father of both speech and breath.

"And don't mistake me," concluded Belding, "just keep out of earshot when Laddy tells us the story of that desert trip, unless you're hankering to have your hair turn *pure* white and stand *curled* on end *and freeze* that way."

A bout the middle of the forenoon on the following day the rangers hobbled out of the kitchen to the porch.

"I'm a sick man, I tell you," Ladd was complaining, "an' I gotta be fed. Soup! Beef tea! That ain't so much as wind to me. I want about a barrel of bread an' butter, an' a whole platter of mashed potatoes with gravy an' green stuff—all kinds of green stuff—an' a whole big apple pie. Give me everythin' an' anythin' to eat but meat. Shore I never, never want to taste meat again, an' sight of a piece of sheep meat would jest about finish me. . . . Jim, you used to be a human bein' that stood up for Charlie Ladd."

"Laddy, I'm lined up beside you with both guns," replied Jim, plaintively. "Hungry? Say, the smell of breakfast in that kitchen made my mouth water so I near choked to death. I reckon we're gettin' most onhuman treatment."

"But I'm a sick man," protested Ladd, "an' I'm agoin' to fall over in a minute if somebody doesn't feed me. Nell, you *used* to be fond of me."

"Oh, Laddy, I am yet," replied Nell.

"Shore I don't believe it. Any girl with a tender heart just couldn't let a man starve under her eyes. . . . Look at Dick, there. I'll bet he's had something to eat, mebbe potatoes an' gravy, an' pie an'—"

"Laddy, Dick has had no more than I gave you—indeed, not nearly so much."

"Shore he's had a lot of kisses then, for he hasn't hollered onct about this treatment."

"Perhaps he has," said Nell, with a blush; "and if you think that—they would help you to be reasonable I might—I'll—"

"Well, powerful fond as I am of you, just now kisses'll have to run second to bread an' butter."

"Oh, Laddy, what a gallant speech!" laughed Nell. "I'm sorry, but I've Dad's orders."

"Laddy," interrupted Belding, "you've got to be broke in gradually to eating. Now you know that. You'd be the severest kind of a boss if you had some starved beggars on your hands."

"But I'm sick—I'm dyin'," howled Ladd.

"You were never sick in your life, and if all the bullet-holes I see in you couldn't kill you, why, you never will die."

"Can I smoke?" queried Ladd, with sudden animation. "My Gawd, I used to smoke. Shore I've forgot. Nell, if you want to be reinstated in my gallery of angels, just find me a pipe an' tobacco."

"I've hung onto my pipe," said Jim, thoughtfully. "I reckon I had it empty in my mouth for seven years or so, wasn't it, Laddy? A long time! I can see the red lava an' the red haze, an' the red twilight creepin' up. It was hot an' some lonely. Then the wind, and always that awful silence! An' always Yaqui watchin' the west, an' Laddy with his checkers, an' Mercedes burnin' up, wastin' away to nothin' but eyes! It's all there—I'll never get rid—"

"Chop that kind of talk," interrupted Belding, bluntly. "Tell us where Yaqui took you—what happened to Rojas—why you seemed lost for so long."

"I reckon Laddy can tell all that best; but when it comes to Rojas's finish I'll tell what I seen, an' so'll Dick an' Thorne. Laddy missed Rojas's finish. Bar none, that was the—"

"I'm a sick man, but I can talk," put in Ladd, "an' shore I don't want the whole story exaggerated none by Jim."

Ladd filled the pipe Nell brought, puffed ecstatically at it, and settled himself upon the bench for a long talk. Nell glanced appealingly at Dick, who tried to slip away. Mercedes did go, and was followed by Thorne. Mr. Gale brought chairs, and in subdued excitement called his wife and daughter. Belding leaned forward, rendered all the more eager by Dick's reluctance to stay, the memory of the quick tragic change in the expression of Mercedes's beautiful eyes, by the strange gloomy cast stealing over Ladd's face.

The ranger talked for two hours—talked till his voice weakened to a husky whisper. At the conclusion of his story there was an impressive silence. Then Elsie Gale stood up, and with her hand on Dick's shoulder, her eyes bright and warm as sunlight, she showed the rangers what a woman thought of them and of the Yaqui. Nell clung to Dick, weeping silently. Mrs. Gale was overcome, and Mr. Gale, very white and quiet, helped her up to her room.

"The Indian! the Indian!" burst out Belding, his voice deep and rolling. "What did I tell you? Didn't I say he'd be a godsend? Remember what I said about Yaqui and some gory Aztec knife work? So he cut Rojas loose from that awful crater wall, foot by foot, finger by finger, slow and terrible? And Rojas didn't hang long on the *cholla* thorns? Thank the Lord for that! . . . Laddy, no story of Camino del Diablo can hold a candle to yours. The flight and the fight were jobs for men. But living through this long hot summer and coming out—that's a miracle. Only the Yaqui could have done it. The Yaqui! the Yaqui!"

"Shore. Charlie Ladd looks up at an Indian these days. But Beldin', as for the comin' out, don't forget the hosses. Without grand old Sol an' Diablo, who I don't hate no more, an' the other Blancos, we'd never have got here. Yaqui *an'* the hosses, that's my story!"

E arly in the afternoon of the next day Belding encountered Dick at the water barrel.

"Belding, this is river water, and muddy at that," said Dick. "Lord knows I'm not kicking. But I've dreamed some of our cool running spring, and I want a drink from it."

"Never again, son. The spring's gone, faded, sunk, dry as dust."

"Dry!" Gale slowly straightened. "We've had rains. The

river's full. The spring ought to be overflowing. What's wrong? Why is it dry?"

"Dick, seeing you're interested, I may as well tell you that a big charge of nitroglycerin choked my spring."

"Nitroglycerin?" echoed Gale. Then he gave a quick start. "My mind's been on home, Nell, my family. But all the same I felt something was wrong here with the ranch, with you, with Nell. . . . Belding, that ditch there is dry. The roses are dead. The little green in that grass has come with the rains. What's happened? The ranch's run down. Now I look around I see a change."

"Some change, yes," replied Belding, bitterly. "Listen, son."

Briefly, but not the less forcibly for that, Belding related his story of the operations of the Chases.

Astonishment appeared to be Gale's first feeling. "Our water gone, our claims gone, our plans forestalled! Why, Belding, it's unbelievable. Forlorn River with promoters, business, railroad, bank, and whatnot!"

Suddenly he became fiery and suspicious. "These Chases—did they do all this on the level?"

"Barefaced robbery! Worse than a Greaser holdup," replied Belding, grimly.

"You say the law upheld them?"

"Sure. Why, Ben Chase has a pull as strong as Diablo's on a downgrade. Dick, we're jobbed, outfigured, beat, tricked, and we can't do a thing."

"Oh, I'm sorry, Belding, most of all for Laddy," said Gale, feelingly. "He's all in. He'll never ride again. He wanted to settle down here on the farm he thought he owned, grow grass and raise horses, and take it easy. Oh, but it's tough! Say, he doesn't know it yet. He was just telling me he'd like to go out and look the farm over. Who's going to tell him? What's he going to do when he finds out about this deal?"

"Son, that's made me think some," replied Belding, with keen eyes fast upon the young man. "And I was kind of wondering how you'd take it."

"I? Well, I'll call on the Chases. Look here, Belding, I'd better do some forestalling myself. If Laddy gets started now there'll be blood spilled. He's not just right in his mind yet. He talks in his sleep sometimes about how Yaqui finished Rojas. If it's left to him—he'll kill these men. But if I take it up—"

"You're talking sense, Dick. Only here, I'm not so sure of you. And there's more to tell. Son, you've Nell to think of, and your mother."

Belding's ranger gave him a long and searching glance.

"You can be sure of me," he said.

"All right, then; listen," began Belding. With deep voice that had many a break and tremor he told Gale how Nell had been hounded by Radford Chase, how her mother had been driven by Ben Chase—the whole sad story.

"So that's the trouble! Poor little girl!" murmured Gale, brokenly. "I felt something was wrong. Nell wasn't natural, like her old self. And when I begged her to marry me soon, while Dad was here, she couldn't talk. She could only cry."

"It *was* hard on Nell," said Belding, simply. "But it'll be better now you're back. Dick, I know the girl. She'll refuse to marry you, and you'll have a hard job to break her down, as hard as the one you just rode in off of. I think I know you, too, or I wouldn't be saying—"

"Belding, what're you hinting at?" demanded Gale. "Do you dare insinuate that—that—if the thing were true it'd make any difference to me?"

"Aw, come now, Dick; I couldn't mean that. I'm only awkward at saying things. And I'm cut pretty deep—"

"For God's sake, you don't *believe* what Chase said?" queried Gale, in passionate haste. "It's a lie. I swear it's a lie. I know it's a lie. And I've got to tell Nell this minute. Come on in with me. I want you, Belding. Oh, why didn't you tell me sooner?"

Belding felt himself dragged by an iron arm into the sitting-room, out into the patio, and across that to where Nell sat in her door. At sight of them she gave a little cry, drooped for an instant, then raised a pale, still face, with eyes beginning to darken.

"Dearest, I know now why you are not wearing my mother's ring," said Gale, steadily and low-voiced.

"Dick, I am not worthy," she replied, and held out a trembling hand with the ring lying in the palm.

Swift as light Gale caught her hand and slipped the ring back upon the third finger.

"Nell! Look at me. It is your engagement ring. . . . Listen. I don't believe this—this that's been torturing you. I know it's a lie. I am absolutely sure your mother will prove it a lie. She must have suffered once—perhaps there was a sad error—but the thing you fear is not true. But, hear me, dearest; even if it *was* true it wouldn't make the slightest difference to me. I'd promise you on my honor I'd never think of it again. I'd love you all the more because you'd suffered. I want you all the more to be my wife—to let me make you forget—to—"

She rose swiftly with the passionate abandon of a woman stirred to her depths, and she kissed him.

"Oh, Dick, you're good—so good! You'll never know—just what those words mean to me. They've saved me—I think."

"Then, dearest, it's all right?" Dick questioned, eagerly. "You will keep your promise? You will marry me?"

The glow, the light faded out of her face, and now the blue eyes were almost black. She drooped and shook her head.

"Nell!" exclaimed Gale, sharply catching his breath.

"Don't ask me, Dick. I—I won't marry you."

"Why?"

"You know. It's true that I—"

"It's a lie," interrupted Gale, fiercely. "But even if it's true—why—why won't you marry me? Between you and me love is the thing. Love, and nothing else! Don't you love me any more?"

They had forgotten Belding, who stepped back into the shade.

"I love you with my whole heart and soul. I'd die for you," whispered Nell, with clenching hands. "But I won't disgrace you."

"Dear, you have worried over this trouble till you're morbid. It has grown out of all proportion. I tell you that I'll not only be the happiest man on earth, but the luckiest, if you marry me."

"Dick, you give not one thought to your family. Would they receive me as your wife?"

"They surely would," replied Gale, steadily.

"No! Oh no!"

"You're wrong, Nell. I'm glad you said that. You give me a chance to prove something. I'll go this minute and tell them all. I'll be back here in less than—"

"Dick, you will not tell her—your mother?" cried Nell, with her eyes streaming. "You will not? Oh, I can't bear it! She's so proud! And Dick, I love her. Don't tell her!

Please, please don't! She'll be going soon. She needn't ever know—about me. I want her always to think well of me. Dick, I beg of you. Oh, the fear of her knowing has been the worst of all! Please don't go!"

"Nell, I'm sorry. I hate to hurt you. But you're wrong. You can't see things clearly. This is your happiness I'm fighting for. And it's my life. . . . Wait here, dear. I won't be long."

Gale ran across the patio and disappeared. Nell sank to the doorstep, and as she met the question in Belding's eyes she shook her head mournfully. They waited without speaking. It seemed a long while before Gale returned. Belding thrilled at sight of him. There was more boy about him than Belding had ever seen. Dick was coming swiftly, flushed, glowing, eager, erect, almost smiling.

"I told them. I swore it was a lie, but I wanted them to decide as if it were true. I didn't have to waste a minute on Elsie. She loves you, Nell. The governor is crazy about you. I didn't have to waste two minutes on him. Mother used up the time. She wanted to know all there was to tell. She is proud, yes; but, Nell, I wish you could have seen how she took the—the story about you. Why, she never thought of me at all, until she had cried over you. Nell, she loves you, too. They all love you. Oh, it's so good to tell you. I think Mother realizes the part you have had in the—what shall I call it?—the regeneration of Richard Gale. Doesn't that sound fine? Darling, Mother not only consents, she wants you to be my wife. Do you hear that? And listen—she had me in a corner and, of course, being my mother, she put on the screws. She made me promise that we'd live in the East half the year. That means Chicago, Cape May, New York—you see, I'm not exactly the lost son any more. Why, Nell, dear, you'll have to learn who Dick Gale really is. But I always want to be the ranger you helped me become, and ride Blanco Sol, and see a little of the desert. Don't let the idea of big cities frighten you. We'll always love the open places best. Now, Nell, say you'll forget this trouble. I know it'll come all right. Say you'll marry me soon. . . . Why, dearest, you're crying . . . Nell!"

"My—heart—is broken," sobbed Nell, "for—I—I can't marry you."

The boyish brightness faded out of Gale's face. Here, Belding saw, was the stern reality arrayed against his dreams.

"That devil Radford Chase—he'll tell my secret," panted Nell. "He swore if you ever came back and married me he'd follow us all over the world to tell it."

Belding saw Gale grow deathly white and suddenly stand stock-still.

"Chase threatened you, then?" asked Dick; and the forced naturalness of his voice struck Belding.

"Threatened me? He made my life a nightmare," replied Nell, in a rush of speech. "At first I wondered how he was worrying Mother sick. But she wouldn't tell me. Then when she went away he began to hint things. I hated him all the more. But when he told me—I was frightened, shamed. Still I did not weaken. He was pretty decent when he was sober. But when he was half drunk he was a devil. He laughed at me and my pride. I didn't dare shut the door in his face. After a while he found out that your mother loved me and that I loved her. Then he began to threaten me. If I didn't give in to him he'd see she learned the truth. That made me weaken. It nearly killed me. I simply could not bear the thought of Mrs. Gale knowing. But I couldn't marry him. Besides, he got so half the time, when he was drunk, he didn't want or ask me to be his wife. I was about ready to give up and go mad when you—you came home."

She ended in a whisper, looking up wistfully and sadly at him. Belding was a raging fire within, cold without. He watched Gale, and believed he could foretell that young man's future conduct. Gale gathered Nell up into his arms and held her to his breast for a long moment.

"Dear Nell, I'm sure the worst of your trouble is over," he said, gently. "I *will* not give you up. Now, won't you lie down, try to rest and calm yourself? Don't grieve any more. This thing isn't so bad as you make it. Trust me. I'll shut Mr. Radford Chase's mouth."

As he released her she glanced quickly up at him, then lifted appealing hands.

"Dick, you won't hunt for him—go after him?"

Gale laughed, and the laugh made Belding jump.

"Dick, I beg of you. Please don't make trouble. The Chases have been hard enough on us. They are rich, powerful. Dick, say you will not make matters worse. Please promise me you'll not go to him."

"You ask me that?" he demanded.

"Yes. Oh yes!"

"But you know it's useless. What kind of a man do you want me to be?"

"It's only that I'm afraid. Oh, Dick, he'd shoot you in the back."

"No, Nell, a man of his kind wouldn't have nerve enough even for that."

"You'll go?" she cried, wildly.

Gale smiled, and the smile made Belding cold.

"Dick, I cannot keep you back?"

"No," he said.

Then the woman in her burst through instinctive fear, and with her eyes blazing black in her white face she lifted parted quivering lips and kissed him.

Gale left the patio, and Belding followed closely at his heels. They went through the sitting room. Outside upon the porch sat the rangers, Mr. Gale, and Thorne. Dick went into his room without speaking.

"Shore somethin's comin' off," said Ladd, sharply; and he sat up with his keen eyes narrowing.

Belding spoke a few words; and, remembering an impression he had wished to make upon Mr. Gale, he made them strong. But now it was with a grim humor that he spoke.

"Better stop that boy," he concluded, looking at Mr. Gale. "He'll do some mischief. He's wilder'n hell."

"Stop him? Why, assuredly," replied Mr. Gale, rising with nervous haste.

Just then Dick came out of his door. Belding eyed him keenly. The only change he could see was that Dick had put on a hat and a pair of heavy gloves.

"Richard, where are you going?" asked his father.

"I'm going over here to see a man."

"No. It is my wish that you remain. I forbid you to go," said Mr. Gale, with a hand on his son's shoulder.

Dick put Mr. Gale aside gently, respectfully, yet forcibly. The old man gasped.

"Dad, I haven't gotten over my bad habit of disobeying you. I'm sorry. Don't interfere with me now. And don't follow me. You might see something unpleasant."

"But my son! What are you going to do?"

"I'm going to beat a dog."

Mr. Gale looked helplessly from this strangely calm and cold son to the restless Belding. Then Dick strode off the porch.

"Hold on!" Ladd's voice would have stopped almost any man. "Dick, you wasn't agoin' without me?"

"Yes, I was. But I'm thoughtless just now, Laddy."

"Shore you was. Wait a minute, Dick. I'm a sick man, but at that nobody can pull any stunts round here without me."

He hobbled along the porch and went into his room. Jim Lash knocked the ashes out of his pipe, and, humming his dance tune, he followed Ladd. In a moment the rangers appeared, and both were packing guns.

Not a little of Belding's grim excitement came from observation of Mr. Gale. At sight of the rangers with their guns the old man turned white and began to tremble.

"Better stay behind," whispered Belding. "Dick's going to beat that two-legged dog, and the rangers get excited when they're packing guns."

"I will not stay behind," replied Mr. Gale, stoutly. "I'll see this affair through. Belding, I've guessed it. Richard is going to fight the Chases, those robbers who have ruined you."

"Well, I can't guarantee any fight on *their* side," returned Belding, dryly. "But maybe there'll be Greasers with a gun or two."

Belding stalked off to catch up with Dick, and Mr. Gale came trudging behind with Thorne.

"Where will we find these Chases?" asked Dick of Belding.

"They've got a place down the road adjoining the inn. They call it their club. At this hour Radford will be there sure. I don't know about the old man. But his office is now just across the way."

They passed several houses, turned a corner into the main street, and stopped at a wide, low adobe structure. A number of saddled horses stood haltered to posts. Mexicans lolled around the wide doorway.

"There's Ben Chase now over on the corner," said Belding to Dick. "See, the tall man with the white hair, and leather band on his hat. He sees us. He knows there's something up. He's got men with him. They'll come over. We're after the young buck, and sure he'll be in here."

They entered. The place was a hall, and needed only a bar to make it a saloon. There were two rickety pool tables. Evidently Chase had fitted up this amusement room for his laborers as well as for the use of his engineers and assistants, for the crowd contained both Mexicans and Americans. A large table near a window was surrounded by a noisy, smoking, drinking circle of card-players.

"Point out this Radford Chase to me," said Gale.

"There! The big fellow with the red face. His eyes stick out a little. See! He's dropped his cards and his face isn't red any more."

Dick strode across the room.

Belding grasped Mr. Gale and whispered hoarsely: "Don't miss anything. It'll be great. Watch Dick and watch Laddy! If there's any gun play, dodge behind me."

Belding smiled with a grim pleasure as he saw Mr. Gale's face turn white.

Dick halted beside the table. His heavy boot shot up, and with a crash the table split, and glasses, cards, chips flew everywhere. As they rattled down and the chairs of the dumbfounded players began to slide Dick called out: "My name is Gale. I'm looking for Mr. Radford Chase."

A tall, heavy-shouldered fellow rose, boldly enough, even swaggeringly, and glowered at Gale.

"I'm Radford Chase," he said. His voice betrayed the boldness of his action.

I t was over in a few moments. The tables and chairs were tumbled into a heap; one of the pool tables had been shoved aside; a lamp lay shattered, with oil running dark upon the floor. Ladd leaned against a post with a smoking gun in his hand. A Mexican crouched close to the wall moaning over a broken arm. In the far corner upheld by comrades another wounded Mexican cried out in pain. These two had attempted to draw weapons upon Gale, and Ladd had crippled them.

In the center of the room lay Radford Chase, a limp, torn, hulking, bloody figure. He was not seriously injured. But he was helpless, a miserable beaten wretch, who knew his condition and felt the eyes upon him. He sobbed and moaned and howled. But no one offered to help him to his feet.

Backed against the door of the hall stood Ben Chase, for once stripped of all authority and confidence and courage. Gale confronted him, and now Gale's mien was in striking contrast to the coolness with which he had entered the place. Though sweat dripped from his face, it was white as chalk. Like dark flames his eyes seemed to leap and dance and burn. His lean jaw hung down and quivered with passion. He shook a huge gloved fist in Chase's face.

"Your gray hairs save you this time. But keep out of my way! And when that son of yours comes to, tell him every time I meet him I'll add some more to what he got today!"

CHAPTER 19

THE SECRET OF
FORLORN RIVER

In the early morning Gale, seeking solitude where he
could brood over his trouble, wandered alone. It was
not easy for him to elude the Yaqui, and just at the moment when he had cast himself down in a secluded shady
corner the Indian appeared, noiseless, shadowy, mysterious as always.

"*Malo,*" he said, in his deep voice.

"Yes, Yaqui, it's bad—very bad," replied Gale.

The Indian had been told of the losses sustained by
Belding and his rangers.

"Go—me!" said Yaqui, with an impressive gesture toward the lofty lilac-colored steps of No Name Mountains.

He seemed the same as usual, but a glance on Gale's
part, a moment's attention, made him conscious of the old
strange force in the Yaqui.

"Why does my brother want me to climb the nameless
mountains with him?" asked Gale.

"Lluvia d'oro," replied Yaqui, and he made motions that Gale found difficult of interpretation.

"Shower of Gold," translated Gale. That was the Yaqui's name for Nell. What did he mean by using it in connection with a climb into the mountains? Were his motions intended to convey an idea of a shower of golden blossoms from that rare and beautiful tree, or a golden rain? Gale's listlessness vanished in a flash of thought. The Yaqui meant gold. Gold! He meant he could retrieve the fallen fortunes of the white brother who had saved his life that evil day at the Papago Well. Gale thrilled as he gazed piercingly into the wonderful eyes of this Indian. Would Yaqui never consider his debt paid?

"Go—me?" repeated the Indian, pointing with the singular directness that always made this action remarkable in him.

"Yes, Yaqui."

Gale ran to his room, put on hobnailed boots, filled a canteen, and hurried back to the corral. Yaqui awaited him. The Indian carried a coiled lasso and a short stout stick. Without a word he led the way down the lane, turned up the river toward the mountains. None of Belding's household saw their departure.

What had once been only a narrow mesquite-bordered trail was now a well-trodden road. A deep irrigation ditch, full of flowing muddy water, ran parallel with the road. Gale had been curious about the operations of the Chases, but a bitterness he could not help had kept him from going out to see the work. He was not surprised to find that the engineers who had constructed the ditches and dam had anticipated him in every particular. The dammed-up gulch made a magnificent reservoir, and Gale could not look upon the long narrow lake without a feeling of gladness.

The dreaded *año seco* of the Mexicans might come again and would come, but never to the inhabitants of Forlorn River. That stonewalled, stone-floored gulch would never leak, and already it contained water enough to irrigate the whole of Altar Valley for two dry seasons.

Yaqui led swiftly along the lake to the upper end, where the stream roared down over unscalable walls. This point was the farthest Gale had ever penetrated into the rough foothills, and he had Belding's word for it that no white man had ever climbed No Name Mountains from the west.

But a white man was not an Indian. The former might have stolen the range and valley and mountain, even the desert, but his possessions would ever remain mysteries. Gale had scarcely faced the great gray ponderous wall of cliff before the old strange interest in the Yaqui seized him again. It recalled the tie that existed between them, a tie almost as close as blood. Then he was eager and curious to see how the Indian would conquer those seemingly insurmountable steps of stone.

Yaqui left the gulch and clambered up over a jumble of weathered slides and traced a slow course along the base of the giant wall. He looked up and seemed to select a point for ascent. It was the last place in that mountainside where Gale would have thought climbing possible. Before him the wall rose, leaning over him, shutting out the light, a dark mighty mountain mass. Innumerable cracks and crevices and caves roughened the bulging sides of dark rock.

Yaqui tied one end of his lasso to the short, stout stick and, carefully disentangling the coils, he whirled the stick round and round and threw it almost over the first rim of the shelf, perhaps thirty feet up. The stick did not lodge.

Yaqui tried again. This time it caught in a crack. He pulled hard. Then, holding to the lasso, he walked up the steep slant, hand over hand on the rope. When he reached the shelf he motioned for Gale to follow. Gale found that method of scaling a wall both quick and easy. Yaqui pulled up the lasso and threw the stick aloft into another crack. He climbed to another shelf, and Gale followed him. The third effort brought them to a more rugged bench a hundred feet above the slides. The Yaqui worked round to the left and turned into a dark fissure. Gale kept close at his heels. They came out presently into lighter space, yet one that restricted any extended view. Broken sections of cliff were on all sides.

Here the ascent became toil. Gale could distance Yaqui going downhill; on the climb, however, he was hard put to it to keep the Indian in sight. It was not a question of strength or lightness of foot. These Gale had beyond the share of most men. It was a matter of lung power, and the Yaqui's life had been spent scaling the desert heights. Moreover, the climbing was infinitely slow, tedious, dangerous. On the way up several times Gale imagined he heard a dull roar of falling water. The sound seemed to be under him, over him, to this side and to that. When he was certain he could locate the direction from which it came then he heard it no more until he had gone on. Gradually he forgot it in the physical sensations of the climb. He burned his hands and knees. He grew hot and wet and winded. His heart thumped so that it hurt, and there were instants when his sight was blurred. When at last he had toiled to where the Yaqui sat awaiting him upon the rim of that great wall, it was none too soon.

Gale lay back and rested for a while without note of anything except the blue sky. Then he sat up. He was amazed to find that after that wonderful climb he was only a thousand feet or so above the valley. Judged by the nature of his effort, he would have said he had climbed a mile. The village lay beneath him, with its new adobe structures and tents and buildings in bright contrast with the older habitations. He saw the green alfalfa fields, and Belding's white horses, looking very small and motionless. He pleased himself by imagining he could pick out Blanco Sol. Then his gaze swept on to the river.

Indeed, he realized now why someone had named it Forlorn River. Even at this season when it was full of water it had a forlorn aspect. It was doomed to fail out there on the desert—doomed never to mingle with the waters of the Gulf. It wound away down the valley, growing wider and shallower, encroaching more and more on the gray flats, until it disappeared on its sad journey toward Sonoyta. That vast shimmering, sun-governed waste recognized its life only at this flood season, and was already with parched tongue and insatiate fire licking and burning up its futile waters.

Yaqui put a hand on Gale's knee. It was a bronzed, scarred, powerful hand, always eloquent of meaning. The Indian was listening. His bent head, his strange dilating eyes, his rigid form, and that close-pressing hand, how these brought back to Gale the terrible lonely night hours on the lava!

"What do you hear, Yaqui?" asked Gale. He laughed a little at the mood that had come over him. But the sound of his voice did not break the spell. He did not want to speak again. He yielded to Yaqui's subtle nameless influence. He listened himself, heard nothing but the scream of an eagle. Often he wondered if the Indian could hear things that made no sound. Yaqui was beyond understanding.

Whatever the Indian had listened to or for, presently he satisfied himself, and, with a grunt that might mean anything, he rose and turned away from the rim. Gale followed, rested now and eager to go on. He saw that the great cliff they had climbed was only a stairway up to the huge looming dark bulk of the plateau above.

Suddenly he again heard the dull roar of falling water. It seemed to have cleared itself of muffled vibrations. Yaqui mounted a little ridge and halted. The next instant Gale stood above a bottomless cleft into which a white stream leaped. His astounded gaze swept backward along this narrow swift stream to its end in a dark, round, boiling pool. It was a huge spring, a bubbling well, the outcropping of an underground river coming down from the vast plateau above.

Yaqui had brought Gale to the source of Forlorn River.

Flashing thoughts in Gale's mind were no swifter than the thrills that ran over him. He would stake out a claim here and never be cheated out of it. Ditches on the benches and troughs on the steep walls would carry water down to the valley. Ben Chase had built a great dam which would be useless if Gale chose to turn Forlorn River from its natural course. The fountainhead of that mysterious desert river belonged to him.

His eagerness, his mounting passion, was checked by Yaqui's unusual action. The Indian showed wonder, hesitation, even reluctance. His strange eyes surveyed this boiling well as if they could not believe the sight they saw. Gale divined instantly that Yaqui had never before seen the source of Forlorn River. If he had ever ascended to this plateau, probably it had been to some other part, for the water was new to him. He stood gazing aloft at peaks, at lower ramparts of the mountain, and at nearer landmarks of prominence. Yaqui seemed at fault. He was not sure of his location.

Then he strode past the swirling pool of dark water and began to ascend a little slope that led up to a shelving cliff. Another object halted the Indian. It was a pile of stones, weathered, crumbled, fallen into ruin, but still retaining shape enough to prove it had been built there by the hands of men. Round and round this the Yaqui stalked, and his curiosity attested a further uncertainty. It was as if he had come upon something surprising. Gale wondered about the pile of stones. Had it once been a prospector's claim?

"Ugh!" grunted the Indian; and, though his exclamation expressed no satisfaction, it surely put an end to doubt. He pointed up to the roof of the sloping yellow shelf of stone. Faintly outlined there in red were the imprints of many human hands with fingers spread wide. Gale had often seen such paintings on the walls of the desert caverns. Manifestly these told Yaqui he had come to the spot for which he had aimed.

Then his actions became swift—and Yaqui seldom moved swiftly. The fact impressed Gale. The Indian searched the level floor under the shelf. He gathered up handfuls of small black stones, and he thrust them at Gale. Their weight made Gale start, and then he trembled. The Indian's next move was to pick up a piece of weathered rock and throw it against the wall. It broke. He snatched up parts, and showed the broken edges to Gale. They contained yellow streaks, dull glints, faint tracings of green. It was gold.

Gale found his legs shaking under him; and he sat down, trying to take all the bits of stone into his lap. His fingers were all thumbs as with knife blade he dug into the black pieces of rock. He found gold. Then he stared down the slope, down into the valley with its river winding forlornly away into the desert. But he did not see any of that. Here was reality as sweet, as wonderful, as saving as a dream come true. Yaqui had led him to a ledge of gold. Gale had learned enough about mineral to know that this was a rich strike. All in a second he was speechless with the joy of it. But his mind whirled in thought about this strange and noble Indian, who seemed never to be able to pay a debt. Belding and the poverty that had come to him! Nell, who had wept over the loss of a spring! Laddy, who never could ride again! Jim Lash, who swore he would always look after his friend! Thorne and Mercedes! All these people, who had been good to him and whom he loved, were poor. But now they would be rich. They would one and all be his partners. He had discovered the source of Forlorn River, and was rich in water. Yaqui had made him rich in gold. Gale wanted to rush down the slope, down into the valley, and tell his wonderful news.

Suddenly his eyes cleared and he saw the pile of stones. His blood turned to ice, then to fire. That was the mark of a prospector's claim. But it was old, very old. The ledge had never been worked. The slope was wild. There was not another single indication that a prospector had ever been there. Where, then, was he who had first staked this claim? Gale wondered with growing hope, with the fire easing, with the cold passing.

The Yaqui uttered the low, strange, involuntary cry so rare with him, a cry somehow always associated with death. Gale shuddered.

The Indian was digging in the sand and dust under the shelving wall. He threw out an object that rang against the stone. It was a belt buckle. He threw out old shrunken, withered boots. He came upon other things, and then he ceased to dig.

The grave of desert prospectors! Gale had seen more than one. Ladd had told him many a story of such gruesome finds. It was grim, hard fact.

Then the keen-eyed Yaqui reached up to a little projecting shelf of rock and took from it a small object. He showed no curiosity and gave the thing to Gale.

How strangely Gale felt when he received into his hands a flat oblong box! Was it only the influence of the Yaqui, or was there a nameless and unseen presence beside that grave? Gale could not be sure. But he knew he had gone back to the old desert mood. He knew something hung in the balance. No accident, no luck, no debt-paying Indian could account wholly for that moment. Gale knew he held in his hands more than gold.

The box was a tin one, and not at all rusty. Gale pried open the reluctant lid. A faint old musty odor penetrated his nostrils. Inside the box lay a packet wrapped in what once might have been oilskin. He took it out and removed this covering. A folded paper remained in his hands.

It was growing yellow with age. But he described a dim tracery of words. A crabbed scrawl, written in blood, hard to read! He held it more to the light, and slowly he deciphered its content.

"We, Robert Burton and Jonas Warren, give half of this gold claim to the man who finds it and half to Nell Burton, daughter and granddaughter."

Gasping, with a bursting heart, overwhelmed by an unutterable joy of divination, Gale fumbled with the paper until he got it open.

It was a certificate twenty-one years old, and recorded the marriage of Robert Burton and Nellie Warren.

CHAPTER 20

DESERT GOLD

A summer day dawned on Forlorn River, a beautiful, still, hot, golden day with huge sail clouds of white motionless over No Name Mountains and the purple of clear air in the distance along the desert horizon.

Mrs. Belding returned that day to find her daughter happy and the past buried forever in two lonely graves. The haunting shadow left her eyes. Gale believed he would never forget the sweetness, the wonder, the passion of her embrace when she called him her boy and gave him her blessing.

The little wrinkled padre who married Gale and Nell performed the ceremony as he told his beads, without interest or penetration, and went his way, leaving happiness behind.

"Shore I *was* a sick man," Ladd said, "an' darn near a dead one, but I'm agoin' to get well. Mebbe I'll be able to ride again some day. Nell, I lay it to you. An' I'm agoin' to kiss you an' wish you all the joy there is in this world. An' Dick, as Yaqui says, she's shore your Shower of Gold."

He spoke of Gale's finding love—spoke of it with the deep and wistful feeling of the lonely ranger who had always yearned for love and had never known it. Belding, once more practical, and important as never before with mining projects and water claims to manage, spoke of Gale's great good fortune in the finding of gold—he called it desert gold.

"Ah, yes. *Desert Gold!*" exclaimed Dick's father, softly, with eyes of pride. Perhaps he was glad Dick had found the rich claim; surely he was happy that Dick had won the girl he loved. But it seemed to Dick himself that his father meant something very different from love and fortune in his allusion to desert gold.

That beautiful happy day, like life or love itself, could not be wholly perfect.

Yaqui came to Dick to say good-by. Dick was startled, grieved, and in his impulsiveness forgot for a moment the nature of the Indian. Yaqui was not to be changed.

Belding tried to overload him with gifts. The Indian packed a bag of food, a blanket, a gun, a knife, a canteen, and no more. The whole household went out with him to the corrals and fields from which Belding bade him choose a horse—any horse, even the loved Blanco Diablo. Gale's heart was in his throat for fear the Indian might choose Blanco Sol, and Gale hated himself for a selfishness he could not help. But without a word he would have parted with the treasured Sol.

Yaqui whistled the horses up—for the last time. Did he care for them? It would have been hard to say. He never looked at the fierce and haughty Diablo, nor at Blanco Sol as he raised his noble head and rang his piercing blast. The Indian did not choose one of Belding's whites. He caught a lean and wiry broncho, strapped a blanket on him, and fastened on the pack.

Then he turned to these friends, the same emotionless, inscrutable dark and silent Indian that he had always been. This parting was nothing to him. He had stayed to pay a debt, and now he was going home.

He shook hands with the men, swept a dark fleeting glance over Nell, and rested his strange eyes upon Mercedes's beautiful and agitated face. It must have been a moment of intense feeling for the Spanish girl. She owed it to him that she had life and love and happiness. She held out those speaking slender hands. But Yaqui did not touch them. Turning away, he mounted the broncho and rode down the trail toward the river.

"He's going home," said Belding.

"*Home!*" whispered Ladd; and Dick knew the ranger had felt the resurging tide of memory. Home—across the cactus and lava, through solemn lonely days, the silent, lonely nights, into the vast and red-hazed world of desolation.

"Thorne, Mercedes, Nell, let's climb the foothill yonder and watch him out of sight," said Dick.

They climbed while the others returned to the house. When they reached the summit of the hill Yaqui was riding up the far bank of the river.

"He will turn to look—to wave good-by?" asked Nell.

"Dear, he is an Indian," replied Gale.

From that height they watched him ride through the mesquites, up over the river bank to enter the cactus. His mount showed dark against the green and white, and for a long time he was plainly in sight. The sun hung red in a golden sky. The last the watchers saw of Yaqui was when he rode across a ridge and stood silhouetted against the gold of desert sky—a wild, lonely, beautiful picture. Then he was gone.

Strangely it came to Gale then that he was glad. Yaqui had returned to his own—the great spaces, the desolation, the solitude—to the trails he had trodden when a child, trails haunted now by ghosts of his people, and ever by his gods. Gale realized that in the Yaqui he had known the spirit of the desert, that this spirit had claimed all which was wild and primitive in him.

Tears glistened in Mercedes's magnificent black eyes and Thorne kissed them away—kissed the fire back to them and the flame to her cheeks.

That action recalled Gale's earlier mood, the joy of the present, and he turned to Nell's sweet face. The desert was there, wonderful, constructive, ennobling, beautiful, terrible, but it was not for him as it was for the Indian. In the light of Nell's tremulous returning smile that strange, deep, clutching shadow faded, lost its hold forever; and he leaned close to her, whispering: *"Lluvia d'oro"*—"Shower of Gold."

THE LIGHT of WESTERN STARS

CHAPTER 1

A GENTLEMAN OF THE RANGE

When Madeline Hammond stepped from the train at El Cajon, New Mexico, it was nearly midnight, and her first impression was of a huge dark space of cool, windy emptiness, strange and silent, stretching away under great blinking white stars.

"Miss, there's no one to meet you," said the conductor, rather anxiously.

"I wired my brother," she replied. "The train being so late—perhaps he grew tired of waiting. He will be here presently. But, if he should not come—surely I can find a hotel?"

"There's lodgings to be had. Get the station agent to show you. If you'll excuse me—this is no place for a lady like you to be alone at night. It's a rough little town—mostly Mexicans, miners, cowboys. And they carouse a lot. Besides, the revolution across the border has stirred up some excitement along the line. Miss, I guess it's safe enough, if you—"

"Thank you. I am not in the least afraid."

As the train started to glide away Miss Hammond walked toward the dimly lighted station. As she was about to enter she encountered a Mexican with sombrero hiding his features and a blanket mantling his shoulders.

"Is there any one here to meet Miss Hammond?" she asked.

"*No sabe,* Señora," he replied from under the muffling blanket, and he shuffled away into the shadow.

She entered the empty waiting-room. An oil-lamp gave out a thick yellow light. The ticket window was open, and through it she saw there was neither agent nor operator in the little compartment. A telegraph instrument clicked faintly.

Madeline Hammond stood tapping a shapely foot on the floor, and with some amusement contrasted her reception in El Cajon with what it was when she left a train at the Grand Central. The only time she could remember ever having been alone like this was once when she had missed her maid and her train at a place outside of Versailles—an adventure that had been a novel and delightful break in the prescribed routine of her much-chaperoned life. She crossed the waiting-room to a window and, holding aside her veil, looked out. At first she could descry only a few dim lights, and these blurred in her sight. As her eyes grew accustomed to the darkness she saw a superbly built horse standing near the window. Beyond was a bare square. Or, if it was a street, it was the widest one Madeline had ever seen. The dim lights shone from low flat buildings. She made out the dark shapes of many horses, all standing motionless with drooping heads.

Through a hole in the window-glass came a cool breeze, and on it breathed a sound that struck coarsely upon her ear—a discordant mingling of laughter and shout, and the tramp of boots to the hard music of a phonograph.

"Western revelry," mused Miss Hammond, as she left the window. "Now, what to do? I'll wait here. Perhaps the station agent will return soon, or Alfred will come for me."

As she sat down to wait she reviewed the causes which accounted for the remarkable situation in which she found herself. That Madeline Hammond should be alone, at a late hour, in a dingy little Western railroad-station, was indeed extraordinary.

The close of her débutante year had been marred by the only unhappy experience of her life—the disgrace of her brother and his leaving home. She dated the beginning of a certain thoughtful habit of mind from that time, and a dissatisfaction with the brilliant life society offered her. The change had been so gradual that it was permanent before she realized it. For a while an active outdoor life— golf, tennis, yachting—kept this realization from becoming morbid introspection. There came a time when even these lost charm for her, and then she believed she was indeed ill in mind. Travel did not help her.

There had been months of unrest, of curiously painful wonderment that her position, her wealth, her popularity no longer sufficed. She believed she had lived through the dreams and fancies of a girl to become a woman of the world. And she had gone on as before, a part of the glittering show, but no longer blind to the truth—that there was nothing in her luxurious life to make it significant.

Sometimes from the depths of her there flashed up at odd moments intimations of a future revolt. She remembered one evening at the opera when the curtain had risen upon a particularly well-done piece of stage scenery—a broad space of deep desolateness, reaching away under an infinitude of night sky, illumined by stars. The suggestion it brought of vast wastes of lonely, rugged earth, of a great, blue-arched vault of starry sky, pervaded her soul with a strange, sweet peace.

When the scene was changed she lost this vague new sense of peace, and she turned away from the stage in irritation. She looked at the long, curved tier of glittering boxes that represented her world. It was a distinguished and splendid world—the wealth, fashion, culture, beauty, and blood of a nation. She, Madeline Hammond, was a part of it. She smiled, she listened, she talked to the men who from time to time strolled into the Hammond box, and she felt that there was not a moment when she was natural, true to herself. She wondered why these people could not somehow, some way be different; but she could not tell what she wanted them to be. If they had been different they would not have fitted the place; indeed, they would not have been there at all. Yet she thought wistfully that they lacked something for her.

And suddenly realizing she would marry one of these men if she did not revolt, she had been assailed by a great weariness, an icy-sickening sense that life had palled upon her. She was tired of fashionable society. She was tired of polished, imperturbable men who sought only to please her. She was tired of being fêted, admired, loved, followed, and importuned; tired of people; tired of houses, noise, ostentation, luxury. She was so tired of herself!

In the lonely distances and the passionless stars of boldly painted stage scenery she had caught a glimpse of something that stirred her soul. The feeling did not last.

She could not call it back. She imagined that the very boldness of the scene had appealed to her; she divined that the man who painted it had found inspiration, joy, strength, serenity in rugged nature. And at last she knew what she needed—to be alone, to brood for long hours, to gaze out on lonely, silent, darkening stretches, to watch the stars, to face her soul, to find her real self.

Then it was she had first thought of visiting the brother who had gone West to cast his fortune with the cattlemen. As it happened, she had friends who were on the eve of starting for California, and she made a quick decision to travel with them. When she calmly announced her intention of going out West her mother had exclaimed in consternation; and her father, surprised into pathetic memory of the black sheep of the family, had stared at her with glistening eyes. "Why, Madeline! You want to see that wild boy!" Then he had reverted to the anger he still felt for his wayward son, and he had forbidden Madeline to go. Her mother forgot her haughty poise and dignity. Madeline, however, had exhibited a will she had never before been known to possess. She stood her ground even to reminding them that she was twenty-four and her own mistress. In the end she had prevailed, and that without betraying the real state of her mind.

Her decision to visit her brother had been too hurriedly made and acted upon for her to write him about it, and so she had telegraphed him from New York, and also, a day later, from Chicago, where her traveling friends had been delayed by illness. Nothing could have turned her back then. Madeline had planned to arrive in El Cajon on October 3d, her brother's birthday, and she had succeeded, though her arrival occurred at the twenty-fourth hour. Her train had been several hours late. Whether or not the message had reached Alfred's hands she had no means of telling, and the thing which concerned her now was the fact that she had arrived and he was not there to meet her.

It did not take long for thought of the past to give way wholly to the reality of the present.

"I hope nothing has happened to Alfred," she said to herself. "He was well, doing splendidly, the last time he wrote. To be sure, that was a good while ago; but, then, he never wrote often. He's all right. Pretty soon he'll come, and how glad I'll be! I wonder if he has changed."

As Madeline sat waiting in the yellow gloom she heard the faint, intermittent click of the telegraph instrument, the low hum of wires, the occasional stamp of an iron-shod hoof, and a distant vacant laugh rising above the sounds of the dance. These commonplace things were new to her. She became conscious of a slight quickening of her pulse. Madeline had only a limited knowledge of the West. Like all of her class, she had traveled Europe and had neglected America. A few letters from her brother had confused her already vague ideas of plains and mountains, as well as of cowboys and cattle. She had been astounded at the interminable distance she had traveled, and if there had been anything attractive to look at in all that journey she had passed it in the night. And here she sat in a dingy little station, with telegraph wires moaning a lonely song in the wind.

A faint sound like the rattling of thin chains diverted Madeline's attention. At first she imagined it was made by the telegraph wires. Then she heard a step. The door swung wide; a tall man entered, and with him came the clinking rattle. She realized then that the sound came from his spurs. The man was a cowboy, and his entrance recalled vividly to her that of Dustin Farnum in the first act of "The Virginian."

"Will you please direct me to a hotel?" asked Madeline, rising.

The cowboy removed his sombrero, and the sweep he made with it and the accompanying bow, despite their exaggeration, had a kind of rude grace. He took two long strides toward her.

"Lady, are you married?"

In the past Miss Hammond's sense of humor had often helped her to overlook critical exactions natural to her breeding. She kept silence, and she imagined it was just as well that her veil hid her face at the moment. She had been prepared to find cowboys rather striking, and she had been warned not to laugh at them.

This gentleman of the range deliberately reached down and took up her left hand. Before she recovered from her start of amaze he had stripped off her glove.

"Fine spark, but no wedding ring," he drawled. "Lady, I'm glad to see you're not married."

He released her hand and returned the glove.

"You see, the only ho-tel in this here town is against boarding married women."

"Indeed?" said Madeline, trying to adjust her wits to the situation.

"It sure is," he went on. "Bad business for ho-tels to have married women. Keeps the boys away. You see, this isn't Reno."

Then he laughed rather boyishly, and from that, and the way he slouched on his sombrero, Madeline realized he was half drunk. As she instinctively recoiled she not only gave him a keener glance, but stepped into a position where a better light shone on his face. It was like red bronze, bold, raw, sharp. He laughed again, as if good-naturedly amused with himself, and the laugh scarcely changed the hard set of his features. Like that of all women whose beauty and charm had brought them much before the world, Miss Hammond's intuition had been developed until she had a delicate and exquisitely sensitive perception of the nature of men and of her effect upon them. This crude cowboy, under the influence of drink, had affronted her; nevertheless, whatever was in his mind, he meant no insult.

"I shall be greatly obliged if you will show me to the hotel," she said.

"Lady, you wait here," he replied, slowly, as if his thought did not come swiftly. "I'll go fetch the porter."

She thanked him, and as he went out, closing the door, she sat down in considerable relief. It occurred to her that she should have mentioned her brother's name. Then she fell to wondering what living with such uncouth cowboys had done to Alfred. He had been wild enough in college, and she doubted that any cowboy could have taught him much. She alone of her family had ever believed in any latent good in Alfred Hammond, and her faith had scarcely survived the two years of silence.

Waiting there, she again found herself listening to the moan of the wind through the wires. The horse outside began to pound with heavy hoofs, and once he whinnied. Then Madeline heard a rapid pattering, low at first and growing louder, which presently she recognized as the galloping of horses. She went to the window, thinking, hoping her brother had arrived. But as the clatter increased to a roar, shadows sped by—lean horses, flying manes and tails, sombreroed riders, all strange and wild in her sight. Recalling what the conductor had said, she was at some pains to quell her uneasiness. Dust-clouds shrouded the dim lights in the windows. Then out of the gloom two figures appeared, one tall, the other slight. The cowboy was returning with a porter.

Heavy footsteps sounded without, and lighter ones dragging along, and then suddenly the door rasped open, jarring the whole room. The cowboy entered, pulling a disheveled figure—that of a priest, a padre, whose mantle had manifestly been disarranged by the rude grasp of his captor. Plain it was that the padre was extremely terrified.

Madeline Hammond gazed in bewilderment at the little man, so pale and shaken, and a protest trembled upon her lips; but it was never uttered, for this half-drunken cowboy now appeared to be a cool, grim-smiling devil; and stretching out a long arm, he grasped her and swung her back to the bench.

"You stay there!" he ordered.

His voice, though neither brutal nor harsh nor cruel, had the unaccountable effect of making her feel powerless to move. No man had ever before addressed her in such a tone. It was the woman in her that obeyed—not the personality of proud Madeline Hammond.

The padre lifted his clasped hands as if supplicating for his life, and began to speak hurriedly in Spanish. Madeline did not understand the language. The cowboy pulled out a huge gun and brandished it in the priest's face. Then he lowered it, apparently to point it at the priest's feet. There was a red flash, and then a thundering report that stunned Madeline. The room filled with smoke and the smell of powder. Madeline did not faint or even shut her eyes, but she felt as if she were fast in a cold vise. When she could see distinctly through the smoke she experienced a sensation of immeasurable relief that the cowboy had not shot the padre. But he was still waving the gun, and now appeared to be dragging his victim toward her. What possibly could be the drunken fool's intention? This must be—this surely was a cowboy trick. She had a vague, swiftly flashing recollection of Alfred's first letters descriptive of the extravagant fun of cowboys. Then she vividly remembered a moving picture she had seen— cowboys playing a monstrous joke on a lone school-teacher. Madeline no sooner thought of it than she made certain her brother was introducing her to a little wild West amusement. She could scarcely believe it, yet it must be true. Alfred's old love of teasing her might have extended even to this outrage. Probably he stood just outside the door or window laughing at her embarrassment.

Anger checked her panic. She straightened up with what composure this surprise had left her and started for the door. But the cowboy barred her passage—grasped her arms. Then Madeline divined that her brother could not have any knowledge of this indignity. It was no trick. It was something that was happening, that was real, that threatened she knew not what. She tried to wrench free, feeling hot all over at being handled by this drunken brute. Poise, dignity, culture—all the acquired habits of character—fled before the instinct to fight. She was athletic. She fought. She struggled desperately. But he forced her back with hands of iron. She had never known a man could be so strong. And then it was the man's coolly smiling face, the paralyzing strangeness of his manner, more than his strength, that weakened Madeline until she sank trembling against the bench.

"What—do you—mean?" she panted.

"Dearie, ease up a little on the bridle," he replied, gaily.

Madeline thought she must be dreaming. She could not think clearly. It had all been too swift, too terrible for her to grasp. Yet she not only saw this man, but also felt his powerful presence. And the shaking priest, the haze of blue smoke, the smell of powder—these were not unreal.

Then close before her eyes burst another blinding red flash, and close at her ears bellowed another report. Unable to stand, Madeline slipped down into the bench. Her drifting faculties refused clearly to record what transpired during the next few moments; presently, however, as her mind steadied somewhat, she heard, though as in a dream, the voice of the padre hurrying over strange words. It ceased, and then the cowboy's voice stirred her.

"Lady, say *Si—Si*. Say it—quick! Say it—*Si!*"

From sheer suggestion, a force irresistible at this moment when her will was clamped by panic, she spoke the word.

"And now, Lady—so we can finish this properly— what's your name?"

Still obeying mechanically, she told him.

He stared for a while, as if the name had awakened associations in a mind somewhat befogged. He leaned back unsteadily. Madeline heard the expulsion of his breath, a kind of hard puff, not unusual in drunken men.

"What name?" he demanded.

"Madeline Hammond. I am Alfred Hammond's sister."

He put his hand up and brushed at an imaginary something before his eyes. Then he loomed over her, and that hand, now shaking a little, reached out for her veil. Before he could touch it, however, she swept it back, revealing her face.

"You're—not—*Majesty* Hammond?"

How strange—stranger than anything that had ever happened to her before—was it to hear that name on the lips of this cowboy! It was a name by which she was familiarly known, though only those nearest and dearest to her had the privilege of using it. And now it revived her dulled faculties, and by an effort she regained control of herself.

"You are *Majesty* Hammond," he replied; and this time he affirmed wonderingly rather than questioned.

Madeline rose and faced him.

"Yes, I am."

He slammed his gun back into its holster.

"Well, I reckon we won't go on with it, then."

"With what, sir? And why did you force me to say *Si* to this priest?"

"I reckon that was a way I took to show him you'd be willing to get married."

"Oh! . . . You—you! . . ." Words failed her.

This appeared to galvanize the cowboy into action. He grasped the padre and led him toward the door, cursing and threatening, no doubt enjoining secrecy. Then he pushed him across the threshold and stood there breathing hard and wrestling with himself.

"Here—wait—wait a minute, Miss—Miss Hammond," he said, huskily. "You could fall into worse company than mine—though I reckon you sure think not. I'm pretty drunk, but I'm—all right otherwise. Just wait—a minute."

She stood quivering and blazing with wrath, and watched this savage fight his drunkenness. He acted like a man who had been suddenly shocked into a rational state of mind, and he was now battling with himself to hold on to it. Madeline saw the dark, damp hair lift from his brows as he held it up to the cool wind. Above him she saw the white stars in the deep-blue sky, and they seemed as unreal to her as any other thing in this strange night. They were cold, brilliant, aloof, distant; and looking at them, she felt her wrath lessen and die, and leave her calm.

The cowboy turned and began to talk.

"You see—I was pretty drunk," he labored. "There was a *fiesta*—and a wedding. I do fool things when I'm drunk. I made a fool bet I'd marry the first girl who came to town. . . . If you hadn't worn that veil—the fellows were joshing me—and Ed Linton was getting married—and everybody always wants to gamble. . . . I must have been pretty drunk."

After the one look at her when she had first put aside her veil he had not raised his eyes to her face. The cool audacity had vanished in what was either excessive emotion or the maudlin condition peculiar to some men when drunk. He could not stand still; perspiration collected in beads upon his forehead; he kept wiping his face with his scarf, and he breathed like a man after violent exertions.

"You see—I was pretty—" he began.

"Explanations are not necessary," she interrupted. "I am very tired—distressed. The hour is late. Have you the slightest idea what it means to be a gentleman?"

His bronzed face burned to a flaming crimson.

"Is my brother here—in town to-night?" Madeline went on.

"No. He's at his ranch."

"But I wired him."

"Like as not the message is over in his box at the P.O. He'll be in town to-morrow. He's shipping cattle for Stillwell."

"Meanwhile I must go to a hotel. Will you please—"

If he heard her last words he showed no evidence of it. A noise outside had attracted his attention. Madeline listened. Low voices of men, the softer liquid tones of a woman, drifted in through the open door. They spoke in Spanish, and the voices grew louder. Evidently the speakers were approaching the station. Footsteps crunching on gravel attested to this, and quicker steps, coming with deep tones of men in anger, told of a quarrel. Then the woman's voice, hurried and broken, rising higher, was eloquent of vain appeal.

The cowboy's demeanor startled Madeline into anticipation of something dreadful. She was not deceived. From outside came the sound of a scuffle—a muffled shot, a groan, the thud of a falling body, a woman's low cry, and footsteps padding away in rapid retreat.

Madeline Hammond leaned weakly back in her seat, cold and sick, and for a moment her ears throbbed to the tramp of the dancers across the way and the rhythm of the cheap music. Then into the open door-place flashed a girl's tragic face, lighted by dark eyes and framed by dusky hair. The girl reached a slim brown hand round the side of the door and held on as if to support herself. A long black scarf accentuated her gaudy attire.

"Señor—Gene!" she exclaimed; and breathless glad recognition made a sudden break in her terror.

"Bonita!" The cowboy leaped to her. "Girl! Are you hurt?"

"No, Señor."

He took hold of her. "I heard—somebody got shot. Was it Danny?"

"No, Señor."

"Did Danny do the shooting? Tell me, girl."

"No, Señor."

"I'm sure glad. I thought Danny was mixed up in that. He had Stillwell's money for the boys—I was afraid. . . . Say, Bonita, but *you'll* get in trouble. Who was with you? What did you do?"

"Señor Gene—they Don Carlos *vacqueros*—they quarrel over me. I only dance a leetle, smile a leetle, and they quarrel. I beg they be good—watch out for Sheriff Hawe . . . and now Sheriff Hawe put me in jail. I so frighten; he try make leetle love to Bonita once, and now he hate me like he hate Señor Gene."

"Pat Hawe won't put you in jail. Take my horse and hit the Peloncillo trail. Bonita, promise to stay away from El Cajon."

"*Si*, Señor."

He led her outside. Madeline heard the horse snort and champ his bit. The cowboy spoke low; only a few words were intelligible—"stirrups . . . wait . . . out of town . . . mountain . . . trail . . . now ride!"

A moment's silence ensued, and was broken by a pounding of hoofs, a pattering of gravel. Then Madeline saw a big, dark horse run into the wide space. She caught a glimpse of wind-swept scarf and hair, a little form low down in the saddle. The horse was outlined in black against the line of dim lights. There was something wild and splendid in his flight.

Directly the cowboy appeared again in the doorway.

"Miss Hammond, I reckon we want to rustle out of here. Been bad goings-on. And there's a train due."

She hurried into the open air, not daring to look back or to either side. Her guide strode swiftly. She had almost to run to keep up with him. Many conflicting emotions confused her. She had a strange sense of this stalking giant beside her, silent except for his jangling spurs. She had a strange feeling of the cool, sweet wind and the white stars. Was it only her disordered fancy, or did these wonderful stars open and shut? She had a queer, disembodied thought that somewhere in ages back, in another life, she had seen these stars. The night seemed dark, yet there was a pale, luminous light—a light from the stars—and she fancied it would always haunt her.

Suddenly aware that she had been led beyond the line of houses, she spoke:

"Where are you taking me?"

"To Florence Kingsley," he replied.

"Who is she?"

"I reckon she's your brother's best friend out here."

Madeline kept pace with the cowboy for a few moments longer, and then she stopped. It was as much from necessity to catch her breath as it was from recurring fear. All at once she realized what little use her training had been for such an experience as this. The cowboy, missing her, came back the few intervening steps. Then he waited, still silent, looming beside her.

"It's so dark, so lonely," she faltered. "How do I know . . . what warrant can you give me that you—that no harm will befall me if I go farther?"

"None, Miss Hammond except that I've seen your face."

CHAPTER 2

A SECRET KEPT

Because of that singular reply Madeline found faith to go farther with the cowboy. But at the moment she really did not think about what he had said. Any answer to her would have served if it had been kind. His silence had augmented her nervousness, compelling her to voice her fear. Still, even if he had not replied at all she would have gone on with him. She shuddered at the idea of returning to the station, where she believed there had been murder; she could hardly have forced herself to go back to those dim lights in the street; she did not want to wander around alone in the dark.

And as she walked on into the windy darkness, much relieved that he had answered as he had, reflecting that he had yet to prove his words true, she began to grasp the deeper significance of them. There was a revival of pride that made her feel that she ought to scorn to think at all about such a man. But Madeline Hammond discovered that thought was involuntary, that there were feelings in her never dreamed of before this night.

Presently Madeline's guide turned off the walk and rapped at a door of a low-roofed house.

"Hullo—who's there?" a deep voice answered.

"Gene Stewart," said the cowboy. "Call Florence—quick!"

Thump of footsteps followed, a tap on a door, and voices. Madeline heard a woman exclaim: "Gene! here when there's a dance in town! Something wrong out on the range." A light flared up and shone bright through a window. In another moment there came a patter of soft steps, and the door opened to disclose a woman holding a lamp.

"Gene! Al's not—"

"Al is all right," interrupted the cowboy.

Madeline had two sensations then: one of wonder at the note of alarm and love in the woman's voice, and the other of unutterable relief to be safe with a friend of her brother's.

"It's Al's sister—came on to-night's train," the cowboy was saying. "I happened to be at the station, and I've fetched her up to you."

Madeline came forward out of the shadow.

"Not—not really *Majesty* Hammond!" exclaimed Florence Kingsley. She nearly dropped the lamp, and she looked and looked, astounded beyond belief.

"Yes, I am really she," replied Madeline. "My train was late, and for some reason Alfred did not meet me. Mr.—Mr. Stewart saw fit to bring me to you instead of taking me to a hotel."

"Oh, I'm so glad to meet you," replied Florence, warmly. "Do come in. I'm so surprised, I forget my manners. Why, Al never mentioned your coming."

"He surely could not have received my messages," said Madeline, as she entered.

The cowboy, who came in with her satchel, had to stoop to enter the door, and, once in, he seemed to fill the room. Florence set the lamp down upon the table. Madeline saw a young woman with a smiling, friendly face, and a profusion of fair hair hanging down over her dressing-gown.

"Oh, but Al will be glad!" cried Florence. "Why, you are white as a sheet. You must be tired. What a long wait you had at the station! I heard the train come in hours ago as I was going to bed. That station is lonely at night. If I had known you were coming! Indeed, you are very pale. Are you ill?"

"No. Only I am very tired. Traveling so far by rail is harder than I imagined. I did have rather a long wait after arriving at the station, but I can't say that it was lonely."

Florence Kingsley searched Madeline's face with keen eyes, and then took a long, significant look at the silent Stewart. With that she deliberately and quietly closed a door leading into another room.

"Miss Hammond, what has happened?" She had lowered her voice.

"I do not wish to recall all that has happened," replied Madeline. "I shall tell Alfred, however, that I would rather have met a hostile Apache than a cowboy."

"Please don't tell Al that!" cried Florence. Then she grasped Stewart and pulled him close to the light. "Gene, you're drunk!"

"I was pretty drunk," he replied, hanging his head.

"Oh, what have you done?"

"Now see here, Flo, I only—"

"I don't want to know. I'd tell it. Gene, aren't you ever going to learn decency? Aren't you ever going to stop drinking? You'll lose all your friends. Stillwell has stuck to you. Al's been your best friend. Molly and I have pleaded with you, and now you've gone and done—God knows what!"

"What do women want to wear veils for?" he growled. "I'd have known her but for that veil."

"And you wouldn't have insulted *her*. But you would the next girl who came along. Gene, you are hopeless. Now, you get out of here and don't ever come back."

"Flo!" he entreated.

"I mean it."

"I reckon then I'll come back to-morrow and take my medicine," he replied.

"Don't you dare!" she cried.

Stewart went out and closed the door.

"Miss Hammond, you—you don't know how this hurts me," said Florence. "What you must think of us! It's so unlucky that you should have had this happen right at first. Now, maybe you won't have the heart to stay. Oh, I've known more than one Eastern girl to go home without ever learning what we really are out here. Miss Hammond, Gene Stewart is a fiend when he's drunk. All the same I *know*, whatever he did, he meant no shame to you. Come now, don't think about it again tonight." She took up the lamp and led Madeline into a little room. "This is out West," she went on, smiling, as she indicated the few furnishings; "but you can rest. You're perfectly safe. Won't you let me help you undress—can't I do anything for you?"

"You are very kind, thank you, but I can manage," replied Madeline.

"Well, then, good night. The sooner I go the sooner

you'll rest. Just forget what happened and think how fine a surprise you're to give your brother to-morrow."

With that she slipped out and softly shut the door.

As Madeline laid her watch on the bureau she noticed that the time was past two o'clock. It seemed long since she had gotten off the train. When she had turned out the lamp and crept wearily into bed she knew what it was to be utterly spent. She was too tired to move a finger. But her brain whirled.

She had at first no control over it, and a thousand thronging sensations came and went and recurred with little logical relation. There was the roar of the train; the feeling of being lost; the sound of pounding hoofs; a picture of her brother's face as she had last seen it five years before; a long, dim line of lights; the jingle of silver spurs; night, wind, darkness, stars. Then the gloomy station, the shadowy blanketed Mexican, the empty room, the dim lights across the square, the tramp of the dancers and vacant laughs and discordant music, the door flung wide and the entrance of the cowboy. She did not recall how he had looked or what he had done. And the next instant she saw him cool, smiling, devilish—saw him in violence; the next his bigness, his apparel, his physical being were vague as outlines in a dream. The white face of the padre flashed along in the train of thought, and it brought the same dull, half-blind, indefinable state of mind subsequent to that last nerve-breaking pistol-shot. That passed, and then clear and vivid rose memories of the rest that had happened—strange voices betraying fury of men, a deadened report, a moan of mortal pain, a woman's poignant cry. And Madeline saw the girl's great tragic eyes and the wild flight of the big horse into the blackness, and the dark, stalking figure of the silent cowboy, and the white stars that seemed to look down remorselessly.

This tide of memory rolled over Madeline again and again, and gradually lost its power and faded. All distress left her, and she felt herself drifting. How black the room was—as black with her eyes open as it was when they were shut! And the silence—it was like a cloak. There was absolutely no sound. She was in another world from that which she knew. She thought of this fair-haired Florence and of Alfred; and, wondering about them, she dropped to sleep.

When she awakened the room was bright with sunlight. A cool wind blowing across the bed caused her to put her hands under the blanket. She was lazily and dreamily contemplating the mud walls of this little room when she remembered where she was and how she had come there.

How great a shock she had been subjected to was manifest in a sensation of disgust that overwhelmed her. She even shut her eyes to try and blot out the recollection. She felt that she had been contaminated.

Presently Madeline Hammond again awoke to the fact she had learned the preceding night—that there were emotions to which she had heretofore been a stranger. She did not try to analyze them, but she exercised her self-control to such good purpose that by the time she had dressed she was outwardly her usual self. She scarcely remembered when she had found it necessary to control her emotions. There had been no trouble, no excitement, no unpleasantness in her life. It had been ordered for her—tranquil, luxurious, brilliant, varied, yet always the same.

She was not surprised to find the hour late, and was going out to make inquiry about her brother when a voice arrested her. She recognized Miss Kingsley's voice addressing some one outside, and it had a sharpness she had not noted before.

"So you came back, did you? Well, you don't look very proud of yourself this mawnin'. Gene Stewart, you look like a coyote."

"Say, Flo, if I am a coyote I'm not going to sneak," he said.

"What'd you come for?" she demanded.

"I said I was coming round to take my medicine."

"Meaning you'll not run from Al Hammond? Gene, your skull is as thick as an old cow's. Al will never know anything about what you did to his sister unless you tell him. And if you do that he'll shoot you. *She* won't give you away. She's a thoroughbred. Why, she was so white last night I thought she'd drop at my feet, but she never blinked an eyelash. I'm a woman, Gene Stewart, and if I couldn't feel like Miss Hammond I know how awful an ordeal she must have had. Why, she's one of the most beautiful, the most sought after, the most exclusive women in New York City. There's a crowd of millionaires and lords and dukes after her. How terrible it'd be for a woman like her to be kissed by a drunken cow-puncher! I say it—"

"Flo, I never insulted her that way," broke out Stewart.

"It was worse, then?" she queried, sharply.

"I made a bet that I'd marry the first girl who came to town. I was on the watch and pretty drunk. When she came—well, I got Padre Marcos and tried to bully her into marrying me."

"Oh, Lord!" Florence gasped. "It's worse than I feared. . . . Gene, Al will kill you."

"That'll be a good thing," replied the cowboy, dejectedly.

"Gene Stewart, it certainly would, unless you turn over

a new leaf," retorted Florence. "But don't be a fool." And here she became earnest and appealing. "Go away, Gene. Go join the rebels across the border—you're always threatening that. Anyhow, don't stay here and run any chance of stirring Al up. He'd kill you just the same as you would kill another man for insulting your sister. Don't make trouble for Al. That'd only make sorrow for *her*, Gene."

The subtle import was not lost upon Madeline. She was distressed because she could not avoid hearing what was not meant for her ears. She made an effort not to listen, and it was futile.

"Flo, you can't see this a man's way," he replied, quietly. "I'll stay and take my medicine."

"Gene, I could sure swear at you or any other pig-head of a cowboy. Listen. My brother-in-law, Jack, heard something of what I said to you last night. He doesn't like you. I'm afraid he'll tell Al. For Heaven's sake, man, go down-town and shut him up and yourself, too."

Then Madeline heard her come into the house, and presently rap on the door and call softly:

"Miss Hammond. Are you awake?"

"Awake and dressed, Miss Kingsley. Come in."

"Oh! You've rested. You look so—so different. I'm sure glad. Come out now. We'll have breakfast, and then you may expect to meet your brother any moment."

"Wait, please. I heard you speaking to Mr. Stewart. It was unavoidable. But I am glad. I must see him. Will you please ask him to come into the parlor a moment?"

"Yes," replied Florence, quickly; and as she turned at the door she flashed at Madeline a woman's meaning glance. "Make him keep his mouth shut!"

Presently there were slow, reluctant steps outside the

front door, then a pause, and the door opened. Stewart stood bareheaded in the sunlight. Madeline remembered with a kind of shudder the tall form, the embroidered buckskin vest, the red scarf, the bright leather wristbands, the wide silver-buckled belt and chaps. Her glance seemed to run over him swift as lightning. But as she saw his face now she did not recognize it. The man's presence roused in her a revolt. Yet something in her, the incomprehensible side of her nature, thrilled in the look of this splendid dark-faced barbarian.

"Mr. Stewart, will you please come in?" she asked, after that long pause.

"I reckon not," he said. The hopelessness of his tone meant that he knew he was not fit to enter a room with her, and did not care or cared too much.

Madeline went to the door. The man's face was hard, yet it was sad, too. And it touched her.

"I shall not tell my brother of your—your rudeness to me," she began. It was impossible for her to keep the chill out of her voice, to speak with other than the pride and aloofness of her class. Nevertheless, despite her loathing, when she had spoken so far it seemed that kindness and pity followed involuntarily. "I choose to overlook what you did because you were not wholly accountable, and because there must be no trouble between Alfred and you. May I rely on you to keep silence and to seal the lips of that priest? And you know, there was a man killed or injured there last night. I want to forget that dreadful thing. I don't want it known that I heard—"

"The Greaser didn't die," interrupted Stewart.

"Ah! then that's not so bad after all. I am glad for the sake of your friend—the little Mexican girl."

A slow scarlet wave overspread his face, and his shame

was painful to see. That fixed in Madeline's mind a conviction that if he was a heathen he was not wholly bad. And it made so much difference that she smiled down at him.

"You will spare me further distress, will you not, please?"

His hoarse reply was incoherent, but she needed only to see his working face to know his remorse and gratitude.

Madeline went back to her room; and presently Florence came for her, and directly they were sitting at breakfast. Madeline Hammond's impression of her brother's friend had to be reconstructed in the morning light. She felt a wholesome, frank, sweet nature. She liked the slow Southern drawl. And she was puzzled to know whether Florence Kingsley was pretty or striking or unusual. She had a youthful glow and flush, the clear tan of outdoors, a face that lacked the soft curves and lines of Eastern women, and her eyes were light gray, like crystal, steady, almost piercing, and her hair was a beautiful bright, waving mass.

Florence's sister was the elder of the two, a stout woman with a strong face and quiet eyes. It was a simple fare and service they gave to their guest; but they made no apologies for that. Indeed, Madeline felt their simplicity to be restful. She was sated with respect, sick of admiration, tired of adulation; and it was good to see that these Western women treated her as very likely they would have treated any other visitor. They were sweet, kind; and what Madeline had at first thought was a lack of expression or vitality she soon discovered to be the natural reserve of women who did not live superficial lives. Florence was breezy and frank, her sister quaint and not given much to speech. Madeline thought she would like to have these women near her if she were ill or in trouble. And she reproached herself for a fastidiousness, a hypercritical sense of refinement that could not help distinguishing what these women lacked.

"Can you ride?" Florence was asking. "That's what a Westerner always asks any one from the East. Can you ride like a man—astride, I mean? Oh, that's fine. You look strong enough to hold a horse. We have some fine horses out here. I reckon when Al comes we'll go out to Bill Stillwell's ranch. We'll have to go whether we want to or not, for when Bill learns you are here he'll just pack us all off. You'll love old Bill. His ranch is run down, but the range and the rides up in the mountains—they are beautiful. We'll hunt and climb, and most of all we'll ride. I love a horse—I love the wind in my face, and a wide stretch with the mountains beckoning. You must have the best horse on the ranges. And that means a scrap between Al and Bill and all the cowboys. We don't all agree about horses, except in case of Gene Stewart's iron-gray."

"Does Mr. Stewart own the best horse in the country?" asked Madeline. Again she had an inexplicable thrill as she remembered the wild flight of Stewart's big dark steed and rider.

"Yes, and that's all he does own," replied Florence. "Gene can't keep even a quirt. But he sure loves that horse and calls him—"

At this juncture a sharp knock on the parlor door interrupted the conversation. Florence's sister went to open it. She returned presently, and said:

"It's Gene. He's been dawdlin' out there on the front porch, and he knocked to let us know Miss Hammond's brother is comin'."

Florence hurried into the parlor, followed by Madeline. The door stood open, and disclosed Stewart sitting on the porch steps. From down the road came a clatter of hoofs. Madeline looked out over Florence's shoulder and saw a cloud of dust approaching, and in it she distinguished outlines of horses and riders. A warmth spread over her, a little tingle of gladness, and the feeling recalled her girlish love for her brother. What would he be like after long years?

"Gene, has Jack kept his mouth shut?" queried Florence; and again Madeline was aware of a sharp ring in the girl's voice.

"No," replied Stewart.

"Gene! You won't let it come to a fight? Al can be managed. But Jack hates you, and he'll have his friends with him."

"There won't be any fight."

"Use your brains now," added Florence; and then she turned to push Madeline gently back into the parlor.

Madeline's glow of warmth changed to a blank dismay. Was she to see her brother act with the violence she now associated with cowboys? The clatter of hoofs stopped before the door. Looking out, Madeline saw a bunch of dusty, wiry horses pawing the gravel and tossing lean heads. Her swift glance ran over the lithe horsemen, trying to pick out the one who was her brother. But she could not. Her glance, however, caught the same rough dress and hard aspect that characterized the cowboy Stewart. Then one rider threw his bridle, leaped from the saddle, and came bounding up the porch steps. Florence met him at the door.

"Hello, Flo. Where is she?" he called, eagerly. With that he looked over her shoulder to espy Madeline. He actually jumped at her. She hardly knew the tall form and the bronzed face, but the warm flash of blue eyes was familiar. As for him, he had no doubt of his sister, it appeared, for with broken welcome he threw his arms around her, then held her off and looked searchingly at her.

"Well, sister," he began, when Florence turned hurriedly from the door and interrupted him.

"Al, I think you'd better stop the wrangling out there."

He stared at her, appeared suddenly to hear the loud voices from the street, and then, releasing Madeline, he said:

"By George! I forgot, Flo. There is a little business to see to. Keep my sister in here, please, and don't be fussed up now."

He went out on the porch and called to his men:

"Shut off your wind, Jack! And you, too, Blaze! I didn't want you fellows to come here. But as you would come, you've got to shut up. This is my business."

Whereupon he turned to Stewart, who was sitting on the fence.

"Hello, Stewart," he said.

It was a greeting; but there was that in the voice which alarmed Madeline.

Stewart leisurely got up and leisurely advanced to the porch.

"Hello, Hammond," he drawled.

"Drunk again last night?"

"Well, if you want to know, and if it's any of your mix, yes, I was—pretty drunk," replied Stewart.

It was a kind of cool speech that showed the cowboy in control of himself and master of the situation—not an easy speech to follow up with undue inquisitiveness. There was a short silence.

"Damn it, Stewart," said the speaker, presently, "here's the situation: It's all over town that you met my sister last night at the station and—and insulted her. Jack's got it in for you, so have these other boys. But it's my affair. Understand, I didn't fetch them here. They can see you square yourself, or else— Gene, you've been on the wrong trail for some time, drinking and all that. You're going to the bad. But Bill thinks, and I think, you're still a man. We never knew you to lie. Now what have you to say for yourself?"

"Nobody is insinuating that I *am* a liar?" drawled Stewart.

"No."

"Well, I'm glad to hear that. You see, Al, I was pretty drunk last night, but not drunk enough to forget the least thing I did. I told Pat Hawe so this morning when he was curious. And that's polite for me to be to Pat. Well, I found Miss Hammond waiting alone at the station. She wore a veil, but I knew she was a lady, of course. I imagine, now that I think of it, that Miss Hammond found my gallantry rather startling, and—"

At this point Madeline, answering to unconsidered impulse, eluded Florence and walked out upon the porch.

Sombreros flashed down and the lean horses jumped.

"Gentlemen," said Madeline, rather breathlessly; and it did not add to her calmness to feel a hot flush in her cheeks, "I am very new to Western ways, but I think you are laboring under a mistake, which, in justice to Mr. Stewart, I want to correct. Indeed, he was rather—rather abrupt and strange when he came up to me last night; but as I understand him now, I can attribute that to his gallantry. He was somewhat wild and sudden and—

sentimental in his demand to protect me—and it was not clear whether he meant his protection for last night or forever; but I am happy to say he offered me no word that was not honorable. And he saw me safely here to Miss Kingsley's home."

CHAPTER 3

SISTER AND BROTHER

Then Madeline returned to the little parlor with the brother whom she had hardly recognized.

"Majesty!" he exclaimed. "To think of your being here!"

The warmth stole back along her veins. She remembered how that pet name had sounded from the lips of this brother who had given it to her.

"Alfred!"

Then his words of gladness at sight of her, his chagrin at not being at the train to welcome her, were not so memorable of him as the way he clasped her, for he had held her that way the day he left home, and she had not forgotten. But now he was so much taller and bigger, so dusty and strange and different and forceful, that she could scarcely think him the same man. She even had a humorous thought that here was another cowboy bullying her, and this time it was her brother.

"Dear old girl," he said, more calmly, as he let her go, "you haven't changed at all, except to grow lovelier. Only you're a woman now, and you've fulfilled the name I gave you. God, how sight of you brings back home! It seems a hundred years since I left. I missed you more than all the rest."

Madeline seemed to feel with his every word that she was remembering him. She was so amazed at the change in him that she could not believe her eyes. She saw a bronzed, strong-jawed, eagle-eyed man, stalwart, superb of height, and, like the cowboys, belted, booted, spurred. And there was something hard as iron in his face that quivered with his words. It seemed that only in those moments when the hard lines broke and softened could she see resemblance to the face she remembered. It was his manner, the tone of his voice, and the tricks of speech that proved to her he was really Alfred. She had bidden good-by to a disgraced, disinherited, dissolute boy. Well she remembered the handsome pale face with its weakness and shadows and careless smile, with the ever-present cigarette hanging between the lips. The years had passed, and now she saw him a man—the West had made him a man. And Madeline Hammond felt a strong, passionate gladness and gratefulness, and a direct check to her suddenly inspired hatred of the West.

"Majesty, it was good of you to come. I'm all broken up. How did you ever do it? But never mind that now. Tell me about that brother of mine."

And Madeline told him, and then about their sister Helen. Question after question he fired at her; and she told him of her mother; of Aunt Grace, who had died a year ago; of his old friends, married, scattered, vanished. But she did not tell him of his father, for he did not ask.

Quite suddenly the rapid-fire questioning ceased; he choked, was silent a moment, and then burst into tears. It seemed to her that a long, stored-up bitterness was flooding away. It hurt her to see him—hurt her more to hear him. And in the succeeding few moments she grew closer to him than she had ever been in the past. Had her father and mother done right by him? Her pulse stirred with unwonted quickness. She did not speak, but she kissed him, which, for her, was an indication of unusual feeling. And when he recovered command over his emotions he made no reference to his breakdown, nor did she. But that scene struck deep into Madeline Hammond's heart. Through it she saw what he had lost and gained.

"Alfred, why did you not answer my last letters?" asked Madeline. "I had not heard from you for two years."

"So long? How time flies! Well, things went bad with me about the last time I heard from you. I always intended to write some day, but I never did."

"Things went wrong? Tell me."

"Majesty, you mustn't worry yourself with my troubles. I want you to enjoy your stay and not be bothered with my difficulties."

"Please tell me. I suspected something had gone wrong. That is partly why I decided to come out."

"All right; if you must know," he began; and it seemed to Madeline that there was a gladness in his decision to unburden himself. "You remember all about my little ranch, and that for a while I did well raising stock? I wrote you all that. Majesty, a man makes enemies anywhere. Perhaps an Eastern man in the West can make, if not so many, certainly more bitter ones. At any rate, I made several. There was a cattleman, Ward by name—he's gone now—and he and I had trouble over cattle. That gave me a back-set. Pat Hawe, the sheriff here, has been instrumental in hurting my business. He's not so much of a rancher, but he has influence at Santa Fe and El Paso and Douglas. I made an enemy of him. I never did anything to him. He hates Gene Stewart, and upon one occasion I spoiled a little plot of his to get Gene in his clutches. The real reason for his animosity toward me is that he loves Florence, and Florence is going to marry me."

"Alfred!"

"What's the matter, Majesty? Didn't Florence impress you favorably?" he asked, with a keen glance.

"Why—yes, indeed. I like her. But I did not think of her in relation to you—that way. I am greatly surprised. Alfred, is she well born? What connections?"

"Florence is just a girl of ordinary people. She was born in Kentucky, was brought up in Texas. My aristocratic and wealthy family would scorn—"

"Alfred, you are still a Hammond," said Madeline, with uplifted head.

Alfred laughed. "We won't quarrel, Majesty. I remember you, and in spite of your pride you've got a heart. If you stay here a month you'll love Florence Kingsley. I want you to know she's had a great deal to do with straightening me up. . . . Well, to go on with my story. There's Don Carlos, a Mexican rancher, and he's my worst enemy. For that matter, he's as bad an enemy of Bill Stillwell and other ranchers. Stillwell, by the way, is my friend and one of the finest men on earth. I got in debt to Don Carlos before I knew he was so mean. In the first place I lost money at faro—I gambled some when I came West—and then I made unwise cattle deals. Don Carlos is a wily Greaser, he knows the ranges, he has the water, and he is dishonest. So he outfigured me. And now I am practically ruined. He has not gotten possession of my ranch, but that's only a matter of time, pending law-suits at Santa Fe. At present I have a few hundred cattle running on Stillwell's range, and I am his foreman."

"Foreman?" queried Madeline.

"I am simply boss of Stillwell's cowboys, and right glad of my job."

Madeline was conscious of an inward burning. It required an effort for her to retain her outward tranquillity. Annoying consciousness she had also of the returning sense of new disturbing emotions. She began to see just how walled in from unusual thought-provoking incident and sensation had been her exclusive life.

"Cannot your property be reclaimed?" she asked. "How much do you owe?"

"Ten thousand dollars would clear me and give me *another start.* But, Majesty, in this country that's a good deal of money, and I haven't been able to raise it. Stillwell's in worse shape than I am."

Madeline went over to Alfred and put her hands on his shoulders.

"We must not be in debt."

He stared at her as if her words had recalled something long forgotten. Then he smiled.

"How imperious you are! I'd forgotten just who my beautiful sister really is. Majesty, you're not going to ask me to take money from you?"

"I am."

"Well, I'll not do it. I never did, even when I was in college, and then there wasn't much beyond me."

"Listen, Alfred," she went on, earnestly, "this is entirely different. I had only an allowance then. You had no way to know that since I last wrote you I had come into my inheritance from Aunt Grace. It was—well, that doesn't matter. Only, I haven't been able to spend half the income. It's mine. It's not Father's money. You will make me very happy if you'll consent. Alfred, I'm so—so amazed at the change in you. I'm so happy. You must never take a backward step from now on. What is ten thousand dollars to me? Sometimes I spend that in a month. I throw money away. If you let me help you it will be doing me good as well as you. Please, Alfred."

He kissed her, evidently surprised at her earnestness. And indeed Madeline was surprised herself. Once started, her speech had flowed.

"You always were the best of fellows, Majesty. And if you really care—if you really want to help me I'll be only too glad to accept. It will be fine. Florence will go wild. And that Greaser won't harass me any more. Majesty, pretty soon some titled fellow will be spending your money; I may as well take a little before he gets it all," he finished, jokingly.

"What do you know about me?" she asked, lightly.

"More than you think. Even if we are lost out here in the woolly West we get news. Everybody knows about Anglesbury. And that Dago duke who chased you all over Europe, that Lord Castleton has the running now and seems about to win. How about it, Majesty?"

Madeline detected a hint that suggested scorn in his gay speech. And deep in his searching glance she saw a flame. She became thoughtful. She had forgotten Castleton, New York, society.

"Alfred," she began, seriously, "I don't believe any titled gentleman will ever spend my money, as you elegantly express it."

"I don't care for that. It's you!" he cried, passionately,

and he grasped her with a violence that startled her. He was white; his eyes were now like fire. "You are so splendid—so wonderful. People called you the American Beauty, but you're more than that. You're the American Girl! Majesty, marry no man unless you love him, and love an *American*. Stay away from Europe long enough to learn to know the men—the real men of your own country."

"Alfred, I'm afraid there are not always real men and real love for American girls in international marriages. But Helen knows this. It'll be her choice. She'll be miserable if she marries Anglesbury."

"It'll serve her just right," declared her brother. "Helen was always crazy for glitter, adulation, fame. I'll gamble she never saw more of Anglesbury than the gold and ribbons on his breast."

"I am sorry. Anglesbury is a gentleman; but it is the money he wanted, I think. Alfred, tell me how you came to know about me, way out here? You may be assured I was astonished to find that Miss Kingsley knew me as Majesty Hammond."

"I imagine it was a surprise," he replied, with a laugh. "I told Florence about you—gave her a picture of you. And, of course, being a woman, she showed the picture and talked. She's in love with you. Then, my dear sister, we do get New York papers out here occasionally, and we can see and read. You may not be aware that you and your society friends are objects of intense interest in the U. S. in general, and the West in particular. The papers are full of you, and perhaps a lot of things you never did."

"That Mr. Stewart knew, too. He said, 'You're not *Majesty* Hammond?'"

"Never mind his impudence!" exclaimed Alfred; and

then again he laughed. "Gene is all right, only you've got to know him. I'll tell you what he did. He got hold of one of those newspaper pictures of you—the one in the *Times;* he took it away from here, and in spite of Florence he wouldn't fetch it back. It was a picture of you in riding-habit with your blue-ribbon horse, White Stockings— remember? It was taken at Newport. Well, Stewart tacked the picture up in his bunk-house, and named his beautiful horse Majesty. All the cowboys knew it. They would see the picture and tease him unmercifully. But he didn't care. One day I happened to drop in on him and found him just recovering from a carouse. I saw the picture, too, and I said to him: 'Gene, if my sister knew you were a drunkard she'd not be proud of having her picture stuck up in your room.' Majesty, he did not touch a drop for a month, and when he did drink again he took the picture down, and he has never put it back."

Madeline smiled at her brother's amusement, but she did not reply. She simply could not adjust herself to these queer free Western ways. Her brother had eloquently pleaded for her to keep herself above a sordid and brilliant marriage, yet he not only allowed a cowboy to keep her picture in his room, but actually spoke of her and used her name in a temperance lecture. Madeline just escaped feeling disgust. She was saved from this, however, by nothing less than her brother's naïve gladness that through subtle suggestion Stewart had been persuaded to be good for a month. Something made up of Stewart's affrontery to her; of Florence Kingsley meeting her, frankly as it were, as an equal; of the elder sister's slow, quiet, easy acceptance of this visitor who had been honored at the courts of royalty; of that faint hint of scorn in Alfred's voice, and his amused statement in regard to her picture

and the name Majesty—something made up of all these
stung Madeline Hammond's pride, alienated her for an instant, and then stimulated her intelligence, excited her
interest, and made her resolve to learn a little about this
incomprehensible West.

"Majesty, I must run down to the siding," he said, consulting his watch. "We're loading a shipment of cattle. I'll
be back by supper-time and bring Stillwell with me. You'll
like him. Give me the check for your trunk."

She went into the little bedroom, and, taking up her
bag, she got out a number of checks.

"Six! Six trunks!" he exclaimed. "Well, I'm very glad
you intend to stay awhile. Say, Majesty, it will take me as
long to realize who you really are as it'll take to break
you of being a tenderfoot. I hope you packed a riding-suit.
If not you'll have to wear trousers! You'll have to do that
anyway when we go up in the mountains."

"No!"

"You sure will, as Florence says."

"We shall see about that. I don't know what's in the
trunks. I never pack anything. My dear brother, what do
I have maids for?"

"How did it come that you didn't travel with a maid?"

"I wanted to be alone. But don't you worry. I shall be
able to look after myself. I dare say it will be good for me."

She went to the gate with him.

"What a shaggy, dusty horse! He's wild, too. Do you
let him stand that way without being haltered? I should
think he would run off."

"Tenderfoot! You'll be great fun, Majesty, especially
for the cowboys."

"Oh, will I?" she asked, constrainedly.

"Yes, and in three days they will be fighting each other

over you. That's going to worry me. Cowboys fall in love with a plain woman, an ugly woman, any woman, so long as she's young. And you! Good Lord! They'll go out of their heads."

"You are pleased to be facetious, Alfred. I think I have had quite enough of cowboys, and I haven't been here twenty-four hours."

"Don't think too much of first impressions. That was my mistake when I arrived here. Good-by. I'll go now. Better rest awhile. You look tired."

The horse started as Alfred put his foot in the stirrup and was running when the rider slipped his leg over the saddle. Madeline watched him in admiration. He seemed to be loosely fitted to the saddle, moving with the horse.

"I suppose that's a cowboy's style. It pleases me," she said. "How different from the seat of Eastern riders!"

Then Madeline sat upon the porch and fell to interested observation of her surrounding. Near at hand it was decidedly not prepossessing. The street was deep in dust, and the cool wind whipped up little puffs. The houses along this street were all low, square, flat-roofed structures made of some kind of red cement. It occurred to her suddenly that this building-material must be the adobe she had read about. There was no person in sight. The long street appeared to have no end, though the line of houses did not extend far. Once she heard a horse trotting at some distance, and several times the ringing of a locomotive bell. Where were the mountains, wondered Madeline. Soon low over the house-roofs she saw a dim, dark-blue, rugged outline. It seemed to charm her eyes and fix her gaze. She knew the Adirondacks, she had seen the Alps from the summit of Mount Blanc, and had stood under the great black, white-tipped shadow of the Himalayas. But they had not drawn her as these remote Rockies. This dim horizon line boldly cutting the blue sky fascinated her. Florence Kingsley's expression "beckoning mountains" returned to Madeline. She could not see or feel so much as that. Her impression was rather that these mountains were aloof, unattainable, that if approached they would recede or vanish like the desert mirage.

Madeline went to her room, intending to rest awhile, and she fell asleep. She was aroused by Florence's knock and call.

"Miss Hammond, your brother has come back with Stillwell."

"Why, how I have slept!" exclaimed Madeline. "It's nearly six o'clock."

"I'm sure glad. You were tired. And the air here makes strangers sleepy. Come, we want you to meet old Bill. He calls himself the last of the cattlemen. He has lived in Texas and here all his life."

Madeline accompanied Florence to the porch. Her brother, who was sitting near the door, jumped up and said:

"Hello, Majesty!" And as he put his arm around her he turned toward a massive man whose broad, craggy face began to ripple and wrinkle. "I want to introduce my friend Stillwell to you. Bill, this is my sister, the sister I've so often told you about—Majesty."

"Wal, wal, Al, this's the proudest meetin' of my life," replied Stillwell, in a booming voice. He extended a huge hand. "Miss—Miss Majesty, sight of you is as welcome as the rain an' the flowers to an old desert cattleman."

Madeline greeted him, and it was all she could do to repress a cry at the way he crunched her hand in a grasp of iron. He was old, white-haired, weather-beaten, with long furrows down his cheeks and with gray eyes almost hidden in wrinkles. If he was smiling she fancied it a most extraordinary smile. The next instant she realized that it had been a smile, for his face appeared to stop rippling, the light died, and suddenly it was like rudely chiseled stone. The quality of hardness she had seen in Stewart was immeasurably intensified in this old man's face.

"Miss Majesty, it's plumb humiliatin' to all of us thet we wasn't on hand to meet you," Stillwell said. "Me an' Al stepped into the P.O. an' said a few mild an' cheerful things. Them messages ought to hev been sent out to the ranch. I'm sure afraid it was a bit unpleasant fer you last night at the station."

"I was rather anxious at first and perhaps frightened," replied Madeline.

"Wal, I'm some glad to tell you thet there's no man in these parts except your brother thet I'd as lief hev met you as Gene Stewart."

"Indeed?"

"Yes, an' thet's takin' into consideration Gene's weakness, too. I'm allus fond of sayin' of myself thet I'm the last of the old cattlemen. Wal, Stewart's not a native Westerner, but he's my pick of the last of the cowboys. Sure, he's young, but he's the last of the old style—the picturesque—an' chivalrous, too, I make bold to say, Miss Majesty, as well as the old hard-ridin' kind. Folks are down on Stewart. An' I'm only sayin' a good word for him because he is down, an' mebbe last night he might hev scared you, you bein' fresh from the East."

Madeline liked the old fellow for his loyalty to the cowboy he evidently cared for; but, as there did not seem anything for her to say, she remained silent.

"Miss Majesty, the day of the cattleman is about over.

An' the day of the cowboy, such as Gene Stewart, *is* over. There's no place for Gene. If these weren't modern days he'd come near bein' a gun-man, same as we had in Texas when I ranched there in the seventies. But he can't fit nowhere now; he can't hold a job, an' he's goin' down."

"I am sorry to hear it," murmured Madeline. "But, Mr. Stillwell, aren't these modern days out here just a little wild—yet? The conductor on my train told me of rebels, bandits, raiders. Then I have had other impressions of— well, that were wild enough for me."

"Wal, it's some more pleasant an' excitin' these days than for many years," replied Stillwell. "The boys hev took to packin' guns again. But thet's owin' to the revolution in Mexico. There's goin' to be trouble along the border. I reckon people in the East don't know there *is* a revolution. Wal, Madero will oust Diaz, an' then some other rebel will oust Madero. It means trouble on the border an' across the border, too. I wouldn't wonder if Uncle Sam hed to get a hand in the game. There's already been holdups on the railroads an' raids along the Rio Grande valley. An' these little towns are full of Greasers, all disturbed by the fightin' down in Mexico. We've been hevin' shootin'-scrapes an' knifin'-scrapes, an' some cattle-raidin'. I hev been losin' a few cattle right along. Reminds me of old times; an' pretty soon, if it doesn't stop, I'll take the old-time way to stop it."

"Yes, indeed, Majesty," put in Alfred, "you have hit upon an interesting time to visit us."

"Wal, thet sure 'pears to be so," rejoined Stillwell. "Stewart got in trouble down heah to-day, an' I'm more than sorry to hev to tell you thet your name figgered in it. But I couldn't blame him, fer I sure would hev done the same myself."

"That so?" queried Alfred, laughing. "Well, tell us about it."

Madeline simply gazed at her brother, and, though he seemed amused at her consternation, there was mortification in his face.

It required no great perspicuity, Madeline thought, *to see that* Stillwell loved to talk, and the way he squared himself and spread his huge hands over his knees suggested that he meant to do this opportunity justice.

"Miss Majesty, I reckon bein' as you're in the West now thet you must take things as they come, an' mind each thing a little less than the one before. If we old fellers hedn't been thet way we'd never hev lasted.

"Last night wasn't particular bad, ratin' with some other nights lately. There wasn't much doin'. But I had a hard knock. Yesterday when we started in with a bunch of cattle I sent one of my cowboys, Danny Mains, along ahead carryin' money I hed to pay off hands an' my bills, an' I wanted thet money to get in town before dark. Wal, Danny was held up. I don't distrust the lad. There's been strange Greasers in town lately, an' mebbe they knew about the money comin'.

"Wal, when I arrived with the cattle I was some put to it to make ends meet. An' to-day I wasn't in no angelic humor. When I hed my business all done I went around pokin' my nose heah an' there, tryin' to get scent of thet money. An' I happened in at a hall we hev thet does duty fer jail an' hospital an' election-post an' whatnot. Wal, just then it was doin' duty as a hospital. Last night was *fiesta* night—these Greasers hev a *fiesta* every week or so—an' one Greaser who hed been bad hurt was layin' in the hall, where he hed been fetched from the station. Somebody hed sent off to Douglas fer a doctor, but he hedn't come yet. I've hed some experience with gun-shot wounds, an' I looked this feller over. He wasn't shot up much, but I thought there was danger of blood-poisonin'. Anyway, I did all I could.

"The hall was full of cowboys, ranchers, Greasers, miners, an' town folks, along with some strangers. I was about to get started up this way when Pat Hawe come in.

"Pat, he's the sheriff. I reckon, Miss Majesty, thet sheriffs are new to you, an' fer sake of the West I'll explain to you thet we don't hev many of the real thing any more. Garrett, who killed Billy the Kid an' was killed himself near a year or so ago—he was the kind of sheriff thet helps to make a self-respectin' country. But this Pat Hawe—wal, I reckon there's no good in me sayin' what I think of him. He come into the hall, an' he was roarin' about things. He was goin' to arrest Danny Mains on sight. Wal, I jest polite-like told Pat thet the money was mine, an' he needn't get riled about it. An' if I wanted to trail the thief I reckon I could do it as well as anybody. Pat howled thet law was law, an' he was goin' to lay down the law. Sure it 'peared to me thet Pat was daid set to arrest the first man he could find excuse to.

"Then he cooled down a bit an' was askin' questions about the wounded Greaser when Gene Stewart come in. Whenever Pat an' Gene come together it reminds me of the early days back in the seventies. Jest naturally everybody shut up. Fer Pat hates Gene, an' I reckon Gene ain't very sweet on Pat. They're jest natural foes in the first place, an' then the course of events here in El Cajon has been aggravatin'.

"'Hullo, Stewart, you're the feller I'm lookin' fer,' said Pat.

"Stewart eyed him an' said mighty cool an' sarcastic:

'Hawe, you look a good deal fer me when I'm hittin' up the dust the other way.'

"Pat went red at thet, but he held in. 'Say, Stewart, you-all think a lot of thet roan horse of your'n, with the aristocratic name?'

"'I reckon I do,' replied Gene, shortly.

"'Wal, where is he?'

"'Thet's none of your business, Hawe.'

"'Oho! it ain't, hey? Wal, I guess I can make it my business. Stewart, there was some queer going's-on last night thet you know somethin' about. Danny Mains robbed— Stillwell's money gone—your roan horse gone—thet little hussy Bonita gone—an' this Greaser near gone, too. Now, seein' thet you was up late an' prowlin' round *the station* where this Greaser was found, it ain't onreasonable to think you might know how he got plugged—is it?'

"Stewart laughed kind of cold, an' he rolled a cigarette, all the time eyin' Pat, an' then he said if he'd plugged the Greaser it'd never hev been sich a bunglin' job.

"'I can arrest you on suspicion, Stewart, but before I go thet far I want some evidence. I want to round up Danny Mains an' thet little Greaser girl. I want to find out what's become of your hoss. You've never lent him since you hed him, an' there ain't enough raiders across the border to steal him from you. It's got a queer look—thet hoss bein' gone.'

"'You sure are a swell detective, Hawe, an' I wish you a heap of luck,' replied Stewart.

"Thet 'peared to nettle Pat beyond bounds, an' he stamped around an' swore. Then he had an idea. It jest stuck out all over him, an' he shook his finger in Stewart's face.

"'You was drunk last night?'

"Stewart never batted an eye.

"'You met some woman on Number Eight, didn't you?' shouted Hawe.

"'I met a lady,' replied Stewart, quiet an' menacin' like.

"'You met Al Hammond's sister, an' you took her up to Kingsley's. An' cinch this, my cowboy cavalier, I'm goin' up there an' ask this grand dame some questions, an' if she's as close-mouthed as you are *I'll arrest her!*'

"Gene Stewart turned white. I fer one expected to see him jump like lightnin', as he does when he's riled sudden. But he was calm an' he was thinkin' hard. Presently he said:

"'Pat, thet's a fool idee, an' if you do the trick it'll hurt you all the rest of your life. There's absolutely no reason to frighten Miss Hammond. An' tryin' to arrest her would be such a damned outrage as won't be stood fer in El Cajon. If you're sore on me send me to jail. I'll go. If you want to hurt Al Hammond, go an' do it some man kind of way. Don't take your spite out on us by insultin' a lady who has come hyar to hev a little visit. We're bad enough without bein' low-down as Greasers.'

"It was a long talk for Gene, an' I was as surprised as the rest of the fellers. Think of Gene Stewart talkin' soft an' sweet to thet red-eyed coyote of a sheriff! An' Pat, he looked so devilishly gleeful thet if somethin' about Gene hedn't held me tight I'd hev got in the game myself. It was plain to me an' others who spoke of it afterwards thet Pat Hawe hed forgotten the law an' the officer in the man an' his hate.

"'I'm a-goin', an' I'm a-goin' right now,' he shouted.

"An after thet any one could hev heerd a clock tick a mile off. Stewart seemed kind of chokin', an' he seemed to hev been bewildered by the idee of Hawe's confrontin' you.

"An' finally he burst out: 'But, man, think who it is! It's Miss Hammond! If you seen her, even if you was locoed or drunk, you—you couldn't do it.'

"'Couldn't I? Wal, I'll show you damn quick. What do I care who she is? Them swell Eastern women—I've heerd of them. They're not so much. This Hammond woman—'

"Suddenly Hawe shut up, an' with his red mug turnin' green he went for his gun."

Stillwell paused in his narrative to get breath, and he wiped his moist brow. And now his face began to lose its cragginess. It changed, it softened, it rippled and wrinkled, and all that strange mobility focused and shone in a wonderful smile.

"An' then, Miss Majesty, then there was somethin' happened. Stewart took Pat's gun away from him and throwed it on the floor. An' what followed was beautiful. Sure it was the beautifulest sight I ever seen. Only it was over so soon! A little while after, when the doctor came, he hed another patient besides the wounded Greaser, an' he said thet this new one would require about four months to be up an' around cheerful-like again. An' Gene Stewart hed hit the trail for the border."

CHAPTER 4

A RIDE FROM SUNRISE
TO SUNSET

Next morning, when Madeline was aroused by her brother, it was not yet daybreak; the air chilled her, and in the gray gloom she had to feel around for matches and lamp. Her usual languid manner vanished at a touch of the cold water. Presently, when Alfred knocked on her door and said he was leaving a pitcher of hot water outside, she replied, with chattering teeth: "Th-thank y-you, b-but I d-don't ne-need any now." She found it necessary, however, to warm her numb fingers before she could fasten hooks and buttons. And when she was dressed she marked in the dim mirror that there were tinges of red in her cheeks.

"Well, if I haven't some color!" she exclaimed.

Breakfast waited for her in the dining-room. The sisters ate with her. Madeline quickly caught the feeling of brisk action that seemed to be in the air. From the back of the house sounded the tramp of boots and voices of men, and from outside came a dull thump of hoofs, the rattle of harness, and creak of wheels. Then Alfred came stamping in.

"Majesty, here's where you get the real thing," he announced, merrily. "We're rushing you off, I'm sorry to say; but we must hustle back to the ranch. The fall round-up begins to-morrow. You will ride in the buck-board with Florence and Stillwell. I'll ride on ahead with the boys and fix up a little for you at the ranch. Your baggage will follow, but won't get there till to-morrow some time. It's a long ride out—nearly fifty miles by wagon-road. Flo, don't forget a couple of robes. Wrap her up well. And hustle getting ready. We're waiting."

A little later, when Madeline went out with Florence, the gray gloom was lightening. Horses were champing bits and pounding gravel.

"Mawnin', Miss Majesty," said Stillwell, gruffly, from the front seat of a high vehicle.

Alfred bundled her up into the back seat, and Florence after her, and wrapped them with robes. Then he mounted his horse and started off. "Gid-eb!" growled Stillwell, and with a crack of his whip the team jumped into a trot. Florence whispered into Madeline's ear:

"Bill's grouchy early in the mawnin'. He'll thaw out soon as it gets warm."

It was still so gray that Madeline could not distinguish objects at any considerable distance, and she left El Cajon without knowing what the town really looked like. She did know that she was glad to get out if it, and found an easier task of dispelling persistent haunting memory.

"Here come the cowboys," said Florence.

A line of horsemen appeared coming from the right and fell in behind Alfred, and gradually they drew ahead, to disappear from sight. While Madeline watched them the gray gloom lightened into dawn. All about her was bare and dark; the horizon seemed close; not a hill nor a tree broke the monotony. The ground appeared to be flat, but the road went up and down over little ridges. Madeline glanced backward in the direction of El Cajon and the mountains she had seen the day before, and she saw only bare and dark ground, like that which rolled before.

A puff of cold wind struck her face and she shivered. Florence noticed her and pulled up the second robe and tucked it closely round her up to her chin.

"If we have a little wind you'll sure feel it," said the Western girl.

Madeline replied that she already felt it. The wind appeared to penetrate the robes. It was cold, pure, nipping. It was so thin she had to breathe as fast as if she were under ordinary exertion. It hurt her nose and made her lungs ache.

"Aren't you co-cold?" asked Madeline.

"I?" Florence laughed. "I'm used to it. I never get cold."

The Western girl sat with ungloved hands on the outside of the robe she evidently did not need to draw up around her. Madeline thought she had never seen such a clear-eyed, healthy, splendid girl.

"Do you like to see the sun rise?" asked Florence.

"Yes, I think I do," replied Madeline, thoughtfully. "Frankly, I have not seen it for years."

"We have beautiful sunrises, and sunsets from the ranch are glorious."

Long lines of pink fire ran level with the eastern horizon, which appeared to recede as day brightened. A bank of thin, fleecy clouds was turning rose. To the south and west the sky was dark; but every moment it changed, the

blue turning bluer. The eastern sky was opalescent. Then
in one place gathered a golden light, and slowly concentrated till it was like fire. The rosy bank of cloud turned
to silver and pearl, and behind it shot up a great circle of
gold. Above the dark horizon gleamed an intensely bright
disk. It was the sun. It rose swiftly, blazing out the darkness between the ridges and giving color and distance to
the sweep of land.

"Wal, wal," drawled Stillwell, and stretched his huge
arms as if he had just awakened, "thet's somethin' like."

Florence nudged Madeline and winked at her.

"Fine mawnin', girls," went on old Bill, cracking his
whip. "Miss Majesty, it'll be some oninterestin' ride all
mawnin'. But when we get up a bit you'll sure like it.
There! Look to the southwest, jest over thet farthest ridge."

Madeline swept her gaze along the gray, sloping horizon line to where dark-blue spires rose far beyond the
ridge.

"Peloncillo Mountains," said Stillwell. "Thet's home,
when we get there. We won't see no more of them till
afternoon, when they rise up sudden-like."

Peloncillo! Madeline murmured the melodious name.
Where had she heard it? Then she remembered. The cowboy Stewart had told the little Mexican girl Bonita to "hit
the Peloncillo trail." Probably the girl had ridden the big,
dark horse over this very road at night, alone. Madeline
had a little shiver that was not occasioned by the cold
wind.

"There's a jack!" cried Florence, suddenly.

Madeline saw her first jack-rabbit. It was as large as a
dog, and its ears were enormous. It appeared to be impu-
dently tame, and the horses kicked dust over it as they
trotted by. From then on old Bill and Florence vied with

each other in calling Madeline's attention to many things along the way. Coyotes stealing away into the brush; buzzards flapping over the carcass of a cow that had been mired in a wash; queer little lizards running swiftly across the road; cattle grazing in the hollows; adobe huts of Mexican herders; wild, shaggy horses, with heads high, watching from the gray ridges—all these things Madeline looked at, indifferently at first, because indifference had become habitual with her, and then with an interest that flourished up and insensibly grew as she rode on. It grew until sight of a little ragged Mexican boy astride the most diminutive burro she had ever seen awakened her to the truth. She became conscious of faint, unmistakable awakening of long-dead feelings—enthusiasm and delight. When she realized that, she breathed deep of the cold, sharp air and experienced an inward joy. And she divined then, though she did not know why, that henceforth there was to be something new in her life, something she had never felt before, something good for her soul in the homely, the commonplace, the natural, and the wild.

Meanwhile, as Madeline gazed about her and listened to her companions, the sun rose higher and grew warm and soared and grew hot; the horses held tirelessly to their steady trot, and mile after mile of rolling land slipped by.

From the top of a ridge Madeline saw down into a hollow where a few of the cowboys had stopped and were sitting round a fire, evidently busy at the noonday meal. Their horses were feeding on the long, gray grass.

"Wal, smell of thet burnin' greasewood makes my mouth water," said Stillwell. "I'm sure hungry. We'll noon hyar an' let the hosses rest. It's a long pull to the ranch."

He halted near the camp-fire, and, clambering down,

began to unharness the team. Florence leaped out and turned to help Madeline.

"Walk round a little," she said. "You must be cramped from sitting still so long. I'll get lunch ready."

Madeline got down, glad to stretch her limbs, and began to stroll about. She heard Stillwell throw the harness on the ground and slap his horses. "Roll, you sons of guns!" he said. Both horses bent their fore legs, heaved down on their sides, and tried to roll over. One horse succeeded on the fourth try, and then heaved up with a satisfied snort and shook off the dust and gravel. The other one failed to roll over, and gave it up, half rose to his feet, and then lay down on the other side.

"He's sure going to feel the ground," said Florence, smiling at Madeline. "Miss Hammond, I suppose that prize horse of yours—White Stockings—would spoil his coat if he were heah to roll in this greasewood and cactus."

During lunch-time Madeline observed that she was an object of manifestly great interest to the three cowboys. She returned the compliment, and was amused to see that a glance their way caused them painful embarrassment.

They were grown men—one of whom had white hair— yet they acted like boys caught in the act of stealing a forbidden look at a pretty girl.

"Cowboys are sure all flirts," said Florence, as if stating an uninteresting fact. But Madeline detected a merry twinkle in her clear eyes. The cowboys heard, and the effect upon them was magical. They fell to shamed confusion and to hurried useless tasks. Madeline found it difficult to see where they had been bold, though evidently they were stricken with conscious guilt. She recalled appraising looks of critical English eyes, impudent French stares, burning Spanish glances—gantlets which any American girl had to run abroad. Compared to foreign eyes the eyes of these cowboys were those of smiling eager babies.

"Haw, haw!" roared Stillwell. "Florence, you jest hit the nail on the haid. Cowboys are all plumb flirts. I was wonderin' why them boys nooned hyar. This aint no place to noon. Ain't no grazin' or wood wuth burnin or nuthin'. Them boys jest held up, throwed the packs an' waited fer us. It ain't so surprisin' fer Booly an' Ned—they're young an' coltish—but Nels there, why, he's old enough to be the paw of both you girls. It sure is amazin strange."

A silence ensued. The white-haired cowboy, Nels, fussed aimlessly over the camp-fire, and then straightened up with a very red face.

"Bill, you're a dog-gone liar," he said. "I reckon I won't stand to be classed with Booly an' Ned. Then ain't no cowboy on this range thet's more appreciatin' of the ladies than me, but I shore ain't ridin' out of my way. I reckon I hev enough ridin' to do. Now, Bill, if you've sich dog-gone good eyes mebbe you seen somethin' on the way out?"

"Nels, I hevn't seen nothin'," he replied, bluntly. His levity disappeared, and the red wrinkles narrowed round his searching eyes.

"Jest take a squint at these hoss-tracks," said Nels, and he drew Stillwell a few paces aside and pointed to large hoof-prints in the dust. "I reckon you know the hoss thet made them?"

"Gene Stewart's roan, or I'm a son of a gun!" exclaimed Stillwell, and he dropped heavily to his knees and began to scrutinize the tracks. "My eyes are sure pore; but, Nels, they ain't fresh."

"I reckon them tracks was made early yesterday mornin'."

"Wal, what if they was?" Stillwell looked at his cowboy. "It's sure as thet red nose of your'n Gene wasn't ridin' the roan."

"Who's sayin' he was? Bill, it's more'n your eyes thet's gittin' old. Jest foller them tracks. Come on."

Stillwell walked slowly, with his head bent, muttering to himself. Some thirty paces or more from the campfire he stopped short and again flopped to his knees. Then he crawled about, evidently examining horse tracks.

"Nels, whoever was straddlin' Stewart's hoss met somebody. An' they hauled up a bit, but didn't git down."

"Tolerable good for you, Bill, thet reasonin'," replied the cowboy.

Stillwell presently got up and walked swiftly to the left for some rods, halted and faced toward the southwest, then retraced his steps. He looked at the imperturbable cowboy.

"Nels, I don't like this a little," he growled. "Them tracks make straight fer the Peloncillo trail."

"Shore," replied Nels.

"Wal?" went on Stillwell, impatiently.

"I reckon you know what hoss made the other tracks?"

"I'm thinkin' hard, but I ain't sure."

"It was Danny Mains's bronch."

"How do you know thet?" demanded Stillwell, sharply.

"Bill, the left front foot of thet little hoss always wears a shoe thet sets crooked. Any of the boys can tell you I'd know thet track if I was blind."

Stillwell's ruddy face clouded, and he kicked at a cactus plant.

"Was Danny comin' or goin'?" he asked.

"I reckon he was hittin' across country fer the Peloncillo trail. But I ain't shore of thet without back-trailing him a ways. I was jest waitin' fer you to come up."

"Nels, you don't think the boy's sloped with thet little hussy, Bonita?"

"Bill, he shore was sweet on Bonita, same as Gene was an' Ed Linton before he got engaged, an' all the boys. She's shore chain-lightnin', that little black-eyed devil. Danny might hev sloped with her all right. Danny was held up on the way to town, an' then in the shame of it he got drunk. But he'll show up soon."

"Wal, mebbe you an' the boys are right. I believe you are. Nels, there ain't no doubt on earth about who was ridin' Stewart's hoss?"

"Thet's as plain as the hoss's tracks."

"Wal, it's all amazin' strange. It beats me. I wish the boys would ease up on drinkin'. I was pretty fond of Danny an' Gene. I'm afraid Gene's done fer, sure. If he crosses the border where he can fight it won't take long fer him to get plugged. I guess I'm gettin' old. I don't stand things like I used to."

"Bill, I reckon I'd better hit the Peloncillo trail. Mebbe I can find Danny."

"I reckon you had, Nels," replied Stillwell. "But don't take more'n a couple of days. We can't do much on the round-up without you. I'm short of boys."

That ended the conversation. Stillwell immediately began to hitch up his team, and the cowboys went out to fetch their strayed horses. Madeline had been curiously interested, and she saw that Florence knew it.

"Things happen, Miss Hammond," she said, soberly, almost sadly.

Madeline thought. And then straightway Florence began brightly to hum a tune and to busy herself repacking what was left of the lunch. Madeline suddenly conceived a strong liking and respect for this Western girl. She admired the consideration or delicacy or wisdom—whatever it was—which kept Florence from asking her what she knew or thought or felt about the events that had taken place.

Soon they were once more bowling along the road down a gradual incline, and then they began to climb a long ridge that had for hours hidden what lay beyond. That climb was rather tiresome, owing to the sun and the dust and the restricted view.

When they reached the summit Madeline gave a little gasp of pleasure. A deep, gray, smooth valley opened below and sloped up on the other side in little ridges like waves, and these led to the foothills, dotted with clumps of brush or trees, and beyond rose dark mountains, pine-fringed and crag-spired.

"Wal, Miss Majesty, now we're gettin' somewhere," said Stillwell, cracking his whip. "Ten miles across this valley an' we'll be in the foothills where the Apaches used to run."

"Ten miles!" exclaimed Madeline. "It looks no more than half a mile to me."

"Wal, young woman, before you go to ridin' off alone you want to get your eyes corrected to Western distance. Now, what 'd you call them black things off there on the slope?"

"Horsemen. No, cattle," replied Madeline, doubtfully.

"Nope. Jest plain, every-day cactus. An' over hyar—look down the valley. Somethin' of a pretty forest, ain't thet?" he asked, pointing.

Madeline saw a beautiful forest in the center of the valley toward the south.

"Wal, Miss Majesty, thet's jest this deceivin' air. There's no forest. It's a mirage."

"Indeed! How beautiful it is!" Madeline strained her gaze on the dark blot, and it seemed to float in the atmosphere, to have no clearly defined margins, to waver and shimmer, and then it faded and vanished.

The mountains dropped down again behind the horizon, and presently the road began once more to slope up. The horses slowed to a walk. There was a mile of rolling ridge, and then came the foothills. The road ascended through winding valleys. Trees and brush and rocks began to appear in the dry ravines. There was no water, yet all along the sandy washes were indications of floods at some periods. The heat and the dust stifled Madeline, and she had already become tired. Still she looked with all her eyes and saw birds, and beautiful quail with crests, and rabbits, and once she saw a deer.

"Miss Majesty," said Stillwell, "in the early days the Indians made this country a bad one to live in. I reckon you never heerd much about them times. Surely you was hardly born then. I'll hev to tell you some day how I fought Comanches in the Panhandle—thet was northern Texas—an' I had some mighty hair-raisin' scares in this country with Apaches."

He told her about Cochise, chief of the Chiricahua Apaches, the most savage and bloodthirsty tribe that ever made life a horror for the pioneer. Cochise befriended the whites once; but he was the victim of that friendliness, and he became the most implacable of foes. Then Geronimo, another Apache chief, had, as late as 1885, gone on the war-path, and had left a bloody trail down the New Mexico and Arizona line almost to the border. Lone ranchmen and cowboys had been killed, and mothers had shot their children and then themselves at the approach of the Apache. The name Apache curdled the blood of any woman of the Southwest in those days.

Madeline shuddered, and was glad when the old frontiersman changed the subject and began to talk of the settling of that country by the Spaniards, the legends of lost gold-mines handed down to the Mexicans, and strange stories of heroism and mystery and religion. The Mexicans had not advanced much in spite of the spread of civilization to the Southwest. They were still superstitious, and believed the legends of treasures hidden in the walls of their missions, and that unseen hands rolled rocks down the gullies upon the heads of prospectors who dared to hunt for the lost mines of the padres.

"Up in the mountains back of my ranch there's a lost mine," said Stillwell. "Mebbe it's only a legend. But somehow I believe it's there. Other lost mines hev been found. An' as fer the rollin' stones, I sure know thet's true, as any one can find out if he goes trailin' up the gulch. Mebbe thet's only the weatherin' of the cliffs. It's a sleepy, strange country, this Southwest, an', Miss Majesty, you're a-goin' to love it. You'll call it romantic. Wal, I reckon ro-mantic is correct. A feller gets lazy out hyar an' dreamy, an' he wants to put off work till to-morrow. Some folks say it's a land of Mañana—a land of to-morrow. Thet's the Mexican of it.

"But I like best to think of what a lady said to me onct—an eddicated lady like you, Miss Majesty. Wal, she said it's a land where it's always afternoon. I liked thet. I always get up sore in the mawnin's, an' don't feel good till noon. But in the afternoon I get sorta warm an' like things. An' sunset is my time. I reckon I don't want nothin' any finer than sunset from my ranch. You look out over a valley that spreads wide between Guadalupe Mountains an' the Chiricahuas, down across the red Arizona desert clear to the Sierra Madres in Mexico. Two hundred miles, Miss Majesty! An' all as clear as print! An' the sun sets behind all thet! When my time comes to die I'd like it to be on my porch smokin' my pipe an' facin' the west."

So the old cattleman talked on while Madeline listened, and Florence dozed in her seat, and the sun began to wane, and the horses climbed steadily. Presently, at the foot of a steep ascent, Stillwell got out and walked, leading the team. During this long climb fatigue claimed Madeline, and she drowsily closed her eyes, to find when she opened them again that the glaring white sky had changed to a steel-blue. The sun had sunk behind the foothills and the air was growing chilly. Stillwell had returned to the driving-seat and was chuckling to the horses. Shadows crept up out of the hollows.

"Wal, Flo," said Stillwell, "I reckon we'd better hev the rest of thet there lunch before dark."

"You didn't leave much of it," laughed Florence, as she produced the basket from under the seat.

While they ate, the short twilight shaded and gloom filled the hollows. Madeline saw the first star, a faint, winking point of light. The sky had now changed to a hazy gray. Madeline saw it gradually clear and darken, to show other faint stars. After that there was perceptible deepening of the gray and an enlarging of the stars and a brightening of new-born ones. Night seemed to come on the cold wind. Madeline was glad to have the robes close around her and to lean against Florence. The hollows were now black, but the tops of the foothills gleamed pale in a soft light. The steady tramp of the horses went on, and the creak of wheels and crunching of gravel. Madeline grew so sleepy that she could not keep her weary eyelids from falling. There were drowsier spells in which she lost a feeling of where she was, and these were disturbed by the jolt of wheels over a rough place. Then came a blank interval, short or long, which ended in a more violent lurch of the buckboard. Madeline awoke to find her head on Florence's shoulder. She sat up laughing and apologizing for her laziness. Florence assured her they would soon reach the ranch.

Madeline observed then that the horses were once more trotting. The wind was colder, the night darker, the foothills flatter. And the sky was now a wonderful deep velvet-blue blazing with millions of stars. Some of them were magnificent. How strangely white and alive! Again Madeline felt the insistence of familiar yet baffling associations. These white stars called strangely to her or haunted her.

CHAPTER 5

THE ROUND-UP

It was a crackling and roaring of fire that awakened Madeline next morning, and the first thing she saw was a huge stone fireplace in which lay a bundle of blazing sticks. Some one had kindled a fire while she slept. For a moment the curious sensation of being lost returned to her. She just dimly remembered reaching the ranch and being taken into a huge house and a huge, dimly lighted room. And it seemed to her that she had gone to sleep at once, and had awakened without remembering how she had gotten to bed.

But she was wide awake in an instant. The bed stood near one end of an enormous chamber. The adobe walls resembled a hall in an ancient feudal castle, stone-floored, stone-walled, with great darkened rafters running across the ceiling. The few articles of furniture were worn out and sadly dilapidated. Light flooded into the room from two windows on the right of the fireplace and two on the

left, and another large window near the bedstead. Looking out from where she lay Madeline saw a dark, slow
up-sweep of mountain. Her eyes returned to the cheery,
snapping fire, and she watched it while gathering courage to get up. The room was cold. When she did slip her
bare feet out upon the stone floor she very quickly put
them back under the warm blankets. And she was still in
bed trying to pluck up her courage when, with a knock
on the door and a cheerful greeting, Florence entered
carrying steaming hot water.

"Good mawnin', Miss Hammond. Hope you slept well.
You sure were tired last night. I imagine you'll find this
old rancho house as cold as a barn. It'll warm up directly.
Al's gone with the boys and Bill. We're to ride down on
the range after a while when your baggage comes."

Florence wore a woolen blouse with a scarf round her
neck, a short corduroy divided skirt, and boots; and while
she talked she energetically heaped up the burning wood
in the fireplace, and laid Madeline's clothes at the foot of
the bed, and heated a rug and put that on the floor by the
bedside. And lastly, with a sweet, direct smile, she said:

"Al told me—and I sure saw myself—that you weren't
used to being without your maid. Will you let me help
you?"

"Thank you, I am going to be my own maid for a while.
I expect I do appear a very helpless individual, but really
I do not feel so. Perhaps I have had just a little too much
waiting on."

"All right. Breakfast will be ready soon, and after that
we'll look about the place."

Madeline was charmed with the old Spanish house, and
the more she saw of it the more she thought what a delightful home it could be made. All the doors opened into

a courtyard, or patio, as Florence called it. The house was low, in the shape of a rectangle, and so immense in size that Madeline wondered if it had been a Spanish barracks. Many of the rooms were dark, without windows, and they were empty. Others were full of ranchers' implements and sacks of grain and bales of hay. Florence called these last alfalfa. The house itself appeared strong and well preserved, and it was very picturesque. But in the living-rooms were only the barest necessities, and these were worn out and comfortless.

However, when Madeline went outdoors she forgot the cheerless, bare interior. Florence led the way out on a porch and waved a hand at a vast, colored void. "That's what Bill likes," she said.

At first Madeline could not tell what was sky and what was land. The immensity of the scene stunned her faculties of conception. She sat down in one of the old rocking-chairs and looked and looked, and knew that she was not grasping the reality of what stretched wondrously before her.

"We're up at the edge of the foothills," Florence said. "You remember we rode around the northern end of the mountain range? Well, that's behind us now, and you look down across the line into Arizona and Mexico. That long slope of gray is the head of the San Bernardino Valley. Straight across you see the black Chiricahua Mountains, and away down to the south the Guadalupe Mountains. That awful red gulf between is the desert, and far, far beyond the dim, blue peaks are the Sierra Madre in Mexico."

Madeline listened and gazed with straining eyes, and wondered if this was only a stupendous mirage, and why it seemed so different from all else that she had seen, and so endless, so baffling, so grand.

"It'll sure take you a little while to get used to being up high and seeing so much," explained Florence. "That's the secret—we're up high, the air is clear, and there's the whole bare world beneath us. Don't it somehow rest you? Well, it will. Now see those specks in the valley. They are stations, little towns. The railroad goes down that way. The largest speck is Chiricahua. It's over forty miles by trail. Here round to the north you can see Don Carlos's rancho. He's fifteen miles off, and I sure wish he were a thousand. That little green square about half-way between here and Don Carlos—that's Al's ranch. Just below us are the adobe houses of the Mexicans. There's a church, too. And here to the left you see Stillwell's corrals and bunkhouses and his stables all falling to pieces. The ranch has gone to ruin. All the ranches are going to ruin. But most of them are little one-horse affairs. And here—see that cloud of dust down in the valley? It's the round-up. The boys are there, and the cattle. Wait, I'll get the glasses."

By their aid Madeline saw in the foreground a great, dense herd of cattle with dark, thick streams and dotted lines of cattle leading in every direction. She saw streaks and clouds of dust, running horses, and a band of horses grazing; and she descried horsemen standing still like sentinels, and others in action.

"The round-up! I want to know all about it—to see it," declared Madeline. "Please tell me what it means, what it's for, and then take me down there."

"It's sure a sight, Miss Hammond. I'll be glad to take you down, but I fancy you'll not want to go close. Few Eastern people who regularly eat their choice cuts of roast beef and porterhouse have any idea of the open range and the struggle cattle have to live and the hard life of cowboys. It'll sure open your eyes, Miss Hammond. I'm glad you care to know. Your brother would have made a big success in this cattle business if it hadn't been for crooked work by rival ranchers. He'll make it yet, in spite of them."

"Indeed he shall," replied Madeline. "But tell me, please, all about the round-up."

"Well, in the first place, every cattleman has to have a brand to identify his stock. Without it no cattleman, nor half a hundred cowboys, if he had so many, could ever recognize all the cattle in a big herd. There are no fences on our ranges. They are all open to everybody. Someday I hope we'll be rich enough to fence a range. The different herds graze together. Every calf has to be caught, if possible, and branded with the mark of its mother. That's no easy job. A maverick is an unbranded calf that has been weaned and shifts for itself. The maverick then belongs to the man who finds it and brands it. These little calves that lose their mothers sure have a cruel time of it. Many of them die. Then the coyotes and wolves and lions prey on them. Every year we have two big round-ups, but the boys do some branding all the year. A calf should be branded as soon as it's found. This is a safeguard against cattle-thieves. We don't have the rustling of herds and bunches of cattle like we used to. But there's always the calf-thief, and always will be as long as there's cattle-raising. The thieves have a good many cunning tricks. They kill the calf's mother or slit the calf's tongue so it can't suck and so loses its mother. They steal and hide a calf and watch it till it's big enough to fare for itself, and then brand it. They make imperfect brands and finish them at a later time.

"We have our big round-up in the fall, when there's plenty of grass and water, and all the riding stock as well as the cattle are in fine shape. The cattlemen in the valley meet with their cowboys and drive in all the cattle they can find. Then they brand and cut out each man's herd and drive it toward home. Then they go on up or down the valley, make another camp, and drive in more cattle. It takes weeks. There are so many Greasers with little bands of stock, and they are crafty and greedy. Bill says he knows Greaser cowboys, *vaqueros*, who never owned a steer or a cow, and now they've got growing herds. The same might be said of more than one white cowboy. But there's not as much of that as there used to be."

"And the horses? I want to know about them," said Madeline, when Florence paused.

"Oh, the cow-ponies! Well, they sure are interesting. Bronchos, the boys call them. Wild! they're wilder than the steers they have to chase. Bill's got bronchos heah that never have been broken and never will be. And not every boy can ride them, either. The *vaqueros* have the finest horses. Don Carlos has a black that I'd give anything to own. And he has other fine stock. Gene Stewart's big roan is a Mexican horse, the swiftest and proudest I ever saw. I was up on him once and—oh, he can run! He likes a woman, too, and that's sure something I want in a horse. I heard Al and Bill talking at breakfast about a horse for you. They were wrangling. Bill wanted you to have one and Al another. It was funny to hear them. Finally they left the choice to me, until the round-up is over. Then I suppose every cowboy on the range will offer you his best mount. Come, let's go out to the corrals and look over the few horses left."

For Madeline the morning hours flew by, with a goodly

part of the time spent on the porch gazing out over that ever-changing vista. At noon a teamster drove up with her trunks. Then while Florence helped the Mexican woman get lunch Madeline unpacked part of her effects and got out things for which she would have immediate need. After lunch she changed her dress for a riding-habit and, going outside, found Florence waiting with the horses.

The Western girl's clear eyes seemed to take stock of Madeline's appearance in one swift, inquisitive glance, and then shone with pleasure.

"You sure look—you're a picture, Miss Hammond. That riding-outfit is a new one. What it'd look like on me or another woman I can't imagine, but on you it's—it's stunning. Bill won't let you go within a mile of the cowboys. If they see you that'll be the finish of the round-up."

While they rode down the slope Florence talked about the open ranges of New Mexico and Arizona.

"Water is scarce," she said. "If Bill could afford to pipe water down from the mountains he'd have the finest ranch in the valley."

She went on to tell that the climate was mild in winter and hot in summer. Warm, sunshiny days prevailed nearly all the year round. Some summers it rained, and occasionally there would be a dry year, the dreaded *ano seco* of the Mexicans. Rain was always expected and prayed for in the midsummer months, and when it came the grama-grass sprang up, making the valleys green from mountain to mountain. The intersecting valleys, ranging between the long slope of foothills, afforded the best pasture for cattle, and these were jealously sought by the Mexicans who had only small herds to look after. Stillwell's cowboys were always chasing these *vaqueros* off land that belonged to Stillwell. He owned twenty thousand acres of unfenced land adjoining the open range. Don Carlos possessed more acreage than that, and his cattle were always mingling with Stillwell's. And in turn Don Carlos's *vaqueros* were always chasing Stillwell's cattle away from the Mexicans' watering-place. Bad feeling had been manifested for years, and now relations were strained to the breaking-point.

As Madeline rode along she made good use of her eyes. The soil was sandy and porous, and she understood why the rain and water from the few springs disappeared so quickly. At a little distance the grama-grass appeared thick, but near at hand it was seen to be sparse. Bunches of greasewood and cactus plants were interspersed here and there in the grass. What surprised Madeline was the fact that, though she and Florence had seemed to be riding quite a while, they had apparently not drawn any closer to the round-up. The slope of the valley was noticeable only after some miles had been traversed. Looking forward, Madeline imagined the valley only a few miles wide. She would have been sure she could walk her horse across it in an hour. Yet that black, bold range of Chiricahua Mountains was distant a long day's journey for even a hard-riding cowboy. It was only by looking back that Madeline could grasp the true relation of things; she could not be deceived by distance she had covered.

Gradually the black dots enlarged and assumed shape of cattle and horses moving round a great dusty patch. In another half-hour Madeline rode behind Florence to the outskirts of the scene of action. They drew rein near a huge wagon in the neighborhood of which were more than a hundred horses grazing and whistling and trotting about and lifting heads to watch the new-comers. Four cowboys

stood mounted guard over this drove of horses. Perhaps a
quarter of a mile farther out was a dusty mêlée. A roar of
tramping hoofs filled Madeline's ears. The lines of marching cattle had merged into a great, moving herd half obscured by dust.

"I can make little of what is going on," said Madeline.
"I want to go closer."

They trotted across half the intervening distance, and
when Florence halted again Madeline was still not satisfied and asked to be taken nearer. This time, before they
reined in again, Al Hammond saw them and wheeled his
horse in their direction. He yelled something which Madeline did not understand, and then halted them.

"Close enough," he called; and in the din his voice was
not very clear. "It's not safe. Wild steers! I'm glad you
came, girls. Majesty, what do you think of that bunch of
cattle?"

Madeline could scarcely reply what she thought, for the
noise and dust and ceaseless action confused her.

"They're milling, Al," said Florence.

"We just rounded them up. They're milling, and that's
bad. The *vaqueros* are hard drivers. They beat us all hollow, and we drove some, too." He was wet with sweat,
black with dust, and out of breath. "I'm off now. Flo, my
sister will have enough of this in about two minutes. Take
her back to the wagon. I'll tell Bill you're here, and run
in whenever I get a minute."

The bawling and bellowing, the crackling of horns and
pounding of hoofs, the dusty whirl of cattle, and the flying cowboys disconcerted Madeline and frightened her a
little; but she was intensely interested and meant to stay
there until she saw for herself what that strife of sound
and action meant. When she tried to take in the whole

scene she did not make out anything clearly and she determined to see it little by little.

"Will you stay longer?" asked Florence; and, receiving an affirmative reply, she warned Madeline: "If a runaway steer or angry cow comes this way let your horse go. He'll get out of the way."

That lent the situation excitement, and Madeline became absorbed. The great mass of cattle seemed to be eddying like a whirlpool, and from that Madeline understood the significance of the range word "milling." But when Madeline looked at one end of the herd she saw cattle standing still, facing outward, and calves cringing close in fear. The motion of the cattle slowed from the inside of the herd to the outside and gradually ceased. The roar and tramp of hoofs and crack of horns and thump of heads also ceased in degree, but the bawling and bellowing continued. While she watched, the herd spread, grew less dense, and stragglers appeared to be about to bolt through the line of mounted cowboys.

From that moment so many things happened, and so swiftly, that Madeline could not see a tenth of what was going on within eyesight. It seemed horsemen darted into the herd and drove out cattle. Madeline pinned her gaze on one cowboy who rode a white horse and was chasing a steer. He whirled a lasso around his head and threw it; the rope streaked out and the loop caught the leg of the steer. The white horse stopped with wonderful suddenness, and the steer slid in the dust. Quick as a flash the cowboy was out of the saddle, and, grasping the legs of the steer before it could rise, he tied them with a rope. It had all been done almost as quickly as thought. Another man came with what Madeline divined was a branding-iron. He applied it to the flank of the steer. Then it seemed the steer was up with a jump, wildly looking for some way to run, and the cowboy was circling his lasso. Madeline saw fires in the background, with a man in charge, evidently heating the irons. Then this same cowboy roped a heifer which bawled lustily when the hot iron seared its hide. Madeline saw the smoke rising from the touch of the iron, and the sight made her shrink and want to turn away, but she resolutely fought her sensitiveness. She had never been able to bear the sight of any animal suffering. The rough work in men's lives was as a sealed book to her; and now, for some reason beyond her knowledge, she wanted to see and hear and learn some of the every-day duties that made up those lives.

"Look, Miss Hammond, there's Don Carlos!" said Florence. "Look at that black horse!"

Madeline saw a dark-faced Mexican riding by. He was too far away for her to distinguish his features, but he reminded her of an Italian brigand. He bestrode a magnificent horse.

Stillwell rode up to the girls then and greeted them in his big voice.

"Right in the thick of it, hey? Wal, thet's sure fine. I'm glad to see, Miss Majesty, thet you ain't afraid of a little dust or smell of burnin' hide an' hair."

"Couldn't you brand the calves without hurting them?" asked Madeline.

"Haw, haw! Why, they ain't hurt none. They jest bawl for their mamas. Sometimes, though, we hev to hurt one jest to find which is his mama."

"I want to know how you tell what brand to put on those calves that are separated from their mothers," asked Madeline.

"Thet's decided by the round-up bosses. I've one boss

an' Don Carlos has one. They decide everything, an' they hev to be obeyed. There's Nick Steele, my boss. Watch him! He's ridin' a bay in among the cattle there. He orders the calves an' steers to be cut out. Then the cowboys do the cuttin' out an' the brandin'. We try to divide up the mavericks as near as possible."

At this juncture Madeline's brother joined the group, evidently in search of Stillwell.

"Bill, Nels just rode in," he said.

"Good. We sure need him. Any news of Danny Mains?"

"No. Nels said he lost the trail when he got on hard ground."

"Wal, wal. Say, Al, your sister is sure takin' to the round-up. An' the boys are gettin' wise. See thet sun of a gun Ambrose cuttin' capers all around. He'll sure do his prettiest. Ambrose is a ladies' man, he thinks."

The two men and Florence joined in a little pleasant teasing of Madeline, and drew her attention to what appeared to be really unnecessary feats of horsemanship all made in her vicinity. The cowboys evinced their interest in covert glances while recoiling a lasso or while passing to and fro. It was all too serious for Madeline to be amused at that moment. She did not care to talk. She sat her horse and watched.

The lithe, dark *vaqueros* fascinated her. They were here, there, everywhere, with lariats flying, horses plunging back, jerking calves and yearlings to the grass. They were cruel to their mounts, cruel to their cattle. Madeline winced as the great silver rowels of the spurs went plowing into the flanks of their horses. She saw these spurs stained with blood, choked with hair. She saw the *vaqueros* break the legs of calves and let them lie till a white cowboy came along and shot them. Calves were jerked down and dragged many yards; steers were pulled by one leg. These *vaqueros* were the most superb horsemen Madeline had ever seen, and she had seen the Cossacks and Tartars of the Russian Steppes. They were swift, graceful, daring; they never failed to catch a running steer, and the lassoes always went true. What sharp dashes the horses made, and wheelings here and there, and sudden stops, and how they braced themselves to withstand the shock!

The cowboys, likewise, showed wonderful horsemanship, and, reckless as they were, Madeline imagined she saw consideration for steed and cattle that was wanting in the *vaqueros*. They changed mounts oftener than the Mexican riders, and the horses they unsaddled for fresh ones were not so spent, so wet, so covered with lather. It was only after an hour or more of observation that Madeline began to realize the exceedingly toilsome and dangerous work cowboys had to perform. There was little or no rest for them. They were continually among wild and vicious and wide-horned steers. In many instances they owed their lives to their horses. The danger came mostly when the cowboy leaped off to tie and brand a calf he had thrown. Some of the cows charged with lowered, twisting horns. Time and again Madeline's heart leaped to her throat for fear a man would be gored. One cowboy roped a calf that bawled loudly. Its mother dashed in and just missed the kneeling cowboy as he rolled over. Then he had to run, and he could not run very fast. He was bowlegged and appeared awkward. Madeline saw another cowboy thrown and nearly run over by a plunging steer. His horse bolted as if it intended to leave the range. Then close by Madeline a big steer went down at the end of a lasso. The cowboy who had thrown it nimbly jumped

THE LIGHT OF WESTERN STARS   ★   439

down, and at that moment his horse began to rear and
prance and suddenly to lower his head close to the ground
and kick high. He ran round in a circle, the fallen steer on
the taut lasso acting as a pivot. The cowboy loosed the rope
from the steer, and then was dragged about on the grass. It
was almost frightful for Madeline to see that cowboy go at
his horse. But she recognized the mastery and skill. Then
two horses came into collision on the run. One horse went
down; the rider of the other was unseated and was kicked
before he could get up. This fellow limped to his mount
and struck at him, while the horse showed his teeth in a
vicious attempt to bite.

All the while this ceaseless activity was going on there
was a strange uproar—bawl and bellow, the shock of
heavy bodies meeting and falling, the shrill jabbering of
the *vaqueros,* and the shouts and banterings of the cowboys. They took sharp orders and replied in jest. They
went about this stern toil as if it were a game to be played
in good humor. One sang a rollicking song, another whistled, another smoked a cigarette. The sun was hot, and
they, like their horses, were dripping with sweat. The
characteristic red faces had taken on so much dust that
cowboys could not be distinguished from *vaqueros* except
by the difference in dress. Blood was not wanting on tireless hands. The air was thick, oppressive, rank with the
smell of cattle and of burning hide.

Madeline began to sicken. She choked with dust, was
almost stifled by the odor. But that made her all the more
determined to stay there. Florence urged her to come
away, or at least move back out of the worst of it. Stillwell seconded Florence. Madeline, however, smilingly refused. Then her brother said: "Here, this is making you
sick. You're pale." And she replied that she intended to

stay until the day's work ended. Al gave her a strange look, and made no more comment. The kindly Stillwell then began to talk.

"Miss Majesty, you're seein' the life of the cattleman an' cowboy—the real thing—same as it was in the early days. The ranchers in Texas an' some in Arizona hev took on style, new-fangled idees thet are good, an' I wish we could follow them. But we've got to stick to the old-fashioned, open-range round-up. It looks cruel to you, I can see thet. Wal, mebbe so, mebbe so. Them Greasers are cruel, thet's certain. Fer thet matter, I never seen a Greaser who wasn't cruel. But I reckon all the strenuous work you've seen to-day ain't any tougher than most any day of a cowboy's life. Long hours on hossback, poor grub, sleepin' on the ground, lonesome watches, dust an' sun an' wind an' thirst, day in an' day out all the year round—thet's what a cowboy has.

"Look at Nels there. See, what little hair he has is snow-white. He's red an' thin an' hard—burned up. You notice thet hump of his shoulders. An' his hands, when he gets close—jest take a peep at his hands. Nels can't pick up a pin. He can't hardly button his shirt or untie a knot in his rope. He looks sixty years—an old man. Wal, Nels ain't seen forty. He's a young man, but he's seen a lifetime fer every year. Miss Majesty, it was Arizona thet made Nels what he is, the Arizona desert an' the work of a cowman. He's seen ridin' at Cañon Diablo an' the Verdi an' Tonto Basin. He knows every mile of Aravaipa Valley an' the Pinaleno country. He's ranged from Tombstone to Douglas. He hed shot bad white men an' bad Greasers before he was twenty-one. He's seen some life, Nels has. My sixty years ain't nothin'; my early days in the Staked Plains an' on the border with Apaches ain't nothin' to what Nels has seen an' lived through. He's just come to be part of the desert; you might say he's stone an' fire an' silence an' cactus an' force. He's a man, Miss Majesty, a wonderful man. Rough he'll seem to you. Wal, I'll show you pieces of quartz from the mountain back of my ranch, an' they're thet rough they'd cut your hands. But there's pure gold in them. An' so it is with Nels an' many of these cowboys.

"An' there's Price, Monty Price. Monty stands fer Montana, where he hails from. Take a good look at him, Miss Majesty. He's been hurt, I reckon. Thet accounts fer him bein' without hoss or rope; an' thet limp. Wal, he's been ripped a little. It's sure rare an' seldom thet a cowboy gets foul of one of them thousands of sharp horns; but it does happen."

Madeline saw a very short, weazened little man, ludicrously bow-legged, with a face the color and hardness of a burnt-out cinder. He was hobbling by toward the wagon, and one of his short, crooked legs dragged.

"Not much to look at, is he?" went on Stillwell. "Wal, I know it's natural thet we're all best pleased by good looks in any one, even a man. It hedn't ought to be thet way. Monty Price looks like hell. But appearances are sure deceivin'. Monty saw years of ridin' along the Missouri bottoms, the big prairies, where there's high grass an' sometimes fires. In Montana they have blizzards thet freeze cattle standin' in their tracks. An' hosses freeze to death. They tell me thet a drivin' sleet in the face with the mercury forty below is somethin' to ride against. You can't get Monty to say much about cold. All you hev to do is to watch him, how he hunts the sun. It never gets too hot fer Monty. Wal, I reckon he was a little more prepossessin' once. The story thet come to us about Monty is this: He got caught out in a prairie fire an' could hev saved himself easy, but there was a lone ranch right in the line of fire, an' Monty knowed the rancher was away, an' his wife an' baby was home. He knowed, too, the way the wind was, thet the ranch-house would burn. It was a long chance he was takin'. But he went over, put the woman up behind him, wrapped the baby an' his hoss's haid in a wet blanket, an' rode away. Thet was sure some ride, I've heerd. But the fire ketched Monty at the last. The woman fell an' was lost, an' then his hoss. An' Monty ran an' walked an' crawled through the fire with thet baby, an' he saved it. Monty was never much good as a cowboy after thet. He couldn't hold no jobs. Wal, he'll have one with me as long as I have a steer left."

CHAPTER 6

A GIFT AND A PURCHASE

For a week the scene of the round-up lay within riding distance of the ranch-house; and Madeline passed most of this time in the saddle, watching the strenuous labors of the *vaqueros* and cowboys. She overestimated her strength, and more than once had to be lifted from her horse. Stillwell's pleasure in her attendance gave place to concern. He tried to persuade her to stay away from the round-up, and Florence grew even more solicitous. Madeline, however, was not moved by their entreaties. She grasped only dimly the truth of what it was she was learning—something infinitely more than the rounding up of cattle by cowboys, and she was loath to lose an hour of her opportunity.

Her brother looked out for her as much as his duties permitted; but for several days he never once mentioned her growing fatigue and the strain of excitement, or suggested that she had better go back to the house with

Florence. Many times she felt the drawing power of his keen, blue eyes on her face. And at these moments she sensed more than brotherly regard. He was watching her, studying her, weighing her, and the conviction was vaguely disturbing. It was disquieting for Madeline to think that Alfred might have guessed her trouble. From time to time he brought cowboys to her and introduced them, and laughed and jested, trying to make the ordeal less embarrassing for these men so little used to women.

Before the week was out, however, Alfred found occasion to tell her that it would be wiser for her to let the round-up go on without gracing it further with her presence. He said it laughingly; nevertheless, he was serious. And when Madeline turned to him in surprise, he said, bluntly:

"I don't like the way Don Carlos follows you around. Bill's afraid that Nels or Ambrose or one of the cowboys will take a fall out of the Mexican. They're itching for the chance. Of course, dear, it's absurd to you, but it's true."

Absurd it certainly was, yet it served to show Madeline how intensely occupied she had been with her own feelings, roused by the tumult and toil of the round-up. She recalled that Don Carlos had been presented to her, and that she had not liked his dark, striking face with its bold, prominent, glittering eyes and sinister lines; and she had not liked his suave, sweet, insinuating voice or his subtle manner, with its slow bows and gestures. She had thought he looked handsome and dashing on the magnificent black horse. However, now that Alfred's words made her think, she recalled that wherever she had been in the field the noble horse, with his silver-mounted saddle and his dark rider, had been always in her vicinity.

"Don Carlos has been after Florence for a long time,"

said Alfred. "He's not a young man by any means. He's fifty, Bill says; but you can seldom tell a Mexican's age from his looks. Don Carlos is well educated and a man we know very little about. Mexicans of his stamp don't regard women as we white men do. Now, my dear, beautiful sister from New York, I haven't much use for Don Carlos; but I don't want Nels or Ambrose to make a wild throw with a rope and pull the Don off his horse. So you had better ride up to the house and stay there."

"Alfred, you are joking, teasing me," said Madeline.

"Indeed not," replied Alfred. "How about it, Flo?"

Florence replied that the cowboys would upon the slightest provocation treat Don Carlos with less ceremony and gentleness than a roped steer. Old Bill Stillwell came up to be importuned by Alfred regarding the conduct of cowboys on occasion, and he not only corroborated the assertion, but added emphasis and evidence of his own.

"An', Miss Majesty," he concluded, "I reckon if Gene Stewart was ridin' fer me, thet grinnin' Greaser would hev hed a bump in the dust before now."

Madeline had been wavering between sobriety and laughter until Stillwell's mention of his ideal of cowboy chivalry decided in favor of the laughter.

"I am not convinced, but I surrender," she said. "You have only some occult motive for driving me away. I am sure that handsome Don Carlos is being unjustly suspected. But as I have seen a little of cowboys' singular imagination and gallantry, I am rather inclined to fear their possibilities. So, good-by."

Then she rode with Florence up the long, gray slope to the ranch-house. That night she suffered from excessive weariness, which she attributed more to the strange working of her mind than to riding and sitting her horse.

Morning, however, found her in no disposition to rest. It was not activity that she craved, or excitement, or pleasure. An unerring instinct, rising clear from the thronging sensations of the last few days, told her that she had missed something in life. It could not have been love, for she loved brother, sister, parents, friends; it could not have been consideration for the poor, the unfortunate, the helpless; she had expressed her sympathy for these by giving freely; it could not have been pleasure, culture, travel, society, wealth, position, fame, for these had been hers all her life. Whatever this something was, she had baffling intimations of it, hopes that faded on the verge of realizations, haunting promises that were unfulfilled. Whatever it was, it had remained hidden and unknown at home, and here in the West it began to allure and drive her to discovery. Therefore she could not rest; she wanted to go and see; she was no longer chasing phantoms; it was a hunt for treasure that held aloof, as intangible as the substance of dreams.

That morning she spoke a desire to visit the Mexican quarters lying at the base of the foothills. Florence protested that this was no place to take Madeline. But Madeline insisted, and it required only a few words and a persuading smile to win Florence over.

From the porch the cluster of adobe houses added a picturesque touch of color and contrast to the waste of gray valley. Near at hand they proved the enchantment lent by distance. They were old, crumbling, broken down, squalid. A few goats climbed around upon them; a few mangy dogs barked announcement of visitors; and then a troop of half-naked, dirty, ragged children ran out. They were very shy, and at first retreated in affright. But kind words and smiles gained their confidence, and then they followed in a body, gathering a quota of new children at each house. Madeline at once conceived the idea of doing something to better the condition of these poor Mexicans, and with this in mind she decided to have a look indoors. She fancied she might have been an apparition, judging from the effect her presence had upon the first woman she encountered. While Florence exercised what little Spanish she had command of, trying to get the women to talk, Madeline looked about the miserable little rooms. And there grew upon her a feeling of sickness, which increased as she passed from one house to another. She had not believed such squalor could exist anywhere in America. The huts reeked with filth; vermin crawled over the dirt floors. There was absolutely no evidence of water, and she believed what Florence told her—that these people never bathed. There was little evidence of labor. Idle men and women smoking cigarettes lolled about, some silent, others jabbering. They did not resent the visit of the American women, nor did they show hospitality. They appeared stupid. Disease was rampant in these houses; when the doors were shut there was no ventilation, and even with the doors open Madeline felt choked and stifled. A powerful penetrating odor pervaded the rooms that were less stifling than others, and this odor Florence explained came from a liquor the Mexicans distilled from a cactus plant. Here drunkenness was manifest, a terrible inert drunkenness that made its victims death-like.

Madeline could not extend her visit to the little mission house. She saw a padre, a starved, sad-faced man who, she instinctively felt, was good. She managed to mount her horse and ride up to the house; but, once there, she weakened, and Florence had almost to carry her indoors. She fought off a faintness, only to succumb to it when alone in her room. Still, she did not entirely lose consciousness, and soon recovered to the extent that she did not require assistance.

Upon the morning after the end of the round-up, when she went out on the porch, her brother and Stillwell appeared to be arguing about the identity of a horse.

"Wal, I reckon it's my old roan," said Stillwell, shading his eyes with his hand.

"Bill, if that isn't Stewart's horse my eyes are going back on me," replied Al. "It's not the color or shape—the distance is too far to judge by that. It's the motion—the swing."

"Al, mebbe you're right. But they ain't no rider up on thet hoss. Flo, fetch my glass."

Florence went into the house, while Madeline tried to discover the object of attention. Presently far up the gray hollow along a foothill she saw dust, and then the dark, moving figure of a horse. She was watching when Florence returned with the glass. Bill took a long look, adjusted the glasses carefully, and tried again.

"Wal, I hate to admit my eyes are gettin' pore. But I guess I'll hev to. Thet's Gene Stewart's hoss, saddled, an' comin' at a fast clip without a rider. It's amazin' strange, an' some in keepin' with other things concernin' Gene."

"Give me the glass," said Al. "Yes, I was right. Bill, the horse is not frightened. He's coming steadily; he's got something on his mind."

"Thet's a trained hoss, Al. He has more sense than some men I know. Take a look with the glasses up the hollow. See anybody?"

"No."

"Swing up over the foothills—where the trail leads.

Higher—along thet ridge where the rocks begin. See any-body?"

"By Jove! Bill—two horses! But I can't make out much for dust. They are climbing fast. One horse gone among the rocks. There—the other's gone. What do you make of that?"

"Wal, I can't make no more'n you. But I'll bet we know somethin' soon, fer Gene's hoss is comin' faster as he nears the ranch."

The wide, hollow sloping up into the foothills lay open to unobstructed view, and less than half a mile distant Madeline saw the riderless horse coming along the white trail at a rapid canter. She watched him, recalling the circumstances under which she had first seen him, and then his wild flight through the dimly lighted streets of El Cajon out into the black night. She thrilled again and believed she would never think of that starry night's adventure without a thrill. She watched the horse and felt more than curiosity. A shrill, piercing whistle pealed in.

"Wal, he's seen us, thet's sure," said Bill.

The horse neared the corrals, disappeared into a lane, and then, breaking his gait again, thundered into the inclosure and pounded to a halt some twenty yards from where Stillwell waited for him.

One look at him at close range in the clear light of day was enough for Madeline to award him a blue ribbon over all horses, even her prize-winner, White Stockings. The cowboy's great steed was no lithe, slender-bodied mustang. He was a charger, almost tremendous of build, with a black coat faintly mottled in gray, and it shone like polished glass in the sun. Evidently, he had been carefully dressed down for this occasion, for there was no dust on him, nor a kink in his beautiful mane, nor a mark on his glossy hide.

"Come hyar, you son of a gun," said Stillwell.

The horse dropped his head, snorted, and came obediently up. He was neither shy nor wild. He poked a friendly nose at Stillwell, and then looked at Al and the women. Unhooking the stirrups from the pommel, Stillwell let them fall and began to search the saddle for something which he evidently expected to find. Presently from somewhere among the trappings he produced a folded bit of paper, and after scrutinizing it handed it to Al.

"Addressed to you; an' I'll bet you two bits I know what's in it," he said.

Alfred unfolded the letter, read it, and then looked at Stillwell.

"Bill, you're a pretty good guesser. Gene's made for the border. He sent the horse by somebody, no names mentioned, and wants my sister to have him if she will accept."

"Any mention of Danny Mains?" asked the rancher.

"Not a word."

"Thet's bad. Gene 'd know about Danny if anybody did. But he's a close-mouthed cuss. So he's sure hittin' for Mexico. Wonder if Danny's goin', too? Wal, there's two of the best cowmen I ever seen gone to hell, an' I'm sorry."

With that he bowed his head and, grumbling to himself, went into the house. Alfred lifted the reins over the head of the horse and, leading him to Madeline, slipped the knot over her arm and placed the letter in her hand.

"Majesty, I'd accept the horse," he said. "Stewart is only a cowboy now, and as tough as any I've known. But he comes of a good family. He was a college man and a gentleman once. He went to the bad out here, like so many fellows go, like I nearly did. Then he had told me about his sister and mother. He cared a good deal for them. I think he has been a source of unhappiness to them. It was mostly when he was reminded of this in some way that he'd get drunk. I have always stuck to him, and I would do so yet if I had the chance. You can see Bill is heartbroken about Danny Mains and Stewart. I think he rather hoped to get good news. There's not much chance of them coming back now, at least not in the case of Stewart. This giving up his horse means he's going to join the rebel forces across the border. What wouldn't I give to see that cowboy break loose on a bunch of Greasers! Oh, damn the luck! I beg your pardon, Majesty. But I'm upset, too. I'm sorry about Stewart. I liked him pretty well before he thrashed that coyote of a sheriff, Pat Hawe, and afterward I guess I liked him more. You read the letter, sister, and accept the horse."

In silence Madeline bent her gaze from her brother's face to the letter:

FRIEND AL,—I'm sending my horse down to you because I'm going away and haven't the nerve to take him where he'd get hurt or fall into strange hands.

If you think it's all right, why, give him to your sister with my respects. But if you don't like the idea, Al, or if she won't have him, then he's for you. I'm not forgetting your kindness to me, even if I never showed it. And, Al, my horse has never felt a quirt or a spur, and I'd like to think you'd never hurt him.

I'm hoping your sister will take him. She'll be good to him, and she can afford to take care of him. And, while I'm waiting to be plugged by a Greaser bullet, if I happen to have a picture in mind of how she'll look up on my horse, why, man, it's not going to make any difference to you. She needn't ever know it.

Between you and me, Al, don't let her or Flo ride alone over Don Carlos's way. If I had time I could tell you something about that slick Greaser. And tell your sister, if there's ever any reason for her to run away from anybody when she's up on that roan, just let her lean over and yell in his ear. She'll find herself riding the wind.

So long,

GENE STEWART.

Madeline thoughtfully folded the letter and murmured: "How he must love his horse!"

"Well, I should say so," replied Alfred. "Flo will tell you. She's the only person Gene ever let ride that horse, unless, as Bill thinks, the little Mexican girl Bonita rode him out of El Cajon the other night. Well, sister mine, how about it—will you accept the horse?"

"Assuredly. And very happy indeed am I to get him. Al, you said, I think, that Mr. Stewart named him after me—saw my nickname in the New York paper?"

"Yes."

"Well, I will not change his name. But, Al, how shall I ever climb up on him? He's taller than I am. What a giant of a horse! Oh, look at him—he's nosing my hand. I really believe he understood what I said. Al, did you ever see such a splendid head and such beautiful eyes? They are so large and dark and soft—and human. Oh, I am a fickle woman, for I am forgetting White Stockings."

"I'll gamble he'll make you forget any other horse," said Alfred. "You'll have to get on him from the porch."

As Madeline was not dressed for the saddle, she did not attempt to mount.

"Come, Majesty—how strange that sounds!—we must get acquainted. You have now a new owner, a very severe young woman who will demand loyalty from you and obedience, and some day, after a decent period, she will expect love."

Madeline led the horse to and fro, and was delighted with his gentleness. She discovered that he did not need to be led. He came at her call, followed her like a pet dog, rubbed his black muzzle against her. Sometimes, at the turns in their walk, he lifted his head and with ears forward looked up the trail by which he had come, and beyond the foothills. He was looking over the range. Some one was calling to him, perhaps, from beyond the mountains. Madeline liked him the better for that memory, and pitied the wayward cowboy who had parted with his only possession for very love of it.

That afternoon when Alfred lifted Madeline to the back of the big roan she felt high in the air.

"We'll have a run out to the mesa," said her brother, as he mounted. "Keep a tight rein on him, and ease up when you want him to go faster. But don't yell in his ear unless you want Florence and me to see you disappear on the horizon."

He trotted out of the yard, down by the corrals, to come out on the edge of a gray, open flat that stretched several miles to the slope of a mesa. Florence led, and Madeline saw that she rode like a cowboy. Alfred drew on to her side, leaving Madeline in the rear. Then the leading horses broke into a gallop. They wanted to run, and Madeline felt with a thrill that she would hardly be able to keep Majesty from running, even if she wanted to. He sawed on the tight bridle as the others drew away, and broke from pace to gallop. Then Florence put her horse into a run. Alfred turned and called to Madeline to come along.

"This will never do. They are running away from us," said Madeline, and she eased up her hold on the bridle. Something happened beneath her just then; she did not know at first exactly what. As much as she had been on horseback she had never ridden at a running gait. In New York it was not decorous or safe. So when Majesty lowered and stretched and changed the stiff, jolting gallop for a wonderful, smooth, gliding run it required Madeline some moments to realize what was happening. It did not take long for her to see the distance diminishing between her and her companions. Still they had gotten a goodly start and were far advanced. She felt the steady, even rush of the wind. It amazed her to find how easily, comfortably she kept to the saddle. The experience was new. The one fault she had heretofore found with riding was the violent shaking-up. In this instance she experienced nothing of that kind, no strain, no necessity to hold on with a desperate awareness of work. She had never felt the wind in her face, the whip of a horse's mane, the buoyant, level spring of a running gait. It thrilled her, exhilarated her, fired her blood. Suddenly she found herself alive, throbbing; and, inspired by she knew not what, she loosened the bridle and, leaning far forward, she cried, "Oh, you splendid fellow, run!"

She heard from under her a sudden quick clattering roar of hoofs, and she swayed back with the wonderfully swift increase in Majesty's speed. The wind stung her face, howled in her ears, tore at her hair. The gray plain swept by on each side, and in front seemed to be waving toward her. In her blurred sight Florence and Alfred appeared to be coming back. But she saw presently, upon nearer view, that Majesty was overhauling the other horses, was going to pass them. Indeed, he did pass them, shooting by so as almost to make them appear standing still. And he ran on, not breaking his gait till he reached the steep side of the mesa, where he slowed down and stopped.

"Glorious!" exclaimed Madeline. She was all in a blaze, and every muscle and nerve of her body tingled and quivered. Her hands, as she endeavored to put up the loosened strands of hair, trembled and failed of their accustomed dexterity. Then she faced about and waited for her companions.

Alfred reached her first, laughing, delighted, yet also a little anxious.

"Holy smoke! But can't he run? Did he bolt on you?"

"No, I called in his ear," replied Madeline.

"So that was it. That's the woman of you and forbidden fruit. Flo said she'd do it the minute she was on him. Majesty, you can ride. See if Flo doesn't say so."

The Western girl came up then with her pleasure bright in her face.

"It was just great to see you. How your hair burned in the wind! Al, she sure can ride. Oh, I'm so glad! I was a little afraid. And that horse! Isn't he grand? Can't he run?"

Alfred led the way up the steep, zigzag trail to the top of the mesa. Madeline saw a beautiful flat surface of short grass, level as a floor. She uttered a little cry of wonder and enthusiasm.

"Al, what a place for golf! This would be the finest links in the world."

"Well, I've thought of that myself," he replied. "The only trouble would be—could anybody stop looking at the scenery long enough to hit a ball? Majesty, look!"

And then it seemed that Madeline was confronted by a spectacle too sublime and terrible for her gaze. The immensity of this red-ridged, deep-gulfed world descending by incalculable distances refused to be grasped, and awed her, shocked her.

"Once, Majesty, when I first came out West I was down and out—determined to end it all," said Alfred. "And I happened to climb up here looking for a lonely place to die. When I saw that I changed my mind."

Madeline was silent. She remained so during the ride around the rim of the mesa and down the steep trail. This time Alfred and Florence failed to tempt her into a race. She had been awe-struck; she had been exalted; she had been confounded; and she recovered slowly without divining exactly what had come to her.

She reached the ranch-house far behind her companions, and at supper-time was unusually thoughtful. Later, when they assembled on the porch to watch the sunset, Stillwell's humorous complainings inspired the inception of an idea which flashed up in her mind swift as lightning. And then by listening sympathetically she encouraged him to recite the troubles of a poor cattleman. They were many and long and interesting, and rather numbing to the life of her inspired idea.

"Mr. Stillwell, could ranching here on a large scale, with up-to-date methods, be made—well, not profitable exactly, but to pay—to run without loss?" she asked, determined to kill her new-born idea at birth or else give it breath and hope of life.

"Wal, I reckon it could," he replied, with a short laugh.

"It'd sure be a money-maker. Why, with all my bad luck an' poor equipment I've lived pretty well an' paid my debts an' haven't really lost any money except the original outlay. I reckon thet's sunk fer good."

"Would you sell—if some one would pay your price?"

"Miss Majesty, I'd jump at the chance. Yet somehow I'd hate to leave hyar. I'd jest be fool enough to go sink the money in another ranch."

"Would Don Carlos and these other Mexicans sell?"

"They sure would. The Don has been after me fer years, wantin' to sell thet old rancho of his; an' these herders in the valley with their stray cattle, they'd fall daid at sight of a little money."

"Please tell me, Mr. Stillwell, exactly what you would do here if you had unlimited means?" went on Madeline.

"Good Lud!" ejaculated the rancher, and started so he dropped his pipe. Then with his clumsy huge fingers he refilled it, relighted it, took a few long pulls, puffed great clouds of smoke, and, squaring round, hands on his knees, he looked at Madeline with piercing intentness. His hard face began to relax and soften and wrinkle into a smile.

"Wal, Miss Majesty, it jest makes my old heart warm up to think of sich a thing. I dreamed a lot when I first come hyar. What would I do if I hed unlimited money? Listen. I'd buy out Don Carlos an' the Greasers. I'd give a job to every good cowman in this country. I'd make them prosper as I prospered myself. I'd buy all the good horses on the ranges. I'd fence twenty thousand acres of the best grazin'. I'd drill fer water in the valley. I'd pipe water down from the mountains. I'd dam up thet draw out there. A mile-long dam from hill to hill would give me a big lake, an' hevin' an eye fer beauty, I'd plant cottonwoods around it. I'd fill that lake full of fish. I'd put in the biggest field of alfalfa in the Southwest. I'd plant fruit trees an' garden. I'd tear down them old corrals an' barns an' bunk-houses to build new ones. I'd make this old rancho some comfortable an' fine. I'd put in grass an' flowers all around an' bring young pine trees down from the mountains. An' when all thet was done I'd sit in my chair an' smoke an' watch the cattle stringin' in fer water an' stragglin' back into the valley. An' I see the cowboys ridin' easy an' heah them singin' in their bunks. An' thet red sun out there wouldn't set on a happier man in the world than Bill Stillwell, last of the old cattlemen."

Madeline thanked the rancher, and then rather abruptly retired to her room, where she felt no restraint to hide the force of that wonderful idea, now full-grown and tenacious and alluring.

Upon the next day, late in the afternoon, she asked Alfred if it would be safe for her to ride out to the mesa.

"I'll go with you," he said, gaily.

"Dear fellow, I want to go alone," she replied.

"Ah!" Alfred exclaimed, suddenly serious. He gave her just a quick glance, then turned away. "Go ahead. I think it's safe. I'll make it safe by sitting here with my glass and keeping an eye on you. Be careful coming down the trail. Let the horse pick his way. That's all."

She rode Majesty across the wide flat, up the zigzag trail, across the beautiful grassy level to the far rim of the mesa, and not till then did she lift her eyes to face the southwest.

Madeline looked from the gray valley at her feet to the blue Sierra Madres, gold-tipped in the setting sun. Her vision embraced in that glance distance and depth and glory hitherto unrevealed to her. The gray valley sloped and widened to the black sentinel Chiricahuas, and beyond was lost in a vast corrugated sweep of earth, reddening down to the west, where a golden blaze lifted the dark, rugged mountains into bold relief. The scene had infinite beauty. But after Madeline's first swift, all-embracing flash of enraptured eyes, thought of beauty passed away. In that darkening desert there was something illimitable. Madeline saw the hollow of a stupendous hand; she felt a mighty hold upon her heart. Out of the endless space, out of silence and desolation and mystery and age, came slow-changing colored shadows, phantoms of peace, and they whispered to Madeline. They whispered that it was a great, grim, immutable earth; that time was eternity; that life was fleeting. They whispered for her to be a woman; to love some one before it was too late; to love any one, every one; to realize the need of work, and in doing it to find happiness.

She rode back across the mesa and down the trail, and, once more upon the flat, she called to the horse and made him run. His spirit seemed to race with hers. The wind of his speed blew her hair from its fastenings. When he thundered to a halt at the porch steps Madeline, breathless and disheveled, alighted with the mass of her hair tumbling around her.

Alfred met her, and his exclamation, and Florence's rapt eyes shining on her face, and Stillwell's speechlessness made her self-conscious. Laughing, she tried to put up the mass of hair.

"I must—look a—fright," she panted.

"Wal, you can say what you like," replied the old cattleman, "but I know what I think."

Madeline strove to attain calmness.

"My hat—and my combs—went on the wind. I thought—my hair would go, too. . . . There is the evening star. . . . I think I am very hungry."

And then she gave up trying to be calm, and likewise to fasten up her hair, which fell again in a golden mass.

"Mr. Stillwell," she began, and paused, strangely aware of a hurried note, a deeper ring in her voice. "Mr. Stillwell, I want to buy your ranch—to engage you as my superintendent. I want to buy Don Carlos's ranch and other property to the extent, say, of fifty thousand acres. I want you to buy horses and cattle—in short, to make all those improvements which you said you had so long dreamed of. Then I have ideas of my own, in the development of which I must have your advice and Alfred's. I intend to better the condition of those poor Mexicans in the valley. I intend to make life a little more worth living for them and for the cowboys of this range. Tomorrow we shall talk it all over, plan all the business details."

Madeline turned from the huge, ever-widening smile that beamed down upon her and held out her hands to her brother.

"Alfred, strange, is it not, my coming out to you? Nay, don't smile. I hope I have found myself—my work, my happiness—here under the light of that western star."

CHAPTER 7

HER MAJESTY'S RANCHO

Five months brought all that Stillwell had dreamed of, and so many more changes and improvements and innovations that it was as if a magic touch had transformed the old ranch. Madeline and Alfred and Florence had talked over a fitting name, and had decided on one chosen by Madeline. But this instance was the only one in the course of developments in which Madeline's wishes were not complied with. The cowboys named the new ranch "Her Majesty's Rancho." Stillwell said the names cowboys bestowed were felicitous, and as unchangeable as the everlasting hills; Florence went over to the enemy; and Alfred, laughing at Madeline's protest, declared the cowboys had elected her queen of the ranges, and that there was no help for it. So the name stood "Her Majesty's Rancho."

The April sun shone down upon a slow-rising green

knoll that nestled in the lea of the foothills, and seemed to center bright rays upon the long ranch-house, which gleamed snow-white from the level summit. The grounds around the house bore no semblance to Eastern lawns or parks; there had been no landscape-gardening; Stillwell had just brought water and grass and flowers and plants to the knoll-top, and there had left them, as it were, to follow nature. His idea may have been crude, but the result was beautiful. Under that hot sun and balmy air, with cool water daily soaking into the rich soil, a green covering sprang into life, and everywhere upon it, as if by magic, many colored flowers rose in the sweet air. Pale wild flowers, lavender daisies, fragile bluebells, white four-petaled lilies, like Eastern Mayflowers, and golden poppies, deep sunset gold, color of the West, bloomed in happy confusion. California roses, crimson as blood, nodded heavy heads and trembled with the weight of bees. Low down in bare places, isolated, open to the full power of the sun, blazed the vermilion and magenta blossoms of cactus plants.

Green slopes led all the way down to where new adobe barns and sheds had been erected, and wide corrals stretched high-barred fences down to the great squares of alfalfa gently inclining to the gray of the valley. The bottom of a dammed-up hollow shone brightly with its slowly increasing acreage of water, upon which thousands of migratory wild fowl whirred and splashed and squawked, as if reluctant to leave this cool, wet surprise so new in the long desert journey to the northland. Quarters for the cowboys—comfortable, roomy adobe houses that not even the lamest cowboy dared designate as crampy bunks— stood in a row upon a long bench of ground above the lake. And down to the edge of the valley the cluster of Mexican habitations and the little church showed the touch of the same renewing hand.

All that had been left of the old Spanish house, which had been Stillwell's home for so long, was the bare, massive structure, and some of this had been cut away for new doors and windows. Every modern convenience, even to hot and cold running water and acetylene light, had been installed; and the whole interior painted and carpentered and furnished. The ideal sought had not been luxury, but comfort. Every door into the patio looked out upon dark, rich grass and sweet-faced flowers, and every window looked down the green slopes.

Madeline's rooms occupied the west end of the building and comprised four in number, all opening out upon the long porch. There was a small room for her maid, another which she used as an office, then her sleeping apartment; and, lastly, the great light chamber which she had liked so well upon first sight, and which now, simply yet beautifully furnished and containing her favorite books and pictures, she had come to love as she had never loved any room at home. In the morning the fragrant, balmy air blew the white curtains of the open windows; at noon the drowsy, sultry quiet seemed to creep in for the siesta that was characteristic of the country; in the afternoon the westering sun peeped under the porch-roof and painted the walls with gold bars that slowly changed to red.

Madeline Hammond cherished a fancy that the transformation she had wrought in the old Spanish house and in the people with whom she had surrounded herself, great as that transformation had been, was as nothing compared to the one wrought in herself. She had found an object in life. She was busy, she worked with her hands as well as mind, yet she seemed to have more time to read and think and study and idle and dream than ever before. She had seen her brother through his difficulties, on the road to all the success and prosperity that he cared for. Madeline had been a conscientious student of ranching and an apt pupil of Stillwell. The old cattleman, in his simplicity, gave her the place in his heart that was meant for the daughter he had never had. His pride in her, Madeline thought, was beyond reason or belief or words to tell. Under his guidance, sometimes accompanied by Alfred and Florence, Madeline had ridden the ranges and had studied the life and work of the cowboys. She had camped on the open range, slept under the blinking stars, ridden forty miles a day in the face of dust and wind. She had taken two wonderful trips down into the desert—one trip to Chiricahua, and from there across the waste of sand and rock and alkali and cactus to the Mexican border-line; and the other through the Aravaipa Valley, with its deep, red-walled cañons and wild fastnesses.

This breaking-in, this training into Western ways, though she had been a so-called outdoor girl, had required great effort and severe pain; but the education, now past its primary grades, had become a labor of love. She had perfect health, abounding spirits. She was so active that she had to train herself into taking the midday siesta, a custom of the country and imperative during the hot summer months. Sometimes she looked in her mirror and laughed with sheer joy at sight of the lithe, audacious, brown-faced, flashing-eyed creature reflected there. It was not so much joy in her beauty as sheer joy of life. Eastern critics had been wont to call her beautiful in those days when she had been pale and slender and proud and cold. She laughed. If they could only see her now! From the tip of her golden head to her feet she was alive, pulsating, on fire.

Sometimes she thought of her parents, sister, friends, of how they had persistently refused to believe she could or would stay in the West. They were always asking her to come home. And when she wrote, which was dutifully often, the last thing under the sun that she was likely to mention was the change in her. She wrote that she would return to her old home sometime, of course, for a visit; and letters such as this brought returns that amused Madeline, sometimes saddened her. She meant to go back East for a while, and after that once or twice every year. But the initiative was a difficult step from which she shrank. Once home, she would have to make explanations, and these would not be understood. Her father's business had been such that he could not leave it for the time required for a Western trip, or else, according to his letter, he would have come for her. Mrs. Hammond could not have been driven to cross the Hudson River; her un-American idea of the wilderness westward was that Indians still chased buffalo on the outskirts of Chicago. Madeline's sister Helen had long been eager to come, as much from curiosity, Madeline thought, as from sisterly regard. And at length Madeline concluded that the proof of her breaking permanent ties might better be seen by visiting relatives and friends before she went back East. With that in mind she invited Helen to visit her during the summer, and bring as many friends as she liked.

No slight task indeed was it to oversee the many business details of Her Majesty's Rancho and to keep a record of them. Madeline found the course of business training upon which her father had insisted to be invaluable to her now. It helped her to assimilate and arrange the practical details of cattle-raising as put forth by the blunt Stillwell. She split up the great stock of cattle into different herds, and when any of these were out running upon the open range she had them closely watched. Part of the time each herd was kept in an inclosed range, fed and watered, and carefully handled by a big force of cowboys. She employed three cowboy scouts whose sole duty was to ride the ranges searching for stray, sick, or crippled cattle or motherless calves, and to bring these in to be treated and nursed. There were two cowboys whose business was to master a pack of Russian staghounds and to hunt down the coyotes, wolves, and lions that preyed upon the herds. The better and tamer milch cows were separated from the ranging herds and kept in a pasture adjoining the dairy. All branding was done in corrals, and calves were weaned from mother-cows at the proper time to benefit both. The old method of branding and classing, that had so shocked Madeline, had been abandoned, and one had been inaugurated whereby cattle and cowboys and horses were spared brutality and injury.

Madeline established an extensive vegetable farm, and she planted orchards. The climate was superior to that of California, and, with abundant water, trees and plants and gardens flourished and bloomed in a way wonderful to behold. It was with ever-increasing pleasure that Madeline walked through acres of ground once bare, now green and bright and fragrant. There were poultry-yards and pigpens and marshy quarters for ducks and geese. Here in the farming section of the ranch Madeline found employment for the little colony of Mexicans. Their lives had been as hard and barren as the dry valley where they had lived. But as the valley had been transformed by the soft, rich touch of water, so their lives had been transformed by help and sympathy and work. The children were wretched no more, and many that had been blind could now see, and Madeline had become to them a new and blessed virgin.

Madeline looked abroad over these lands and likened the change in them and those who lived by them to the change in her heart. It may have been fancy, but the sun seemed to be brighter, the sky bluer, the wind sweeter. Certain it was that the deep green of grass and garden was not fancy, nor the white and pink of blossom, nor the blaze and perfume of flower, nor the sheen of lake and the fluttering of new-born leaves. Where there had been monotonous gray there was now vivid and changing color. Formerly there had been silence both day and night; now during the sunny hours there was music. The whistle of prancing stallions pealed in from the grassy ridges. Innumerable birds had come and, like the northward-journeying ducks, they had tarried to stay. The song of meadow-lark and blackbird and robin, familiar to Madeline from childhood, mingled with the new and strange heart-throbbing song of mocking-bird and the piercing blast of the desert eagle and the melancholy moan of turtle-dove.

One April morning Madeline sat in her office wrestling with a problem. She had problems to solve every day. The majority of these were concerned with the management of twenty-seven incomprehensible cowboys. This particular problem involved Ambrose Mills, who had eloped with her French maid, Christine.

Stillwell faced Madeline with a smile almost as huge as his bulk.

"Wal, Miss Majesty, we ketched them; but not before Padre Marcos had married them. All thet speedin' in the autoomoobile was jest a-scarin' of me to death fer nothin'. I tell you Link Stevens is crazy about runnin' thet car. Link never hed no sense even with a hoss. He ain't afraid of the devil hisself. If my hair hedn't been white it'd be white now. No more rides in thet thing fer me! Wal, we ketched Ambrose an' the girl too late. But we fetched them back, an' they're out there now, spoonin', sure oblivious to their shameless conduct."

"Stillwell, what shall I say to Ambrose? How shall I punish him? He has done wrong to deceive me. I never was so surprised in my life. Christine did not seem to care any more for Ambrose than for any of the other cowboys. What does my authority amount to? I must do something. Stillwell, you must help me."

Whenever Madeline fell into a quandary she had to call upon the old cattleman. No man ever held a position with greater pride than Stillwell, but he had been put to tests that steeped him in humility. Here he scratched his head in great perplexity.

"Dog-gone the luck! What's this elopin' bizness to do with cattle-raisin'? I don't know nothin' but cattle. Miss Majesty, it's amazin' strange what these cowboys hev come to. I never seen no cowboys like these we've got hyar now. I don't know them any more. They dress swell an' read books, an' some of them hev actooly stopped cussin' an' drinkin'. I ain't sayin' all this is against them. Why, now they're jest the finest bunch of cow-punchers I ever seen or dreamed of. But managin' them now is beyond me. When cowboys begin to play thet game gol-lof an' run off with French maids I reckon Bill Stillwell has got to resign."

"Stillwell! Oh, you will not leave me? What in the world would I do?" exclaimed Madeline, in great anxiety.

"Wal, I sure won't leave you, Miss Majesty. No, I never'll do thet. I'll run the cattle bizness fer you an' see after the hosses an' other stock. But I've got to hev a foreman who can handle this amazin' strange bunch of cowboys."

"You've tried half a dozen foremen. Try more until you find the man who meets your requirements," said Madeline. "Never mind that now. Tell me how to impress Ambrose—to make him an example, so to speak. I must have another maid. And I do not want a new one carried off in this summary manner."

"Wal, if you fetch pretty maids out hyar you can't expect nothin' else. Why, thet black-eyed little French girl, with her white skin an' pretty airs an' smiles an' shrugs, she had the cowboys crazy. It'll be wuss with the next one."

"Oh, dear," sighed Madeline.

"An' as fer impressin' Ambrose, I reckon I can tell you how to do thet. Jest give it to him good an' say you're goin' to fire him. That'll fix Ambrose, an' mebbe scare the other boys fer a spell."

"Very well, Stillwell, bring Ambrose in to see me, and tell Christine to wait in my room."

It was a handsome, debonair, bright-eyed cowboy that came tramping into Madeline's presence. His accustomed shyness and awkwardness had disappeared in an excited manner. He was a happy boy. He looked straight into Madeline's face as if he expected her to wish him joy. And Madeline actually found that expression trembling to her lips. She held it back until she could be severe. But Madeline feared she would fail of much severity.

Something warm and sweet, like a fragrance, had entered the room with Ambrose.

"Ambrose, what have you done?" she asked.

"Miss Hammond, I've been and gone and got married," replied Ambrose, his words tumbling over one another. His eyes snapped, and there was a kind of glow upon his clean-shaven brown cheek. "I've stole a march on the other boys. There was Frank Slade pushin' me close, and I was havin' some runnin' to keep Jim Bell back in my dust. Even old man Nels made eyes at Christine! So I wasn't goin' to take any chances. I just packed her off to El Cajon and married her."

"Oh, so I heard," said Madeline, slowly, as she watched him. "Ambrose, do you—love her?"

He reddened under her clear gaze, dropped his head, and fumbled with his new sombrero, and there was a catch in his breath. Madeline saw his powerful brown hand tremble. It affected her strangely that this stalwart cowboy, who could rope and throw and tie a wild steer in less than one minute, should tremble at a mere question. Suddenly he raised his head, and at the beautiful blaze of his eyes Madeline turned her own away.

"Yes, Miss Hammond, I love her," he said. "I think I love her in the way you're askin' about. I know the first time I saw her I thought how wonderful it'd be to have a girl like that for my wife. It's all been so strange—her comin' an' how she made me feel. Sure I never knew many girls, and I haven't seen any girls at all for years. But when she came! A girl makes a wonderful difference in a man's feelin's and thoughts. I guess I never had any before. Leastways, none like I have now. My—it—well, I guess I have a little understandin' now of Padre Marcos's blessin'."

"Ambrose, have you nothing to say to me?" asked Madeline.

"I'm sure sorry I didn't have time to tell you. But I was in some hurry."

"What did you intend to do? Where were you going when Stillwell found you?"

"We'd just been married. I hadn't thought of anything after that. Suppose I'd have rustled back to my job. I'll sure have to work now and save my money."

"Oh, well, Ambrose, I am glad you realize your responsibilities. Do you earn enough—is your pay sufficient to keep a wife?"

"Sure it is! Why, Miss Hammond, I never before earned half the salary I'm gettin' now. It's some fine to work for you. I'm goin' to fire the boys out of my bunk-house and fix it up for Christine and me. Say, won't they be jealous?"

"Ambrose, I—I congratulate you. I wish you joy," said Madeline. "I—I shall make Christine a little wedding-present. I want to talk to her for a few moments. You may go now."

It would have been impossible for Madeline to say one severe word to that happy cowboy. She experienced difficulty in hiding her own happiness at the turn of events. Curiosity and interest mingled with her pleasure when she called to Christine.

"Mrs. Ambrose Mills, please come in."

No sound came from the other room.

"I should like very much to see the bride," went on Madeline.

Still there was no stir or reply.

"Christine!" called Madeline.

Then it was as if a little whirlwind of flying feet and

entreating hands and beseeching eyes blew in upon Madeline. Christine was small, graceful, plump, with very white skin and very dark hair. She had been Madeline's favorite maid for years, and there was sincere affection between the two. Whatever had been the blissful ignorance of Ambrose, it was manifestly certain that Christine knew how she had transgressed. Her fear and remorse and appeal for forgiveness were poured out in an incoherent storm. Plain it was that the little French maid had been overwhelmed. It was only after Madeline had taken the emotional girl in her arms and had forgiven and soothed her that her part in the elopement became clear. Christine was in a maze. But gradually, as she talked and saw that she was forgiven, calmness came in some degree, and with it a story which amused, yet shocked Madeline. The unmistakable, shy, marveling love, scarcely realized by Christine, gave Madeline relief and joy. If Christine loved Ambrose there was no harm done. Watching the girl's eyes, wonderful with their changes of thought, listening to her attempts to explain what it was evident she did not understand, Madeline gathered that if ever a caveman had taken unto himself a wife, if ever a barbarian had carried off a Sabine woman, then Ambrose Mills had acted with the violence of such ancient forebears. Just how it all happened seemed to be beyond Christine.

"He say he love me," repeated the girl, in a kind of rapt awe. "He ask me to marry him—he kees me—he hug me—he lift me on ze horse—he ride with me all night—he marry me."

And she exhibited a ring on the third finger of her left hand. Madeline saw that, whatever had been the state of Christine's feeling for Ambrose before this marriage, she loved him now. She had been taken forcibly, but she was won.

After Christine had gone, comforted and betraying her shy eagerness to get back to Ambrose, Madeline was haunted by the look in the girl's eyes, and her words. Assuredly the spell of romance was on this sunny land. For Madeline there was a nameless charm, a nameless thrill combating her sense of the violence and unfitness of Ambrose's wooing. Something, she knew not what, took arms against her intellectual arraignment of the cowboy's method of getting himself a wife. He had said straight out that he loved the girl—he had asked her to marry him— he kissed her—he hugged her—he lifted her upon his horse—he rode away with her through the night—and he married her. In whatever light Madeline reviewed this thing she always came back to her first natural impression; it thrilled her, charmed her. It went against all the precepts of her training; nevertheless, it was somehow splendid and beautiful. She imagined it stripped another artificial scale from her over-sophisticated eyes.

Scarcely had she settled again to the task on her desk when Stillwell's heavy tread across the porch interrupted her. This time when he entered he wore a look that bordered upon the hysterical; it was difficult to tell whether he was trying to suppress grief or glee.

"Miss Majesty, there's another amazin' strange thing sprung on me. Hyar's Jim Bell come to see you, an' when I taxed him, sayin' you was tolerable busy, he up an' says he was hungry an' he ain't a-goin' to eat any more bread made in a wash-basin! Says he'll starve first. Says Nels hed the gang over to his bunk an' feasted them on bread you taught him how to make in some new-fangled bucket-machine with a crank. Jim says thet bread beat any cake he ever eat, an' he wants you to show him how to make some. Now, Miss Majesty, as superintendent of this ranch I ought to know what's goin' on. Mebbe Jim is jest a-joshin' me. Mebbe he's gone clean dotty. Mebbe I hev. An' beggin' your pardon, I want to know if there's any truth in what Jim says Nels says."

Whereupon it became necessary for Madeline to stifle her mirth and to inform the sadly perplexed old cattleman that she had received from the East a patent bread-mixer, and in view of the fact that her household women had taken fright at the contrivance, she had essayed to operate it herself. This had turned out to be so simple, so saving of time and energy and flour, so much more cleanly than the old method of mixing dough with the hands, and particularly it had resulted in such good bread, that Madeline had been pleased. Immediately she ordered more of the bread-mixers. One day she had happened upon Nels making biscuit dough in his wash-basin, and she had delicately and considerately introduced to him the idea of her new method. Nels, it appeared, had a great reputation as a bread-maker, and he was proud of it. Moreover, he was skeptical of any clap-trap thing with wheels and cranks. He consented, however, to let her show how the thing worked and to sample some of the bread. To that end she had him come up to the house, where she won him over. Stillwell laughed loud and long.

"Wal, wal, wal!" he exclaimed, at length. "Thet's fine, an' it's powerful funny. Mebbe you don't see how funny? Wal, Nels has jest been lordin' it over the boys about how you showed *him,* an' now you'll hev to show every last cowboy on the place the same thing. Cowboys are the jealousest kind of fellers. They're all crazy about you, anyway. Take Jim out hyar. Why, thet lazy cow-puncher jest never would make bread. He's notorious fer shirkin' his share of the grub deal. I've knowed Jim to trade off washin' the pots an' pans fer a lonely watch on a rainy night. All he wants is to see you show him the same as Nels is crowin' over. Then he'll crow over his bunkie, Frank Slade, an' then Frank'll get lonely to know all about this wonderful bread-machine. Cowboys are amazin' strange critters, Miss Majesty. An' now thet you've begun with them this way, you'll hev to keep it up. I will say I never seen such a bunch to work. You've sure put heart in them."

"Indeed, Stillwell, I am glad to hear that," replied Madeline. "And I shall be pleased to teach them all. But may I not have them all up here at once—at least those off duty?"

"Wal, I reckon you can't onless you want to hev them scrappin'," rejoined Stillwell, dryly. "What you've got on your hands now, Miss Majesty, is to let 'em come one by one, an' make each cowboy think you're takin' more especial pleasure in showin' him than the feller who came before him. Then mebbe we can go on with cattle-raisin'."

Madeline protested, and Stillwell held inexorably to what he said was wisdom. Several times Madeline had gone against his advice, to her utter discomfiture and rout. She dared not risk it again, and resigned herself gracefully and with subdued merriment to her task. Jim Bell was ushered into the great, light, spotless kitchen, where presently Madeline appeared to put on an apron and roll up her sleeves. She explained the use of the several pieces of aluminum that made up the bread-mixer and fastened the bucket to the table-shelf. Jim's life might have depended upon this lesson, judging from his absorbed manner and his desire to have things explained over and over, especially the turning of the crank. When Madeline had to take Jim's hand three times to show him the simple mechanism and then he did not understand, she began to have faint misgivings as to his absolute sincerity. She guessed that as long as she touched Jim's hand he never would understand. Then as she began to measure out flour and milk and lard and salt and yeast she saw with despair that Jim was not looking at the ingredients, was not paying the slightest attention to them. His eyes were covertly upon her.

"Jim, I am not sure about you," said Madeline, severely. "How can you learn to make bread if you do not watch me mix it?"

"I am a-watchin' you," replied Jim, innocently.

Finally Madeline sent the cowboy on his way rejoicing with the bread-mixer under his arm. Next morning, true to Stillwell's prophecy, Frank Slade, Jim's bunk-mate, presented himself cheerfully to Madeline and unbosomed himself of a long-deferred and persistent desire to relieve his overworked comrade of some of the housekeeping in their bunk.

"Miss Hammond," said Frank, "Jim's orful kind wantin' to do it all hisself. But he ain't very bright, an' I didn't believe him. You see, I'm from Missouri, an' you'll *have* to show me."

For a whole week Madeline held clinics where she expounded the scientific method of modern bread-making. She got a good deal of enjoyment out of her lectures. What boys these great hulking fellows were! She saw through their simple ruses. Some of them were grave as deacons; others wore expressions important enough to have fitted the faces of statesmen signing government treaties. These cowboys were children; they needed to be governed; but in order to govern them they had to be humored. A more light-hearted, fun-loving crowd of boys could not have been found. And they were grown men. Stillwell explained that the exuberance of spirits lay in the difference in their fortunes. Twenty-seven cowboys, in relays of nine, worked eight hours a day. That had never been heard of before in the West. Stillwell declared that cowboys from all points of the compass would head their horses toward Her Majesty's Rancho.

CHAPTER 8

EL CAPITAN

Stillwell's interest in the revolution across the Mexican line had manifestly increased with the news that Gene Stewart had achieved distinction with the rebel forces. Thereafter the old cattleman sent for El Paso and Douglas newspapers, wrote to ranchmen he knew on the big bend of the Rio Grande, and he would talk indefinitely to any one who would listen to him. There was not any possibility of Stillwell's friends at the ranch forgetting his favorite cowboy. Stillwell always prefaced his eulogy with an apologetic statement that Stewart had gone to the bad. Madeline liked to listen to him, though she was not always sure which news was authentic and which imagination.

There appeared to be no doubt, however, that the cowboy had performed some daring feats for the rebels. Madeline found his name mentioned in several of the border papers. When the rebels under Madero stormed and captured the city of Juarez, Stewart did fighting that won him the name of El Capitan. This battle apparently ended the revolution. The capitulation of President Diaz followed shortly, and there was a feeling of relief among ranchers on the border from Texas to California. Nothing more was heard of Gene Stewart until April, when a report reached Stillwell that the cowboy had arrived in El Cajon, evidently hunting trouble. The old cattleman saddled a horse and started post-haste for town. In two days he returned depressed in spirit. Madeline happened to be present when Stillwell talked to Alfred.

"I got there too late, Al," said the cattleman. "Gene was gone. An' what do you think of this? Danny Mains hed jest left with a couple of burros packed. I couldn't find what way he went, but I'm bettin' he hit the Peloncillo trail."

"Danny will show up some day," replied Alfred. "What did you learn about Stewart? Maybe he left with Danny."

"Not much," said Stillwell, shortly. "Gene's hell-bent ter election! No mountains fer him."

"Well, tell us about him."

Stillwell wiped his sweaty brow and squared himself to talk.

"Wal, it's sure amazin' strange about Gene. It's got me locoed. He arrived in El Cajon a week or so ago. He was trained down like as if he'd been ridin' the range all winter. He hed plenty of money—Mex, they said. An' all the Greasers was crazy about him. Called him El Capitan. He got drunk an' went roarin' round fer Pat Hawe. You remember that Greaser who was plugged last October— the night Miss Majesty arrived? Wal, he's daid. He's daid, an' people says thet Pat is a-goin' to lay thet killin' onto Gene. I reckon thet's jest talk, though Pat is mean enough to do it, if he hed the nerve. Anyway, if he was in El Cajon he kept mighty much to hisself. Gene walked up an' down, up an' down, all day an' night lookin' fer Pat. But he didn't find him. An', of course, he kept gettin' drunker. He jest got plumb bad. He made lots of trouble, but there wasn't no gun-play. Mebbe thet made him sore, so he went an' licked Flo's brother-in-law. Thet wasn't so bad. Jack sure needed a good lickin'. Wal, then Gene met Danny an' tried to get Danny drunk. An' he couldn't! What do you think of that? Danny hedn't been drinkin'—wouldn't touch a drop. I'm sure glad of thet, but it's so amazin' strange. Why, Danny was a fish fer red liquor. I guess he an' Gene had some pretty hard words, though I'm not sure about thet. Anyway, Gene went down to the railroad an' he got on an engine, an' he was in the engine when it pulled out. Lord, I hope he doesn't hold up the train! If he gets gay over in Arizona he'll go to the pen at Yuma. An' thet pen is a graveyard fer cowboys. I wired to agents along the railroad to look out fer Stewart, an' to wire back to me if he's located."

"Suppose you do find him, Stillwell, what can you do?" inquired Alfred.

The old man nodded gloomily.

"I straightened him up once. Mebbe I can do it again." Then brightening somewhat, he turned to Madeline. "I jest hed an idee, Miss Majesty. If I can get him, Gene Stewart is the cowboy I want fer my foreman. *He* can manage this bunch of cow-punchers thet are drivin' me dotty. What's more, since he's fought fer the rebels an' got that name El Capitan all the Greasers in the country will kneel to him. Now, Miss Majesty, we hevn't got rid of Don Carlos an' his *vaqueros* yet. To be sure, he sold you his house an' ranch an' stock. But you remember nothin' was

put in black and white about when he should get out. An'
Don Carlos ain't gettin' out. I don't like the looks of things
a little bit. I'll tell you now thet Don Carlos knows
somethin' about the cattle I lost, an' thet you've been losin'
right along. Thet Greaser is hand an' glove with the
rebels. I'm willin' to gamble thet when he does get out he
an' his *vaqueros* will make another one of the bands of
guerrillas thet are harassin' the border. This revolution
ain't over yet. It's jest commenced. An' all these gangs of
outlaws are goin' to take advantage of it. We'll see some
old times, mebbe. Wal, I need Gene Stewart. I need him
bad. Will you let me hire him, Miss Majesty, if I can get
him straightened up?"

The old cattleman ended huskily.

"Stillwell, by all means find Stewart, and do not wait
to straighten him up. Bring him to the ranch," replied
Madeline.

Thanking her, Stillwell led his horse away.

"Strange how he loves that cowboy!" murmured Madeline.

"Not so strange, Majesty," replied her brother. "Not
when you know. Stewart has been with Stillwell on some
hard trips into the desert alone. There's no middle
course·of feeling between men facing death in the desert.
Either they hate each other or love each other. I don't
know, but I imagine Stewart did something for Stillwell.
Saved his life, perhaps. Besides, Stewart's a lovable chap
when he's going straight. I hope Stillwell brings him back.
We do need him, Majesty. He's a born leader. Once I saw
him ride into a bunch of Mexicans whom we suspected
of rustling. It was fine to see him. Well, I'm sorry to tell
you that we are worried about Don Carlos. Some of his
vaqueros came into my yard the other day when I had left

Flo alone. She had a bad scare. These *vaqueros* have been different since Don Carlos sold the ranch. For that matter, I never would have trusted a white woman alone with them. But they are bolder now. Something's in the wind. They've got assurance. They can ride off any night and cross the border."

During the succeeding week Madeline discovered that a good deal of her sympathy for Stillwell in his hunt for the reckless Stewart had insensibly grown to be sympathy for the cowboy. It was rather a paradox, she thought, that opposed to the continual reports of Stewart's wildness as he caroused from town to town were the continual expressions of good will and faith and hope universally given out by those near her at the ranch. Stillwell loved the cowboy; Florence was fond of him; Alfred liked and admired him, pitied him; the cowboys swore their regard for him the more he disgraced himself. The Mexicans called him *el grande Capitan*. Madeline's personal opinion of Stewart had not changed in the least since the night it had been formed. But certain attributes of his, not clearly defined in her mind, and the gift of his beautiful horse, his valor with the fighting rebels, and all this strange regard for him, especially that of her brother, made her exceedingly regret the cowboy's present behavior.

Meanwhile Stillwell was so earnest and zealous that one not familiar with the situation would have believed he was trying to find and reclaim his own son. He made several trips to little stations in the valley, and from these he returned with a gloomy face. Madeline got the details from Alfred. Stewart was going from bad to worse—drunk, disorderly, savage, sure to land in the penitentiary. Then came a report that hurried Stillwell off to Rodeo. He returned on the third day, a crushed man. He had been so bitterly hurt that no one, not even Madeline, could get out of him what had happened. He admitted finding Stewart, failing to influence him; and when the old cattleman got so far he turned purple in the face and talked to himself, as if dazed: "But Gene was drunk. He was *drunk*, or he couldn't hev treated old Bill like thet!"

Madeline was stirred with an anger toward the brutal cowboy that was as strong as her sorrow for the loyal old cattleman. And it was when Stillwell gave up that she resolved to take a hand. The persistent faith of Stillwell, his pathetic excuses in the face of what must have been Stewart's violence, perhaps baseness, actuated her powerfully, gave her new insight into human nature. She honored a faith that remained unshaken. And the strange thought came to her that Stewart must somehow be worthy of such a faith, or he never could have inspired it. Madeline discovered that she wanted to believe that somewhere deep down in the most depraved and sinful wretch upon earth there was some grain of good. She yearned to have the faith in human nature that Stillwell had in Stewart.

She sent Nels, mounted upon his own horse, and leading Majesty, to Rodeo in search of Stewart. Nels had instructions to bring Stewart back to the ranch. In due time Nels returned, leading the roan without a rider.

"Yep, I shore found him," replied Nels, when questioned. "Found him half sobered up. He'd been in a scrap, an' somebody hed put him to sleep, I guess. Wal, when he seen thet roan hoss he let out a yell an' grabbed him round the neck. The hoss knowed him, all right. Then Gene hugged the hoss an' cried—cried like—I never seen no one who cried like he did. I waited awhile, an' was jest goin' to say somethin' to him when he turned on me red-eyed, mad as fire. 'Nels,' he said, 'I care a hell of a lot fer thet hoss, an' I liked you pretty well, but if you don't take him away quick I'll shoot you both.' Wal, I lit out. I didn't even git to say howdy to him."

"Nels, you think it useless—any attempt to see him—persuade him?" asked Madeline.

"I shore do, Miss Hammond," replied Nels, gravely. "I've seen a few sun-blinded an' locoed an' snake-poisoned an' skunk-bitten cow-punchers in my day, but Gene Stewart beats 'em all. He's shore runnin' wild fer the divide."

Madeline dismissed Nels, but before he got out of earshot she heard him speak to Stillwell, who awaited him on the porch.

"Bill, put this in your pipe an' smoke it—none of them scraps Gene has hed was over a woman! It used to be thet when he was drunk he'd scrap over every pretty Greaser girl he'd run across. Thet's why Pat Hawe thinks Gene plugged the strange *vaquero* who was with little Bonita thet night last fall. Wal, Gene's scrappin' now jest to git shot up hisself, for some reason thet only God Almighty knows."

Nels's story of how Stewart wept over his horse influenced Madeline powerfully. Her next move was to persuade Alfred to see if he could not do better with this doggedly bent cowboy. Alfred needed only a word of persuasion, for he said he had considered going to Rodeo of his own accord. He went, and returned alone.

"Majesty, I can't explain Stewart's singular actions," said Alfred. "I saw him, talked with him. He knew me, but nothing I said appeared to get to him. He has changed terribly. I fancy his once magnificent strength is breaking. It—it actually hurt me to look at him. I couldn't have fetched him back here—not as he is now. I heard all about him, and if he isn't downright out of his mind he's hell-bent, as Bill says, on getting killed. Some of his escapades are—are not for your ears. Bill did all any man could do for another. We've all done our best for Stewart. If you'd been given a chance perhaps you could have saved him. But it's too late. Put it out of mind now, dear."

Madeline, however, did not forget nor give it up. If she had forgotten or surrendered, she felt that she would have been relinquishing infinitely more than hope to aid one ruined man. But she was at a loss to know what further steps to take. Days passed, and each one brought additional gossip of Stewart's headlong career toward the Yuma penitentiary. For he had crossed the line into Cochise County, Arizona, where sheriffs kept a stricter observance of law. Finally a letter came from a friend of Nels's in Chiricahua saying that Stewart had been hurt in a brawl there. His hurt was not serious, but it would probably keep him quiet long enough to get sober, and this opportunity, Nels's informant said, would be a good one for Stewart's friends to take him home before he got locked up. This epistle inclosed a letter to Stewart from his sister. Evidently, it had been found upon him. It told a story of illness and made an appeal for aid. Nels's friend forwarded this letter without Stewart's knowledge, thinking Stillwell might care to help Stewart's family. Stewart had no money, he said.

The sister's letter found its way to Madeline. She read it, tears in her eyes. It told Madeline much more than its brief story of illness and poverty, and wonder why Gene had not written home for so long. It told of motherly love, sisterly love, brotherly love—dear family ties that had not been broken. It spoke of pride in this El Capitan brother who had become famous. It was signed "your loving sister Letty."

Not improbably, Madeline revolved in mind, this letter was one reason for Stewart's headstrong, long-continued abasement. It had been received too late—after he had squandered the money that would have meant so much to mother and sister. Be that as it might, Madeline immediately sent a bank-draft to Stewart's sister with a letter explaining that the money was drawn in advance on Stewart's salary. This done, she impulsively determined to go to Chiricahua herself.

The horseback-rides Madeline had taken to this little Arizona hamlet had tried her endurance to the utmost; but the journey by automobile, except for some rocky bits of road and sandy stretches, was comfortable, and a matter of only a few hours. The big touring-car was still a kind of seventh wonder to the Mexicans and cowboys; not that automobiles were very new and strange, but because this one was such an enormous machine and capable of greater speed than an express-train. The chauffeur who had arrived with the car found his situation among the jealous cowboys somewhat far removed from a bed of roses. He had been induced to remain long enough to teach the operating and mechanical technique of the car. And choice fell upon Link Stevens, for the simple reason that of all the cowboys he was the only one with any knack for mechanics. Now Link had been a hard-riding, hard-driving cowboy, and that winter he had sustained an injury to his leg, caused by a bad fall, and was unable to sit his horse. This had been gall and wormwood to him. But when the big white automobile came and he was elected to drive it, life was once more worth living for him. But all the other cowboys regarded Link and his machine as some correlated species of demon. They were deathly afraid of both.

It was for this reason that Nels, when Madeline asked

him to accompany her to Chiricahua, replied reluctantly that he would rather follow on his horse. However, she prevailed over his hesitancy, and with Florence also in the car they set out. For miles and miles the valley road was smooth, hard-packed, and slightly downhill. And when speeding was perfectly safe, Madeline was not averse to it. The grassy plain sailed backward in gray sheets, and the little dot in the valley grew larger and larger. From time to time Link glanced round at unhappy Nels, whose eyes were wild and whose hands clutched his seat. While the car was crossing the sandy and rocky places, going slowly, Nels appeared to breathe easier. And when it stopped in the wide, dusty street of Chiricahua Nels gladly tumbled out.

"Nels, we shall wait here in the car while you find Stewart," said Madeline.

"Miss Hammond, I reckon Gene'll run when he sees us, if he's able to run," replied Nels. "Wal, I'll go find him an' make up my mind then what we'd better do."

Nels crossed the railroad track and disappeared behind the low, flat houses. After a little time he reappeared and hurried up to the car. Madeline felt his gray gaze searching her face.

"Miss Hammond, I found him," said Nels. "He was sleepin'. I woke him. He's sober an' not bad hurt; but I don't believe you ought to see him. Mebbe Florence—"

"Nels, I want to see him myself. Why not? What did he say when you told him I was here?"

"Shore I didn't tell him that. I jest says 'Hullo, Gene,' an' he says, 'My Gawd, Nels, mebbe I ain't glad to see a human bein'.' He asked me who was with me, an' I told him Link an' some friends. I said I'd fetch them in. He hollered at thet. But I went, anyway. Now, if you really *will* see him, Miss Hammond, it's a good chance. But shore it's a touchy matter, an' you'll be some sick at sight of him. He's layin' in a Greaser hole over here. Likely the Greasers hev been kind to him. But they're shore a poor lot."

Madeline did not hesitate a moment.

"Thank you, Nels. Take me at once. Come, Florence."

They left the car, now surrounded by gaping-eyed Mexican children, and crossed the dusty space to a narrow lane between red adobe walls. Passing by several houses, Nels stopped at the door of what appeared to be an alley-way leading back. It was filthy.

"He's in there, around thet first corner. It's a patio, open an' sunny. An', Miss Hammond, if you don't mind, I'll wait here for you. I reckon Gene wouldn't like any fellers around when he sees you girls."

It was that which made Madeline hesitate then and go forward slowly. She had given no thought at all to what Stewart might feel when suddenly surprised by her presence.

"Florence, you wait also," said Madeline, at the door-way, and turned in alone.

And she had stepped into a broken-down patio littered with alfalfa straw and debris, all clear in the sunlight. Upon a bench, back toward her, sat a man looking out through the rents in the broken wall. He had not heard her. The place was not quite so filthy and stifling as the passages Madeline had come through to get there. Then she saw that it had been used as a corral. A rat ran boldly across the dirt floor. The air swarmed with flies, which the man brushed at with weary hand. Madeline did not recognize Stewart. The side of his face exposed to her gaze was black, bruised, bearded. His clothes were ragged and soiled. There were bits of alfalfa in his hair. His shoulders sagged. He made a wretched and hopeless figure sitting there. Madeline divined something of why Nels shrank from being present.

"Mr. Stewart. It is I, Miss Hammond, come to see you," she said.

He grew suddenly perfectly motionless, as if he had been changed to stone. She repeated her greeting.

His body jerked. He moved violently as if instinctively to turn and face this intruder; but a more violent movement checked him.

Madeline waited. How singular that this ruined cowboy had pride which kept him from showing his face! And was it not shame more than pride?

"Mr. Stewart, I have come to talk with you, if you will let me."

"Go away," he muttered.

"Mr. Stewart!" she began, with involuntary hauteur. But instantly she corrected herself, became deliberate and cool, for she saw that she might fail to be even heard by this man. "I have come to help you. Will you let me?"

"For God's sake! You—you—" he choked over the words. "Go away!"

"Stewart, perhaps it was for God's sake that I came," said Madeline, gently. "Surely it was for yours—and your sister's—" Madeline bit her tongue, for she had not meant to betray her knowledge of Letty.

He groaned, and, staggering up to the broken wall, he leaned there with his face hidden. Madeline reflected that perhaps the slip of speech had been well.

"Stewart, please let me say what I have to say?"

He was silent. And she gathered courage and inspiration.

"Stillwell is deeply hurt, deeply grieved that he could

not turn you back from this—this fatal course. My brother is also. They wanted to help you. And so do I. I have come, thinking somehow I might succeed where they have failed. Nels brought your sister's letter. I—I read it. I was only the more determined to try to help you, and indirectly help your mother and Letty. Stewart, we want you to come to the ranch. Stillwell needs you for his foreman. The position is open to you, and you can name your salary. Both Al and Stillwell are worried about Don Carlos, the *vaqueros*, and the raids down along the border. My cowboys are without a capable leader. Will you come?"

"No," he answered.

"But Stillwell wants you so badly."

"No."

"Stewart. I want you to come."

"No."

His replies had been hoarse, loud, furious. They disconcerted Madeline, and she paused, trying to think of a way to proceed. Stewart staggered away from the wall, and, falling upon the bench, he hid his face in his hands. All his motions, like his speech, had been violent.

"Will you please go away?" he asked.

"Stewart, certainly I cannot remain here longer if you insist upon my going. But why not listen to me when I want so much to help you? Why?"

"I'm a damned blackguard," he burst out. "But I was a gentleman once, and I'm not so low that I can stand for you seeing me here."

"When I made up my mind to help you I made it up to see you wherever you were. Stewart, come away, come back with us to the ranch. You are in a bad condition now. Everything looks black to you. But that will pass. When you are among friends again you will get well. You will be your old self. The very fact that you were once a gentleman, that you come of good family, makes you owe so much more to yourself. Why, Stewart, think how young you are! It is a shame to waste your life. Come back with me."

"Miss Hammond, this was my last plunge," he replied, despondently. "It's too late."

"Oh no, it is not so bad as that."

"It's too late."

"At least make an effort, Stewart. Try!"

"No. There's no use. I'm done for. Please leave me—thank you for—"

He had been savage, then sullen, and now he was grim. Madeline all but lost power to resist his strange, deadly, cold finality. No doubt he knew he was doomed. Yet something halted her—held her even as she took a backward step. And she became conscious of a subtle change in her own feeling. She had come into that squalid hole, Madeline Hammond, earnest enough, kind enough in her own intentions; but she had been almost imperious—a woman habitually, proudly used to being obeyed. She divined that all the pride, blue blood, wealth, culture, distinction, all the impersonal condescending persuasion, the fatuous philanthropy on earth would not avail to turn this man a single hair's breath from his downward career to destruction. Her coming had terribly augmented his bitter hate of himself. She was going to fail to help him. She experienced a sensation of impotence that amounted almost to distress. The situation assumed a tragic keenness. She had set forth to reverse the tide of a wild cowboy's fortunes; she faced the swift wasting of his life, the damnation of his soul. The subtle consciousness of change in her was the birth of that faith she had revered in Stillwell.

And all at once she became merely a woman, brave and sweet and indomitable.

"Stewart, look at me," she said.

He shuddered. She advanced and laid a hand on his bent shoulder. Under the light touch he appeared to sink.

"Look at me," she repeated.

But he could not lift his head. He was abject, crushed. He dared not show his swollen, blackened face. His fierce, cramped posture revealed more than his features might have shown; it betrayed the torturing shame of a man of pride and passion, a man who had been confronted in his degradation by the woman he had dared to enshrine in his heart. It betrayed his love.

"Listen, then," went on Madeline; and her voice was unsteady. "Listen to me, Stewart. The greatest men are those who have fallen deepest into the mire, sinned most, suffered most, and then have fought their evil natures and conquered. I think you can shake off this desperate mood and be a man."

"No!" he cried.

"Listen to me again. Somehow I know you're worthy of Stillwell's love. Will you come back with us—for his sake?"

"No. It's too late, I tell you."

"Stewart, the best thing in life is faith in human nature. I have faith in you. I believe you are worth it."

"You're only kind and good—saying that. You can't mean it."

"I mean it with all my heart," she replied, a sudden rich warmth suffusing her body as she saw the first sign of his softening. "Will you come back—if not for your own sake or Stillwell's—then for mine?"

"What am I to such a woman as you?"

"A man in trouble, Stewart. But I have come to help you, to show my faith in you."

"If I believed that I might try," he said.

"Listen," she began, softly, hurriedly. "My word is not lightly given. Let it prove my faith in you. Look at me now and say you will come."

He heaved up his big frame as if trying to cast off a giant's burden, and then slowly he turned toward her. His face was a blotched and terrible thing. The physical brutalizing marks were there, and at that instant all that appeared human to Madeline was the dawning in dead, furnace-like eyes of a beautiful light.

"I'll come," he whispered, huskily. "Give me a few days to straighten up, then I'll come."

CHAPTER 9

THE NEW FOREMAN

Toward the end of the week Stillwell informed Madeline that Stewart had arrived at the ranch and had taken up quarters with Nels.

"Gene's sick. He looks bad," said the old cattleman. "He's so weak an' shaky he can't lift a cup. Nels says that Gene has hed some bad spells. A little liqour would straighten him up now. But Nels can't force him to drink a drop, an' has hed to sneak some liquor in his coffee. Wal, I think we'll pull Gene through. He's forgotten a lot. I was goin' to tell him what he did to me up at Rodeo. But I know if he'd believe it he'd be sicker than he is. Gene's losin' his mind, or he's got somethin' powerful strange on it."

From that time Stillwell, who evidently found Madeline his most sympathetic listener, unburdened himself daily of his hopes and fears and conjectures.

Stewart was really ill. It became necessary to send Link

Stevens for a physician. Then Stewart began slowly to mend and presently was able to get up and about. Stillwell said the cowboy lacked interest and seemed to be a broken man. This statement, however, the old cattleman modified as Stewart continued to improve. Then presently it was a good augury of Stewart's progress that the cowboys once more took up the teasing relation which had been characteristic of them before his illness. A cowboy was indeed out of sorts when he could not vent his peculiar humor on somebody or something. Stewart had evidently become a broad target for their badinage.

"Wal, the boys are sure after Gene," said Stillwell, with his huge smile. "Joshin' him all the time about how he sits around an' hangs around an' loafs around jest to get a glimpse of you, Miss Majesty. Sure all the boys hev a pretty bad case over their pretty boss, but none of them is a marker to Gene. He's got it so bad, Miss Majesty, thet he actooly don't know they are joshin' him. It's the amazinest strange thing I ever seen. Why, Gene was always a feller thet you could josh. An' he'd laugh an' get back at you. But he was never before deaf to talk, an' there was a certain limit no feller cared to cross with him. Now he takes every word an' smiles dreamy like, an' jest looks an' looks. Why, he's beginnin' to make me tired. He'll never run thet bunch of cowboys if he doesn't wake up quick."

Madeline smiled her amusement and expressed a belief that Stillwell wanted too much in such short time from a man who had done body and mind a grievous injury.

It had been impossible for Madeline to fail to observe Stewart's singular behavior. She never went out to take her customary walks and rides without seeing him somewhere in the distance. She was aware that he watched for her and avoided meeting her. When she sat on the porch during the afternoon or at sunset Stewart could always be descried at some point near. He idled listlessly in the sun, lounged on the porch of his bunk-house, sat whittling the top bar of the corral fence, and always it seemed to Madeline he was watching her. Once, while going the rounds with her gardener, she encountered Stewart and greeted him kindly. He said little, but he was not embarrassed. She did not recognize in his face any feature that she remembered. In fact, on each of the few occasions when she had met Stewart he had looked so different that she had no consistent idea of his facial appearance. He was now pale, haggard, drawn. His eyes held a shadow through which shone a soft, subdued light; and, once having observed this, Madeline fancied it was like the light in Majesty's eyes, in the dumb, worshiping eyes of her favorite staghound. She told Stewart that she hoped he would soon be in the saddle again, and passed on her way.

That Stewart loved her Madeline could not help but see. She endeavored to think of him as one of the many who, she was glad to know, liked her. But she could not regulate her thoughts to fit the order her intelligence prescribed. Thought of Stewart dissociated itself from thought of the other cowboys. When she discovered this she felt a little surprise and annoyance. Then she interrogated herself, and concluded that it was not that Stewart was so different from his comrades, but that circumstances made him stand out from them. She recalled her meeting with him that night when he had tried to force her to marry him. This was unforgettable in itself. She called subsequent mention of him, and found it had been peculiarly memorable. The man and his actions seemed to hinge on events. Lastly, the fact standing clear of all others in its relation to her interest was that he had been almost ruined, almost lost, and she had saved him. That alone was sufficient to explain why she thought of him differently. She had befriended, uplifted the other cowboys; she had saved Stewart's life. To be sure, he had been a ruffian, but a woman could not save the life of even a ruffian without remembering it with gladness. Madeline at length decided her interest in Stewart was natural, and that her deeper feeling was pity. Perhaps the interest had been forced from her; however, she gave the pity as she gave everything.

Stewart recovered his strength, though not in time to ride at the spring round-up; and Stillwell discussed with Madeline the advisability of making the cowboy his foreman.

"Wal, Gene seems to be gettin' along," said Stillwell. "But he ain't like his old self. I think more of him at thet. But where's his spirit? The boys 'd ride roughshod all over him. Mebbe I'd do best to wait longer now, as the slack season is on. All the same, if those *vaqueros* of Don Carlos's don't lay low I'll send Gene over there. Thet'll wake him up."

A few days afterward Stillwell came to Madeline, rubbing his big hands in satisfaction and wearing a grin that was enormous.

"Miss Majesty, I reckon before this I've said things was amazin' strange. But *now* Gene Stewart has gone an' done it! Listen to me. Them Greasers down on our slope hev been gettin' prosperous. They're growin' like bad weeds. An' they got a new padre—the little old feller from El Cajon, Padre Marcos. Wal, this was all right, all the boys thought, except Gene. An' he got blacker'n thunder an' roared round like a dehorned bull. I was sure glad to see he could get mad again. Then Gene haids down the slope fer the church. Nels an' me follered him, thinkin' he might hev been took sudden with a crazy spell or somethin'. He hasn't never been jest right yet since he left off drinkin'. Wal, we run into him comin' out of the church. We never was so dumfounded in our lives. Gene was crazy all right—he sure hed a spell. But it was the *kind* of a spell he hed thet paralyzed us. He ran past us like a streak, an' we follered. We couldn't ketch him. We heerd him laugh—the strangest laugh I ever heerd! You'd thought the feller was suddenly made a king. He was like thet feller who was tied in a buryin'-sack an' throwed into the sea, an' cut his way out, an' swam to the island where the treasures was, an' stood up yellin': 'The world is mine!' Wal, when we got up to his bunk-house he was gone. He didn't come back all day an' all night. Frankie Slade, who has a sharp tongue, says Gene hed gone crazy fer liquor an' thet was his finish. Nels was some worried. An' I was sick.

"Wal, this mawnin' I went over to Nels's bunk. Some of the fellers was there, all speculatin' about Gene. Then big as life Gene struts round the corner. He wasn't the same Gene. His face was pale an' his eyes burned like fire. He hed thet old mockin', cool smile, an' somethin' besides thet I couldn't understand. Frankie Slade up an' made a remark—no wuss than he'd been makin' fer days—an' Gene tumbled him out of his chair, punched him good, walked all over him. Frankie wasn't hurt so much as he was bewildered. 'Gene,' he says, 'what the hell struck you?' An' Gene says, kind of sweet like, 'Frankie, you may be a nice feller when you're alone, but your talk's offensive to a gentleman.'

"After thet what was said to Gene was with a nice smile. Now, Miss Majesty, it's beyond me what to allow for

Gene's sudden change. First off, I thought Padre Marcos had converted him. I actooly thought thet. But I reckon it's only Gene Stewart come back—the old Gene Stewart *an'* some. Thet's all I care about. I'm rememberin' how I once told you thet Gene was the last of the cowboys. Perhaps I should hev said he's the last of my *kind* of cowboys. Wal, Miss Majesty, you'll be appreciatin' of what I meant from now on."

It was also beyond Madeline to account for Gene Stewart's antics, and, making allowance for the old cattleman's fancy, she did not weigh his remarks very heavily. She guessed why Stewart might have been angry at the presence of Padre Marcos. Madeline supposed that it was rather an unusual circumstance for a cowboy to be converted to religious belief. But it was possible. And she knew that religious fervor often manifested itself in extremes of feeling and action. Most likely, in Stewart's case, his real manner had been both misunderstood and exaggerated. However, Madeline had a curious desire, which she did not wholly admit to herself, to see the cowboy and make her own deductions.

The opportunity did not present itself for nearly two weeks. Stewart had taken up his duties as foreman, and his activities were ceaseless. He was absent most of the time, ranging down toward the Mexican line. When he returned Stillwell sent for him.

This was late in the afternoon of a day in the middle of April. Alfred and Florence were with Madeline on the porch. They saw the cowboy turn his horse over to one of the Mexican boys at the corral and then come with weary step up to the house, beating the dust out of his gauntlets. Little streams of gray sand trickled from his sombrero as he removed it and bowed to the women.

Madeline saw the man she remembered, but with a singularly different aspect. His skin was brown; his eyes were piercing and dark and steady; he carried himself erect; he seemed preoccupied, and there was not a trace of embarrassment in his manner.

"Wal, Gene, I'm sure glad to see you," Stillwell was saying. "Where do you hail from?"

"Guadalupe Cañon," replied the cowboy.

Stillwell whistled.

"Way down there! You don't mean you follered them hoss tracks thet far?"

"All the way from Don Carlos's rancho across the Mexican line. I took Nick Steele with me. Nick is the best tracker in the outfit. This trail we were on led along the foothill valleys. First we thought whoever made it was hunting for water. But they passed two ranches without watering. At Seaton's Wash they dug for water. Here they met a pack-train of burros that came down the mountain trail. The burros were heavily loaded. Horse and burro tracks struck south from Seaton's to the old California emigrant road. We followed the trail through Guadalupe Cañon and across the border. On the way back we stopped at Slaughter's ranch, where the United States Cavalry are camping. There we met foresters from the Peloncillo forest reserve. If these fellows knew anything they kept it to themselves. So we hit the trail home."

"Wal, I reckon you know enough?" inquired Stillwell, slowly.

"I reckon," replied Stewart.

"Wal, out with it, then," said Stillwell, gruffly. "Miss Hammond can't be kept in the dark much longer. Make your report to her."

The cowboy shifted his dark gaze to Madeline. He was cool and slow.

"We're losing a few cattle on the open range. Night-drives by *vaqueros*. Some of these cattle are driven across the valley, others up into the foothills. So far as I can find out no cattle are being driven south. So this raiding is a blind to fool the cowboys. Don Carlos is a Mexican rebel. He located his rancho here a few years ago and pretended to raise cattle. All that time he has been smuggling arms and ammunition across the border. He was for Madero against Diaz. Now he is against Madero because he and all the rebels think Madero failed to keep his promises. There will be another revolution. And all the arms go from the States across the border. Those burros I told about were packed with contraband goods."

"That's a matter for the United States Cavalry. They are patrolling the border," said Alfred.

"They can't stop the smuggling of arms, not down in that wild corner," replied Stewart.

"What is my—my duty? What has it to do with me?" inquired Madeline, somewhat perturbed.

"Wal, Miss Majesty, I reckon it hasn't nothing to do with you," put in Stillwell. "Thet's my bizness an' Stewart's. But I jest wanted you to know. There might be some trouble follerin' my orders."

"Your orders?"

"I want to send Stewart over to fire Don Carlos an' his *vaqueros* off the range. They've got to go. Don Carlos is breakin' the law of the United States, an' doin' it on our property an' with our hosses. Hev I your permission, Miss Hammond?"

"Why, assuredly you have. Stillwell, you know what to do. Alfred, what do you think best?"

"It'll make trouble, Majesty, but it's got to be done," replied Alfred. "Here you have a crowd of Eastern friends due next month. We want the range to ourselves then. But, Stillwell, if you drive those *vaqueros* off, won't they hang around in the foothills? I declare they are a bad lot."

Stillwell's mind was not at ease. He paced the porch with a frown clouding his brow.

"Gene, I reckon you got this Greaser deal figgered better'n me," said Stillwell. "Now what do you say?"

"He'll have to be forced off," replied Stewart, quietly. "The Don's pretty slick, but his *vaqueros* are bad actors. It's just this way. Nels said the other day to me: 'Gene, I haven't packed a gun for years until lately, and it feels good whenever I meet any of those strange Greasers.' You see, Stillwell, Don Carlos has *vaqueros* coming and going all the time. They're guerrilla bands, that's all. And they're getting uglier. There have been several shooting scrapes lately. A rancher named White, who lives up the valley, was badly hurt. It's only a matter of time till something stirs up the boys here. Stillwell, you know Nels and Monty and Nick."

"Sure, I know 'em. An' you're not mentionin' one more particular cowboy in my outfit," said Stillwell, with a dry chuckle and a glance at Stewart.

Madeline divined the covert meaning, and a slight chill passed over her, as if a cold wind had blown in from the hills.

"Stewart, I see you carry a gun," she said, pointing to a black handle protruding from a sheath swinging low along his leather chaps.

"Yes, ma'am."

"Why do you carry it?" she asked.

"Well," he said, "it's not a pretty gun—and it's heavy."

She caught the inference. The gun was not an ornament. His keen, steady, dark gaze caused her vague alarm.
What had once seemed cool and audacious about this
cowboy was now cold and powerful and mystical. Both
her instinct and her intelligence realized the steel fiber of
the man's nature. As she was his employer, she had the
right to demand that he should not do what was so chill-
ingly manifest that he might do. But Madeline could not
demand. She felt curiously young and weak, and the five
months of Western life were as if they had never been.
She now had to do with a question involving human life.
And the value she placed upon human life and its spiritual significance was a matter far from her cowboy's
thoughts. A strange idea flashed up. Did she place too
much value upon all human life? She checked that, wondering, almost horrified at herself. And then her intuition
told her that she possessed a far stronger power to move
these primitive men than any woman's stern rule or
order.

"Stewart, I do not fully understand what you hint that
Nels and his comrades might do. Please be frank with me.
Do you mean Nels would shoot upon little provocation?"

"Miss Hammond, as far as Nels is concerned, shooting
is now just a matter of his meeting Don Carlos's *vaqueros*. It's wonderful what Nels has stood from them,
considering the Mexicans he's already killed."

"Already killed! Stewart, you are not in earnest?" cried
Madeline, shocked.

"I am. Nels has seen hard life along the Arizona border. He likes peace as well as any man. But a few years
of that doesn't change what the early days made of him.
As for Nick Steele and Monty, they're just bad men, and
looking for trouble."

"How about yourself, Stewart? Stillwell's remark was not lost upon me," said Madeline, prompted by curiosity.

Stewart did not reply. He looked at her in respectful silence. In her keen earnestness Madeline saw beneath his cool exterior and was all the more baffled. Was there a slight inscrutable mocking light in his eyes, or was it only her imagination? However, the cowboy's face was as hard as flint.

"Stewart, I have come to love my ranch," said Madeline, slowly, "and I care a great deal for my—my cowboys. It would be dreadful if they were to kill anybody, or especially if one of them should be killed."

"Miss Hammond, you've changed things considerable out here, but you can't change these men. All that's needed to start them is a little trouble. And this Mexican revolution is bound to make rough times along some of the wilder passes across the border. We're in line, that's all. And the boys are getting stirred up."

"Very well, then, I must accept the inevitable. I am facing a rough time. And some of my cowboys cannot be checked much longer. But, Stewart, whatever you have been in the past, you have changed." She smiled at him, and her voice was singularly sweet and rich. "Stillwell has so often referred to you as the last of his kind of cowboy. I have just a faint idea of what a wild life you have led. Perhaps that fits you to be a leader of such rough men. I am no judge of what a leader should do in this crisis. My cowboys are entailing risk in my employ; my property is not safe; perhaps my life even might be endangered. I want to rely upon you, since Stillwell believes, and I, too, that you are the man for this place. I shall give you no orders. But is it too much to ask that you be *my* kind of a cowboy?"

Madeline remembered Stewart's former brutality and shame and abject worship, and she measured the great change in him by the contrast afforded now in his dark, changeless, intent face.

"Miss Hammond, what kind of a cowboy is that?" he asked.

"I—I don't exactly know. It is that kind which I feel you *might* be. But I do know that in the problem at hand I want your actions to be governed by reason, not passion. Human life is not for any man to sacrifice unless in self-defense or in protecting those dependent upon him. What Stillwell and you hinted makes me afraid of Nels and Nick Steele and Monty. Cannot they be controlled? I want to feel that they will not go gunning for Don Carlos's men. I want to avoid all violence. And yet when my guests come I want to feel that they will be safe from danger or fright or even annoyance. May I not rely wholly upon you, Stewart? Just trust you to manage these obstreperous cowboys and protect my property and Alfred's, and take care of us—of me, until this revolution is ended? I have never had a day's worry since I bought the ranch. It is not that I want to shirk my responsibilities; it is that I like being happy. May I put so much faith in you?"

"I hope so, Miss Hammond," replied Stewart. It was an instant response, but none the less fraught with consciousness of responsibility. He waited a moment, and then, as neither Stillwell nor Madeline offered further speech, he bowed and turned down the path, his long spurs clinking in the gravel.

"Wal, wal," exclaimed Stillwell, "thet's no little job you give him, Miss Majesty."

"It was a woman's cunning, Stillwell," said Alfred. "My sister used to be a wonder at getting her own way when we were kids. Just a smile or two, a few sweet words or turns of thought, and she had what she wanted."

"Al, what a character to give me!" protested Madeline. "Indeed, I was deeply in earnest with Stewart. I do not understand just why, but I trust him. He seems like iron and steel. Then I was a little frightened at the prospect of trouble with the *vaqueros*. Both you and Stillwell have influenced me to look upon Stewart as invaluable. I thought it best to confess my utter helplessness and to look to him for support."

"Majesty, whatever actuated you, it was a stroke of diplomacy," replied her brother. "Stewart has got good stuff in him. He was down and out. Well, he's made a game fight, and it looks as if he'd win. Trusting him, giving him responsibility, relying upon him was the surest way to strengthen his hold upon himself. Then that little touch of sentiment about being your kind of cowboy and protecting you—well, if Gene Stewart doesn't develop into an Argus-eyed knight I'll say I don't know cowboys. But, Majesty, remember, he's a composite of tiger-breed and forked lightning, and don't imagine he has failed you if he gets into a fight."

"I'll sure tell you what Gene Stewart will do," said Florence. "Don't I know cowboys? Why, they used to take me up on their horses when I was a baby. Gene Stewart will be the kind of cowboy your sister said he *might* be, whatever that is. She may not know and we may not guess, but he knows."

"Wal, Flo, there you hit plumb center," replied the old cattleman. "An' I couldn't be gladder if he was my own son."

CHAPTER 10

DON CARLOS'S *VAQUEROS*

Early the following morning Stewart, with a company of cowboys, departed for Don Carlos's rancho. As the day wore on without any report from him, Stillwell appeared to grow more at ease; and at nightfall he told Madeline that he guessed there was now no reason for concern.

"Wal, though it's sure amazin' strange," he continued, "I've been worryin' some about how we was goin' to fire Don Carlos. But Gene has a way of doin' things."

Next day Stillwell and Alfred decided to ride over to Don Carlos's place, taking Madeline and Florence with them, and upon the return trip to stop at Alfred's ranch. They started in the cool, gray dawn, and after three hours' riding, as the sun began to get bright, they entered a mesquite grove surrounding corrals and barns, and a number of low, squat buildings and a huge, rambling structure, all built of adobe and mostly crumbling to ruin. Only one green spot relieved the bald red of grounds and walls; and this evidently was made by the spring which had given both value and fame to Don Carlos's range. The approach to the house was through a wide courtyard, bare, stony, hard-packed, with hitching-rails and watering-troughs in front of a long porch. Several dusty, tired horses stood with drooping heads and bridles down, their wet flanks attesting to travel just ended.

"Wal, dog-gone it, Al, if there ain't Pat Hawe's hoss I'll eat it," exclaimed Stillwell.

"What's Pat want here, anyhow?" growled Alfred.

No one was in sight; but Madeline heard loud voices _____ from the house. Stillwell dismounted at the porch and stalked in at the door. Alfred leaped off his horse, helped Florence and Madeline down, and, bidding them rest and wait on the porch, he followed Stillwell.

"I hate these Greaser places," said Florence, with a grimace. "They're so mysterious and creepy. Just watch now! There'll be dark-skinned, beady-eyed, soft-footed Greasers slip right up out of the ground! There'll be an ugly face in every door and window and crack."

"It's like a huge barn with its characteristic odor permeated by tobacco smoke," replied Madeline, sitting down beside Florence. "I don't think very much of this end of my purchase. Florence, isn't that Don Carlos's black horse over there in the corral?"

"It sure is. Then the Don's heah yet. I wish we hadn't been in such a hurry to come over. There! that doesn't sound encouraging."

From the corridor came the rattling of spurs, tramping of boots, and loud voices. Madeline detected Alfred's quick notes when he was annoyed: "We'll rustle back home, then," he said. The answer came: "No!" Madeline recognized Stewart's voice, and she quickly straightened up. "I won't have them in here," went on Alfred. "Outdoors or in they've got to be with us!" replied Stewart, sharply. "Listen, Al," came the boom of Stillwell's big voice, "now that we've butted in over hyar with the girls, you let Stewart run things."

Then a crowd of men tramped pell-mell out upon the porch. Stewart, dark-browed and somber, was in the lead. Nels hung close to him, and Madeline's quick glance saw that Nels had undergone some indescribable change. The grinning, brilliant-eyed Don Carlos came jostling out beside a gaunt, sharp-featured man wearing a silver shield. This no doubt was Pat Hawe. In the background behind Stillwell and Alfred stood Nick Steele, head and shoulders over a number of *vaqueros* and cowboys.

"Miss Hammond, I'm sorry you came," said Stewart, bluntly. "We're in a muddle here. I've insisted that you and Flo be kept close to us. I'll explain later. If you can't stop your ears I beg you to overlook rough talk."

With that he turned to the men behind him: "Nick, take Booly, go back to Monty and the boys. Fetch out that stuff. All of it. Rustle, now!"

Stillwell and Alfred disengaged themselves from the crowd to take up positions in front of Madeline and Florence. Pat Hawe leaned against a post and insolently ogled Madeline and then Florence. Don Carlos pressed forward. His whole figure filled Madeline's reluctant but fascinated eyes. He wore tight velveteen breeches, with a heavyfold down the outside seam, which was ornamented with silver buttons. Round his waist was a sash, and a belt with fringed holster, from which protruded a pearl-handled gun. A vest or waistcoat, richly embroidered, partly concealed a blouse of silk, and wholly revealed a silken scarf round his neck. His swarthy face showed dark lines, like cords, under the surface. His little eyes were exceedingly prominent and glittering. To Madeline his face seemed to be a bold, handsome mask through which his eyes piercingly betrayed the evil nature of the man.

He bowed low with elaborate and sinuous grace. His smile revealed brilliant teeth, enhanced the brilliance of his eyes. He slowly spread deprecatory hands.

"Señoritas, I beg a thousand pardons," he said. How strange it was for Madeline to hear English spoken in a soft, whiningly sweet accent! "The gracious hospitality of Don Carlos has passed with his house."

Stewart stepped forward, and, thrusting Don Carlos aside, he called, "Make way, there!"

The crowd fell back to the tramp of heavy boots. Cowboys appeared staggering out of the corridor with long boxes. These they placed side by side upon the floor of the porch.

"Now, Hawe, we'll proceed with our business," said Stewart. "You see these boxes, don't you?"

"I reckon I see a good many things round hyar," replied Hawe, meaningly.

"Well, do you intend to open these boxes upon my say-so?"

"No!" retorted Hawe. "It's not my place to meddle with property as come by express an' all accounted fer regular."

"You call yourself a sheriff!" exclaimed Stewart, scornfully.

"Mebbe you'll think so before long," rejoined Hawe, sullenly.

"I'll open them. Here, one of you boys, knock the tops

off these boxes," ordered Stewart. "No, not you, Monty. You use your eyes. Let Booly handle the ax. Rustle, now!"

Monty Price had jumped out of the crowd into the middle of the porch. The manner in which he gave way to Booly and faced the *vaqueros* was not significant of friendliness or trust.

"Stewart, you're dead wrong to bust open them boxes. Thet's agin the law," protested Hawe, trying to interfere.

Stewart pushed him back. Then Don Carlos, who had been stunned by the appearance of the boxes, suddenly became active in speech and person. Stewart thrust him back also. The Mexican's excitement increased. He wildly gesticulated; he exclaimed shrilly in Spanish. When, however, the lids were wrenched open and an inside packing torn away he grew rigid and silent. Madeline raised herself behind Stillwell to see that the boxes were full of rifles and ammunition.

"There, Hawe! What did I tell you?" demanded Stewart. "I came over here to take charge of this ranch. I found these boxes hidden in an unused room. I suspected what they were. Contraband goods!"

"Wal, supposin' they are? I don't see any call fer sech all-fired fuss as you're makin'. Stewart, I calkilate you're some stuck on your new job an' want to make a big show before—"

"Hawe, stop slinging that kind of talk," interrupted Stewart. "You got too free with your mouth once before! Now here, I'm supposed to be consulting an officer of the law. Will you take charge of these contraband goods?"

"Say, you're holdin' on high an' mighty," replied Hawe, in astonishment that was plainly pretended. "What're you drivin' at?"

Stewart muttered an imprecation. He took several swift strides across the porch; he held out his hands to Stillwell as if to indicate the hopelessness of intelligent and reasonable arbitration; he looked at Madeline with a glance eloquent of his regret that he could not handle the situation to please her. Then as he wheeled he came face to face with Nels, who had slipped forward out of the crowd.

Madeline gathered serious import from the steel-blue meaning flash of eyes whereby Nels communicated something to Stewart. Whatever that something was, it dispelled Stewart's impatience. A slight movement of his hand brought Monty Price forward with a jump. In these sudden jumps of Monty's there was a suggestion of restrained ferocity. Then Nels and Monty lined up behind Stewart. It was a deliberate action, even to Madeline, unmistakably formidable. Pat Hawe's face took on an ugly look; his eyes had a reddish gleam. Don Carlos added a pale face and extreme nervousness to his former expressions of agitation. The cowboys edged away from the *vaqueros*, and the bronzed, bearded horsemen who were evidently Hawe's assistants.

"I'm driving at this," spoke up Stewart, presently; and now he was slow and caustic. "Here's contraband of war! Hawe, do you get that? Arms and ammunition for the rebels across the border! I charge you as an officer to confiscate these goods and to arrest the smuggler—Don Carlos."

These words of Stewart's precipitated a riot among Don Carlos and his followers, and they surged wildly around the sheriff. There was an upflinging of brown, clenching hands, a shrill, jabbering babel of Mexican voices. The crowd around Don Carlos grew louder and denser with the addition of armed *vaqueros* and barefooted stable-boys and dusty-booted herdsmen and blanketed Mexicans, the last of whom suddenly slipped from doors and windows and round corners. It was a motley assemblage. The laced, fringed, ornamented *vaqueros* presented a sharp contrast to the bare-legged, sandal-footed boys and the ragged herders. Shrill cries, evidently from Don Carlos, somewhat quieted the commotion. Then Don Carlos could be heard addressing Sheriff Hawe in an exhortation of mingled English and Spanish. He denied, he avowed, he proclaimed, and all in rapid, passionate utterance. He tossed his black hair in his vehemence; he waved his fists and stamped the floor; he rolled his glittering eyes; he twisted his thin lips into a hundred different shapes, and like a cornered wolf showed snarling white teeth.

It seemed to Madeline that Don Carlos denied knowledge of the boxes of contraband goods, then knowledge of their real contents, then knowledge of their destination, and, finally, everything except that they were there in sight, damning witnesses to somebody's complicity in the breaking of neutrality laws. Passionate as had been his denial of all this, it was as nothing compared to his denunciation of Stewart.

"Señor Stewart, he keel my *vaquero!*" shouted Don Carlos, as, sweating and spent, he concluded his arraignment of the cowboy. "Him you must arrest! Señor Stewart a bad man! He keel my *vaquero!*"

"Do you hear thet?" yelled Hawe. "The Don's got you figgered fer thet little job at El Cajon last fall."

The clamor burst into a roar. Hawe began shaking his finger in Stewart's face and hoarsely shouting. Then a lithe young *vaquero*, swift as an Indian, glided under Hawe's uplifted arm. Whatever the action he intended, he was too late for its execution. Stewart lunged out, struck the *vaquero*, and knocked him off the porch. As he fell a dagger glittered in the sunlight and rolled clinking over the stones. The man went down hard and did not move. With the same abrupt violence, and a manner of contempt, Stewart threw Hawe off the porch, then Don Carlos, who, being less supple, fell heavily. Then the mob backed before Stewart's rush until all were down in the courtyard.

The shuffling of feet ceased, the clanking of spurs, and the shouting. Nels and Monty, now reinforced by Nick Steele, were as shadows of Stewart, so closely did they follow him. Stewart waved them back and stepped down into the yard. He was absolutely fearless; but what struck Madeline so keenly was his magnificent disdain. Manifestly, he knew the nature of the men with whom he was dealing. From the look of him it was natural for Madeline to expect them to give way before him, which they did, even Hawe and his attendants sullenly retreating.

Don Carlos got up to confront Stewart. The prostrate *vaquero* stirred and moaned, but did not rise.

"You needn't jibber Spanish to me," said Stewart. "You can talk American, and you can understand American. If you start a rough-house here you and your Greasers will be cleaned up. You've got to leave this ranch. You can have the stock, the packs and traps in the second corral. There's grub, too. Saddle up and hit the trail. Don Carlos, I'm dealing more than square with you. You're lying about these boxes of guns and cartridges. You're breaking the laws of my country, and you're doing it on property in my charge. If I let smuggling go on here I'd be implicated myself. Now, you get off the range. If you don't I'll have the United States Cavalry here in six hours, and you can gamble they'll get what my cowboys leave of you."

Don Carlos was either a capital actor and gratefully relieved at Stewart's leniency, or else he was thoroughly cowed by reference to the troops.

"*Si*, Señor! *Gracias*, Señor!" he exclaimed; and then, turning away, he called to his men. They hurried after him, while the fallen *vaquero* got to his feet with Stewart's help and staggered across the courtyard. In a moment they were gone, leaving Hawe and his several comrades behind.

Hawe was spitefully ejecting a wad of tobacco from his mouth and swearing in an undertone about "white-livered Greasers." He cocked his red eye speculatively at Stewart.

"Wal, I reckon as you're so hell-bent on doin' it up brown, thet you'll try to fire me off'n the range, too?"

"If I ever do, Pat, you'll need to be carried off," replied Stewart. "Just now I'm politely inviting you and your deputy sheriffs to leave."

"We'll go; but we're comin' back one of these days, an' when we do we'll put you in irons."

"Hawe, if you've got it in that bad for me, come over here in the corral and let's fight it out."

"I'm an officer, an' I don't fight outlaws an' sich except when I hev to make arrests."

"Officer! You're a disgrace to the county. If you ever did get irons on me you'd take me some place out of sight, shoot me, and then swear you killed me in self-defense. It wouldn't be the first time you pulled that trick, Pat Hawe."

"Ho, ho!" laughed Hawe, derisively. Then he started toward the horses.

Stewart's long arm shot out, his hand clapped on Hawe's shoulder, spinning him round like a top.

"You're leaving, Pat, but before you leave you'll come out with your play, or you'll crawl," said Stewart. "You've got it in for me, man to man. Speak up now, and prove you're not the cowardly skunk I've always thought you. I've called your hand."

Pat Hawe's face turned a blackish-purple hue.

"You can jest bet thet I've got it in fer you," he shouted, hoarsely. "You're only a low-down cow-puncher. You never hed a dollar of a decent job till you was mixed up with thet Hammond woman—"

Stewart's hand flashed out and hit Hawe's face in a ringing slap. The sheriff's head jerked back, his sombrero fell to the ground. As he bent over to reach it his hand shook, his arm shook, his whole body shook.

Monty Price jumped straight forward and crouched down with a strange, low cry.

Stewart seemed all at once rigid, bending a little.

"*Say Miss Hammond*, if there's occasion to use her name," said Stewart, in a voice that seemed coolly pleasant, yet had a deadly undernote.

Hawe did a moment's battle with strangling fury, which he conquered in some measure.

"I said you was a low-down, drunken cow-puncher, a tough as damn near a desperado as we ever hed on the border," went on Hawe, deliberately. His speech appeared to be addressed to Stewart, although his flame-pointed eyes were riveted upon Monty Price. "I know you plugged that *vaquero* last fall, an' when I git my proof I'm comin' after you."

"That's all right, Hawe. You can call me what you like, and you can come after me when you like," replied Stewart. "But you're going to get in bad with me. You're in bad now with Monty and Nels. Pretty soon you'll queer yourself with all the cowboys and the ranchers, too. If that don't put sense into you— Here, listen to this. You knew what these boxes contained. You know Don Carlos has been smuggling arms and ammunition across the border. You know he is hand and glove with the rebels. You've been wearing blinders, and it has been to your interest. Take a hunch from me. That's all. Light out now, and the less we see of your handsome mug the better we'll like you."

Muttering, cursing, pallid of face, Hawe climbed astride his horse. His comrades followed suit. Certain it appeared that the sheriff was contending with more than fear and wrath. He must have had an irresistible impulse to fling more invective and threat upon Stewart, but he was speechless. Savagely he spurred his horse, and as it snorted and leaped he turned in his saddle, shaking his fist. His comrades led the way, with their horses clattering into a canter. They disappeared through the gate.

When, later in the day, Madeline and Florence, accompanied by Alfred and Stillwell, left Don Carlos's ranch it was not any too soon for Madeline. The inside of the Mexican's home was more unprepossessing and uncomfortable than the outside. The halls were dark, the rooms huge, empty, and musty; and there was an air of silence and secrecy and mystery about them most fitting to the character Florence had bestowed upon the place.

On the other hand, Alfred's ranch-house, where the party halted to spend the night, was picturesquely located,

small and cozy, camp-like in its arrangement, and altogether agreeable to Madeline.

The day's long rides and the exciting events had wearied
her. She rested while Florence and the two men got supper. During the meal Stillwell expressed satisfaction over
the good riddance of the *vaqueros,* and with his usual
optimism trusted he had seen the last of them. Alfred, too,
took a decidedly favorable view of the day's proceedings.
However, it was not lost upon Madeline that Florence
appeared unusually quiet and thoughtful. Madeline wondered a little at the cause. She remembered that Stewart
had wanted to come with them, or detail a few cowboys
to accompany them, but Alfred had laughed at the idea
and would have none of it.

After supper Alfred monopolized the conversation by
describing what he wanted to do to improve his home before he and Florence were married.

Then at an early hour they all retired.

Madeline's deep slumbers were disturbed by a pounding upon the wall, and then by Florence's crying out in
answer to a call:

"Get up! Throw some clothes on and come out!"

It was Alfred's voice.

"What's the matter?" asked Florence, as she slipped out
of bed.

"Alfred, is there anything wrong?" added Madeline,
sitting up.

The room was dark as pitch, but a faint glow seemed
to mark the position of the window.

"Oh, nothing much," replied Alfred. "Only Don Carlos's rancho going up in smoke."

"Fire!" cried Florence, sharply.

"You'll think so when you see it. Hurry out. Majesty,

old girl, now you won't have to tear down that heap of adobe, as you threatened. I don't believe a wall will stand after that fire."

"Well, I'm glad of it," said Madeline. "A good healthy fire will purify the atmosphere over there and save me expense. Ugh, that haunted rancho got on my nerves! Florence, I do believe you've appropriated part of my riding-habit. Doesn't Alfred have lights in this house?"

Florence laughingly helped Madeline to dress. Then they hurriedly stumbled over chairs, and, passing through the dining-room, went out upon the porch.

Away to the westward, low down along the horizon, she saw leaping red flames and wind-swept columns of smoke.

Stillwell appeared greatly perturbed.

"Al, I'm lookin' fer that ammunition to blow up," he said. "There was enough of it to blow the roof off the rancho."

"Bill, surely the cowboys would get that stuff out the first thing," replied Alfred, anxiously.

"I reckon so. But all the same, I'm worryin'. Mebbe there wasn't time. Supposin' that powder went off as the boys was goin' fer it or carryin' it out! We'll know soon. If the explosion doesn't come quick now we can figger the boys got the boxes out."

For the next few moments there was a silence of sustained and painful suspense. Florence gripped Madeline's arm. Madeline felt a fullness in her throat and a rapid beating of her heart. Presently she was relieved with the others when Stillwell declared the danger of an explosion needed to be feared no longer.

"Sure you can gamble on Gene Stewart," he added.

The night happened to be partly cloudy, with broken rifts showing the moon, and the wind blew unusually strong. The brightness of the fire seemed subdued. It was like a huge bonfire smothered by some great covering, penetrated by different, widely separated points of flame. These corners of flame flew up, curling in the wind, and then died down. Thus the scene was constantly changing from dull light to dark. There came a moment when a blacker shade overspread the wide area of flickering gleams and then obliterated them. Night enfolded the scene. The moon peeped a curved yellow rim from under broken clouds. To all appearances the fire had burned itself out. But suddenly a pinpoint of light showed where all had been dense black. It grew and became long and sharp. It moved. It had life. It leaped up. Its color warmed from white to red. Then from all about it burst flame on flame, to leap into a great changing pillar of fire that climbed high and higher. Huge funnels of smoke, yellow, black, white, all tinged with the color of fire, slanted skyward, drifting away on the wind.

"Wal, I reckon we won't hev the good of them two thousand tons of alfalfa we was figgerin' on," remarked Stillwell.

"Ah! Then that last outbreak of fire was burning hay," said Madeline. "I do not regret the rancho. But it's too bad to lose such a quantity of good feed for the stock."

"It's lost, an' no mistake. The fire's dyin' as quick as she flared up. Wal, I hope none of the boys got risky to save a saddle or blanket. Monty—he's hell on runnin' the gantlet of fire. He's like a hoss that's jest been dragged out of a burnin' stable an' runs back sure locoed. There! She's smolderin' down now. Reckon we-all might jest as well turn in again. It's only three o'clock."

"I wonder how the fire originated?" remarked Alfred. "Some careless cowboy's cigarette, I'll bet."

Stillwell rolled out his laugh.

"Al, you sure are a free-hearted, trustin' feller. I'm some doubtin' the cigarette idee; but you can gamble if it was a cigarette it belonged to a cunnin' *vaquero*, an' wasn't dropped accident-like."

"Now, Bill, you don't mean Don Carlos burned the rancho?" ejaculated Alfred, in mingled amaze and anger.

Again the old cattleman laughed.

"Powerful strange to say, my friend, ole Bill means jest that."

"Of course Don Carlos set that fire," put in Florence, with spirit. "Al, if you live out heah a hundred years you'll never learn that Greasers are *treacherous*. I know Gene Stewart suspected something underhand. That's why he wanted us to hurry away. That's why he put me on the black horse of Don Carlos's. He wants that horse for himself, and feared the Don would steal or shoot him. And you, Bill Stillwell, you're as bad as Al. You never distrust anybody till it's too late. You've been singing ever since Stewart ordered the *vaqueros* off the range. But you sure haven't been thinking."

"Wal, now, Flo, you needn't pitch into me jest because I hev a natural Christian spirit," replied Stillwell, much aggrieved. "I reckon I've hed enough trouble in my life so's not to go lookin' fer more. Wal, I'm sorry about the hay burnin'. But mebbe the boys saved the stock. An' as fer that ole adobe house of dark holes an' underground passages, so long's Miss Majesty doesn't mind, I'm darn glad it burned. Come, let's all turn in again. Somebody'll ride over early an' tell us what's what."

Madeline awakened early, but not so early as the others, who were up and had breakfast ready when she went into the dining-room. Stillwell was not in an amiable frame of mind. The furrows of worry lined his broad brow, and he continually glanced at his watch, and growled because the cowboys were so late in riding over with the news. He gulped his breakfast, and while Madeline and the others ate theirs he tramped up and down the porch. Madeline noted that Alfred grew nervous and restless. Presently he left the table to join Stillwell outside.

"They'll slope off to Don Carlos's rancho and leave us to ride home alone," observed Florence.

"Do you mind?" questioned Madeline.

"No, I don't exactly mind; we've got the fastest horses in this country. I'd like to run that big black devil off his legs. No, I don't mind; but I've no hankering for a situation Gene Stewart thinks—"

Florence began disconnectedly, and she ended evasively. Madeline did not press the point, although she had some sense of misgiving. Stillwell tramped in, shaking the floor with his huge boots; Alfred followed him, carrying a field-glass.

"Not a hoss in sight," complained Stillwell. "Somethin' wrong over Don Carlos's way. Miss Majesty, it'll be jest as well fer you an' Flo to hit the home trail. We can telephone over an' see that the boys know you're comin'."

Alfred, standing in the door, swept the gray valley with his field-glass.

"Bill, I see running stock-horses or cattle; I can't make out which. I guess we'd better rustle over there."

Both men hurried out, and while the horses were being brought up and saddled Madeline and Florence put away the breakfast dishes, then speedily donned spurs, sombreros, and gauntlets.

"Here are the horses ready," called Alfred. "Flo, that black Mexican horse is a prince."

The girls went out in time to hear Stillwell's good-by as he mounted and spurred away. Alfred went through the motions of assisting Madeline and Florence to mount, which assistance they always flouted, and then he, too, swung up astride.

"I guess it's all right," he said, rather dubiously. "You really must not go over toward Don Carlos's. It's only a few miles home."

"Sure it's all right. We can ride, can't we?" retorted Florence. "Better have a care for yourself, going off over there to mix in goodness knows what."

Alfred said good-by, spurred his horse, and rode away.

"If Bill didn't forget to telephone!" exclaimed Florence. "I declare he and Al were sure rattled."

Florence dismounted and went into the house. She left the door open. Madeline had some difficulty in holding Majesty. It struck Madeline that Florence stayed rather long indoors. Presently she came out with sober face and rather tight lips.

"I couldn't get anybody on the 'phone. No answer. I tried a dozen times."

"Why, Florence!" Madeline was more concerned by the girl's looks than by the information she imparted.

"The wire's been cut," said Florence. Her gray glance swept swiftly after Alfred, who was now far out of ear-shot. "I don't like this a little bit. Heah's where I've got to 'figger,' as Bill says."

She pondered a moment, then hurried into the house, to return presently with the field-glass that Alfred had used. With this she took a survey of the valley, particularly in the direction of Madeline's ranch-house. This was hidden by low, rolling ridges which were quite close by.

"Anyway, nobody in that direction can see us leave

heah," she mused. "There's mesquite on the ridges. We've got cover long enough to save us till we can see what's ahead."

"Florence, what—what do you expect?" asked Madeline, nervously.

"I don't know. There's never any telling about Greasers. I wish Bill and Al hadn't left us. Still, come to think of that, they couldn't help us much in case of a chase. We'd run right away from them. Besides, they'd shoot. I guess I'm as well satisfied that we've got the job of getting home on our own hands. We don't dare follow Al toward Don Carlos's ranch. We know there's trouble over there. So all that's left is to hit the trail for home. Come, let's ride. You stick like a Spanish needle to me."

A heavy growth of mesquite covered the top of the first ridge, and the trail went through it. Florence took the lead, proceeding cautiously, and as soon as she could see over the summit she used the field-glass. Then she went on. Madeline, following closely, saw down the slope of the ridge to a bare, wide, grassy hollow, and onward to more rolling land, thick with cactus and mesquite. Florence appeared cautious, deliberate, yet she lost no time. She was ominously silent. Madeline's misgivings took definite shape in the fear of *vaqueros* in ambush.

Upon the ascent of the third ridge, which Madeline remembered was the last uneven ground between the point she had reached and home, Florence exercised even more guarded care in advancing. Before she reached the top of this ridge she dismounted, looped her bridle round a dead snag, and, motioning Madeline to wait, she slipped ahead through the mesquite out of sight. Madeline waited, anxiously listening and watching. Certain it was that she could not see or hear anything alarming. The sun began to have a touch of heat; the morning breeze rustled the thin mesquite foliage; the deep magenta of a cactus flower caught her eye; a long-tailed, cruel-beaked, brown bird sailed so close to her she could have touched it with her whip. But she was only vaguely aware of these things. She was watching for Florence, listening for some sound fraught with untoward meaning. All of a sudden she saw Majesty's ears were held straight up. Then Florence's face, now strangely white, showed round the turn of the trail.

"'S-s-s-sh!" whispered Florence, holding up a warning finger. She reached the black horse and petted him, evidently to still an uneasiness he manifested. "We're in for it," she went on. "A whole bunch of *vaqueros* hiding among the mesquite over the ridge! They've not seen or heard us yet. We'd better risk riding ahead, cut off the trail, and beat them to the ranch. Madeline, you're white as death! Don't faint *now!*"

"I shall not faint. But you frighten me. Is there danger? What shall we do?"

"There's danger. Madeline, I wouldn't deceive you," went on Florence, in an earnest whisper. "Things have turned out just as Gene Stewart hinted. Oh, we should—Al should have listened to Gene! I believe—I'm afraid Gene *knew!*"

"Knew what?" asked Madeline.

"Never mind now. Listen. We daren't take the back trail. We'll go on. I've a scheme to fool that grinning Don Carlos. Get down, Madeline—hurry."

Madeline dismounted.

"Give me your white sweater. Take it off— And that white hat! Hurry, Madeline."

"Florence, what on earth do you mean?" cried Madeline.

"Not so loud," whispered the other. Her gray eyes snapped. She had divested herself of sombrero and jacket, which she held out to Madeline. "Heah. Take these. Give me yours. Then get up on the black. I'll ride Majesty. Rustle now, Madeline. This is no time to talk."

"But, dear, why—why do you want—? Ah! You're going to make the *vaqueros* take you for me!"

"You guessed it. Will you—"

"I shall not allow you to do anything of the kind," returned Madeline.

It was then that Florence's face, changing, took on the hard, stern sharpness so typical of a cowboy's. Madeline had caught glimpses of that expression in Alfred's face, and on Stewart's when he was silent, and on Stillwell's always. It was a look of iron and fire—unchangeable, unquenchable will. There was even much of violence in the swift action whereby Florence compelled Madeline to the change of apparel.

"It'd been my idea, anyhow, if Stewart hadn't told me to do it," said Florence, her words as swift as her hands. "Don Carlos is after you—*you, Miss Madeline Hammond!* He wouldn't ambush a trail for any one else. He's not killing cowboys these days. He wants you for some reason. So Gene thought, and now I believe him. Well, we'll know for sure in five minutes. You ride the black; I'll ride Majesty. We'll slip round through the brush, out of sight and sound, till we can break out into the open. Then we'll split. You make straight for the ranch. I'll cut loose for the valley where Gene said positively the cowboys were with the cattle. The *vaqueros* will take me for you. They all know those striking white things you wear. They'll chase me. They'll never get anywhere near me. And you'll be on a fast horse. He can take you home ahead of any *vaqueros*. But you won't be chased. I'm staking all on that. Trust me, Madeline. If it were only my calculation maybe I'd— It's because I remember Stewart. That cowboy knows things. Come, this heah's the safest and smartest way to fool Don Carlos."

Madeline felt herself more forced than persuaded into acquiescence. She mounted the black and took up the bridle. In another moment she was guiding her horse off the trail in the tracks of Majesty. Florence led off at right angles, threading a slow passage through the mesquite. She favored sandy patches and open aisles between the trees, and was careful not to break a branch. Often she stopped to listen. This detour of perhaps half a mile brought Madeline to where she could see open ground, the ranch-house only a few miles off, and the cattle dotting the valley. She had not lost her courage, but it was certain that these familiar sights somewhat lightened the pressure upon her breast. Excitement gripped her. The shrill whistle of a horse made both the black and Majesty jump. Florence quickened the gait down the slope. Soon Madeline saw the edge of the brush, the gray-bleached grass and level ground.

Florence waited at the opening between the low trees. She gave Madeline a quick, bright glance.

"All over but the ride! That'll sure be easy. Bolt now and keep your nerve!"

When Florence wheeled the fiery roan and screamed in his ear Madeline seemed suddenly to grow lax and helpless. The big horse leaped into thundering action. This was memorable of Bonita of the flying dark hair and the wild night ride. Florence's hair streamed on the wind and shone gold in the sunlight. Yet Madeline saw her with the same thrill with which she had seen the wild-riding

Bonita. Then hoarse shouts unclamped Madeline's power of movement, and she spurred the black into the open.

He wanted to run, and he was swift. Madeline loosened the reins—laid them loose upon his neck. His action was strange to her. He was hard to ride. But he was fast, and she cared for nothing else. Madeline knew horses well enough to realize that the black had found he was free and carrying a light weight. A few times she took up the bridle and pulled to right or left, trying to guide him. He kept a straight course, however, and crashed through small patches of mesquite and jumped the cracks and washes. Uneven ground offered no perceptible obstacle to his running. To Madeline there was now a thrilling difference in the lash of wind and the flash of the gray ground underneath. She was running away from something; what that was she did not know. But she remembered Florence, and she wanted to look back, yet hated to do so for fear of the nameless danger Florence had mentioned.

Madeline listened for the pounding of pursuing hoofs in her rear. Involuntarily she glanced back. On the mile or more of gray level between her and the ridge there was not a horse, a man, or anything living. She wheeled to look back on the other side, down the valley slope.

The sight of Florence riding Majesty in zigzag flight before a whole troop of *vaqueros* blanched Madeline's cheek and made her grip the pommel of her saddle in terror. That strange gait of her roan was not his wonderful stride. Could Majesty be running wild? Madeline saw one *vaquero* draw closer, whirling his lasso round his head, but he did not get near enough to throw. So it seemed to Madeline. Another *vaquero* swept across in front of the first one. Then, when Madeline gasped in breathless expectancy, the roan swerved to elude the attack. It flashed over Madeline that Florence was putting the horse to some such awkward flight as might have been expected of an Eastern girl frightened out of her wits. Madeline made sure of this when, after looking again, she saw that Florence, in spite of the horse's breaking gait and the irregular course, was drawing slowly and surely down the valley.

Madeline had not lost her head to the extent of forgetting her own mount and the nature of the ground in front. When, presently, she turned again to watch Florence, uncertainty ceased in her mind. The strange features of that race between girl and *vaqueros* were no longer in evidence. Majesty was in his beautiful, wonderful stride, low down along the ground, stretching, with his nose level and straight for the valley. Between him and the lean horses in pursuit lay an ever-increasing space. He was running away from the *vaqueros*. Florence was indeed "riding the wind," as Stewart had aptly expressed his idea of flight upon the fleet roan.

A dimness came over Madeline's eyes, and it was not all owing to the sting of the wind. She rubbed it away, seeing Florence as a flying dot in a strange blur. What a daring, intrepid girl! This kind of strength—and aye, splendid thought for a weaker sister—was what the West inculcated in a woman.

The next time Madeline looked back Florence was far ahead of her pursuers and going out of sight behind a low knoll. Assured of Florence's safety, Madeline put her mind to her own ride and the possibilities awaiting at the ranch. She remembered the failure to get any of her servants or cowboys on the telephone. To be sure, a windstorm had once broken the wire. But she had little real hope of such being the case in this instance. She rode on, pulling the black as she neared the ranch. Her approach was from the south and off the usual trail, so that she went up the long slope of the knoll toward the back of the house. Under these circumstances she could not consider it out of the ordinary that she did not see any one about the grounds.

It was perhaps fortunate for her, she thought, that the climb up the slope cut the black's speed so she could manage him. He was not very hard to stop. The moment she dismounted, however, he jumped and trotted off. At the edge of the slope, facing the corrals, he halted to lift his head and shoot up his ears. Then he let out a piercing whistle and dashed down the lane.

Madeline, prepared by that warning whistle, tried to fortify herself for a new and unexpected situation; but as she espied an unfamiliar company of horsemen rapidly riding down a hollow leading from the foothills she felt the return of fears gripping at her like cold hands, and she fled precipitously into the house.

CHAPTER 11

A BAND OF GUERRILLAS

Madeline bolted the door, and, flying into the kitchen, she told the scared servants to shut themselves in. Then she ran to her own rooms. It was only a matter of a few moments for her to close and bar the heavy shutters, yet even as she was fastening the last one in the room she used as an office a clattering roar of hoofs seemed to swell up to the front of the house. She caught a glimpse of wild, shaggy horses and ragged, dusty men. She had never seen any *vaqueros* that resembled these horsemen. *Vaqueros* had grace and style; they were fond of lace and glitter and fringe; they dressed their horses in silvered trappings. But the riders now trampling into the driveway were uncouth, lean, savage. They were guerrillas, a band of the raiders who had been harassing the border since the beginning of the revolution. A second glimpse assured Madeline that they were not all Mexicans.

The presence of outlaws in that band brought home to

Madeline her real danger. She remembered what Stillwell had told her about recent outlaw raids along the Rio Grande. These flying bands, operating under the excitement of the revolution, appeared here and there, everywhere, in remote places, and were gone as quickly as they came. Mostly they wanted money and arms, but they would steal anything, and unprotected women had suffered at their hands.

Madeline, hurriedly collecting her securities and the considerable money she had in her desk, ran out, closed and locked the door, crossed the patio to the opposite side of the house, and, entering again, went down a long corridor, trying to decide which of the many unused rooms would be best to hide in. And before she made up her mind she came to the last room. Just then a battering on door or window in the direction of the kitchen and shrill screams from the servant women increased Madeline's alarm.

She entered the last room. There was no lock or bar upon the door. But the room was large and dark, and it was half full of bales of alfalfa hay. Probably it was the safest place in the house; at least, time would be necessary to find any one hidden there. She dropped her valuables in a dark corner and covered them with loose hay. That done, she felt her way down a narrow aisle between the piled-up bales and presently crouched in a niche.

With the necessity of action over for the immediate present, Madeline became conscious that she was quivering and almost breathless. Her skin felt tight and cold. There was a weight on her chest; her mouth was dry, and she had a strange tendency to swallow. Her listening faculty seemed most acute. Dull sounds came from parts of the house remote from her. In the intervals of silence between these sounds she heard the squeaking and rustling of mice in the hay. A mouse ran over her hand.

She listened, waiting, hoping yet dreading to hear the clattering approach of her cowboys. There would be fighting—blood—men injured, perhaps killed. Even the thought of violence of any kind hurt her. But perhaps the guerrillas would run in time to avoid a clash with her men. She hoped for that, prayed for it. Through her mind flitted what she knew of Nels, of Monty, of Nick Steele; and she experienced a sensation that left her somewhat chilled and sick. Then she thought of the dark-browed, fire-eyed Stewart. She felt a thrill drive away the cold nausea. And her excitement augmented.

Waiting, listening increased all her emotions. Nothing appeared to be happening. Yet hours seemed to pass while she crouched there. Had Florence been overtaken? Could any of those lean horses outrun Majesty? She doubted it; she knew it could not be true. Nevertheless, the strain of uncertainty was torturing.

Suddenly the bang of the corridor door pierced her through and through with the dread of uncertainty. Some of the guerrillas had entered the east wing of the house. She heard a babel of jabbering voices, the shuffling of boots and clinking of spurs, the slamming of doors and ransacking of rooms.

Madeline lost faith in her hiding-place. Moreover, she found it impossible to take the chance. The idea of being caught in that dark room by those ruffians filled her with horror. She must get out into the light. Swiftly she rose and went to the window. It was rather more of a door than window, being a large aperture closed by two wooden doors on hinges. The iron hook yielded readily to her grasp, and one door stuck fast while the other opened a few inches. She looked out upon a green slope covered with flowers and bunches of sage and bushes. Neither man nor horse showed in the narrow field of her vision. She believed she would be safer hidden out there in the shrubbery than in the house. The jump from the window would be easy for her. And with her quick decision came a rush and stir of spirit that warded off her weakness.

She pulled at the door. It did not budge. It had caught at the bottom. Pulling with all her might proved to be in vain. Pausing, with palms hot and bruised, she heard a louder, closer approach of the invaders of her home. Fear, wrath, and impotence contested for supremacy over her and drove her to desperation. She was alone here, and she must rely on herself. And as she strained every muscle to move that obstinate door and heard the quick, harsh voices of men and the sounds of a hurried search she suddenly felt sure that they were hunting for her. She knew it. She did not wonder at it. But she wondered if she were really Madeline Hammond, and if it were possible that brutal men would harm her. Then the tramping of heavy feet on the floor of the adjoining room lent her the last strength of fear. Pushing with hands and shoulders, she moved the door far enough to permit the passage of her body. Then she stepped up on the sill and slipped through the aperture. She saw no one. Lightly she jumped down and ran in among the bushes. But these did not afford her the cover she needed. She stole from one clump to another, finding too late that she had chosen with poor judgment. The position of the bushes had drawn her closer to the front of the house rather than away from it, and just before her were horses, and beyond a group of excited men. With her heart in her throat Madeline crouched down.

A shrill yell, followed by running and mounting guer-

THE LIGHT OF WESTERN STARS ★ 535

rillas, roused her hope. They had sighted the cowboys and were in flight. Rapid thumping of boots on the porch told of men hurrying from the house. Several horses dashed past her, not ten feet distant. One rider saw her, for he turned to shout back. This drove Madeline into a panic. Hardly knowing what she did, she began to run away from the house. Her feet seemed leaden. She felt the same horrible powerlessness that sometimes came over her when she dreamed of being pursued. Horses with shouting riders streaked past her in the shrubbery. There was a thunder of hoofs behind her. She turned aside, but the thundering grew nearer. She was being run down.

As Madeline shut her eyes, and, staggering, was about to fall, apparently right under pounding hoofs, a rude, powerful hand clapped round her waist, clutched deep and strong, and swung her aloft. She felt a heavy blow when the shoulder of the horse struck her, and then a wrenching of her arm as she was dragged up. A sudden blighting pain made sight and feeling fade from her.

But she did not become unconscious to the extent that she lost the sense of being rapidly borne away. She seemed to hold that for a long time. When her faculties began to return the motion of the horse was no longer violent. For a few moments she could not determine her position. Apparently she was upside down. Then she saw that she was facing the ground, and must be lying across a saddle with her head hanging down. She could not move a hand; she could not tell where her hands were. Then she felt the touch of soft leather. She saw a high-topped Mexican boot, wearing a huge silver spur, and the reeking flank and legs of a horse, and a dusty narrow trail. Soon a kind of red darkness veiled her eyes, her head swam, and she felt motion and pain only dully.

After what seemed a thousand weary hours some one lifted her from the horse and laid her upon the ground, where, gradually, as the blood left her head and she could see, she began to get the right relation of things.

She lay in a sparse grove of firs, and the shadows told of late afternoon. She smelled wood smoke, and she heard the sharp crunch of horses' teeth nipping grass. Voices caused her to turn her face. A group of men stood and sat round a camp-fire eating like wolves. The looks of her captors made Madeline close her eyes, and the fascination, the fear they roused in her made her open them again. Mostly they were thin-bodied, thin-bearded Mexicans, black and haggard and starved. Whatever they might be, they surely were hunger-stricken and squalid. Not one had a coat. A few had scarfs. Some wore belts in which were scattered cartridges. Only a few had guns, and these were of diverse patterns. Madeline could see no packs, no blankets, and only a few cooking-utensils, all battered and blackened. Her eyes fastened upon men she believed were white men; but it was from their features and not their color that she judged. Once she had seen a band of nomad robbers in the Sahara, and somehow was reminded of them by this motley outlaw troop.

They divided attention between the satisfying of ravenous appetites and a vigilant watching down the forest aisles. They expected some one, Madeline thought, and, manifestly, if it were a pursuing posse, they did not show anxiety. She could not understand more than a word here and there that they uttered. Presently, however, the name of Don Carlos revived keen curiosity in her, and realization of her situation, and then once more dread possessed her breast.

A low exclamation and a sweep of arm from one of the

guerrillas caused the whole band to wheel and concentrate their attention in the opposite direction. They heard something. They saw some one. Grimy hands sought weapons, and then every man stiffened. Madeline saw what hunted men looked like at the moment of discovery, and the sight was terrible. She closed her eyes, sick with what she saw, fearful of the moment when the guns would leap out.

There were muttered curses, a short period of silence followed by whisperings, and then a clear voice rang out, "El Capitan!"

A strong shock vibrated through Madeline, and her eyelids swept open. Instantly she associated the name El Capitan with Stewart and experienced a sensation of strange regret. It was not pursuit or rescue she thought of then, but death. These men would kill Stewart. But surely he had not come alone. The lean, dark faces, corded and rigid, told her in what direction to look. She heard the slow, heavy thump of hoofs. Soon into the wide aisle between the trees moved the form of a man, arms flung high over his head. Then Madeline saw the horse, and she recognized Majesty, and she knew it was really Stewart who rode the roan. When doubt was no longer possible she felt a suffocating sense of gladness and fear and wonder.

Many of the guerrillas leaped up with drawn weapons. Still Stewart approached with his hands high, and he rode right into the camp-fire circle. Then a guerrilla, evidently the chief, waved down the threatening men and strode up to Stewart. He greeted him. There was amaze and pleasure and respect in the greeting. Madeline could tell that, though she did not know what was said. At the moment Stewart appeared to her as cool and careless as if he were dismounting at her porch steps. But when he got down she saw that his face was white. He shook hands with the guerrilla, and then his glittering eyes roved over the men and around the glade until they rested upon Madeline. Without moving from his tracks he seemed to leap, as if a powerful current had shocked him. Madeline tried to smile to assure him she was alive and well; but the intent in his eyes, the power of his controlled spirit telling her of her peril and his, froze the smile on her lips.

With that he faced the chief and spoke rapidly in the Mexican jargon Madeline had always found so difficult to translate. The chief answered, spreading wide his hands, one of which indicated Madeline as she lay there. Stewart drew the fellow a little aside and said something for his ear alone. The chief's hands swept up in a gesture of surprise and acquiescence. Again Stewart spoke swiftly. His hearer then turned to address the band. Madeline caught the words "Don Carlos" and "pesos." There was a brief muttering protest which the chief thundered down. Madeline guessed her release had been given by this guerrilla and bought from the others of the band.

Stewart strode to her side, leading the roan. Majesty reared and snorted when he saw his mistress prostrate. Stewart knelt, still holding the bridle.

"Are you all right?" he asked.

"I think so," she replied, essaying a laugh that was rather a failure. "My feet are tied."

Dark blood blotted out all the white from his face, and lightning shot from his eyes. She felt his hands, like steel tongs, loosening the bonds round her ankles. Without a word he lifted her upright and then upon Majesty. Madeline reeled a little in the saddle, held hard to the pommel with one hand, and tried to lean on Stewart's shoulder with the other.

"Don't give up," he said.

She saw him gaze furtively into the forest on all sides. And it surprised her to see the guerrillas riding away. Putting the two facts together, Madeline formed an idea that neither Stewart nor the others desired to meet with some one evidently due shortly in the glade. Stewart guided the roan off to the right and walked beside Madeline, steadying her in the saddle. At first Madeline was so weak and dizzy that she could scarcely retain her seat. The dizziness left her presently, and then she made an effort to ride without help. Her weakness, however, and a pain in her wrenched arm made the task laborsome.

Stewart had struck off the trail, if there were one, and was keeping to denser parts of the forest. The sun sank low, and the shafts of gold fell with a long slant among the firs. Majesty's hoofs made no sound on the soft ground, and Stewart strode on without speaking. Neither his hurry nor vigilance relaxed until at least two miles had been covered. Then he held to a straighter course and did not send so many glances into the darkening woods. The level of the forest began to be cut up by little hollows, all of which sloped and widened. Presently the soft ground gave place to bare, rocky soil. The horse snorted and tossed his head. A sound of splashing water broke the silence. The hollow opened into a wider one through which a little brook murmured its way over the stones. Majesty snorted again and stopped and bent his head.

"He wants a drink," said Madeline. "I'm thirsty, too, and very tired."

Stewart lifted her out of the saddle, and as their hands parted she felt something moist and warm. Blood was running down her arm and into the palm of her hand.

"I'm—bleeding," she said, a little unsteadily. "Oh, I remember. My arm was hurt."

She held it out, the blood making her conscious of her weakness. Stewart's fingers felt so firm and sure. Swiftly he ripped the wet sleeve. Her forearm had been cut or scratched. He washed off the blood.

"Why, Stewart, it's nothing. I was only a little nervous. I guess that's the first time I ever saw my own blood."

He made no reply as he tore her handkerchief into strips and bound her arm. His swift motions and his silence gave her a hint of how he might meet a more serious emergency. She felt safe. And because of that impression, when he lifted his head and she saw that he was pale and shaking, she was surprised. He stood before her folding his scarf, which was still wet, and from which he made no effort to remove the red stains.

"Miss Hammond," he said, hoarsely, "it was a man's hands—a Greaser's finger-nails that cut your arm. I know who he was. I could have killed him. But I mightn't have got your freedom. You understand? I didn't dare."

Madeline gazed at Stewart, astounded more by his speech than his excessive emotion.

"My dear boy!" she exclaimed. And then she paused. She could not find words.

He was making an apology to her for not killing a man who had laid a rough hand upon her person. He was ashamed and seemed to be in a torture that she would not understand why he had not killed the man. There seemed to be something of passionate scorn in him that he had not been able to avenge her as well as free her.

"Stewart, I understand. You were being *my* kind of cowboy. I thank you."

But she did not understand so much as she implied. She

had heard many stories of this man's cool indifference to
peril and death. He had always seemed as hard as gran-
ite. Why should the sight of a little blood upon her arm
pale his cheek and shake his hand and thicken his voice?
What was there in his nature to make him implore her to
see the only reason he could not kill an outlaw? The answer to the first question was that he loved her. It was beyond her to answer the second. But the secret of it lay in
the same strength from which his love sprang—an intensity of feeling which seemed characteristic of these Western men of simple, lonely, elemental lives. All at once
over Madeline rushed a tide of realization of how greatly
it was possible for such a man as Stewart to love her. The
thought came to her in all its singular power. All her Eastern lovers who had the graces that made them her equals
in the sight of the world were without the only great essential that a lonely hard life had given to Stewart. Nature here struck a just balance. Something deep and dim
in the future, an unknown voice called to Madeline and
disturbed her. And because it was not a voice to her intelligence she deadened the ears of her warm and throbbing
life and decided never to listen.

"Is it safe to rest a little?" she asked. "I am so tired.
Perhaps I'll be stronger if I rest."

"We're all right now," he said. "The horse will be better, too. I ran him out. And uphill, at that."

"Where are we?"

"Up in the mountains ten miles and more from the
ranch. There's a trail just below here. I can get you home by
midnight. They'll be some worried down there."

"What happened?"

"Nothing much to any one but you. That's the—the
hard luck of it. Florence caught us out on the slope. We

were returning from the fire. We were dead beat. But we got to the ranch before any damage was done. We sure had trouble in finding a trace of you. Nick spotted the prints of your heels under the window. And then we knew. I had to fight the boys. If they'd come after you we'd never have gotten you without a fight. I didn't want that. Old Bill came out packing a dozen guns. He was crazy. I had to rope Monty. Honest, I tied him to the porch. Nels and Nick promised to stay and hold him till morning. That was the best I could do. I was sure lucky to come up with the band so soon. I had figured right. I knew that guerrilla chief. He's a bandit in Mexico. It's a business with him. But he fought for Madero, and I was with him a good deal. He may be a Greaser, but he's white."

"How did you effect my release?"

"I offered them money. That's what the rebels all want. They need money. They're a lot of poor hungry devils."

"I gathered that you offered to pay ransom. How much?"

"Two thousand dollars Mex. I gave my word. I'll have to take the money. I told them when and where I'd meet them."

"Certainly. I'm glad I've got the money." Madeline laughed. "What a strange thing to happen to me! I wonder what Dad would say to that? Stewart, I'm afraid he'd say two thousand dollars is more than I'm worth. But tell me. That rebel chieftain did not demand money?"

"No. The money is for his men."

"What did you say to him? I saw you whisper in his ear."

Stewart dropped his head, averting her direct gaze.

"We were comrades before Juarez. One day I dragged

him out of a ditch. I reminded him. Then I—I told him something I—I thought—"

"Stewart, I know from the way he looked at me that you spoke of me."

Her companion did not offer a reply to this, and Madeline did not press the point.

"I heard Don Carlos's name several times. That interests me. What have Don Carlos and his *vaqueros* to do with this?"

"That Greaser has all to do with it," replied Stewart, grimly. "He burned his ranch and corrals to keep us from getting them. But he also did it to draw all the boys away from your home. They had a deep plot, all right. I left orders for some one to stay with you. But Al and Stillwell, who're both hot-headed, rode off this morning. Then the guerrillas came down."

"Well, what was the idea—the plot—as you call it?"

"To get you," he said, bluntly.

"Me! Stewart, you do not mean my capture—whatever you call it—was anything more than mere accident?"

"I do mean that. But Stillwell and your brother think the guerrillas wanted money and arms, and they just happened to make off with you because you ran under a horse's nose."

"You do not incline to that point of view?"

"I don't. Neither does Nels or Nick Steele. And *we* know Don Carlos and the Greasers. Look how the *vaqueros* chased Flo for you!"

"What do you think, then?"

"I'd rather not say."

"But, Stewart, I would like to know. If it is about me, surely I ought to know," protested Madeline. "What reason have Nels and Nick to suspect Don Carlos of plotting to abduct me?"

"I suppose they've no reason you'd take. Once I heard Nels say he'd seen the Greaser look at you, and if he ever saw him do it again he'd shoot him."

"Why, Stewart, that is ridiculous. To shoot a man for looking at a woman! This is a civilized country."

"Well, maybe it would be ridiculous in a civilized country. There's some things about civilization I don't care for."

"What, for instance?"

"For one thing, I can't stand for the way men let other men treat women."

"But, Stewart, this is strange talk from you, who, that night I came—"

She broke off, sorry that she had spoken. His shame was not pleasant to see. Suddenly he lifted his head, and she felt scorched by flaming eyes.

"Suppose I was drunk. Suppose I had met some ordinary girl. Suppose I had really made her marry me. Don't you think I would have stopped being a drunkard and have been good to her?"

"Stewart, I do not know what to think about you," replied Madeline.

Then followed a short silence. Madeline saw the last bright rays of the setting sun glide up over a distant crag. Stewart rebridled the horse and looked at the saddle-girths.

"I got off the trail. About Don Carlos I'll say right out, not what Nels and Nick think, but what *I know.* Don Carlos hoped to make off with you for himself, the same as if you had been a poor peon slave-girl down in Sonora. Maybe he had a deeper plot than my rebel friend told me. Maybe he even went so far as to hope for American troops to chase him. The rebels are trying to stir up the United States. They'd welcome intervention. But, however that may be, the Greaser meant evil to you, and has meant it ever since he saw you first. That's all."

"Stewart, you have done me and my family a service we can never hope to repay."

"I've done the service. Only don't mention pay to me. But there's one thing I'd like you to know, and I find it hard to say. It's prompted, maybe, by what I know you think of me and what I imagine your family and friends would think if they knew. It's not prompted by pride or conceit. And it's this: Such a woman as you should never have come to this God-forsaken country, unless she meant to forget herself. But as you *did* come, and as you *were* dragged away by those devils, I want you to know that all your wealth and position and influence—all that power behind you—would never have saved you from hell to-night. Only such a man as Nels or Nick Steele or I could have done that."

Madeline Hammond felt the great leveling force of the truth. Whatever the difference between her and Stewart, or whatever the imagined difference set up by false standards of class and culture, the truth was that here on this wild mountainside she was only a woman and he was simply a man. It was a man that she needed, and if her choice could have been considered in this extremity it would have fallen upon him who had just faced her in quiet, bitter speech. Here was food for thought.

"I reckon we'd better start now," he said, and drew the horse close to a large rock. "Come."

Madeline's will greatly exceeded her strength. For the first time she acknowledged to herself that she had been hurt. Still, she did not feel much pain except when she moved her shoulder. Once in the saddle, where Stewart lifted her, she drooped weakly. The way was rough; every step the horse took hurt her; and the slope of the ground threw her forward on the pommel. Presently, as the slope grew rockier and her discomfort increased, she forgot everything except that she was suffering.

"Here is the trail," said Stewart, at length.

Not far from that point Madeline swayed, and but for Stewart's support would have fallen from the saddle. She heard him swear under his breath.

"Here, this won't do," he said. "Throw your leg over the pommel. The other one—there."

Then, mounting, he slipped behind her and lifted and turned her, and then held her with his left arm so that she lay across the saddle and his knees, her head against his shoulder.

As the horse started into a rapid walk Madeline gradually lost all pain and discomfort when she relaxed her muscles. Presently she let herself go and lay inert, greatly to her relief. For a little while she seemed to be half drunk with the gentle swaying of a hammock. Her mind became at once dreamy and active, as if it thoughtfully recorded the slow, soft impressions pouring in from all her senses.

A red glow faded in the west. She could see out over the foothills, where twilight was settling gray on the crests, dark in the hollows. Cedar and piñon trees lined the trail, and there were no more firs. At intervals huge drab-colored rocks loomed over her. The sky was clear and steely. A faint star twinkled. And lastly, close to her, she saw Stewart's face, once more dark and impassive, with the inscrutable eyes fixed on the trail.

His arm, like a band of iron, held her, yet it was flexible and yielded her to the motion of the horse. One instant she felt the brawn, the bone, heavy and powerful; the next the stretch and ripple, the elasticity of muscles. He held her as easily as if she were a child. The roughness of his flannel shirt rubbed her cheek, and beneath that she felt the dampness of the scarf he had used to bathe her arm, and deeper still the regular pound of his heart. Against her ear, filling it with strong, vibrant beat, his heart seemed a mighty engine deep within a great cavern. Her head had never before rested on a man's breast, and she had no liking for it there; but she felt more than the physical·contact. The position was mysterious and fascinating, and something natural in it made her think of life. Then as the cool wind blew down from the heights, loosening her tumbled hair, she was compelled to see strands of it curl softly into Stewart's face, before his eyes, across his lips. She was unable to reach it with her free hand, and therefore could not refasten it. And when she shut her eyes she felt those loosened strands playing against his cheeks.

In the keener press of such sensations she caught the smell of dust and a faint, wild, sweet tang on the air. There was a low, rustling sigh of wind in the brush along the trail. Suddenly the silence ripped apart to the sharp bark of a coyote, and then, from far away, came a long wail. And then Majesty's metal-rimmed hoof rang on a stone.

These later things lent probability to that ride for Madeline. Otherwise it would have seemed like a dream. Even so it was hard to believe. Again she wondered if this woman who had begun to think and feel so much was Madeline Hammond. Nothing had ever happened to her. And here, playing about her like her hair played about Stewart's face, was adventure, perhaps death, and surely life. She could not believe the evidence of the day's happenings. Would any of her people, her friends, ever believe it? Could she tell it? How impossible to think that a cunning Mexican might have used her to further the interests of a forlorn revolution! She remembered the ghoulish visages of those starved rebels, and marveled at her blessed fortune in escaping them. She was safe, and now self-preservation had some meaning for her. Stewart's arrival in the glade, the courage with which he had faced the outlawed men, grew as real to her now as the iron arm that clasped her. Had it been an instinct which had importuned her to save this man when he lay ill and hopeless in the shack at Chiricahua? In helping him had she hedged round her forces that had just operated to save her life, or if not that, more than life was to her? She believed so.

Madeline opened her eyes after a while and found that night had fallen. The sky was a dark, velvety blue blazing with white stars. The cool wind tugged at her hair, and through waving strands she saw Stewart's profile, bold and sharp against the sky.

Then, as her mind succumbed to her bodily fatigue, again her situation became unreal and wild. A heavy languor, like a blanket, began to steal upon her. She wavered and drifted. With the last half-conscious sense of a muffled throb at her ear, a something intangibly sweet, deep-toned, and strange, like a distant calling bell she fell asleep with her head on Stewart's breast.

CHAPTER 12

FRIENDS FROM THE EAST

Three days after her return to the ranch Madeline could not discover any physical discomfort as a reminder of her adventurous experiences. This surprised her, but not nearly so much as the fact that after a few weeks she found she scarcely remembered the adventures at all. If it had not been for the quiet and persistent guardianship of her cowboys she might almost have forgotten Don Carlos and the raiders. Madeline was assured of the splendid physical fitness to which this ranch life had developed her, and that she was assimilating something of the Western disregard of danger. A hard ride, an accident, a day in the sun and dust, an adventure with outlaws—these might once have been matters of large import, but now for Madeline they were in order with all the rest of her changed life.

There was never a day that something interesting was not brought to her notice. Stillwell, who had ceaselessly reproached himself for riding away the morning Madeline was captured, grew more like an anxious parent than a faithful superintendent. He was never at ease regarding her unless he was near the ranch or had left Stewart there, or else Nels and Nick Steele. Naturally, he trusted more to Stewart than to any one else.

"Miss Majesty, it's sure amazin' strange about Gene," said the old cattleman, as he tramped into Madeline's office.

"What's the matter now?" she inquired.

"Wal, Gene has rustled off into the mountains again."

"Again? I did not know he had gone. I gave him money for that band of guerrillas. Perhaps he went to take it to them."

"No. He took that a day or so after he fetched you back home. Then in about a week he went a second time. An' he packed some stuff with him. Now he's sneaked off, an' Nels, who was down to the lower trail, saw him meet somebody that looked like Padre Marcos. Wal, I went down to the church, and, sure enough, Padre Marcos is gone. What do you think of that, Miss Majesty?"

"Maybe Stewart is getting religious," laughed Madeline. "You told me so once."

Stillwell puffed and wiped his red face.

"If you'd heerd him cuss Monty this mawnin' you'd never guess it was religion. Monty an' Nels hev been givin' Gene a lot of trouble lately. They're both sore an' in fightin' mood ever since Don Carlos hed you kidnapped. Sure they're goin' to break soon, an' then we'll hev a couple of wild Texas steers ridin' the range. I've a heap to worry me."

"Let Stewart take his·mysterious trips into the mountains. Here, Stillwell, I have news for you that may give you reason for worry. I have letters from home. And my sister, with a party of friends, is coming out to visit me. They are society folk, and one of them is an English lord."

"Wal, Miss Majesty, I reckon we'll all be glad to see them," said Stillwell. "Onless they pack you off back East."

"That isn't likely," replied Madeline, thoughtfully. "I must go back sometime, though. Well, let me read you a few extracts from my mail."

Madeline took up her sister's letter with a strange sensation of how easily sight of a crested monogram and scent of delicately perfumed paper could recall the brilliant life she had given up. She scanned the pages of beautiful handwriting. Helen's letter was in turn gay and brilliant and lazy, just as she was herself; but Madeline detected more of curiosity in it than of real longing to see the sister and brother in the Far West. Much of what Helen wrote was enthusiastic anticipation of the fun she expected to have with bashful cowboys. Helen seldom wrote letters, and she never read anything, not even popular novels of the day. She was as absolutely ignorant of the West as the Englishman who, she said, expected to hunt buffalo and fight Indians. Moreover, there was a satiric note in the letter that Madeline did not like, and which roused her spirit. Manifestly, Helen was reveling in the prospect of new sensation.

When she finished reading aloud a few paragraphs the old cattleman snorted, and his face grew redder.

"Did your sister write that?" he asked.

"Yes."

"Wal, I—I beg pawdin, Miss Majesty. But it doesn't seem like you. Does she think we're a lot of wild men from Borneo?"

"Evidently she does. I rather think she is in for a surprise. Now, Stillwell, you are clever, and you can see the situation. I want my guests to enjoy their stay here, but I do not want that to be at the expense of the feelings of all of us, or even any one. Helen will bring a lively crowd. They'll crave excitement—the unusual. Let us see that they are not disappointed. You take the boys into your confidence. Tell them what to expect, and tell them how to meet it. I shall help you in that. I want the boys to be on dress-parade when they are off duty. I want them to be on their most elegant behavior. I do not care what they do, what measures they take to protect themselves, what tricks they contrive, so long as they do not overstep the limit of kindness and courtesy. I want them to play their parts seriously, naturally, as if they had lived no other way. My guests expect to have fun. Let us meet them with fun. Now, what do you say?"

Stillwell rose, his great bulk towering, his huge face beaming.

"Wal, I say it's the most amazin' fine idee I ever heerd in my life."

"Indeed, I am glad you like it," went on Madeline. "Come to me again, Stillwell, after you have spoken to the boys. But, now that I have suggested it, I am a little afraid. You know what cowboy fun is. Perhaps—"

"Don't you go back on that idee," interrupted Stillwell. He was assuring and bland, but his hurry to convince Madeline betrayed him. "Leave the boys to me. Why, don't they all swear by you, same as the Mexicans do to the Virgin? They won't disgrace you, Miss Majesty. They'll be simply immense. It'll beat any show you ever seen."

"I believe it will," replied Madeline. She was still doubtful of her plan, but the enthusiasm of the old cattleman was infectious and irresistible. "Very well, we will consider it settled. My guests will arrive on May ninth. Meanwhile let us get Her Majesty's Rancho in shape for this invasion."

On the afternoon of the ninth of May, perhaps half an hour after Madeline had received a telephone message from Link Stevens announcing the arrival of her guests at El Cajon, Florence called her out upon the porch. Stillwell was there with his face wrinkled by his wonderful smile and his eagle eyes riveted upon the distant valley. Far away, perhaps twenty miles, a thin streak of white dust rose from the valley floor and slanted skyward.

"Look!" said Florence, excitedly.

"What is that?" asked Madeline.

"Link Stevens and the automobile!"

"Oh no! Why it's only a few minutes since he telephoned saying the party had just arrived."

"Take a look with the glasses," said Florence.

One glance through the powerful binoculars convinced Madeline that Florence was right. And another glance at Stillwell told her that he was speechless with delight. She remembered a little conversation she had had with Link Stevens a short while previous.

"Stevens, I hope the car is in good shape," she had said.

"Now, Miss Hammond, she's as right as the best-trained hoss I ever rode," he had replied.

"The valley road is perfect," she had gone on, musingly. "I never saw such a beautiful road, even in France. No fences, no ditches, no rocks, no vehicles. Just a lonely road on the desert."

"Shore, it's lonely," Stevens had answered, with slowly brightening eyes. "An' safe, Miss Hammond."

"My sister used to like fast riding. If I remember correctly, all of my guests were a little afflicted with the speed mania. It is a common disease with New-Yorkers. I hope, Stevens, that you will not give them reason to think we are altogether steeped in the slow, dreamy *mañana* languor of the Southwest."

Link doubtfully eyed her, and then his bronze face changed its dark aspect and seemed to shine.

"Beggin' your pardon, Miss Hammond, thet's shore tall talk fer Link Stevens to savvy. You mean—as long as I drive careful an' safe I can run away from my dust, so to say, an' get here in somethin' less than the Greaser's to-morrow?"

Madeline had laughed her assent. And now, as she watched the thin streak of dust, at that distance moving with snail pace, she reproached herself. She trusted Stevens; she had never known so skilful, daring, and iron-nerved a driver as he was. If she had been in the car herself she would have had no anxiety. But, imagining what Stevens would do on forty miles and more of that desert road, Madeline suffered a prick of conscience.

"Oh, Stillwell!" she exclaimed. "I am afraid I will go back on my wonderful idea. What made me do it?"

"Your sister wanted the *real thing*, didn't she? Said they all wanted it. Wal, I reckon they've begun gettin' it," replied Stillwell.

That statement from the cattleman allayed Madeline's pangs of conscience. She understood just what she felt, though she could not have put it in words. She was hungry for a sight of well-remembered faces; she longed to hear the soft laughter and gay repartee of old friends; she was eager for gossipy first-hand news of her old world. Nevertheless, something in her sister's letter, in messages from the others who were coming, had touched Madeline's pride. In one sense the expected guests were hostile, inasmuch as they were scornful and curious about the West that had claimed her. She imagined what they would expect in a Western ranch. They would surely get the real thing, too, as Stillwell said; and in that certainty was satisfaction for a small grain of something within Madeline which approached resentment. She wistfully wondered, however, if her sister or friends would come to see the West even a little as she saw it. That, perhaps, would be hoping too much. She resolved once and for all to do her best to give them the sensation their senses craved, and equally to show them the sweetness and beauty and wholesomeness and strength of life in the Southwest.

"Wal, as Nels says, I wouldn't be in that there ottomobile right now for a million pesos," remarked Stillwell.

"Why? Is Stevens driving fast?"

"Good Lord! Fast? Miss Majesty, there hain't ever been anythin' except a streak of lightnin' run so fast in this country. I'll bet Link for once is in heaven. I can jest see him now, the grim, crooked-legged little devil, hunchin' down over that wheel as if it was a hoss's neck."

"I told him not to let the ride be hot or dusty," remarked Madeline.

"Haw, haw!" roared Stillwell. "Wal, I'll be goin'. I reckon I'd like to be hyar when Link drives up, but I want to be with the boys down by the bunks. It'll be some fun to see Nels an' Monty when Link comes flyin' along."

"I wish Al had stayed to meet them," said Madeline.

Her brother had rather hurried a shipment of cattle to California; and it was Madeline's supposition that he had welcomed the opportunity to absent himself from the ranch.

"I am sorry he wouldn't stay," replied Florence. "But Al's all business now. And he's doing finely. It's just as well, perhaps."

"Surely. That was my pride speaking. I would like to have all my family and all my old friends see what a man Al has become. Well, Link Stevens is running like the wind. The car will be here before we know it. Florence, we've only a few moments to dress. But first I want to order many and various and exceedingly cold refreshments for that approaching party."

Less than a half-hour later Madeline went again to the porch and found Florence there.

"Oh, you look just lovely!" exclaimed Florence, impulsively, as she gazed wide-eyed up at Madeline. "And somehow so different!"

Madeline smiled a little sadly. Perhaps when she had put on that exquisite white gown something had come to her of the manner which befitted the wearing of it. She could not resist the desire to look fair once more in the eyes of these hypercritical friends. The sad smile had been for the days that were gone. For she knew that what society had once been pleased to call her beauty had trebled since it had last been seen in a drawing-room. Madeline wore no jewels, but at her waist she had pinned two great crimson roses. Against the dead-white they had the life and fire and redness of the desert.

"Link's hit the old round-up trail," said Florence, "and, oh, isn't he riding that car!"

With Florence, as with most of the cowboys, the car was never driven, but ridden.

A white spot with a long trail of dust showed low down

in the valley. It was now headed almost straight for the ranch. Madeline watched it growing larger moment by moment, and her pleasurable emotion grew accordingly. Then the rapid beat of a horse's hoofs caused her to turn.

Stewart was riding in on his black horse. He had been absent on an important mission, and his duty had taken him to the international boundary line. His presence home long before he was expected was particularly gratifying to Madeline, for it meant that his mission had been brought to a successful issue. Once more, for the hundredth time, the man's reliability struck Madeline. He was a doer of things. The black horse halted wearily without the usual pound of hoofs on the gravel, and the dusty rider dismounted wearily. Both horse and rider showed the heat and dust and wind of many miles.

Madeline advanced to the porch steps. And Stewart, after taking a parcel of papers from a saddle-bag, turned toward her.

"Stewart, you are the best of couriers," she said. "I am pleased."

Dust streamed from his sombrero as he doffed it. His dark face seemed to rise as he straightened weary shoulders.

"Here are the reports, Miss Hammond," he replied.

As he looked up to see her standing there, dressed to receive her Eastern guests, he checked his advance with a violent action which recalled to Madeline the one he had made on the night she had met him, when she disclosed her identity. It was not fear nor embarrassment nor awkwardness. And it was only momentary. Yet slight as had been his pause, Madeline received from it an impression of some strong halting force. A man struck by a bullet might have had an instant jerk of muscular control such as convulsed Stewart. In that instant, as her keen gaze searched his dust-caked face, she met the full, free look of his eyes. Her own did not fall, though she felt a warmth steal to her cheeks. Madeline very seldom blushed. And now, conscious of her sudden color, a genuine blush flamed on her face. It was irritating because it was incomprehensible. She received the papers from Stewart and thanked him. He bowed, then led the black down the path toward the corrals.

"When Stewart looks like that he's been riding," said Florence. "But when his horse looks like that he's sure been burning the wind."

Madeline watched the weary horse and rider limp down the path. What had made her thoughtful? Mostly it was something new or sudden or inexplicable that stirred her mind to quick analysis. In this instance the thing that had struck Madeline was Stewart's glance. He had looked at her, and the old burning, inscrutable fire, the darkness, had left his eyes. Suddenly they had been beautiful. The look had not been one of surprise or admiration; nor had it been one of love. She was familiar, too familiar with all three. It had not been a gaze of passion, for there was nothing beautiful in that. Madeline pondered. And presently she realized that Stewart's eyes had expressed a strange joy of pride. That expression Madeline had never before encountered in the look of any man. Probably its strangeness had made her notice it and accounted for her blushing. The longer she lived among these outdoor men the more they surprised her. Particularly, how incomprehensible was this cowboy Stewart! Why should he have pride or joy at sight of her?

Florence's exclamation made Madeline once more attend to the approaching automobile. It was in the slope now, some miles down the long gradual slant. Two yellow funnel-shaped clouds of dust seemed to shoot out from behind the car and roll aloft to join the column that stretched down the valley.

"I wonder what riding a mile a minute would be like," said Florence. "I'll sure make Link take me. Oh, but look at him come!"

The giant car resembled a white demon, and but for the dust would have appeared to be sailing in the air. Its motion was steadily forward, holding to the road as if on rails. And its velocity was astounding. Long, gray veils, like pennants, streamed in the wind. A low rushing sound became perceptible, and it grew louder, became a roar. The car shot like an arrow past the alfalfa-field, by the bunk-houses, where the cowboys waved and cheered. The horses and burros in the corrals began to snort and tramp and race in fright. At the base of the long slope of the foothill Link cut the speed more than half. Yet the car roared up, rolling the dust, flying capes and veils and ulsters, and crashed and cracked to a halt in the yard before the porch.

Madeline descried a gray, disheveled mass of humanity packed inside the car. Besides the driver there were seven occupants, and for a moment they appeared to be coming to life, moving and exclaiming under the veils and wraps and dust-shields.

Link Stevens stepped out and, removing helmet and goggles, coolly looked at his watch.

"An hour an' a quarter, Miss Hammond," he said. "It's sixty-three miles by the valley road, an' you know there's a couple of bad hills. I reckon we made fair time, considerin' you wanted me to drive slow an' safe."

From the mass of dusty-veiled humanity in the car came low exclamations and plaintive feminine wails.

Madeline stepped to the front of the porch. Then the deep voices of men and softer voices of women united in one glad outburst, as much a thanksgiving as a greeting, "MAJESTY!"

Helen Hammond was three years younger than Madeline, and a slender, pretty girl. She did not resemble her sister, except in whiteness and fineness of skin, being more of a brown-eyed, brown-haired type. Having recovered her breath soon after Madeline took her to her room, she began to talk.

"Majesty, old girl, I'm here; but you can bet I would never have gotten here if I had known about that ride from the railroad. You never wrote that you had a car. I thought this was out West—stage-coach, and all that sort of thing. Such a tremendous car! And the road! And that terrible little man with the leather trousers! What kind of a chauffeur is he?"

"He's a cowboy. He was crippled by falling under his horse, so I had him instructed to run the car. He can drive, don't you think?"

"Drive? Good gracious! He scared us to death, except Castleton. Nothing could scare that cold-blooded little Englishman. I am dizzy yet. Do you know, Majesty, I was delighted when I saw the car. Then your cowboy driver met us at the platform. What a queer-looking individual! He had a big pistol strapped to those leather trousers. That made me nervous. When he piled us all in with our grips, he put me in the seat beside him, whether I liked it or not. I was fool enough to tell him I loved to travel fast. What do you think he said? Well, he eyed me in a rather cool and speculative way and said, with a smile: 'Miss, I reckon anything you love an' want bad will be coming to you out here!' I didn't know whether it was delightful candor or impudence. Then he said to all of us: 'Shore you had better wrap up in the veils an' dusters. It's a long, slow, hot, dusty ride to the ranch, an' Miss Hammond's order was to drive safe.' He got our baggage checks and gave them to a man with a huge wagon and a four-horse team. Then he cranked the car, jumped in, wrapped his arms round the wheel, and sunk down low in his seat. There was a crack, a jerk, a kind of flash around us, and that dirty little town was somewhere on the map behind. For about five minutes I had a lovely time. Then the wind began to tear me to pieces. I couldn't hear anything but the rush of wind and roar of the car. I could see only straight ahead. What a road! I never saw a road in my life till to-day. Miles and miles and miles ahead, with not even a post or tree. That big car seemed to leap at the miles. It hummed and sang. I was fascinated, then terrified. We went so fast I couldn't catch my breath. The wind went through me, and I expected to be disrobed by it any minute. I was afraid I couldn't hold any clothes on. Presently all I could see was a flashing gray wall with a white line in the middle. Then my eyes blurred. My face burned. My ears grew full of a hundred thousand howling devils. I was about ready to die when the car stopped. I looked and looked, and when I could see, there you stood!"

"Helen, I thought you were fond of speeding," said Madeline, with a laugh.

"I was. But I assure you I never before was in a fast car; I never saw a road; I never met a driver."

"Perhaps I may have a few surprises for you out here in the wild and woolly West."

Helen's dark eyes showed a sister's memory of possibilities.

"You've started well," she said. "I am simply stunned. I expected to find you old and dowdy. Majesty, you're the handsomest thing I ever laid eyes on. You're so splendid and strong, and your skin is like white gold. What's happened to you? What's changed you? This beautiful room, those glorious roses out there, the cool, dark sweetness of this wonderful house! I know you, Majesty, and, though you never wrote it, I believe you have made a home out here. That's the most stunning surprise of all. Come, confess. I know I've always been selfish and not much of a sister; but if you are happy out here I am glad. You were not happy at home. Tell me about yourself and about Alfred. Then I shall give you all the messages and news from the East."

It afforded Madeline exceeding pleasure to have from one and all of her guests varied encomiums of her beautiful home, and a real and warm interest in what promised to be a delightful and memorable visit.

Of them all Castleton was the only one who failed to show surprise. He greeted her precisely as he had when he had last seen her in London. Madeline, rather to her astonishment, found meeting him again pleasurable. She discovered she liked this imperturbable Englishman. Manifestly, her capacity for liking any one had immeasurably enlarged. Quite unexpectedly her old girlish love for her younger sister sprang into life, and with it interest in these half-forgotten friends, and a warm regard for Edith Wayne, a chum of college days.

Helen's party was smaller than Madeline had expected it to be. Helen had been careful to select a company of good friends, all of whom were well known to Madeline. Edith Wayne was a patrician brunette, a serious, soft-voiced woman, sweet and kindly, despite a rather bitter experience that had left her worldly wise. Mrs. Carrollton Beck, a plain, lively person, had chaperoned the party. The fourth and last of the feminine contingent was Miss Dorothy Coombs—Dot, as they called her—a young woman of attractive blond prettiness.

For a man Castleton was of very small stature. He had a pink-and-white complexion, a small golden mustache, and his heavy eyelids, always drooping, made him look dull. His attire, cut to what appeared to be an exaggerated English style, attracted attention to his diminutive size. He was immaculate and fastidious. Robert Weede was a rather large florid young man, remarkable only for his good nature. Counting Boyd Harvey, a handsome, pale-faced fellow, with the careless smile of the man for whom life had been easy and pleasant, the party was complete.

Dinner was a happy hour, especially for the Mexican women who served it and who could not fail to note its success. The mingling of low voices and laughter, the old, gay, superficial talk, the graciousness of a class which lived for the pleasure of things and to make time pass pleasurably for others—all took Madeline far back into the past. She did not care to return to it, but she saw that it was well she had not wholly cut herself off from her people and friends.

When the party adjourned to the porch the heat had markedly decreased, and the red sun was sinking over the red desert. An absence of spoken praise, a gradually deepening silence attested to the impression on the visitors of that noble sunset. Just as the last curve of red rim vanished beyond the dim Sierra Madres and the golden lightning began to flare brighter Helen broke the silence with an exclamation.

"It wants only life. Ah, there's a horse climbing the hill! See, he's up! He has a rider!"

Madeline knew before she looked the identity of the man riding up the mesa. But she did not know until that moment how the habit of watching for him at this hour had grown upon her. He rode along the rim of the mesa and out to the point where, against the golden background, horse and rider stood silhouetted in bold relief.

"What's he doing there? Who is he?" inquired the curious Helen.

"That is Stewart, my right-hand man," replied Madeline. "Every day when he is at the ranch he rides up there at sunset. I think he likes the ride and the scene; but he goes to take a look at the cattle in the valley."

"Is he a cowboy?" asked Helen.

"Indeed, yes," replied Madeline, with a little laugh. "You will think so when Stillwell gets hold of you and begins to talk."

Madeline found it necessary to explain who Stillwell was, and what he thought of Stewart, and, while she was about it, of her own accord she added a few details of Stewart's fame.

"El Capitan. How interesting!" mused Helen. "What does he look like?"

"He is superb."

Florence handed the field-glass to Helen and bade her look.

"Oh, thank you," said Helen, as she complied. "There. I see him. Indeed, he is superb. What a magnificent horse! How still he stands! Why, he seems carved in stone."

"Let me look?" said Dorothy Coombs, eagerly.

Helen gave her the glass.

"You can look, Dot, but that's all. He's mine. I saw him first."

Whereupon Madeline's feminine guests held a spirited contest over the field-glass, and three of them made gay, bantering boasts not to consider Helen's self-asserted rights. Madeline laughed with the others while she watched the dark figure of Stewart and his black outline against the sky. There came over her a thought not by any means new or strange—she wondered what was in Stewart's mind as he stood there in the solitude and faced the desert and the darkening west. Some day she meant to ask him. Presently he turned the horse and rode down into the shadow creeping up the mesa.

"Majesty, have you planned any fun, any excitement for us?" asked Helen. She was restless, nervous, and did not seem to be able to sit still a moment.

"You will think so when I get through with you," replied Madeline.

"What, for instance?" inquired Helen and Dot and Mrs. Beck, in unison. Edith Wayne smiled her interest.

"Well, I am not counting rides and climbs and golf; but these are necessary to train you for trips over into Arizona. I want to show you the desert and the Aravaipa Cañon. We have to go on horseback and pack our outfit. If any of you are alive after those trips and want more we shall go up into the mountains. I should like very much to know what you each want particularly."

"I'll tell you," replied Helen, promptly. "Dot will be the same out here as she was in the East. She wants to look bashfully down at her hand—a hand imprisoned in another, by the way—and listen to a man talk poetry about her eyes. If cowboys don't make love that way Dot's visit will be a failure. Now, Elsie Beck wants solely to be revenged upon us for dragging her out here. She wants some dreadful thing to happen to us. I don't know what's in Edith's head, but it isn't fun. Bobby wants to be near Elsie, and no more. Boyd wants what he has always wanted—the only thing he ever wanted that he didn't get. Castleton has a horrible bloodthirsty desire to kill something."

"I declare now, I want to ride and camp out, also," protested Castleton.

"As for myself," went on Helen, "I want—Oh, if I only knew what it is that I want! Well, I know I want to be outdoors, to get into the open, to feel sun and wind, to burn some color into my white face. I want some flesh and blood and life. I am tired out. Beyond all that I don't know very well. I'll try to keep Dot from attaching all the cowboys to her train."

"What a diversity of wants," said Madeline.

"Above all, Majesty, we want something to happen," concluded Helen, with passionate finality.

"My dear sister, maybe you will have your wish fulfilled," replied Madeline, soberly. "Edith, Helen has made me curious about your especial yearning."

"Majesty, it is only that I wanted to be with you for a while," replied this old friend.

There was in the wistful reply, accompanied by a dark and eloquent glance of eyes, what told Madeline of Edith's understanding, of her sympathy, and perhaps a betrayal of her own unquiet soul. It saddened Madeline. How many women might there not be who had the longing to break down the bars of their cage, but had not the spirit.

CHAPTER 13

COWBOY GOLF

In the whirl of the succeeding days it was a mooted question whether Madeline's guests or her cowboys or herself got the keenest enjoyment out of the flying time. Considering the sameness of the cowboys' ordinary life, she was inclined to think they made the most of the present. Stillwell and Stewart, however, had found the situation trying. The work of the ranch had to go on, and some of it got sadly neglected. Stillwell could not resist the ladies any more than he could resist the fun in the extraordinary goings-on of the cowboys. Stewart alone kept the business of cattle-raising from a serious set-back. Early and late he was in the saddle, driving the lazy Mexicans whom he had hired to relieve the cowboys.

One morning in June Madeline was sitting on the porch with her merry friends when Stillwell appeared on the corral path. He had not come to consult Madeline for several days—an omission so unusual as to be remarked.

"Here comes Bill—in trouble," laughed Florence.

Indeed, he bore some faint resemblance to a thunder-cloud as he approached the porch; but the greetings he got from Madeline's party, especially from Helen and Dorothy, chased away the blackness from his face and brought the wonderful wrinkling smile.

"Miss Majesty, sure I'm a sad demoralized old cattleman," he said, presently. "An' I'm in need of a heap of help."

"What's wrong now?" asked Madeline, with her encouraging smile.

"Wal, it's so amazin' strange what cowboys will do. I jest am about to give up. Why, you might say my cowboys were all on strike for vacations. What do you think of that? We've changed the shifts, shortened hours, let one an' another off duty, hired Greasers, an', in fact, done everythin' that could be thought of. But this vacation idee growed worse. When Stewart set his foot down, then the boys begin to get sick. Never in my born days as a cattleman have I heerd of so many diseases. An' you ought to see how lame an' crippled an' weak many of the boys have got all of a sudden. The idee of a cowboy comin' to me with a sore finger an' askin' to be let off for a day! There's Booly. Now I've knowed a hoss to fall all over him, an' onct he rolled down a cañon. Never bothered him at all. He's got a blister on his heel, a ridin' blister, an' he says it's goin' to blood-poisonin' if he doesn't rest. There's Jim Bell. He's developed what he says is spinal-mengalootis, or some such like. There's Frankie Slade. He swore he had scarlet fever because his face burnt so red, I guess, an' when I hollered that scarlet fever was contagious an' he must be put away somewhere, he up an' says he guessed it wasn't that. But he was sure awful sick an' needed to loaf around an' be amused. Why, even Nels doesn't want to work these days. If it wasn't for Stewart, who's had Greasers with the cattle, I don't know what I'd do."

"Why all this sudden illness and idleness?" asked Madeline.

"Wal, you see, the truth is every blamed cowboy on the range except Stewart thinks it's his bounden duty to entertain the ladies."

"I think that is just fine!" exclaimed Dorothy Coombs; and she joined in the general laugh.

"Stewart, then, doesn't care to help entertain us?" inquired Helen, in curious interest.

"Wal, Miss Helen, Stewart is sure different from the other cowboys," replied Stillwell. "Yet he used to be like them. There never was a cowboy fuller of the devil than Gene. But he's changed. He's foreman here, an' that must be it. All the responsibility rests on him. He sure has no time for amusin' the ladies."

"I imagine that is our loss," said Edith Wayne, in her earnest way. "I admire him."

"Stillwell, you need not be so distressed with what is only gallantry in the boys, even if it does make a temporary confusion in the work," said Madeline.

"Miss Majesty, all I said is not the half, nor the quarter, nor nuthin' of what's troublin' me," answered he, sadly.

"Very well; unburden yourself."

"Wal, the cowboys, exceptin' Gene, have gone plumb batty, jest plain crazy over this heah game of gol-lof."

A merry peal of mirth greeted Stillwell's solemn assertion.

"Oh, Stillwell, you are in fun," replied Madeline.

"I hope to die if I'm not in daid earnest," declared the cattleman. "It's an amazin' strange fact. Ask Flo. She'll tell you. She knows cowboys, an' how if they ever start on somethin' they ride it as they ride a hoss."

Florence being appealed to, and evidently feeling all eyes upon her, modestly replied that Stillwell had scarcely misstated the situation.

"Cowboys play like they work or fight," she added. "They give their whole souls to it. They are great big simple boys."

"Indeed they are," said Madeline. "Oh, I'm glad if they like the game of golf. They have so little play."

"Wal, somethin's got to be did if we're to go on raisin' cattle at Her Majesty's Rancho," replied Stillwell. He appeared both deliberate and resigned.

Madeline remembered that despite Stillwell's simplicity he was as deep as any of his cowboys, and there was absolutely no gauging him where possibilities of fun were concerned. Madeline fancied that his exaggerated talk about the cowboys' sudden craze for golf was in line with certain other remarkable tales that had lately emanated from him. Some very strange things had occurred of late, and it was impossible to tell whether or not they were accidents, mere coincidents, or deep-laid, skilfully worked-out designs of the fun-loving cowboys. Certainly there had been great fun, and at the expense of her guests, particularly Castleton. So Madeline was at a loss to know what to think about Stillwell's latest elaboration. From mere force of habit she sympathized with him and found difficulty in doubting his apparent sincerity.

"To go back a ways," went on Stillwell, as Madeline looked up expectantly, "you recollect what pride the boys took in fixin' up that gol-lof course out on the mesa? Wal, they worked on that job, an', though I never seen any other course, I'll gamble yours can't be beat. The boys was sure curious about that game. You recollect also how they all wanted to see you an' your brother play, an' be caddies for you? Wal, whenever you'd quit they'd go to work tryin' to play the game. Monty Price, he was the leadin' spirit. Old as I am, Miss Majesty, an' used as I am to cowboy excentrikities, I nearly dropped daid when I heered that little hobble-footed, burned-up Montana cow-puncher say there wasn't any game too swell for him, an' gol-lof was just his speed. Serious as a preacher, mind you, he was. An' he was always practisin'. When Stewart gave him charge of the course an' the club-house an' all them funny sticks, why, Monty was tickled to death. You see, Monty is sensitive that he ain't much good any more for cowboy work. He was glad to have a job that he didn't feel he was hangin' to by kindness. Wal, he practised the game, an' he read the books in the club-house, an' he got the boys to doin' the same. That wasn't very hard, I reckon. They played early an' late an' in the moonlight. For a while Monty was coach, an' the boys stood it. But pretty soon Frankie Slade got puffed on his game, an' he had to have it out with Monty. Wal, Monty beat him bad. Then one after another the other boys tackled Monty. He beat them all. After that they split up an' begin to play matches, two on a side. For a spell this worked fine. But cowboys can't never be satisfied long onless they win all the time. Monty an' Link Stevens, both cripples, you might say, joined forces an' elected to beat all comers. Wal, they did, an' that's the trouble. Long an' patient the other cowboys tried to beat them two game-legs, an' hevn't done it. Mebbe if Monty an' Link was perfectly sound in their legs like the other cowboys there wouldn't hev been such a holler. But no sound cowboys'll ever stand for a disgrace like that. Why, down at the bunks in the evenin's it's some mortifyin' the way Monty an' Link crow over the rest of the outfit. They've taken on superior airs. You couldn't reach up to Monty with a trimmed spruce pole. An' Link—wal, he's just amazin' scornful.

"'It's a swell game, ain't it?' says Link, powerful sarcastic. 'Wal, what's hurtin' you low-down common cowmen? You keep harpin' on Monty's game-leg an' on my game-leg. If we hed good legs we'd beat you all the wuss. It's brains that wins in gol-lof. Brains an' airstoocratik blood, which of the same you fellers sure hev little.'

"An' then Monty he blows smoke powerful careless an' superior, an' he says:

"'Sure it's a swell game. You cow-headed gents think beef an' brawn ought to hev the call over skill an' graymatter. You'll all hev to back up an' get down. Go out an' learn the game. You don't know a baffy from a Chinee sandwich. All you can do is waggle with a club an' fozzle the ball.'

"Whenever Monty gets to usin' them queer names the boys go round kind of dotty. Monty an' Link hev got the books an' directions of the game, an' they won't let the other boys see them. They show the rules, but that's all. An', of course, every game ends in a row almost before it's started. The boys are all turrible in earnest about this gol-lof. An' I want to say, for the good of ranchin', not to mention a possible fight, that Monty an' Link hev got to be beat. There'll be no peace round this ranch till that's done."

Madeline's guests were much amused. As for herself, in spite of her scarcely considered doubt, Stillwell's tale of woe occasioned her anxiety. However, she could hardly control her mirth.

"What in the world can *I* do?"

"Wal, I reckon I couldn't say. I only come to you for advice. It seems that a queer kind of game has locoed my cowboys, an' for the time bein' ranchin' is at a standstill. Sounds ridiculous, I know, but cowboys are as strange as wild cattle. All I'm sure of is that the conceit has got to be taken out of Monty an' Link. Onct, just onct, will square it, an' then we can resoome our work."

"Stillwell, listen," said Madeline, brightly. "We'll arrange a match game, a four-some, between Monty and Link and your best picked team. Castleton, who is an expert golfer, will umpire. My sister, and friends, and I will take turns as caddies for your team. That will be fair, considering yours is the weaker. Caddies may coach, and perhaps expert advice is all that is necessary for your team to defeat Monty's."

"A grand idee," declared Stillwell, with instant decision. "When can we have this match game?"

"Why, to-day—this afternoon. We'll all ride out to the links."

"Wal, I reckon I'll be some indebted to you, Miss Majesty, an' all your guests," replied Stillwell, warmly. He rose with sombrero in hand, and a twinkle in his eye that again prompted Madeline to wonder. "An' now I'll be goin' to fix up for the game of cowboy gol-lof. *Adios.*"

The idea was as enthusiastically received by Madeline's guests as it had been by Stillwell. They were highly amused and speculative to the point of taking sides and making wagers on their choice. Moreover, this situation so frankly revealed by Stillwell had completed their deep mystification. They were now absolutely nonplussed by the singular character of American cowboys. Madeline was pleased to note how seriously they had taken the old cattleman's story. She had a little throb of wild expectancy that made her both fear and delight in the afternoon's prospect.

The June days had set in warm; in fact, hot during the noon hours; and this had inculcated in her insatiable visitors a tendency to profit by the experience of those used to the Southwest. They indulged in the restful siesta during the heated term of the day.

Madeline was awakened by Majesty's well-known whistle and pounding on the gravel. Then she heard the other horses. When she went out she found her party assembled in gala golf attire, and with spirits to match their costumes. Castleton, especially, appeared resplendent in a golf coat that beggared description. Madeline had faint misgivings when she reflected on what Monty and Nels and Nick might do under the influence of that blazing garment.

"Oh, Majesty," cried Helen, as Madeline went up to her horse, "don't make him kneel! Try that flying mount. We all want to see it. It's so stunning."

"But that way, too, I must have him kneel," said Madeline, "or I can't reach the stirrup. He's so tremendously high."

Madeline had to yield to the laughing insistence of her friends, and after all of them except Florence were up she made Majesty go down on one knee. Then she stood on his left side, facing back, and took a good firm grip on the bridle and pommel and his mane. After she had slipped the toe of her boot firmly into the stirrup she called to Majesty. He jumped and swung her up into the saddle.

"Now just to see how it ought to be done watch Florence," said Madeline.

The Western girl was at her best in riding-habit and with her horse. It was beautiful to see the ease and grace with which she accomplished the cowboys' flying mount. Then she led the party down the slope and across the flat to climb the mesa.

Madeline never saw a group of her cowboys without looking them over, almost unconsciously, for her foreman, Gene Stewart. This afternoon, as usual, he was not present. However, she now had a sense—of which she was wholly conscious—that she was both disappointed and irritated. He had really not been attentive to her guests, and he, of all her cowboys, was the one of whom they wanted most to see something. Helen, particularly, had asked to have him attend the match. But Stewart was with the cattle. Madeline thought of his faithfulness, and was ashamed of her momentary lapse into that old imperious habit of desiring things irrespective of reason.

Stewart, however, immediately slipped out of her mind as she surveyed the group of cowboys on the links. By actual count there were sixteen, not including Stillwell. And the same number of splendid horses, all shiny and clean, grazed on the rim in care of Mexican lads. The cowboys were on dress-parade, looking very different in Madeline's eyes, at least, from the way cowboys usually appeared. But they were real and natural to her guests; and they were so picturesque that they might have been stage cowboys instead of real ones. Sombreros with silver buckles and horse-hair bands were in evidence; and bright silk scarfs, embroidered vests, fringed and ornamented chaps, huge swinging guns, and clinking silver spurs lent a festive appearance.

Madeline and her party were at once eagerly surrounded by the cowboys, and she found it difficult to repress a smile. If these cowboys were still remarkable to her, what must they be to her guests?

"Wal, you-all raced over, I seen," said Stillwell, taking Madeline's bridle. "Get down—get down. We're sure amazin' glad an' proud. An', Miss Majesty, I'm offerin' to beg pawdin for the way the boys are packin' guns. Mebbe it ain't polite. But it's Stewart's orders."

"Stewart's orders!" echoed Madeline. Her friends were suddenly silent.

"I reckon he won't take no chances on the boys bein' surprised sudden by raiders. An' there's raiders operatin' in from the Guadalupes. That's all. Nothin' to worry over. I was just explainin'."

Madeline, with several of her party, expressed relief, but Helen showed excitement and then disappointment.

"Oh, I want something to happen!" she cried.

Sixteen pairs of keen cowboy eyes fastened intently upon her pretty, petulant face; and Madeline divined, if Helen did not, that the desired consummation was not far off.

"So do I," said Dot Coombs. "It would be perfectly lovely to have a real adventure."

The gaze of the sixteen cowboys shifted and sought the demure face of this other discontented girl. Madeline laughed, and Stillwell wore his strange, moving smile.

"Wal, I reckon you ladies sure won't have to go home unhappy," he said. "Why, as boss of this heah outfit I'd feel myself disgraced forever if you didn't have your wish. Just wait. An' now, ladies, the matter on hand may not be amusin' or excitin' to you; but to this heah cowboy outfit it's powerful important. An' all the help you can give us will sure be thankfully received. Take a look across the links. Do you-all see them two apologies for human bein's prancin' like a couple of hobbled bronchs? Wal, you're gazin' at Monty Price an' Link Stevens, who have of a sudden got too swell to associate with their old bunkies. They're practisin' for the toornament. They don't want my boys to see how they handle them crooked clubs."

"Have you picked your team?" inquired Madeline.

Stillwell mopped his red face with an immense bandana, and showed something of confusion and perplexity.

"I've sixteen boys, an' they all want to play," he replied. "Pickin' the team ain't goin' to be an easy job. Mebbe it won't be healthy, either. There's Nels and Nick. They just stated cheerful-like that if they didn't play we won't have any game at all. Nick never tried before, an' Nels, all he wants is to get a crack at Monty with one of them crooked clubs."

"I suggest you let all your boys drive from the tee and choose the two who drive the farthest," said Madeline.

Stillwell's perplexed face lighted up.

"Wal, that's a plumb good idee. The boys'll stand for that."

Wherewith he broke up the admiring circle of cowboys round the ladies.

"Grab a rope—I mean a club—all you cow-punchers, an' march over hyar, an' take a swipe at this little white bean."

The cowboys obeyed with alacrity. There was considerable difficulty over the choice of clubs and who should try first. The latter question had to be adjusted by lot. However, after Frankie Slade made several ineffectual attempts to hit the ball from the teeing-ground, at last to send it only a few yards, the other players were not so eager to follow. Stillwell had to push Booly forward, and Booly executed a most miserable shot and retired to the laughing comments of his comrades. The efforts of several succeeding cowboys attested to the extreme difficulty of making a good drive.

"Wal, Nick, it's your turn," said Stillwell.

"Bill, I ain't so all-fired particular about playin'," replied Nick.

"Why? You was roarin' about it a little while ago. Afraid to show how bad you'll play?"

"Nope, jest plain consideration for my feller cowpunchers," answered Nick, with spirit. "I'm appreciatin' how bad they play, an' I'm not mean enough to show them up."

"Wal, you've got to show me," said Stillwell. "I know you never seen a gol-lof stick in your life. What's more, I'll bet you can't hit that little ball square—not in a dozen cracks at it."

"Bill, I'm also too much of a gent to take your money. But you know I'm from Missouri. Gimme a club."

Nick's angry confidence seemed to evaporate as one after another he took up and handled the clubs. It was plain that he had never before wielded one. But, also, it was plain that he was not the kind of a man to give in. Finally he selected a driver, looked doubtfully at the small knob, and then stepped into position on the teeing-ground.

Nick Steele stood six feet four inches in height. He had the rider's wiry slenderness, yet he was broad of shoulder. His arms were long. Manifestly, he was an exceedingly powerful man. He swung the driver aloft and whirled it down with a tremendous swing. Crack! The white ball disappeared, and from where it had been rose a tiny cloud of dust.

Madeline's quick sight caught the ball as it lined somewhat to the right. It was shooting low and level with the speed of a bullet. It went up and up in swift, beautiful flight, then lost its speed and began to sail, to curve, to drop; and it fell out of sight beyond the rim of the mesa. Madeline had never seen a drive that approached this one. It was magnificent, beyond belief except for actual evidence of her own eyes.

The yelling of the cowboys probably brought Nick Steele out of the astounding spell with which he beheld his shot. Then Nick, suddenly alive to the situation, recovered from his trance and, resting nonchalantly upon his club, he surveyed Stillwell and the boys. After their first surprised outburst they were dumb.

"You-all seen thet?" Nick grandly waved his hand. "Thought I was joshin', didn't you? Why, I used to go to St. Louis an' Kansas City to play this here game. There was some talk of the golf clubs takin' me down East to play the champions. But I never cared fer the game. Too easy fer me! Them fellers back in Missouri were a lot of cheap dubs, anyhow, always kickin' because whenever I hit a ball hard I *always lost it.* Why, I hed to hit sort of left-handed to let 'em stay in my class. Now you-all can go ahead an' play Monty an' Link. I could beat 'em both, playin' with one hand, if I wanted to. But I ain't interested. I jest hit thet ball off the mesa to show you. I sure wouldn't be seen playin' on your team."

With that Nick sauntered away toward the horses. Stillwell appeared crushed. And not a scornful word was hurled after Nick, which fact proved the nature of his victory. Then Nels strode into the limelight. As far as it was possible for this iron-faced cowboy to be so, he was bland and suave. He remarked to Stillwell and the other cowboys that sometimes it was painful for them to judge of the gifts of superior cowboys such as belonged to Nick and himself. He picked up the club Nick had used and called for a new ball. Stillwell carefully built up a little mound of sand and, placing the ball upon it, squared away to watch. He looked grim and expectant.

Nels was not so large a man as Nick, and did not look so formidable as he waved his club at the gaping cowboys. Still he was lithe, tough, strong. Briskly, with a debonair manner, he stepped up and then delivered a mighty swing at the ball. He missed. The power and momentum of his swing flung him off his feet, and he actually turned upside down and spun round on his head. The cowboys howled. Stillwell's stentorian laugh rolled across the mesa. Madeline and her guests found it impossible to restrain their mirth. And when Nels got up he cast a reproachful glance at Madeline. His feelings were hurt.

His second attempt, not by any means so violent, resulted in as clean a miss as the first, and brought jeers from the cowboys. Nels's red face flamed redder. Angrily he swung again. The mound of sand spread over the teeing-ground and the exasperating little ball rolled a few inches. This time he had to build up the sand mound and replace the ball himself. Stillwell stood scornfully by, and the boys addressed remarks to Nels.

"Take off them blinders," said one.

"Nels, your eyes are shore bad," said another.

"You don't hit where you look."

"Nels, your left eye has sprung a limp."

"Why, you dog-goned old fule, you cain't hit thet bawl."

Nels essayed again, only to meet ignominious failure. Then carefully he gathered himself together, gauged distance, balanced the club, swung cautiously. And the head of the club made a beautiful curve round the ball.

"Shore it's jest thet crooked club," he declared.

He changed clubs and made another signal failure. Rage suddenly possessing him, he began to swing wildly. Always, it appeared, the illusive little ball was not where he aimed. Stillwell hunched his huge bulk, leaned hands on knees, and roared his riotous mirth. The cowboys leaped up and down in glee.

"You cain't hit thet bawl," sang out one of the noisiest. A few more whirling, desperate lunges on the part of Nels, all as futile as if the ball had been thin air, finally brought to the dogged cowboy a realization that golf was beyond him.

Stillwell bawled: "Oh, haw, haw, haw! Nels, you're—too old—eyes no good!"

Nels slammed down the club, and when he straightened up with the red leaving his face, then the real pride and fire of the man showed. Deliberately he stepped off ten paces and turned toward the little mound upon which rested the ball. His arm shot down, elbow crooked, hand like a claw.

"Aw, Nels, this is fun!" yelled Stillwell.

But swift as a gleam of light Nels flashed his gun, and the report came with the action. Chips flew from the golf-ball as it tumbled from the mound. Nels had hit it without raising the dust. Then he dropped the gun back in its sheath and faced the cowboys.

"Mebbe my eyes ain't so orful bad," he said, coolly, and started to walk off.

"But look a-heah, Nels," yelled Stillwell, "we come out to play gol-lof! We can't let you knock the ball around with your gun. What'd you want to get mad for? It's only fun. Now you an' Nick hang round heah an' be sociable. We ain't depreciatin' your company none, nor your usefulness on occasions. An' if you just hain't got inborn politeness sufficient to do the gallant before the ladies, why, remember Stewart's orders."

"Stewart's orders?" queried Nels, coming to a sudden halt.

"That's what I said," replied Stillwell, with asperity. "His orders. Are you forgettin' orders? Wal, you're a fine cowboy. You an' Nick an' Monty, 'specially, are to obey orders."

Nels took off his sombrero and scratched his head. "Bill, I reckon I'm some forgetful. But I was mad. I'd'a remembered pretty soon, an' mebbe my manners."

"Sure you would," replied Stillwell. "Wal, now, we don't seem to be proceedin' much with my gol-lof team. Next ambitious player step up."

In Ambrose, who showed some skill in driving, Stillwell found one of his team. The succeeding players, however, were so poor and so evenly matched that the earnest Stillwell was in despair. He lost his temper just as speedily as Nels had. Finally Ed Linton's wife appeared riding up with Ambrose's wife, and perhaps this helped, for Ed suddenly disclosed ability that made Stillwell single him out.

"Let me coach you a little," said Bill.

"Sure, if you like," replied Ed. "But I know more about this game than you do."

"Wal, then, let's see you hit a ball straight. Seems to me you got good all-fired quick. It's amazin' strange." Here Bill looked around to discover the two young wives modestly casting eyes of admiration upon their husbands. "Haw, haw! It ain't so darned strange. Mebbe that'll help some. Now, Ed, stand up and don't sling your club as if you was ropin' a steer. Come round easylike an' hit straight."

Ed made several attempts which, although better than

those of his predecessors, were rather discouraging to the exacting coach. Presently, after a particularly atrocious shot, Stillwell strode in distress here and there, and finally stopped a dozen paces or more in front of the teeing-ground. Ed, who for a cowboy was somewhat phlegmatic, calmly made ready for another attempt.

"Fore!" he called.

Stillwell stared.

"Fore!" yelled Ed.

"Why're you hollerin' that way at me?" demanded Bill.

"I mean for you to lope off the horizon. Get back from in front."

"Oh, that was one of them durned crazy words Monty is always hollerin'. Wal. I reckon I'm safe enough hyar. You couldn't hit me in a million years."

"Bill, ooze away," urged Ed.

"Didn't I say you couldn't hit me? What am I coach-in' you for? It's because you hit crooked, ain't it? Wal, go ahaid an' break your back."

Ed Linton was a short, heavy man, and his stocky build gave evidence of considerable strength. His former strokes had not been made at the expense of exertion, but now he got ready for a supreme effort. A sudden silence clamped down upon the exuberant cowboys. It was one of those fateful moments when the air was charged with disaster. As Ed swung the club it fairly whistled.

Crack! Instantly came a thump. But no one saw the ball until it dropped from Stillwell's shrinking body. His big hands went spasmodically to the place that hurt, and a terrible groan rumbled from him.

Then the cowboys broke into a frenzy of mirth that seemed to find adequate expression only in dancing and rolling accompaniment to their howls. Stillwell recovered his dignity as soon as he caught his breath, and he advanced with a rueful face.

"Wal, boys, it's on Bill," he said. "I'm a livin' proof of the pig-headedness of mankind. Ed, you win. You're captain of the team. You hit straight, an' if I hadn't been obstructin' the general atmosphere that ball would sure have gone clear to the Chiricahuas."

Then making a megaphone of his huge hands, he yelled a loud blast of defiance at Monty and Link.

"Hey, you swell gol-lofers! We're waitin'. Come on if you ain't scared."

Instantly Monty and Link quit practising, and like two emperors came stalking across the links.

"Guess my bluff didn't work much," said Stillwell. Then he turned to Madeline and her friends. "Sure I hope, Miss Majesty, that you-all won't weaken an' go over to the enemy. Monty is some eloquent, an', besides, he has a way of gettin' people to agree with him. He'll be plumb wild when he heahs what he an' Link are up against. But it's a square deal, because he wouldn't help us or lend the book that shows how to play. An', besides, it's policy for us to beat him. Now, if you'll elect who's to be caddies an' umpire I'll be powerful obliged."

Madeline's friends were hugely amused over the prospective match; but, except for Dorothy and Castleton, they disclaimed any ambition for active participation. Accordingly, Madeline appointed Castleton to judge the play, Dorothy to act as caddie for Ed Linton, and she herself to be caddie for Ambrose. While Stillwell beamingly announced this momentous news to his team and supporters Monty and Link were striding up.

Both were diminutive in size, bow-legged, lame in one foot, and altogether unprepossessing. Link was young, and Monty's years, more than twice Link's, had left their mark. But it would have been impossible to tell Monty's age. As Stillwell said, Monty was burned to the color and hardness of a cinder. He never minded the heat, and always wore heavy sheepskin chaps with the wool outside. This made him look broader than he was long. Link, partial to leather, had, since he became Madeline's chauffeur, taken to leather altogether. He carried no weapon, but Monty wore a huge gun-sheath and gun. Link smoked a cigarette and looked coolly impudent. Monty was dark-faced, swaggering, for all the world like a barbarian chief.

"That Monty makes my flesh creep," said Helen, low-voiced. "Really, Mr. Stillwell, is he so bad—desperate—as I've heard? Did he ever kill anybody?"

"Sure. Most as many as Nels," replied Stillwell, cheerfully.

"Oh! And is that nice Mr. Nels a desperado, too? I wouldn't have thought so. He's so kind and old-fashioned and soft-voiced."

"Nels is sure an example of the dooplicity of men, Miss Helen. Don't you listen to his soft voice. He's really as bad as a side-winder rattlesnake."

At this juncture Monty and Link reached the teeing-ground, and Stillwell went out to meet them. The other cowboys pressed forward to surround the trio. Madeline heard Stillwell's voice, and, evidently, he was explaining that his team was to have skilled advice during the play. Suddenly there came from the center of the group a loud, angry roar that broke off as suddenly. Then followed excited voices all mingled together. Presently Monty appeared, breaking away from restraining hands, and he strode toward Madeline.

Monty Price was a type of cowboy who had never been

known to speak to a woman unless he was first addressed, and then he answered in blunt, awkward shyness. Upon this great occasion, however, it appeared that he meant to protest or plead with Madeline, for he showed stress of emotion. Madeline had never gotten acquainted with Monty. She was a little in awe, if not in fear of him, and now she found it imperative for her to keep in mind that more than any other of the wild fellows on her ranch this one should be dealt with as if he were a big boy.

Monty removed his sombrero—something he had never done before—and the single instant when it was off was long enough to show his head entirely bald. This was one of the hall-marks of that terrible Montana prairie fire through which he had fought to save the life of a child. Madeline did not forget it, and all at once she wanted to take Monty's side. Remembering Stillwell's wisdom, however, she forbore yielding to sentiment, and called upon her wits.

"Miss—Miss Hammond," began Monty, stammering, "I'm extendin' admirin' greetin's to you an' your friends. Link an' me are right down proud to play the match game with you watchin'. But Bill says you're goin' to caddy for his team an' coach 'em on the fine points. An' I want to ask, all repectful, if thet's fair an' square?"

"Monty, that is for you to say," replied Madeline. "It was my suggestion. But if you object in the least, of course, we shall withdraw. It seems fair to me, because you have learned the game; you are expert, and I understand the other boys have no chance with you. Then you have coached Link. I think it would be sportsman-like of you to accept the handicap."

"Aw, a handicap! Thet was what Bill was drivin' at. Why didn't he say so? Every time Bill comes to a word thet's pie to us old golfers he jest stumbles. Miss Majesty, you've made it all clear as print. An' I may say with becomin' modesty thet you wasn't mistaken none about me bein' sportsmanlike. Me an' Link was born thet way. An' we accept the handicap. Lackin' thet handicap, I reckon Link an' me would have no ambish to play our most be-ootiful game. An' thankin' you, Miss Majesty, an' all your friends, I want to add thet if Bill's outfit couldn't beat us before, they've got a swell chanct now, with you ladies a-watchin' me an' Link."

Monty had seemed to expand with pride as he delivered this speech, and at the end he bowed low and turned away. He joined the group round Stillwell. Once more there was animated discussion and argument and expostulation. One of the cowboys came for Castleton and led him away to exploit upon ground rules.

It seemed to Madeline that the game never would begin. She strolled on the rim of the mesa, arm in arm with Edith Wayne, and while Edith talked she looked out over the gray valley leading to the rugged black mountains and the vast red wastes. In the foreground on the gray slope she saw cattle in movement and cowboys riding to and fro. She thought of Stewart. Then Boyd Harvey came for them, saying all details had been arranged. Stillwell met them half-way, and this cool, dry, old cattleman, whose face and manner scarcely changed at the announcement of a cattle-raid, now showed extreme agitation.

"Wal, Miss Majesty, we've gone an' made a foozle right at the start," he said, dejectedly.

"A foozle? But the game has not yet begun," replied Madeline.

"A bad start, I mean. It's amazin' bad, an' we're licked already."

"What in the world is wrong?"

She wanted to laugh, but Stillwell's distress restrained her.

"Wal, it's this way. That darn Monty is as cute an' slick as a fox. After he got done declaimin' about the handicap he an' Link was so happy to take, he got Castleton over hyar an' drove us all dotty with his crazy gol-lof names. Then he borrowed Castleton's gol-lof coat. I reckon borrowed is some kind word. He just about took that blazin' coat off the Englishman. Though I ain't sayin' but that Castleton was agreeable when he tumbled to Monty's meanin'. Which was nothin' more'n to break Ambrose's heart. That coat dazzles Ambrose. You know how vain Ambrose is. Why, he'd die to get to wear that Englishman's gol-lof coat. An' Monty forestalled him. It's plumb pitiful to see the look in Ambrose's eyes. He won't be able to play much. Then what do you think? Monty fixed Ed Linton, all right. Usually Ed is easy-goin' an' cool. But now he's on the rampage. Wal, mebbe it's news to you to learn that Ed's wife is powerful, turrible jealous of him. Ed was somethin' of a devil with the wimmen. Monty goes over an' tells Beulah—that's Ed's wife—that Ed is goin' to have for caddie the lovely Miss Dorothy with the goo-goo eyes. I reckon this was some disrespectful, but with all doo respect to Miss Dorothy, she has got a pair of unbridled eyes. Mebbe it's just natural for her to look at a feller like that. Oh, it's all right; I'm not sayin' anythin'! I know it's all proper an' regular for girls back East to use their eyes. But out hyar it's bound to result disastrous. All the boys talk about among themselves is Miss Dot's eyes, an' all they brag about is which feller is the luckiest. Anyway, sure Ed's wife knows it.

An' Monty up an' told her that it was fine for her to come out an' see how swell Ed was prancin' round under the light of Miss Dot's brown eyes. Beulah calls over Ed, fig- gertively speakin', ropes him for a minnit. Ed comes back huggin' a grouch as big as a hill. Oh, it was funny! He was goin' to punch Monty's haid off. An' Monty stands there an' laughs. Says Monty, sarcastic as alkali water: 'Ed, we- all knowed you was a heap married man, but you're some locoed to give yourself away.' That settled Ed. He's some touchy about the way Beulah hen-pecks him. He lost his spirit. An' now he couldn't play marbles, let alone gol-lof. Nope, Monty was too smart. An' I reckon he was right about brains bein' what wins."

The game began. At first Madeline and Dorothy es- sayed to direct the endeavors of their respective players. But all they said and did only made their team play the worse. At the third hole they were far behind and hope- lessly bewildered. What with Monty's borrowed coat, with its dazzling effect upon Ambrose, and Link's oft-repeated allusion to Ed's matrimonial state, and Still- well's vociferated disgust, and the clamoring good in- tention and pursuit of the cowboy supporters, and the embarrassing presence of the ladies, Ambrose and Ed wore through all manner of strange play until it be- came ridiculous.

"Hey, Link," came Monty's voice booming over the links, "our esteemed rivals are playin' shinny."

Madeline and Dorothy gave up, presently, when the game became a rout; and they sat down with their follow- ers to watch the fun. Whether by hook or crook, Ed and Ambrose forged ahead to come close upon Monty and Link. Castleton disappeared in a mass of gesticulating, shouting cowboys. When that compact mass disintegrated Castleton came forth rather hurriedly, it appeared, to stalk back toward his hostess and friends.

"Look!" exclaimed Helen, in delight. "Castleton is actually excited. Whatever did they do to him? Oh, this is immense!"

Castleton was excited, indeed, and also somewhat disheveled.

"By Jove, that was a rum go," he said, as he came up.

"Never saw such blooming golf! I resigned my office as umpire."

Only upon considerable pressure did he reveal the reason.

"It was like this, don't you know. They were all together over there watching each other. Monty Price's ball dropped into a hazard, and he moved it to improve the lie. By Jove, they've all been doing that. But over there the game was waxing hot. Stillwell and his cowboys saw Monty move the ball, and there was a row. They appealed to me. I corrected the play, showed the rules. Monty agreed he was in the wrong. However, when it came to moving his ball back to its former lie in the hazard there was more blooming trouble. Monty placed the ball to suit him, and then he transfixed me with an evil eye.

"'Dook,' he said. I wish the bloody cowboy would not call me that. 'Dook, mebee this game ain't as important as international politics or some other things relatin', but there's some health an' peace dependin' on it. Savvy? For some space our opponents have been dead to honor an' sportsmanlike conduct. I calculate the game depends on my next drive. I'm placin' my ball as near to where it was as human eyesight could. You seen where it was same as I seen it. You're the umpire, an', Dook, I take you as a honorable man. Moreover, never in my born days has my word been doubted without sorrow. So I'm askin' you, wasn't my ball layin' just about here?'

"The bloody little desperado smiled cheerfully, and he dropped his right hand down to the butt of his gun. By Jove, he did! Then I had to tell a blooming lie!"

Castleton even caught the tone of Monty's voice, but it was plain that he had not the least conception that Monty had been fooling. Madeline and her friends divined it, however; and, there being no need of reserve, they let loose the fountains of mirth.

CHAPTER 14

BANDITS

When Madeline and her party recovered composure, they sat up to watch the finish of the match. It came with spectacular suddenness. A sharp yell pealed out, and all the cowboys turned attentively in its direction. A big, black horse had surmounted the rim of the mesa and was just breaking into a run. His rider yelled sharply to the cowboys. They wheeled to dash toward their grazing horses.

"That's Stewart. There is something wrong," said Madeline, in alarm.

Castleton stared. The other men exclaimed uneasily. The women sought Madeline's face with anxious eyes.

The black got into his stride and bore swiftly down upon them.

"Oh, look at that horse run!" cried Helen. "Look at that fellow ride!"

Helen was not alone in her admiration, for Madeline

divided her emotions between growing alarm of some danger menacing and a thrill and quickening of pulse-beat that tingled over her whenever she saw Stewart in violent action. No action of his was any longer insignificant, but violent action meant so much. It might mean anything. For one moment she remembered Stillwell and all his talk about fun, and plots, and tricks to amuse her guests. Then she discountenanced the thought. Stewart might lend himself to a little fun, but he cared too much for a horse to run him at that speed unless there was imperious need. That alone sufficed to answer Madeline's questioning curiosity. And her alarm mounted to fear not so much for herself as for her guests. But what danger could there be? She could think of nothing except the guerrillas.

Whatever threatened, it would be met and checked by this man Stewart, who was thundering up on his fleet horse; and as he neared her, so that she could see the dark gleam of face and eyes, she had a strange feeling of trust in her dependence upon him.

The big black was so close to Madeline and her friends that when Stewart pulled him, the dust and sand kicked up by his pounding hoofs flew in their faces.

"Oh, Stewart, what is it?" cried Madeline.

"Guess I scared you, Miss Hammond," he replied. "But I'm pressed for time. There's a gang of bandits hiding on the ranch, most likely in a deserted hut. They held up a train near Agua Prieta. Pat Hawe is with the posse that's trailing them, and you know Pat has no use for us. I'm afraid it wouldn't be pleasant for you or your guests to meet either the posse or the bandits."

"I fancy not," said Madeline, considerably relieved. "We'll hurry back to the house."

They exchanged no more speech at the moment, and

Madeline's guests were silent. Perhaps Stewart's actions and looks belied his calm words. His piercing eyes roved round the rim of the mesa, and his face was as hard and stern as chiseled bronze.

Monty and Nick came galloping up, each leading several horses by the bridles. Nels appeared behind them with Majesty, and he was having trouble with the roan. Madeline observed that all the other cowboys had disappeared.

One sharp word from Stewart calmed Madeline's horse; the other horses, however, were frightened and not inclined to stand. The men mounted without trouble, and likewise Madeline and Florence. But Edith Wayne and Mrs. Beck, being nervous and almost helpless, were with difficulty gotten into the saddle.

"Beg pardon, but I'm pressed for time," said Stewart, coolly, as with iron arm he forced Dorothy's horse almost to its knees. Dorothy, who was active and plucky, climbed astride; and when Stewart loosed his hold on bit and mane the horse doubled up and began to buck. Dorothy screamed as she shot into the air. Stewart, as quick as the horse, leaped forward and caught Dorothy in his arms. She had slipped head downward and, had he not caught her, would have had a serious fall. Stewart, handling her as if she were a child, turned her right side up to set her upon her feet. Dorothy evidently thought only of the spectacle she presented, and made startled motions to readjust her riding-habit. It was no time to laugh, though Madeline felt as if she wanted to. Besides, it was impossible to be anything but sober with Stewart in violent mood. For he had jumped at Dorothy's stubborn mount. All cowboys were masters of horses. It was wonderful to see him conquer the vicious animal. He was cruel, perhaps, yet it was from necessity. When, presently, he led the horse back to Dorothy, she mounted without further trouble. Meanwhile, Nels and Nick had lifted Helen into her saddle.

"We'll take the side trail," said Stewart, shortly, as he swung upon the big black. Then he led the way, and the other cowboys trotted in the rear.

It was only a short distance to the rim of the mesa, and when Madeline saw the steep trail, narrow and choked with weathered stone, she felt that her guests would certainly flinch.

"That's a jolly bad course," observed Castleton.

The women appeared to be speechless.

Stewart checked his horse at the deep cut where the trail started down.

"Boys, drop over, and go slow," he said, dismounting. "Flo, you follow. Now, ladies, let your horses loose and hold on. Lean forward and hang to the pommel. It looks bad. But the horses are used to such trails."

Helen followed closely after Florence; Mrs. Beck went next, and then Edith Wayne. Dorothy's horse balked.

"I'm not so—so frightened," said Dorothy. "If only he would behave!"

She began to urge him into the trail, making him rear, when Stewart grasped the bit and jerked the horse down.

"Put your foot in my stirrup," said Stewart. "We can't waste time."

He lifted her upon his horse and started him down over the rim.

"Go on, Miss Hammond. I'll have to lead this nag down. It'll save time."

Then Madeline attended to the business of getting down herself. It was a loose trail. The weathered slopes seemed to slide under the feet of the horses. Dust-clouds formed; rocks rolled and rattled down; cactus spikes tore at horse and rider. Mrs. Beck broke into laughter, and there was a note in it that suggested hysteria. Once or twice Dorothy murmured plaintively. Half the time Madeline could not distinguish those ahead through the yellow dust. It was dry and made her cough. The horses snorted. She heard Stewart close behind, starting little avalanches that kept rolling on Majesty's fetlocks. She feared his legs might be cut or bruised, for some of the stones cracked by and went rattling down the slope. At length the clouds of dust thinned, and Madeline saw the others before her ride out upon a level. Soon she was down, and Stewart also.

Here there was a delay, occasioned by Stewart changing Dorothy from his horse to her own. This struck Madeline as being singular, and made her thoughtful. In fact, the alert, quiet manner of all the cowboys was not reassuring. As they resumed the ride it was noticeable that Nels and Nick were far in advance, Monty stayed far in the rear, and Stewart rode with the party. Madeline heard Boyd Harvey ask Stewart if lawlessness such as he had mentioned was not unusual. Stewart replied that, except for occasional deeds of outlawry such as might break out in any isolated section of the country, there had been peace and quiet along the border for years. It was the Mexican revolution that had revived wild times, with all the attendant raids and hold-ups and gun-packing. Madeline knew that they were really being escorted home under armed guard.

When they rounded the head of the mesa, bringing into view the ranch-house and the valley, Madeline saw dust or smoke hovering over a hut upon the outskirts of the

Mexican quarters. As the sun had set and the light was fading, she could not distinguish which it was. Then Stewart set a fast pace for the house. In a few minutes the party was in the yard, ready and willing to dismount.

Stillwell appeared, ostensibly cheerful, too cheerful to deceive Madeline. She noted also that a number of armed cowboys were walking with their horses just below the house.

"Wal, you-all had a nice little run," Stillwell said, speaking generally. "I reckon there wasn't much need of it. Pat Hawe thinks he's got some outlaws corralled on the ranch. Nothin' at all to be fussed up about. Stewart's that particular he won't have you meetin' with any rowdies."

Many and fervent were the expressions of relief from Madeline's feminine guests as they dismounted and went into the house. Madeline lingered behind to speak with Stillwell and Stewart.

"Now, Stillwell, out with it," she said, briefly.

The old cattleman stared, and then he laughed, evidently pleased with her keenness.

"Wal, Miss Majesty, there's goin' to be a fight somewhere, an' Stewart wanted to get you-all in before it come off. He says the valley's overrun by *vaqueros* an' guerrillas an' robbers, an' Lord knows what else."

He stamped off the porch, his huge spurs rattling, and started down the path toward the waiting men.

Stewart stood in his familiar attentive position, erect, silent, with a hand on pommel and bridle.

"Stewart, you are exceedingly—thoughtful of my interests," she said, wanting to thank him, and not readily finding words. "I would not know what to do without you. Is there danger?"

"I'm not sure. But I want to be on the safe side."

She hesitated. It was no longer easy for her to talk to him, and she did not know why.

"May I know the special orders you gave Nels and Nick and Monty?" she asked.

"Who said I gave those boys special orders?"

"I heard Stillwell tell them so."

"Of course I'll tell you if you insist. But why should you worry over something that'll likely never happen?"

"I insist, Stewart," she replied, quietly.

"My orders were that at least one of them must be on guard near you day and night—never to be out of hearing of your voice."

"I thought as much. But why Nels or Monty or Nick? That seems rather hard on them. For that matter, why put any one to keep guard over me? Do you not trust any other of my cowboys?"

"I'd trust their honesty, but not their ability."

"Ability? Of what nature?"

"With guns."

"Stewart!" she exclaimed.

"Miss Hammond, you have been having such a good time entertaining your guests that you forget. I'm glad of that. I wish you had not questioned me."

"Forget what?"

"Don Carlos and his guerrillas."

"Indeed I have not forgotten. Stewart, you still think Don Carlos tried to make off with me—may try it again?"

"I don't think. I know."

"And besides all your other duties you have shared the watch with these three cowboys?"

"Yes."

"It has been going on without my knowledge?"

"Yes."

"Since when?"

"Since I brought you down from the mountains last month."

"How long is it to continue?"

"That's hard to say. Till the revolution is over, anyhow."

She mused a moment, looking away to the west, where the great void was filling with red haze. She believed implicitly in him, and the menace hovering near her fell like a shadow upon her present happiness.

"What must I do?" she asked.

"I think you ought to send your friends back East—and go with them, until this guerrilla war is over."

"Why, Stewart, they would be broken-hearted, and so would I."

He had no reply for that.

"If I do not take your advice it will be the first time since I have come to look to you for so much," she went on. "Cannot you suggest something else? My friends are having such a splendid visit. Helen is getting well. Oh, I should be sorry to see them go before they want to."

"We might take them up into the mountains and camp out for a while," he said, presently. "I know a wild place up among the crags. It's a hard climb, but worth the work. I never saw a more beautiful spot. Fine water, and it will be cool. Pretty soon it'll be too hot here for your party to go out-of-doors."

"You mean to hide me away among the crags and clouds?" replied Madeline, with a laugh.

"Well, it'd amount to that. Your friends need not know. Perhaps in a few weeks this spell of trouble on the border will be over till fall."

"You say it's a hard climb up to this place?"

"It surely is. Your friends will get the real thing if they make that trip."

"That suits me. Helen especially wants something to happen. And they are all crazy for excitement."

"They'd get it up there. Bad trails, cañons to head, steep climbs, wind-storms, thunder and lightning, rain, mountain-lions and wildcats."

"Very well, I am decided. Stewart, of course you will take charge? I don't believe I— Stewart, isn't there something more you could tell me—why you think, why you know my own personal liberty is in peril?"

"Yes. But do not ask me what it is. If I hadn't been a rebel soldier I would never have known."

"If you had not been a rebel soldier, where would Madeline Hammond be now?" she asked, earnestly.

He made no reply.

"Stewart," she continued, with warm impulse, "you once mentioned a debt you owed me—" And seeing his dark face pale, she wavered, then went on. "It is paid."

"No, no," he answered, huskily.

"Yes. I will not have it otherwise."

"No. That never can be paid."

Madeline held out her hand.

"It is paid, I tell you," she repeated.

Suddenly he drew back from the outstretched white hand that seemed to fascinate him.

"I'd kill a man to touch your hand. But I won't touch it on the terms you offer."

His unexpected passion disconcerted her.

"Stewart, no man ever before refused to shake hands with me, for any reason. It—it is scarcely flattering," she said, with a little laugh. "Why won't you? Because you think I offer it as mistress to servant—rancher to cowboy?"

"No."

"Then why? The debt you owed me is paid. I cancel it. So why not shake hands upon it, as men do?"

"I won't. That's all."

"I fear you are ungracious, whatever your reason," she replied. "Still, I may offer it again some day. Good night."

He said good night and turned. Madeline wonderingly watched him go down the path with his hand on the black horse's neck.

She went in to rest a little before dressing for dinner, and, being fatigued from the day's riding and excitement, she fell asleep. When she awoke it was twilight. She wondered why her Mexican maid had not come to her, and she rang the bell. The maid did not put in an appearance, nor was there any answer to the ring. The house seemed unusually quiet. It was a brooding silence, which presently broke to the sound of footsteps on the porch. Madeline recognized Stillwell's tread, though it appeared to be light for him. Then she heard him call softly in at the open door of her office. The suggestion of caution in his voice suited the strangeness of his walk. With a boding sense of trouble she hurried through the rooms. He was standing outside her office door.

"Stillwell!" she exclaimed.

"Anybody with you?" he asked, in a low tone.

"No."

"Please come out on the porch," he added.

She complied, and, once out, was enabled to see him. His grave face, paler than she had ever beheld it, caused her to stretch an appealing hand toward him. Stillwell intercepted it and held it in his own.

"Miss Majesty, I'm amazin' sorry to tell worrysome news." He spoke almost in a whisper, cautiously looked about him, and seemed both hurried and mysterious. "If you'd heered Stewart cuss you'd sure know how we hate to hev to tell you this. But it can't be avoided. The fact is we're in a bad fix. If your guests ain't scared out of their skins it'll be owin' to your nerve an' how you carry out Stewart's orders."

"You can rely upon me," replied Madeline, firmly, though she trembled.

"Wal, what we're up against is this: that gang of bandits Pat Hawe was chasin'—they're hidin' in the house!"

"In the house?" echoed Madeline, aghast.

"Miss Majesty, it's the amazin' truth, an' shamed indeed am I to admit it. Stewart—why, he's wild with rage to think it could hev happened. You see, it couldn't hev happened if I hedn't sloped the boys off to the gol-lof links, an' if Stewart hedn't rid out on the mesa after us. It's my fault. I've hed too much femininity around fer my old haid. Gene cussed me—he cussed me sure scandalous. But now we've got to face it—to figger."

"Do you mean that a gang of hunted outlaws—bandits—have actually taken refuge somewhere in my house?" demanded Madeline.

"I sure do. Seems powerful strange to me why you didn't find somethin' was wrong, seein' all your servants hev sloped."

"Gone? Ah, I missed my maid! I wondered why no lights were lit. Where did my servants go?"

"Down to the Mexican quarters, an' scared half to death. Now listen. When Stewart left you an hour or so ago he follered me direct to where me an' the boys was tryin' to keep Pat Hawe from tearin' the ranch to pieces.

At that we was helpin' Pat all we could to find them bandits. But when Stewart got there he made a difference. Pat was nasty before, but seein' Stewart made him wuss. I reckon Gene to Pat is the same as red to a Greaser bull. Anyway, when the sheriff set fire to an old adobe hut Stewart called him an' called him hard. Pat Hawe hed six fellers with him, an' from all appearances bandit-huntin' was some *fiesta*. There was a row, an' it looked bad fer a little. But Gene was cool, an' he controlled the boys. Then Pat an' his tough de-pooties went on huntin'. That huntin', Miss Majesty, petered out into what was only a farce. I reckon Pat could hev kept on foolin' me an' the boys, but as soon as Stewart showed up on the scene—wal, either Pat got to blunderin' or else we-all shed our blinders. Anyway, the facts stood plain. Pat Hawe wasn't lookin' hard fer any bandits; he wasn't daid set huntin' anythin', unless it was trouble fer Stewart. Finally, when Pat's men made fer our storehouse, where we keep ammunition, grub, liquors, an' sich, then Gene called a halt. An' he ordered Pat Hawe off the ranch. It was hyar Hawe an' Stewart locked horns. An' hyar the truth come out. There was a gang of bandits hid somewheres, an' at fust Pat Hawe hed been powerful active an' earnest in his huntin'. But sudden-like he'd fetched a pecooliar change of heart. He had been some flustered with Stewart's eyes a-pryin' into his moves, an' then, mebbe to hide somethin', mebbe jest nat'rul, he got mad. He hollered law. He pulled down off the shelf his old stock grudge on Stewart, accusin' him over again of that Greaser murder last fall. Stewart made him look like a fool—showed him up as bein' scared of the bandits or hevin' some reason fer slopin' off the trail. Anyway, the row started all right, an' but fer Nels it might hev amounted to a fight. In the thick of it, when Stewart was drivin' Pat an' his crowd off the place, one of them de-pooties lost his head an' went fer his gun. Nels threw his gun an' crippled the feller's arm. Monty jumped then an' threw two forty-fives, an' fer a second or so it looked ticklish. But the bandit-hunters crawled, an' then lit out."

Stillwell paused in the rapid delivery of his narrative; he still retained Madeline's hand, as if by that he might comfort her.

"After Pat left we put our haids together," began the old cattleman, with a long respiration. "We rounded up a lad who hed seen a dozen or so fellers—he wouldn't say they was Greasers—breakin' through the shrubbery to the back of the house. That was while Stewart was ridin' out to the mesa. Then this lad seen your servants all runnin' down the hill toward the village. Now, heah's the way Gene figgers. There sure was some deviltry down along the railroad, an' Pat Hawe trailed bandits up to the ranch. He hunts hard an' then all to onct he quits. Stewart says Pat Hawe wasn't scared, but he discovered signs or somethin', or got wind in some strange way, that there was in the gang of bandits some fellers he didn't want to ketch. *Sabe?* Then Gene, quicker'n a flash, springs his plan on me. He'd go down to Padre Marcos an' hev him help to find out all possible from your Mexican servants. I was to hurry up hyar an' tell you—give you orders, Miss Majesty. Ain't that amazin' strange? Wal, you're to assemble all your guests in the kitchen. Make a grand bluff an' pretend, as your help has left, that it'll be great fun fer your guests to cook dinner. The kitchen is the safest room in the house. While you're joshin' your party along, makin' a kind of picnic out of it, I'll place cowboys in the long corridor, an' also outside in the corner where the kitchen joins on to the main house. It's pretty sure the bandits think no one's wise to where they're hid. Stewart says they're in that end room where the alfalfa is, an' they'll slope in the night. Of course, with me an' the boys watchin', you-all will be safe to go to bed. An' we're to rouse your guests early before daylight, to hit the trail up into the mountains. Tell them to pack outfits before goin' to bed. Say as your servants hev sloped, you might as well go campin' with the cowboys. That's all. If we hev any luck your friends'll never know they've been sittin' on a powder-mine."

"Stillwell, do you advise that' trip up into the mountains?" asked Madeline.

"I reckon I do, considerin' everythin'. Now, Miss Majesty, I've used up a lot of time explainin'. You'll sure keep your nerve?"

"Yes," Madeline replied, and was surprised at herself.

"Better tell Florence. She'll be a power of comfort to you. I'm goin' now to fetch up the boys."

Instead of returning to her room Madeline went through the office into the long corridor. It was almost as dark as night. She fancied she saw a slow-gliding figure darker than the surrounding gloom; and she entered upon the ful-filment of her part of the plan in something like trepida-tion. Her footsteps were noiseless. Finding the door to the kitchen, and going in, she struck lights. Upon passing out again she made certain she discerned a dark shape, now motionless, crouching along the wall. But she mistrusted her vivid imagination. It took all her boldness to enable her unconcernedly and naturally to strike the corridor light. Then she went on through her own rooms and thence into the patio.

Her guests laughingly and gladly entered into the spirit

of the occasion. Madeline fancied her deceit must have been perfect, seeing that it deceived even Florence. They trooped merrily into the kitchen. Madeline, delaying at the door, took a sharp but unobtrusive glance down the great, barn-like hall. She saw nothing but blank dark space. Suddenly from one side, not a rod distant, protruded a pale, gleaming face breaking the even blackness. Instantly it flashed back out of sight. Yet that time was long enough for Madeline to see a pair of glittering eyes, and to recognize them as Don Carlos's.

Without betraying either hurry or alarm, she closed the door. It had a heavy bolt which she slowly, noiselessly shot. Then the cold amaze that had all but stunned her into inaction throbbed into wrath. How dared that Mexican steal into her home! What did he mean? Was he one of the bandits supposed to be hidden in her house? She was thinking herself into greater anger and excitement, and probably would have betrayed herself had not Florence, who had evidently seen her bolt the door and now read her thoughts, come toward her with a bright, intent, questioning look. Madeline caught herself in time.

Thereupon she gave each of her guests a duty to perform. Leading Florence into the pantry, she unburdened herself of the secret in one brief whisper. Florence's reply was to point out of the little open window, passing which was a file of stealthily moving cowboys. Then Madeline lost both anger and fear, retaining only the glow of excitement.

Madeline could be gay, and she initiated the abandonment of dignity by calling Castleton into the pantry, and, while interesting him in some pretext or other, imprinting the outlines of her flour-covered hands upon the back of his black coat. Castleton innocently returned to the kitchen to be greeted with a roar. That surprising act of the hostess set the pace, and there followed a merry noisy time. Everybody helped. The miscellaneous collection of dishes so confusingly contrived made up a dinner which they all heartily enjoyed. Madeline enjoyed it herself, even with the feeling of a sword hanging suspended over her.

The hour was late when she rose from the table and told her guests to go to their rooms, don their riding-clothes, pack what they needed for the long and adventurous camping trip that she hoped would be the climax of their Western experience, and to snatch a little sleep before the cowboys roused them for the early start.

Madeline went immediately to her room, and was getting out her camping apparel when a knock interrupted her. She thought Florence had come to help her pack. But this knock was upon the door opening out in the porch. It was repeated.

"Who's there?" she questioned.

"Stewart," came the reply.

She opened the door. He stood on the threshold. Beyond him, indistinct in the gloom, were several cowboys.

"May I speak to you?" he asked.

"Certainly." She hesitated a moment, then asked him in and closed the door. "Is—is everything all right?"

"No. These bandits stick to cover pretty close. They must have found out we're on the watch. But I'm sure we'll get you and your friends away before anything starts. I wanted to tell you that I've talked with your servants. They were just scared. They'll come back to-morrow, soon as Bill gets rid of this gang. You need not worry about them or your property."

"Do you have any idea who is hiding in the house?"

"I was worried some at first. Pat Hawe acted queer.

I imagined he'd discovered he was trailing bandits who might turn out to be his smuggling guerrilla cronies. But talking with your servants, finding a bunch of horses hidden down in the mesquite behind the pond—several things have changed my mind. My idea is that a cowardly handful of riffraff outcasts from the border have hidden in your house, more by accident than design. We'll let them go—get rid of them without even a shot. If I didn't think so—well, I'd be considerably worried. It would make a different state of affairs."

"Stewart, you are wrong," she said.

He started, but his reply did not follow swiftly. The expression of his eyes altered. Presently he spoke:

"How so?"

"I saw one of these bandits. I distinctly recognized him."

One long step brought him close to her.

"Who was he?" demanded Stewart.

"Don Carlos."

He muttered low and deep, then said: "Are you sure?"

"Absolutely. I saw his figure twice in the hall, then his face in the light. I could never mistake his eyes."

"Did he know you saw him?"

"I am not positive, but I think so. Oh, he must have known! I was standing full in the light. I had entered the door, then purposely stepped out. His face showed from around a corner, and swiftly flashed out of sight."

Madeline was tremblingly conscious that Stewart underwent a transformation. She saw as well as felt the leaping passion that changed him.

"Call your friends—get them in here!" he ordered, tersely, and wheeled toward the door.

"Stewart, wait!" she said.

He turned. His white face, his burning eyes, his presence now charged with definite, fearful meaning, influenced her strangely, weakened her.

"What will you do?" she asked.

"That needn't concern you. Get your party in here. Bar the windows and lock the doors. You'll be safe."

"Stewart! Tell me what you intend to do."

"I won't tell you," he replied, and turned away again.

"But I will know," she said. With a hand on his arm she detained him. She saw how he halted—felt the shock in him as she touched him. "Oh, I do know. You mean to fight!"

"Well, Miss Hammond, isn't it about time?" he asked. Evidently, he overcame a violent passion for instant action. There was weariness, dignity, even reproof in his question. "The fact of that Mexican's presence here in your house ought to prove to you the nature of the case. These *vaqueros,* these guerrillas, have found out you won't stand for any fighting on the part of your men. Don Carlos is a sneak, a coward, yet he's not afraid to hide in your own house. He has learned you won't let your cowboys hurt anybody. He's taking advantage of it. He'll rob, burn, and make off with you. He'll murder, too, if it falls his way. These Greasers use knives in the dark. So I ask— isn't it about time we stop him?"

"Stewart, I forbid you to fight, unless in self-defense. I forbid you."

"What I mean to do is self-defense. Haven't I tried to explain to you that just now we've wild times along this stretch of border? Must I tell you again that Don Carlos is hand and glove with the revolution? The rebels are crazy to stir up the United States. You are a woman of prominence. Don Carlos would make off with you. If he got you, what little matter to cross the border with you! Well, where would the hue and cry go? Through the troops along the border! To New York! To Washington! Why, it would mean what the rebels are working for—United States intervention. In other words, war!"

"Oh, surely you exaggerate!" she cried.

"Maybe so. But I'm beginning to see the Don's game. And, Miss Hammond, I—it's awful for me to think what you'd suffer if Don Carlos got you over the line. I know these low-caste Mexicans. I've been among the peons— the slaves."

"Stewart, don't let Don Carlos get me," replied Madeline, in sweet directness.

She saw him shake, saw his throat swell as he swallowed hard, saw the hard fierceness return to his face.

"I won't. That's why I'm going after him."

"But I forbade you to start a fight deliberately."

"Then I'll go ahead and start one without your permission," he replied, shortly, and again he wheeled.

This time, when Madeline caught his arm, she held to it, even after he stopped.

"No," she said, imperiously.

He shook off her hand and strode forward.

"Please don't go!" she called, beseechingly. But he kept on. "Stewart!"

She ran ahead of him, intercepted him, faced him with her back against the door. He swept out a long arm as if to brush her aside. But it wavered and fell. Haggard, troubled, with working face, he stood before her.

"It's for your sake," he expostulated.

"If it is for my sake, then do what pleases me."

"These guerrillas will knife somebody. They'll burn

the house. They'll make off with you. They'll do something bad unless we stop them."

"Let us risk all that," she importuned.

"But it's a terrible risk, and it oughtn't be run," he exclaimed, passionately. "I know best here. Stillwell upholds me. Let me out, Miss Hammond. I'm going to take the boys and go after these guerrillas."

"No!"

"Good Heavens!" exclaimed Stewart. "Why not let me go? It's the thing to do. I'm sorry to distress you and your guests. Why not put an end to Don Carlos's badgering? Is it because you're afraid a rumpus will spoil your friends' visit?"

"It isn't—not this time."

"Then it's the idea of a little shooting at these Greasers?"

"No."

"You're sick to think of a little Greaser blood staining the halls of your home?"

"No!"

"Well, then, why keep me from doing what I know is best?"

"Stewart, I—I—" she faltered, in growing agitation. "I'm frightened—confused. All this is too—too much for me. I'm not a coward. If you *have* to fight you'll see I'm not a coward. But your way seems so reckless—that hall is so dark—the guerrillas would shoot from behind doors. You're so wild, so daring, you'd rush right into peril. Is that necessary? I think—I mean—I don't know just why I feel so—so about you doing it. But I believe it's because I'm afraid you—you might be hurt."

"You're afraid I—*I* might be hurt?" he echoed,

wonderingly, the hard whiteness of his face warming, flushing, glowing.

"Yes."

The single word, with all it might mean, with all it might not mean, softened him as if by magic, made him gentle, amazed, shy as a boy, stifling under a torrent of emotions.

Madeline thought she had persuaded him—worked her will with him. Then another of his startlingly sudden moves told her that she had reckoned too quickly. This move was to put her firmly aside so he could pass; and Madeline, seeing he would not hesitate to lift her out of the way, surrendered the door. He turned on the threshold. His face was still working, but the flame-pointed gleam of his eyes indicated the return of that cowboy ruthlessness.

"I'm going to drive Don Carlos and his gang out of the house," declared Stewart. "I think I may promise you to do it without a fight. But if it takes a fight, off he goes!"

CHAPTER 15

THE MOUNTAIN TRAIL

As Stewart departed from one door Florence knocked upon another; and Madeline, far shaken out of her usual serenity, admitted the cool Western girl with more than gladness. Just to have her near helped Madeline to get back her balance. She was conscious of Florence's sharp scrutiny, then of a sweet, deliberate change of manner. Florence might have been burning with curiosity to know more about the bandits hidden in the house, the plans of the cowboys, the reason for Madeline's suppressed emotion; but instead of asking Madeline questions she introduced the important subject of what to take on the camping trip. For an hour they discussed the need of this and that article, selected those things most needful, and then packed them in Madeline's duffle-bags.

That done, they decided to lie down, fully dressed as they were in riding-costume, and sleep, or at least rest, the little remaining time left before the call to saddle.

Madeline turned out the light and, peeping through her window, saw dark forms standing sentinel-like in the gloom. When she lay down she heard soft steps on the path. This fidelity to her swelled her heart, while the need of it presaged that fearful something which, since Stewart's passionate appeal to her, haunted her as inevitable.

Madeline did not expect to sleep, yet she did sleep, and it seemed to have been only a moment until Florence called her. She followed Florence outside. It was the dark hour before dawn. She could discern saddled horses being held by cowboys. There was an air of hurry and mystery about the departure. Helen, who came tiptoeing out with Madeline's other guests, whispered that it was like an escape. She was delighted. The others were amused. To Madeline it was indeed an escape.

In the darkness Madeline could not see how many escorts her party was to have. She heard low voices, the champing of bits and thumping of hoofs, and she recognized Stewart when he led up Majesty for her to mount. Then came a pattering of soft feet and the whining of dogs. Cold noses touched her hands, and she saw the long, gray, shaggy shapes of her pack of Russian wolfhounds. That Stewart meant to let them go with her was indicative of how he studied her pleasure. She loved to be out with the hounds and her horse.

Stewart led Majesty out into the darkness past a line of mounted horses.

"Guess we're ready," he said. "I'll make the count." He went back along the line, and on the return Madeline heard him say several times: "Now, everybody ride close to the horse in front, and keep quiet till daylight." Then the snorting and pounding of the big black horse in front of her told Madeline that Stewart had mounted.

"All right, we're off," he called.

Madeline lifted Majesty's bridle and let the roan go. There was a crack and crunch of gravel, fire struck from stone, a low whinny, a snort, and then steady, short, clip-clop of iron hoofs on hard ground. Madeline could just discern Stewart and his black outlined in shadowy gray before her. Yet they were almost within touching distance. Once or twice one of the huge stag-hounds leaped up at her and whined joyously. A thick belt of darkness lay low, and seemed to thin out above to a gray fog, through which a few wan stars showed. It was altogether an unusual departure from the ranch; and Madeline, always susceptible even to ordinary incident that promised well, now found herself thrillingly sensitive to the soft beat of hoofs, the feel of cool, moist air, the dim sight of Stewart's dark figure. The caution, the early start before dawn, the enforced silence—these lent the occasion all that was needful to make it stirring.

Majesty plunged into a gully, where sand and rough going made Madeline stop romancing to attend to riding. In the darkness Stewart was not so easy to keep close to even on smooth trails, and now she had to be watchfully attentive to do it. Then followed a long march through dragging sand. Meantime the blackness gradually changed to gray. At length Majesty climbed out of the wash, and once more his iron shoes rang on stone. He began to climb. The figure of Stewart and his horse loomed more distinctly in Madeline's sight. Bending over, she tried to see the trail, but could not. She wondered how Stewart could follow a trail in the dark. His eyes must be as piercing as they sometimes looked. Over her shoulder Madeline could not see the horse behind her, but she heard him.

As Majesty climbed steadily Madeline saw the gray darkness grow opaque, change and lighten, lose its substance, and yield the grotesque shapes of yucca and ocotillo. Dawn was about to break. Madeline imagined she was facing east, still she saw no brightening of sky. All at once, to her surprise, Stewart and his powerful horse stood clear in her sight. She saw the characteristic rock and cactus and brush that covered the foothills. The trail was old and seldom used, and it zigzagged and turned and twisted. Looking back, she saw the short, squat figure of Monty Price humped over his saddle. Monty's face was hidden under his sombrero. Behind him rode Dorothy Coombs, and next loomed up the lofty form of Nick Steele. Madeline and the members of her party were riding between cowboy escorts.

Bright daylight came, and Madeline saw the trail was leading up through foothills. It led in a roundabout way through shallow gullies full of stone and brush washed down by floods. At every turn now Madeline expected to come upon water and the waiting pack-train. But time passed, and miles of climbing, and no water or horses were met. Expectation in Madeline gave place to desire; she was hungry.

Presently Stewart's horse went splashing into a shallow pool. Beyond that damp places in the sand showed here and there, and again more water in rocky pockets. Stewart kept on. It was eight o'clock by Madeline's watch when, upon turning into a wide hollow, she saw horses grazing on spare grass, a great pile of canvas-covered bundles, and a fire round which cowboys and two Mexican women were busy.

Madeline sat her horse and reviewed her followers as

they rode up single file. Her guests were in merry mood, and they all talked at once.

"Breakfast—and rustle," called out Stewart, without ceremony.

"No need to tell me to rustle," said Helen. "I am simply ravenous. This air makes me hungry."

For that matter, Madeline observed Helen did not show any marked contrast to the others. The hurry order, however, did not interfere with the meal being somewhat in the nature of a picnic. While they ate and talked and laughed the cowboys were packing horses and burros and throwing the diamond-hitch, a procedure so interesting to Castleton that he got up with coffee-cup in hand and tramped from one place to another.

"Heard of that diamond-hitch-up," he observed to a cowboy. "Bally nice little job!"

As soon as the pack-train was in readiness Stewart started it off in the lead to break trail. A heavy growth of shrub interspersed with rock and cactus covered the slopes; and now all the trail appeared to be uphill. It was not a question of comfort for Madeline and her party, for comfort was impossible; it was a matter of making the travel possible for them. Florence wore corduroy breeches and high-top boots, and the advantage of this masculine garb was at once in evidence. The riding-habits of the other ladies suffered considerably from the sharp spikes. It took all Madeline's watchfulness to save her horse's legs, to pick the best bits of open ground, to make cut-offs from the trail, and to protect herself from outreaching thorny branches, so that the time sped by without her knowing it. The pack-train forged ahead, and the trailing couples grew farther apart. At noon they got out of the foothills to face the real ascent of the mountains. The sun beat down hot. There was little breeze, and the dust rose thick and hung in a pall. The view was restricted, and what scenery lay open to the eye was dreary and drab, a barren monotony of slow-mounting slopes ridged by rocky cañons.

Once Stewart waited for Madeline, and as she came up he said:

"We're going to have a storm."

"That will be a relief. It's so hot and dusty," replied Madeline.

"Shall I call a halt and make camp?"

"Here? Oh no! What do you think best?"

"Well, if we have a good healthy thunder-storm it will be something new for your friends. I think we'd be wise to keep on the go. There's no place to make a good camp. The wind would blow us off this slope if the rain didn't wash us off. It'll take all-day travel to reach a good camp-site, and I don't promise that. We're making slow time. If it rains, let it rain. The pack outfit is well covered. We will have to get wet."

"Surely," replied Madeline; and she smiled at his inference. She knew what a storm was in that country, and her guests had yet to experience one. "If it rains, let it rain."

Stewart rode on, and Madeline followed. Up the slope toiled and nodded the pack-animals, the little burros going easily where the horses labored. Their packs, like the humps of camels, bobbed from side to side. Stones rattled down; the heat-waves wavered black; the dust puffed up and sailed. The sky was a pale blue, like heated steel, except where dark clouds peeped over the mountain crests. A heavy, sultry atmosphere made breathing difficult. Down the slope the trailing party stretched out in twos and threes, and it was easy to distinguish the weary riders.

Half a mile farther up Madeline could see over the foothills to the north and west and a little south, and she forgot the heat and weariness and discomfort for her guests in wide, unlimited prospects of sun-scorched earth. She marked the gray valley and the black mountains and the wide, red gateway of the desert, and the dim, shadowy peaks, blue as the sky they pierced. She was sorry when the bleak, gnarled cedar-trees shut off her view.

Then there came a respite from the steep climb, and the way led in a winding course through a matted, storm-wrenched forest of stunted trees. Even up to this elevation the desert reached with its gaunt hand. The clouds overspreading the sky, hiding the sun, made a welcome change. The pack-train rested, and Stewart and Madeline waited for the party to come up. Here he briefly explained to her that Don Carlos and his bandits had left the ranch sometime in the night. Thunder rumbled in the distance, and a faint wind rustled the scant foliage of the cedars. The air grew oppressive; the horses panted.

"Sure it'll be a hummer," said Stewart. "The first storm almost always is bad. I can feel it in the air."

The air, indeed, seemed to be charged with a heavy force that was waiting to be liberated.

One by one the couples mounted to the cedar forest, and the feminine contingent declaimed eloquently for rest. But there was to be no permanent rest until night, and then that depended upon reaching the crags. The pack-train wagged onward, and Stewart fell in behind. The storm-center gathered slowly around the peaks; low rumble and bowl of thunder increased in frequence; slowly the light shaded as smoky clouds rolled up; the air grew sultrier, and the exasperating breeze puffed a few times and then failed.

An hour later the party had climbed high, and was rounding the side of a great bare ridge that long had hidden the crags. The last burro of the pack-train plodded over the ridge out of Madeline's sight. She looked backward down the slope, amused to see her guests change wearily from side to side in their saddles. Far below lay the cedar flat and the foothills. Far to the west the sky was still clear, with shafts of sunlight shooting down from behind the encroaching clouds.

Stewart reached the summit of the ridge and, though only a few rods ahead, he waved to her, sweeping his hand round to what he saw beyond. It was an impressive gesture, and Madeline, never having climbed as high as this, anticipated much.

Majesty surmounted the last few steps and, snorting, halted beside Stewart's black. To Madeline the scene was as if the world had changed. The ridge was a mountaintop. It dropped before her into a black, stone-ridged, shrub-patched, many-cañoned gulf. Eastward, beyond the gulf, round, bare mountain-heads loomed up. Upward, on the right, led giant steps of cliff and bench and weathered slope to the fir-bordered and pine-fringed crags standing dark and bare against the stormy sky. Massed inky clouds were piling across the peaks, obscuring the highest ones. A fork of white lightning flashed, and, like the booming of an avalanche, thunder followed.

That bold world of broken rock under the slow mustering of storm-clouds was a grim, awe-inspiring spectacle. It had beauty, but beauty of the sublime and majestic kind. The fierce desert had reached up to meet the magnetic heights where heat and wind and frost and lightning and flood contended in everlasting strife. And before their on-slaught this mighty up-flung world of rugged stone was crumbling, splitting, wearing to ruin.

Madeline glanced at Stewart. He had forgotten her presence. Immovable as stone he sat his horse, dark-faced, dark-eyed, and, like an Indian unconscious of thought, he watched and watched. To see him thus, to divine the strange affinity between the soul of this man become primitive, and the savage environment that had developed him, were powerful helps to Madeline Hammond in her strange desire to understand his nature.

A cracking of iron-shod hoofs behind her broke the spell. Monty had reached the summit.

"Gene, what it won't all be doin' in a minnut Moses his-self couldn't tell," observed Monty.

Then Dorothy climbed to his side and looked.

"Oh, isn't it just perfectly lovely!" she exclaimed. "But I wish it wouldn't storm. We'll all get wet."

Once more Stewart faced the ascent, keeping to the slow heave of the ridge as it rose southward toward the looming spires of rock. Soon he was off smooth ground, and Mad-eline, some rods behind him, looked back with concern at her friends. Here the real toil, the real climb began, and a mountain storm was about to burst in all its fury.

The slope that Stewart entered upon was a magnificent monument to the ruined crags above. It was a southerly slope, and therefore semi-arid, covered with cercocarpus and yucca and some shrub that Madeline believed was manzanita. Every foot of the trail seemed to slide under

Majesty. What hard ground there was could not be traveled upon owing to the spiny covering or masses of shattered rocks. Gullies lined the slope.

Then the sky grew blacker; the slow-gathering clouds appeared to be suddenly agitated; they piled and rolled and mushroomed and obscured the crags. The air moved heavily, and seemed to be laden with sulphurous smoke, and sharp lightning flashes began to play. A distant roar of wind could be heard between the peals of thunder.

Stewart waited for Madeline under the lee of a shelving cliff, where the cowboys had halted the pack-train. Majesty was sensitive to the flashes of lightning. Madeline patted his neck and softly called to him. The weary burros nodded; the Mexican women covered their heads with their mantles. Stewart untied the slicker at the back of Madeline's saddle and helped her on with it. Then he put on his own. The other cowboys followed suit. Presently Madeline saw Monty and Dorothy rounding the cliff, and hoped the others would come soon.

A blue-white, knotted rope of lightning burned down out of the clouds, and instantly a thunder-clap crashed, seeming to shake the foundations of the earth. Then it rolled, as if banging from cloud to cloud, and boomed along the peaks, and reverberated from deep to low, at last to rumble away into silence. Madeline felt the electricity in Majesty's mane, and it seemed to tingle through her nerves. The air had a weird, bright cast. The ponderous clouds swallowed more and more of the eastern domes. This moment of the breaking of the storm, with the strange growing roar of wind, like a moaning monster, was pregnant with a hcart-disturbing emotion for Madeline Hammond. Glorious it was to be free, healthy, out in the open, under the shadow of the mountain and cloud, in the teeth of the wind and rain and storm.

Another dazzling blue blaze showed the bold mountainside and the storm-driven clouds. In the flare of light Madeline saw Stewart's face.

"Are you afraid?" she asked.

"Yes," he replied, simply.

Then the thunderbolt racked the heavens, and as it boomed away in lessening power Madeline reflected with surprise upon Stewart's answer. Something in his face had made her ask him what she considered a foolish question. His reply amazed her. She loved a storm. Why should he fear it—he, with whom she could not associate fear?

"How strange! Have you not been out in many storms?"

A smile that was only a gleam flitted over his dark face.

"In hundreds of them. By day, with the cattle stampeding. At night, alone on the mountain, with the pines crashing and the rocks rolling—in flood on the desert."

"It's not only the lightning, then?" she asked.

"No. All the storm."

Madeline felt that henceforth she would have less faith in what she had imagined was her love of the elements. What little she knew! If this iron-nerved man feared a storm, then there was something about a storm to fear.

And suddenly, as the ground quaked under her horse's feet, and all the sky grew black and criss-crossed by flaming streaks, and between thunderous reports there was a strange hollow roar sweeping down upon her, she realized how small was her knowledge and experience of the mighty forces of nature. Then, with that perversity of character of which she was wholly conscious, she was humble, submissive, reverent, and fearful even while she gloried in

the grandeur of the dark, cloud-shadowed crags and cañons, the stupendous strife of sound, the wonderful driving
lances of white fire.

With blacker gloom and deafening roar came the torrent of rain. It was a cloud-burst. It was like solid water
tumbling down. For long Madeline sat her horse, head
bent to the pelting rain. When its force lessened, and she
heard Stewart call for all to follow, she looked up to see
that he was starting once more. She shot a glimpse at Dorothy and as quickly glanced away. Dorothy, who would
not wear a hat suitable for inclement weather, nor one of
the horrid yellow, sticky slickers, was a drenched and disheveled spectacle. Madeline did not trust herself to look
at the other girls. It was enough to hear their lament. So
she turned her horse into Stewart's trail.

Rain fell steadily. The fury of the storm, however, had
passed, and the roll of thunder diminished in volume. The
air had wonderfully cleared and was growing cool. Madeline began to feel uncomfortably cold and wet. Stewart
was climbing faster than formerly, and she noted that
Monty kept at her heels, pressing her on. Time had been
lost, and the camp-site was a long way off. The stag-
hounds began to lag and get footsore. The sharp rocks of
the trail were cruel to their feet. Then, as Madeline began to tire, she noticed less and less around her. The ascent grew rougher and steeper—slow toil for panting
horses. The thinning rain grew colder, and sometimes a
stronger whip of wind lashed stingingly in Madeline's
face. Her horse climbed and climbed, and brush and sharp
corners of stone everlastingly pulled and tore at her wet
garments. A gray gloom settled down around her. Night
was approaching. Majesty heaved upward with a snort,
the wet saddle creaked; and an even motion told Madeline

she was on level ground. She looked up to see looming crags and spires, like huge pipe-organs, dark at the base and growing light upward. The rain had ceased, but the branches of fir-trees and juniper were water-soaked arms reaching out for her. Through an opening between crags Madeline caught a momentary glimpse of the west. Red sun-shafts shone through the murky, broken clouds. The sun had set.

Stewart's horse was on a jog-trot now, and Madeline left the trail more to Majesty than to her own choosing. The shadows deepened, and the crags grew gloomy and spectral. A cool wind moaned through the dark trees. Coyotes, scenting the hounds, kept apace of them, and barked and howled off in the gloom. But the tired hounds did not appear to notice.

As black night began to envelop her surroundings, Madeline marked that the fir-trees had given place to pine forest. Suddenly a pin-point of light pierced the ebony blackness. Like a solitary star in dark sky it twinkled and blinked. She lost sight of it—found it again. It grew larger. Black tree-trunks crossed her line of vision. The light was a fire. She heard a cowboy song and the wild chorus of a pack of coyotes. Drops of rain on the branches of trees glittered in the rays of the fire. Stewart's tall figure, with sombrero slouched down, was now and then outlined against a growing circle of light. And by the aid of that light she saw him turn every moment or so to look back, probably to assure himself that she was close behind.

With a prospect of fire and warmth, and food and rest, Madeline's enthusiasm revived. What a climb! There was promise in this wild ride and lonely trail and hidden craggy height, not only in the adventure her friends yearned for, but in some nameless joy and spirit for herself.

CHAPTER 16

THE CRAGS

Glad indeed was Madeline to be lifted off her horse beside a roaring fire—to see steaming pots upon red-hot coals. Except about her shoulders, which had been protected by the slicker, she was wringing wet. The Mexican women came quickly to help her change in a tent near by; but Madeline preferred for the moment to warm her numb feet and hands and to watch the spectacle of her arriving friends.

Dorothy plumped off her saddle into the arms of several waiting cowboys. She could scarcely walk. Far removed in appearance was she from her usual stylish self. Her face was hidden by a limp and lopsided hat. From under the disheveled brim came a plaintive moan: "O-h-h! what a-an a-awful ride!" Mrs. Beck was in worse condition; she had to be taken off her horse. "I'm paralyzed—I'm a wreck. Bobby, get a roller-chair." Bobby was solicitous and willing, but there were no roller-chairs. Florence dismounted easily, and but for her mass of hair, wet and tumbling, would have been taken for a handsome cowboy. Edith Wayne had stood the physical strain of the ride better than Dorothy; however, as her mount was rather small, she had been more at the mercy of cactus and brush. Her habit hung in tatters. Helen had preserved a remnant of style, as well as of pride, and perhaps a little strength. But her face was white, her eyes were big, and she limped. "Majesty!" she exclaimed. "What did you want to do to us? Kill us outright or make us homesick?" Of all of them, however, Ambrose's wife, Christine, the little French maid, had suffered the most in that long ride. She was unaccustomed to horses. Ambrose had to carry her into the big tent. Florence persuaded Madeline to leave the fire, and when they went in with the others Dorothy was wailing because her wet boots would not come off, Mrs. Beck was weeping and trying to direct a Mexican woman to unfasten her bedraggled dress, and there was general pandemonium.

"Warm clothes—hot drinks and grub—warm blankets," rang out Stewart's sharp order.

Then, with Florence helping the Mexican women, it was not long until Madeline and the feminine side of the party were comfortable, except for the weariness and aches that only rest and sleep could alleviate.

Neither fatigue nor pains, however, nor the strangeness of being packed sardine-like under canvas, nor the howls of coyotes kept Madeline's guests from stretching out with long, grateful sighs, and one by one dropping into deep slumber. Madeline whispered a little to Florence, and laughed with her once or twice, and then the light flickering on the canvas faded and her eyelids closed. Darkness and roar of camp life, low voices of men, thump of horses' hoofs, coyote serenade, the sense of warmth and sweet rest—all drifted away.

When she awakened shadows of swaying branches moved on the sunlit canvas above her. She heard the ringing strokes of an ax, but no other sound from outside. Slow, regular breathing attested to the deep slumbers of her tent comrades. She observed presently that Florence was missing from the number. Madeline rose and peeped out between the flaps.

An exquisitely beautiful scene surprised and enthralled her gaze. She saw a level space, green with long grass, bright with flowers, dotted with groves of graceful firs and pines and spruces, reaching to superb crags, rosy and golden in the sunlight. Eager to get out where she could enjoy an unrestricted view, she searched for her pack, found it in a corner, and then hurriedly and quietly dressed.

Her favorite stag-hounds, Russ and Tartar, were asleep before the door, where they had been chained. She awakened them and loosened them, thinking the while that it must have been Stewart who had chained them near her. Close at hand also was a cowboy's bed rolled up in a tarpaulin.

The cool air, fragrant with pine and spruce and some subtle nameless tang, sweet and tonic, made Madeline stand erect and breathe slowly and deeply. It was like drinking of a magic draught. She felt it in her blood, that it quickened its flow. Turning to look in the other direction, beyond the tent, she saw the remnants of last night's temporary camp, and farther on a grove of beautiful pines from which came the sharp ring of the ax. Wider gaze took in a wonderful park, not only surrounded by lofty crags, but full of crags of lesser height, many lifting their heads from dark-green groves of trees. The morning sun, not yet above the eastern elevations, sent its rosy and golden shafts in between the towering rocks, to tip the pines.

Madeline, with the hounds beside her, walked through the nearest grove. The ground was soft and springy and brown with pine-needles. Then she saw that a clump of trees had prevented her from seeing the most striking part of this natural park. The cowboys had selected a camp-site where they would have the morning sun and after-noon shade. Several tents and flys were already up; there was a huge lean-to made of spruce boughs; cowboys were busy round several camp-fires; piles of packs lay covered with tarpaulins, and beds were rolled up under the trees. This space was a kind of rolling meadow, with isolated trees here and there, and other trees in aisles and circles; and it mounted up in low, grassy banks to great towers of stone five hundred feet high. Other crags rose behind these. From under a mossy cliff, huge and green and cool, bubbled a full, clear spring. Wild flowers fringed its banks. Out in the meadow the horses were knee-deep in grass that waved in the morning breeze.

Florence espied Madeline under the trees and came running. She was like a young girl, with life and color and joy. She wore a flannel blouse, corduroy skirt, and moc-casins. And her hair was fastened under a band like an Indian's.

"Castleton's gone with a gun, for hours it seems," said Florence. "Gene just went to hunt him up. The other gen-tlemen are still asleep. I imagine they sure will sleep up heah in this air."

Then, businesslike, Florence fell to questioning Madeline about details of camp arrangement which Stewart, and Florence herself, could hardly see to without suggestion.

Before any of Madeline's sleepy guests awakened the camp was completed. Madeline and Florence had a tent under a pine-tree, but they did not intend to sleep in it except during stormy weather. They spread a tarpaulin, made their bed on it, and elected to sleep under the light of the stars. After that, taking the hounds with them, they explored. To Madeline's surprise, the park was not a little half-mile nook nestling among the crags, but extended farther than they cared to walk, and was rather a series of parks. They were no more than small valleys between gray-toothed peaks. As the day advanced the charm of the place grew upon Madeline. Even at noon, with the sun beating down, there was comfortable warmth rather than heat. It was the kind of warmth that Madeline liked to feel in the spring. And the sweet, thin, rare atmosphere began to affect her strangely. She breathed deeply of it until she felt light-headed, as if her body lacked substance and might drift away like a thistle-down. All at once she grew uncomfortably sleepy. A dreamy languor possessed her, and, lying under a pine with her head against Florence, she went to sleep. When she opened her eyes the shadows of the crags stretched from the west, and between them streamed a red-gold light. It was hazy, smoky sunshine losing its fire. The afternoon had far advanced. Madeline sat up. Florence was lazily reading. The two Mexican women were at work under the fly where the big stone fireplace had been erected. No one else was in sight.

Florence, upon being questioned, informed Madeline that incident about camp had been delightfully absent.

Castleton had returned and was profoundly sleeping with the other men. Presently a chorus of merry calls attracted Madeline's attention, and she turned to see Helen limping along with Dorothy, and Mrs. Beck and Edith supporting each other. They were all rested, but lame, and delighted with the place, and as hungry as bears awakened from a winter's sleep. Madeline forthwith escorted them round the camp, and through the many aisles between the trees, and to the mossy, pine-matted nooks under the crags.

Then they had dinner, sitting on the ground after the manner of Indians; and it was a dinner that lacked merriment only because everybody was too busily appeasing appetite.

Later Stewart led them across a neck of the park, up a rather steep climb between towering crags, to take them out upon a grassy promontory that faced the great open West—a vast, ridged, streaked, and reddened sweep of earth rolling down, as it seemed, to the golden sunset end of the world. Castleton said it was a jolly fine view; Dorothy voiced her usual languid enthusiasm; Helen was on fire with pleasure and wonder; Mrs. Beck appealed to Bobby to see how he liked it before she ventured, and she then reiterated his praise; and Edith Wayne, like Madeline and Florence, was silent. Boyd was politely interested; he was the kind of man who appeared to care for things as other people cared for them.

Madeline watched the slow transformation of the changing west, with its haze of desert dust, through which mountain and cloud and sun slowly darkened. She watched until her eyes ached, and scarcely had a thought of what she was watching. When her eyes shifted to encounter the tall form of Stewart standing motionless on the rim, her mind became active again. As usual, he stood apart from the others, and now he seemed aloof and unconscious. He made a dark, powerful figure, and he fitted that wild promontory.

She experienced a strange, annoying surprise when she discovered both Helen and Dorothy watching Stewart with peculiar interest. Edith, too, was alive to the splendid picture the cowboy made. But when Edith smiled and whispered in her ear, "It's so good to look at a man like that," Madeline again felt the surprise, only this time the accompaniment was a vague pleasure rather than annoyance. Helen and Dorothy were flirts, one deliberate and skilled, the other unconscious and natural. Edith Wayne, occasionally—and Madeline reflected that the occasions were infrequent—admired a man sincerely. Just here Madeline might have fallen into a somewhat revealing state of mind if it had not been for the fact that she believed Stewart was only an object of deep interest to her, not as a man, but as a part of this wild and wonderful West which was claiming her. So she did not inquire of herself why Helen's coquetry and Dorothy's languishing allurement annoyed her, or why Edith's eloquent smile and words had pleased her. She got as far, however, as to think scornfully how Helen and Dorothy would welcome and meet a flirtation with this cowboy and then go back home and forget him as utterly as if he had never existed. She wondered, too, with a curious twist of feeling that was almost eagerness, how the cowboy would meet their advances. Obviously, the situation was unfair to him; and if by some strange accident he escaped unscathed by Dorothy's beautiful eyes he would never be able to withstand Helen's subtle and fascinating and imperious personality.

They returned to camp in the cool of the evening and

made merry round a blazing camp-fire. But Madeline's guests soon succumbed to the persistent and irresistible desire to sleep.

Then Madeline went to bed with Florence under the pine-tree. Russ lay upon one side and Tartar upon the other. The cool night breeze swept over her, fanning her face, waving her hair. It was not strong enough to make any sound through the branches, but it stirred a faint, silken rustle in the long grass. The coyotes began their weird bark and howl. Russ raised his head to growl at their impudence.

Madeline faced upward, and it seemed to her that under those wonderful white stars she would never be able to go to sleep. They blinked down through the black-barred, delicate crisscross of pine foliage, and they looked so big and so close. Then she gazed away to open space, where an expanse of sky glittered with stars, and the longer she gazed the larger they grew and the more she saw.

It was her belief that she had come to love all the physical things from which sensations of beauty and mystery and strength poured into her responsive mind; but best of all she loved these Western stars, for they were to have something to do with her life, were somehow to influence her destiny.

For a few days the prevailing features of camp life for Madeline's guests were sleep and rest. Dorothy Coombs slept through twenty-four hours, and then was so difficult to awaken that for a while her friends were alarmed. Helen almost fell asleep while eating and talking. The men were more visibly affected by the mountain air than the women. Castleton, however, would not succumb to the strange drowsiness while he had a chance to prowl around with a gun.

This languorous spell disappeared presently, and then the days were full of life and action. Mrs. Beck and Bobby and Boyd, however, did not go in for anything very strenuous. Edith Wayne, too, preferred to walk through the groves or sit upon the grassy promontory. It was Helen and Dorothy who wanted to explore the crags and cañons, and when they could not get the others to accompany them they went alone, giving the cowboy guides many a long climb.

Necessarily, of course, Madeline and her guests were now thrown much in company with the cowboys. And the party grew to be like one big family. Her friends not only adapted themselves admirably to the situation, but came to revel in it. As for Madeline, she saw that outside of a certain proclivity of the cowboys to be gallant and on dress-parade and alive to possibilities of fun and excitement, they were not greatly different from what they were at all times. If there were a leveling process here it was made by her friends coming down to meet the Westerners. Besides, any class of people would tend to grow natural in such circumstances and environment.

Madeline found the situation one of keen and double interest for her. If before she had cared to study her cowboys, particularly Stewart, now, with the contrasts afforded by her guests, she felt by turns she was amused and mystified and perplexed and saddened, and then again subtly pleased.

Monty, once he had overcome his shyness, became a source of delight to Madeline, and, for that matter, to everybody. Monty had suddenly discovered that he was a success among the ladies. Either he was exalted to heroic heights by this knowledge or he made it appear so. Dorothy had been his undoing, and in justice to her Madeline believed her innocent. Dorothy thought Monty hideous to look at, and, accordingly, if he had been a hero a hundred times and had saved a hundred poor little babies' lives, he could not have interested her. Monty followed her around, reminding her, she told Madeline, of a little adoring dog one moment and the next of a huge, devouring gorilla.

Nels and Nick stalked at Helen's heels like grenadiers on duty, and if she as much as dropped her glove they almost came to blows to see who should pick it up.

In a way Castleton was the best feature of the camping party. He was such an absurd-looking little man, and his abilities were at such tremendous odds with what might have been expected of him from his looks. He could ride, tramp, climb, shoot. He liked to help around the camp, and the cowboys could not keep him from it. He had an insatiable desire to do things that were new to him. The cowboys played innumerable tricks upon him, not one of which he ever discovered. He was serious, slow in speech and action, and absolutely imperturbable. If imperturbability could ever be good humor, then he was always good-humored. Presently the cowboys began to understand him, and then to like him. When they liked a man it meant something. Madeline had been sorry more than once to see how little the cowboys chose to speak to Boyd Harvey. With Castleton, however, they actually became friends. They did not know it, and certainly such a thing never occurred to him; all the same, it was a fact. And it grew solely out of the truth that the Englishman was manly in the only way cowboys could have interpreted manliness. When, after innumerable attempts, he succeeded in throwing the diamond-hitch on a pack-horse the cowboys began to respect him. Castleton needed only one more accomplishment to claim their hearts, and he kept trying that—to ride a bucking broncho. One of the cowboys had a broncho that they called Devil. Every day for a week Devil threw the Englishman all over the park, ruined his clothes, bruised him, and finally kicked him. Then the cowboys solicitously tried to make Castleton give up; and this was remarkable enough, for the spectacle of an English lord on a bucking broncho was one that any Westerner would have ridden a thousand miles to see. Whenever Devil threw Castleton the cowboys went into spasms. But Castleton did not know the meaning of the word fail, and there came a day when Devil could not throw him. Then it was a singular sight to see the men line up to shake hands with the cool Englishman. Even Stewart, who had watched from the background, came forward with a warm and pleasant smile on his dark face. When Castleton went to his tent there was much characteristic cowboy talk, and this time vastly different from the former persiflage.

"By Gawd!" ejaculated Monty Price, who seemed to be the most amazed and elated of them all. "Thet's the fust Englishman I ever seen! He's orful deceivin' to look at, but I know now why England rules the wurrld. Jest take a peek at thet broncho. His spirit is broke. Rid by a leetle English dook no bigger'n a grasshopper! Fellers, if it hain't dawned on you yit, let Monty Price give you a hunch. There's no flies on Castleton. An' I'll bet a million steers to a rawhide rope thet next he'll be throwin' a gun as good as Nels."

It was a distinct pleasure for Madeline to realize that she liked Castleton all the better for the traits brought out so forcibly by his association with the cowboys. On the other hand, she liked the cowboys better for something in them that contact with Easterners brought out. This was especially true in Stewart's case. She had been wholly wrong when she had imagined he would fall an easy victim to Dorothy's eyes and Helen's lures. He was kind, helpful, courteous, and watchful. But he had no sentiment. He did not see Dorothy's charms or feel Helen's fascination. And their efforts to captivate him were now so obvious that Mrs. Beck taunted them, and Edith smiled knowingly, and Bobby and Boyd made playful remarks. All of which cut Helen's pride and hurt Dorothy's vanity. They essayed open conquest of Stewart.

So it came about that Madeline unconsciously admitted the cowboy to a place in her mind never occupied by any other. The instant it occurred to her why he was proof against the wiles of the other women she drove that amazing and strangely disturbing thought from her. Nevertheless, as she was human, she could not help thinking and being pleased, and enjoying a little the discomfiture of the two coquettes.

Moreover, from this thought of Stewart, and the watchfulness growing out of it, she discovered more about him. He was not happy; he often paced up and down the grove at night; he absented himself from camp sometimes during the afternoon when Nels and Nick and Monty were there; he was always watching the trails, as if he expected to see some one come riding up. He alone of the cowboys did not indulge in the fun and talk around the camp-fire. He remained preoccupied and sad, and was always looking away into distance. Madeline had a strange sense of his guardianship over her; and, remembering Don Carlos, she imagined he worried a good deal over his charge, and, indeed, over the safety of all the party.

But, if he did worry about possible visits from wandering guerrillas, why did he absent himself from camp? Suddenly into Madeline's inquisitive mind flashed a remembrance of the dark-eyed Mexican girl Bonita, who had never been heard of since that night she rode Stewart's big horse out of El Cajon. The remembrance of her brought an idea. Perhaps Stewart had a rendezvous in the mountains, and these lonely trips of his were to meet Bonita. With the idea hot blood flamed into Madeline's cheek. Then she was amazed at her own feelings—amazed because her swiftest succeeding thought was to deny the idea—amazed that its conception had fired her cheek with shame. Then her old self, the one aloof from this red-blooded new self, gained control over her emotions.

But Madeline found that new-born self a creature of strange power to return and govern at any moment. She found it fighting loyally for what intelligence and wisdom told her was only her romantic conception of a cowboy. She reasoned: If Stewart were the kind of man her feminine skepticism wanted to make him, he would not have been so blind to the coquettish advances of Helen and Dorothy. He had once been—she did not want to recall what he had once been. But he had been uplifted. Madeline Hammond declared that. She was swayed by a strong, beating pride, and her instinctive woman's faith told her that he could not stoop to such dishonor. She reproached herself for having momentarily thought of it.

One afternoon a huge storm-cloud swooped out of the sky and enveloped the crags. It obscured the westering sun and laid a mantle of darkness over the park. Madeline was uneasy, because several of her party, including

Helen and Dorothy, had ridden off with the cowboys that afternoon and had not returned. Florence assured her that even if they did not get back before the storm broke there was no reason for apprehension. Nevertheless, Madeline sent for Stewart and asked him to go or send some one in search of them.

Perhaps half an hour later Madeline heard the welcome pattering of hoofs on the trail. The big tent was brightly lighted by several lanterns. Edith and Florence were with her. It was so black outside that Madeline could not see a rod before her face. The wind was moaning in the trees, and big drops of rain were pelting upon the canvas.

Presently, just outside the door, the horses halted, and there was a sharp bustle of sound, such as would naturally result from a hurried dismounting and confusion in the dark. Mrs. Beck came running into the tent out of breath and radiant because they had beaten the storm. Helen entered next, and a little later came Dorothy, but long enough to make her entrance more noticeable. The instant Madeline saw Dorothy's blazing eyes she knew something unusual had happened. Whatever it was might have escaped comment had not Helen caught sight of Dorothy.

"Heavens, Dot, but you're handsome occasionally," remarked Helen. "When you get some life in your face and eyes!"

Dorothy turned her face away from the others, and perhaps it was only accident that she looked into a mirror hanging on the tent wall. Swiftly she put her hand up to feel a wide red welt on her cheek. Dorothy had been assiduously careful of her soft, white skin, and here was an ugly mark marring its beauty.

"Look at that!" she cried, in distress. "My complexion's ruined!"

"How did you get such a splotch?" inquired Helen, going closer.

"I've been kissed!" exclaimed Dorothy, dramatically.

"What?" queried Helen, more curiously, while the others laughed.

"I've been kissed—hugged and kissed by one of those shameless cowboys! It was so pitch-dark outside I couldn't see a thing. And so noisy I couldn't hear. But somebody was trying to help me off my horse. My foot caught in the stirrup, and away I went—right into somebody's arms. Then he did it, the wretch! He hugged and kissed me in a most awful bearish manner. I couldn't budge a finger. I'm simply boiling with rage!"

When the outburst of mirth subsided Dorothy turned her big, dilated eyes upon Florence.

"Do these cowboys really take advantage of a girl when she's helpless and in the dark?"

"Of course they do," replied Florence, with her frank smile.

"Dot, what in the world could you expect?" asked Helen. "Haven't you been dying to be kissed?"

"No."

"Well, you acted like it, then. I never before saw you in a rage over being kissed."

"I—I wouldn't care so much if the brute hadn't scoured the skin off my face. He had whiskers as sharp and stiff as sandpaper. And when I jerked away he rubbed my cheek with them."

This revelation as to the cause of her outraged dignity almost prostrated her friends with glee.

"Dot, I agree with you; it's one thing to be kissed, and quite another to have your beauty spoiled," replied Helen, presently. "Who was this particular savage?"

"I don't know!" burst out Dorothy. "If I did I'd—I'd—"

Her eyes expressed the direful punishment she could not speak.

"Honestly now, Dot, haven't you the least idea who did it?" questioned Helen.

"I hope—I think it was Stewart," replied Dorothy.

"Ah! Dot, your hope is father to the thought. My dear, I'm sorry to riddle your little romance. Stewart did not—could not have been the offender or hero."

"How do you know he couldn't?" demanded Dorothy, flushing.

"Because he was clean-shaven to-day at noon, before we rode out. I remember perfectly how nice and smooth and brown his face looked."

"Oh, do you? Well, if your memory for faces is so good, maybe you can tell me which one of these cowboys wasn't clean-shaven."

"Merely a matter of elimination," replied Helen, merrily. "It was not Nick; it was not Nels; it was not Frankie. There was only one other cowboy with us, and he had a short, stubby growth of black beard, much like that cactus we passed on the trail."

"Oh, I was afraid of it," moaned Dorothy. "I *knew* he was going to do it. That horrible little smiling demon, Monty Price!"

A favorite lounging spot of Madeline's was a shaded niche under the lee of crags facing the east. Here the outlook was entirely different from that on the western side. It was not red and white and glaring, nor so changeable that it taxed attention. This eastern view was one of the mountains and valleys, where, to be sure, there were arid patches; but the restful green of pine and fir was there, and the cool gray of crags. Bold and rugged indeed were these mountain features, yet they were companionably close, not immeasurably distant and unattainable like the desert. Here in the shade of afternoon Madeline and Edith would often lounge under a low-branched tree. Seldom they talked much, for it was afternoon and dreamy with the strange spell of this mountain fastness. There was smoky haze in the valleys, a fleecy cloud resting over the peaks, a sailing eagle in the blue sky, silence that was the unbroken silence of the wild heights, and a soft wind laden with incense of pine.

One afternoon, however, Edith appeared prone to talk seriously.

"Majesty, I must go home soon. I cannot stay out here forever. Are you going back with me?"

"Well, maybe," replied Madeline, thoughtfully. "I have considered it. I shall have to visit home some time. But this summer Mother and Father are going to Europe."

"See here, Majesty Hammond, do you intend to spend the rest of your life in this wilderness?" asked Edith, bluntly.

Madeline was silent.

"Oh, it is glorious! Don't misunderstand me, dear," went on Edith, earnestly, as she laid her hand on Madeline's. "This trip has been a revelation to me. I did not tell you, Majesty, that I was ill when I arrived. Now I'm well. So well! Look at Helen, too. Why, she was a ghost when we got here. Now she is brown and strong and beautiful. If it were for nothing else than this wonderful gift of health I would love the West. But I have come to love it for other things—even spiritual things. Majesty, I have been studying you. I see and feel what this life has made of you. When I came I wondered at your strength, your virility, your serenity, your happiness. And I was stunned.

I wondered at the causes of your change. Now I know. You were sick of idleness, sick of uselessness, if not of society—sick of the horrible noises and smells and contacts one can no longer escape in the cities. I am sick of all that, too, and I could tell you many women of our kind who suffer in a like manner. You have done what many of us want to do but have not the courage. You have left it. I am not blind to the splendid difference you have made in your life. I think I would have discovered, even if your brother had not told me, what good you have done to the Mexicans and cattlemen of your range. Then you have work to do. That is much the secret of your happiness, is it not? Tell me. Tell me something of what it means to you?"

"Work, of course, has much to do with any one's happiness," replied Madeline. "No one can be happy who has no work. As regards myself—for the rest I can hardly tell you. I have never tried to put it in words. Frankly, I believe, if I had not had money that I could not have found such contentment here. That is not in any sense a judgment against the West. But if I had been poor I could not have bought and maintained my ranch. Stillwell tells me there are many larger ranches than mine, but none just like it. Then I am almost paying my expenses out of my business. Think of that! My income, instead of being wasted, is mostly saved. I think—I hope I am useful. I have been of some little good to the Mexicans—eased the hardships of a few cowboys. For the rest, I think my life is a kind of dream. Of course my ranch and range are real, my cowboys are typical. If I were to tell you how I feel about them it would simply be a story of how Madeline Hammond sees the West. They are true to the West. It is I who am strange, and what I feel for them may be strange, too. Edith, hold to your own impressions."

"But, Majesty, my impressions have changed. At first I did not like the wind, the dust, the sun, the endless open stretches. But now I do like them. Where once I saw only terrible wastes of barren ground, now I see beauty and something noble. Then, at first, your cowboys struck me as dirty, rough, loud, crude, savage—all that was primitive. I did not want them near me. I imagined them callous, hard men, their only joy a carouse with their kind. But I was wrong. I have changed. The dirt was only dust, and this desert dust is clean. They are still rough, loud, crude, and savage in my eyes, but with a difference. They are natural men. They are little children. Monty Price is one of nature's noblemen. The hard thing is to discover it. All his hideous person, all his actions and speech are masks of his real nature. Nels is a joy, a simple, sweet, kindly, quiet man whom some woman should have loved. What would love have meant to him! He told me that no woman ever loved him except his mother, and he lost her when he was ten. Every man ought to be loved—especially such a man as Nels. Somehow his gun record does not impress me. I never could believe he killed a man. Then take your foreman, Stewart. He is a cowboy, his work and life the same as the others. But he has education, and most of the graces we are in the habit of saying make a gentleman. Stewart is a strange fellow, just like this strange country. He's a man, Majesty, and I admire him. So, you see, my impressions are developing with my stay out here."

"Edith, I am so glad you told me that," replied Madeline, warmly.

"I like the country, and I like the men," went on Edith. "One reason I want to go home soon is because I am discontented enough at home now, without falling in love with the West. For, of course, Majesty, I would. I *could* not live out here. And that brings me to my point. Admitting all the beauty and charm and wholesomeness and good of this wonderful country, still it is no place for *you,* Madeline Hammond. You have your position, your wealth, your name, your family. You must marry. You must have children. You must not give up all that for a quixotic life in a wilderness."

"I am convinced, Edith, that I shall live here all the rest of my life."

"Oh, Majesty! I hate to preach this way. But I promised your mother I would talk to you. And the truth is I hate—I *hate* what I'm saying. I envy you your courage and wisdom. I know you have refused to marry Boyd Harvey. I could see that in his face. I believe you will refuse Castleton. Whom will you marry? What chance is there for a woman of your position to marry out here? What in the world will become of you?"

"*Quien sabe!*" replied Madeline, with a smile that was almost sad.

Not so many hours after this conversation with Edith, Madeline sat with Boyd Harvey upon the grassy promontory overlooking the west, and she listened once again to his suave courtship.

Suddenly she turned to him and said: "Boyd, if I married you would you be willing—glad to spend the rest of your life here in the West?"

"Majesty!" he exclaimed. There was amaze in the voice usually so even and well modulated—amaze in the handsome face usually so indifferent. Her question had startled him. She saw him look down the iron-gray cliffs, over the barren slopes and cedared ridges, beyond the cactus-covered foothills to the grim and ghastly desert. Just then, with its red veils of sunlit dust-clouds, its illimitable waste of ruined and up-heaved earth, it was a sinister spectacle.

"No," he replied, with a tinge of shame in his cheek.

Madeline said no more, nor did he speak. She was spared the pain of refusing him, and she imagined he would never ask her again. There was both relief and regret in the conviction. Humiliated lovers seldom made good friends.

It was impossible not to like Boyd Harvey. The thought of that, and why she could not marry him, concentrated her never-satisfied mind upon the man. She looked at him, and she thought of him.

He was handsome, young, rich, well born, pleasant, cultivated—he was all that made a gentleman of his class. If he had any vices she had not heard of them. She knew he had no thirst for drink or craze for gambling. He was considered a very desirable and eligible young man. Madeline admitted all this.

Then she thought of things that were perhaps exclusively her own strange ideas. Boyd Harvey's white skin did not tan even in this Southwestern sun and wind. His hands were whiter than her own, and as soft. They were really beautiful, and she remembered what care he took of them. They were a proof that he never worked. His frame was tall, graceful, elegant. It did not bear evidence of ruggedness. He had never indulged in a sport more strenuous than yachting. He hated effort and activity. He rode horseback very little, disliked any but moderate motoring, spent much time in Newport and Europe, never walked when he could help it, and had no ambition unless it were to pass the days pleasantly. If he ever had any sons they would be like him, only a generation more toward the inevitable extinction of his race.

Madeline returned to camp in just the mood to make a sharp, deciding contrast. It happened—fatefully, perhaps—that the first man she saw was Stewart. He had just ridden into camp, and as she came up he explained that he had gone down to the ranch for the important mail, about which she had expressed anxiety.

"Down and back in one day!" she exclaimed.

"Yes," he replied. "It wasn't so bad."

"But why did you not send one of the boys, and let him make the regular two-day trip?"

"You were worried about your mail," he answered, briefly, as he delivered it. Then he bent to examine the fetlocks of his weary horse.

It was midsummer now, Madeline reflected, and exceedingly hot and dusty on the lower trail. Stewart had ridden down the mountain and back again in twelve hours. Probably no horse in the outfit, except his big black or Majesty, could have stood that trip. And his horse showed the effects of a grueling day. He was caked with dust and lame and weary.

Stewart looked as if he had spared the horse his weight on many a mile of that rough ascent. His boots were evidence of it. His heavy flannel shirt, wet through with perspiration, adhered closely to his shoulders and arms, so that every ripple of muscle plainly showed. His face was black, except round the temples and forehead, where it was bright red. Drops of sweat, running off his blackened hands, dripped to the ground. He got up from examining the lame foot, and then threw off the saddle. The black horse snorted and lunged for the watering-pool. Stewart let him drink a little, then with iron arms dragged him away. In·this action the man's lithe, powerful form impressed Madeline with a wonderful sense of muscular force. His brawny wrist was bare; his big, strong hand, first clutching the horse's mane, then patting his neck, had a bruised knuckle, and one finger was bound up. That hand expressed as much gentleness and thoughtfulness for the horse as it had strength to drag him back from too much drinking at a dangerous moment.

Stewart was a combination of fire, strength, and action. These attributes seemed to cling about him. There was something vital and compelling in his presence. Worn and spent and drawn as he was from the long ride, he thrilled Madeline with his potential youth and unused vitality and promise of things to be, red-blooded deeds, both of flesh and spirit. In him she saw the strength of his forefathers unimpaired. The life in him was marvelously significant. The dust, the dirt, the sweat, the soiled clothes, the bruised and bandaged hand, the brawn and bone— these had not been despised by the knights of ancient days, nor by modern women whose eyes shed soft light upon coarse and bloody toilers.

Madeline Hammond compared the man of the East with the man of the West; and that comparison was the last parting regret for her old standards.

CHAPTER 17

THE LOST MINE OF THE PADRES

In the cool, starry evenings the campers sat around a blazing fire and told and listened to stories thrillingly fitted to the dark crags and the wild solitude.

Monty Price had come to shine brilliantly as a story-teller. He was an atrocious liar, but this fact would not have been evident to his enthralled listeners if his cowboy comrades, in base jealousy, had not betrayed him. The truth about his remarkable fabrications, however, had not become known to Castleton, solely because of the Englishman's obtuseness. And there was another thing much stranger than this and quite as amusing. Dorothy Coombs knew Monty was a liar; but she was so fascinated by the glittering, basilisk eyes he riveted upon her, so taken in by his horrible tales of blood, that despite her knowledge she could not help believing them.

Manifestly, Monty was very proud of his suddenly acquired gift. Formerly he had hardly been known to open his lips in the presence of strangers. Monty had developed more than one singular and hitherto unknown trait since his supremacy at golf had revealed his possibilities. He was as sober and vain and pompous about his capacity for lying as about anything else. Some of the cowboys were jealous of him because he held the attention and, apparently, the admiration of the ladies; and Nels was jealous, not because Monty made himself out to be a wonderful gun-man, but because Monty could tell a story. Nels really had been the hero of a hundred fights; he had never been known to talk about them; but Dorothy's eyes and Helen's smile had somehow upset his modesty. Whenever Monty would begin to talk Nels would growl and knock his pipe on a log, and make it appear he could not stay and listen, though he never really left the charmed circle of the camp-fire. Wild horses could not have dragged him away.

One evening at twilight, as Madeline was leaving her tent, she encountered Monty. Evidently, he had waylaid her. With the most mysterious of signs and whispers he led her a little aside.

"Miss Hammond, I'm makin' bold to ask a favor of you," he said.

Madeline smiled her willingness.

"To-night, when they've all shot off their chins, an' it's quiet-like, I want you to ask me, jest this way: 'Monty, seein' as you've hed more adventures than all them cow-punchers put together, tell us about the most turrible time you ever hed.' Will you ask me, Miss Hammond, jest kinda sincere like?"

"Certainly I will, Monty," she replied.

His dark, seared face had no more warmth than a piece of cold, volcanic rock, which it resembled. Madeline appreciated how monstrous Dorothy found this burned and distorted visage, how deformed the little man looked to a woman of refined sensibilities. It was difficult for Madeline to look into his face. But she saw behind the blackened mask. And now she saw in Monty's deep eyes a spirit of pure fun.

So, true to her word, Madeline remembered at an opportune moment, when conversation had hushed and only the long, dismal wail of coyotes broke the silence, to turn toward the little cowboy.

"Monty," she said, and paused for effect—"Monty, seeing that you have had more adventures than all the cowboys together, tell us about the most terrible time *you* ever had."

Monty appeared startled at the question that fastened all eyes upon him. He waved a deprecatory hand.

"Aw, Miss Hammond, thankin' you all modest-like fer the compliment, I'll hev to refuse," replied Monty, laboring in distress. "It's too harrowin' fer tender-hearted gurls to listen to."

"Go on!" cried everybody except the cowboys. Nels began to nod his head as if he, as well as Monty, understood human nature. Dorothy hugged her knees with a kind of shudder. Monty had fastened the hypnotic eyes upon her. Castleton ceased smoking, adjusted his eyeglass, and prepared to listen in great earnestness.

Monty changed his seat to one where the light from the blazing logs fell upon his face; and he appeared plunged into melancholy and profound thought.

"Now I tax myself, I can't jest decide which was the orfulest time I ever hed," he said, reflectively.

Here Nels blew forth an immense cloud of smoke, as if he desired to hide himself from sight. Monty pondered, and then when the smoke rolled away, he turned to Nels:

"See hyar, old pard, me an' you seen somethin' of each other in the Panhandle, more'n thirty years ago—"

"Which we didn't," interrupted Nels, bluntly. "Shore you can't make me out an ole man."

"Mebbe it wasn't so darn long. Anyhow, Nels, you recollect them three hoss-thieves I hung all on one cottonwood tree, an' likewise thet boo-tiful blonde gurl I rescooed from a band of cutthroats who murdered her paw, ole Bill Warren, the buffalo-hunter? Now, which of them two scraps was the turriblest, in your idee?"

"Monty, my memory's shore bad," replied the unimpeachable Nels.

"Tell us about the beautiful blonde," cried at least three of the ladies. Dorothy, who had suffered from nightmare because of a former story of hanging men on trees, had voicelessly appealed to Monty to spare her more of that.

"All right, we'll hev the blonde gurl," said Monty, settling back, "though I ain't thinkin' her story is most turrible of the two, an' it'll rake over tender affections long slumberin' in my breast."

As he paused there came a sharp, rapping sound. This appeared to be Nels knocking the ashes out of his pipe on a stump—a true indication of the passing of content from that jealous cowboy.

"It was down in the Panhandle, way over in the west end of thet Comanche huntin'-ground, an' all the redskins an' outlaws in thet country were hidin' in the river-bottoms, an' chasin' some of the last buffalo herds thet hed wintered in there. I was a young buck them days, an' purty much of a desperado, I'm thinkin'. Though of all the seventeen notches on my gun—an' each notch meant a man killed face to face—there was only one thet I was ashamed of. Thet one was fer an express messenger who I hit on the head most unprofessional like, jest because he wouldn't hand over a leetle package. I hed the kind of a reputashun thet made all the fellers in saloons smile an' buy drinks.

"Well, I dropped into a place named Taylor's Bend, an' was peaceful standin' to the bar when three cowpunchers come in, an', me bein' with my back turned, they didn't recognize me, an' got playful. I didn't stop drink-in', an' I didn't turn square round; but when I stopped shootin' under my arm the saloon-keeper hed to go over to the sawmill an' fetch a heap of sawdust to cover up what was left of them three cow-punchers, after they was hauled out. You see, I was rough them days, an' would shoot ears off an' noses off an' hands off; when in later days I'd jest kill a man quick, same as Wild Bill.

"News drifts into town thet night thet a gang of cutthroats hed murdered ole Bill Warren, an' carried off his gurl. I gathers up a few good gun-men, an' we rid out an' down the river-bottom, to an' ole log-cabin, where the outlaws hed a rondevoo. We rid up bold like, an' made a hell of a racket. Then the gang began to throw lead from the cabin, an' we all hunted cover. Fightin' went on all night. In the mornin' all my outfit was killed but two, an' they was shot up bad. We fought all day without eatin' or drinkin', except some whisky I hed, an' at night I was on the job by my lonesome.

"Bein' bunged up some myself, I laid off an' went down to the river to wash the blood off, tie up my wounds, an' drink a leetle. While I was down there along comes one of the cutthroats with a bucket. Instead of gettin' water he got lead, an' as he was about to croak he tells me a whole bunch of outlaws was headin' in there, doo tomorrer. An' if I wanted to rescoo the gurl I hed to be hurryin'. There was five fellers left in the cabin.

"I went back to the thicket where I hed left my hoss, an' loaded up with two more guns an' another belt, an' busted a fresh box of shells. If I recollect proper, I got some cigarettes, too. Well, I mozied back to the cabin. It was a boo-tiful moonshiny night, an' I wondered if ole Bill's gurl was as purty as I'd heerd. The grass growed long round the cabin, an' I crawled up to the door without startin' anythin'. Then I figgered. There was only one door in thet cabin, an' it was black dark inside. I jest grabbed open the door an' slipped in quick. It worked all right. They heerd me, but hedn't been quick enough to ketch me in the light of the door. Of course there was some shots, but I ducked too quick, an' changed my position.

"Ladies an' gentlemen, thet there was some dool by night. An' I wasn't often in the place where they shot. I was most wonderful patient, an' jest waited until one of them darned ruffians would get so nervous he'd hev to hunt me up. When mornin' come there they was all piled up on the floor, all shot to pieces. I found the gurl. Purty! Say, she was boo-tiful. We went down to the river, where she begun to bathe my wounds. I'd collected a dozen more or so, an' the sight of tears in her lovely eyes, an' my blood a-stainin' of her little hands, jest nat'rally wakened a trembly spell in my heart. I seen she was took the same way, an' thet settled it.

"We was comin' up from the river, an' I hed jest straddled my hoss, with the gurl behind, when we run right into thet cutthroat gang thet was doo about then. Bein' some handicapped, I couldn't drop more'n one gun-round of them, an' then I hed to slope. The whole gang follered me, an' some miles out chased me over a ridge right into a big herd of buffalo. Before I knowed what was what thet herd broke into a stampede with me in the middle. Purty soon the buffalo closed in tight. I knowed I was in some peril then. But the gurl trusted me somethin' pitiful. I seen again thet she hed fell in love with me. I could tell from the way she hugged me an' yelled. Before long I was some put to it to keep my hoss on his feet. Far as I could see was dusty, black, bobbin', shaggy humps. A huge cloud of dust went along over our heads. The roar of tramplin' hoofs was turrible. My hoss weakened, went down, an' was carried along a leetle while I slipped off with the gurl onto the backs of the buffalo.

"Ladies, I ain't denyin' that then Monty Price was some scairt. Fust time in my life! But the trustin' face of thet boo-tiful gurl, as she lay in my arms an' hugged me an' yelled, made my spirit leap like a shootin' star. I just began to jump from buffalo to buffalo. I must hev jumped a mile of them bobbin' backs before I come to open places. An' here's where I performed the greatest stunts of my life. I hed on my big spurs, an' I jest sit down an' rid an' spurred till thet pertickler buffalo I was on got near another, an' then I'd flop over. Thusly I got to the edge of the herd, tumbled off'en the last one, an' rescooed the gurl.

"Well, as my memory takes me back, thet was a most affectin' walk home to the little town where she lived. But she wasn't troo to me, an' married another feller. I was too much a sport to kill him. But thet low-down trick rankled in my breast. Gurls is strange. I've never stopped wonderin' how any gurl who has been hugged an' kissed by one man could marry another. But matoor experience teaches me thet sich is the case."

The cowboys roared; Helen and Mrs. Beck and Edith laughed till they cried; Madeline found repression absolutely impossible; Dorothy sat hugging her knees, her horror at the story no greater than at Monty's unmistakable reference to her and to the fickleness of women; and Castleton for the first time appeared to be moved out of his imperturbability, though not in any sense by humor. Indeed, when he came to notice it, he was dumfounded by the mirth.

"By Jove! You Americans are an extraordinary people," he said. "I don't see anything blooming funny in Mr. Price's story of his adventure. By Jove! That was a bally warm occasion. Mr. Price, when you speak of being frightened for the only time in your life, I appreciate what you mean. I have experienced that. I was frightened once."

"Dook, I wouldn't hev thought it of you," replied Monty. "I'm sure tolerable curious to hear about it."

Madeline and her friends dared not break the spell, for fear that the Englishman might hold to his usual modest reticence. He had explored in Brazil, seen service in the Boer War, hunted in India and Africa—matters of experience of which he never spoke. Upon this occasion, however, evidently taking Monty's recital word for word as literal truth, and excited by it into a Homeric mood, he might tell a story. The cowboys almost fell upon their knees in their importunity. There was a suppressed eagerness in their solicitations, a hint of something that meant more than desire, great as it was, to hear a story told by an English lord. Madeline divined instantly that the cowboys had suddenly fancied that Castleton was not the dense and easily fooled person they had made such game of; that he had played his part well; that he was having fun at their expense; that he meant to tell a story, a lie which would simply dwarf Monty's. Nels's keen, bright expectation suggested how he would welcome the joke turned upon Monty. The slow closing of Monty's cavernous smile, the gradual sinking of his proud bearing, the doubt with which he began to regard Castleton—these were proofs of his fears.

"I have faced charging tigers and elephants in India, and charging rhinos and lions in Africa," began Castleton, his quick and fluent speech so different from the drawl of his ordinary conversation; "but I never was frightened but once. It will not do to hunt those wild beasts if you are easily balled up. This adventure I have in mind happened in British East Africa, in Uganda. I was out with Safari, and we were in a native district much infested by man-eating lions. Perhaps I may as well state that man-eaters are very different from ordinary lions. They are always matured beasts, and sometimes—indeed, mostly—are old. They become man-eaters most likely by accident or necessity. When old they find it more difficult to make a kill, being slower, probably, and with poorer teeth. Driven by hunger, they stalk and kill a native, and, once having tasted human blood, they want no other. They become absolutely fearless and terrible in their attacks.

"The natives of this village near where we camped were in a terrorized state owing to depredations of two or more man-eaters. The night of our arrival a lion leaped a stockade fence, seized a native from among others sitting round a fire, and leaped out again, carrying the screaming fellow away into the darkness. I determined to kill these lions, and made a permanent camp in the village for that purpose. By day I sent beaters into the brush and rocks of the river-valley, and by night I watched. Every night the lions visited us, but I did not see one. I discovered that when they roared around the camp they were not so liable to attack as when they were silent. It was indeed remarkable how silently they could stalk a man. They could creep through a thicket so dense you would not believe a rabbit could get through, and do it without the slightest sound. Then, when ready to charge, they did so with terrible onslaught and roar. They leaped right into a circle of fires, tore down huts, even dragged natives from the low trees. There was no way to tell at which point they would make an attack.

"After ten days or more of this I was worn out by loss of sleep. And one night, when tired out with watching, I fell asleep. My gun-bearer was alone in the tent with me. A terrible roar awakened me, then an unearthly scream pierced right into my ears. I always slept with my rifle in my hands, and, grasping it, I tried to rise. But I could not for the reason that a lion was standing over me. Then I lay still. The screams of my gun-bearer told me that the lion had him. I was fond of this fellow, and wanted to save him. I thought it best, however, not to move while the lion stood over me. Suddenly he stepped, and I felt poor Luki's feet dragging across me. He screamed, 'Save me, master!' And instinctively I grasped at him and caught his foot. The lion walked out of the tent dragging me as I held to Luki's foot. The night was bright moonlight. I could see the lion distinctly. He was a huge, black-maned brute, and he held Luki by the shoulder. The poor lad kept screaming frightfully. The man-eater must have dragged me forty yards before he became aware of a double encumbrance to his progress. Then he halted and turned. By Jove! He made a devilish fierce object with his shaggy, massive head, his green-fire eyes, and his huge jaws holding Luki. I let go of Luki's foot and bethought myself of the gun. But as I lay there on my side, before attempting to rise, I made a horrible discovery. I did not have my rifle at all. I had Luki's iron spear, which he always had near him. My rifle had slipped out of the hollow of my arm, and when the lion awakened me, in my confusion I picked up Luki's spear instead. The bloody brute dropped Luki and uttered a roar that shook the ground. It was then I felt frightened. For an instant I was almost paralyzed. The lion meant to charge, and in one spring he could reach me. Under circumstances like those a man can think many things in little time. I knew to try to run would be fatal. I remembered how strangely lions had been known to act upon occasion. One had been frightened by an umbrella; one had been frightened by a blast from a cow-horn; another had been frightened by a native who in running from one lion ran right at the other which he had not seen. Accordingly, I wondered if I could frighten the lion that meant to leap at me. Acting upon wild impulse, I prodded him in the hind quarters with the spear. Ladies and gentlemen, I am a blooming idiot if that lion did not cower like a whipped dog, put his tail down, and begin to slink away. Quick to see my chance, I jumped up yelling, and made after him, prodding him again. He let out a bellow such as you could imagine would come from an outraged king of beasts. I prodded again, and then he loped off. I found Luki not badly hurt. In fact, he got well. But I've never forgotten that scare."

When Castleton finished his narrative there was a trenchant silence. All eyes were upon Monty. He looked beaten, disgraced, a disgusted man. Yet there shone from his face a wonderful admiration for Castleton.

"Dook, you win!" he said; and, dropping his head, he left the camp-fire circle with the manner of a deposed emperor.

Then the cowboys exploded. The quiet, serene, low-voiced Nels yelled like a madman, and he stood upon his head. All the other cowboys went through marvelous contortions. Mere noise was insufficient to relieve their joy at what they considered the fall and humiliation of the tyrant Monty.

The Englishman stood there and watched them in amused consternation. They baffled his understanding. Plain it was to Madeline and her friends that Castleton had told the simple truth. But never on the earth, or anywhere else, could Nels and his comrades have been persuaded that Castleton had not lied deliberately to humble their great exponent of Ananias.

Everybody seemed reluctant to break the camp-fire spell. The logs had burned out to a great heap of opal and gold and red coals, in the heart of which quivered a glow alluring to the spirit of dreams. As the blaze subsided the shadows of the pines encroached darker and darker upon the circle of fading light. A cool wind fanned the embers, whipped up flakes of white ashes, and moaned through the trees. The wild yelps of coyotes were dying in the distance, and the sky was a wonderful dark-blue dome spangled with white stars.

"What a perfect night!" said Madeline. "This is a night to understand the dream, the mystery, the wonder of the Southwest. Florence, for long you have promised to tell us the story of the lost mine of the padres. It will give us all pleasure, make us understand something of the thrall in which this land held the Spaniards who discovered it so many years ago. It will be especially interesting now, because this mountain hides somewhere under its crags the treasures of the lost mine of the padres."

"In the sixteenth century," Florence began, in her soft, slow voice so suited to the nature of the legend, "a poor young padre of New Spain was shepherding his goats upon a hill when the Virgin appeared before him. He prostrated himself at her feet, and when he looked up she was gone. But upon the maguey plant near where she had stood there were golden ashes of a strange and wonderful substance. He took the incident as a good omen, and went again to the hilltop. Under the maguey had sprung up slender stalks of white, bearing delicate gold flowers, and as these flowers waved in the wind a fine golden dust, as fine as powdered ashes, blew away toward the north. Padre Juan was mystified, but believed that great fortune attended upon him and his poor people. So he went again and again to the hilltop in hope that the Virgin would appear to him.

"One morning, as the sun rose gloriously, he looked across the windy hill toward the waving grass and golden flowers under the maguey, and he saw the Virgin beckoning to him. Again he fell upon his knees; but she lifted him, and gave him of the golden flowers, and bade him leave his home and people to follow where these blowing golden ashes led. There he would find gold—pure gold—wonderful fortune to bring back to his poor people to build a church for them, and a city.

"Padre Juan took the flowers and left his home, promising to return, and he traveled northward over the hot and dusty desert, through the mountain passes, to a new country where fierce and warlike Indians menaced his life. He was gentle and good, and of a persuasive speech. Moreover, he was young and handsome of person. The Indians were Apaches, and among them he became a missonary, while always he was searching for the flowers of gold. He heard of gold lying in pebbles upon the mountain slopes, but he never found any. A few of the Apaches he converted; the most of them, however, were prone to be hostile to him and his religion. But Padre Juan prayed and worked on.

"There came a time when the old Apache chief, imagining the padre had designs upon his influence with the tribe, sought to put him to death by fire. The chief's daughter, a beautiful, dark-eyed maiden, secretly loved Juan and believed in his mission, and she interceded for his life and saved him. Juan fell in love with her. One day she came to him wearing golden flowers in her dark hair, and as the wind blew the flowers a golden dust blew upon it. Juan asked her where to find such flowers, and she told him that upon a certain day she would take him to the mountain to look for them. And upon the day she led up to the mountaintop from which they could see beautiful valleys and great trees and cool waters. There, at the top of a wonderful slope that looked down upon the world, she showed Juan the flowers. And Juan found gold in such abundance that he thought he would go out of his mind. Dust of gold! Grains of gold! Pebbles of gold! Rocks of gold! He was rich beyond all dreams. He remembered the Virgin and her words. He must return to his people and build their church, and the great city that would bear his name.

"But Juan tarried. Always he was going *mañana*. He loved the dark-eyed Apache girl so well that he could not leave her. He hated himself for his infidelity to his Virgin, to his people. He was weak and false, a sinner. But he could not go, and he gave himself up to love of the Indian maiden.

"The old Apache chief discovered the secret love of his daughter and the padre. And, fierce in his anger, he took her up into the mountains and burned her alive, and cast her ashes upon the wind. He did not kill Padre Juan. He was too wise, and perhaps too cruel, for he saw the strength of Juan's love. Besides, many of his tribe had learned much from the Spaniard.

"Padre Juan fell into despair. He had no desire to live. He faded and wasted away. But before he died he went to the old Indians who had burned the maiden, and he begged them, when he was dead, to burn his body and to cast his ashes to the wind from that wonderful slope, where they would blow away to mingle forever with those of his Indian sweetheart.

"The Indians promised, and when Padre Juan died they burned his body and took his ashes to the mountain heights and cast them to the wind, where they drifted and fell to mix with the ashes of the Indian girl he had loved.

"Years passed. More padres traveled across the desert to the home of the Apaches, and they heard the story of Juan. Among their number was a padre who in his youth had been one of Juan's people. He set forth to find Juan's grave, where he believed he would also find the gold. And he came back with pebbles of gold and flowers that shed a golden dust, and he told a wonderful story. He had climbed and climbed into the mountains, and he had come to a wonderful slope under the crags. That slope was yellow with golden flowers. When he touched them golden ashes drifted from them and blew down among the rocks. There the padre found dust of gold, grains of gold, pebbles of gold, rocks of gold.

"Then all the padres went into the mountains. But the discoverer of the mine lost his way. They searched and searched until they were old and gray, but never found the wonderful slope and flowers that marked the grave and the mine of Padre Juan.

"In the succeeding years the story was handed down from father to son. But of the many who hunted for the lost mine of the padres there was never a Mexican or an Apache. For the Apache the mountain slopes were haunted by the spirit of an Indian maiden who had been false to her tribe and forever accursed. For the Mexican the mountain slopes were haunted by the spirit of the false padre, who rolled stones upon the heads of those adventurers who sought to find his grave and his accursed gold."

CHAPTER 18

BONITA

Florence's story of the lost mine fired Madeline's guests with the fever for gold-hunting. But after they had tried it a few times and the glamour of the thing wore off they gave up and remained in camp. Having exhausted all the resources of the mountain, such that had interest for them, they settled quietly down for a rest, which Madeline knew would soon end in a desire for civilized comforts. They were almost tired of roughing it. Helen's discontent manifested itself in her remark, "I guess nothing is going to happen, after all."

Madeline awaited their pleasure in regard to the breaking of camp; and meanwhile, as none of them cared for more exertion, she took her walks without them, sometimes accompanied by one of the cowboys, always by the stag-hounds. These walks furnished her exceeding pleasure. And, now that the cowboys would talk to her without reserve, she grew fonder of listening to their simple stories. The more she knew of them the more she doubted the wisdom of shut-in lives. Companionship with Nels and most of the cowboys was in its effect like that of the rugged pines and crags and the untainted wind. Humor, their predominant trait when a person grew to know them, saved Madeline from finding their hardness trying. They were dreamers, as all men who lived lonely lives in the wilds were dreamers.

The cowboys all had secrets. Madeline learned some of them. She marveled most at the strange way in which they hid emotions, except of violence of mirth and temper so easily aroused. It was all the more remarkable in view of the fact that they felt intensely over little things to which men of the world were blind and dead. Madeline had to believe that a hard and perilous life in a barren and wild country developed great principles in men. Living close to earth, under the cold, bleak peaks, on the dust-veiled desert, men grew like the nature that developed them—hard, fierce, terrible, perhaps, but big—big with elemental force.

But one day, while out walking alone, before she realized it she had gone a long way down a dim trail winding among the rocks. It was the middle of a summer afternoon, and all about her were shadows of the crags crossing the sunlit patches. The quiet was undisturbed. She went on and on, not blind to the fact that she was perhaps going too far from camp, but risking it because she was sure of her way back, and enjoying the wild, craggy recesses that were new to her. Finally she came out upon a bank that broke abruptly into a beautiful little glade. Here she sat down to rest before undertaking the return trip.

Suddenly Russ, the keener of the stag-hounds, raised his head and growled. Madeline feared he might have scented a mountain-lion or wildcat. She quieted him and carefully looked around. To each side was an irregular line of massive blocks of stone that had weathered from the crags. The little glade was open and grassy, with here a pine-tree, there a boulder. The outlet seemed to go down into a wilderness of cañons and ridges. Looking in this direction, Madeline saw the slight, dark figure of a woman coming stealthily along under the pines. Madeline was amazed, then a little frightened, for that stealthy walk from tree to tree was suggestive of secrecy, if nothing worse.

Presently the woman was joined by a tall man who carried a package, which he gave to her. They came on up the glade and appeared to be talking earnestly. In another moment Madeline recognized Stewart. She had no greater feeling of surprise than had at first been hers. But for the next moment she scarcely thought at all—merely watched the couple approaching. In a flash came back her former curiosity as to Stewart's strange absences from camp, and then with the return of her doubt of him the recognition of the woman. The small, dark head, the brown face, the big eyes—Madeline now saw distinctly—belonged to the Mexican girl Bonita. Stewart had met her there. This was the secret of his lonely trips, taken ever since he had come to work for Madeline. This secluded glade was a rendezvous. He had her hidden there.

Quietly Madeline arose, with a gesture to the dogs, and went back along the trail toward camp. Succeeding her surprise was a feeling of sorrow that Stewart's regeneration had not been complete. Sorrow gave place to insufferable disgust that while she had been romancing about this cowboy, dreaming of her good influence over him, he had been merely base. Somehow it stung her. Stewart had been nothing to her, she thought, yet she had been proud of him. She tried to revolve the thing, to be fair to him, when every instinctive tendency was to expel him, and all pertaining to him, from her thoughts. And her effort at sympathy, at extenuation, failed utterly before her pride. Exerting her will-power, she dismissed Stewart from her mind.

Madeline did not think of him again till late that afternoon when, as she was leaving her tent to join several of her guests, Stewart appeared suddenly in her path.

"Miss Hammond, I saw your tracks down the trail," he began, eagerly, but his tone was easy and natural. "I'm thinking—well, maybe you sure got the idea—"

"I do not wish for an explanation," interrupted Madeline.

Stewart gave a slight start. His manner had a semblance of the old, cool audacity. As he looked down at her it subtly changed.

What effrontery, Madeline thought, to face her before her guests with an explanation of his conduct! Suddenly she felt an inward flash of fire that was pain, so strange, so incomprehensible that her mind whirled. Then anger possessed her, not at Stewart, but at herself, that anything could rouse in her a raw emotion. She stood there, outwardly cold, serene, with level, haughty eyes upon Stewart; but inwardly she was burning with rage and shame.

"I'm sure not going to have you think—" He began passionately, but he broke off, and a slow dull crimson blotted over the healthy red-brown of his neck and cheeks.

"What you do or think, Stewart, is no concern of mine."

"Miss—Miss Hammond! You don't believe—" faltered Stewart.

The crimson receded from his face, leaving it pale. His eyes were appealing. They had a kind of timid look that struck Madeline even in her anger. There was something boyish about him then. He took a step forward and reached out with his hand open-palmed in a gesture that was humble, yet held a certain dignity.

"But listen. Never mind now what you—you think about me. There's a good reason—"

"I have no wish to hear your reason."

"But you ought to," he persisted.

"Sir!"

Stewart underwent another swift change. He started violently. A dark tide shaded his face, and a glitter leaped to his eyes. He took two long strides—loomed over her.

"I'm not thinking about myself," he thundered. "Will you listen?"

"No," she replied; and there was freezing hauteur in her voice. With a slight gesture of dismissal, unmistakable in its finality, she turned her back upon him. Then she joined her guests.

Stewart stood perfectly motionless. Then slowly he began to lift his right hand in which he held his sombrero. He swept it up and up, high over his head. His tall form towered. With fierce suddenness he flung his sombrero down. He leaped at his black horse and dragged him to where his saddle lay. With one pitch he tossed the saddle upon the horse's back. His strong hands flashed at girths and straps. Every action was swift, decisive, fierce. Bounding for his bridle, which hung over a bush, he ran against a cowboy who awkwardly tried to avoid the onslaught.

"Get out of my way!" he yelled.

Then with the same savage haste he adjusted the bridle on his horse.

"Mebbe you better hold on a minnit, Gene, ole feller," said Monty Price.

"Monty, do you want me to brain you?" said Stewart, with the short, hard ring in his voice.

"Now, considerin' the high class of my brains, I oughter be real careful to keep 'em," replied Monty. "You can betcher life, Gene, I ain't goin' to git in front of you. But I jest says— Listen!"

Stewart raised his dark face. Everybody listened. And everybody heard the rapid beat of a horse's hoofs. The sun had set, but the park was light. Nels appeared down the trail, and his horse was running. In another moment he was in the circle, pulling his bay back to a sliding halt. He leaped off abreast of Stewart.

Madeline saw and felt a difference in Nels's presence.

"What's up, Gene?" he queried, sharply.

"I'm leaving camp," replied Stewart, thickly. His black horse began to stamp as Stewart grasped bridle and mane and kicked the stirrup round.

Nels's long arm shot out, and his hand fell upon Stewart, holding him down.

"Shore I'm sorry," said Nels, slowly. "Then you was goin' to hit the trail?"

"I am going to. Let go, Nels."

"Shore you ain't goin', Gene?"

"Let go, damn you!" cried Stewart, as he wrestled free.

"What's wrong?" asked Nels, lifting his hand again.

"Man! Don't touch me!"

Nels stepped back instantly. He seemed to become aware of Stewart's white, wild passion. Again Stewart moved to mount.

"Nels, don't make me forget we've been friends," he said.

"Shore I ain't fergettin'," replied Nels. "An' I resign my job right here an' now!"

His strange speech checked the mounting cowboy. Stewart stepped down from the stirrup. Then their hard faces were still and cold while their eyes locked glances.

Madeline was as much startled by Nels's speech as Stewart. Quick to note a change in these men, she now sensed one that was unfathomable.

"Resign?" questioned Stewart.

"Shore. What'd you think I'd do under circumstances sich as has come up?"

"But see here, Nels, I won't stand for it."

"You're not my boss no more, an' I ain't beholdin' to Miss Hammond, neither. I'm my own boss, an' I'll do as I please. *Sabe*, señor?"

Nels's words were at variance with the meaning in his face.

"Gene, you sent me on a little scout down in the mountains, didn't you?" he continued.

"Yes, I did," replied Stewart, with a new sharpness in his voice.

"Wal, shore you was so good an' right in your figgerin', as opposed to mine, that I'm sick with admirin' of you. If you hedn't sent me—wal, I'm reckonin' somethin' might hev happened. As it is we're shore up against a hell of a proposition!"

How significant was the effect of his words upon all the cowboys! Stewart made a fierce and violent motion, terrible where his other motions had been but passionate. Monty leaped straight up into the air in a singular action

as suggestive of surprise as it was of wild acceptance of
menace. Like a stalking giant Nick Steele strode over to
Nels and Stewart. The other cowboys rose silently, without a word.

Madeline and her guests, in a little group, watched and
listened, unable to divine what all this strange talk and
action meant.

"Hold on, Nels, they don't need to hear it," said Stewart, hoarsely, as he waved a hand toward Madeline's silent
group.

"Wal, I'm sorry, but I reckon they'd as well know fust
as last. Mebbe thet yearnin' wish of Miss Helen's fer
somethin' to happen will come true. Shore I—"

"Cut out the joshin'," rang out Monty's strident voice.

It had as decided an effect as any preceding word or
action. Perhaps it was the last thing needed to transform
thcsc men, doing unaccustomed duty as escorts of beautiful women, to their natural state as men of the wild.

"Tell us what's what," said Stewart, cool and grim.

"Don Carlos an' his guerrillas are campin' on the trails
thet lead up here. They've got them trails blocked. By tomorrer they'd hed us corralled. Mebbe they meant to surprise us. He's got a lot of Greasers an' outlaws. They're
well armed. Now what do they mean? You-all can figger
it out to suit yourselves. Mebbe the Don wants to pay a
sociable call on our ladies. Mebbe his gang is some hungry, as usual. Mebbe they want to steal a few hosses, or
anythin' they can lay hands on. Mebbe they mean wuss,
too. Now, my idee is this, an' mebbe it's wrong. I long
since separated from love with Greasers. Thet black-faced
Don Carlos has got a deep game. Thet two-bit of a revolution is hevin' hard times. The rebels want American
intervention. They'd stretch any point to make trouble.

We're only ten miles from the border. Suppose them guer-rillas got our crowd across thet border? The U. S. cavalry would foller. You-all know what thet'd mean. Mebbe Don Carlos's mind works thet way. Mebbe it don't. I reckon we'll know soon. An' now, Stewart, whatever the Don's game is, shore you're the man to outfigger him. Mebbe it's just as well you're good an' mad about somethin'. An' I resign my job because I want to feel unbeholdin' to any-body. Shore it struck me long since thet the old days hed come back fer a little spell, an' there I was trailin' a prom-ise not to hurt any Greaser."

CHAPTER 19

DON CARLOS

Stewart took Nels, Monty, and Nick Steele aside out of earshot, and they evidently entered upon an earnest colloquy. Presently the other cowboys were called. They all talked more or less, but the deep voice of Stewart predominated over the others. Then the consultation broke up, and the cowboys scattered.

"Rustle, you Indians!" ordered Stewart.

The ensuing scene of action was not reassuring to Madeline and her friends. They were quiet, awaiting some one to tell them what to do. At the offset the cowboys appeared to have forgotten Madeline. Some of them ran off into the woods, others into the open, grassy places, where they rounded up the horses and burros. Several cowboys spread tarpaulins upon the ground and began to select and roll small packs, evidently for hurried travel. Nels mounted his horse to ride down the trail. Monty and Nick Steele went off into the grove leading their horses. Stewart climbed up a steep jumble of stones between two sections of low, cracked cliff back of the camp.

Castleton offered to help the packers, and was curtly told he would be in the way. Madeline's friends all importuned her: Was there real danger? Were the guerrillas coming? Would a start be made at once for the ranch? Why had the cowboys suddenly become so different? Madeline answered as best she could; but her replies were only conjecture, and modified to allay the fears of her guests. Helen was in a white glow of excitement.

Soon cowboys appeared riding barebacked horses, driving in others and the burros. Some of these horses were taken away and evidently hidden in deep recesses between the crags. The string of burros were packed and sent off down the trail in charge of a cowboy. Nick Steele and Monty returned. Then Stewart appeared clambering down the break between the cliffs.

His next move was to order all the baggage belonging to Madeline and her guests taken up the cliff. This was strenuous toil, requiring the need of lassoes to haul up the effects.

"Get ready to climb," said Stewart, turning to Madeline's party.

"Where?" asked Helen.

He waved his hand at the ascent to be made. Exclamations of dismay followed his gesture.

"Mr. Stewart, is there danger?" asked Dorothy; and her voice trembled.

This was the question Madeline had upon her lips to ask Stewart, but she could not speak it.

"No, there's no danger," replied Stewart, "but we're taking precautions we all agreed on as best."

Dorothy whispered that she believed Stewart lied.

Castleton asked another question, and then Harvey followed suit. Mrs. Beck made a timid query.

"Please keep quiet and do as you're told," said Stewart, bluntly.

At this juncture, when the last of the baggage was being hauled up the cliff, Monty approached Madeline and removed his sombrero. His black face seemed the same, yet this was a vastly changed Monty.

"Miss Hammond, I'm givin' notice I resign my job," he said.

"Monty! What do you mean? What does Nels mean now, when danger threatens?"

"We jest quit. Thet's all," replied Monty, tersely. He was stern and somber; he could not stand still; his eyes roved everywhere.

Castleton jumped up from the log where he had been sitting, and his face was very red.

"Mr. Price, does all this blooming fuss mean we are to be robbed or attacked or abducted by a lot of ragmuffin guerrillas?"

"You've called the bet."

Dorothy turned a very pale face toward Monty.

"Mr. Price, you wouldn't—you couldn't desert us now? You and Mr. Nels—"

"Desert you?" asked Monty, blankly.

"Yes, desert us. Leave us when we may need you so much, with something dreadful coming."

Monty uttered a short, hard laugh as he bent a strange look upon the girl.

"Me an' Nels is purty much scared, an' we're goin' to slope. Miss Dorothy, bein' as we've rustled round so much, it sorta hurts us to see nice young girls dragged off by the hair."

Dorothy uttered a little cry and then became hysterical. Castleton for once was fully aroused.

"By Gad! You and your partner are a couple of blooming cowards. Where now is that courage you boasted of?"

Monty's dark face expressed extreme sarcasm.

"Dook, in my time I've seen some bright fellers, but you take the cake. It's most marvelous how bright you are. Figger'n' me an' Nels so correct. Say, Dook, if you don't git rustled off to Mexico an' roped to a cactus bush you'll hev a swell story fer your English chums. Bah Jove! You'll tell 'em how you seen two old-time gun-men run like scared jack-rabbits from a lot of Greasers. Like hell you will! Unless you lie like the time you told about proddin' the lion. That there story allus—"

"Monty, shut up!" yelled Stewart, as he came hurriedly up. Then Monty slouched away, cursing to himself.

Madeline and Helen, assisted by Castleton, worked over Dorothy, and with some difficulty quieted her. Stewart passed several times without noticing them, and Monty, who had been so ridiculously eager to pay every little attention to Dorothy, did not see her at all. Rude it seemed; in Monty's case more than that. Madeline hardly knew what to make of it.

Stewart directed cowboys to go to the head of the open place in the cliff and let down lassoes. Then, with little waste of words, he urged the women toward this rough ladder of stones.

"We want to hide you," he said, when they demurred. "If the guerrillas come we'll tell them you've all gone down to the ranch. If we have to fight you'll be safe up there."

Helen stepped boldly forward and let Stewart put the loop of a lasso round her and tighten it. He waved his hand to the cowboys above.

"Just walk up, now," he directed Helen.

It proved to the watchers to be an easy, safe, and rapid means of scaling the steep passage. The men climbed up without assistance. Mrs. Beck, as usual, had hysteria; she half walked and was half dragged up. Stewart supported Dorothy with one arm, while with the other he held to the lasso. Ambrose had to carry Christine. The Mexican women required no assistance. Edith Wayne and Madeline climbed last; and once up, Madeline saw a narrow bench, thick with shrubs, and overshadowed by huge, leaning crags. There were holes in the rock, and dark fissures leading back. It was a rough, wild place. Tarpaulins and bedding were then hauled up, and food and water. The cowboys spread comfortable beds in several of the caves, and told Madeline and her friends to be as quiet as possible, not to make a light, and to sleep dressed, ready for travel at a moment's notice.

After the cowboys had gone down it was not a cheerful group left there in the darkening twilight. Castleton prevailed upon them to eat.

"This is simply great," whispered Helen.

"Oh, it's awful!" moaned Dorothy. "It's your fault, Helen. You prayed for something to happen."

"I believe it's a horrid trick those cowboys are playing," said Mrs. Beck.

Madeline assured her friends that no trick was being played upon them, and that she deplored the discomfort and distress, but felt no real alarm. She was more inclined to evasive kindness here than to sincerity, for she had a decided uneasiness. The swift change in the manner and looks of her cowboys had been a shock to her. The last glance she had of Stewart's face, then stern, almost sad,

and haggard with worry, remained to augment her foreboding.

Darkness appeared to drop swiftly down; the coyotes
began their haunting, mournful howls; the stars showed
and grew brighter; the wind moaned through the tips of
the pines. Castleton was restless. He walked to and fro
before the overhanging shelf of rock, where his companions sat lamenting, and presently he went out to the ledge
of the bench. The cowboys below had built a fire, and the
light from it rose in a huge, fan-shaped glow. Castleton's
little figure stood out black against this light. Curious and
anxious also, Madeline joined him and peered down from
the cliff. The distance was short, and occasionally she
could distinguish a word spoken by the cowboys. They
were unconcernedly cooking and eating. She marked the
absence of Stewart, and mentioned it to Castleton. Silently
Castleton pointed almost straight down, and there in the
gloom stood Stewart, with the two stag-hounds at his feet.

Presently Nick Steele silenced the camp-fire circle by
raising a warning hand. The cowboys bent their heads, listening. Madeline listened with all her might. She heard
one of the hounds whine, then the faint beat of a horse's
hoofs. Nick spoke again, and turned to his supper, and the
other men seemed to slacken in attention. The beat of
hoofs grew louder, entered the grove, then the circle of
light. The rider was Nels. He dismounted, and the sound
of his low voice just reached Madeline.

"Gene, it's Nels. Somethin' doin'," Madeline heard one
of the cowboys call softly.

"Send him over," replied Stewart.

Nels stalked away from the fire.

"See here, Nels, the boys are all right, but I don't want

them to know everything about this mix-up," said Stewart, as Nels came up. "Did you find the girl?"

Madeline guessed that Stewart referred to the Mexican girl Bonita.

"No. But I met"—Madeline did not catch the name—"an' he was wild. He was with a forest-ranger. An' they said Pat Hawe had trailed her, an' was takin' her down under arrest."

Stewart muttered deep under his breath, evidently cursing.

"Wonder why he didn't come on up here?" he queried, presently. "He can see a trail."

"Wal, Gene, Pat knowed you was here all right, fer thet ranger said Pat hed wind of the guerrillas, an' Pat said if Don Carlos didn't kill you—which he hoped he'd do—then it'd be time enough to put you in jail when you come down."

"He's dead set to arrest me, Nels."

"An' he'll do it, like the old lady who kept tavern out West. Gene, the reason thet red-faced coyote didn't trail you up here is because he's scared. He allus was scared of you. But I reckon he's shore scared to death of me an' Monty."

"Well, we'll take Pat in his turn. The thing now is, when will that Greaser stalk us, and what'll we do when he comes?"

"My boy, there's only one way to handle a Greaser. I shore told you thet. He means rough toward us. He'll come smilin' up, all soci'ble like, insinuatin' an' sweeter'n a woman. But he's treacherous; he's wuss than an Indian. An', Gene, we know for a positive fact how his gang hev been operatin' between these hills an' Agua Prieta. They're no nervy gang of outlaws like we used to hev. But they're plumb bad. They've raided and murdered through the San Luis Pass an' Guadalupe Cañon. They've murdered women, an' wuss than thet both north an' south of Agua Prieta. Mebbe the U. S. cavalry don't know it, an' the good old States; but we, *you* an' *me* an' *Monty* an' *Nick, we* know it. We know jest about what thet rebel war down there amounts to. It's guerrilla war, an' shore some harvest time fer a lot of cheap thieves an' outcasts."

"Oh, you're right, Nels. I'm not disputing that," replied Stewart. "If it wasn't for Miss Hammond and the other women, I'd rather enjoy seeing you and Monty open up on that bunch. I'm thinking I'd be glad to meet Don Carlos. But Miss Hammond! Why, Nels, such a woman as she is would *never* recover from the sight of real gun-play, let alone any stunts with a rope. These Eastern women are different. I'm not belittling our Western women. It's in the blood. Miss Hammond is—is—"

"Shore she is," interrupted Nels; "but she's got a damn sight more spunk than you think she has, Gene Stewart. I'm no thick-skulled cow. I'd hate somethin' powerful to hev Miss Hammond see any rough work, let alone me an' Monty startin' somethin'. An' me an' Monty'll stick to you, Gene, as long as seems reasonable. Mind, ole feller, beggin' your pardon, you're shore stuck on Miss Hammond, an' over-tender not to hurt her feelin's or make her sick by lettin' some blood. We're in bad here, an' mebbe we'll *hev* to fight. *Sabe,* señor? Wal, if we do you can jest gamble thet Miss Hammond'll be game. An' I'll bet you a million pesos thet if you got goin' onct, an' she seen you as I've seen you—wal, I know what she'd think of you. This old world ain't changed much. Some women may be white-skinned an' soft-eyed an' sweet-voiced an' high-souled, but they all like to see a man! Gene, here's your game. Let Don Carlos come along. Be civil. If he an' his gang are hungry, feed 'em. Take even a little over-bearin' Greaser talk. Be blind if he wants his gang to steal somethin'. Let him think the women hev mosied down to the ranch. But if he says you're lyin'—if he as much as looks round to see the women—jest jump him same as you jumped Pat Hawe. Me an' Monty'll hang back fer thet, an' if your strong bluff don't go through, if the Don's gang even *thinks* of flashin' guns, then we'll open up. An' all I got to say is if them Greasers stand fer real gun-play they'll be the fust I ever seen."

"Nels, there are white men in that gang," said Stewart.

"Shore. But me an Monty'll be thinkin' of thet. If they start anythin' it'll hev to be shore quick."

"All right, Nels, old friend, and thanks," replied Stewart.

Nels returned to the camp-fire, and Stewart resumed his silent guard.

Madeline led Castleton away from the brink of the wall.

"By Jove! Cowboys are blooming strange folk!" he exclaimed. "They are not what they pretend to be."

"Indeed, you are right," replied Madeline. "I cannot understand them. Come, let us tell the others that Nels and Monty were only talking, and do not intend to leave us. Dorothy, at least, will be less frightened if she knows."

Dorothy was somewhat comforted. The others, however, complained of the cowboys' singular behavior. More than once the idea was advanced that an elaborate trick had been concocted. Upon general discussion this idea gained ground. Madeline did not combat it, because she saw it tended to a less perturbed condition of mind among her guests. Castleton for once proved that he was not absolutely obtuse, and helped along the idea.

They sat talking in low voices until a late hour. The incident now began to take on the nature of Helen's long-yearned-for adventure. Some of the party even grew merry in a subdued way. Then, gradually, one by one they tired and went to bed. Helen vowed she could not sleep in a place where there were bats and crawling things. Madeline fancied, however, that they all went to sleep while she lay wide-eyed, staring up at the black bulge of overhanging rock and beyond to the starry sky.

To keep from thinking of Stewart and the burning anger he had caused her to feel for herself, Madeline tried to keep her mind on other things. But thought of him recurred, and each time there was a hot commotion in her breast hard to stifle. Intelligent reasoning seemed out of her power. In the daylight it had been possible for her to be oblivious to Stewart's deceit after the moment of its realization. At night, however, in the strange silence and hovering shadows of gloom, with the speaking stars seeming to call to her, with the moan of the wind in the pines, and the melancholy mourn of coyotes in the distance, she was not able to govern her thought and emotion. The day was practical, cold; the night was strange and tense. In the darkness she had fancies wholly unknown to her in the bright light of the sun. She battled with a haunting thought. She had inadvertently heard Nels's conversation with Stewart; she had listened, hoping to hear some good news or to hear the worst; she had learned both, and, moreover, enlightenment on one point of Stewart's complex motives. He wished to spare her any sight that might offend, frighten, or disgust her. Yet this Stewart, who showed a fineness of feeling that might have been wanting even in Boyd Harvey, maintained a secret rendezvous with that pretty, abandoned Bonita. Here, always the hot shame, like a live, stinging, internal fire, abruptly ended Madeline's thought. It was intolerable, and it was the more so because she could neither control nor understand it. The hours wore on, and at length, as the stars began to pale and there was no sound whatever, she fell asleep.

She was called out of her slumber. Day had broken bright and cool. The sun was still below the eastern crags. Ambrose, with several other cowboys, had brought up buckets of spring-water, and hot coffee and cakes. Madeline's party appeared to be none the worse for the night's experience. Indeed, the meager breakfast might have been as merrily partaken of as it was hungrily had not Ambrose enjoined silence.

"They're expectin' company down below," he said.

This information and the summary manner in which the cowboys soon led the party higher up among the ruined shelves of rock caused a recurrence of anxiety. Madeline insisted on not going beyond a projection of cliff from which she could see directly down into the camp. As the vantage-point was one affording concealment, Ambrose consented, but he placed the frightened Christine near Madeline and remained there himself.

"Ambrose, do you really think the guerrillas will come?" asked Madeline.

"Sure. We know. Nels just rode in and said they were on their way up. Miss Hammond, can I trust you? You won't let out a squeal if there's a fight down there? Stewart told me to hide you out of sight or keep you from lookin'."

"I promise not to make any noise," replied Madeline.

Madeline arranged her coat so that she could lie upon it, and settled down to wait developments. There came a slight rattling of stones in the rear. She turned to see Helen sliding down a bank with a perplexed and troubled cowboy. Helen came stooping low to where Madeline lay and said: "I am going to see what happens if I die in the attempt! I can stand it if you can." She was pale and big-eyed. Ambrose promptly swore at the cowboy who had let her get away from him. "Take a half-hitch on her yourself an' see where you end up," replied the fellow, and disappeared in the jumble of rocks. Ambrose, finding words useless, sternly and heroically prepared to carry Helen back to the others. He laid hold of her. In a fury, with eyes blazing, Helen whispered:

"Let go of me! Majesty, what does this fool mean?"

Madeline laughed. She knew Helen, and had marked the whisper, when ordinarily Helen would have spoken imperiously, and not low. Madeline explained to her the exigency of the situation. "I might run, but I'll never scream," said Helen. With that Ambrose had to be content to let her stay. However, he found her a place somewhat farther back from Madeline's position, where he said there was less danger of her being seen. Then he sternly bound her to silence, tarried a moment to comfort Christine, and returned to where Madeline lay concealed. He had been there scarcely a moment when he whispered:

"I hear hosses. The guerrillas are comin'."

Madeline's hiding-place was well protected from possible discovery from below. She could peep over a kind of parapet, through an opening in the tips of the pines that reached up to the cliff, and obtain a commanding view of the camp circle and its immediate surroundings. She could not, however, see far either to right or left of the camp, owing to the obstructing foliage. Presently the sound of horses' hoofs quickened the beat of her pulse and caused her to turn keener gaze upon the cowboys below.

Although she had some inkling of the course Stewart and his men were to pursue, she was not by any means prepared for the indifference she saw. Frank was asleep, or pretended to be. Three cowboys were lazily and unconcernedly attending to camp-fire duties, such as baking biscuits, watching the ovens, and washing tins and pots. The elaborate set of aluminum plates, cups, etc., together with the other camp fixtures that had done service for Madeline's party, had disappeared. Nick Steele sat with his back to a log, smoking his pipe. Another cowboy had just brought the horses closer into camp, where they stood waiting to be saddled. Nels appeared to be fussing over a pack. Stewart was rolling a cigarette. Monty had apparently nothing to do for the present except whistle, which he was doing much more loudly than melodiously. The whole ensemble gave an impression of careless indifference.

The sound of horses' hoofs grew louder and slowed its beat. One of the cowboys pointed down the trail, toward which several of his comrades turned their heads for a moment, then went on with their occupations.

Presently a shaggy, dusty horse bearing a lean, ragged, dark rider rode into camp and halted. Another followed, and another. Horses with Mexican riders came in single file and stopped behind the leader.

The cowboys looked up, and the guerrillas looked down.

"*Buenas dias,* señor," ceremoniously said the foremost guerrilla.

By straining her ears Madeline heard that voice, and she recognized it as belonging to Don Carlos. His graceful bow to Stewart was also familiar. Otherwise she would never have recognized the former elegant *vaquero* in this uncouth, roughly dressed Mexican.

Stewart answered the greeting in Spanish, and, waving his hand toward the camp-fire, added in English, "Get down and eat."

The guerrillas were anything but slow in complying. They crowded to the fire, then spread in a little circle and squatted upon the ground, laying their weapons beside them. In appearance they tallied with the band of guerrillas that had carried Madeline up into the foothills, only this band was larger and better armed. The men, moreover, were just as hungry and as wild and beggarly. The cowboys were not cordial in their reception of this visit, but they were hospitable. The law of the desert had always been to give food and drink to wayfaring men, whether lost or hunted or hunting.

"There's twenty-three in that outfit," whispered Ambrose, "includin' four white men. Pretty rummy outfit."

"They appear to be friendly enough," whispered Madeline.

"Things down there ain't what they seem," replied Ambrose.

"Ambrose, tell me—explain to me. This is my opportunity. As long as you will let me watch them please let me know the—the real thing."

"Sure. But recollect, Miss Hammond, that Gene'll give it to me good if he ever knows I let you look and told you what's what. Well, decent-like Gene is seein' them poor devils get a square meal. They're only a lot of calf-thieves in this country. Across the border they're bandits, some of them, the others just riffraff outlaws. That rebel bluff doesn't go down with us. I'd have to see first before I'd believe them Greasers would fight. They're a lot of hard-ridin' thieves, and they'd steal a fellow's blanket or to-bacco. Gene thinks they're after you ladies—to carry you off. But Gene— Oh! Gene's some highfalutin in his ideas lately. Most of us boys think the guerrillas are out to rob—that's all."

Whatever might have been the secret motive of Don Carlos and his men, they did not allow it to interfere with a hearty appreciation of a generous amount of food. Plainly, each individual ate all that he was able to eat at the time. They jabbered like a flock of parrots; some were even merry, in a kind of wild way. Then, as each and every one began to roll and smoke the inevitable cigarette of the Mexican, there was a subtle change in manner. They smoked and looked about the camp, off into the woods, up at the crags, and back at the leisurely cowboys. They had the air of men waiting for something.

"Señor," began Don Carlos, addressing Stewart. As he spoke he swept his sombrero to indicate the camp circle.

Madeline could not distinguish his words, but his gesture plainly indicated a question in regard to the rest of the camping party. Stewart's reply and the wave of his hand down the trail meant that his party had gone home. Stewart turned to some task, and the guerrilla leader quietly smoked. He looked cunning and thoughtful. His men gradually began to manifest a restlessness, noticeable in the absence of former languor and slow puffing of ciga-rette smoke. Presently a big-boned man with a bullet-head and a blistered red face of evil coarseness got up and threw away his cigarette. He was an American.

"Hey, cull," he called, in loud voice, "ain't ye goin' to cough up a drink?"

"My boys don't carry liquor on the trail," replied Stewart. He turned now to face the guerrillas.

"Haw, haw! I heerd over in Rodeo thet ye was gittin' to be shore some fer temperance," said this fellow. "I hate to drink water, but I guess I've gotter do it."

He went to the spring, sprawled down to drink, and all of a sudden he thrust his arm down in the water to bring forth a basket. The cowboys in the hurry of packing had neglected to remove this basket; and it contained bottles of wine and liquors for Madeline's guests. They had been submerged in the spring to keep them cold. The guerrilla fumbled with the lid, opened it, and then got up, uttering a loud roar of delight.

Stewart made an almost imperceptible motion, as if to leap forward; but he checked the impulse, and after a quick glance at Nels he said to the guerrilla:

"Guess my party forgot that. You're welcome to it."

Like bees the guerrillas swarmed around the lucky finder of the bottles. There was a babel of voices. The drink did not last long, and it served only to liberate the spirit of recklessness. The several white outlaws began to prowl around the camp; some of the Mexicans did likewise; others waited, showing by their ill-concealed expectancy the nature of their thoughts.

It was the demeanor of Stewart and his comrades that puzzled Madeline. Apparently, they felt no anxiety or even particular interest. Don Carlos, who had been covertly watching them, now made his scrutiny open, even aggressive. He looked from Stewart to Nels and Monty, and then to the other cowboys. While some of his men prowled around the others watched him, and the waiting attitude had taken on something sinister. The guerrilla leader seemed undecided, but not in any sense puzzled. When he turned his cunning face upon Nels and Monty he had the manner of a man in whom decision was lacking.

In her growing excitement Madeline had not clearly heard Ambrose's low whispers and she made an effort to distract some of her attention from those below to the cowboy crouching beside her.

The quality, the note of Ambrose's whisper had changed. It had a slight, sibilant sound.

"Don't be mad if sudden-like I clap my hands over your eyes, Miss Hammond," he was saying. "Somethin's brewin' below. I never seen Gene so cool. That's a dangerous sign in him. And look, see how the boys are workin' together! Oh! It's slow and accident-like, but I know it's sure not accident. That foxy Greaser knows, too. But maybe his men don't. If they are wise they haven't sense enough to care. The Don, though—he's worried. He's not payin' so much attention to Gene, either. It's Nels and Monty he's watchin'. And well he need do it! There, Nick and Frank have settled down on that log with Booly. They don't seem to be packin' guns. But look how heavy their vests hang. A gun in each side! Those boys can pull a gun and flop over that log quicker than you can think. Do you notice how Nels and Monty and Gene are square between them guerrillas and the trail up here? It doesn't seem on purpose, but it *is*. Look at Nels and Monty. How quiet they are confabin' together, payin' no attention to the guerrillas. I see Monty look at Gene, then I see Nels look at Gene. Well, it's up to Gene. And they're goin' to back him. I reckon, Miss Hammond, there'd be dead Greasers round that camp long ago if Nels and Monty were foot-loose. They're beholdin' to Gene. That's plain. And Lord, how it tickles me to watch them! Both packin' two forty-fives, butts swingin' clear. There's twenty-four shots in them four guns. And there's twenty-three guerrillas. If Nels and Monty ever throw guns at that close range, why, before you'd know what was up there'd be a pile of Greasers. There! Stewart said something to the Don. I wonder what. I'll gamble it was something to get the Don's outfit all close together. Sure! Greasers have no sense. But them white guerrillas, they're lookin' some dubious. Whatever's comin' off will come soon, you can bet. I wish I was down there. But maybe it won't come to a scrap. Stewart's set on avoidin' that. He's a wonderful chap to get his way. Lord, though, I'd like to see him go after that overbearin' Greaser! See! The Don can't stand prosperity. All this strange behavior of cowboys is beyond his pulque-soaked brains. Then he's a Greaser. If Gene doesn't knock him on the head presently he'll begin to get over his scare, even of Nels and Monty. But Gene'll pick out the right time. And I'm gettin' nervous. I want somethin' to start. Never saw Nels in but one fight, then he just shot a Greaser's arm off for tryin' to draw on him. But I've heard all about him. And Monty! Monty's the real old-fashioned gun-man. Why, none of them stories, them lies he told to entertain the Englishman, was a marker to what Monty has done. What I don't understand is how Monty keeps so quiet and easy and peaceful-like. That's not his way, with such an outfit lookin' for trouble. O-ha! Now for the grand bluff. Looks like no fight at all!"

The guerrilla leader had ceased his restless steps and glances, and turned to Stewart with something of bold resolution in his aspect.

"*Gracias*, señor," he said. "*Adios*." He swept his sombrero in the direction of the trail leading down the mountain to the ranch; and as he completed the gesture a smile, crafty and jeering, crossed his swarthy face.

Ambrose whispered so low that Madeline scarcely heard him. "If the Greaser goes that way he'll find our horses and get wise to the trick. Oh, he's wise now! But I'll gamble he never even starts on that trail."

Neither hurriedly nor guardedly Stewart rose out of his leaning posture and took a couple of long strides toward Don Carlos.

"Go back the way you came," he fairly yelled; and his voice had the ring of a bugle.

Ambrose nudged Madeline; his whisper was tense and rapid: "Don't miss nothin'. Gene's called him. Whatever's comin' off will be here quick as lightnin'. See! I guess maybe that Greaser don't savvy good U. S. lingo. Look at that durty yaller face turn green. Put one eye on Nels and Monty! That's great—just to see 'em. Just as quiet and easy. But oh, the difference! Bent and stiff—that means every muscle is like a rawhide riata. They're watchin' with eyes that can see the workin's of them Greasers' minds. Now there ain't a hoss-hair between them Greasers and hell!"

Don Carlos gave Stewart one long malignant stare; then he threw back his head, swept up the sombrero, and his evil smile showed gleaming teeth.

"Señor," he began.

With magnificent bound Stewart was upon him. The guerrilla's cry was throttled in his throat. A fierce wrestling ensued, too swift to see clearly; then heavy, sodden blows, and Don Carlos was beaten to the ground. Stewart leaped back. Then, crouching with his hands on the butts of guns at his hips, he yelled, he thundered at the guerrillas. He had been quicker than a panther, and now his voice was so terrible that it curdled Madeline's blood, and the menace of deadly violence in his crouching position made her shut her eyes. But she had to open them. In that single instant Nels and Monty had leaped to Stewart's side. Both were bent down with hands on the butts of guns at their hips. Nels's piercing yell seemed to divide Monty's roar of rage. Then they ceased, and echoes clapped from the crags. The silence of those three men crouching like tigers about to leap was more menacing than the nerve-racking yells.

Then the guerrillas wavered and broke and ran for their horses. Don Carlos rolled over, rose, and staggered away, to be helped upon his mount. He looked back, his pale and bloody face that of a thwarted demon. The whole band got into action and were gone in a moment.

"I knew it," declared Ambrose. "Never seen a Greaser who could face gun-play. That was some warm. And Monty Price never flashed a gun! He'll never get over that. I reckon, Miss Hammond, we're some lucky to avoid trouble. Gene had his way, as you seen. We'll be makin' tracks for the ranch in about two shakes."

"Why?" whispered Madeline, breathlessly. She became conscious that she was weak and shaken.

"Because the guerrillas sure will get their nerve back, and come sneakin' on our trail or try to head us off by ambushin'," replied Ambrose. "That's their way. Otherwise three cowboys couldn't bluff a whole gang like that. Gene knows the nature of Greasers. They're white-livered. But I reckon we're in more danger now than before, unless we get a good start down the mountain. There! Gene's callin'. Come! Hurry!"

Helen had slipped down from her vantage-point, and therefore had not seen the last act in that little camp-fire drama. It seemed, however, that her desire for excitement was satisfied, for her face was pale and she trembled when she asked if the guerrillas were gone.

"I didn't see the finish, but those horrible yells were enough for me."

Ambrose hurried the three women over the rough rocks down to the cliff. The cowboys below were saddling horses in haste. Evidently, all the horses had been brought out of hiding. Swiftly, with regard only for life and limb, Madeline, Helen, and Christine were lowered by lassoes and half carried down to the level. By the time they were safely down the other members of the party appeared on the cliff above. They were in excellent spirits, appearing to treat the matter as a huge joke.

Ambrose put Christine on a horse and rode away through the pines; Frankie Slade did likewise with Helen. Stewart led Madeline's horse up to her, helped her to mount, and spoke one stern word, "Wait!" Then as fast as one of the women reached the level she was put upon a horse and taken away by a cowboy escort. Few words were spoken. Haste seemed to be the great essential. The horses were urged, and, once in the trail, spurred and led into a swift trot. One cowboy drove up four pack-horses, and these were hurriedly loaded with the party's baggage. Castleton and his companions mounted, and galloped off to catch the others in the lead. This left Madeline behind with Stewart and Nels and Monty.

"They're goin' to switch off at the holler thet heads near the trail a few miles down," Nels was saying, as he tightened his saddle-girth. "Thet holler heads into a big cañon. Once in thet, it'll be every man fer hisself. I reckon there won't be anythin' wuss than a rough ride."

Nels smiled reassuringly at Madeline, but he did not

speak to her. Monty took her canteen and filled it at the spring and hung it over the pommel of her saddle. He put a couple of biscuits in the saddle-bag.

"Don't fergit to take a drink an' a bite as you're ridin' along," he said. "An' don't worry, Miss Majesty. Stewart'll be with you, an' me an' Nels hangin' on the back-trail."

His somber and sullen face did not change in its strange intensity, but the look in his eyes Madeline felt she would never forget. Left alone with these three men, now stripped of all pretense, she realized how fortune had favored her and what peril still hung in the balance. Stewart swung astride his big black, spurred him, and whistled. At the whistle Majesty jumped, and with swift canter followed Stewart. Madeline looked back to see Nels already up and Monty handing him a rifle. Then the pines hid her view.

Once in the trail, Stewart's horse broke into a gallop. Majesty changed his gait and kept at the black's heels. Stewart called back a warning. The low, wide-spreading branches of trees might brush Madeline out of the saddle. Fast riding through the forest along a crooked, obstructed trail called forth all her alertness. Likewise the stirring of her blood, always susceptible to the spirit and motion of a ride, let alone one of peril, now began to throb and burn away the worry, the dread, the coldness that had weighted her down.

Before long Stewart wheeled at right angles off the trail and entered a hollow between two low bluffs. Madeline saw tracks in the open patches of ground. Here Stewart's horse took to a brisk walk. The hollow deepened, narrowed, became rocky, full of logs and brush. Madeline exerted all her keenness, and needed it, to keep close to Stewart. She did not think of him, nor her own safety, but of keeping Majesty close in the tracks of the black, of eluding the sharp spikes in the dead brush, of avoiding the treacherous loose stones.

At last Madeline was brought to a dead halt by Stewart and his horse blocking the trail. Looking up, she saw they were at the head of a cañon that yawned beneath and widened its gray-walled, green-patched slopes down to a black forest of fir. The drab monotony of the foothills made contrast below the forest, and away in the distance, rosy and smoky, lay the desert. Retracting her gaze, Madeline saw pack-horses cross an open space a mile below, and she thought she saw the stag-hounds. Stewart's dark eyes searched the slopes high up along the craggy escarpments. Then he put the black to the descent.

If there had been a trail left by the leading cowboys, Stewart did not follow it. He led off to the right, zigzagging an intricate course through the roughest ground Madeline had ever ridden over. He crashed through cedars, threaded a tortuous way among boulders, made his horse slide down slanting banks of soft earth, picked a slow and cautious progress across weathered slopes of loose rock. Madeline followed, finding in this ride a tax on strength and judgment. On an ordinary horse she never could have kept in Stewart's trail. It was dust and heat, a parching throat, that caused Madeline to think of time; and she was amazed to see the sun sloping to the west. Stewart never stopped; he never looked back; he never spoke. He must have heard the horse close behind him. Madeline remembered Monty's advice about drinking and eating as she rode along. The worst of that rough travel came at the bottom of the cañon. Dead cedars and brush and logs were easy to pass compared with the miles, it seemed, of loose boulders. The horses slipped and stumbled. Stewart proceeded here with exceeding care. At last, when the cañon opened into a level forest of firs, the sun was setting red in the west.

Stewart quickened the gait of his horse. After a mile or so of easy travel the ground again began to fall decidedly, sloping in numerous ridges, with draws between. Soon night shadowed the deeper gullies. Madeline was refreshed by the cooling of the air.

Stewart traveled slowly now. The barks of coyotes seemed to startle him. Often he stopped to listen. And during one of those intervals the silence was broken by sharp rifle-shots. Madeline could not tell whether they were near or far, to right or left, behind or before. Evidently, Stewart was both alarmed and baffled. He dismounted. He went cautiously forward to listen. Madeline fancied she heard a cry, low and far away. It was only that of a coyote, she convinced herself, yet it was so wailing, so human that she shuddered. Stewart came back. He slipped the bridles of both horses, and he led them. Every few paces he stopped to listen. He changed his direction several times, and the last time he got among rough, rocky ridges. The iron shoes of the horses cracked on the rocks. That sound must have penetrated far into the forest. It perturbed Stewart, for he searched for softer ground. Meanwhile the shadows merged into darkness. The stars shone. The wind rose. Madeline believed hours passed.

Stewart halted again. In the gloom Madeline discerned a log cabin, and beyond it pear-pointed dark trees piercing the sky-line. She could just make out Stewart's tall form as he leaned against his horse. Either he was listening or debating what to do—perhaps both. Presently he went inside the cabin. Madeline heard the scratching of a match; then she saw a faint light. The cabin appeared to be deserted. Probably it was one of the many habitations belonging to prospectors and foresters who lived in the mountains. Stewart came out again. He walked around the horses, out into the gloom, then back to Madeline. For a long moment he stood as still as a statue and listened. Then she heard him mutter: "If we have to start quick I can ride bareback." With that he took the saddle and blanket off his horse and carried them into the cabin.

"Get off," he said, in a low voice, as he stepped out of the door.

He helped her down and led her inside, where again he struck a match. Madeline caught a glimpse of a rude fireplace and rough-hewn logs. Stewart's blanket and saddle lay on the hard-packed earthen floor.

"Rest a little," he said. "I'm going into the woods a piece to listen. Gone only a minute or so."

Madeline had to feel round in the dark to locate the saddle and blanket. When she lay down it was with a grateful sense of ease and relief. As her body rested, however, her mind became the old thronging maze for sensation and thought. All day she had attended to the alert business of helping her horse. Now, what had already happened, the night, the silence, the proximity of Stewart and his strange, stern caution, the possible happenings to her friends—all claimed their due share of her feeling. She went over them all with lightning swiftness of thought. She believed, and she was sure Stewart believed, that her friends, owing to their quicker start down the mountain, had not been headed off in their travel by any of the things which had delayed Stewart. This conviction lifted the suddenly returning dread from her breast; and as for herself, somehow she had no fear. But she could not sleep; she did not try to.

Stewart's soft steps sounded outside. His dark form

loomed in the door. As he sat down Madeline heard the thump of a gun that he laid beside him on the sill; then the thump of another as he put that down, too. The sounds thrilled her. Stewart's wide shoulders filled the door; his finely shaped head and strong, stern profile showed clearly in outline against the sky; the wind waved his hair. He turned his ear to that wind and listened. Motionless he sat for what to her seemed hours.

Then the stirring memory of the day's adventure, the feeling of the beauty of the night, and a strange, deep-seated, sweetly vague consciousness of happiness portending, were all burned out in hot, pressing pain at the remembrance of Stewart's disgrace in her eyes. Something had changed within her so that what had been anger at herself was sorrow for him. He was such a splendid man. She could not feel the same; she knew her debt to him, yet she could not thank him, could not speak to him. She fought an unintelligible bitterness.

Then she rested with closed eyes, and time seemed neither short nor long. When Stewart called her she opened her eyes to see the gray of dawn. She rose and stepped outside. The horses whinnied. In a moment she was in the saddle, aware of cramped muscles and a weariness of limbs. Stewart led off at a sharp trot into the fir forest. They came to a trail into which he turned. The horses traveled steadily; the descent grew less steep; the firs thinned out; the gray gloom brightened.

When Madeline rode out of the firs the sun had arisen, and the foothills rolled beneath her; and at their edge, where the gray of valley began, she saw a dark patch that she knew was the ranch-house.

CHAPTER 20

THE SHERIFF OF EL CAJON

About the middle of the forenoon of that day Madeline reached the ranch. Her guests had all arrived there late the night before, and wanted only her presence and the assurance of her well-being to consider the last of the camping trip a rare adventure. Likewise, they voted it the cowboys' masterpiece of a trick. Madeline's delay, they averred, had been only a clever coup to give a final effect. She did not correct their impression, nor think it needful to state that she had been escorted home by only one cowboy.

Her guests reported an arduous ride down the mountain, with only one incident to lend excitement. On the descent they had fallen in with Sheriff Hawe and several of his deputies, who were considerably under the influence of drink and very greatly enraged by the escape of the Mexican girl Bonita. Hawe had used insulting language to the ladies and, according to Ambrose, would have inconvenienced the party on some pretext or other if he had not been sharply silenced by the cowboys.

Madeline's guests were two days in recovering from the hard ride. On the third day they leisurely began to prepare for departure. This period was doubly trying for Madeline. She had her own physical need of rest, and, moreover, had to face a mental conflict that could scarcely be postponed further. Her sister and friends were kindly and earnestly persistent in their entreaties that she go back East with them. She desired to go. It was not going that mattered; it was how and when and under what circumstances she was to return that roused in her disturbing emotion. Before she went East she wanted to have fixed in mind her future relation to the ranch and the West. When the crucial hour arrived she found that the West had not claimed her yet. These old friends had warmed cold ties.

It turned out, however, that there need be no hurry about making the decision. Madeline would have welcomed any excuse to procrastinate; but, as it happened, a letter from Alfred made her departure out of the question for the present. He wrote that his trip to California had been very profitable, that he had a proposition for Madeline from a large cattle company, and, particularly, that he wanted to marry Florence soon after his arrival home, and would bring a minister from Douglas for that purpose.

Madeline went so far, however, as to promise Helen and her friends that she would go East soon, at the very latest by Thanksgiving. With that promise they were reluctantly content to say good-by to the ranch and to her. At the last moment there seemed a great likelihood of a hitch in plans for the first stage of that homeward journey. All of

Madeline's guests held up their hands, Western fashion, when Link Stevens appeared with the big white car. Link protested innocently, solemnly, that he would drive slowly and safely; but it was necessary for Madeline to guarantee Link's word and to accompany them before they would enter the car. At the station good-bys were spoken and repeated, and Madeline's promise was exacted for the hundredth time.

Dorothy Coombs's last words were: "Give my love to Monty Price. Tell him I'm—I'm *glad* he kissed me!"

Helen's eyes had a sweet, grave, yet mocking light as she said:

"Majesty, bring Stewart with you when you come. He'll be the rage."

Madeline treated the remark with the same merry lightness with which it was received by the others; but after the train had pulled out and she was on her way home she remembered Helen's words and looks with something almost amounting to a shock. Any mention of Stewart, any thought of him displeased her.

"What did Helen mean?" mused Madeline. And she pondered. That mocking light in Helen's eyes had been simply an ironical glint, a cynical gleam from that worldly experience so suspicious and tolerant in its wisdom. The sweet gravity of Helen's look had been a deeper and more subtle thing. Madeline wanted to understand it, to divine in it a new relation between Helen and herself, something fine and sisterly that might lead to love. The thought, however, revolving around a strange suggestion of Stewart, was poisoned at its inception, and she dismissed it.

Upon the drive in to the ranch, as she was passing the lower lake, she saw Stewart walking listlessly along the shore. When he became aware of the approach of the car he suddenly awakened from his aimless sauntering and disappeared quickly in the shade of the shrubbery. This was not by any means the first time Madeline had seen him avoid a possible meeting with her. Somehow the act had pained her, though affording her a relief. She did not want to meet him face to face.

It was annoying for her to guess that Stillwell had something to say in Stewart's defense. The old cattleman was evidently distressed. Several times he had tried to open a conversation with Madeline relating to Stewart; she had evaded him until the last time, when his persistence had brought a cold and final refusal to hear another word about the foreman. Stillwell had been crushed.

As days passed Stewart remained at the ranch without his old faithfulness to his work. Madeline was not moved to a kinder frame of mind to see him wandering dejectedly around. It hurt her, and because it hurt her she grew all the harder. Then she could not help hearing snatches of conversation which strengthened her suspicions that Stewart was losing his grip on himself, that he would soon take the downward course again. Verification of her own suspicion made it a belief, and belief brought about a sharp conflict between her generosity and some feeling that she could not name. It was not a question of justice or mercy or sympathy. If a single word could have saved Stewart from sinking his splendid manhood into the brute she had recoiled from at Chiricahua, she would not have spoken it. She could not restore him to his former place in her regard; she really did not want him at the ranch at all. Once, considering in wonder her knowledge of men, she interrogated herself to see just why she could not overlook Stewart's transgression. She never wanted to speak to him again, or see him, or think of him. In some way, through her interest in Stewart, she had come to feel for herself an inexplicable thing close to scorn.

A telegram from Douglas, heralding the coming of Alfred and a minister, put an end to Madeline's brooding; and she shared something of Florence Kingsley's excitement. The cowboys were as eager and gossipy as girls. It was arranged to have the wedding ceremony performed in Madeline's great hall-chamber, and the dinner in the cool, flower-scented patio.

Alfred and his minister arrived at the ranch in the big white car. They appeared considerably wind-blown. In fact, the minister was breathless, almost sightless, and certainly hatless. Alfred, used as he was to wind and speed, remarked that he did not wonder at Nels's aversion to riding a fleeting cannon-ball. The imperturbable Link took off his cap and goggles and, consulting his watch, made his usual apologetic report to Madeline, deploring the fact that a teamster and a few stray cattle on the road had held him down to the *mañana* time of only a mile a minute.

Arrangements for the wedding brought Alfred's delighted approval. When he had learned all Florence and Madeline would tell him he expressed a desire to have the cowboys attend; and then he went on to talk about California, where he was going to take Florence on a short trip. He was curiously interested to find out all about Madeline's guests and what had happened to them. His keen glance at Madeline grew softer as she talked.

"I breathe again," he said, and laughed. "I was afraid. Well, I must have missed some sport. I can just fancy what Monty and Nels did to that Englishman. So you went up to the crags. That's a wild place. I'm not surprised at guerrillas falling in with you up there. The crags were a famous rendezvous for Apaches—it's near the border—almost inaccessible—good water and grass. I wonder what the U. S. cavalry would think if they knew these guerrillas crossed the border right under their noses. Well, it's practically impossible to patrol some of that border line. It's desert, mountain, and cañon, exceedingly wild and broken. I'm sorry to say that there seems to be more trouble in sight with these guerrillas than at any time heretofore. Orozco, the rebel leader, has failed to withstand Madero's army. The Federals are occupying Chihuahua now, and are driving the rebels north. Orozco has broken up his army into guerrilla bands. They are moving north and west, intending to carry on guerrilla warfare in Sonora. I can't say just how this will affect us here. But we're too close to the border for comfort. These guerrillas are nightriding hawks; they can cross the border, raid us here, and get back the same night. Fighting, I imagine, will not be restricted to northern Mexico. With the revolution a failure the guerrillas will be more numerous, bolder, and hungrier. Unfortunately we happen to be favorably situated for them down here in this wilderness corner of the state."

On the following day Alfred and Florence were married. Florence's sister and several friends from El Cajon were present, besides Madeline, Stillwell, and his men. It was Alfred's express wish that Stewart attend the ceremony. Madeline was amused when she noticed the painfully suppressed excitement of the cowboys. For them a wedding must have been an unusual and impressive event. She began to have a better understanding of the nature of it when they cast off restraint and pressed forward to kiss the bride. In all her life Madeline had never seen a bride kissed so much and so heartily, nor one so flushed and disheveled and happy. This indeed was a joyful occasion. There was nothing of the "effete East" about Alfred Hammond; he might have been a Westerner all his days. When Madeline managed to get through the press of cowboys to offer her congratulations Alfred gave her a bear hug and a kiss. This appeared to fascinate the cowboys. With shining eyes and faces aglow, with smiling, boyish boldness, they made a rush at Madeline. For one instant her heart leaped to her throat. They looked as if they could most shamelessly kiss and maul her. That little, ugly-faced, soft-eyed, rude, tender-hearted ruffian, Monty Price, was in the lead. He resembled a dragon actuated by sentiment. All at once Madeline's instinctive antagonism to being touched by strange hands or lips battled with a real, warm, and fun-loving desire to let the cowboys work their will with her. But she saw Stewart hanging at the back of the crowd, and something—some fierce, dark expression of pain amazed her, while it froze her desire to be kind. Then she did not know what change must have come to her face and bearing; but she saw Monty fall back sheepishly and the other cowboys draw aside to let her lead the way into the patio.

The dinner began quietly enough with the cowboys divided between embarrassment and voracious appetites that they evidently feared to indulge. Wine, however, loosened their tongues, and when Stillwell got up to make the speech everybody seemed to expect of him, they greeted him with a roar.

Stillwell was now one huge, mountainous smile. He was so happy that he appeared on the verge of tears. He rambled on ecstatically till he came to raise his glass.

"An' now, girls an' boys, let's all drink to the bride an' groom; to their sincere an' lastin' love; to their happiness an' prosperity; to their good health an' long life. Let's drink to the unitin' of the East with the West. No man full of red blood an' the real breath of life could resist a Western girl an' a good hoss an' God's free hand—that open country out there. So we claim Al Hammond, an' may we be true to him. An', friends, I think it fittin' that we drink to his sister an' to our hopes. Heah's to the lady we hope to make *our* Majesty! Heah's to the man who'll come ridin' out of the West, a fine, big-hearted man with a fast hoss an' a strong rope, an' may he win an' hold her! Come, friends, drink."

A heavy pound of horses' hoofs and a yell outside arrested Stillwell's voice and halted his hand in midair.

The patio became as silent as an unoccupied room.

Through the open doors and windows of Madeline's chamber burst the sounds of horses stamping to a halt, then harsh speech of men, and a low cry of a woman in pain.

Rapid steps crossed the porch, entered Madeline's room. Nels appeared in the doorway. Madeline was surprised to see that he had not been at the dinner-table. She was disturbed at sight of his face.

"Stewart, you're wanted outdoors," called Nels, bluntly. "Monty, you slope out here with me. You, Nick, an' Stillwell—I reckon the rest of you hed better shut the doors an' stay inside."

Nels disappeared. Quick as a cat Monty glided out. Madeline heard his soft, swift steps pass from her room into her office. He had left his guns there. Madeline trembled. She saw Stewart get up quietly and, without any change of expression on his dark, sad face, leave the patio. Nick Steele followed him. Stillwell dropped his wineglass. As it broke, shivering the silence, his huge smile vanished. His face set into the old cragginess, and the red slowly thickened into black. Stillwell went out and closed the door behind him.

Then there was a blank silence. The enjoyment of the moment had been rudely disrupted. Madeline glanced down the lines of brown faces to see the pleasure fade into the old familiar hardness.

"What's wrong?" asked Alfred, rather stupidly. The change of mood had been too rapid for him. Suddenly he awakened, thoroughly aroused at the interruption. "I'm going to see who's butted in here to spoil our dinner," he said, and strode out.

He returned before any one at the table had spoken or moved, and now the dull red of anger mottled his forehead.

"It's the sheriff of El Cajon!" he exclaimed, contemptuously. "Pat Hawe with some of his tough deputies come to arrest Gene Stewart. They've got that poor little Mexican girl out there tied on a horse. Confound that sheriff!"

Madeline calmly rose from the table, eluding Florence's entreating hand, and started for the door. The cowboys jumped up. Alfred barred her progress.

"Alfred, I am going out," she said.

"No, I guess not," he replied. "That's no place for you."

"I am going." She looked straight at him.

"Madeline! Why, what is it? You look— Dear, there's pretty sure to be trouble outside. Maybe there'll be a fight. You can do nothing. You must not go."

"Perhaps I can prevent trouble," she replied.

As she left the patio she was aware that Alfred, with Florence at his side and the cowboys behind, were starting to follow her. When she got out of her room upon the porch she heard several men in loud, angry discussion. Then, at sight of Bonita helplessly and cruelly bound upon a horse, pale and disheveled and suffering, Madeline experienced the thrill that sight or mention of this girl always gave her. It yielded to a hot pang in her breast—that live pain which so shamed her. But almost instantly, as a second glance showed an agony in Bonita's face, her bruised arms where the rope bit deep into the flesh, her little brown hands stained with blood, Madeline was overcome by pity for the unfortunate girl and a woman's righteous passion at such barbarous treatment of one of her own sex.

The man holding the bridle of the horse on which Bonita had been bound was at once recognized by Madeline as the big-bodied, bullet-headed guerrilla who had found the basket of wine in the spring at camp. Redder of face, blacker of beard, coarser of aspect, evidently under the influence of liquor, he was as fierce-looking as a gorilla and as repulsive. Besides him there were three other men present, all mounted on weary horses. The one in the foreground, gaunt, sharp-featured, red-eyed, with a pointed beard, she recognized as the sheriff of El Cajon.

Madeline hesitated, then stopped in the middle of the porch. Alfred, Florence, and several others followed her out; the rest of the cowboys and guests crowded the windows and doors. Stillwell saw Madeline, and, throwing up his hands, roared to be heard. This quieted the gesticulating, quarreling men.

"Wal now, Pat Hawe, what's drivin' you like a locoed steer on the rampage?" demanded Stillwell.

"Keep in the traces, Bill," replied Hawe. "You savvy what I come fer. I've been bidin' my time. But I'm ready now. I'm hyar to arrest a criminal."

The huge frame of the old cattleman jerked as if he had been stabbed. His face turned purple.

"What criminal?" he shouted, hoarsely.

The sheriff flicked his quirt against his dirty boot, and he twisted his thin lips into a leer. The situation was agreeable to him.

"Why, Bill, I knowed you hed a no-good outfit ridin' this range; but I wasn't wise thet you hed more'n one criminal."

"Cut that talk! Which cowboy are you wantin' to arrest?"

Hawe's manner altered.

"Gene Stewart," he replied, curtly.

"On what charge?"

"Fer killin' a Greaser one night last fall."

"So you're still harpin' on that? Pat, you're on the wrong trail. You can't lay that killin' onto Stewart. The thing's ancient by now. But if you insist on bringin' him to court let the arrest go to-day—we're hevin' some *fiesta* hyar—an' I'll fetch Gene in to El Cajon."

"Nope. I reckon I'll take him when I got the chance, before he slopes."

"I'm givin' you my word," thundered Stillwell.

"I reckon I don't hev to take your word, Bill, or anybody else's."

Stillwell's great bulk quivered with his rage, yet he made a successful effort to control it.

"See hyar, Pat Hawe, I know what's reasonable. Law is law. But in this country there always has been an' is now a safe an' sane way to proceed with the law. Mebbe you've forgot that. The law as invested in one man in a wild country is liable, owin' to that man's weaknesses an' onlimited authority, to be disputed even by a decent ole cattleman like myself. I'm a-goin' to give you a hunch. Pat, you're not overliked in these parts. You've rid too much with a high hand. Some of your deals hev been shady, an' don't you overlook what I'm sayin'. But you're the sheriff, an' I'm respectin' your office. I'm respectin' it this much. If the milk of human decency is so soured in your breast that you can't hev a kind feelin', then try to avoid the onpleasantness that'll result from any contrary move on your part to-day. Do you get that hunch?"

"Stillwell, you're threatenin' an officer," replied Hawe, angrily.

"Will you hit the trail quick out of hyar?" queried Stillwell, in strained voice. "I guarantee Stewart's appearance in El Cajon any day you say."

"No. I come to arrest him, an' I'm goin' to."

"So that's your game!" shouted Stillwell. "We-all are glad to get you straight, Pat. Now listen, you cheap, red-eyed coyote of a sheriff! You don't care how many enemies you make. You know you'll never get office again in this county. What do you care now? It's amazin' strange how earnest you are to hunt down the man who killed that particular Greaser. I reckon there's been some dozen or more killin's of Greasers in the last year. Why don't you take to trailin' some of them killin's? I'll tell you why. You're afraid to go near the border. An' your hate of Gene Stewart makes you want to hound him an' put him where he's never been yet—in jail. You want to spite his friends. Wal, listen, you lean-jawed, skunk-bitten coyote! Go ahead an' try to arrest him!"

Stillwell took one mighty stride off the porch. His last words had been cold. His rage appeared to have been transferred to Hawe. The sheriff had begun to stutter and shake a lanky red hand at the cattleman when Stewart stepped out.

"Here, you fellows, give me a chance to say a word."

As Stewart appeared the Mexican girl suddenly seemed vitalized out of her stupor. She strained at her bonds, as if to lift her hands beseechingly. A flush animated her haggard face, and her big dark eyes lighted.

"Señor Gene!" she moaned. "Help me! I so seek. They beat me, rope me, mos' keel me. Oh, help me, Señor Gene!"

"Shut up, er I'll gag you," said the man who held Bonita's horse.

"Muzzle her, Sneed, if she blabs again," called Hawe.

Madeline felt something tense and strained working in the short silence. Was it only a phase of her thrilling excitement? Her swift glançe showed the faces of Nels and Monty and Nick to be brooding, cold, watchful. She wondered why Stewart did not look toward Bonita. He, too, was now dark-faced, cool, quiet, with something ominous about him.

"Hawe, I'll submit to arrest without any fuss," he said, slowly, "if you'll take the ropes off that girl."

"Nope," replied the sheriff. "She got away from me onct. She's hawg-tied now, an' she'll stay hawg-tied."

Madeline thought she saw Stewart give a slight start. But an unaccountable dimness came over her eyes, at brief intervals obscuring her keen sight. Vaguely she was conscious of a clogged and beating tumult in her breast.

"All right, let's hurry out of here," said Stewart. "You've made annoyance enough. Ride down to the corral with me. I'll get my horse and go with you."

"Hold on!" yelled Hawe, as Stewart turned away. "Not so fast. Who's doin' this? You don't come no El Capitan stunts on me. You'll ride one of my pack-horses, an' you'll go in irons."

"You want to handcuff me?" queried Stewart, with sudden swift start of passion.

"Want to? Haw, haw! Nope, Stewart, thet's jest my way with hoss-thieves, raiders, Greasers, murderers, an' sich. See hyar, you Sneed, git off an' put the irons on this man."

The guerrilla called Sneed slid off his horse and began to fumble in his saddle-bags.

"You see, Bill," went on Hawe, "I swore in a new depooty fer this particular job. Sneed is some handy. He rounded up thet little Mexican cat fer me."

Stillwell did not hear the sheriff; he was gazing at Stewart in a kind of imploring amaze.

"Gene, you ain't goin' to stand fer them handcuffs?" he pleaded.

"Yes," replied the cowboy. "Bill, old friend, I'm an outsider here. There's no call for Miss Hammond and—and her brother and Florence to be worried further about me. Their happy day has already been spoiled on my account. I want to get out quick."

"Wal, you might be too damn considerate of Miss Hammond's sensitive feelin's." There was now no trace of the courteous, kindly old rancher. He looked harder than stone. "How about my feelin's? I want to know if you're goin' to let this sneakin' coyote, this last gasp of the old rum-guzzlin' frontier sheriffs put you in irons an' hawg-tie you an' drive you off to jail?"

"Yes," replied Stewart, steadily.

"Wal, by Gawd! *You, Gene Stewart!* What's come over you? Why, man, go in the house, an' I'll tend to this feller. Then to-morrow you can ride in an' give yourself up like a gentleman."

"No. I'll go. Thanks, Bill, for the way you and the

boys would stick to me. Hurry, Hawe, before my mind *changes*."

His voice broke at the last, betraying the wonderful control he had kept over his passions. As he ceased speaking he seemed suddenly to become spiritless. He dropped his head.

Madeline saw in him then a semblance to the hopeless, shamed Stewart of earlier days. The vague riot in her breast leaped into conscious fury—a woman's passionate repudiation of Stewart's broken spirit. It was not that she would have him be a law-breaker; it was that she could not bear to see him deny his manhood. Once she had entreated him to become her kind of a cowboy—a man in whom reason tempered passion. She had let him see how painful and shocking any violence was to her. And the idea had obsessed him, softened him, had grown like a stultifying lichen upon his will, had shorn him of a wild, bold spirit she now strangely longed to see him feel. When the man Sneed came forward, jingling the iron fetters, Madeline's blood turned to fire. She would have forgiven Stewart then for lapsing into the kind of cowboy it had been her blind and sickly sentiment to abhor. This was a man's West—a man's game. What right had a woman reared in a softer mold to use her beauty and her influence to change a man who was bold and free and strong? At that moment, with her blood hot and racing, she would have gloried in the violence which she had so deplored; she would have welcomed the action that had characterized Stewart's treatment of Don Carlos; she had in her the sudden dawning temper of a woman who had been assimilating the life and nature around her, and who would not have turned her eyes away from a harsh and bloody deed.

But Stewart held forth his hands to be manacled. Then Madeline heard her own voice burst out in a ringing imperious, *"Wait!"*

In the time it took her to make the few steps to the edge of the porch, facing the men, she not only felt her anger and justice and pride summoning forces to her command, but there was something else calling—a deep, passionate, mysterious thing not born of the moment.

Sneed dropped the manacles. Stewart's face took on a chalky whiteness. Hawe, in a slow, stupid embarrassment beyond his control, removed his sombrero in a respect that seemed wrenched from him.

"Mr. Hawe, I can prove to you that Stewart was not concerned in any way whatever with the crime for which you want to arrest him."

The sheriff's stare underwent a blinking change. He coughed, stammered, and tried to speak. Manifestly, he had been thrown completely off his balance. Astonishment slowly merged into discomfiture.

"It was absolutely impossible for Stewart to have been connected with that assault," went on Madeline, swiftly, "for he was with me in the waiting-room of the station at the moment the assault was made outside. I assure you I have a distinct and vivid recollection. The door was open. I heard the voices of quarreling men. They grew louder. The language was Spanish. Evidently, these men had left the dance-hall opposite and were approaching the station. I heard a woman's voice mingling with the others. It, too, was Spanish, and I could not understand. But the tone was beseeching. Then I heard footsteps on the gravel. I knew Stewart heard them. I could see from his face that something dreadful was about to happen. Just outside the door then there were hoarse, furious voices, a scuffle, a muffled shot, a woman's cry, the thud of a falling body, and rapid footsteps of a man running away. Next, the girl Bonita staggered into the door. She was white, trembling, terror-stricken. She recognized Stewart, appealed to him. Stewart supported her and endeavored to calm her. He was excited. He asked her if Danny Mains had been shot, or if he had done the shooting. The girl said no. She told Stewart that she had danced a little, flirted a little with *vaqueros*, and they had quarreled over her. Then Stewart took her outside and put her upon his horse. I saw the girl ride that horse down the street to disappear in the darkness."

While Madeline spoke another change appeared to be working in the man Hawe. He was not long disconcerted, but his discomfiture wore to a sullen fury, and his sharp features fixed in an expression of craft.

"Thet's mighty interestin', Miss Hammond, most as interestin' as a story book," he said. "Now, since you're so obligin' a witness, I'd sure like to put a question or two. What time did you arrive at El Cajon thet night?"

"It was after eleven o'clock," replied Madeline.

"Nobody there to meet you?"

"No."

"The station agent an' operator both gone?"

"Yes."

"Wal, how soon did this feller Stewart show up?" Hawe continued, with a wry smile.

"Very soon after my arrival. I think—perhaps fifteen minutes, possibly a little more."

"Some dark an' lonesome around thet station, wasn't it?"

"Indeed yes."

"An' what time was the Greaser shot?" queried Hawe, with his little eyes gleaming like coals.

"Probably close to half past one. It was two o'clock when I looked at my watch at Florence Kingsley's house. Directly after Stewart sent Bonita away he took me to Miss Kingsley's. So, allowing for the walk and a few minutes' conversation with her, I can pretty definitely say the shooting took place at about half past one."

Stillwell heaved his big frame a step closer to the sheriff.

"What're you drivin' at?" he roared, his face black again.

"Evidence," snapped Hawe.

Madeline marveled at this interruption; and as Stewart irresistibly drew her glance she saw him gray-faced as ashes, shaking, utterly unnerved.

"I thank you, Miss Hammond," he said, huskily. "But you needn't answer any more of Hawe's questions. He's—he's—it's not necessary. I'll go with him now, under arrest. Bonita will corroborate your testimony in court, and that will save me from this—this man's spite."

Madeline, looking at Stewart, seeing a humility she at first took for cowardice, suddenly divined that it was not fear for himself which made him dread further disclosures of that night, but fear for her—fear of shame she might suffer through him.

Pat Hawe cocked his head to one side, like a vulture about to strike with his beak, and cunningly eyed Madeline.

"Considered as testimony, what you've said is sure important an' conclusive. But I'm calculatin' thet the court will want to hev explained *why* you stayed from eleven-thirty till one-thirty in thet waitin'-room alone with Stewart."

His deliberate speech met with what Madeline imagined a remarkable reception from Stewart, who gave a tigerish start; from Stillwell, whose big hands tore at the neck of his shirt, as if he was choking; from Alfred, who now strode hotly forward to be stopped by the cold and silent Nels; from Monty Price, who uttered a violent. "*Aw!*" which was both a hiss and a roar.

In the rush of her thought Madeline could not interpret the meaning of these things which seemed so strange at that moment. But they were portentous. Even as she was forming a reply to Hawe's speech she felt a chill creep over her.

"Stewart detained me in the waiting-room," she said, clear-voiced as a bell. "But we were not alone—all the time."

For a moment the only sound following her words was a gasp from Stewart. Hawe's face became transformed with a hideous amaze and joy.

"Detained?" he whispered, craning his lean and corded neck. "How's thet?"

"Stewart was drunk. He—"

With sudden, passionate gesture of despair Stewart appealed to her:

"Oh, Miss Hammond, don't! *don't!* DON'T! . . ."

Then he seemed to sink down, head lowered upon his breast, in utter shame. Stillwell's great hand swept to the bowed shoulder, and he turned to Madeline.

"Miss Majesty, I reckon you'd be wise to tell all," said the old cattleman, gravely. "There ain't one of us who *could* misunderstand any motive or act of yours. Mebbe a stroke of lightnin' might clear this murky air. Whatever Gene Stewart did that onlucky night—you tell it."

Madeline's dignity and self-possession had been disturbed by Stewart's importunity. She broke into swift, disconnected speech:

"He came into the station—a few minutes after I got there. I asked—to be shown to a hotel. He said there wasn't any that would accommodate married women. He grasped my hand—looked for a wedding ring. Then I saw he was—he was intoxicated. He told me he would go for a hotel porter. But he came back with a padre—Padre Marcos. The poor priest was—terribly frightened. So was I. Stewart had turned into a devil. He fired his gun at the padre's feet. He pushed me into a bench. Again he shot—right before my face. I—I nearly fainted. But I heard him cursing the padre—heard the padre praying or chanting—I didn't know what. Stewart tried to make me say things in Spanish. All at once he asked my name. I told him. He jerked at my veil. I took it off. Then he threw his gun down—pushed the padre out of the door. That was just before the *vaqueros* approached with Bonita. Padre Marcos must have seen them—must have heard them. After that Stewart grew quickly sober. He was mortified— distressed—stricken with shame. He told me he had been drinking at a wedding—I remember, it was Ed Linton's wedding. Then he explained—the boys were always gambling—he wagered he would marry the first girl who arrived at El Cajon. I happened to be the first one. He tried to force me to marry him. The rest—relating to the assault on the *vaquero*—I have already told you."

Madeline ended, out of breath and panting, with her hands pressed upon her heaving bosom. Revelation of that secret liberated emotion; those hurried outspoken words had made her throb and tremble and burn. Strangely then she thought of Alfred and his wrath. But he stood motionless, as if dazed. Stillwell was trying to bolster up the crushed Stewart.

Hawe rolled his red eyes and threw back his head.

"Ho, ho, ho! Ho, ho, ho! Say, Sneed, you didn't miss any of it, did ye? Haw, haw! Best I ever heerd in all my born days. Ho, ho!"

Then he ceased laughing, and with glinting gaze upon Madeline, insolent and vicious and savage, he began to drawl:

"Wal now, my lady, I reckon your story, if it tallies with Bonita's an' Padre Marcos's, will clear Gene Stewart in the eyes of the court." Here he grew slower, more biting, sharper and harder of face. "But you needn't expect Pat Hawe or the court to swaller thet part of your story— *about bein' detained unwillin'!*"

Madeline had not time to grasp the sense of his last words. Stewart had convulsively sprung upward, white as chalk. As he leaped at Hawe Stillwell interposed his huge bulk and wrapped his arms around Stewart. There was a brief, whirling, wrestling struggle. Stewart appeared to be besting the old cattleman.

"Help, boys, help!" yelled Stillwell. "I can't hold him. Hurry, or there's goin' to be blood spilled!"

Nick Steele and several cowboys leaped to Stillwell's assistance. Stewart, getting free, tossed one aside and then another. They closed in on him. For an instant a furious straining wrestle of powerful bodies made rasp and shock and blow. Once Stewart heaved them from him. But they plunged back upon him—conquered him.

"Gene! Why, Gene!" panted the old cattleman. "Sure you're locoed—to act this way. Cool down! Cool down! Why, boy, it's all right. Jest stand still—give us a chance to talk to you. It's only ole Bill, you know—your ole pal who's tried to be a daddy to you. He's only wantin' you to hev sense—to be cool—to wait."

"Let me go! Let me go!" cried Stewart; and the poignancy of that cry pierced Madeline's heart. "Let me go, Bill, if you're my friend. I saved your life once—over in the desert. You swore you'd never forget. Boys, make him let me go! Oh, I don't care what Hawe's said or done to me! It was that about *her!* Are you all a lot of Greasers? How can you stand it? Damn you for a lot of cowards! There's a limit, I tell you." Then his voice broke, fell to a whisper. "Bill, dear old Bill, let me go. *I'll kill him! You know I'll kill him!*"

"Gene, I know you'd kill him if you hed an even break," replied Stillwell, soothingly. "But, Gene, why you ain't even packin' a gun! An' there's Pat lookin' nasty, with his hand nervous-like. He seen you hed no gun. He'd jump at the chance to plug you now, an' then holler about opposition to the law. Cool down, son; it'll all come right."

Suddenly Madeline was transfixed by a terrible sound. Her startled glance shifted from the anxious group round Stewart to see that Monty Price had leaped off the porch. He crouched down with his hands below his hips, where the big guns swung. From his distorted lips issued that sound which was combined roar and bellow and Indian war-whoop, and, more than all, a horrible warning cry. He resembled a hunchback about to make the leap of a demon. He was quivering, vibrating. His eyes, black and hot, were fastened with most piercing intentness upon Hawe and Sneed.

"Git back, Bill, git back!" he roared. "Git 'em back!"

With one lunge Stillwell shoved Stewart and Nick and the other cowboys up on the porch. Then he crowded Madeline and Alfred and Florence to the wall, tried to force them farther. His motions were rapid and stern. But failing to get them through door and windows, he planted his wide person between the women and danger. Madeline grasped his arm, held on, and peered fearfully from behind his broad shoulder.

"You, Hawe! You, Sneed!" called Monty, in that same wild voice. "Don't you move a finger er an eyelash!"

Madeline's faculties nerved to keen, thrilling divination. She grasped the relation between Monty's terrible cry and the strange hunched posture he had assumed. Stillwell's haste and silence, too, were pregnant of catastrophe.

"Nels, git in this!" yelled Monty; and all the time he never shifted his intent gaze as much as a hair's breadth from Hawe and his deputy. "Nels, chase away them two fellers hangin' back there. Chase 'em, quick!"

These men, the two deputies who had remained in the background with the pack-horses, did not wait for Nels. They spurred their mounts, wheeled, and galloped away.

"Now, Nels, cut the gurl loose," ordered Monty.

Nels ran forward, jerked the halter out of Sneed's hand, and pulled Bonita's horse in close to the porch. As he slit the rope which bound her she fell into his arms.

"Hawe, git down!" went on Monty. "Face front an' stiff!"

The sheriff swung his leg, and, never moving his hands, with his face now a deathly, sickening white, he slid to the ground.

"Line up there beside your gerrilla pard. There! You two make a damn fine pictoor, a damn fine team of pizened coyote an' a cross between a wild mule an' a Greaser. Now listen!"

Monty made a long pause, in which his breathing was plainly audible.

Madeline's eyes were riveted upon Monty. Her mind,

swift as lightning, had gathered the subtleties in action and word succeeding his domination of the men. Violence, terrible violence, the thing she had felt, the thing she had feared, the thing she had sought to eliminate from among her cowboys, was, after many months, about to be enacted before her eyes. It had come at last. She had softened Stillwell, she had influenced Nels, she had changed Stewart; but this little black-faced, terrible Monty Price now rose, as it were, out of his past wild years, and no power on earth or in heaven could stay his hand. It was the hard life of wild men in a wild country that was about to strike this blow at her. She did not shudder; she did not wish to blot out from sight this little man, terrible in his mood of wild justice. She suffered a flash of horror that Monty, blind and dead to her authority, cold as steel toward her presence, understood the deeps of a woman's soul. For in this moment of strife, of insult to her, of torture to the man she had uplifted and then broken, the passion of her reached deep toward primitive hate. With eyes slowly hazing red, she watched Monty Price; she listened with thrumming ears; she waited, slowly sagging against Stillwell.

"Hawe, if you an' your dirty pard hev loved the sound of human voice, then listen an' listen hard," said Monty. "Fer I've been goin' contrary to my ole style jest to hev a talk with you. You all but got away on your nerve, didn't you? 'Cause why? You roll in here like a mad steer an' flash yer badge an' talk mean, then almost bluff away with it. You heerd all about Miss Hammond's cowboy outfit stoppin' drinkin' an' cussin' an' packin' guns. They've took on religion an' decent livin', an' sure they'll be easy to hobble an' drive to jail. Hawe, listen. There was a good an' noble an' be-ootiful woman come out of the East somewheres, an' she brought a lot of sunshine an' happiness an' new idees into the tough lives of cowboys. I reckon it's beyond you to know what she come to mean to them. Wal, I'll tell you. They-all went clean out of their heads. They-all got soft an' easy an' sweet-tempered. They got so they couldn't kill a coyote, a crippled calf in a mud-hole. They took to books, an' writin' home to mother an' sister, an' to savin' money, an' to gittin' married. Onct they was only a lot of poor cowboys, an' then sudden-like they was human bein's, livin' in a big world thet hed somethin' sweet even fer them. Even fer me— an ole, worn-out, hobble-legged, burned-up cowman like me! Do you git thet? An' you, Mister Hawe, you come along, not satisfied with ropin' an' beatin', an' Gawd knows what else, of thet friendless little Bonita; you come along an' face the lady we fellers honor an' love an' reverence, an' you—you— *Hell's fire!*"

With whistling breath, foaming at the mouth, Monty Price crouched lower, hands at his hips, and he edged inch by inch farther out from the porch, closer to Hawe and Sneed. Madeline saw them only in the blurred fringe of her sight. They resembled specters. She heard the shrill whistle of a horse and recognized Majesty calling her from the corral.

"Thet's all!" roared Monty, in a voice now strangling. Lower and lower he bent, a terrible figure of ferocity. "Now, both you armed ocifers of the law, come on! Flash your guns! Throw 'em, an' be quick! Monty Price is done! There'll be daylight through you both before you fan a hammer! But I'm givin' you a chanst to sting me. You holler law, an' my way is the ole law."

His breath came quicker, his voice grew hoarser, and

he crouched lower. All his body except his rigid arms quivered with a wonderful muscular convulsion.

"Dogs! Skunks! Buzzards! Flash them guns, er I'll flash mine! *Aha!*"

To Madeline it seemed the three stiff, crouching men leaped into instant and united action. She saw streaks of fire—streaks of smoke. Then a crashing volley deafened her. It ceased as quickly. Smoke veiled the scene. Slowly it drifted away to disclose three fallen men, one of whom, Monty, leaned on his left hand, a smoking gun in his right. He watched for a movement from the other two. It did not come. Then, with a terrible smile, he slid back and stretched out.

CHAPTER 21

UNBRIDLED

In waking and sleeping hours Madeline Hammond could not release herself from the thralling memory of that tragedy. She was haunted by Monty Price's terrible smile. Only in action of some kind could she escape; and to that end she worked, she walked and rode. She even overcame a strong feeling, which she feared was unreasonable disgust, for the Mexican girl Bonita, who lay ill at the ranch, bruised and feverish, in need of skilful nursing.

Madeline felt there was something inscrutable changing her soul. That strife—the struggle to decide her destiny for East or West—held still further aloof. She was never spiritually alone. There was a step on her trail. Indoors she was oppressed. She required the open—the light and wind, the sight of endless slope, the sounds of corral and pond and field, physical things, natural things.

One afternoon she rode down to the alfalfa fields, round

them, and back up to the spillway of the lower lake, where a group of mesquite-trees, owing to the water that seeped through the sand to their roots, had taken on bloom and beauty of renewed life. Under these trees there was shade enough to make a pleasant place to linger. Madeline dismounted, desiring to rest a little. She liked this quiet, lonely spot. It was really the only secluded nook near the house. If she rode down into the valley or out to the mesa or up on the foothills she could not go alone. Probably now Stillwell or Nels knew her whereabouts. But as she was comparatively hidden here, she imagined a solitude that was not actually hers.

Her horse, Majesty, tossed his head and flung his mane and switched his tail at the flies. He would rather have been cutting the wind down the valley slope. Madeline sat with her back against a tree, and took off her sombrero. The soft breeze, fanning her hot face, blowing strands of her hair, was refreshingly cool. She heard the slow tramp of cattle going in to drink. That sound ceased, and the grove of mesquites appeared to be lifeless, except for her and her horse. It was, however, only after moments of attention that she found the place was far from being dead. Keen eyes and ears brought reward. Desert quail, as gray as the bare earth, were dusting themselves in a shady spot. A bee, swift as light, hummed by. She saw a horned toad, the color of stone, squatting low, hiding fearfully in the sand within reach of her whip. She extended the point of the whip, and the toad quivered and swelled and hissed. It was instinct with fight. The wind faintly stirred the thin foliage of the mesquites, making a mournful sigh. From far up in the foothills, barely distinguishable, came the scream of an eagle. The bray of a burro brought a brief, discordant break. Then a brown bird darted down from an unseen perch and made a swift, irregular flight after a fluttering winged insect. Madeline heard the sharp snapping of a merciless beak. Indeed, there was more than life in the shade of the mesquites.

Suddenly Majesty picked up his long ears and snorted. Then Madeline heard a slow pad of hoofs. A horse was approaching from the direction of the lake. Madeline had learned to be wary, and, mounting Majesty, she turned him toward the open. A moment later she felt glad of her caution, for, looking back between the trees, she saw Stewart leading a horse into the grove. She would as lief have met a guerrilla as this cowboy.

Majesty had broken into a trot when a shrill whistle rent the air. The horse leaped and, wheeling so swiftly that he nearly unseated Madeline, he charged back straight for the mesquites. Madeline spoke to him, cried angrily at him, pulled with all her strength upon the bridle, but was helplessly unable to stop him. He whistled a piercing blast. Madeline realized then that Stewart, his old master, had called him and that nothing could turn him. She gave up trying, and attended to the urgent need of intercepting mesquite boughs that Majesty thrashed into motion. The horse thumped into an aisle between the trees and, stopping before Stewart, whinnied eagerly.

Madeline, not knowing what to expect, had not time for any feeling but amaze. A quick glance showed her Stewart in rough garb, dressed for the trail, and leading a wiry horse, saddled and packed. When Stewart, without looking at her, put his arm around Majesty's neck and laid his face against the flowing mane Madeline's heart suddenly began to beat with unwonted quickness. Stewart seemed oblivious to her presence. His eyes were closed. His dark face softened, lost its hardness and fierceness and sadness, and for an instant became beautiful.

Madeline instantly divined what his action meant. He was leaving the ranch; this was his good-by to his horse. How strange, sad, fine was this love between man and beast! A dimness confused Madeline's eyes; she hurriedly brushed it away, and it came back wet and blurring. She averted her face, ashamed of the tears Stewart might see. She was sorry for him. He was going away, and this time, judging from the nature of his farewell to his horse, it was to be forever. Like a stab from a cold blade a pain shot through Madeline's heart. The wonder of it, the incomprehensibility of it, the utter newness and strangeness of this sharp pain that now left behind a dull pang, made her forget Stewart, her surroundings, everything except to search her heart. Maybe here was the secret that had eluded her. She trembled on the brink of something unknown. In some strange way the emotion brought back her girlhood. Her mind revolved swift queries and replies; she was living, feeling, learning; happiness mocked at her from behind a barred door, and the bar of that door seemed to be an inexplicable pain. Then like lightning strokes shot the questions: Why should pain hide her happiness? What was her happiness? What relation had it to this man? Why should she feel strangely about his departure? And the voices within her were silenced, stunned, unanswered.

"I want to talk to you," said Stewart.

Madeline started, turned to him, and now she saw the earlier Stewart, the man who reminded her of their first meeting at El Cajon, of that memorable meeting at Chiricahua.

"I want to ask you something," he went on. "I've been wanting to know something. That's why I've hung on here. You never spoke to me, never noticed me, never gave me a chance to ask you. But now I'm going over—over the border. And I want to know. Why did you refuse to listen to me?"

At his last words that hot shame, tenfold more stifling than when it had before humiliated Madeline, rushed over her, sending the scarlet in a wave to her temples. It seemed that his words made her realize she was actually face to face with him, that somehow a shame she would rather have died than revealed was being liberated. Biting her lips to hold back speech, she jerked on Majesty's bridle, struck him with her whip, spurred him. Stewart's iron arm held the horse. Then Madeline, in a flash of passion, struck at Stewart's face, missed it, struck again, and hit. With one pull, almost drawing her from the saddle, he tore the whip from her hands. It was not that action on his part, or the sudden strong masterfulness of his look, so much as the livid mark on his face where the whip had lashed that quieted, if it did not check her fury.

"That's nothing," he said, with something of his old audacity. "That's nothing to how you've hurt me."

Madeline battled with herself for control. This man would not be denied. Never before had the hardness of his face, the flinty hardness of these desert-bred men, so struck her with its revelation of the unbridled spirit. He looked stern, haggard, bitter. The dark shade was changing to gray—the gray to ash-color of passion. About him now there was only the ghost of that finer, gentler man she had helped to bring into being. The piercing dark eyes he bent upon her burned her, went through her as if he were looking into her soul. Then Madeline's quick sight

caught a fleeting doubt, a wistfulness, a surprised and saddened certainty in his eyes, saw it shade and pass away.
Her woman's intuition, as keen as her sight, told her Stewart in that moment had sustained a shock of bitter, final
truth.

For the third time he repeated his question to her. Madeline did not answer; she could not speak.

"You don't know I love you, do you?" he continued,
passionately. "That ever since you stood before me in that
hole at Chiricahua I've loved you? You can't see I've been
another man, loving you, working for you, living for you?
You won't believe I've turned my back on the old wild life,
that I've been decent and honorable and happy and
useful—*your kind of a cowboy?* You couldn't tell, though
I loved you, that I never wanted you to know it, that I never
dared to think of you except as my angel, my holy Virgin? What do you know of a man's heart and soul? How
could you tell of the love, the salvation of a man who's
lived his life in the silence and loneliness? Who could
teach you the actual truth—that a wild cowboy, faithless
to mother and sister, except in memory, riding a hard,
drunken trail straight to hell, had looked into the face, the
eyes of a beautiful woman infinitely beyond him, above
him, and had so loved her that he was saved—that he became faithful again—that he saw her face in every flower
and her eyes in the blue heaven? Who could tell you, when
at night I stood alone under these Western stars, how deep
in my soul I was glad just to be alive, to be able to do something for you, to be near you, to stand between you and
worry, trouble, danger, to feel somehow that I was a part,
just a little part of the West you had come to love?"

Madeline was mute. She heard her heart thundering in
her ears.

Stewart leaped at her. His powerful hand closed on her arm. She trembled. His action presaged the old instinctive violence.

"No; but you think I kept Bonita up in the mountains, that I went secretly to meet her, that all the while I served you I was— Oh, I *know* what you think! I know *now*. I never knew till I made you look at me. Now, say it! *Speak!*"

White-hot, blinded, utterly in the fiery grasp of passion, powerless to stem the rush of a word both shameful and revealing and fatal, Madeline cried:

"Yes!"

He had wrenched that word from her, but he was not subtle enough, not versed in the mystery of woman's motive enough, to divine the deep significance of her reply.

For him the word had only literal meaning confirming the dishonor in which she held him. Dropping her arm, he shrank back, a strange action for the savage and crude man she judged him to be.

"But that day at Chiricahua you spoke of faith," he burst out. "You said the greatest thing in the world was faith in human nature. You said the finest men had been those who had fallen low and had risen. You said you had faith in me! *You made me have faith in myself!*"

His reproach, without bitterness or scorn, was a lash to her old egoistic belief in her fairness. She had preached a beautiful principle that she had failed to live up to. She understood his rebuke, she wondered and wavered, but the affront to her pride had been too great, the tumult within her breast had been too startlingly fierce; she could not speak, the moment passed, and with it his brief, rugged splendor of simplicity.

"You think I am vile," he said. "You think that about

Bonita! And all the time I've been . . . I could make you ashamed—I could tell you—"

His passionate utterance ceased with a snap of his teeth. His lips set in a thin, bitter line. The agitation of his face preceded a convulsive wrestling of his shoulders. All this swift action denoted an inner combat, and it nearly overwhelmed him.

"No, no!" he panted. Was it his answer to some mighty temptation? Then, like a bent sapling released, he sprang erect. "But I'll be the man—the dog—you think me!"

He laid hold of her arm with rude, powerful clutch. One pull drew her sliding half out of the saddle into his arms. She fell with her breast against his, not wholly free of stirrups or horse, and there she hung, utterly powerless. Maddened, writhing, she tore to release herself. All she could accomplish was to twist herself, raise herself high enough to see his face. That almost paralyzed her. Did he mean to kill her? Then he wrapped his arms around her and crushed her tighter, closer to him. She felt the pound of his heart; her own seemed to have frozen. Then he pressed his burning lips to hers. It was a long, terrible kiss. She felt him shake.

"Oh, Stewart! I—implore—you—let—me—go!" she whispered.

His white face loomed over hers. She closed her eyes. He rained kisses upon her face, but no more upon her mouth. On her closed eyes, her hair, her cheeks, her neck he pressed swift lips—lips that lost their fire and grew cold. Then he released her, and, lifting and righting her in the saddle, he still held her arm to keep her from falling.

For a moment Madeline sat on her horse with shut eyes. She dreaded the light.

"Now you can't say you've never been kissed," Stewart said. His voice seemed a long way off. "But that was coming to you, so be game. Here!"

She felt something hard and cold and metallic thrust into her hand. He made her fingers close over it, hold it. The feel of the thing revived her. She opened her eyes. Stewart had given her his gun. He stood with his broad breast against her knee, and she looked up to see that old mocking smile on his face.

"Go ahead! Throw my gun on me! Be a thoroughbred!"

Madeline did not yet grasp his meaning.

"You can put me down in that quiet place on the hill— beside Monty Price."

Madeline dropped the gun with a shuddering cry of horror. The sense of his words, the memory of Monty, the certainty that she would kill Stewart if she held the gun an instant longer tortured the self-accusing cry from her.

Stewart stooped to pick up the weapon.

"You might have saved me a hell of a lot of trouble," he said, with another flash of the mocking smile. "You're beautiful and sweet and proud, but you're no thoroughbred! *Majesty Hammond, adios!*"

Stewart leaped for the saddle of his horse, and with the flying mount crashed through the mesquites to disappear.

CHAPTER 22

THE SECRET TOLD

In the shaded seclusion of her room, buried face-down deep among the soft cushions on her couch, Madeline Hammond lay prostrate and quivering under the outrage she had suffered.

The afternoon wore away; twilight fell; night came; and then Madeline rose to sit by the window to let the cool wind blow upon her hot face. She passed through hours of unintelligible shame and impotent rage and futile striving to reason away her defilement.

The train of brightening stars seemed to mock her with their unattainable passionless serenity. She had loved them, and now she imagined she hated them and everything connected with this wild, fateful, and abrupt West.

She would go home.

Edith Wayne had been right; the West was no place for Madeline Hammond. The decision to go home came easily, naturally, she thought, as the result of events. It caused her no mental strife. Indeed, she fancied she felt relief. The great stars, blinking white and cold over the dark crags, looked down upon her, and, as always, after she had watched them for a while they enthralled her. "Under Western stars," she mused, thinking a little scornfully of the romantic destiny they had blazed for her idle sentiment. But they were beautiful; they were speaking; they were mocking; they drew her. "Ah!" she sighed. "It will not be so very easy to leave them, after all."

Madeline closed and darkened the window. She struck a light. It was necessary to tell the anxious servants who knocked that she was well and required nothing. A soft step on the walk outside arrested her. Who was there—Nels or Nick Steele or Stillwell? Who shared the guardianship over her now that Monty Price was dead and that other— that savage—? It was monstrous and unfathomable that she regretted him.

The light annoyed her. Complete darkness fitted her strange mood. She retired and tried to compose herself to sleep. Sleep for her was not a matter of will. Her cheeks burned so hotly that she rose to bathe them. Cold water would not alleviate this burn, and then, despairing of forgetfulness, she lay down again with a shameful gratitude for the cloak of night. Stewart's kisses were there, scorching her lips, her closed eyes, her swelling neck. They penetrated deeper and deeper into her blood, into her heart, into her soul—the terrible farewell kisses of a passionate, hardened man. Despite his baseness he had loved her.

Late in the night Madeline fell asleep. In the morning she was pale and languid, but in a mental condition that promised composure.

It was considerably after her regular hour that Madeline repaired to her office. The door was open, and just outside, tipped back in a chair, sat Stillwell.

"Mawnin', Miss Majesty," he said, as he rose to greet her with his usual courtesy. There were signs of trouble in his lined face. Madeline shrank inwardly, fearing his old lamentations about Stewart. Then she saw a dusty, ragged pony in the yard and a little burro drooping under a heavy pack. Both animals bore evidence of long, arduous travel.

"To whom do they belong?" asked Madeline.

"Them critters? Why, Danny Mains," replied Stillwell, with a cough that betrayed embarrassment.

"Danny Mains?" echoed Madeline, wonderingly.

"Wal, I said so."

Stillwell was indeed not himself.

"Is Danny Mains here?" she asked, in sudden curiosity.

The old cattleman nodded gloomily.

"Yep, he's hyar, all right. Sloped in from the hills, an' he hollered to see Bonita. He's locoed, too, about that little black-eyed hussy. Why, he hardly said 'Howdy, Bill,' before he begun to ask wild an' eager questions. I took him in to see Bonita. He's been there more'n a half-hour now."

Evidently, Stillwell's sensitive feelings had been ruffled. Madeline's curiosity changed to blank astonishment, which left her with a thrilling premonition. She caught her breath. A thousand thoughts seemed thronging for clear conception in her mind.

Rapid footsteps with an accompaniment of clinking spurs sounded in the hallway. Then a young man ran out upon the porch. He resembled a cowboy in his lithe build, his garb and action, in the way he wore his gun; but his face, instead of being red, was clear, brown tan. His eyes were blue; his hair was light and curly. He was a handsome, frank-faced boy. At sight of Madeline he slammed down his sombrero, and, leaping at her, he possessed himself of her hands. His swift violence not only alarmed her, but painfully reminded her of something she wished to forget.

This cowboy bent his head and kissed her hands, and wrung them, and when he straightened up he was crying.

"Miss Hammond, she's safe an' almost well, an' what I feared most ain't so, thank God," he cried. "Sure I'll never be able to pay you for all you've done for her. She's told me how she was dragged down here, how Gene tried to save her, how you spoke up for Gene an' her, too, how Monty at the last throwed his guns. Poor Monty! We were good friends, Monty an' I. But it wasn't friendship for me that made Monty stand in there. He would have saved her anyway. Monty Price was the whitest man I ever knew. There's Nels an' Nick an' Gene, he's been some friend to me; but Monty Price was—he was grand. He never knew, any more than you or Bill, here, or the boys, what Bonita was to me."

Stillwell's kind and heavy hand fell upon the cowboy's shoulder.

"Danny, what's all this queer gab?" he asked. "An' you're takin' some liberty with Miss Hammond, who never seen you before. Sure I'm makin' allowance fer amazin' strange talk. I see you're not drinkin'. Mebbe you're plumb locoed. Come, ease up now an' talk sense."

The cowboy's fine, frank face broke into a smile. He dashed the tears from his eyes. Then he laughed. His laugh had a pleasant, boyish ring—a happy ring.

"Bill, old pal, stand bridle-down a minute, will you?" Then he bowed to Madeline. "I beg your pardon, Miss Hammond, for seemin' rudeness. I'm Danny Mains.

An' Bonita is my wife. I'm so crazy glad she's safe an' unharmed—so grateful to you that—why, sure it's a wonder I didn't kiss you outright."

"Bonita's your wife!" ejaculated Stillwell.

"Sure. We've been married for months," replied Danny, happily. "Gene Stewart did it. Good old Gene, he's hell on marryin'. I guess maybe I haven't come to pay him up for all he's done for me! You see, I've been in love with Bonita for two years. An' Gene—you know, Bill, what a way Gene has with girls—he was—well, he was tryin' to get Bonita to have me."

Madeline's quick, varying emotions were swallowed up in a boundless gladness. Something dark, deep, heavy, and somber was flooded from her heart. She had a sudden rich sense of gratitude toward this smiling, clean-faced cowboy whose blue eyes flashed through tears.

"Danny Mains!" she said, tremulously and smilingly. "If you are as glad as your news has made me—if you really think I merit such a reward—you *may* kiss me outright."

With a bashful wonder, but with right hearty will, Danny Mains availed himself of this gracious privilege.

Stillwell snorted. The signs of his phenomenal smile were manifest, otherwise Madeline would have thought that snort an indication of furious disapproval.

"Bill, straddle a chair," said Danny. "You've gone back a heap these last few months, frettin' over your bad boys, Danny an' Gene. You'll need support under you while I'm throwin' my yarn. Story of my life, Bill." He placed a chair for Madeline. "Miss Hammond, beggin' your pardon again, I want you to listen, also. You've the face an' eyes of a woman who loves to hear of other people's happiness. Besides, somehow, it's easy for me to talk lookin' at you."

His manner subtly changed them. Possibly it took on a little swagger; certainly he lost the dignity that he had shown under stress of feeling; he was now more like a cowboy about to boast or affect some stunning manœuver. Walking off the porch, he stood before the weary horse and burro.

"Played out!" he exclaimed.

Then with the swift violence so characteristic of men of his class he slipped the pack from the burro and threw saddle and bridle from the horse.

"There! See 'em! Take a look at the last dog-gone weight you ever packed! You've been some faithful to Danny Mains. An' Danny Mains pays! Never a saddle again or a strap or a halter or a hobble so long as you live! So long as you live nothin' but grass an' clover, an' cool water in shady places, an' dusty swales to roll in an' rest an' sleep!"

Then he untied the pack, and, taking a small, heavy sack from it, he came back upon the porch. Deliberately he dumped the contents of the sack at Stillwell's feet. Piece after piece of rock thumped upon the floor. The pieces were sharp, ragged, evidently broken from a ledge; the body of them was white in color, with yellow veins and bars and streaks. Stillwell grasped up one rock after another, stared and stuttered, put the rocks to his lips, dug into them with his shaking fingers; then he lay back in his chair, head against the wall, and as he gaped at Danny the old smile began to transform his face.

"Lord, Danny, if you hevn't been an' gone an' struck it rich!"

Danny regarded Stillwell with lofty condescension.

"Some rich," he said. "Now, Bill, what've we got here, say, offhand?"

"Oh, Lord, Danny! I'm afraid to say. Look, Miss Majesty, jest look at the gold. I've lived among prospectors an' gold-mines fer thirty years, an' I never seen the beat of this."

"The Lost Mine of the Padres!" cried Danny, in stentorian voice. *"An' it belongs to me!"*

Stillwell made some incoherent sound as he sat up fascinated, quite beside himself.

"Bill, it was some long time ago since you saw me," said Danny. "Fact is, I know how you felt, because Gene kept me posted. I happened to run across Bonita, an' I wasn't goin' to let her ride away alone, when she told me she was in trouble. We hit the trail for the Peloncillos. Bonita had Gene's horse, an' she was to meet him up on the trail. We got to the mountains all right, an' nearly starved for a few days till Gene found us. He had got in trouble himself an' couldn't fetch much with him.

"We made for the crags an' built a cabin. I come down that day Gene sent his horse Majesty to you. Never saw Gene so broken-hearted. Well, after he sloped for the border Bonita an' I were hard put to it to keep alive. But we got along, an' I think it was then she began to care a little for me. Because I was decent. I killed cougars an' went down to Rodeo to get bounties for the skins, an' bought grub an' supplies I needed. Once I went to El Cajon an' run plumb into Gene. He was back from the revolution an' cuttin' up some. But I got away from him after doin' all I could to drag him out of town. A long time after that Gene trailed up to the crags an' found us. Gene had stopped drinkin', he'd changed wonderful, was fine an' dandy. It was then he began to pester the life out of me to make me marry Bonita. I was happy, so was she, an' I was some scared of spoilin' it. Bonita had been a little flirt, an' I was afraid she'd get shy of a halter, so I bucked against Gene. But I was all locoed, as it turned out. Gene would come up occasionally packin' supplies for us, an' always he'd get after me to do the right thing by Bonita. Gene's so dog-gone hard to buck against! I had to give in, an' I asked Bonita to marry me. Well, she wouldn't at first—said she wasn't good enough for me. But I saw the marriage idea was workin' deep, an' I just kept on bein' as decent as I knew how. So it was my wantin' to marry Bonita—my bein' glad to marry her—that made her grow soft an' sweet an' pretty as—as a mountain quail. Gene fetched up Padre Marcos, an' he married us."

Danny paused in his narrative, breathing hard, as if the memory of the incident described had stirred strong and thrilling feeling in him. Stillwell's smile was rapturous. Madeline leaned toward Danny with her eyes shining.

"Miss Hammond, an' you, Bill Stillwell, now listen, for this is strange I've got to tell you. The afternoon Bonita an' I were married, when Gene an' the padre had gone, I was happy one minute an' low-hearted the next. I was miserable because I had a bad name. I couldn't buy even a decent dress for my pretty wife. Bonita heard me, an' she was some mysterious. She told me the story of the lost mine of the padres, an' she kissed me an' made joyful over me in the strangest way. I knew marriage went to women's heads, an' I thought even Bonita had a spell.

"Well, she left me for a little, an' when she came back she wore some pretty yellow flowers in her hair. Her eyes were big an' black an' beautiful. She said some queer things about spirits rollin' rocks down the cañon. Then she said she wanted to show me where she always sat an' waited an' watched for me when I was away. She led me around under the crags to a long slope. It was some pretty there—clear an' open, with a long sweep, an' the desert yawnin' deep an' red. There were yellow flowers on that slope, the same kind she had in her hair—*the same kind that Apache girl wore hundreds of years ago when she led the padre to the gold-mine.*

"When I thought of that, an' saw Bonita's eyes, an' then heard the strange crack of rollin' rocks—heard them rattle down an' roll an' grow faint—I was some out of my head. But not for long. Them rocks were rollin' all right, only it was the weatherin' of the cliffs.

"An' there under the crags was a gold pocket.

"Then I was worse than locoed. I went gold-crazy. I worked like seventeen burros. Bill, I dug a lot of gold-bearin' quartz. Bonita watched the trails for me, brought me water. That was how she come to get caught by Pat Hawe an' his guerrillas. Sure! Pat Hawe was so set on doin' Gene dirt that he mixed up with Don Carlos. Bonita will tell you some staggerin' news about that outfit. Just now my story is all gold."

Danny Mains got up and kicked back his chair. Blue lightning gleamed from his eyes as he thrust a hand toward Stillwell.

"Bill, old pal, put her there—give me your hand," he said. "You were always my friend. You had faith in me. Well, Danny Mains owes you, an' he owes Gene Stewart a good deal, an' Danny Mains pays! I want two pardners to help me work my gold-mine. You an' Gene. If there's any ranch hereabouts that takes your fancy I'll buy it. If Miss Hammond ever gets tired of her range an' stock an' home I'll buy them for Gene. If there's any railroad or town round here that she likes I'll buy it. If I see anythin' myself that I like I'll buy it. Go out; find Gene for me. I'm achin' to see him, to tell him. Go fetch him; an' right here in this house, with my wife an' Miss Hammond as witnesses, we'll draw up a pardnership. Go find him, Bill. I want to show him this gold, show him how Danny Mains pays! An' the only bitter drop in my cup to-day is that I can't ever pay Monty Price."

Madeline's lips tremblingly formed to tell Danny Mains and Stillwell that the cowboy they wanted so much had left the ranch; but the flame of fine loyalty that burned in Danny's eyes, the happiness that made the old cattleman's face at once amazing and beautiful, stiffened her lips. She watched the huge Stillwell and the little cowboy, both talking wildly, as they walked off arm in arm to find Stewart. She imagined something of what Danny's disappointment would be, of the elder man's consternation and grief, when he learned Stewart had left for the border. At this juncture she looked up to see a strange, yet familiar figure approaching. Padre Marcos! Certain it was that Madeline felt herself trembling. What did his presence mean on this day? He had always avoided meeting her whenever possible. He had been exceedingly grateful for all she had done for his people, his church, and himself; but he had never thanked her in person. Perhaps he had come for that purpose now. But Madeline did not believe so.

Mention of Padre Marcos, sight of him had always occasioned Madeline a little indefinable shock; and now, as he stepped to the porch, a shrunken, stooped, and sad-faced man, she was startled.

The padre bowed low to her.

"Señora, will you grant me audience?" he asked, in perfect English, and his voice was low-toned and grave.

"Certainly, Padre Marcos," replied Madeline; and she led him into her office.

"May I beg to close the doors?" he asked. "It is a matter of great moment, which you might not care to have any one hear."

Wonderingly Madeline inclined her head. The padre gently closed one door and then the other.

"Señora, I have come to disclose a secret—my own sinfulness in keeping it—and to implore your pardon. Do you remember that night Señor Stewart dragged me before you in the waiting-room at El Cajon?"

"Yes," replied Madeline.

"Señora, since that night you have been Señor Stewart's wife!"

Madeline became as motionless as stone. She seemed to feel nothing, only to hear.

"You are Señor Stewart's wife. I have kept the secret under fear of death. But I could keep it no longer. Señor Stewart may kill me now. Ah! Señora, it is very strange to you. You were so frightened that night, you knew not what happened. Señor Stewart threatened me. He forced you. He made me speak the service. He made you speak the Spanish yes. And I, Señora, knowing the deeds of these sinful cowboys, fearing worse than disgrace to one so beautiful and so good as you, I could not do less than marry you truly. At least you should be his wife. So I married you, truly, in the service of my church."

"My God!" cried Madeline, rising.

"Hear me! I implore you, Señora, hear me out! Do not leave me! Do not look so—so— Ah, Señora, let me speak a word for Señor Stewart. He was drunk that night. He did not know what he was about. In the morning he came to me, made me swear by my cross that I would not reveal the disgrace he had put upon you. If I did he would kill me. Life is nothing to the American *vaquero*, Señora. I promised to respect his command. But I did not tell him you were his wife. He did not dream I had truly married you. He went to fight for the freedom of my country— Señora, he is one splendid soldier—and I brooded over the sin of my secret. If he were killed I need never tell you. But if he lived I knew that I must some day.

"Strange indeed that Señor Stewart and Padre Marcos should both come to this ranch together. The great change your goodness wrought in my beloved people was no greater than the change in Señor Stewart. Señora, I feared you would go away one day, go back to your Eastern home ignorant of the truth. The time came when I confessed to Stewart—said I must tell you. Señora, the man went mad with joy. I have never seen so supreme a joy. He threatened no more to kill me! That strong, cruel *vaquero* begged me not to tell the secret—never to reveal it. He confessed his love for you—a love something like the desert storm. He swore by all that was once sacred to him, and by my cross and my church, that he would be a good man, that he would be worthy to have you secretly his wife for the little time life left him to worship at your shrine. You needed never to know. So I held my tongue, half pitying him, half fearing him, and praying for some God-sent light.

"Señora, it was a fool's paradise that Stewart lived in. I saw him often. When he took me up into the mountains to have me marry that wayward Bonita and her lover I came to have respect for a man whose ideas about nature and life and God were at a variance with mine. But the man is a worshiper of God in all material things. He is a part of the wind and sun and desert and mountain that have made him. I have never heard more beautiful words than those in which he persuaded Bonita to accept Señor Mains, to forget her old lovers, and henceforth to be happy. He is their friend. I wish I could tell you what that means. It sounds so simple. It *is* really simple. All great things are so. For Señor Stewart it was natural to be loyal to his friend, to have a fine sense of the honor due to a woman who had loved and given, to bring about their marriage, to succor them in their need and loneliness. It was natural for him never to speak of them. It would have been natural for him to give his life in their defense if peril menaced them. Señora, I want you to understand that to me the man has the same stability, the same strength, the same elements which I am in the habit of attributing to the physical life around me in this wild and rugged desert."

Madeline listened as one under a spell. It was not only that this soft-voiced, eloquent priest knew how to move the heart, stir the soul; but his defense, his praise of Stewart, if they had been couched in the crude speech of cowboys, would have been a glory to her.

"Señora, I pray you, do not misunderstand my mission. Beyond my confession to you I have only a duty—to tell you of the man whose wife you are. But I am a priest, and I can read the soul. The ways of God are inscrutable. I am only a humble instrument. You are a noble woman, and Señor Stewart is a man of desert iron forged anew in the crucible of love. *Quien sabe?* Señor Stewart swore he would kill me if I betrayed him. But he will not lift his hand against me. For the man bears you a very great and pure love, and it has changed him. I no longer fear his threat, but I do fear his anger, should he ever know I spoke

of his love, of his fool's paradise. I have watched his dark
face turned to the sun setting over the desert. I have
watched him lift it to the light of the stars. Think, my gracious and noble lady, think what *is* his paradise? To love
you above the spirit of the flesh; to know you arc his wife,
his, never to be another's except by *his* sacrifice; to watch
you with a secret glory of joy and pride; to stand, while
he might, between you and evil; to find his happiness in
service; to wait, with never a dream of telling you, for the
hour to come when to leave you free he must go out and
get himself shot! Señora, that is beautiful, it is sublime, it
is terrible. It has brought me to you with my confession. I
repeat, Señora, the ways of God are inscrutable. What is
the meaning of your influence upon Señor Stewart?
Once he was merely an animal, brutal, unquickened; now
he is a man—I have not seen his like! So I beseech you
in my humble office as priest, as a lover of mankind, before you send Stewart to his death, to be sure there is here
no mysterious dispensation of God. Love, that mighty and
blessed and unknown thing, might be at work. Señora, I
have heard that somewhere in the rich Eastern cities you
are a very great lady. I know you are good and noble. That
is all I want to know. To me you are only a woman, the
same as Senōr Stewart is only a man. So I pray you, Señora, before you let Stewart give you freedom at such
cost be sure you do not want his love, lest you cast away
something sweet and ennobling which you yourself have
created."

CHAPTER 23

THE LIGHT OF WESTERN STARS

Blinded, like a wild creature, Madeline Hammond ran to her room. She felt as if a stroke of lightning had shattered the shadowy substance of the dream she had made of real life. The wonder of Danny Mains's story, the strange regret with which she had realized her injustice to Stewart, the astounding secret as revealed by Padre Marcos—these were forgotten in the sudden consciousness of her own love.

Madeline fled as if pursued. With trembling hands she locked the doors, drew the blinds of the windows that opened on the porch, pushed chairs aside so that she could pace the length of her room. She was now alone, and she walked with soft, hurried, uneven steps. She could be herself here; she needed no mask; the long habit of serenely hiding the truth from the world and from herself could be broken. The seclusion of her darkened chamber made possible that betrayal of herself to which she was impelled.

She paused in her swift pacing to and fro. She liberated the thought that knocked at the gates of her mind. With quivering lips she whispered it. Then she spoke aloud:

"I will say it—hear it. I—I love him!"

"I love him!" she repeated the astounding truth, but she doubted her identity.

"Am I still Madeline Hammond? What has happened? Who am I?" She stood where the light from one unclosed window fell upon her image in the mirror. "Who is this woman?"

She expected to see a familiar, dignified person, a quiet, unruffled figure, a tranquil face with dark, proud eyes and calm, proud lips. No, she did not see Madeline Hammond. She did not see any one she knew. Were her eyes, like her heart, playing her false? The figure before her was instinct with pulsating life. The hands she saw, clasped together, pressed deep into a swelling bosom that heaved with each panting breath. The face she saw—white, rapt, strangely glowing, with parted, quivering lips, with great, staring, tragic eyes—this could not be Madeline Hammond's face.

Yet as she looked she knew no fancy could really deceive her, that she was only Madeline Hammond come at last to the end of brooding dreams. She swiftly realized the change in her, divined its cause and meaning, accepted it as inevitable, and straightway fell back again into the mood of bewildering amaze.

Calmness was unattainable. The surprise absorbed her. She could not go back to count the innumerable, imperceptible steps of her undoing. Her old power of reflecting, analyzing, even thinking at all, seemed to have vanished in a pulse-stirring sense of one new emotion. She only felt all her instinctive outward action that was a physical relief, all her involuntary inner strife that was maddening, yet unutterably sweet; and they seemed to be just one bewildering effect of surprise.

In a nature like hers, where strength of feeling had long been inhibited as a matter of training, such a transforming surprise as sudden consciousness of passionate love required time for its awakening, time for its sway.

By and by that last enlightening moment came, and Madeline Hammond faced not only the love in her heart, but the thought of the man she loved.

Suddenly, as she raged, something in her—this dauntless new personality—took arms against indictment of Gene Stewart. Her mind whirled about him and his life. She saw him drunk, brutal; she saw him abandoned, lost. Then out of the picture she had of him thus slowly grew one of a different man—weak, sick, changed by shock, growing strong, strangely spiritually altered, silent, lonely like an eagle, secretive, tireless, faithful, soft as a woman, hard as iron to endure, and at the last noble.

She softened. In a flash her complex mood changed to one wherein she thought of the truth, the beauty, the wonder of Stewart's uplifting. Humbly she trusted that she had helped him to climb. That influence had been the best she had ever exerted. It had wrought magic in her own character. By it she had reached some higher, nobler plane of trust in man. She had received infinitely more than she had given.

Her swiftly flying memory seemed to assort a vast mine of treasures of the past. Of that letter Stewart had written to her brother she saw vivid words. But ah! she had known, and if it had not made any difference then, now it made all in the world. She recalled how her loosened hair had blown across his lips that night he had ridden down from the mountains carrying her in his arms. She recalled the strange joy of pride in Stewart's eyes when he had suddenly come upon her dressed to receive her Eastern guests in the white gown with the red roses at her breast.

Swiftly as they had come these dreamful memories departed. There was to be no rest for her mind. All she had thought and felt seemed only to presage a tumult.

Heedless, desperate, she cast off the last remnant of self-control, turned from the old proud, pale, cold, self-contained ghost of herself to face this strange, strong, passionate woman. Then, with hands pressed to her beating heart, with eyes shut, she listened to the ringing trip-hammer voice of circumstance, of truth, of fatality. The whole story was revealed, simple enough in the sum of its complicated details, strange and beautiful in part, remorseless in its proof of great love on Stewart's side, in dreaming blindness on her own, and, from the first fatal moment to the last, prophetic of tragedy.

Madeline, like a prisoner in a cell, began again to pace to and fro.

"Oh, it is all terrible!" she cried. "I am his wife. His wife! That meeting with him—the marriage—then his fall, his love, his rise, his silence, his pride! And I can never be anything to him. Could I be anything to him? I, Madeline Hammond? But I am his wife, and I love him! His wife! I am the wife of a cowboy! That might be undone. Can my love be undone? Ah, do I want anything undone? He is gone. *Gone!* Could he have meant— I will not, dare not think of that. He will come back. No, he never will come back. Oh, what shall I do?"

For Madeline Hammond the days following that storm of feeling were leaden-footed, endless, hopeless—a long succession of weary hours, sleepless hours, passionate hours, all haunted by a fear slowly growing into torture, a fear that Stewart had crossed the border to invite the bullet which would give her freedom. The day came when she knew this to be true. The spiritual tidings reached her, not subtly as so many divinations had come, but in a clear, vital flash of certainty. Then she suffered. She burned inwardly, and the nature of that deep fire showed through her eyes. She kept to herself, waiting, waiting for her fears to be confirmed.

At times she broke out in wrath at the circumstances she had failed to control, at herself, at Stewart.

"He might have learned from Ambrose!" she exclaimed, sick with a bitterness she knew was not consistent with her pride. She recalled Christine's trenchant exposition of Ambrose's wooing: "He tell me he love me; he kees me; he hug me; he put me on his horse; he ride away with me; he marry me!"

Then in the next breath Madeline denied this insistent clamoring of a love that was gradually breaking her spirit. Like a somber shadow remorse followed her, shading blacker. She had been blind to a man's honesty, manliness, uprightness, faith, and striving. She had been dead to love, to nobility that she had herself created. Padre Marcos's grave, wise words returned to haunt her. She fought her bitterness, scorned her intelligence, hated her pride, and, weakening, gave up more and more to a yearning, hopeless hope.

She had shunned the light of the stars as she had violently dismissed every hinting suggestive memory of Stewart's kisses. But one night she went deliberately to her window. There they shone. Her stars! Beautiful, passionless as always, but strangely closer, warmer, speaking a kinder language, helpful as they had never been, teaching her now that regret was futile, revealing to her in their one grand, blazing task the supreme duty of life—to be true.

Those shining stars made her yield. She whispered to them that they had claimed her—the West claimed her—Stewart claimed her forever, whether he lived or died. She gave up to her love. And it was as if he was there in person, dark-faced, fire-eyed, violent in his action, crushing her to his breast in that farewell moment, kissing her with one burning kiss of passion, then with cold, terrible lips of renunciation.

"I am your wife!" she whispered to him. In that moment, throbbing, exalted, quivering in her first sweet, tumultuous surrender to love, she would have given her all, her life, to be in his arms again, to meet his lips, to put forever out of his power any thought of wild sacrifice.

A nd on the morning of the next day, when Madeline went out upon the porch, Stillwell, haggard and stern, with a husky, incoherent word, handed her a message from El Cajon. She read:

"El Capitan Stewart captured by rebel soldiers in fight at Agua Prieta yesterday. He was a sharpshooter in the Federal ranks. Sentenced to death Thursday at sunset."

CHAPTER 24

THE RIDE

"**S**tillwell!" Madeline's cry was more than the utterance of a breaking heart. It was full of agony. But also it uttered the shattering of a structure built of false pride, of old beliefs, of bloodless standards, of ignorance of self. It betrayed the final conquest of her doubts, and out of their darkness blazed the unquenchable spirit of a woman who had found herself, her love, her salvation, her duty to a man, and who would not be cheated.

The old cattleman stood mute before her, staring at her white face, at her eyes of flame.

"Stillwell! I am Stewart's wife!"

"My Gawd, Miss Majesty!" he burst out. "I knowed somethin' turrible was wrong. Aw, sure it's a pity—"

"Do you think I'll let him be shot when I know him now, when I'm no longer blind, when I love him?" she asked, with passionate swiftness. "I will save him. This is Wednesday morning. I have thirty-six hours to save his life. Stillwell, send for Link and the car!"

She went into her office. Her mind worked with extraordinary rapidity and clearness. Her plan, born in one lightning-like flash of thought, necessitated the careful wording of telegrams to Washington, to New York, to San Antonio. These were to Senators, Representatives, men high in public and private life, men who would remember her and who would serve her to their utmost. Never before had her position meant anything to her comparable with what it meant now. Never in all her life had money seemed the power that it was then. If she had been poor! A shuddering chill froze the thought at its inception. She dispelled heartbreaking thoughts. She had power. She had wealth. She would set into operation all the unlimited means these gave her—the wires and pulleys and strings underneath the surface of political and international life, the open, free, purchasing value of money or the deep, underground, mysterious, incalculably powerful influence moved by gold. She could save Stewart. She must await results—deadlocked in feeling, strained perhaps almost beyond endurance, because the suspense would be great; but she would allow no possibility of failure to enter her mind.

When she went outside, the car was there with Link, helmet in hand, a cool, bright gleam in his eyes, and with Stillwell, losing his haggard misery, beginning to respond to Madeline's spirit.

"Link, drive Stillwell to El Cajon in time for him to catch the El Paso train," she said. "Wait there for his return, and if any message comes from him, telephone it at once to me."

Then she gave Stillwell the telegrams to send from El Cajon and drafts to cash in El Paso. She instructed him to go before the rebel junta, then stationed at Juarez, to explain the situation, to bid them expect communications from Washington officials requesting and advising Stewart's exchange as a prisoner of war, to offer to buy his release from the rebel authorities.

When Stillwell had heard her through his huge, bowed form straightened, a ghost of his old smile just moved his lips. He was no longer young, and hope could not at once drive away stern and grim realities. As he bent over her hand his manner appeared courtly and reverent. But either he was speechless or felt the moment not one for him to break silence.

He climbed to a seat beside Link, who pocketed the watch he had been studying and leaned over the wheel. There was a crack, a muffled sound bursting into a roar, and the big car jerked forward to bound over the edge of the slope, to leap down the long incline, to shoot out upon the level valley floor and disappear in moving dust.

For the first time in days Madeline visited the gardens, the corrals, the lakes, the quarters of the cowboys. Though imagining she was calm, she feared she looked strange to Nels, to Nick, to Frankie Slade, to those boys best known to her. The situation for them must have been one of tormenting pain and bewilderment. They acted as if they wanted to say something to her, but found themselves spellbound. She wondered—did they know she was Stewart's wife? Stillwell had not had time to tell them; besides, he would not have mentioned the fact. These cowboys only knew that Stewart was sentenced to be shot; they knew if Madeline had not been angry with him he would not have gone in desperate fighting mood across the border. She spoke of the weather, of the horses and cattle, asked Nels when he was to go on duty, and turned away from the wide, sunlit, adobe-arched porch where the cowboys stood silent and bareheaded. Then one of her subtle impulses checked her.

"Nels, you and Nick need not go on duty to-day," she said. "I may want you. I—I—"

She hesitated, paused, and stood lingering there. Her glance had fallen upon Stewart's big black horse prancing in a near-by corral.

"I have sent Stillwell to El Paso," she went on, in a low voice she failed to hold steady. "He will save Stewart. I have to tell you—I am Stewart's wife!"

She felt the stricken amaze that made these men silent and immovable. With level gaze averted she left them. Returning to the house and her room, she prepared for something—for what? To wait!

Then a great invisible shadow seemed to hover behind her. She essayed many tasks, to fail of attention, to find that her mind held only Stewart and his fortunes. Why had he become a Federal? She reflected that he had won his title, El Capitan, fighting for Madero, the rebel. But Madero was now a Federal, and Stewart was true to him. In crossing the border had Stewart any other motive than the one he had implied to Madeline in his mocking smile and scornful words, "You might have saved me a hell of a lot of trouble!" What trouble? She felt again the cold shock of contact with the gun she had dropped in horror. He meant the trouble of getting himself shot in the only way a man could seek death without cowardice. But had he any other motive? She recalled Don Carlos and his guerrillas. Then the thought leaped up in her mind with gripping power that Stewart meant to hunt Don Carlos, to meet him, to kill him. It would be the deed of a silent, vengeful, implacable man driven by wild justice such as had been the deadly leaven in Monty

Price. It was a deed to expect of Nels or Nick Steele—and aye, of Gene Stewart. Madeline felt regret that Stewart, as he had climbed so high, had not risen above deliberate seeking to kill his enemy, however evil that enemy.

The local newspapers, which came regularly a day late from El Paso and Douglas, had never won any particular interest from Madeline; now, however, she took up any copies she could find and read all the information pertaining to the revolution. Every word seemed vital to her, of moving significant force.

AMERICANS ROBBED BY MEXICAN REBELS

MADERA, State of Chihuahua, Mexico, July 17.— Having looted the Madera Lumber Company's storehouses of $25,000 worth of goods and robbed scores of foreigners of horses and saddles, the rebel command of Gen. Antonio Rojas, comprising a thousand men, started westward to-day through the state of Sonora for Aguaymas and Pacific coast points.

The troops are headed for Dolores, where a mountain pass leads into the state of Sonora. Their entrance will be opposed by 1,000 Maderista volunteers, who are reported to be waiting the rebel invasion.

The railroad south of Madera is being destroyed and many Americans who were traveling to Chihuahua from Juarez are marooned here.

General Rojas executed five men while here for alleged offenses of a trivial character. Gen. Rosalio y Hernandez, Lieut. Cipriano Amador, and three soldiers were the unfortunates.

————

WASHINGTON, July 17.—Somewhere in Mexico Patrick Dunne, an American citizen, is in prison under sentence of death. This much and no more the State Department learned through Representative Kinkaid of Nebraska. Consular officers in various sections of Mexico have been directed to make every effort to locate Dunne and save his life.

JUAREZ, Mexico, July 31.—General Orozco, chief of the rebels, declared to-day:

"If the United States will throw down the barriers and let us have all the ammunition we can buy, I promise in sixty days to have peace restored in Mexico and a stable government in charge."

CASAS GRANDES, Chihuahau, July 31.—Rebel soldiers looted many homes of Mormons near here yesterday. All the Mormon families have fled to El Paso. Although General Salazar had two of his soldiers executed yesterday for robbing Mormons, he has not made any attempt to stop his men looting the unprotected homes of Americans.

Last night's and to-day's trains carried many Americans from Pearson, Madera, and other localities outside the Mormon settlements. Refugees from Mexico continued to pour into El Paso. About one hundred came last night, the majority of whom were men. Heretofore few men came.

Madeline read on in feverish absorption. It was not a real war, but a starving, robbing, burning, hopeless revolution. Five men executed for alleged offenses of a trivial nature! What chance had, then, a Federal prisoner, an enemy to be feared, an American cowboy in the clutches of those crazed rebels?

Madeline endured patiently, endured for long interminable hours while holding to her hope with indomitable will.

No message came. At sunset she went outdoors, suffering a torment of accumulating suspense. She faced the desert, hoping, praying for strength. The desert did not influence her as did the passionless, unchangeable stars that had soothed her spirit. It was red, mutable, shrouded in shadows, terrible like her mood. A dust-veiled sunset colored the vast, brooding, naked waste of rock and sand. The grim Chiricahua frowned black and sinister. The dim, blue domes of the Guadalupes seemed to whisper, to beckon to her. Beyond them somewhere was Stewart awaiting the end of a few brief hours—hours that to her were boundless, endless, insupportable.

Night fell. But now the white, pitiless stars failed her. Then she sought the seclusion and darkness of her room, there to lie with wide eyes, waiting, waiting. She had always been susceptible to the somber, mystic unrealities of the night, and now her mind slowly revolved round a vague and monstrous gloom. Nevertheless, she was acutely sensitive to outside impressions. She heard the measured tread of a guard, the rustle of wind stirring the window-curtain, the remote, mournful wail of a coyote. By and by the dead silence of the night insulated her with leaden oppression. There was silent darkness for so long that when the window casements showed gray she believed it was only fancy and that dawn would never come. She prayed for the sun not to rise, not to begin its short twelve-hour journey toward what might be a fatal setting for Stewart. But the dawn did lighten, swiftly she thought, remorselessly. Daylight had broken, and this was Thursday!

Sharp ringing of the telephone bell startled her, roused her into action. She ran to answer the call.

"Hello—hello—Miss Majesty!" came the hurried reply. "This's Link talkin'. Messages for you. Favorable, the operator said. I'm to ride out with them. I'll come a-hummin'."

That was all. Madeline heard the bang of the receiver as Stevens threw it down. She passionately wanted to know more, but was immeasurably grateful for so much! Favorable! Then Stillwell had been successful. Her heart leaped. Suddenly she became weak, and her hands failed of their accustomed morning deftness. It took her what seemed a thousand years to dress. Breakfast meant nothing to her except that it helped her to pass dragging minutes.

Finally a low hum, mounting swiftly to a roar and ending with a sharp report, announced the arrival of the car. If her feet had kept pace with her heart she would have raced out to meet Link. She saw him, helmet thrown back, watch in hand, and he looked up at her with his cool, bright smile, with his familiar apologetic manner.

"Fifty-three minutes, Miss Majesty," he said, "but I hed to ride round a herd of steers an' bump a couple off the trail."

He gave her a packet of telegrams. Madeline tore them open with shaking fingers, began to read with swift, dim eyes. Some were from Washington, assuring her of every possible service; some were from New York; others written in Spanish were from El Paso; and these she could not wholly translate in a brief glance. Would she never find Stillwell's message? It was the last. It was lengthy. It read:

Bought Stewart's release. Also arranged for his transfer as prisoner of war. Both matters official. He's safe if we can get notice to his captors. Not sure I've reached them by wire. Afraid to trust it. You go with Link to Agua Prieta. Take the messages sent you in Spanish. They will protect you and secure Stewart's freedom. Take Nels with you. Stop for nothing. Tell Link all—trust him—let him drive that car.

STILLWELL.

The first few lines of Stillwell's message lifted Madeline to the heights of thanksgiving and happiness. Then, reading on, she experienced a check, a numb, icy, sickening pang. At the last line she flung off doubt and dread, and in white, cold passion faced the issue.

"Read," she said, briefly, handing the telegram to Link. He scanned it and then looked blankly up at her.

"Link, do you know the roads, the trails—the desert between here and Agua Prieta?" she asked.

"Thet's sure my old stampin'-ground. An' I know Sonora, too."

"We must reach Agua Prieta before sunset—long before, so if Stewart is in some near-by camp we can get to it in—in time."

"Miss Majesty, it ain't possible!" he exclaimed. "Stillwell's crazy to say thet."

"Link, can an automobile be driven from here into northern Mexico?"

"Sure. But it'd take time."

"We must do it in little time," she went on, in swift eagerness. "Otherwise Stewart may be—probably will be—be shot."

Link Stevens appeared suddenly to grow lax, shriveled, to lose all his peculiar pert brightness, to weaken and age.

"I'm only a—a cowboy, Miss Majesty." He almost faltered. It was a singular change in him. "Thet's an awful ride—down over the border. If by some luck I didn't smash the car I'd turn your hair gray. You'd never be no good after thet ride!"

"I am Stewart's wife," she answered him, and she looked at him, not conscious of any motive to persuade or allure, but just to let him know the greatness of her dependence upon him.

He started violently—the old action of Stewart, the memorable action of Monty Price. This man was of the same wild breed.

Then Madeline's words flowed in a torrent. "I am Stewart's wife. I love him; I have been unjust to him; I must save him. Link, I have faith in you. I beseech you to do your best for Stewart's sake—for my sake. I'll risk the ride gladly—bravely. I'll not care where or how you drive. I'd far rather plunge into a cañon—go to my death on the rocks—than not try to save Stewart."

How beautiful the response of this rude cowboy—to realize his absolute unconsciousness of self, to see the haggard shade burn out of his face, the old, cool, devil-may-care spirit return to his eyes, and to feel something wonderful about him then! It was more than will or daring or sacrifice. A blood-tie might have existed between him and Madeline. She sensed again that indefinable brother-like quality, so fine, so almost invisible, which seemed to be an inalienable trait in these wild cowboys.

"Miss Majesty, thet ride figgers impossible, but I'll do it!" he replied. His cool, bright glance thrilled her. "I'll need mebbe half an hour to go over the car an' to pack on what I'll want."

She could not thank him, and her reply was merely a request that he tell Nels and other cowboys off duty to come up to the house. When Link had gone Madeline gave a moment's thought to preparations for the ride. She placed what money she had and the telegrams in a satchel. The gown she had on was thin and white, not suitable for travel, but she would not risk the losing of one moment in changing it. She put on a long coat and wound veils round her head and neck, arranging them in a hood so she could cover her face when necessary. She remembered to take an extra pair of goggles for Nels's use, and then, drawing on her gloves, she went out ready for the ride.

A number of cowboys were waiting. She explained the situation and left them in charge of her home. With that she asked Nels to accompany her down into the desert. He turned white to his lips, and this occasioned Madeline to remember his mortal dread of the car and Link's driving.

"Nels, I'm sorry to ask you," she added. "I know you hate the car. But I need you—may need you, oh! so much."

"Why, Miss Majesty, thet's shore all a mistaken idee of yours about me hatin' the car," he said, in his slow, soft drawl. "I was only jealous of Link; an' the boys, they made thet joke up on me about bein' scared of ridin' fast. Shore I'm powerful proud to go. An' I reckon if you hedn't asked me my feelin's might hev been some hurt Because if you're goin' down among the Greasers you want me."

His cool, easy speech, his familiar swagger, the smile with which he regarded her did not in the least deceive

Madeline. The gray was still in his face. Incomprehensible as it seemed, Nels had a dread, an uncanny fear, and it was of that huge white automobile. But he lied about it. Here again was that strange quality of faithfulness.

Madeline heard the buzz of the car. Link appeared driving up the slope. He made a short, sliding turn and stopped before the porch. Link had tied two long, heavy planks upon the car, one on each side, and in every available space he had strapped extra tires. A huge cask occupied one back seat, and another seat was full of tools and ropes. There was just room in this rear part of the car for Nels to squeeze in. Link put Madeline in front beside him, then bent over the wheel. Madeline waved her hand at the silent cowboys on the porch. Not an audible good-by was spoken.

The car glided out of the yard, leaped from level to slope, and started swiftly down the road, out into the open valley. Each stronger rush of dry wind in Madeline's face marked the increase of speed. She took one glance at the winding cattle-road, smooth, unobstructed, disappearing in the gray of distance. She took another at the leather-garbed, leather-helmeted driver beside her, and then she drew the hood of veils over her face and fastened it round her neck so there was no possibility of its blowing loose.

Harder and stronger pressed the wind till it was like sheeted lead forcing her back in her seat. There was a ceaseless, intense, inconceivably rapid vibration under her; occasionally she felt a long swing, as if she were to be propelled aloft; but no jars disturbed the easy celerity of the car. The buzz, the roar of wheels, of heavy body in flight, increased to a continuous droning hum. The wind became an insupportable body moving toward her, crushing her breast, making the task of breathing most difficult. To Madeline the time seemed to fly with the speed of miles. A moment came when she detected a faint difference in hum and rush and vibration, in the ceaseless sweeping of the invisible weight against her. This difference became marked. Link was reducing speed. Then came swift change of all sensations, and she realized the car had slowed to normal travel.

Madeline removed her hood and goggles. It was a relief to breathe freely, to be able to use her eyes. To her right, not far distant, lay the little town of Chiricahua. Sight of it made her remember Stewart in a way strange to her constant thought of him. To the left inclined the gray valley. The red desert was hidden from view, but the Guadalupe Mountains loomed close in the southwest.

Opposite Chiricahua, where the road forked, Link Stevens headed the car straight south and gradually increased speed. Madeline faced another endless gray incline. It was the San Bernardino Valley. The singing of the car, the stinging of the wind warned her to draw the hood securly down over her face again, and then it was as if she was riding at night. The car lurched ahead, settled into that driving speed which wedged Madeline back as in a vise. Again the moments went by fleet as the miles. Seemingly, there was an acceleration of the car till it reached a certain swiftness—a period of time in which it held that pace, and then a diminishing of all motion and sound which contributed to Madeline's acute sensation. Uncovering her face, she saw Link was passing another village. Could it be Bernardino? She asked Link—repeated the question.

"Sure," he replied. "Eighty miles."

Link did not this time apologize for the work of his machine. Madeline marked the omission with her first thrill of the ride. Leaning over, she glanced at Link's watch, which he had fastened upon the wheel in front of his eyes. A quarter to ten! Link had indeed made short work of the valley miles.

Beyond Bernardino Link sheered off the road and put the car to a long, low-rising slope. Here the valley appeared to run south under the dark brows of the Guadalupes. Link was heading southwest. Madeline observed that the grass began to fail as they climbed the ridge; bare, white, dusty spots appeared; there were patches of mesquite and cactus and scattering areas of broken rock.

She might have been prepared for what she saw from the ridge-top. Beneath them the desert blazed. Seen from afar, it was striking enough, but riding down into its red jaws gave Madeline the first affront to her imperious confidence. All about her ranch had been desert, the valleys were desert; but this was different. Here began the red desert, extending far into Mexico, far across Arizona and California to the Pacific. She saw a bare hummocky ridge, down which the car was gliding, bounding, swinging, and this long slant seemed to merge into a corrugated world of rock and sand, patched by flats and basins, streaked with cañons and ranges of ragged, saw-toothed stone. The distant Sierra Madres were clearer, bluer, less smoky and suggestive of mirage than she had ever seen them. Madeline's sustaining faith upheld her in the face of this appalling obstacle. Then the desert that had rolled its immensity beneath her gradually began to rise, to lose its distant margins, to condense its varying lights and shades, at last to hide its yawning depths and looming heights behind red ridges, which were only little steps, little outposts, little landmarks at its gates.

The bouncing of the huge car, throwing Madeline up,

directed her attention and fastened it upon the way Link Stevens was driving and upon the immediate foreground. Then she discovered that he was following an old wagon-road. At the foot of that long slope they struck into rougher ground, and here Link took to a cautious zigzag course. The wagon-road disappeared and then presently reappeared. But Link did not always hold to it. He made cuts, detours, crosses, and all the time seemed to be getting deeper into a maze of low, red dunes, of flat cañon-beds lined by banks of gravel, of ridges mounting higher. Yet Link Stevens kept on and never turned back. He never headed into a place that he could not pass. Up to this point of travel he had not been compelled to back the car; and Madeline began to realize that it was the cowboy's wonderful judgment of ground that made advance possible. He knew the country; he was never at a loss; after making a choice of direction he never hesitated.

Then at the bottom of a wide cañon he entered a wash where the wheels just barely turned in dragging sand. The sun beat down white-hot, the dust arose, there was not a breath of wind; and no sound save the slide of a rock now and then down the weathered slopes and the labored chugging of the machine. The snail pace, like the sand at the wheels, began to drag at Madeline's faith. Link gave over the wheel to Madeline, and, leaping out, he called Nels. When they untied the long planks and laid them straight in front for the wheels to pass over, Madeline saw how wise had been Link's forethought. With the aid of those planks they worked the car through sand and gravel otherwise impossible to pass.

This cañon widened and opened into space affording an unobstructed view for miles. The desert sloped up in steps, and in the morning light, with the sun bright on the mesas and escarpments, it was gray, drab, stone, slate, yellow, pink, and, dominating all, a dull rust-red. There was level ground ahead, a wind-swept floor as hard as rock. Link rushed the car over this free distance. Madeline's ears filled with a droning hum like the sound of a monstrous, hungry bee and with a strange, incessant crinkle which she at length guessed to be the spreading of sheets of gravel from under the wheels. The giant car attained such a speed that Madeline could only distinguish the colored landmarks to the fore, and these faded as the wind stung her eyes.

Then Link began the ascent of the first step, a long, sweeping, barren waste with dunes of wonderful violet and heliotrope hues. Here were well-defined marks of an old wagon-road lately traversed by cattle. The car climbed steadily, surmounted the height, faced another long bench that had been cleaned smooth by desert winds. The sky was an intense, light, steely blue, hard on the eyes. Madeline veiled her face, and did not uncover it until Link had reduced the racing speed. From the summit of the next ridge she saw more red ruin of desert.

A deep wash crossing the road caused Link Stevens to turn due south. There was a narrow space along the wash just wide enough for the car. Link seemed oblivious to the fact that the outside wheels were perilously close to the edge. Madeline heard the rattle of loosened gravel and earth sliding into the gully. The wash widened and opened out into a sandy flat. Link crossed this and turned up on the opposite side. Rocks impeded the progress of the car, and these had to be rolled out of the way. The shelves of silt, apparently ready to slide with the slightest weight, the little tributary washes, the boulder-strewn stretches of slope, the narrow spaces allowing no more than a foot for the outside wheels, the spear-pointed cactus that had to be avoided—all these obstacles were as nothing to the cowboy driver. He kept on, and when he came to the road again he made up for the lost time by speed.

Another height was reached, and here Madeline fancied that Link had driven the car to the summit of a high pass between two mountain ranges. The western slope of that pass appeared to be exceedingly rough and broken. Below it spread out another gray valley, at the extreme end of which glistened a white spot that Link grimly called Douglas. Part of that white spot was Agua Prieta, the sister town across the line. Madeline looked with eyes that would fain have pierced the intervening distance.

The descent of the pass began under difficulties. Sharp stones and cactus spikes penetrated the front tires, bursting them with ripping reports. It took time to replace them. The planks were called into requisition to cross soft places. A jagged point of projecting rock had to be broken with a sledge. At length a huge stone appeared to hinder any further advance. Madeline caught her breath. There was no room to turn the car. But Link Stevens had no intention of such a thing. He backed the car to a considerable distance, then walked forward. He appeared to be busy around the boulder for a moment and returned down the road on the run. A heavy explosion, a cloud of dust, and rattle of falling fragments told Madeline that her indomitable driver had cleared a passage with dynamite. He seemed to be prepared for every emergency. Madeline looked to see what effect the discovery of Link carrying dynamite would have upon the silent Nels.

"Shore, now, Miss Majesty, there ain't nothin' goin' to stop Link," said Nels, with a reassuring smile. The significance of the incident had not dawned upon Nels, or else he was heedless of it. After all, he was afraid only of the car and Link, and that fear was an idiosyncrasy. Madeline began to see her cowboy driver with clearer eyes, and his spirit awoke something in her that made danger of no moment. Nels likewise subtly responded, and, though he was gray-faced, tight-lipped, his eyes took on the cool, bright gleam of Link's.

Cactus barred the way, rocks barred the way, gullies barred the way, and these Nels addressed in the grim humor with which he was wont to view tragic things. A mistake on Link's part, a slip of a wheel, a bursting of a tire at a critical moment, an instant of the bad luck which might happen a hundred times on a less perilous ride— any one of these might spell disaster for the car, perhaps death to the occupants. Again and again Link used the planks to cross washes in sand. Sometimes the wheels ran all the length of the planks, sometimes slipped off. Presently Link came to a ditch where water had worn deep into the road. Without hesitation he placed them, measuring distance carefully, and then started across. The danger was in ditching the machine. One of the planks split, sagged a little, but Link made the crossing without a slip.

The road led round under an overhanging cliff and was narrow, rocky, and slightly downhill. Bidding Madeline and Nels walk round this hazardous corner, Link drove the car. Madeline expected to hear it crash down into the cañon, but presently she saw Link waiting to take them aboard again. Then came steeper parts of the road, places that Link could run down if he had space below to control the car, and on the other hand places where the little inclines ended in abrupt ledges upon one side or a declivity upon the other. Here the cowboy with ropes on the wheels and half-hitches upon the spurs of rock let the car slide down.

Once at a particularly bad spot Madeline exclaimed involuntarily, "Oh, time is flying!" Link Stevens looked up at her as if he had been reproved for his care. His eyes shone like the glint of steel on ice. Perhaps that utterance of Madeline's was needed to liberate his recklessness to its utmost. Certainly he put the car to seemingly impossible feats. He rimmed gullies, he hurdled rising ground, he leaped little breaks in the even road. He made his machine cling like a goat to steep inclines; he rounded corners with the inside wheels higher than the outside; he passed over banks of soft earth that caved in the instant he crossed weak places. He kept on and on, threading tortuous passages through rock-strewn patches, keeping to the old road where it was clear, abandoning it for open spaces, and always going down.

At length a mile of clean, brown slope, ridged and grooved like a wash-board, led gently down to meet the floor of the valley, where the scant grama-grass struggled to give a tinge of gray. The road appeared to become more clearly defined, and could be seen striking straight across the valley.

To Madeline's dismay, that road led down to a deep, narrow wash. It plunged on one side, ascended on the other at a still steeper angle. The crossing would have been laborsome for a horse; for an automobile it was impassable. Link turned the car to the right along the rim and drove as far along the wash as the ground permitted. The gully widened, deepened all the way. Then he took the other direction. When he made this turn Madeline observed that the sun had perceptibly begun its slant westward. It shone in her face, glaring and wrathful. Link drove back to the road, crossed it, and kept on down the line of the wash. It was a deep cut in red earth, worn straight down by swift water in the rainy seasons. It narrowed. In some places it was only five feet wide. Link studied these points and looked up the slope, and seemed to be making deductions. The valley was level now, and there were nothing but little breaks in the rim of the wash. Link drove mile after mile looking for a place to cross, and there was none. Finally progress to the south was obstructed by impassable gullies where the wash plunged into the head of a cañon. It was necessary to back the car a distance before there was room to turn. Madeline looked at the imperturbable driver. His face revealed no more than the same old hard, immutable character. When he reached the narrowest points, which had so interested him, he got out of the car and walked from place to place. Once, with a little jump, he cleared the wash. Then Madeline noted that the farther rim was somewhat lower. In a flash she divined Link's intention. He was hunting a place to jump the car over the crack in the ground.

Soon he found one that seemed to suit him, for he tied his red scarf upon a greasewood bush. Then, returning to the car, he clambered in, and, muttering, broke his long silence: "This ain't no air-ship, but I've outfiggered thet damn wash!" He backed up the gentle slope and halted just short of steeper ground. His red scarf waved in the wind. Hunching low over the wheel, he started, slowly at first, then faster, and then faster. The great car gave a spring like a huge tiger. The impact of suddenly formed wind almost tore Madeline out of her seat. She felt Nels's powerful hands on her shoulders. She closed her eyes. The jolting headway of the car gave place to a gliding rush.

This was broken by a slight jar, and then above the hum and roar rose a cowboy yell. Madeline waited with strained nerves for the expected crash. It did not come. Opening her eyes, she saw the level valley floor without a break. She had not even noticed the instant when the car had shot over the wash.

A strange breathlessness attacked her, and she attributed it to the celerity with which she was being carried along. Pulling the hood down over her face, she sank low in the seat. The whir of the car now seemed to be a world-filling sound. Again the feeling of excitement, the poignancy of emotional heights, the ever-present impending sense of catastrophe became held in abeyance to the sheer intensity of physical sensations. There came a time when all her strength seemed to unite in an effort to lift her breast against the terrific force of the wind—to draw air into her flattened lungs. She became partly dazed. The darkness before her eyes was not all occasioned by the hood that pressed like a stone mask on her face. She had a sense that she was floating, sailing, drifting, reeling, even while being borne swiftly as a thunderbolt. Her hands and arms were immovable under the weight of mountains. There was a long, blank period from which she awakened to feel an arm supporting her. Then she rallied. The velocity of the car had been cut to the speed to which she was accustomed. Throwing back the hood, she breathed freely again, recovered fully.

The car was bowling along a wide road upon the outskirts of a city. Madeline asked what place it could be.

"Douglas," replied Link. "An' jest around is Agua Prieta!"

That last name seemed to stun Madeline. She heard no more, and saw little until the car stopped. Nels spoke to some one. Then sight of khaki-clad soldiers quickened Madeline's faculties. She was on the boundary line between the United States and Mexico, and Agua Prieta, with its white and blue walled houses, it brown-tiled roofs, lay before her. A soldier, evidently despatched by Nels, returned and said an officer would come at once. Madeline's attention was centered in the foreground, upon the guard over the road, upon the dry, dusty town beyond; but she was aware of noise and people in the rear. A cavalry officer approached the car, stared, and removed his sombrero.

"Can you tell me anything about Stewart, the American cowboy who was captured by rebels a few days ago?" asked Madeline.

"Yes," replied the officer. "There was a skirmish over the line between a company of Federals and a large force of guerrillas and rebels. The Federals were driven west along the line. Stewart is reported to have done reckless fighting, and was captured. He got a Mexican sentence. He is known here along the border, and the news of his capture stirred up excitement. We did all we could to get his release. The guerrillas feared to execute him here, and believed he might be aided to escape. So a detachment departed with him for Mezquital."

"He was sentenced to be shot Thursday at sunset—tonight?"

"Yes. It was rumored there was a personal resentment against Stewart. I regret that I can't give you definite information. If you are friends of Stewart's—relatives—I might find—"

"I am his wife," interrupted Madeline. "Will you please read these." She handed him the telegrams. "Advise me—help me, if you can?"

With a wondering glance at her the officer received the telegrams. He read several, and whistled low in amaze. His manner became quick, alert, serious.

"I can't read these written in Spanish, but I know the names signed." Swiftly he ran through the others. "Why, these mean Stewart's release has been authorized. They explain mysterious rumors we have heard here. Greaser treachery! For some strange reason messages from the rebel junta have failed to reach their destination. We heard reports of an exchange for Stewart, but nothing came of it. No one departed for Mezquital with authority. What an outrage! Come, I'll go with you to General Salazar, the rebel chief in command. I know him. Perhaps we can find out something."

Nels made room for the officer. Link sent the car whirring across the line into Mexican territory. Madeline's sensibilities were now exquisitely alive. The white road led into Agua Prieta, a town of colored walls and roofs. Goats and pigs and buzzards scattered before the roar of the machine. Native women wearing black mantles peeped through iron-barred windows. Men wearing huge sombreros, cotton shirts and trousers, bright sashes round their waists, and sandals, stood motionless watching the car go by. The road ended in an immense plaza, in the center of which was a circular structure that in some measure resembled a corral. It was a bull-ring, where the national sport of bull-fighting was carried on. Just now it appeared to be quarters for a considerable army. Ragged, unkempt rebels were everywhere, and the whole square was littered with tents, packs, wagons, arms. There were horses, mules, burros, and oxen.

The place was so crowded that Link was compelled to drive slowly up to the entrance to the bull-ring. Madeline caught a glimpse of tents inside, then her view was obstructed by a curious pressing throng. The cavalry officer leaped from the car and pushed his way into the entrance.

"Link, do you know the road to this Mezquital?" asked Madeline.

"Yes, I've been there."

"How far is it?"

"Aw, not so very far," he mumbled.

"Link! How many miles?" she implored.

"I reckon only a few."

Madeline knew that he lied. She asked him no more, nor looked at him, nor at Nels. How stifling was this crowded, ill-smelling plaza! The sun, red and lowering, had sloped far down in the west, but still burned with furnace-heat. A swarm of flies whirled over the car. The shadows of low-sailing buzzards crossed Madeline's sight. Then she saw a row of the huge, uncanny black birds sitting upon the tiled roof of a house. They had neither an air of sleeping nor resting. They were waiting. She fought off a horrible ghastly idea before its full realization. These rebels and guerrillas—what lean, yellow, bearded wretches! They curiously watched Link as he went working over the car. No two were alike, and all were ragged. They had glittering eyes sunk deep in their heads. They wore huge sombreros of brown and black felt, of straw, of cloth. Every man wore a belt or sash, into which was thrust some kind of weapon. Some wore boots, some shoes, some moccasins, some sandals, and many were barefooted. They were an excited, jibbering, gesticulating mob. Madeline shuddered to think how a frenzy to spill blood could run through these poor revolutionists. If it was liberty they fought for they did not show the intelligence in their faces. They were like wolves upon a scent.

They affronted her, shocked her. She wondered if their officers were men of the same class. What struck her at last and stirred pity in her was the fact that every man of the horde her swift glance roamed over, however dirty and bedraggled he was, wore upon him some ornament, some tassel or fringe or lace, some ensign, some band, bracelet, badge or belt, some twist of scarf, something that betrayed the vanity which was the poor jewel of their souls. It was in the race.

Suddenly the crowd parted to let the cavalry officer and a rebel of striking presence get to the car.

"Madam, it is as I suspected," said the officer, quickly. "The messages directing Stewart's release never reached Salazar. They were intercepted. But even without them we might have secured Stewart's exchange if it had not been for the fact that one of his captors wanted him shot. This guerrilla intercepted the orders, and then was instrumental in taking Stewart to Mezquital. It is exceedingly sad. Why, he should be a free man this instant. I regret—"

"Who did this—this thing?" cried Madeline, cold and sick. "Who is the guerrilla?"

"Señor Don Carlos Martinez. He has been a bandit, a man of influence in Sonora. He is more of a secret agent in the affairs of the revolution than an active participator. But he has seen guerrilla service."

"Don Carlos! Stewart in his power! Oh, God!" Madeline sank down, almost overcome. Then two great hands, powerful, thrilling, clasped her shoulders, and Nels bent over her.

"Miss Majesty, shore we're wastin' time here," he said. His voice, like his hands, was uplifting. She wheeled to him in trembling importunity. How cold, bright, blue the flash of his eyes! They told Madeline she must not weaken.

But she could not speak her thought to Nels—could only look at Link.

"It figgers impossible, but I'll do it!" said Link Stevens, in answer to her voiceless query. The cold, grim, wild something about her cowboys blanched Madeline's face, steeled her nerve, called to the depths of her for that last supreme courage of a woman. The spirit of the moment was nature with Link and Nels; with her it must be passion.

"Can I get a permit to go into the interior—to Mezquital?" asked Madeline, of the officer.

"You are going on? Madam, it's a forlorn hope. Mezquital is a hundred miles away. But there's a chance—the barest chance if your man can drive this car. The Mexicans are either murderous or ceremonious in their executions. The arrangements for Stewart's will be elaborate. But, barring unusual circumstances, it will take place precisely at the hour designated. You need no permit. Your messages are official papers. But to save time, perhaps delay, I suggest you take this Mexican, Señor Montes, with you. He outranks Don Carlos and knows the captain of the Mezquital detachment."

"Ah! Then Don Carlos is not in command of the forces holding Stewart?"

"No."

"I thank you, sir. I shall not forget your kindness," concluded Madeline.

She bowed to Señor Montes, and requested him to enter the car. Nels stowed some of the paraphernalia away, making room in the rear seat. Link bent over the wheel. The start was so sudden, with such crack and roar, that the crowd split in wild disorder. Out of the plaza the car ran, gathering headway; down a street lined by white and blue walls; across a square where rebels were building barricades; along a railroad track full of iron flat-cars that carried mounted pieces of artillery; through the outlying guards, who waved to the officer Montes.

Madeline bound her glasses tightly over her eyes, and wound veils round the lower part of her face. She was all in a strange glow, she had begun to burn, to throb, to thrill, to expand, and she meant to see all that was possible. The sullen sun, red as fire, hung over the mountain range in the west. How low it had sunk! Before her stretched a narrow, white road, dusty, hard as stone—a highway that had been used for centuries. If it had been wide enough to permit passing a vehicle it would have been a magnificent course for automobiles. But the weeds and the dusty flowers and the mesquite boughs and arms of cactus brushed the car as it sped by.

Faster, faster, faster! That old resistless weight began to press Madeline back; the old incessant bellow of wind filled her ears. Link Stevens hunched low over the wheel. His eyes were hidden under leather helmet and goggles, but the lower part of his face was unprotected. He resembled a demon, so dark and stone-hard and strangely grinning was he. All at once Madeline realized how matchless, how wonderful a driver was this cowboy. She divined that weakening could not have been possible to Link Stevens. He was a cowboy, and he really was riding that car, making it answer to his will, as it had been born in him to master a horse. He had never driven to suit himself, had never reached an all-satisfying speed until now. Beyond that his motive was to save Stewart—to make Madeline happy. Life was nothing to him. That fact gave him the superhuman nerve to face the peril of this ride. Because of his disregard of self he was able to operate the machine, to choose the power, the speed, the guidance, the going with the best judgment and highest efficiency possible. Madeline knew he would get her to Mezquital in time to save Stewart, or he would kill her in the attempt.

The white, narrow road flashed out of the foreground, slipped with inconceivable rapidity under the car. When she marked a clump of cactus far ahead it seemed to shoot at her, to speed behind her even the instant she noticed it. Nevertheless, Madeline knew Link was not putting the car to its limit. Swiftly as he was flying, he held something in reserve. But he took the turns of the road as if he knew the way was cleared before him. He trusted to a cowboy's luck. A wagon in one of those curves, a herd of cattle, even a frightened steer, meant a wreck. Madeline never closed her eyes at these fateful moments. If Link could stake himself, the others, and her upon such chance, what could not she stake with her motive? So while the great car hummed and thrummed, and darted round the curves on two wheels, and sped on like a bullet, Madeline lived that ride, meant to feel it to the uttermost.

But it was not all swift going. A stretch of softer ground delayed Link, made the car labor and pant and pound and grind through gravel. Moreover, the cactus plants assumed an alarming ability to impede progress. Long, slender arms of the ocotillo encroached upon the road; broad, round leaves did likewise; fluted columns, fallen like timbers in a forest, lay along the narrow margins; the bayonet cactus and the hisnagi leaned threateningly; clusters of maguey, shadowed by the huge, looming saguaro, infringed upon the highway to Mezquital. And every leaf and blade and branch of cactus bore wicked thorns, any one of which would be fatal to a tire.

It came at length, the bursting report. The car lurched,

went on like a crippled thing and halted, obedient to the master hand at the wheel. Swift as Link was in replacing the tire, he lost time. The red sun, more sullen, duskier as it neared the black, bold horizon, appeared to mock Madeline, to eye her in derision.

Link leaped in, and the car sprang ahead. The roadbed changed, the trees changed—all the surroundings changed except the cactus. There were miles of rolling ridges, rough in the hollows, and short rocky bits of road, and washes to cross, and a low, sandy swale where mesquites grouped a forest along a trickling inch-deep sheet of water. Green things softened the hard, dry aspect of the desert. There were birds and parrots and deer and wild boars. All these Madeline remarked with clear eyes, with remarkable susceptibility of attention; but what she strained to see, what she yearned for, prayed for, was straight, unobstructed road.

But the road began to wind up; it turned and twisted in tantalizing lazy curves; it was in no hurry to surmount a hill that began to assume proportions of a mountain; it was leisurely, as were all things in Mexcio except strife. That was quick, fierce, bloody—it was Spanish.

The descent from that elevation was difficult, extremely hazardous, yet Link Stevens drove fast. At the base of the hill rocks and sand all but halted him for good. Then in taking an abrupt curve a grasping spear ruined another tire. This time the car rasped across the road into the cactus, bursting the second front-wheel tire. Like demons indeed Link and Nels worked. Shuddering, Madeline felt the declining heat of the sun, saw with gloomy eyes the shading of the red light over the desert. She did not look back to see how near the sun was to the horizon. She wanted to ask Nels. Strange as anything on this terrible ride was the absence of speech. As yet no word had been spoken. Madeline wanted to shriek to Link to hurry. But he was more than humanly swift in all his actions. So with mute lips, with the fire in her beginning to chill, with a lifelessness menacing her spirit, she watched, hoped against hope, prayed for a long, straight, smooth road.

Quite suddenly she saw it, seemingly miles of clear, narrow lane disappearing like a thin, white streak in distant green. Perhaps Link Stevens's heart leaped like Madeline's. The huge car, with a roar and a jerk, seemed to answer Madeline's call, a cry no less poignant because it was silent.

Faster, faster, faster! The roar became a whining hum. Then for Madeline sound ceased to be anything—she could not hear. The wind was now heavy, imponderable, no longer a swift, plastic thing, but solid, like an on-rushing wall. It bore down upon Madeline with such resistless weight that she could not move. The green of desert plants along the road merged in two shapeless fences, sliding at her from the distance. Objects ahead began to blur, the white road to grow streaky, like rays of light, the sky to take on more of a reddening haze.

Madeline, realizing her sight was failing her, turned for one more look at Link Stevens. It had come to be his ride almost as much as it was hers. He hunched lower than ever, rigid, strained to the last degree, a terrible, implacable driver. This was his hour, and he was great. If he so much as brushed a flying tire against one of the millions of spikes clutching out, striking out from the·cactus, there would be a shock, a splitting wave of air—an end. Madeline thought she saw that Link's bulging cheek and jaw were gray, that his tight-shut lips were white, that the smile was gone. Then he really was human—not a demon. She felt a strange sense of brotherhood. He understood a woman's soul as Monty Price had understood it. Link was the lightning-forged automaton, the driving, relentless, unconquerable instrument of a woman's will. He was a man whose force was directed by a woman's passion. He reached up to her height, felt her love, understood the nature of her agony. These made him heroic. But it was the hard life, the wild years of danger on the desert, the companionship of ruthless men, the elemental that made possible his physical achievement. Madeline loved his spirit then and gloried in the man.

She had pictured upon her heart, never to be forgotten, this little hunched, deformed figure of Link's hanging with dauntless, with deathless grip over the wheel, his gray face like a marble mask.

That was Madeline's last clear sensation upon the ride. Blinded, dazed, she succumbed to the demands upon her strength. She reeled, fell back, only vaguely aware of a helping hand. Confusion seized her senses. All about her was a dark chaos through which she was rushing, rushing, rushing under the wrathful red eye of a setting sun. Then, as there was no more sound or sight for her, she felt there was no color. But the rush never slackened—a rush through opaque, limitless space. For moments, hours, ages she was propelled with the velocity of a shooting star. The earth seemed a huge automobile. And it sped with her down an endless white track through the universe. Looming, ghostly, ghastly, spectral forms of cacti plants, large as pine-trees, stabbed her with giant spikes. She became an unstable being in a shapeless, colorless, soundless cosmos of unrelated things, but always rushing, even to meet the darkness that haunted her and never reached her.

But at an end of infinite time that rush ceased. Madeline lost the queer feeling of being disembodied by a frightfully swift careening through boundless distance. She distinguished voices, low at first, apparently far away. Then she opened her eyes to blurred but conscious sight.

The car had come to a stop. Link was lying face down over the wheel. Nels was rubbing her hands, calling to her. She saw a house with clean whitewashed wall and brown-tiled roof. Beyond, over a dark mountain range, peeped the last red curve, the last beautiful ray of the setting sun.

CHAPTER 25

AT THE END OF THE ROAD

Madeline saw that the car was surrounded by armed Mexicans. They presented a contrast to the others she had seen that day; she wondered a little at their silence, at their respectful front.

Suddenly a sharp spoken order opened up the ranks next to the house. Señor Montes appeared in the break coming swiftly. His dark face wore a smile; his manner was courteous, important, authoritative.

"Señora, it is not too late!"

He spoke her language with an accent strange to her, so that it seemed to hinder understanding.

"Señora, you got here in time," he went on. "El Capitan Stewart will be free."

"Free!" she whispered.

She rose, reeling.

"Come," replied Montes, taking her arm. "*Perdoneme*, Señora."

Without his assistance she would have fallen wholly upon Nels, who supported her on the other side. They helped her alight from the car. For a moment the white walls, the hazy red sky, the dark figures of the rebels, whirled before Madeline's eyes. She took a few steps, swaying between her escorts; then the confusion of her sight and mind passed away. It was as if she quickened with a thousand vivifying currents, as if she could see and hear and feel everything in the world, as if nothing could be overlooked, forgotten, neglected.

She turned back, remembering Link. He was lurching from the car, helmet and goggles thrust back, the gray shade gone from his face, the cool, bright gleam of his eyes disappearing for something warmer.

Señor Montes led Madeline and her cowboys through a hall to a patio, and on through a large room with flooring of rough, bare boards that rattled, into a smaller room full of armed quiet rebels facing an open window.

Madeline scanned the faces of these men expecting to see Don Carlos. But he was not present. A soldier addressed her in Spanish too swiftly uttered, too voluble for her to translate. But, like Señor Montes, he was gracious, and, despite his ragged garb and uncouth appearance, he bore the unmistakable stamp of authority.

Montes directed Madeline's attention to a man standing at the window. A loose scarf of vivid red hung from his hand.

"Señora, they were waiting for the sun to set when we arrived," said Montes. "The signal was about to be given for Señor Stewart's walk to death."

"Stewart's walk!" echoed Madeline.

"Ah, Señora, let me tell you his sentence—the sentence I have had the honor and happiness to revoke for you."

Stewart had been court-martialed and sentenced according to a Mexican custom observed in cases of brave soldiers to whom honorable and fitting executions were due. His hour had been set for Thursday when the sun had sunk. Upon signal he was to be liberated and was free to walk out into the road, to take any direction he pleased. He knew his sentence; knew that death awaited him, that every possible avenue of escape was blocked by men with rifles ready. But he had not the slightest idea at what moment or from what direction the bullets were to come.

"Señora, we have sent messengers to every squad of waiting soldiers—an order that El Capitan is not to be shot. He is ignorant of his release. I shall give the signal for his freedom."

Montes was ceremonious, gallant, emotional. Madeline saw his pride, and divined that the situation was one which brought out the vanity, the ostentation, as well as the cruelty of his race. He would keep her in an agony of suspense, let Stewart start upon that terrible walk in ignorance of his freedom. It was the motive of a Spaniard. Suddenly Madeline had a horrible quaking fear that Montes lied, that he meant her to be a witness of Stewart's execution. But, no, the man was honest; he was only barbarous. He would satisfy certain instincts of his nature—sentiment, romance, cruelty—by starting Stewart upon that walk, by watching Stewart's actions in the face of seeming death; by seeing Madeline's agony of doubt, fear, pity, love. Almost Madeline felt that she could not endure the situation. She was weak and tottering.

"Señora! Ah, it will be one beautiful thing!" Montes caught the scarf from the rebel's hand. He was glowing, passionate; his eyes had a strange, soft, cold flash; his voice was low, intense. He was living something splendid to him. "I'll wave the scarf, Señora. That will be the signal. It will be seen down at the other end of the road. Señor Stewart's jailer will see the signal, take off Stewart's irons, release him, open the door for his walk. Stewart will be free. But he will not know. He will expect death. As he is a brave man, he will face it. He will walk this way. Every step of that walk he will expect to be shot from some unknown quarter. But he will not be afraid. Señora, I have seen El Capitan fighting in the field. What is death to him? Ah, will it not be magnificent to see him come forth—to walk down? Señora, you will see what a man he is. All the way he will expect cold, swift death. Here at this end of the road he will meet his beautiful lady!"

"Is there no—no possibility of a mistake?" faltered Madeline.

"None. My order included unloading of rifles."

"Don Carlos?"

"He is in irons, and must answer to General Salazar," replied Montes.

Madeline looked down the deserted road. How strange to see the last ruddy glow of the sun over the brow of the mountain range! The thought of that sunset had been torture for her. Yet it had passed, and now the afterlights were luminous, beautiful, prophetic.

With a heart stricken by both joy and agony, she saw Montes wave the scarf.

Then she waited. No change manifested itself down the length of that lonely road. There was absolute silence in the room behind her. How terribly, infinitely long seemed the waiting! Never in all her future life would she forget the quaint pink, blue, and white walled houses with their colored roofs. That dusty, bare road resembled one of the uncovered streets of Pompeii with its look of centuries of solitude.

Suddenly a door opened and a tall man stepped out.

Madeline recognized Stewart. She had to place both hands on the window-still for support, while a storm of emotion swayed her. Like a retreating wave it rushed away. Stewart lived. He was free. He had stepped out into the light. She had saved him. Life changed for her in that instant of realization, and became sweet, full, strange.

Stewart shook hands with someone in the doorway. Then he looked up and down the road. The door closed behind him. Leisurely he rolled a cigarette, stood close to the wall while he scratched a match. Even at that distance Madeline's keen eyes caught the small flame, the first little puff of smoke.

Stewart then took to the middle of the road and leisurely began his walk.

To Madeline he appeared natural, walked as unconcernedly as if he were strolling for pleasure; but the absence of any other living thing, the silence, the red haze, the surcharged, atmosphere—these were all unnatural. From time to time Stewart stopped to turn face forward toward houses and corners. Only silence greeted these significant moves of his. Once he halted to roll and light another cigarette. After that his step quickened.

Madeline watched him, with pride, love, pain, glory combating for a mastery over her. This walk of his seemingly took longer than all her hours of awakening, of strife, of remorse, longer than the ride to find him. She felt that it would be impossible for her to wait till he reached the end of the road. Yet in the hurry and riot of her feelings she had fleeting panics. What could she say to him? How meet him? Well she remembered the tall, powerful form now growing close enough to distinguish its dress. Stewart's face was yet only a dark gleam. Soon she would see it—long before he could know she was there. She wanted to run to meet him. Nevertheless, she stood rooted to her covert behind the window, living that terrible walk with him to the uttermost thought of home, sister, mother, sweetheart, wife, life itself—every thought that could come to a man stalking to meet his executioners. With all that tumult in her mind and heart Madeline still fell prey to the incomprehensible variations of emotion possible to a woman. Every step Stewart took thrilled her. She had some strange, subtle intuition that he was not unhappy, and that he believed beyond shadow of doubt that he was walking to his death. His steps dragged a little, though they had begun to be swift. The old, hard, physical, wild nerve of the cowboy was perhaps in conflict with spiritual growth of the finer man, realizing too late that life ought not to be sacrificed.

Then the dark gleam that was his face took shape, grew sharper and clearer. He was stalking now, and there was a suggestion of impatience in his stride. It took these hidden Mexicans a long time to kill him! At a point in the middle of the road, even with the corner of a house and opposite to Madeline's position, Stewart halted stock-still. He presented a fair, bold mark to his executioners, and he stood there motionless a full moment.

Only silence greeted him. Plain it was to Madeline, and she thought to all who had eyes to see, that to Stewart, since for some reason he had been spared all along his walk, this was the moment when he ought to be mercifully shot. But as no shots came a rugged dignity left him for a reckless scorn manifest in the way he strolled across to the corner of the house, rolled yet another cigarette, and, presenting a broad breast to the window, smoked and waited.

That wait was almost unendurable for Madeline. Perhaps it was only a moment, several moments at the longest, but the time seemed a year. Stewart's face was scornful, hard. Did he suspect treachery on the part of his captors, that they meant to play with him as a cat with a mouse, to murder him at leisure? Madeline was sure she caught the old inscrutable, mocking smile fleeting across his lips. He held that position for what must have been a reasonable time to his mind, then with a laugh and a shrug he threw the cigarette into the road. He shook his head as if at the incomprehensible motives of men who could have no fair reasons now for delay.

He made a sudden violent action that was more than a straightening of his powerful frame. It was the old instinctive violence. Then he faced north. Madeline read his thought, knew he was thinking of her, calling her a last silent farewell. He would serve her to his last breath, leave her free, keep his secret. That picture of him, dark-browed, fire-eyed, strangely sad and strong, sunk indelibly into Madeline's heart of hearts.

The next instant he was striding forward, to force by bold and scornful presence a speedy fulfilment of his sentence.

Madeline stepped into the door, crossed the threshold.

Stewart staggered as if indeed the bullets he expected had pierced him in mortal wound. His dark face turned white. His eyes had the rapt stare, the wild fear of a man who saw an apparition, yet who doubted his sight. Perhaps he had called to her as the Mexicans called to their Virgin; perhaps he imagined sudden death had come unawares, and this was her image appearing to him in some other life.

"Who—are—you?" he whispered, hoarsely.

She tried to lift her hands, failed, tried again, and held them out, trembling.

"It is I. Majesty. Your wife!"